St. Teresa.

(FROM AN OLD PRINT.)

THE LIFE OF SAINT TERESA

TAKEN FROM THE FRENCH OF "A CARMELITE NUN" BY ALICE LADY LOVAT WITH A PREFACE BY MGR. ROBERT HUGH BENSON

HERBERT & DANIEL,
21 MADDOX STREET,
LONDON, W.

B. HERDER,
17 SOUTH BROADWAY,
ST. LOUIS, MO.

1912

Alice Mary (Weld-Blundell) Fraser (1845 - 1938)
Birthdate: March 1, 1846 (92)
Birthplace: Ince Blundell Hall, Liverpool, Merseyside, England, United Kingdom
Death: June 3, 1938 (92)
Immediate Family:
Daughter of Thomas Weld-Blundell and Theresa Mary Eleanora Weld-Blundell
Wife of Simon Fraser, 13th Baron Lovat
Mother of Mary Laura Scott; Alice Mary Charlotte Constable-Maxwell; Simon Joseph Fraser, 14th Baron Lovat; Hon. Etheldreda Mary Lindley, Lady Lindley; Alastair Thomas Joseph Fraser and 4 others
Sister of Edith Mary Caroline Weld-Blundell; Mary Elizabeth Frances Weld-Blundell; Teresa Mary Anne Weld-Blundell; Charles Joseph Weld-Blundell; Henry Joseph Weld-Blundell and 7 others…

Robert Hugh Benson AFSC KC*SG KGCHS (18 November 1871 – 19 October 1914) was an English Anglican priest who in 1903 was received into the Roman Catholic Church in which he was ordained priest in 1904. He was a prolific writer of fiction and wrote the notable dystopian novel Lord of the World (1907). His output encompassed historical, horror and science fiction, contemporary fiction, children's stories, plays, apologetics, devotional works and articles. He continued his writing career at the same time as he progressed through the hierarchy to become a Chamberlain to the Pope in 1911 and subsequently titled Monsignor.
Early life: Benson was the youngest son of Edward White Benson (Archbishop of Canterbury) and his wife, Mary, and the younger brother of Edward Frederic Benson and A. C. Benson. Benson was educated at Eton College and then studied classics and theology at Trinity College, Cambridge, from 1890 to 1893.
In 1895, Benson was ordained a priest in the Church of England by his father, who was the then Archbishop of Canterbury.
Career: After his father died suddenly in 1896, Benson was sent on a trip to the Middle East to recover his own health. While there he began to question the status of the Church of England and to consider the claims of the Roman Catholic Church. His own piety began to tend toward the High Church tradition, and he started exploring religious life in various Anglican communities, eventually obtaining permission to join the Community of the Resurrection.
Benson made his profession as a member of the community in 1901, at which time he had no thoughts of leaving the Church of England. As he continued his studies and began writing, however, he became more and more uneasy with his own doctrinal position and, on 11 September 1903, he was received into the Catholic Church. He was awarded the Dignitary of Honour of the Order of the Holy Sepulchre.
Benson was ordained as a Roman Catholic priest in 1904 and sent to Cambridge. He continued his writing career along with his ministry as a priest.
Novelist: Like both his brothers, Edward Frederic Benson ("Fred") and Arthur Christopher Benson, Robert wrote many ghost and horror stories, as well as children's stories and historical fiction. His horror and ghost fiction are collected in The Light Invisible (1903) and A Mirror of Shallott (1907). His novel, Lord of the World (1907), is generally regarded as one of the first modern dystopian novels (see List of dystopian literature). The bibliography below reveals a prodigious output.

PREFACE

PERHAPS the most remarkable symptom of IT modern religious thought lies in the attempt to penetrate behind the differences of religious creeds to the common inheritance of spiritual experience which, it is thought, surely underlies them. The real spiritual facts, we are told, are the same for all alike ; it is but the play of individual or national or class temperaments—in a word, purely human limitations—that have produced the unhappy clash of dogmas which has divided for so long religiously minded men and women. Gradually we are learning, our modern prophets tell us, that our agreements are more considerable than our variations, that our attitudes are more important than our tenets ; and it will not be long before we come fearlessly to acknowledge that historical events (or supposed events), and still more the doctrines deduced from them, which have formed up to now the principal features of every faith, are comparatively if not wholly negligible ; and that real religion consists in a " will-attitude " towards the Supreme Will rather than in an intellectual appreciation of any particular facts, historical or dogmatic.

It is not worth while analysing this position very closely, since, like the earlier theories as to the evolution of physical life, it evades, as a matter of fact, the whole point at issue— namely, the question as to how,

if spiritual experience is really all one, these variations ever came into existence. For religion, it must be remembered, is not one department of life (like art or biology); it cannot be segregated from the rest of our experience without ceasing to be true to itself: it is, on the contrary, either the sum of the whole of life, affecting and being affected by every single incident of life, or it is not true religion at all. To attempt, therefore, to frame a " spiritual religion " that is independent of fact and event and tradition and record, or, (which is the same thing), to believe that it is the object, not of the senses or of the intellect or the affections, but rather of a special and individual " religious sense," is to dethrone it from its proper place and to set it in the department of merely human activities.

Argument, however, is very nearly useless in such a matter; since argument is believed, as by more than one characteristically modern sect, to be itself carnal and external. If the tide of false spirituality is to be stemmed at all, it must be by other means, and, perhaps most of all, by the presentation to the world of those giants of spiritual experience whose achievements in the deep things of the spirit are beyond all dispute, and who yet, repeatedly and professedly, base all that they know upon the despised facts and dogmas and historical events of the religion which they follow. For by studying such lives as these it becomes possible to compare religion with religion, to understand not only that dogmas affect the spiritual interior attitude, but how they affect it, and with what results— not only, that is, to discern the common possessions of those who under the shadow of various creeds are yet all enlightened in various degrees by the One Light of

the World, but, what is even more important, the differences that divide them, and the consequent claim of one Religion distinguished from the rest as being the actual historical revelation of Almighty God. No Christian, least of all a Catholic, desires to minimize the portion of truth to which every sincere soul can attain by a conscientious fidelity to the Light within her; but it is the most superficial and shallow intellectual laziness to be content with this, and to assume as a matter of course that since there are various competitors in the field, none of them is legitimate.

Now, in the long list of Christian seers, the name of Teresa of Jesus is perhaps the best known of all. Other figures stand out brilliantly in this or that light —Saint Francis of Assisi, as the all-but-perfect imitator of the Poor Man of Galilee ; Saint Benedict, as the father of a holy family beyond all reckoning ; Saint Ignatius, as a veritable captain of an army of Christ; but, so far as the interior life is concerned — the knowledge and sovereignty of that inner realm where, as in a magic mirror, the historical and external life of Christ is reproduced and re-enacted, where His Birth, His Passion, His Resurrection, Ascension, and Session are seen to be not merely exterior happenings, but the antitypes of actual individual experience — in all this strange region known as the scene of the mystical life, Saint Teresa, with two or three of her contemporaries— Saint John of the Cross, Saint Peter of Alcantara — reigns supreme".

She was born into circumstances which to our modern eyes are the most romantic that can be imagined, of a noble Spanish family, in the town of Avila, and at

the period which is perhaps the most significant in the Christian era ; for she came into the world almost exactly as the " Reformation " began, and left it within a year or two of the defeat of the Spanish Armada. Nearly the whole of her life was, however, spent within convent walls, and the news of all the world-shaking movements and incidents of the time came to her through the strange atmosphere engendered by her life —an atmosphere which the world would say was one of obscurantism, and herself, no doubt, one of extraordinary luminousness. For, with her marvellous knowledge of the realm of motive and fundamental principles and spiritual realities, she would understand and interpret those exterior portents in a manner altogether impossible to those who strove with them in the dust and din of the conflict; and her exceptionally practical abilities, as illustrated by her schemes of reform and her numerous religious foundations, as well as by the strong common sense and sanity of her writings—these preclude the possibility of regarding her merely as a dreamer or visionary to whom the world seems but a phantom.

First, then, we may look upon her as one of God's answers to the charge brought against the Church of the sixteenth century, to the effect that true Christianity was dead, that the old spiritual tradition was lost, and that a burdensome and Pharisaic code of observances and formalities had taken its place. For, at the very time that Teresa was born—along with the other souls who, with her, formed one of the most brilliant cluster of spiritual lights to which Christianity has ever given rise—Luther was already beginning his thunders against the " papal system"; and within a year or

two of her entry into Religion Henry VIII of England was beginning to contemplate his final assault upon the Religious Houses of his realm. History has since vindicated monasticism from the charge of corruption and superstition, even though the world may not be yet—and, of course, never will be—converted to a sense of the utility of the enclosed contemplative life; but if any further answer were needed to the accusation that the Religious Life involves a sacrifice of common sense and intelligence as well as of the nobler faculties of human nature, it would surely be found in the fact that Teresa of Jesus not only embraced the Life with a full and deliberate consent, but persevered in it, illuminated it, and extolled it as the highest vocation to which a soul can come.

Here, then, in the very midst of a period concerning which even defenders of the Church are found sometimes to speak deprecatingly and almost apologetically, in the very heart of the life of a nation most characteristically and passionately Catholic, and therefore most generally considered to be the type and acme of degeneration and ignorance—under these circumstances we find a soul, intensely human—crammed, we might almost say, with exactly those attributes and gifts that go to make a brilliant social figure—humour, shrewdness, delicacy of insight and instinct, virile common sense, and practical abilities—a soul of strong humanity no less than of a genius for divine things, entering into that very state of life which, normally, ought to have extinguished her name for ever, and yet, from the remoteness and silence of her cell, influencing the world as perhaps no woman and scarcely any man has ever yet succeeded in influencing it. Not one man

in ten thousand, probably, knows the name of the builder of the Pyramids, or of the founder of a Mexican Dynasty, or of the inventor of the pulley ; and probably not one in that same ten thousand but has at least heard the name of Teresa, if no more.

On what, then, rests her claim to fame ?

Certainly she accomplished many practical works. She reformed the Order into which she had entered, she founded over thirty monastic establishments, she managed the lives of a great many individuals; yet it is scarcely at all in these outward works that she is known to the world. It is rather in that inner life of hers, "hid with Christ in God," that life which we know, so far as we know it, from her books and letters, that life lived within walls, in silence and solitude, that she burns to-day, like a star, in the heaven even of those who deny its existence. She has made herself known, that is, by the sheer force of her inner life, amongst those who are most apt to question its reality.

Now the inner life is, from its very nature, inexpressible in its essence — inexpressible, that is, as art or love or beauty are inexpressible. We can learn something of the limits, or the conditions, or the results of these things ; but we cannot experience life except by living it, any more than a mathematician can understand Beethoven through the process of reckoning up vibrations. The utmost, then, that can be done towards making the inner life analysable or intelligible is by presenting analogies proportionate to their originals. (It was this method, we may note in passing, which our Divine Lord Himself employed in His revelation of the kingdom of God — that final embodiment of all organized spiritual life. In one aspect it is like a net,

in another like a pearl, in another like a city seen against the sky.) No analogy is complete in itself; each illustrates one fact only. To gain even an approximately adequate idea of the original it is necessary to have a number of illustrations.

This, then, was Saint Teresa's plan. She wrote, it might almost be said, voluminously, considering the nature of her life, and almost entirely under obedience to her spiritual directors ; and she employed analogies not merely for the details of her theme, but for the whole framework itself in which she presented it. The fullest example of this method is to be found in that which is perhaps her best-known work, the "Spiritual Mansions." Here she displays before us the scheme of deepening spirituality through which the developing soul must pass in its gradual approach towards, and final union with, God, under the allegory of a castle where two dwell together, the Creator and the creature. She shows us, under the name of "mansions," or, in the Italian phrase, "apartments" or suites of rooms, the various stages in which this growth in holiness consists, describing the temptations, the delusions, the graces, the consolations common to each, up to the "nuptial chamber" itself (and beyond it), in which the union of the soul with God is made perfect. Again and again, it need hardly be said, the analogy wavers, and sometimes even breaks in her strong hand ; she flings it aside, and catches up another ; she runs off for page after page into disquisitions, and shrewd counsels, and warnings and encouragements; but the reader, stumbling after, bewildered by her movements, yet becomes more and more conscious as he perseveres that here is a soul who knows indeed of what she is

speaking, who has experienced all that she relates, and far more, with a vividness compared to which the keenness of sensation in other realms of being is but a very faded and nerveless experience—above all, that here is a soul who has " found the one thing needful," and who " knows in Whom she has believed.'*

In other writings of hers it is the same. She uses sometimes analogies of the Godhead, let us say, which appear fantastic and indeed ludicrously inadequate, until we reflect that all analogies of the Godhead must be so. Even Christ Himself, Who reveals to us the Father, is compelled, not by His limitations, but our own, to liken Him to an " unjust judge," an "austere man," a "nobleman taking a journey/' an observer of trapped sparrows. For, owing to these limitations of ours, there is simply no possible way by which we can learn spiritual all-truths except by seeing them reflected in a many-facetted mirror of half-truths. Saint Teresa, then, as a "wise steward" of spiritual experience, is perfectly fearless in what she brings out of her storehouse. God is a kind of "globe" ; He is also her Spouse ; He is also a sort of Darkness. . . .

All this, of course, appears like hysterical raving to those minds that sedulously confine themselves to material phenomena, and judge of a thing's reality according to its approximation to inert matter. The man who regards a table as more "real" than an emotion or a virtue, who thinks that the bread that perishes is more solid and permanent than the Bread which never perishes, who regards human love as the effect of a condition of material particles—this man is as little capable of understanding Saint Teresa as his opposite, the man who does not regard a table as real

at all. The fact is that Saint Teresa, like every real genius, is a perfectly balanced personality, and she is thought, therefore, too realistic by the idealists, and too idealistic by the realists. She has found out, by the aid of grace acting upon a selected nature, that there is but one thing in the world really worth pursuing—the knowledge of God ; that this qiiesF~ls one which ~ verifies itself as it is pursued—that it increases, that is to say, the sense of reality in the soul that follows it, instead of, as the materialist thinks, leading to mere visionariness and abstraction—and that while, on the one side its reality is so great as to make all else insignificant, on the other it must use images of created things in order to express itself; and that it develops rather than retards the administration of even the most practical concerns.

It is this balance and sanity in Saint Teresa, then, that constitute, as it would appear, her claim to be heard in the present generation. We live, largely, in an age of over-specialization. Men tend at present to devote themselves not to living in general, but to doing one thing in particular, to " know all about one thing," but to neglect all knowledge whatever about other things. Religion, art, science—as was said just now— each has its votaries, but the number of those who attempt to live religiously, artistically, and healthily, all at the same time—in a word, to live as complete and not fragmentary human beings—seems steadily on the decrease. Many causes contribute to this : competition, in one way ; attention to temperament, in another; and the result is that mysticism or, in other words, an intelligent and conscious attention to the spiritual life—is thought to be as faddish and peculiar

as a careful attention to diet or health-clothing—a possible but slightly contemptible vocation suitable only for those who have nothing else more important with which to occupy themselves. And this condition of public opinion has its inevitable result even upon those who ought most to resent it: even those who have by nature or grace that temperament at once introspective and generous, self-knowing and self-sacrificing, which constitutes the " mystical" nature, little by little come to look upon themselves as exceptional and peculiar, to cultivate an attitude of remoteness and abstraction, and to regard their citizenship in the company of the saints às in inverse ratio to their companionableness on earth.

Into this stifling and perfumed unreality the personality of Saint Teresa enters like a morning breeze of summer. She too has her perfumes, but they are the scents of the fields of nature and grace ; she too has her ecstasies, her embraces, her aspirations, her communications, but they are the dealings of a real soul with a Divine Lover, not of an anaemic sentimentalist with a god made in her own image and likeness. She too soars up into darkness, but it is the realm of the clouds and darkness that are about the throne of the uncreated Light, not the miasma that rises from the earth. She soars, but she never loses her head ; she is drunken, but not with wine.

For those things make her more, and not less, real than the rest of us. Never for one hour does she lose her shrewdness, her gaiety, her almost divine gift of humour. " Distrust yourselves," she tells her sisters in effect, " when you begin to faint in the arms of your Beloved : when such and such symptoms occur, your

ecstasy proceeds not from an excess of spirit, but a defect of body. Sleep well ; eat well. It is infinitely more pleasing to God to see a convent of quiet and healthy children who do what they are told than a mob of hysterical young women who fancy themselves privileged. ..."

And yet her encouragement is even greater than her criticism, as must be the case with every friend of God. She too had headaches, as she sat in her cell far into the night, with her spectacles on, tracing with her painful pen the marvellous account of her voyagings to the Bosom of God ; she too, as month after month went by, turned from her fruitless attempts at meditation to reading in a book, unable to fix her mind for three minutes together upon Him Whom she loved more than all the world ; she too found it necessary to sit at bodily ease, when a less humble worshipper would have knelt in agony; she too, describing the " person whom she once knew," found herself " very wicked indeed " at such and such a time, very worldly-minded, very unsatisfactory in all her relations both with God and man. And yet she too " went on trying," fulfilling by that trying the one essential of sanctity and of union with Him without whose grace and mercy every success is a failure, and by whose love every failure can be transmuted into triumph.

Finally it must be remarked how, in a line with what has already been said of her, Saint Teresa offers one more answer to one more fallacy common in our own days.

It is generally believed, as has already been implied, that Mysticism is the religion of the vaguely-minded, that high spiritual religion has something in it incom-b

patible with dogmatism, and that it is, in fact, an initiation into a unity so high as to be incapable of precise statement, and that intense, or, in other words, personal feeling cannot easily co-exist with defined statements of fact, or be subjected to ordinary rules of discipline. Here, once and for all, Saint Teresa speaks plainly. Not only is she a rigid Catholic, first and last (that perhaps might be explained away by the circumstances of her life and her period), but she is an enthusiastic dogmatist, and an humble and obedient disciple of the rather incompetent spiritual directors by whom Providence for a time tested her capacity for docility. For indeed, in the mysticism of the disciples of Jesus Christ, teaching as He did that the very virtues which we ourselves demand of children are the virtues which He demands from us, there can be no greater criterion of a true submission to God (and hence of a true union with Him) than a true submission to those whom the Catholic holds to be His representatives and vicegerents. And, after all, this is but natural, since Christian mysticism is not primarily (as are certain forms of pagan mysticism) an initiation into truths of the intellectual order, but rather of the moral; it is not in order to learn new facts about the supernatural that Saint Teresa and St. John of the Cross enter into contemplation, but to dwell upon facts already known, to correlate them, to perceive their inwardness, to embody them into the realm of experience, and by this process to pass into an ever closer and more intimate union with Him of whom they are true. Humility, then — obedience to those whose spiritual insight is not so deep as her own —so far from being an obstacle, may become in itself a

positive progress for the soul, far more elevating than the brilliant excursions and adventures in which a less obedient spirit imperils her own self-knowledge and self-contempt.

So too was it with Saint Teresa in regard even to what might be called the dogmatic details of the Catholic system. It is a constant danger to the soul which enjoys a high degree of insight to despise as merely elementary helps to beginners those comparatively small and optional devotions with which the Church furnishes her children ; and, even more than this, to regard as almost negligible familiar truths delivered by authority when contrasted with personal discoveries that have the charm of novelty and individuality. This, in short, was the exact process by which Quietism fell; the earlier Quietists, beginning by acts of intense spiritual insight (of a nature whose perils were not understood), so much over-valued these, and the sensations that followed from them, that little by little the most weighty means of grace, instituted by Christ Himself, began first to be under-valued, and then neglected. It is a constant temptation to certain kinds of intuitive souls to regard, as has been remarked, " everything as sacramental, except the sacraments."

Never for one instant did Saint Teresa even approach in the direction of this spiritual trap. Not only was her fervour nourished steadily and consistently by those ordinary and familiar means of grace accessible to us all, but she laid the strongest possible emphasis upon what are comparatively optional observances, such as an ardent devotion to Saint Joseph and a frequent use of holy water. There never appears in

her story from beginning to end even the faintest trace of that spiritual snobbery in which so many souls, otherwise capable of real progress, hinder their own sanctification. She was so far advanced as never to forget that she was a child, so wise as never to ignore "the foolishness of God," so strong as fearlessly to condescend to that "weakness" in which the Divine Strength is made manifest.

Such then, in short, are a few of the most prominent characteristics and significances of the soul whose history is here related, up to the point when she passed from Contemplation to the Beatific Vision, that last and final Mansion of the soul that received her in her Father's House. Of what she has done in the past, the story of Mysticism is already eloquent; of what she will do in the present and in the future, now that once more the nightmare of materialism seems passing, and guides who have themselves traversed the ground of the interior life are once more being eagerly demanded, we may be confident and expectant.

ROBERT HUGH BENSON.

CONTENTS

CHAPTER XXVIII

PAGE

CHAPTER XXIX

CHAPTER XXX

PAGE

CHAPTER XXXI

CHAPTER XXXII

THE LIFE OF SAINT TERESA

CHAPTER I

" THIS day, Wednesday, March 28th, 1515, my JL daughter Teresa was born about half-past five in the morning with the first dawn of day. She was baptized, having for godfather Vela Nunez, and for godmother Dona Maria de PAguila."

These are the words in which Alonso Sanchez de Cepeda, in a memorandum which he drew up of his childrenV history, acquaints us with the date of his daughter's birth.

Alonso Sanchez de Cepeda was descended on both his father and mother's side from two of those ancient Castilian families in which purity of faith and morals was transmitted with that of blood. His father numbered amongst his ancestors a king of Leon. His mother, Agnes de Cepeda, bore a name which was also one of the most distinguished in the kingdom of the two Castiles. She came of a branch of the Tordesillas family, " a name honoured for its nobility," Ribera tells us, " throughout Spain." John Sanchez and Agnes de Cepeda had four sons, Francis—grandfather of the ! Ocampo family, of whom we shall hear more later—

Peter, Rodriguez, and Alonso. Alonso, after some years of marriage with Catalina del Peso y Enao, was left a widower in the prime of life, with three young children, at the age when they were most in need of a mother's care. He found a second mother for them in the gentle companion who was to give birth to our saint, Beatriz Davila de Ahumada.

Teresa, according to the Spanish custom, bore the name of her mother, not of her father, and was called Teresa de Ahumada until the hour when she exchanged it for the immortal one of Teresa of Jesus. Without wandering into long digressions on the history of the Ahumada family, let us take one incident from its annals which doubtless was dearer to Teresa than the thought of all her family glories.

The name Ahumada, says an ancient historian, was derived from the word Ahumar, smoke. A tradition, from ages so remote that the exact date of the incident is unknown, relates that the illustrious knight, Ferdinand, head of the family, whilst fighting against the Moors, was besieged with his three sons in a tower which he held valiantly against the infidel troops. The enemy, unable in spite of their number to overcome the resistance of its brave defenders, set fire to the tower. God came to the protection of His servants, and permitted that the smoke should envelop the Moors in an impenetrable darkness, which facilitated the escape of Ferdinand and his sons, so that a heap of ruins was all that fell into the enemy's hands.

From that time the Castilians gave Ferdinand the name of Ahumada, and, by order of the King of Castile, he and his descendants were given the right of quartering a tower on their arms surrounded with flames. This device, which had been in former days

carved on the entrance of the house of Teresa's parents, is now to be seen on the entablature of the principal entrance of the chapel built on the spot of her birthplace.

The documents collected by the learned researches of the Bollandists would allow of a much deeper insight into the genealogy of our saint, but she cuts us short herself by a remark such as we shall often have occasion to chronicle : " As we are all made of the same clay, to dispute on nobility of birth is the same as to wrangle about whether one kind of clay or another was best fitted for making bricks or potsherds; a fine question indeed ! For my part, I am satisfied with being a daughter of the Church. A venial sin would be a greater- cause of humiliation to me than that my origin was an ignoble one." Let it suffice, therefore, in deference to historic truth, to record the fact that Teresa's birth was no less illustrious than it was Christian. Providence had selected the spot of her birthplace with scarcely less care.

Avila is built in the shape of an amphitheatre on a soil which is fertile in spite of great rocks which crop up on all parts of its surface. It is situated to the south of Old Castile, on the picturesque bank of the Adaja, affluent of the Douro, in the midst of innumerable hillocks forming the westerly spurs of the Guadarrama mountains. Peak-shaped rocks to the south and north form a majestic framework to the town, and their harshness serves to bring out in more vivid contrast the blue waters of the river which bathes the foot of the cliffs to the westward. Fortified by Raymond, a French prince and companion of Henry of Burgundy, in the eleventh century, during the Castilian crusade, Avila preserves to the present day the imposing walls which made her impregnable to the

Moors. Her high portals protected by turrets, her bastions, towers and portcullis must have, in the year 1515, told many a story of the doings of their ancestors to the children who lived in those days ; for the little city which stood like an outpost at the foot of the mountains had repulsed continual attacks made upon it. Celebrated for the bravery of its inhabitants, of its women as well as of its men, it gained the name of Avila of the knights. These loyal knights, faithful to their king as to their God, gained from the former, in grateful recognition, the name of Avila of the King. A last title which effaced both the previous ones fell to its lot. Royal and knightly as it had ever been, Avila gave even more to heaven than it had done to country or prince. Saints multiplied within its precincts, and thus it became known as the holy city, and when the glory of Teresa had completed its own, Avila would brook no lower title than that of " Avila of the saints." Avila cantosy santos was a popular saying in allusion to the rocky eminences which we have already mentioned : Avila of the stones, and the saints.

In this city—Catholic before everything—and with the blood of heroes in her veins, Teresa first saw daylight. The bells were ringing for Angelus; possibly one bell was heard above the rest, and soothed the infant's slumbers from afar. It was that of the Carmelites. Two years before, they had begun to build the convent of the Incarnation. It had just been completed, and the community had chosen the 28th of March, eve of the feast of St. Berthold (first general of the Latin branch of the Carmelite order) to inaugurate their church by the first celebration of the divine sacrifice. The bells announced this great solemnity to the inhabitants of Avila, and by a singular coincidence they rang out at the same time

the tidings of the birth of the future Reformer of Carmel.

The name of Teresa had also its glories of old, forgotten as they now are in the fame of the great saint who has eclipsed them. The holy companion of St. Paulinus of Nola appears first to have brought it to Spain. After her a sister of Alfonso, King of Leon, and a Queen of Portugal rendered it illustrious by their virtues ; the Church venerates their memory. The history of the first of these two princesses is another record of the triumph of faith over the brutality of the Moors ; but it was of a triumph far more sublime than that of arms, it was that of innocence over brute force, and of weakness made invincible by love of virginity. The choice of Alonso and Beatriz of a patron saint for their child was therefore a wise one, and we gladly recognize these incidents in the lives of the servants of God, which, though insignificant in themselves, seem to foreshadow their future greatness.

An elder sister and four little brothers were grouped round Teresa's cradle. Her mother was but twenty-one years of age when she was born. Married at fifteen, Dona Beatriz had, as we have already observed, to take upon herself at once the care of the three orphan children bequeathed to Alonso by his first wife, and it is said of her that she made no distinction between her own children and those she had adopted before God's altar. Maria de Cepeda, the eldest of the family, responded fully to her stepmother's devotion, and the young mother soon found in her a prop and support in her many cares. The delicate health brought on by her maternal duties obliged Beatrice to devolve by degrees much of the government of the house on her stepdaughter. She had six more children after giving birth to Teresa : Lorenzo, Antonio, Pedro, Geronimo, Augustin, and Juana.

Let us give a glance into this truly patriarchal home. Doubtless we shall hear the noise of children—lively voices, great gaiety and animation, especially at moments when play takes the place of work; but we are conscious of a firm hand governing the little company. It was kept in order by the discipline of strict submission to parents, and by the " give and take" of a large family bound by a tie of strong natural affections.

Alonso de Cepeda was a second Jacob in inculcating virtuous habits on his children by his example, and guiding them by his wise counsels. If his stately height, his austere appearance and the dignity of his manner inspired the respect of the citizens of Avila, it is in the character of an affectionate father that we realize him best, and we know that, without losing any part of his parental authority, he succeeded in making himself loved as well as obeyed. In Beatriz, his gentle helpmate, we see a Rachel in beauty and a Leah in fecundity, whilst in modesty she resembles both one and the other; the olive plants growing up round their table speak of God's blessing on their union.

Teresa tells us that she can never thank God enough for such parents. " This," she says, " would have been enough to make me good if I had not been so wicked. My father was very much given to the reading of good books ; and so he had them in Spanish that his children might read them. ... It helped me too that I never saw my father and mother respect anything but goodness. They were very good themselves. My father was a man of great charity towards the poor and compassion for the sick, and also for servants, so much so that he never could be persuaded to keep slaves, for he pitied them so much, and a slave belonging to one of his brothers being once in his house was treated by him with as much tenderness as one of his own children. . . . He was a man of great truthfulness ; nobody ever heard him swear or speak ill of anyone ; his life was most pure. My mother also was a woman of great goodness, and her life was spent in great infirmities. She was singularly pure in all her ways. Though possessing great beauty, yet was it never known that she gave reason to suspect that she made any account whatever of it; for though she was only three-and-thirty years of age when she died, her apparel already was that of a woman advanced in years. She was very calm, and had great sense. The sufferings she went through during her life were grievous, her death most Christian." We can have no difficulty in guessing the education such a father and mother would give to their children. Alonso with his love of solid books doubtless imbued his family with his literary tastes. We may safely conclude that he encouraged the development of his children's ideas, listened to their remarks, and to the impression made upon them by his favourite books—many of which were eagerly devoured by them. Nor would he allow any purely frivolous occupation to absorb their time. Worldly concerns being thus kept at arm's length peace reigned in the home. The Church's feasts in honour of God and His saints were those most highly honoured in this family, its canticles were their songs, and for dances they had the joyous games of the children. Dona Beatriz took a large share in the important work of directing the early education of her family. Her love for them and the grace of the maternal vocation gave her the key to their hearts. She had no difficulty in teaching them to

pray who prayed so well herself; or to inspire them with her own love for our Lady, for the angels and the saints. The robust faith, the austere virtues of the father, the tender devotion and gentle goodness of the mother seemed to belong to their children by divine right of inheritance; all in mind and heart took after their parents. Teresa is our authority for this statement, and she adds, "all with the exception of myself."

Naturally there were differences of character in so numerous a family; we can distinguish them even at this distance of time. In Maria de Cepeda, the eldest sister, we recognize the reasonable woman, possibly only too grave in manner, but sweet and calm and given up to her duties with a precocious wisdom semi-maternal. The brothers are distinguished by their chivalrous tastes to an extent which causes little surprise in the sons of Avila. With hardly an exception they will take to the Army, and seek the glory in a New World which in the preceding century they would have acquired beside the walls of the city of their birth. In the meantime, whilst awaiting the battle-fields of the future—the exploits they already see in their youthful imaginations—doubtless they exercise themselves in passages of arms, and their recreations are spent in mimic tournaments. What becomes of Teresa in these days? For it is with her, in the midst of this family group, of which she is the pearl and centre, that we are most concerned.

At the time we speak of she is scarcely seven years of age. Her first studies chosen, directed by her father have already made a deep impression on her mind. Her mother has taught her to pray, and if her brothers and sisters have likewise come under the sweet influence of maternal piety, upon not one of them has

such an impression been made as upon her. She is eager to hear Dona Beatriz speak of Heaven, of our Lord, and of the Blessed Virgin. Her child's heart has opened to the love which is later on to take entire possession of it; though so young she willingly sacrifices the pleasures which belong to her years, and appear natural to them, in order to give herself up to God's service. Sometimes she takes her mother's beads from her hands and recites them with her. Possibly the child who is already so thoughtful, and preternaturally wise, lingers over the words of the "Our Father" which she is afterwards to comment upon in such eloquent words. And our Divine Saviour, who loves to attract children to His feet and takes pleasure in their coming to Him, encourages her first fervours by ever-increasing graces and blessings. Teresa, in spite of her affection for her family, now goes in search of solitude. She hides herself in the most remote parts of the garden, where for a short time she can remain undisturbed, united to her God whom she loves so much that she would fain know Him better in order to love Him more. This youthful fervour, far from making her sad and morose, does but add to the charm of her character and that delightful simplicity which endears her so much to her parents. She gives gladly all that she possesses: her alms to the poor, kind words and deeds to neighbours and servants, and to her family her deepest affections. But young as she was she had already begun to find that all were not capable of understanding the secrets of her heart. Moreover, there are thoughts so intimate that they can be only breathed low into one ear, that of a loved confidant. Teresa found this intimate friend in one of her brothers who was four years older than herself, and for whom she had a special affection.

"He and I," she says, " used to read the lives of saints together. When I read of martyrdom undergone by the saints for the love of God, it struck me that the vision of God was very cheaply purchased by it, and I had a great desire to die a martyr's death, not out of any love of Him of which I was conscious, but that I might the more quickly attain to the fruition of those great joys of which I read that they were reserved for Heaven."

Teresa's character shows itself in every line of this narrative ; we see her childish ardour, and the courage no difficulty could daunt. She communicates her longings to Rodriguez, and the two children deliberate together how they can soonest carry out their intentions. "We settled," she says, "to go together to the country of the Moors, begging our way there for the love of God, that we might be beheaded there ; and I believe our Lord would have given us courage enough, even at that tender age, if we could have found the means to proceed. But our greatest difficulty seemed to be our father and mother."

Teresa overcomes this obstacle, which from every point of view was little less than insurmountable, by desires which became daily more ardent to see God. Would not — she doubtless thought — the glory of their martyrdom cast a reflected halo over their parents which would console them for their loss, and very soon would they not be re-united in paradise? What, indeed, are the sacrifices, the separations, the tears shed here below in comparison with eternity?

" It astonished us greatly to find it said in the books we read that pain and bliss were everlasting. We frequently talked about this, and we took pleasure in repeating, ' for ever, ever, ever !' Through the constant uttering of these words our Lord was pleased

that I should receive an abiding impression of the way of truth when I was yet a child."

Finally they agreed to carry out the plan without further delay. One morning at the earliest dawn of day brother and sister slipped quietly out of the paternal abode. They proceeded on their way, proposing to beg as they went along, taking some pieces of bread only with them for all provision for their grand journey to Paradise ! But God had other designs on our youthful pilgrims, and their loving impetuosity was not permitted to take them much beyond the gates of Avila. When they had got a short way outside the town and were rapidly crossing the bridge over the Adaja, they fell into the arms of one of their uncles who was returning from the country, and who soon brought the fugitives back to their mother, who, already much alarmed, was searching for them far and wide. Needless to say they were well scolded; Rodriguez, in excuse, pleads that " la nina had overpersuaded him." Teresa, appealed to for her justification, answers with a frankness which was to be her characteristic to her dying day. "I ran away because I wanted to see God, and one cannot do that without first dying."

Doubtless there was an interior joy in the heart of the mother mingled with her displeasure, though she allowed the latter only to be seen. She recognized the treasure God had confided to her care in this ardent child so full of faith and so prompt to carry into action the loving impulses of her heart. Accordingly she explained to Teresa's inexperience, that the reward she was in such haste to gain was not to be won in the easy way she dreamt of, but by a life spent in God's service. Teresa had some difficulty in consoling herself for the loss of a happiness which she had thought

almost within her grasp. But, as it seemed that the martyrs were not open to imitation, she set her mind to work at another form of sanctity, and again in concert with Rodriguez, she proposed that they should become hermits. The garden attached to their home was to be their Thebaid. Thus the brother and sister set to work to build themselves hermitages " by piling little stones one upon the other," she tells us in her life, " which fell down immediately, and so it came to pass that we found no means of accomplishing our wish." Teresa, grieved but not discouraged, consoled herself by offering up her ardent desires to God, and understands by these failures that she is to seek Him under the guidance of her excellent parents. She redoubles her fervour, and strives to do still better the little that is given her to do. To quote her words, speaking of these youthful days : " Even now I have a feeling of devotion when I consider how God gave me in my early youth what I afterwards lost by my own fault. I gave alms when I could—and I could but little. I contrived to be alone for the sake of saying my prayers — and they were many — especially the rosary, to which my mother had a great devotion, and had made us also in this like herself. I used to delight exceedingly when playing with other children in the building of convents as if we were nuns; and I think I wished to be a nun, though not so much as I did to be a martyr or a hermit."

Thus passed this touching and beautiful childhood. Were we to sum up its most prominent qualities, they would be but a description of what we shall see later on in Teresa's character as exemplified in her life. Already the germs of her vivid faith, her ardent love, her tenderness of heart, and her strong generous will are visible; all these characteristics we shall find again,

fully developed, in the history of the great saint. Perhaps we have lingered too long over the early scenes of the dawn of a life which has so much stronger claims at a later period to our admiration. But, apart from the charm of Teresa's early life, it seems to us that the wondrous facts which are to follow require an attentive examination of the minutest ones which preceded them. "It is a pleasing task," says an ancient writer, "after contemplating a great river to trace back its waters to their source."

We find a similar satisfaction in this budding sanctity ; in these first outpourings of grace in the heart of a little child, and in the appeals to Teresa, from the Divine lover of her soul, and her response to them.

CHAPTER II

NOTHING definite is known about Teresa's first Communion. It was not usual in those days for the Church to accompany that great act with an outward observance customary in these. Children were prepared for it either in the seclusion of their own families, or in a convent or monastery, and the father and mother and brothers and sisters were alone witnesses of the joys and fervour of that day of benediction. We can at best conjecture, in the absence of precise information, that it was at the church of St. John where our saint had already received the Sacrament of Baptism, that her young heart was united with unspeakable delight and consolation to Him whom she had before gone forth to seek in the country of the Moors.

Teresa's first Communion was possibly her mother's last joy on earth. Dona Beatriz, who had long suffered from premature disease and infirmity, died in the year 1528, leaving to her nine orphaned children, besides a great sorrow, the memory of a spotless life, and an example of much patience and holiness. Teresa felt deeply the extent of her loss. "I went in my affliction," she writes, "to an image of our Lady, and with many tears implored her to be my mother. I did this in my simplicity, and I believe that it was of service to me ; for I have by experience found that she has helped me whenever I recommended myself to her ; and at last she has brought me back to herself."

Teresa had great need of help from our blessed Lady. She was left an orphan at the age when the inexperienced heart of a young girl requires all the vigilant care and solicitude of a mother to guide it aright. It is a mother's part, at this age to invite confidence, to guess the newly formed ideas passing through her child's brain, and to respond by her maternal affection to the cravings of the child's heart. The more ardent the character of the young girl, the richer and more spontaneous her nature, so much the more necessary will it be for the mother to display both prudence and resolution in giving a right direction to her child's desires and aspirations. It was at this critical time —one which frequently decides a girl's character for life — that God chose for depriving Teresa of Dona Beatriz's love and good counsels. Let us adore the designs of His Providence. God may have intended, by taking away from our saint the prop on which she leant, and letting her fall into defects which were to be a cause of lifelong mourning to her, to dig still deeper the foundations of His great work in her soul, by thus planting them on the bed-rock of humility and repentance.

Teresa was at this time thirteen years of age. She was tall and well developed, and her beauty was already beginning to attract attention in her native town. Her forehead was large and high, and crowned with black tresses ; her pale and colourless complexion was marked on the left side of her face by three small dimples which added to its attraction ; whilst a candid smile playing frequently on her lips allowed her beautiful teeth to be seen. Her eyes were of medium size and set rather deep in her head; they were black and very bright and expressive ; her figure was supple, her hands long and well formed, her walk dignified and graceful ; an innate distinction which her education

had developed, a nobility of manner which she had inherited from her father, an amiability which recalled her mother—such were her characteristics as reported by her contemporaries. 1 " When she spoke," remarks one of them, " nothing could exceed the charm and vivacity of her conversation." From the first it was prognosticated that Doila Teresa de Ahumada would be no ordinary person. Surely a young girl with such gifts was exposed to more than ordinary perils !

Before her mother's death Teresa had already opened a door to the temptations by which she was afterwards to be assailed. We will allow her to tell the story of her errors in her own words. Speaking of her mother, she says: " She was very fond of books of chivalry ; but this pastime did not hurt her so much as it hurt me, because she never wasted her time on them ; only we, her children, were left at liberty to read them; and perhaps she did this to distract her thoughts from her great sufferings and occupy her children that they might not go astray in other ways. It annoyed my father so much that we had to be careful he never saw us. I contracted a habit of reading these books ; and this little fault which I observed in my mother was the beginning of lukewarmness in my good desires and the occasion of my falling away in other respects. I thought there was no harm in it when I wasted many hours night and day in so vain an occupation, even when I kept it a secret from my father. So completely was I mastered by this passion that I thought I could never be happy without a new book."

What kind of books were these of which Teresa speaks? Books were still rare at the beginning of the sixteenth century. Those best known were doubtless the Old and New Testament, the works of the Fathers,

1 Yepes, Ribera, History of the Carmelites.

the lives of saints, and a few similar productions of a moral or spiritual tendency; these were the choice of grave and well-balanced minds. But the greater number of people, who ask, as Teresa reminds us, for recreation and amusement in what they read, found these qualities more readily in romances in which the exploits of knights errant were mingled with sentimental adventures of, frequently, a very dangerous character. Dona Beatriz probably selected for her own reading, and still more for that of her children, those histories which were least objectionable. Nevertheless, the judgment St. Francis of Sales pronounces on balls might be applied with equal truth to romances: " Believe me, Philothea, it is the case with them as with mushrooms, the best of them are good for nothing."

The " passion " for reading of which Teresa speaks had no evil results with her whilst the mother was there to watch over her child. The gentle gravity of Dona Beatriz, her modesty of attire, and unworldli-ness, held out a living example to Teresa's soul which spoke more vividly to it than any folly derived from imaginary heroes or heroines. But no sooner was she left an orphan than, in spite of the confidence with which we have seen her throw herself into the arms of Mary, our saint felt the effects of her imprudence. We will take the touching avowal of her faults from her own words. But before opening those tear-stained pages (similar to those we read in the Confessions of St. Augustine\'7d it will be as well to point out the sense in which we should accept them.

Are we right in drawing the conclusion from Teresa's words that she was a great sinner? If we were required to make this admission in the interests of truth, we should do so without the smallest fear of dimming the

halo which encircles her name. Do Magdalen's sins, the errors and falls of Augustine to which we have just alluded, take away any portion of their glory? Would they, possibly, not even have loved so much if so many sins had not been forgiven them ? With the parable of the debts remitted before our eyes we are inclined to doubt it. Sanctity shows itself under a thousand different forms, and thus in writing the life of our saint we are not going in search of a kind whose beauty we may think suitable to her ; our object is rather to recognize that which is truly hers. What that was the Church's judgment does not leave us for a moment in doubt. 1 Teresa, when quitting the world at the age of sixty-seven, took with her to Heaven an angelic purity of body and soul which she had preserved intact from her childhood till her death. If in her profound humility she makes the most, in her life, of the faults she had committed, never had she sinned grievously. She had faithfully preserved the nuptial robe of innocence which she received in baptism ; our Saviour found a virginal and spotless heart in the spouse He had chosen in order to make of her a victim of His love. How then is it possible that Teresa should have been thus self-deceived? Her candour would surely not permit of her feigning, out of humility, a horror of self such as there was no cause for her experiencing ? We are conscious in these confessions of a sorrow-laden heart, of anguish, and repentance which love of God renders wellnigh inconsolable, of outpourings which come from the very depths of the soul, leaving it torn and transfixed. Why such anguish for a few trifling faults? Later on we hope to clear up this mystery. Meanwhile we would call attention to one fact: Teresa did not write

1 See Acts of Canonization of St. Teresa (Boll., 1241).

the history of her life, with all its faults, till after she had seen in vision our Lord and His angels, and had been given a glimpse of the glories of Heaven.

Now let us hear her speak : "I am filled with sorrow whenever I think of the good desires with which our Lord inspired me, and what a wretched use I made of them. O my Lord, since

Thou art determined to save me—may it be the pleasure of Thy Majesty to effect it!—and to bestow on me so many graces, why has it not been Thy pleasure also, not for my advantage but for Thy greater honour, that this habitation in which Thou hast continually to dwell should have contracted so much defilement? It distresses me even to say this, O my Lord, because I know the fault is all my own, seeing Thou hast left nothing undone to make me, even from my youth, wholly Thine. When I would complain of my parents I cannot do it, for I saw nothing in them but good and carefulness for my welfare. Then, growing up, I began to discover the natural gifts which our Lord had given me—they were said to be many; and when I should have given Him thanks for them, I made use of every one of them, as I shall now explain, to offend Him. ... I began to make much of dress, to wish to please others by my appearance. I took pains with my hands, and my hair, used perfumes, and all vanities within my reach—and they were many, for I was very much given to them. I had no evil intention, for I never wished any one to offend God for me. This fastidiousness of excessive neatness lasted some years ; and so also did other practices which I thought then were not at all sinful : now I see how wrong all this must have been. I had some cousins, for no others were allowed an entrance into my father's house. In this he was very cautious ; and would to God he had been as cautious about

them ! for I see now the danger of conversing at an age when virtue should begin to grow, with persons who, knowing nothing themselves of the vanity of the world, provoke others to throw themselves into the midst of it. These cousins were nearly of mine own age—a little older, perhaps. We were always together, and they had a great affection for me. In everything that gave them pleasure I kept the conversation alive, listened to the stories of their affections and childish follies—all good-for-nothing ; and what was still worse, my soul began to give itself up to that which was the cause of all its disorders. If I were to give advice, I should say to parents that they ought to be very careful whom they allow to mix with their children when young ; for much mischief thence ensues, and our natural inclinations are for evil rather than for good. So it was with me ; for I had a sister much older than myself, from whose modesty and goodness I learned nothing and learned every evil from a relative who was often in the house. Shewas solight and frivolous that my mother took great pains to keep her out of the house, as if she foresaw the evil I should learn from her, but she could not succeed, there being so many reasons for her coming. I was very fond of this person's company, and talked and gossiped with her; for she helped me in all the amusements I liked, and what is more, found some for me, and communicated to me her own conversations and vanities. Until I knew her, I mean until she became friendly with me, and communicated to me her own affairs—I was then fourteen years of age, a little more I think—I do not believe that I turned away from God in mortal sin, or lost the fear of Him, though I had a greater fear of disgrace. This latter fear had such sway over me that I never wholly forfeited my good name—and as to that

there was nothing in the world for which I would have bartered it, and nobody in the world I liked well enough who could have persuaded me to do it. Thus I might have had the strength never to do anything against the honour of God, as I had it by nature not to fail in that wherein I thought the honour of the world consisted, and I never observed that I was failing in many other ways. In vainly seeking after it I was extremely careful, but in the use of the means necessary for preserving it I was utterly careless. I was anxious only not to be lost altogether. This friendship distressed my father and sister exceedingly. They often blamed me for it; but as they could not hinder that person from coming into the house, all their efforts were in vain ; for I was very adroit in doing anything that was wrong. Sometimes I am amazed at the evil one bad companion can do—nor could I believe it if I did not know it by experience—especially when we are young ; then is it that the evil is the greatest. Oh that parents would take warning by me, and look carefully to this ! So it was ; the conversation of this person so changed me, that no trace was left of my soul's natural disposition to virtue, and I became a reflection of her, and of another who was given to the same kind of amusements.

" I know from this the great advantage of good companions ; and I am certain if at that tender age I had been thrown among good people I should have persevered in virtue ; for if at that time I had found anyone to teach me the fear of God, my soul would have grown strong enough not to fall away. Afterwards, when the fear of God had utterly departed from me, the fear of dishonour alone remained, and was a torment to me in all I did. When I thought that nobody would ever know, I ventured on things that were neither honourable nor pleasing unto God. In the beginning these conversations did me harm. I believe so. The fault was perhaps not hers, but mine ; for afterwards my own wickedness was enough to lead me astray, together with the servants about me, whom I found ready enough for evil. If any one of these had given me good advice, I might perhaps have profited by it; but they were blinded by interest as I was by passion. Still I was never inclined to much evil—for I hated naturally anything dishonourable—but only to the amusement of a pleasant conversation. The occasion of sin, however, being present, danger was at hand, and I exposed to it my father and brothers. God delivered me out of it all, so that I should not be lost."

We make a point of giving Teresa's confession in full, leaving it to her to word it in her own simple and natural style. She accuses herself of her faults, but the charm of her personality, the strong and energetic character with which God had endowed her, shows itself in every line, in spite of the efforts she makes to bring out only her defects. We see also how her kindness of heart wins the affection of all around her. A dangerous ascendency for one who would exercise it for selfish ends, instead of in God's service, but a power nothing short of apostolic when used with that object.

It is thus that we may represent to ourselves Teresa at the age of fourteen. She is for the moment forgetful of the aspirations of her childhood, and the graces she had received, and carried away by the charm of loving and being loved. The knowledge gained by the books she has imprudently read, the flattery of the world, the admiration excited by her beauty and charm in those around her, the innocent but too ardent affec-

tion shown her by her cousins, above all the influence of frivolous friends, all contribute to blind her ; her fervour is stifled, and the grave thoughts on which her mind had dwelt in childhood lose their hold upon her. Martyrdom is no longer the object of her desires, nor the Paradise which was to follow martyrdom ; her thoughts turn upon personal adornment, and upon pleasures and entertainments. What she now asks of life are its earthly joys.

The perils to which Teresa was exposed at this time of her life were undoubtedly great. Childlike, she played at the edge of an abyss into which a careless footstep might at any moment have precipitated her. Everything combined against her : her orphan isolation (for' neither father nor sister could take a mother's place), the charm of her brilliant youth, her glowing and expressive countenance, the ardour of her imagination fed upon the thrilling diet of tales of knightly adventure, and the flattery of the little court which had formed itself round her, of which she was the acknowledged queen !

Rodriguez, her pious brother, who had been the confidant of her past fervours, followed her still, but by a very different path. His sympathies were now enlisted in her studies of romances, and Teresa (to whom he was still dearer than her other brothers and sisters), persuading him to act as her secretary, they composed together a romance in the approved style of the day. This tale had, at once, a great success amongst Teresa's friends and admirers. Naturally it shared the defects of the class of literature to which it belonged, but the young girl's talents found such scope for them in a work of imagination, that she now added to her other attractions that of a claim to literary distinction. We have no difficulty therefore in realizing the adulation with

which it was greeted ; thus every day her situation became more dangerous.

And yet, in spite of the pitfalls by which she was surrounded, Teresa escaped with the bloom of her innocence upon her. Mary watched over the child who had thrown herself, as it were, into her arms, and asked her to take the place of a mother to her. For can we believe that Teresa would have found a sufficiently solid rampart in her natural inclination towards goodness, the pride which belonged to her race and nation, her sense of honour, without a very special grace from Heaven? Assuredly not. What strength would a girl of fifteen get from such motives as pride, natural virtue, regard for her good name, to oppose to forces such as we have seen arrayed against her—a current which every moment threatened to carry her away?

God, by the interposition of His divine Providence, safeguarded Teresa through this trial. Her fervour, however, suffered serious loss, and Don Alonso noticed with inward misgiving that his beloved child neglected her prayers, and left off frequenting the churches, whilst she multiplied her pleasures and amusements. Another, and an even more sharp-sighted eye because it was that of a woman— a less indulgent and yet a kindly one too—that of her eldest sister, Maria de Cepeda, was directed upon Teresa. Maria, ever since the death of her stepmother, fulfilled the double duty of mistress of the house and of mother with equal wisdom and firmness. In this twofold capacity, and actuated by a deeply Christian spirit, she longed to banish the germs of worldliness which had found entrance into the home, and to induce Teresa to change her way of life. It was necessary to take a decisive step, and Maria, perceiving this, did not hesitate, after taking the preliminary steps of offering

advice, and even administering gentle rebukes to resort to it. Circumstances lent themselves to a change. Maria was about to be married to an excellent and wellborn gentleman of Castellanos of the name of Martino de Guzman Barrientos. Alonso, in concert with his eldest daughter, therefore took occasion of this event to send Teresa away from home. The sacrifice was a severe one to the father's tender'heart, for Teresa was the joy, the sunshine of his house. But to remain alone with her brothers (the little Juana being her only female companion) was impossible; above all, it was an occasion to break with the bad habits of which we have spoken. It was settled accordingly that Teresa should become a boarder at the convent of the Augustinians of Our Lady of Grace. It was but a short period— three months — which our saint had given up to these- " great vanities," as she was later on to call them. 1 Three months, however, sufficed to weary her of pleasures unworthy of her character. Accordingly her father and sister's wishes not only found her submissive, but ready to fall in with all the arrangements they had made for her. Nothing was said till the last moment of a plan which, when carried out, probably gave rise to some gossip amongst Teresa's friends and relations. Maria de Cepeda's marriage was no sooner celebrated than Teresa quietly disappeared from their midst; and Don Alonso gave her into the hands of the Augustinian Canonesses, recommending her to their care as the greatest treasure he possessed.

1 Teresa adds these words, which are sufficiently explicit: Informada dc con quien me confesaba y de otras personas en muchas cosas me decean no iba contra Dios.

CHAPTER III

THE Monastery of Our Lady of Grace, built in 1508 on the site of an ancient mosque, enjoyed a deserved reputation in Avila for sanctity. The highest families in the city confided their daughters to the Canonesses, in cases when domestic difficulties interfered with a home bringing-up, which, always preferable to any other, was especially so in those ages of faith. A community of forty nuns divided between them the duties required by the education of their pupils and the exercises of religious life. Everything in this holy retreat—the regular observance, the fervour of the religious, and the recent direction of a saint 1 -contributed to render it worthy of the mission which Providence had confided to it of completing Teresa's training and education.

The first few days must have appeared somewhat dreary to the young schoolgirl. Accustomed to the sweetness of home-life and the free use of her own time, and having had three months of constant change and distraction, she probably looked upon the convent grille almost in the light of the bars of a prison. The silence of the convent, in addition to the yoke of obedience, the uniformity of life and recollection of the nuns, all contributed to surround her with an atmosphere of peace which was almost like that of the grave. It was then that her conscience awoke, and no sooner had she emerged from the toils in which her friends

1 St. Peter of Alcantara. 26

had held her captive than she saw her past faults, and exaggerating them she became uneasy, alarmed, and not content with a first confession—a humble avowal of her faults having obtained her forgiveness—she desires to be allowed to humble herself again. This time of anguish was not of long duration. God permitted it in order that the break with the past might be the more entire and complete, but a weak scrupulosity was impossible to one of Teresa's innate sincerity and just judgment. After eight days of interior suffering her conscience resumed its tranquillity, and she soon succumbed to the charm of a convent life from the schoolgirl point of view; u for," she tells us, "I had then only a feeling of dread and dislike to the religious life." But if the prospect of tying herself down for life in a narrow circle bound by strict rules offered her no attraction, she found it pleasant to sojourn for a time, away from worldly noise and distraction, in the company of these holy and peaceful nuns. The calm which at first had alarmed her and the silence which had wearied her were both now a source of pleasure to her, for they allowed her to give herself up more completely to her thoughts and studies.

Maria Briceno, a religious of singular merit, occupied the position of first mistress in the school. Her insight into character soon showed her the treasure hidden in the soul of the new pupil. She lavished upon her a care and solicitude which Teresa responded to by giving her a large share in her affections and confidence. Teresa's heart having been gained, nothing more was necessary than to let her follow its inspirations. She attached herself to Maria Briceno in the same way as she had previously attached herself to her cousin, seeking her company, and every opportunity of talking to her ; and as Maria Briceno was not only a superior

woman but a very holy one, her influence over Teresa was as salutary as that of the other woman had been disastrous. We will learn from Teresa's own words how this transformation was effected : —

"One of the nuns slept with us who were seculars, and through her it pleased our Lord to give me light, as I shall now explain. I began gradually to like the good and holy conversation of this nun. How well she used to speak of God—for she was a person of great discretion and sanctity. I listened to her with delight. I think there never was a time when I was not glad to listen to her. She began by telling me how she came to be a nun through the mere reading of the words of the Gospel. 'Many are called, but few are chosen.' She would speak of the reward which our Lord gives to those who forsake all for His sake. This good companionship began to root out the habits which bad companionship had formed, and to bring my thoughts back to the desire of eternal things as well as to banish in some measure the great dislike I had to be a nun, which had been very great, and if I saw anyone weep in prayer, or devout in any other way, I envied her very much, for my heart was now so hard that I could not shed a tear, even if I read the Psalms through. This was a grief to me. I remained in the convent a year and a half and was very much the better for it. I began to say many vocal prayers, and to ask all the nuns to pray for me, that God would place me in that state wherein I was to serve Him; but for all this I wished not to be a nun, and that God would not be pleased I should be one, though at the same time I was afraid of marriage. At the end of my stay there I had a greater inclination to be a nun, yet not there, on account of certain devotional practices which I understood prevailed there and which I thought overstrained.

Some of the younger ones encouraged me in this my wish, and if all had been of one mind I might have profited by it. I had also a great friend in another monastery, and this made me resolve, if I was to be a nun, not to be one in any other house than where she was. I then looked more to the pleasure of sense and vanity than to the good of my soul. These good thoughts of being a nun came to me from time to time. They left me very soon, and I could not persuade myself to become one. At this time, though I was not careless about my own good, our Lord was much more careful to dispose me for that state of life which was best for me."

After having been a year and a half at the convent Teresa was attacked by a serious illness, which was the cause of her having to leave it. This illness was the beginning of the constant sufferings which she was to endure with cheerful resignation for the space of fifty years. Teresa was then sixteen and a half years of age. She returned to the paternal roof sobered by a solid education, her taste for frivolous pleasures gone, pious enough even to satisfy her excellent father, and as amiable, bright, and ardent in mind and heart as ever. Don Alonso, overjoyed to get his beloved child home again, devoted himself to the restoration of her health ; and to hasten her convalescence took her, himself, to stay with her sister Maria de Cepeda, now the wife of Don Martino Guzman, at their country house at Castellanos.

Teresa enjoyed greatly the beautiful scenery and country life at Castellanos; her health gained by being in the fresh air, and her sister's affection for her created an atmosphere around her which seemed almost too pleasant to last. Teresa says of Maria: " Her love for me was so great that if she had had her will I

should never have left her. Her husband also had a great affection for me, at least he showed me all kindness. This too I owe rather to our Lord, for I have received kindness everywhere, and all my service in return is that I am what I am." The sisters had at last to part, Don Alonso not wishing to be a second time deprived of his daughter's society. On their return journey Teresa and her father stopped for a time at Hortigosa, a place about four leagues out of Avila, where Pedro Sanchez, a brother of Don Alonso, lived. Don Pedro was very desirous of keeping his niece with him a little while, so that Don Alonso having to hurry home on business of importance consented, finally, to leave his daughter with her uncle for a few weeks whilst he returned to Avila. What were these important affairs? Probably they were connected with the grave paternal anxieties which must have preoccupied Don Alonso's mind at this time. We know that Rodriguez, Teresa's beloved brother, solicited his father's leave to join the troops of Pizarro, the conqueror of Peru, and that Don Alonso allowed him to go with his elder brother Hernando. These two brothers by their brilliant success as soldiers were to pave the way in that career for their younger brothers, nearly all of whom were to follow in their footsteps. Rodriguez before leaving Spain drew up a will in Teresa's favour by which she was to inherit all he possessed, as well as his rights to the paternal succession. We regret that our saint should not have related the story of their farewells, when parting for what was to be a lifelong separation. We know, however, that her heart was ever faithful to her dear Rodriguez ; that she sustained him during life by constant prayers, and never ceased honouring him as a martyr when the

brave young man died a glorious death at Rio de la Plata, because, as she believed, he died in the cause of the Faith.

Whilst Rodriguez pursued the dream of his youth across the ocean, Teresa, unknown to him, was preparing to realize the same dream in a very different manner at home.

Don Alonso had left Teresa at Hortigosa in his brother's house. The life of this venerable old man ever since he became a widower had been spent in study and prayer. Our saint, though now very pious, still enjoyed the innocent pleasures of life, so that she found the contrast between the solitude and mortified life led by her uncle and the happy days she had been spending with her sister exceedingly trying. His only conversation was upon the greatness of God and the vanity of earthly things; all his time was employed in studying the works of the Fathers or the mystic treatises of contemporaneous authors. He used to beg of Teresa to be his reader. " Though," as she tells us in her Life, " I did not much like them, yet I appeared as if I did, for in giving pleasure to others I have been most particular, though it might be painful to myself, so much so that what in others might have been a virtue was in me a great fault, because I was often extremely indiscreet."

Teresa's desire to give pleasure was on this occasion amply rewarded. For she had not read Don Pedro's books long before she succumbed to the attraction of a literature which she had so long abandoned. Though Maria Briceno's influence had been exerted with the happiest results in bringing Teresa back to her former practices of piety, she had not been equally successful in inspiring her with a taste for spiritual reading. The rosary was her favourite form of prayer

at this period of her life, and that and a number of vocal prayers filled the hours she reserved for her exercises of devotion. This was not enough for the wants of Teresa's soul, and her aged uncle had the consolation of putting her on another and a more satisfactory path. Thirty years later our saint made use of these words in a transport of gratitude: "I thank God with all my soul (and all women and ignorant people ought to join in thanking Him without ceasing, with me) that men have been found who, by dint of labour, have fought their way to the truth, and have enriched us with their treasures. I have often reflected with astonishment how much the pursuit of knowledge has cost these learned men, whilst for our part we have only to interrogate them to share in all their wisdom. And there are people who do not take the trouble even to profit by it. Please God that may not be the case with us."

Teresa preserved all her life a great love for true knowledge and wisdom, as exemplified in the works of the great doctors of the Church. Later on we shall be given frequent proofs of this fact. Meanwhile, we can picture her to ourselves in the garden of Hortigosa reading, and leisurely enjoying the epistles of St. Jerome, St. Gregory's Morals, and the treatises of St. Augustine. Her uncle, delighted with the interest displayed by his young reader, makes comments on the finest passages of these works. Thus the fascinating scenes of our saint's childhood, the conversations of Rodriguez and his little sister, are renewed between the old man and his niece—the elder already with one foot in the grave, at the decline of a well-spent life, perfected by a great sorrow ; the younger at the dawn of a life which seemed to announce a bright and joyous future. The eyes of both are fixed on one

object: and that is Paradise. They contemplate the nothingness of life ; the rapidity with which it passes, with all its vanities. Eternal life is all they ask for, or desire. How are they to attain to it? Which is the most direct road to Heaven ? This is not the first time this problem had presented itself to Teresa, and we know the ready solution of it in the mind of the would-be martyr of seven years ; but now another is put before her which will test her courage to the utmost, nor will she accept it without long and severe mental struggle.

To offer to God the sacrifice of her life, and thus at the cost of a few hours' agony to gain an eternal crown seemed to the ardent imagination of the child an easy matter, the exchange a wholly desirable one. But to make the same sacrifice by a daily immolation of self, and to continue the work without pause or relaxation, year after year for the rest of her life, was a fate so distasteful to Teresa that it took her three months of inward conflict before she could force her will to make it.

The first encounters only of this interior warfare took place at Hortigosa. Don Alonso came a little later to take away his daughter from his brother's care. Shortly afterwards the latter, notwithstanding his great age, embraced the religious life. His death was the death of a saint, and amongst the merits for which his Saviour rewarded him perhaps not the least was the impetus which he gave to the heart of Teresa towards the cloister.

Thus our saint found on returning to her father's house that her thoughts had taken an entirely fresh direction. The subject of Teresa's vocation is such an interesting one that it cannot be dismissed in a single paragraph.

The world, in the days in which we live, is strangely at fault with regard to a vocation to a religious life. It disposes of the matter as a rule in a summary manner. The young girl (for it is question here of a woman's vocation) who breaks with her relations, and gives up a promising future in order to bury herself in an impenetrable cloister, and clothe her youth and beauty in the rough garments of religion, such a girl, the world decides, is labouring under a fit of enthusiasm which she will pay for dearly by bitter tears in the long years of solitude and subjection which are in store for her.

If this is the ordinary verdict, passed by the crowd on an act of heroism which it is incapable of appreciating, no less unjust is that of the family unless it happens to be a truly Christian one. The girl, the object up td this time of tender care and affection, is now looked upon as a dreamer, a victim of egotism ; her firmness is treated as obstinate pride, her fervour as fanaticism. Probably similar instances are known to us all, in which women with true vocations have been subjected to accusations of this sort and have lived them down by their firmness and constancy. We have followed them to the cloister, and there, possibly after years of religious life, we have found them calm and contented, happier far than they would have thought it possible to be here below ; the family reconciled, friends won over to their cause, and even the world almost ready to own that there are aspirations in the human soul which God alone can satisfy and which cannot be lightly classed under the heading of folly or delusion.

To return to Teresa, let us follow her step by step, and notice what share reason and faith, as opposed to imagination, had in her choice of her vocation. She had had an opportunity whilst at the convent of the

Augustinians of studying closely a religious life. The intimate relations in which she stood to Maria Briceno had enabled her to appreciate the serenity and austere joys which God instils into the heart of those in whom He reigns alone. In spite of the edification she received there her nature rebelled against the life of a nun, and the lesson and example of her mistress had had but little effect in rooting out the invincible repugnance she was conscious of feeling to a cloistered life. The problem of her future, however, had to be solved.

Her spirit of independence made her shrink no less from the ties of married life than from those of monastic vows. An inward monitor warned her that to think of an independent existence was but to indulge in idle dreams ; 'nor did the prospect of such a life offer her any attraction. Between the two vocations, matrimony and the cloister, which was she to choose? Notwithstanding the repugnance she still bore to the latter, all her prayers were directed to imploring our Lord to cause her to embrace the vocation most pleasing to Him, and in which she could best serve Him. When a soul throws itself absolutely on the mercy of God, it is not long kept in suspense; thus Teresa was soon enlightened.

Her thoughts before she left the Augustinians had more than once turned to the religious life, but these were but passing thoughts. They came and went without her giving any assent to them. It was whilst staying with her aged uncle Don Pedro that the Divine Will began to manifest itself in a more distinct and persistent manner to her soul. And in what manner? By extraordinary graces or irresistible attractions? By a Divine summons which would admit of no refusal? We read of nothing of the sort in the history of Teresa's vocation, and if anyone is tempted to regret that the

spiritual espousals of one so eminent in sanctit)^ should have been celebrated in so simple a manner, we on the other hand rejoice that God should have seen fit to give a model to His humblest little ones to follow, rather than a prodigy for their admiration.

A few pious lectures commented on by an old man ; the voice of the mortified hermit of Bethlehem, and of the holy Bishop of Hippo, preaching each in their different style of the vanity of all earthly ambitions, and of the greatness of God ; a few days' retreat in the solitude of Hortigosa: these were the blessed influences which led Teresa to reflect seriously on herself and her destiny in life. She shuddered at the thought that death might have surprised her in the midst of her former frivolities. If the same dangers presented themselves again under another form, would she be stronger to resist them ? It was under these aspects of repentance and fear that she faced the future. Was she going to expose her hopes of eternal welfare to the risks, the snares, the pitfalls of a life in the world? On the other hand, the cloister offered her a shelter where her days would flow peacefully, and where she would pass, in the end, from her cell into Paradise. In short, the religious life was the highest and the safest. Was that not sufficient? Teresa, faithfully corresponding with divine grace which told her that Heaven was worthy of every sacrifice she could make for it, resolved to conquer her distaste for the cloister. She decides she will become a nun, cost her what it may. In Teresa's vocation nothing partakes of the visionary; faith and reason alone influence her decision. Faith submits the grave premisses, to which reason draws an inevitable deduction.

But before Teresa carried out her determination she had still to fight unceasingly the enemy from within.

The fear of God had been the source of her vocation, the enemy of man would fain inspire her with other fears. Brought up delicately as she had been, would she be able to stand the austerities of the cloister? Will she not break down under the yoke of obedience? Is there not reason to fear that after a vain attempt she may have to return to her friends, humbled and confused by her failure? Teresa trod these vain apprehensions underfoot. She contemplated her Saviour's cross, His wounds, His crown of thorns ; it appeared to her that she could well " suffer a little for Him who had suffered so much for love of her." At the same time she told herself that Jesus would be her strength, and that He would give her the courage necessary to support'the trials of a life chosen and embraced for His sake.

St. Jerome, her favourite author, sustained her resolution ; she read and re-read his epistles to Paula, Eustochium, and Heliodorus. Doubtless her thoughts lingered on the following page whence many souls, even less ardent than hers, have imbibed a supernatural strength:—

"O desert, enamelled with the flowers of Christ! Solitude which has given birth to those mysterious stones of which the Apocalypse of the city of the great King is built! Holy retreat where it is given to man to enjoy the familiarities of God Himself! Brother, what have you to do in the world—you who are greater than the world? How much longer will the weight of a roof oppress your head ? How much longer will the prison of towns hold you ? Believe me, I know not how it is, but here there is more light. Here, delivered from the weight of bodily care, the soul takes its flight to Heaven. What do you fear here? Poverty? Jesus has said, * Blessed are the poor.' Work? What

athlete is crowned without a struggle? Are you troubled about what you will eat? He who has faith in Providence is not afraid of hunger. Do you fear to extend your bare limbs, worn with fasting, on the ground? Think! our Lord will repose by your side. . . . Does solitude strike terror in your heart? Let your spirit soar to Heaven ; when your soul is there you are no longer in the desert. In short, the apostle sums up all in a single sentence. He says: * The sufferings of this time are not to be compared to the glory that awaits us.' You ask too much, my brother, if you wish to enjoy the pleasures here below, and then expect to reign with Jesus Christ in Heaven." 1

The prospect of the austerities of a cloistered life was that which affected Teresa least. The loss of her independence attacked her on a more tender point, but what she felt more deeply than anything was the sacrifice of the joys of home-life, and of the paternal tenderness—a sacrifice which cost her much to make, and still more, much more, to impose upon those dear to her. The heart must truly be shattered before it can be given wholly to God. How would it be possible to encounter similar trials were it not that God whispers in the ear those words: " He that loveth father or mother more than me is not worthy of me, and he that taketh not up his cross and followeth me is not worthy of me. . . . Hearken, daughter, and consider and incline thine ear, and forget also thine own people, and thy father's house."

Teresa listened to these words and understood their significance. On the first occasion when she broke the news to her father her words made no impression on him. God, in order possibly to increase the merit of Teresa's sacrifice, permitted that he should refuse to

1 Ep. : St. Jerome to Heliodorus.

hear of her making it. He insisted on his right to retain the daughter whose presence charmed and sanctified his fireside, and after a long struggle, in which Teresa sought to veil her inflexible determination under a cloak of filial love and piety, the father and daughter separated, both with anguish in their hearts, and both inflexible—Don Alonso determined that nothing should induce him to part with his daughter, and Teresa equally determined to belong to God alone. Desirous of using loving and gentle methods only, our saint then applied to her uncle, Don Pedro, and to her sister, Maria, to intercede for her with her father ; her brothers also, in spite of their love for her, pleaded her cause. It was all in vain. The hapless father protested that he could not deprive himself of the society of the best-beloved of his children, and that she must wait for his death in order to be free to carry out her wishes.

" I now began," Teresa tells us, "to be afraid of my own weakness, for I felt I might go back. So considering that such waiting was not safe for me, I obtained my end in another way."

CHAPTER IV

SAN MIGUEL, the hereditary domain of Dona Elvira de Medina, was situated to the northerly side of Avila, at the foot of the hill crowned by that city, in a wooded valley, which like all the rest of that neighbourhood has a beauty and picturesqueness of its own. Dona Elvira, we are told by Lezana in the Carmelite Annals, made over her patrimony to the Blessed Virgin, and built the Carmelite monastery of the Incarnation upon it. The first Mass in the monastery chapel, as we have already mentioned, was celebrated on the very day of Teresa's birth. Again, it was close to this holy spot that our little seven-year-old heroine was arrested in her flight, and whence she had sorrowfully to retrace her steps, and follow the uncle who brought her back to her mother's arms. A double coincidence which the future was to render even more striking, for it was here that Teresa was to endure her martyrdom of love united to Jesus hidden beneath the sacramental veil.

The monastery was a large one, as Dofia Elvira de Medina's generosity enabled the Carmelites to add more than once to the size of their buildings, so that they had room for a great number of nuns. Lezana relates that in the year 1550 they counted 190 in the community, but in 1533, the period to which we refer, they were probably far short of this number. A friend of Teresa's had taken the veil at the monastery but a few years before. Juana Suarez was a true sister of

Maria Briceno, in the sense that she was a model religious, remarkable for her fidelity to her Rule. Teresa was so deeply attached to her that she almost feared for a moment that her choice of the monastery of the Incarnation in preference for the Augustinian convent was influenced by her affection for her. Accordingly, she tells us that this was " the monastery where that friend of mine lived for whom I had so great an affection ; though I would have gone to any other if I had thought I should serve God better in it, or to any one my father liked, so strong was my resolution now to become a nun, for I thought more of the salvation of my soul now, and made no account whatever of mine own ease."

Juana Suarez on her side seconded Teresa's wishes with her own fervent prayers, recommending her also to those of her companions. Teresa found comfort and support also in one of her brothers; not her dear Rodriguez, who had departed to the New World, but in Antonio, who, younger than her by two years, was worthy of understanding his sister and taking example of her. Let us now listen to her account of the manner in which she carried out her design.

"In those days when I was thus resolved, I had persuaded one of my brothers, by speaking of the vanity of the world, to become a friar, and we agreed to set out one day very early in the morning for the monastery. ... I remember perfectly well (and it is quite true) that the pain I felt when I left my father's house was so great that I do not believe the pain of dying will be greater, for it seemed to me as if every bone in my body were wrenched asunder ; for as I had no love of God to destroy the love of father, and of kindred, this latter love came upon me with a violence

so great that if our Lord had not been my Keeper, my own resolution to go on would have failed me. But He gave me courage to fight against myself, so that I executed my purpose."

Antonio, faithful to his promise, accompanied Teresa to the door of the monastery of the Incarnation. Leaving her there, in the hands of the Prioress and Juana Suarez, he proceeded on his way to the Fathers of St. Thomas, to ask of them the habit of St. Dominic.

The brother and sister had made a wise choice of the day of their sacrifice. The bells of Avila were tolling for the dead, and the sound of the sad and peaceful requiem was the first that greeted Teresa's ears when she entered the chapel. It was the feast of All Souls' ; who on that day does not feel how little anything matters which concerns this world only—how much all that concerns the next? Soon the prayers for the dead ceased ; and according to the custom of those times, Teresa exchanged that same day her secular dress for the monastic habit. Happy to be delivered from vanities which she still feared but had ceased to care for, she allowed her beautiful hair—true Spanish ornament—to be cut off, and humbly wrapping herself up in the folds of her white veil, she took the last place amongst the postulants, buried herself in prayer, and passed the rest of the day in peaceful and joyous seclusion, a prelude to the happy days which were to come in her holy noviceship. Shortly afterwards Don Alonso came to the monastery to give her in person the permission he had till then withheld. All Teresa's wishes were now fulfilled, and the effort she had made to part with her father was compensated by the increased love and sympathy which was ever afterwards to subsist between them. By degrees their affection for each

other assumed a still more supernatural and touching character. For Teresa's natural ascendancy showing itself in spite of all she could do, it was the father who put himself under the spiritual guidance of the young novice, and learnt from her the way of perfection : a first conquest for the Carmelite in a field where she was to make so many more for the glory of God and the good of souls. The brothers also soon found their way to the convent parlour. They were at the age when the great question of their careers had to be decided on, and each had his secret trials and difficulties. Teresa had a kind and loving word for all ; and who could resist her burning words when she spoke of the love of God, or of the happiness of serving Him in the person of their'neighbour? Lorenzo, under her influence, grew up to be a model Christian, and worthy son of Don Alonso. Geronimo, " our excellent Geronimo," as Teresa loved to call him, though his heart was in his martial exercises, did not on that account neglect his work nor his religious duties. Augustine, ambitious though he was by nature, learned to set a higher value on the things of eternity than upon worldly honours. Antonio, the young Dominican, even came from time to time to excite his soul to fresh fervour by the side of her who had done so much to help him on the path to Heaven. As for Juana, her greatest pleasure was to visit her sister, and Don Alonso, desiring to give her the benefit of having her education directed by Teresa, imposed yet another sacrifice upon himself, and brought his little Benjamin to the monastery to be educated.

Having given one glance over the family history, let us follow Teresa through the exercises of her novice-ship. The history of saints is above all the history of their souls : of their intercourse with God through

prayer and love and with their brethren through charity. If this axiom holds good with regard to all saints it is more especially applicable to Teresa, who was hereafter to attain in so eminent a degree that state of perfect detachment in which the human ego becomes wholly effaced, and the soul can say with the apostle, " I live, not I, but Christ lives in me."

We are still at the foot of this holy mountain—that of perfection—which Teresa was to ascend, not at one bound, but at first with alternate steps of fervour and tepidity. A moment will come when the dove will mount with the wings of an eagle up to the very summit. At present she is still threading her way through the valleys, where it is necessary to advance slowly before attempting a long flight.

If we give a general survey of the first year of Teresa's religious life, we see her sustained by divine grace and encouraged by sensible devotion. She readily submits to monastic observance, she prays much, and puts her willing aid at the service of all, with a goodness and amiability which is peculiar to her. She is satisfied with small things, which her practical good sense makes her appreciate at their true worth ; and feeling incapable as yet of offering God great and overwhelming proofs of her love for Him, or of her zeal for His service, she loses no occasion of making the utmost of the lesser ones. Again, when, in spite of her persevering efforts to conquer herself, she is conscious that nature, her instincts and inclinations, are not to be mastered at a single blow, she suffers, she struggles against them, and by this interior combat she prepares for the day when she will give herself wholly to God in her religious profession. With her usual delightful simplicity our saint gives us every detail of her new life. Her first start was at the cost

of an unspeakable effort. It seemed to her at the time like passing through the portal of death ; but she had not to wait long before reaping her reward.

" When I took the habit our Lord at once made me understand how He helps those who do violence to themselves in order to serve Him. No one observed this violence in me ; they saw nothing but the greatest good will. At that moment because I was entering on that state I was filled with a joy so great, that it has never failed me to this day, and God converted the aridity of my soul into the greatest tenderness. Everything in religion was a delight unto me, and it is true that now and then I used to sweep the house during those hours of the day which I had formerly spent on my dress and amusements, and calling to mind that I was delivered from such follies, I was filled with a new joy that surprised me, nor could I understand whence it came. Whenever I remember this, there is nothing in the world, however hard it may be, that, if it were proposed to me, I would not undertake without any hesitation whatever, for I know now by experience in many things that if from the first I resolutely persevere in my purpose, even in this life His Majesty rewards it in a way which he only understands who has tried it. When the act is done for God only, it is His will before we begin it that the soul, in order to the increase of its merits, should be afraid, and the greater the fear if we do but succeed, the greater the reward, and the sweetness thence afterwards resulting."

Overwhelmed with spiritual favours, Teresa found in the much feared cloister the ante-room to Paradise. Not satisfied with the prayers specified by the Rule, all her spare time was spent in praying. She used to be constantly seen prostrate before the Tabernacle wrapt in contemplation, whilst tears of ardent love, and re-

pentance for her past infidelities flowed from her eyes. Teresa's behaviour probably did not pass without comment ; the fervent who were in sympathy with her prophesied that God had many graces in store for the holy novice ; the lukewarm and indifferent were probably inclined to find fault with what they looked upon as an exaggeration of piety. Teresa was silent, and though, as we shall see later on, she was not indifferent to what was said about her, she kept straight on towards the goal she had in view, looking neither to right nor to left. To seek God, to go to Him ; this was the object of all her thoughts and her desires.

Teresa's deepest study was given to the Rule of her Order, and all her efforts were directed to keeping it in its integrity. She was especially attentive to her duties in choir, and the elder nuns were edified to observe that she was ever amongst the first to take her place there, and that her recollected behaviour, and fidelity to the ceremonies prescribed, were those of a professed nun rather than that of a youthful novice. If any slight breach of the Rule escaped her vigilance, she made haste to repair her fault by the usual penances, with a simplicity and humility which touched and delighted all who saw her. Religious life, however, is not only the life of a soul with her God, it is also community life; the life of a daughter with her mother, the life of a sister with sisters. Teresa sought, in the sanctified affections of the cloister, food for a heart which divine love had never cooled, nor for a moment narrowed in its love for those around her. To realize this it is only necessary to study the history of her life.

To live without loving, without giving, without devoting oneself to some living object:

that is not to be alive at all. And should this page come before

the eye of some prejudiced individual who entertains the strange theory that the cloister is the death of human affections, we would recall to him the fundamental rule of the Divine Teacher's doctrine : " Thou shalt love the Lord thy God above all things, and thy neighbour as thyself. " One who enters holy Religion— be it man or woman—who pronounces his vows, abandons the world, and keeps the Counsels of perfection, does so only in order to fulfil more integrally this supreme law ; that is, in order to love and serve God better, and to love man, and love him more wisely, for God's sake.

It was in this sense undoubtedly that Teresa understood her vocation. If she excelled in one virtue more than another whilst in the noviceship, it was in her ardent and watchful love for her neighbour. Happy to be the last in the house, she took advantage of the fact to claim various privileges which she would on no account surrender to anyone else. If there was any disaster that had to be repaired, any menial or distasteful work to be undertaken, the young novice was always the first on the spot, either to acquit herself quietly of the task, or to claim it as her special duty. If one of the older sisters was engaged in carrying a load of any sort, Teresa was at once at her side, dividing the labour with her; and these services were given in so affectionate and cheerful a manner as to leave the impression on the recipient that she was conferring rather than receiving a favour. One of her resolutions was never to allow a day to pass without performing some act of charity. Sometimes when kneeling at her night-prayers, and going over in thought her day's occupation, she reproached herself with not having assisted her companions as much as she might have done ; perhaps whilst thus engaged

she would hear an uncertain and tottering step in the cloisters, revealing the fact that a sister was groping her way in the dark to her cell. Instantly Teresa would take her lamp and, going to the nun's assistance, light up her way for her, and escort her to bed. 1 Then she would thank God for the opportunity He had given her of thus repairing a little the negligences of the day. It was in truth a flower in the wreath of her good actions which her angel guardian wove for her that day. These things were doubtless trifles, but God knows their value, and He recognizes that the love which lies below them is no trifle. Again, as the occasions grew for the exercise of this great virtue, the novice's charity grew and kept pace with them. To satisfy her desire to devote herself to the service of her neighbour she had been employed in the infirmary work, which was generally given to professed nuns only. Neither fatigue, nor night watching, nor services, sometimes of the most trying and revolting nature, appeared to cost her anything. The sick cheered up the moment they saw the flutter of her white veil in the distance. All felt that they could ask what they liked of Teresa without risk of exhausting her patience ; and however weary she might be, she would still have a gentle and loving word or thought to give to those whose sufferings even her charitable care had not sufficed to alleviate. There was one nun amongst the inmates of the infirmary who had been attacked by a disease of which the sight alone was a trial to all around her. Her body was covered with ulcers of a nature so terrible and deep-seated that the little nourishment she contrived to take used to be forcibly ejected, with much pain, through them. The unfortunate patient, resigned to the Divine Will,

1 Ribera.

blessed God, and endured her cross in silence. Teresa, witness of her resignation, and of the involuntary horror produced by her malady, obtained leave to devote herself entirely to her service. Her power over herself enabled her to triumph over every feeling of natural fastidiousness. She used to kiss the hands of her dear patient, sit near her, and take her meals at her bedside ; in short, she manifested in every possible way that, far from feeling any sort of disgust for her, she took the utmost pleasure in serving her. "All the sisters," Teresa tells us, "were afraid of her malady. I envied her patience very much, and I prayed to God that He would give me a like patience ; and then, whatever sickness it might be His pleasure to send, I do not think I was afraid of any, for I was resolved on gaining eternal good, and determined to gain it by any and by every means. I am surprised at myself now, because I had not then, as I believe, that love of God which I think 1 had after I began to pray. Then I had only light to see that all things that pass away are to be lightly esteemed, and that the good things to be gained by despising these are of great price, because they are eternal." Shortly afterwards the holy nun went to her reward, and God heard Teresa's prayers by sending her an illness which, though it differed in its nature from that of her patient, equalled it in severity. In order to enable her to receive the graces of her profession, God gave her sufficient health to enable her to follow the Rule until the day arrived for her to pronounce her vows. The change of life and of food brought on faintness, it is true, and other symptoms of failing health, but the novice endured these troubles with such courage and equanimity that her superior attached but little importance to them, and Teresa still less. Providence

allowed her to pass through other trials which touched her far more deeply ; these we will give in her own words :—

" I forgot to say how in the year of my novitiate I suffered much uneasiness about things in themselves of no importance, but I was found fault with very often when I was blameless. I bore it painfully and with imperfection, however. I went through it all because of the joy I had in being a nun. . . . All religious observances had an attraction for me, but I could not endure any which seemed to make me contemptible. I delighted in being thought well of by others, and was very exact in everything I had to do. All this I thought was a virtue, though it will not serve as any excuse for me, because I knew what it was to procure my own satisfaction in everything."

These are the shadows cast by nature upon the work of grace. Teresa was still sensitive on the point of her reputation and of the confidence and affection in which she was held. She suffered because the hearts of those around her to whom she tendered a sister's love did not always respond to it, nor understand her. She felt herself neglected, who at home had ever been accustomed to having her smallest desires complied with by father, brothers, and friends, and was the object of their tender sympathy and affection. What was she to do ? Retreat ? Go back to joys which she had been prepared to renounce for ever? No! Her courage tramples upon these feeble obstacles, and ever advancing in the paths of perfection, humbling herself before her weakness, and deploring her too sensitive nature, Teresa, on the 3rd of November, 1534, with equal resolution and joy, pronounces the solemn words of her profession. Thirty years later, when she had received signal graces from God, the recollection of

her profession was still dearer 1 to her than any other, and she will even then look upon this day of her spiritual espousals as the greatest in her life.

1 Later on Teresa, in a time of special trial, says : " I do not think my sufferings were greater even on the day of my profession." But we need see no contradiction in these two statements. The saint enjoyed spiritual consolation in proportion to the sacrifice she was making-, and the sacrifice was one she felt most deeply.

CHAPTER V

TERESA, referring to the year of her profession, says: "Though my happiness was great, that was not enough ; 1 the fainting-fits began to be more frequent, and my heart was so seriously affected that everyone who saw me was alarmed, and I had also other ailments. And thus it was that I spent the first year, having very bad health, though I do not think I offended God in it much."

Our Lord answered Teresa's prayer, addressed to Him from the bedside of the dying nun the previous year. He sent her equal suffering, and the grace of bearing her suffering with equal patience.

The hours appear long in the infirmary when bodily pangs and the weariness of bad health are combined with the deprivation of the monastic exercises which alone fill and animate community life. The young nun with her natural energy and her love of the Rule found in her enforced inaction a grand occasion for the practice of patience. She accepted it; she received the services of her sisters with a gratitude only equal to the eagerness with which she had, when she had been able, offered her own. Her great weakness frequently prevented her from having recourse to spiritual reading, which was the one recreation for which she longed. She could supply this great privation only by recalling to mind passages in books she had previously read. The works of the Fathers were familiar

1 e.g. Not enough to cure her body.

to her, and no doubt when reading St. Gregory the Great's commentary on Job her mind dwelt on the words of that holy patriarch: " If we have received good things at the hand of God, why should we not receive evil? Blessed be the name of the Lord." Her patience edified the whole community, and if anyone had asked her the secret of her peace of mind she might possibly have answered in the words we have already quoted from her life: "It seems to me that I did not offend God in it much." Don Alonso, distressed by the state of his daughter's health, took one doctor after another to see her, but after trying their skill upon her they all declared that she was suffering from an incurable disease. In despair at their want of success Alonso determined to try what a quack doctress, to whom marvellous cures were attributed, could do for Teresa. This woman lived at Becedas, at a considerable distance from Avila, but with the superior's permission (the convent of the Incarnation not being enclosed), Alonso made up his mind to take his daughter to consult her. Accordingly Teresa was confided to her father's care, and, accompanied by Juana Sanchez, she set out on this long journey with little expectation on the part of those she left behind that they would ever see her again.

It was the month of November, 1535, and the fatigues of the journey were rendered more trying by the cold of early winter. The travellers' first halting-place was at Hortigosa. Here her uncle, Don Pedro, surrounded her with every care and attention ; he also presented her with "an excellent book on Recollection," Teresa tells us, by Fr. Osuna. "I did not know how to make my prayer nor how to recollect myself. I was therefore much pleased with the book,

and resolved to follow the way of prayer it described with all my might."

From Hortigosa Teresa was taken by her father to Castellanos, where she was anxiously awaited by Dofia Maria de Cepeda and Don Martino de Guzman. The travellers decided on spending the winter here, and postponing the cure till the spring. We see, therefore, the holy nun once more restored to her family.

Teresa's sufferings would have served in the case of many as a plea for the suspension of a regular course of devotional exercises, and, moreover, would have permitted the enjoyment of attentions such as are ever lavished on invalids. But Teresa's cross was too dear to her to admit of her losing any particle of it. She seized the opportunity accordingly of her residence at Castellanos to begin to lead the life of recollection and prayer recommended in the treatise given to her by her uncle. This book became her guide and her master. It prescribed solitude and silence, accompanied by great purity of heart. Teresa found that these precepts were compatible with the life she was forced to lead, and she contrived to give some hours daily to recollection. Neither her father nor sister tried to interfere with her purpose. Both recognized that she belonged more to God than to them, and venerated in their dear invalid the spouse of Jesus Christ. The winter passed quickly for all except Teresa, whose sufferings increased daily in severity.

It was decided that the doctress should begin her course of treatment in April; accordingly the travellers resumed their journey early in that month, accompanied by Dofia Maria. They travelled slowly out of consideration for Teresa's health ; her weakness was so great that she fainted repeatedly on the road. This was but the Way of the Cross: Teresa found her

Calvary at Becedas. Confided by her father into the hands of a woman whose foolhardiness was only equalled by her ignorance, Teresa became a victim of desperate remedies applied without knowledge or discrimination. She was consumed day and night by fever, and unable to digest any food. An interior fire appeared to prey on her vitals, and so acute were the pains she endured that it seemed as if her heart was being torn on the teeth of a rack. Finally a universal contraction of nerves, the result of her sufferings and weakness, left her, to use her own expression, in torture from head to foot. Don Alonso, in despair at the state to which she was reduced, brought her back three months later to Avila. Before taking up her history again, we will let our saint tell us in her own words how God was carrying out His great work in her soul at a period when, joyous and calm as ever, she had surrendered herself to pains worse than those of martyrdom. The treatment she went through at Becedas had had no effect in making her relax her fervour; all this time she never ceased applying her mind to prayer and spiritual reading.

" From the beginning God was most gracious to me," Teresa says. " At the end of my stay there (I spent nearly nine months in the practice of solitude) our Lord began to comfort me so much in this way of prayer as in His mercy to raise me to the prayer of quiet, and now and then to that of union, though I understood not what either the one or the other was nor the great esteem I ought to have had of them. I believe it would have been a great blessing to me if I had understood the matter. It is true that the prayer of union lasted but a short time. I know not if it continued for the space of an Ave Maria; but the fruits of it remained ; and these were such that though I was

then not twenty years of age I seemed to despise the world utterly; and so I remember how sorry I was for those who followed its ways, though only in things lawful. I used to labour with all my might to imagine Jesus Christ, our God and our Lord, present within me. And this was the way I prayed. If I meditated on any mystery of His life, I represented it to myself as within me, though the greater part of my time I spent in reading good books, in which I took all my comfort."

Teresa drew from this spirit of prayer the actual graces of which she was so greatly in need, such as an unfailing patience amidst her pains. At the same time the unbroken union between her innocent soul and God developed in her the distinctive marks of her sanctity, which was that of love: divine love and love of souls ; the ardent, self-effacing, zealous love of which her name has become almost a symbol. Circumstances of a very delicate nature were the cause at this time of her beginning her first mission for the conversion of sinners. Up to this moment we have only seen her exert her influence over the pure and the good, in short such who asked her advice and were prepared to follow it; we shall now see her rescuing a sinner from the degradation of a bad life, and bringing him back to God.

On her first arrival at Becedas, Teresa, according to her custom, asked for a confessor in order to approach the Sacraments. A priest was brought to her who, though of good birth (she mentions) and naturally intelligent, was no theologian. She soon perceived his ignorance, and deeply regretted it, for she had a strong predilection for enlightened confessors. Still, as she had been brought into relations with him she did not judge it necessary, considering the short time

she was to spend at Becedas, to apply for another priest. Accordingly she went to confession to him. This unfortunate man, however, bore a greater stain on his conscience than that of ignorance; and no sooner had Teresa revealed her soul to him, and he saw her shedding tears of contrition over the trifling faults which had escaped her watchfulness over herself, that he noted her humility, her union with God, than he was overcome by a sense of his own degradation. Unable to master his feelings, he allowed an admission of the scandalous and sacrilegious life he had been leading for seven years to escape him. Teresa, taken by surprise and no less distressed than horrified, was determined to do her utmost to save him at all costs. The undertaking was not without its perils ; and the saint, later on recognizing them, accused herself of rashness—such as her inexperience alone excused. Her single-mindedness and simplicity, however, the ardour of her zeal, and God's protection enabled her to surmount all difficulties. She prayed with all her heart for this soul whom she saw on the point of shipwrecking, and adjured him to turn to God, whose servant he was, and repent while there was still time. Faith was not extinct in the man's heart, though his passions had over-mastered it. Teresa's words awakened it anew. Before long he broke the disgraceful ties that bound him, humbly sought to repair the scandal he had given, and earned by the fervour of his repentance the grace, a year after he had made the acquaintance with our saint, of a holy and contrite death.

Teresa needed all the consolation such a triumph of divine grace must have given her in the ever-increasing sufferings which followed this event, accompanied as they were by great spiritual desolation. The resigna-

tion with which she bore all these trials was not shared by Don Alonso, who, in despair at the consequences of her medical treatment at Becedas, brought her back a few weeks later to Avila. The return journey was again followed by fresh fatigues and greater suffering. Finally Teresa reached the paternal roof in the month of July in a wellnigh dying condition. The vigil of the feast of the Assumption arrived, and Teresa asked for her confessor in order to prepare for receiving Holy Communion the following day. She expressed this desire with so much earnestness, and her father was so forcibly struck with the idea that she believed herself to be at the point of death, that to dispel this impression, by proving to her that he did not share it, he refused to send for a priest.

" That very night," she says, " my sickness became so acute that for four days I remained insensible. They administered the Sacrament of the last Anointing, and every hour, or rather every moment, thought I was dying ; they did nothing but repeat the Credo— as if I could understand anything they said. They must have regarded me as dead more than once, for I found afterwards drops of wax on my eyelids. My father, because he had not allowed me to go to confession, was grievously distressed, and many prayers were made to God ; blessed be He Who heard them ! "

So alarmingly ill was our saint that the report of her death was spread in the town of Avila. The nuns of the convent of the Incarnation prepared her grave, and sent two sisters of the Order to render the last services to her body and watch beside it in the coffin. The Carmelites in a neighbouring monastery celebrated a solemn requiem for the repose of her soul. Her family felt that they were but watching beside a corpse ;

her father alone preserved hope in the midst of his anguish. Love and sorrow united in the cry which he sent up in his heart to the Throne of Grace to implore God's mercy on his beloved daughter that she might not suffer from the effects of his too great paternal tenderness. He sought to warm Teresa's icy hands in his own, and to those who wished to lead him away from her bedside he repeated emphatically the same words: " She is not dead. I know it. She is not going to die. Leave me here." 1

At last, on the fourth day of her illness, Teresa opened her eyes, and, with a smile for her father and brothers, quietly reproached them for recalling her to earth after she had begun to taste the joys of Heaven. Other words also fell from her lips which revealed some part of the mysteries into which she had been initiated during her long sleep. She had not only been given a glimpse of the joys of Paradise, but she had also sounded with one look the abysses of hell ; and God, before restoring her to life, had in part revealed to her the great destiny He had reserved for her, and which He had sent her back to the world to accomplish. Such were some of the words and impressions which Teresa allowed to escape her in waking from her slumber, perhaps hardly realizing what she said. When those around her recalled them to her later, she blushed and treated all she had then said as idle dreams. Her humility ever found a good excuse for passing lightly over anything which would raise her in the estimation of others. We shall also see at a later period the extreme caution and diffidence with which she received visions, and various other supernatural manifestations, which at different times were vouchsafed to her, in spite of the indubitable marks which they

carried with them of their divine origin. Humility apart, it is quite possible that our saint at that time should have taken the extraordinary favours she received from God, whilst lying in an unconscious state, for idle phantoms of her brain. The future, however, was to show her whence they came ; and Teresa, enlightened then by years of experience, and better instructed in the secrets of the supernatural life, admitted to her spiritual daughters that in her youth, when in extreme danger, God had showed her heaven and hell in a vision, and had foretold to her the good she was to effect in her Order, the holy death she was to obtain for her father and Juana Sanchez by her prayers, and finally the happy one which was to terminate her own existence, and the halo with which posterity was to surround her name.

As soon as she recovered consciousness Teresa asked once more for the Sacraments. When the priest brought her holy Viaticum she shed tears of devotion, and after having communicated she remained long absorbed in sentiments of ardent love and compunction, to which the sufferings, which lost no time in returning, appeared to contribute rather than to diminish. Her throat was dried up to such an extent that it was not possible for her to swallow a drop of water ; she could only breathe with extreme pain and difficulty ; her contracted nerves distorted all her body, her helpless limbs refused to render her any service, so that without assistance she could neither use hands nor feet, nor arms nor head. She remained in this state from the Feast of Assumption, 1526, to the Easter of the following year. A slight improvement then rendered her removal possible, though she was still bedridden, to her monastery. The grief of being away from it added to her other sufferings, and Don Alonso found himself obliged

to agree with her wishes; the poor father could no longer dispute the possession of his child with God.

Accordingly the Carmelites received once more the victim who, four years previously, had brought her youth and happiness to immolate it at the foot of the altar. The sacrifice had been accepted, and consummated. Teresa was but a shadow of her former self, and it was with profound compassion that the nuns perceived the awful ravages that illness had made on the frame of the humble and patient sufferer. Eight months passed before she was able to leave her bed. She began early in the following year, 1538 (as she says in her Life) to drag herself about; a huge progress, and one which filled her with joy, because she could then help herself in many ways and thus save trouble to her sisters. She now believed that her illness would be chronic ; her limbs remained ever in the same helpless and incapable state, and the doctors judged that she was suffering from incurable paralysis. In this state, always infirm, nearly always in bed, the years 1538 and 1539 rolled by for our saint without giving her any reason to hope for any favourable change in the future. It was not without a hidden purpose that God thus kept Teresa on the Cross. He was completing the inner education and training of her soul and preparing her for her future mission. She was to suffer much in order to comprehend at the same time the price of suffering and its severity, in order to know what she had to offer to God, and what she had to ask of souls in the time when she was to devote her Order to the sacrifices and immolations of an apostleship of expiation.

But this design of God's, though she had a glimpse of it for one moment in the great crisis of her illness, was nevertheless still hidden from her. She suffered

in patience, abandoning herself to God's good pleasure without thought of the morrow, only intent on praying and practising the solid Christian virtues—above all that favourite one of hers, charity. Let us hear her impressions of those days from her own lips; her straightforward, simple character, full alike of love and ardour, reveals itself in every line :—

"I bore all this with great resignation and, if I except the beginning of my illness, with great joy ; for all this was nothing in comparison with the pains and tortures I had to bear at first. I was resigned to the Will of God, even if He left me in this state for ever. My anxiety about the recovery of my health seemed to be grounded on my desire to pray in solitude as I had been taught; for there was no means of doing so in the infirmary. . . . They all marvelled at the patience which our Lord gave me—for if it had not come from the hand of His Majesty it seemed impossible to endure so great an affliction with so great joy. It was a great thing for me to have had the grace of prayer, which God had wrought in me ; it made me understand what it is to'love Him. In a little while I saw these virtues renewed within me ; still they were not strong, for they were not sufficient to sustain me in justice. I never spoke ill in the slightest degree whatever of anyone, and my ordinary practice was to avoid all detraction ; for I used to keep most carefully in mind that I ought not to assent to, nor say of another, anything I should not like said of myself. I was extremely careful to keep this resolution on all occasions ; though not so perfectly upon some great occasions that presented themselves sometimes. But my ordinary practice was this; and those who were about me, and those with whom I conversed, became so convinced that it was right that they adopted it as a habit. It came to be understood

that where I was, absent persons were safe; so they were also with my friends and kindred, and with those whom I instructed. Still, for all this I have a strict account to give unto God for the bad example I gave in other respects. May it please His Majesty to forgive me, for I have been the cause of much evil ; though not with intentions as perverse as were the acts that followed. The longing for solitude remained, and I loved to discourse and speak of God ; for if I found anyone with whom I could do so, it was a greater joy and satisfaction to me than all the refinements, or rather, to speak more correctly, the impertinences, of the world's conversation. I communicated and confessed more frequently still, and desired to do so. I was most extremely fond of reading good books ; I was deeply penitent for having offended God ; and I remember that very often I did not dare to pray, because I was afraid of that most bitter anguish which I felt for having offended God—dreading it as a great chastisement."

We shall learn more, later on, about these faults with which Teresa reproaches herself. Meanwhile, let us sum up in a few words the effect of the picture she presents to us of her interior life. Prayer is the principle, the foundation stone, and the food of her life, and that life unfolds itself under the aspects of an ever-patient resignation, a charity, and burning zeal for souls. This is Teresa at the age of twenty-four. Do we not recognize Rodriguez's little sister, the child in love with martyrdom, in the description ? What harmony there is in every event of this astounding life ! To go to God ; to be united to Him, and lead souls to His feet. This is the predominant idea, or, to put it in other words, the sublime passion of this valiant soul. From childhood to the grave Teresa knew no other.

These years of acute suffering had borne their fruit. It was time the patient victim, who up to this could only merit by her sufferings and her prayers, should be restored to her community and to the Church. Though Teresa would have wished to be cured in order better to serve her divine Spouse, yet she had never asked this grace of Him, desiring only to abandon herself in all things to His good pleasure. A secret inspiration caused her to change her mind. Thus she tells us in her Life : " When I saw how helpless I was through paralysis, being still so young, and how the physicians of this world had dealt with me, I determined to ask those of Heaven to heal me, for 1 wished to be well, though nevertheless I bore my illness with great joy. I began by having masses and prayers said for my intention-prayers that were highly sanctioned—for I never liked those other devotions which some people, especially women, make use of with a ceremoniousness to me intolerable, but which move them to devotion. I have since learnt that they were unseemly and superstitious. And I took for my patron and lord the glorious St. Joseph, and recommended myself earnestly to him. ... I cannot call to mind that I have ever asked him at any time for anything that he has not granted ; and I am filled with amazement when I consider the great favours which God hath given me through this great saint—the danger from which he hath delivered me, both of body and soul. To other saints our Lord seems to have given grace to succour men in some special necessity, but to this glorious saint, I know by experience, to help us in all."

We should have much wished to have heard from our saint how she was cured. But carried away by filial piety to him whom she never ceased to describe as her " beloved Father St. Joseph," she leaves her

story unfinished, and gives herself up to the joy of glorifying the saint of her predilection. Two pages of that natural eloquence of the heart for which she is distinguished are the tribute of gratitude which Teresa lays at the feet of St. Joseph, little dreaming that they would be the text of many devout works written in succeeding ages in praise of the saint. We shall see how Teresa's devotion to St. Joseph increases with the growth of her sanctity, and we shall see her later on, in gratitude of the favour she had received from him, dedicating chapels and monasteries to his name.

" I do not know how anyone," she says, " can think of the Queen of Angels, during the time she suffered so much with the Infant Jesus, without giving thanks to St. Joseph for the service he has rendered them. He who cannot find anyone to teach him how to pray, let him take this glorious saint for his master, and he will not wander out of the way."

Coming back to her own history, two words suffice her to show the miraculous nature of her cure: " Though I publicly profess my devotion to him, I have always failed in my service to him, and imitation of him. He was like himself when he made me able to rise and walk—no longer a paralytic—and I too am like myself when I make so bad a use of this grace."

Teresa wishe(j to testify her gratitude to God for her cure by taking up at once with renewed fervour the exercises of community life. Those who have gone through a similar experience will easily represent to themselves Teresa's joy in returning to life after having been held in the clutches of what might be called a living death for so long. Teresa was not insensible to this happiness ; her love of God grew with it, and she longed, now that she was restored to life, to realize the fervent desires of her sick bed. And yet,

notwithstanding all this, sixteen long years were to elapse before her soul was to take that astounding flight to the heights of perfection and contemplation in which her later years were to be consummated. A great distance still lies before us which separates Teresa de Ahumada from Teresa of Jesus.

CHAPTER VI

THE period of Teresa's history which we have now reached requires more than a passing comment. As we have said once before, we are not engaged in writing Teresa's panegyric, but her life. It is undoubtedly true that a saint's biographer is sometimes apt to allow his enthusiasm to colour his story, but it is of the utmost importance that he should preserve its historic character intact, and not pass the limits of scrupulous veracity. The period to which we allude is the one she afterwards called " the time of her great dissipation, of her vanity." She accuses herself of lukewarmness, and of resistance to grace, and, to believe her, these faults were of a grave character. Against her own testimony we must set that of her biographers Yepes and Ribera, both of whom were intimately acquainted with her and had heard her confessions. We have in addition to their affirmations—which were worded in the strongest terms—the decisions of the process of canonization, the judgments of Gregory XV and Urban VIII, and finally the unanimous opinion of the Church, and (with the exception of a few writers tainted with Jansenism) of all Catholic theologians.

Teresa's historian, therefore, backed up by such an array of authorities, need have no hesitation in declaring that the faults she bewailed with the sorrow and repentance of an Augustine or a Magdalen were not of a serious nature. Thus the Bollandists apply to Teresa St. Gregory's comment on Job in his treatise on

the holy patriarch: " Let all admire the virtues to be found in this great saint ; as for me, I see sublimity in his very defects." That Teresa was not without defects at this period of her life is doubtless true. But if the human element still clung to her, and her actions showed marks of imperfection, no less does her loving nature, the attraction she exercised on all around her, and the holy use she made of this influence to draw souls to God, and to initiate them into the secrets of prayer, reveal itself in every page of her history.

Let us therefore turn to Teresa's confessions and allow her to humble herself, in her own words, to her heart's content. We will sum up afterwards the arguments which may be used on the other side.

" Who could have said that I was so soon to fall," she says, "after such great consolations from God; after His Majesty had implanted virtues in me which of themselves made me serve Him ; after I had been as it were dead, and in such extreme peril of eternal damnation-after He had raised me up soul and body so that all who saw me marvelled to see me alive ? What can it mean, O my Lord? Truly the life we live is full of dangers. . . . I think that it did me much harm to be in a monastery not enclosed. The liberty which those who were good might have with advantage (they not being obliged to do more than they do, because they had not bound themselves to enclosure) would certainly have led me, who am wicked, straight to hell, if our Lord, by so many remedies and means of His most singular mercy, had not delivered me out of that danger. ... So then going on from vanity to vanity, from one occasion of sin to another, I began to expose myself exceedingly to the very greatest dangers ; my soul was so distracted by many vanities that I was ashamed to draw near unto God in an act of special friendship such as prayer. As

my sins multiplied, I began to lose the pleasure and comfort I had in virtuous things, and that loss contributed to the abandonment of prayer. I see now most clearly, O my Lord, that this comfort departed from me because I had departed from Thee. It was the most fatal delusion into which Satan could plunge me to give up prayer under the pretext of humility. I began to be afraid of giving myself to prayer, because I saw myself so lost. I thought it would be better for me—seeing that in my wickedness I was one of the most wicked—to live like the multitude, to say the prayers I was bound to say, and that vocally; not to practise mental prayer, nor commune with God so much. For I deserved to be with the devils, and was deceiving those who were about me because I made an outward show of goodness. And therefore the community in which I dwelt is not to be blamed, for with my cunning I so arranged matters that all had a good opinion of me ; and yet I did not seek this deliberately by simulating devotion; for in all that relates to hypocrisy and ostentation—glory be to God—I do not remember that I ever offended Him, so far as I know. The very first movement herein gave me such pain, that the devil would depart from me with loss, and the gain remained with me, and thus he never tempted me much in this way. Perhaps, however, if God had permitted Satan to tempt me as sharply herein as he tempted me in other things, I should have fallen also in this, but His Majesty has preserved me until now. May He be blessed for evermore. Rather it was a heavy affliction to me that I should be thought so well of, for I knew my own secret. The reason why they thought I was not so wicked was this: they saw that I who was so young, and exposed to so many occasions of sin, withdrew myself so often into solitude for prayer, read so

much, and spoke of God ; that I liked to have His image painted in so many places, to have an oratory of my own, and furnish it with objects of devotion, that I spoke ill of no one, and other things of the same kind in me which had the appearance of virtue. Yet all the while (I was so vain) I knew how to procure respect for myself by doing those things which in the world are usually regarded with respect. In consequence of this they gave me as much liberty as they did to the oldest nuns, and even more, and had great confidence in me, for as to taking liberty for myself, or doing anything without leave, I never did it—for our Lord held me back."

Let us pause here for a moment. Can we, judging the " appearances of virtue " to which Teresa is forced to own from an independent standpoint, see them in the same light as she, in her humility, sees them? The obedient nun who, in spite of an exceptional liberty lawfully granted by her superior, does nothing without their knowledge and permission ; the charitable nun who has ever kind and amiable words on her lips for her neighbours, whether absent or present; the fervent nun who gives much time to prayer : can a nun who does all this be virtuous in appearance only? Is she not performing the duties necessary to her state of life ? Possibly she is not free from imperfections ; but these may weaken her union with God and the light of grace in her, and yet not destroy either the one or the other. Full weight will have to be given to these admissions of Teresa's in the discussion on the subject with which we propose terminating the history of her wanderings.

After some reflections of a general character upon the inconveniences entailed by the absence of the enclosure in a monastery, Teresa takes up once more the thread of her confessions.

" I was once with a person — it was at the very beginning of my acquaintance with her — when our Lord was pleased to show me that these friendships were not good for me, to warn me also, and in my blindness, which was so great, to give me light. Christ stood before me stern and grave, giving me to understand in what my conduct was displeasing to Him. I saw Him with the eyes of the soul more distinctly than I could have seen Him with the eyes of the body. The vision made so deep an impression upon me that, though it is more than twenty-six years ago, I seem to see Him present even now. I was greatly astonished and disturbed, and I resolved not to see that person again. It did me much harm that I did not then know that it was possible to see anything otherwise than with the eyes of the body, so did Satan too, in that he helped me to think so. He made me understand it to be impossible, and suggested that I had imagined the vision : that it might be Satan himself, and other suppositions of that kind. For all this the impression remained with me that the vision was from God, and not an imagination ; but as it was not to my liking I forced myself to lie to myself, and as I did not dare to discuss the matter with anyone, and as great importunity was used, I went back to my conversation with the same person, and with others also, at different times ; for I was assured that there was no harm in seeing such a person, and that I gained instead of losing in reputation by doing so. I spent many years in this pestilent amusement, for it never appeared when I was engaged in it to be so bad as it really was, though at times I saw clearly that it was not good. But no one caused me the same distraction as that person did of whom I am speaking ; and that was because I had a great affection for her.

"At another time when I was with that person we saw, both of us, something like a great toad crawling towards us, more rapidly than such creatures have the habit of moving. I cannot understand how a reptile of that kind could, in the middle of the day, have come forth from that place. It never had done so before, but the impression it made upon me was such that I think it must have had a meaning ; neither have I ever forgotten it. Oh, the greatness of God ! With what care and tenderness didst Thou warn me in every way, and how little I profited by those warnings."

These were not the only means chosen by Providence to warn Teresa. She was closely watched by an aged relative, a nun revered for her virtues and her years. Teresa says of her: " She warned me from time to time, but I not only did not listen to her, but I was even offended, thinking she was scandalized without cause." Her father's talks with her, when they met, touched a more tender chord. Don Alonso, ever since making the sacrifice of his child to God, had vowed himself, though still living in the world, to a life of perfection. He frequently visited Teresa, and under her direction and with the help of the books she procured for him, he gave himself up with ever increasing fervour to the practice of prayer. The holy man had a profound veneration for his beloved child, and looked upon her as being far advanced in the paths of sanctity, and in the ways of that interior life in which she had long conducted him. Teresa, who was already troubled at finding herself the object of universal esteem, would not suffer her father to be long under this delusion. " I told him that I did not pray, but I did not give him the reason. I put my infirmities forward as an excuse ; for though I had recovered from that which was so troublesome I have always been

weak, even very much so ; and though my infirmities are somewhat less troublesome now, they still afflict me in many ways. . . . Neither was it a sufficient reason for giving up a practice which does not require of necessity bodily strength, but only love and a habit thereof;

yet our Lord always furnishes an opportunity for it, if we but seek it. But my father having that opinion of me which he had, and because of the love he bore me, believed all I told him. And moreover he was sorry for me, and as he had now risen to great heights of prayer himself, he never remained with me long; for when he had seen me he went his way, saying that he was wasting his time. As I was wasting it in other vanities I cared little about this."

In spite of these excuses which Teresa made to herself, she suffered cruelly from her infidelities to grace. She had had sufficient experience of divine joys, and of interior consolations, to be athirst for them even in the midst of the empty distractions of which she speaks. These she submitted to, more from an innate amiability which inclined her to yield to those around her, than from any personal satisfaction she found in them. She had, moreover, imposed upon herself as punishment of her faults the abandonment of the practice of mental prayer, as long as her state of lukewarmness and dissipation should last. Teresa had thus tied herself up in a vicious circle. She makes these admirable remarks on the subject in the nineteenth chapter of her Life: " In this the devil turned his batteries against me, and I suffered so much because I thought it showed but little humility if I persevered in prayer when I was so wicked (as I have already said). I gave it up for a year and a half—at least for a year, but I do not remember distinctly the other six months. This could not have been—neither

was it—anything else, but to throw myself down to hell ; there was no need of devils to drag me thither. Oh, my God, was there ever blindness so great as this? How well Satan prepares his measures for his purpose when he pursues us in this way ! The traitor knows that he has already lost that soul which perseveres in prayer, and that every fall that he can bring about helps it by the goodness of God to make greater progress in His service."

These last words contain an apparent mystery which the saint hastens to explain. The page which follows is worthy of comparison with the Confessions of St. Augustine: "O my Lord and Saviour, what a sight that must be—a soul so highly exalted falling into sin, and raised up again by Thee—Who in Thy mercy stretched forth Thy Hand to save. How such a soul confesses Thy greatness and compassion and its own wretchedness ! It looks upon itself as nothingness, and confesses Thy power. It dares not lift up its eyes—it raises them indeed, but it is to acknowledge how much it oweth to Thee. It comes direct to the Queen of Heaven that she may propitiate Thee. It invokes the saints who fell after Thou hadst called them, for succour. Thou seemest to be now too bountiful in Thy gifts, because it feels itself to be unworthy of the ground it treads on. It has recourse to the Sacraments, to a quickened faith, which abides in it at the contemplation of the power which Thou hast lodged in them. It pains Thee because Thou hast left us such medicines and ointments for our wounds, which not only heal them on the surface, but remove all traces whatever of them. The soul is amazed at it. Who is there, O Lord of my soul, that is not amazed at compassion so great and mercy so surpassing, after treason so foul and so hateful ? I know not how it is that mv heart

does not break when I write this, for I am wicked. With these scanty tears which I am weeping, but yet Thy gift—water out of a well, which as far as it is mine is so impure— I seem to make Thee some amends for treachery so great as mine, in that I was always doing evil, labouring to make void the graces Thou hast given me. Do Thou, O Lord, make my tears avail, purify the troubled waters. . . . Was there ever blindness so great as mine? Where could I think I should find help but in Thee? What folly to run away from the light, to be for ever stumbling ! What a proud humility was that which Satan devised for me, when I ceased to lean upon the pillar, and threw the staff away which supported me, in order that my fall might not be great. . . .

But how could my spirit be tranquil? It was going away in its misery from its true rest. I remembered the graces and mercies I had received, and felt that the joys of this world were loathsome. I am astonished that I was able to bear it. It must have been the hope I had, for as well as I can remember, it was twenty-one years ago. I do not think I ever gave up my purpose of resuming my prayer, but I was waiting to be free from sin first. Oh, how deluded I was in this expectation ! The devil would have held it out before me till the day of judgment, that he might then take me with him to hell. Then when I applied myself to prayer and to spiritual reading whereby I might perceive these truths and the evil nature of the way in which I was walking, and used often to importunate our Lord with tears, I was so wicked it availed me nothing." 1

These are the bewailings of the great saint and the touching story of her repentance. Putting aside those passages of her life in which, in spite of all her efforts,

she allows glimpses of her unalterable goodness and piety to be perceived, we have chosen those in which she accuses herself with the greatest vehemence. Let us now lift the veil, one of tears and confusion, in which she loves to cover herself, and see what lies beneath : in other words, what were really the errors and shortcomings of which she accuses herself. In the first place, we should note two points after reading and analysing the passages we have just quoted. The first, that Teresa not only kept the divine precepts most faithfully, but also the observance of the Rule ; doubtless one relaxed by authorized mitigations, yet sufficiently strict to maintain the greater number of the community of the monastery of the Incarnation in their primitive fervour—for Teresa loves to record the regular and edifying life led in the house. Again, Teresa, though one of its youngest members, enjoyed the same confidence and liberty as her elders. She was esteemed, even venerated, and a trust was reposed in her which (as she herself owns) she never abused ; and it is under the shadow of this peaceful cloister that the days of her "great vanity" were spent ! Protected by her religious habit, and even more so by the virtues which rendered her worthy of it; surrounded by companions whom she looked upon as guardian angels, attached to the tie that bound her, by her tastes and natural attraction, and by a firm will to fulfil its duties : it is thus that Teresa presents herself to our gaze at the very time when she brands herself in her humility with every abusive epithet. This is the first conclusion to which we are led by her own admissions.

In the second place, we are conscious of imperfections or, even more, of weaknesses, under the rich growth of natural virtues and supernatural gifts. What then are these weaknesses? It is difficult to dis-

cover any amongst the saint's accusations, except possibly a too great readiness to yield to the demands made upon her time, her help, and her counsels. Teresa, though of undaunted courage when it was a question of imposing sacrifices upon herself, or facing the trials involved in physical suffering, was weak indeed before a suppliant word, or the expression of a wish from her sisters and friends. Her great and loving heart longed to find a vent in helping others and working for their happiness. Nor was it possible for her to ignore the ascendancy she possessed amongst those by whom she was surrounded. She had the gift of persuasiveness ; a born leader, she takes advantage of this power to lead to God all those with whom she comes in contact. Her delightful company, which attracted so many to visit her, was in her hands but a means by which she might gain souls to Him, for she loses no opportunity of bringing round the conversation to the love of God and the happiness of serving Him. But to this truly apostolic work, other results, such as the praise of the crowd, their admiration, and the pursuit of her society, mingle with disastrous effect. She is run after by the gay world of Avila and has not strength to fight against the current. With her charming simplicity, she is ready to see all who ask for her; she delights them without intending it, and thus becomes absorbed in occupations and engagements which take up all the leisure left her after a strict fulfilment of her religious duties—for in the performance of these we know she never fails. These are the vanities to which our saint gave way in the early days of her religious life and bewailed to her dying day.

That these imperfections and weaknesses were not without a graver side to them we may acknowledge

with Teresa, but in what sense ? Every one at the last day will have to render an account of the gifts God has given them ; and of those to whom much has been given much will be required. That is the code of divine justice as formulated by our Divine Saviour Himself.

Now Teresa from her earliest infancy had been overwhelmed with favours from Heaven. Interior lights, profound graces, supernatural attractions, and finally the trial of great suffering had disposed her to enter, according to God's designs, on the paths of great sanctity and heights of prayer. God had called her to His service from the first moment of her existence, and had given her, more than once, some glimpse of His infinite beauty and perfections. She had seen enough to go in pursuit of martyrdom in order the sooner to possess the Sovereign Good Who had taken possession of her heart. But before long a battle rages within her. The world and the devil do their utmost, first with the young girl, then with the religious, to arrest her flight heavenward. They try to lead her away by means of giddy companions, to make her lose her time, to lessen her fervour. They hide their plot under appearances well fitted to deceive her. They drag her into a succession of visits—of conversations— under which the poor saint loses her recollection, and all in the name and under the guise of gratitude, consideration for her neighbours, or on the plea of the good she can do to others by her advice. She leaves the path appointed for her by God ; she gives up mental prayer. Her dissipation of mind puts an obstacle to grace, which leaves her plunged in interior desolation. Truly we have no difficulty in understanding her tears. She weeps, and she is right to bewail long hours thrown away in the company of creatures which she had been invited to spend with God and His

angels. She weeps, and it is right she should weep at having found pleasure in worldly vanities after having been fed on heavenly manna. Infidelities which would have been trifling in others had a double gravity in her case ; that of divine love abandoned, and an exceptional vocation neglected.

This is the extent of her wrongdoing, and he who would give it a wider significance but mistakes the nature of her repentance. If anyone is deceived by the vividness of Teresa's expressions into doubting the spotless character of our saint, we have but to answer with the admissions wrung from her by her strict sense of truth. Let us call to mind her sweetness, her charity, the success with which she avoided anything in the shape of detraction in her conversation. Let us remember her victories over self-love, her fidelity to her Rule, her numberless pious practices — practices which she did not intermit, let it be noted, when she gave up mental prayer. Again, let us add one detail which she gives us later. " Notwithstanding all my miseries," she says, "I had always the fear of the Lord before me." Whcre are the great sins in such a life ? It is in vain we search for them ; and the strictest scrutiny, enlightened by holy Church, sounding the veriest depths of this sublime character, has never found a stain on it which could sully Teresa's baptismal innocence. There is also another consideration which we should like to put to our readers before concluding our review of this portion of Teresa's life. As we have said in a previous chapter, it was written after she had been drawn into closest union with her Divine Master, and had even been allowed to gaze for a moment on His glorified Humanity. Does not this fact alone throw great light on the saint's confessions? Spiritual writers have said that though it is

probable that saints such as the Magdalene and St. Francis of Assisi equalled the Blessed in Heaven in their love of God, not one has ever equalled them in humility. The reason of this is not far to seek. The disembodied soul that has gazed on the Beatific vision, and beheld Him before Whom the angels tremble and veil their faces, sees his past life in a light in which he has never seen it before. It was in this light, less vivid indeed than that of one who has u gone beyond the veil," but incomparably greater than that vouchsafed to common humanity, in which Teresa saw the heinousness of her imperfections, her ingratitude to God for His favours, and her infidelity to grace. Can we be astonished at the depth of her anguish, or wonder at the burning words wrung from her by her repentance? It has been customary to explain away the force of her expressions by attributing them to pious exaggeration. Would it not be nearer the mark to say that truths were visible to her which are hidden, as a rule, in this life, to man? The Psalmist says: Delicta quis intelligit? Teresa could have answered, had her humility allowed her, that through the mercy of God she had been given some knowledge of sin, for the enlightenment of mankind. For can we doubt that this Life, which is one of the masterpieces of spirituality, and in which the guiding Hand of the Holy Spirit is revealed in every page, was written for our instruction as well as for our edification? And could a lesson of deeper significance be given to us than that of the heinousness of what we are accustomed to call so lightly "little sins," or of the terrible misfortune to the soul (one which none but the greatest servants of God, such as St. Teresa, have realized this side of the grave) of neglect of divine grace and want of correspondence to it?

CHAPTER VII

TERESA'S relations with her family, as we have already had occasion to notice, were ever of the most affectionate character; and if her conscience reproached her for her too frequent conversations with seculars, she could not entertain the same scruples with regard to her intercourse with her father, and brothers, and sisters. For many years God had reigned alone in the hearts of that holy household, and Don Alonso's chief object in his visits to the Convent of the Incarnation seems to have been that he might receive good advice and edification from his daughter. He was in the habit of rendering her account with touching simplicity of the graces he had received in prayer. He used to confide the fruits of his meditations to her, and invite her to help him in the path in which she had been the first to set his footsteps. The progress made by her father was a source of profound humiliation to Teresa, though it was at the same time one of great consolation to her. For here she felt, at least, that she was making amends to her Divine Saviour for her own infidelities.

"Alas," she cries, "I was well aware that I was resisting the voice of conscience, which was ever telling me that I was not serving God as I should have done, so in order not to lose the entire profit of the light which His Divine Majesty had accorded me, I G 81

endeavoured to communicate them to fervent souls who were able to benefit by them in my place."

Don Alonso took the first place amongst this number. Under Teresa's direction his piety, which though always solid, had till then been of a timid and rigorous character, expanded with a new perception of the wonders of Divine love. He read less, and prayed more, and already he tasted in prayer the joys of Heaven. It was, as it were, the crowning consolation of a patriarchal life, which had been spent in good works and in the exercise of the duties of the head of a family.

One day a sad message arrived at the monastery of the Incarnation : Don Alonso was dying and asked for his daughter. Teresa, with her superior's permission, at once betook herself to her father's side, and she soon perceived that death was not far distant. Alonso's last wish was to die in the company of her whom he looked upon as the angel of his house, and to hear once more that dearly loved voice speaking to him of eternal joys.

"Though in losing him," Teresa says, "I was to lose all the comfort and good of my life, for he was all this to me, I had the courage never to betray my sorrows, concealing them till he was dead, as if I felt none at all. It seemed as if my very soul were wrenched when I saw him at the point of death, my love for him was so deep. It was a matter for which we ought to praise our Lord the death that he died and the desire that he had to die. So also was the advice he gave us after the last anointing ; how he charged us to recommend him to God, and to pray for mercy for him, how he bade us serve God always, and consider how all things come to an end. He told us, with tears, how grieved he was that he had not better served Him himself, for he wished he had been a friar in one of the strictest

Orders. . . . His chief suffering was a most acute pain in the shoulders, which never left him ; it was so sharp at times that it put him to acute torture. I said to him that as he had so great a devotion to our Lord carrying His Cross on His shoulders, he should now think that His Majesty wished him to feel somewhat of the pain which He then suffered Himself. This so comforted him that I do not think I heard him complain afterwards. He remained three days without consciousness; but on the day he died our Lord restored him so completely that it astonished us all. He preserved his understanding to the last, for in the middle of the credo, which he repeated himself, he died. He lay there like an angel, and such he seemed to me, if I may say so, in soul and disposition. . . . His confessor, a most learned Dominican, used to say he had no doubt he went straight to Heaven."

It was perhaps the blessing of her dying father which obtained for Teresa the decisive graces which recalled her to her rightful path. Father Vincent Barren, the above mentioned friar, assisted the dying man in his last moments with a devotion and piety which deeply touched the daughter's heart. She begged him to hear her confession ; and her soul, lacerated by sorrow, broke asunder her " chains" (as she was accustomed to call them) and found relief in humbling admissions such as those which we have already read in her life. Father Barren, who was not only a good theologian but a holy and enlightened man, perceived at once the nature of the soul which Providence had confided to him for direction. Teresa, on her side, felt herself for the first time in her life understood. Till then she had never made a spiritual manifestation of her conscience except to those who, in her opinion, judged her too leniently, who had reassured her on the state of her

soul, approved of her relations with seculars, and found nothing blameworthy in her conversations in the parlour. Their sole error, doubtless, was to lead Teresa in the path of the ordinary nun desirous of leading a good life, without taking into consideration the exceptional designs God had upon her, nor the very exceptional graces she had received. The Dominican, with greater spiritual insight, solved the question by insisting upon her resuming her meditations. "I obeyed," she said, "and from that moment never have I abandoned the practice of prayer." This was the prudent director's first injunction. He knew that in bringing Teresa back to God's feet, in obliging her to give herself up anew to the attraction of her Divine Master, he could ensure the speedy triumph of grace in this generous soul which was ever more open to the appeal of love than to the threat of punishment. Thus, without insisting on her making a sacrifice of habits in which he saw nothing to condemn, he was satisfied with committing her into God's hands by means of the practice of mental prayer.

Teresa accordingly now entered into another phasa of her existence. It was a period of suffering and warfare, and at times of inexpressible bitterness ; in short, a crucifixion lasting from twelve to thirteen years, which had for its object the formation of a great saint, with all her natural beauty of character preserved, and a supernatural beauty added to it.

It would be far from our purpose to give the history of this interior conflict, which Teresa has described in terms as vivid as were her sufferings. But before listening to her account, let us give one moment to the consideration of the real state of her soul at a time when her humility had sought to hide it under a cloak of shame and repentance.

Should we even admit that she had been unfaithful to God during the preceding years of her life, we can do so no longer now that she was faithful to the practice of prayer. Nevertheless she had not yet acquired that degree of purity of conscience to which He Who had chosen her for the confidant of His Heart, and for the contemplation of His unspeakable Beauty, wished to raise her. She had not broken those ties, legitimate though they were, which yet bound her to creatures, and impeded her flight heavenward. She desired to give herself wholly to her beloved Master, but she still trembled before certain sacrifices, which she feared for herself only because she imposed them at the same time upon others. These trials to her loving heart were a torture indeed, but this process of purification disposed her, unconsciously, to enter into that intimate and close union with God which was to follow, when grace had completed its work in her soul. As Teresa's heart was her vulnerable point, it is there that God's hand is raised to strike her.

" My life," she tells us, " became most wretched, because I learned in prayer more and more of my faults. On one side God was calling me, on the other I was following the world. All the things of God gave me much pleasure, yet I was captive to the things of the world. . . . Oh, Lord of my soul ! how shall I be able to magnify the graces which Thou in those years didst bestow on me ! O how didst Thou prepare me at the very time that I offended Thee most, in a moment by a most profound compunction to taste of the sweetness of Thy consolations and mercies ! In truth, O my King, Thou didst administer to me the most delicate and painful chastisement it was possible for me to bear ; for Thou knewest well what would have given me most pain. Thou didst chastise my sins with great

consolations. I trust I am not saying foolish things, though it may well be that I am beside myself whenever I call to mind my ingratitude and my wickedness. It was more painful for me, in the state I was in, to receive graces, when I had fallen into grievous faults, than it would have been to receive chastisements; for one of those faults I am sure used to bring me low, shame and distress me more than many diseases, together with many heavy trials, could have done. For as to the latter I saw that I deserved them, and it seemed to me that by them I was making some slight reparation for my sins—though it was but slight, for my sins were many. But when I see myself receive graces anew, after being so ungrateful for those already received, that is to me—and I believe to all who have any knowledge or love of God—a fearful kind of torment. Hence my tears and trouble of mind when I reflected on what I felt, seeing myself in a condition to fall at every moment, though my resolutions and desires then were strong."

Soon, however, Heaven appeared to have sided with our saint, and her martyrdom took another form. Celestial joys deserted her, consolations disappeared, her sweetness in prayer was changed for aridity. Her prayer became a long torture, when her sad and downcast soul had to endure the weariness of " remaining long in the company of One who has nothing in common with us."

" For some years," she goes on to say, " I was very often more occupied with the wish to see the end of the time I had appointed for myself to spend in prayer, and in watching the hour-glass, than with other thoughts that were good. If a sharp penance had been laid upon me, I know of none that I would not very often have willingly undertaken, rather than prepare myself for prayer, by self-recollection. And certainly the violence with which Satan assailed me was so irresistible, or my evil habits were so strong, that I did not betake myself to prayer ; and the sadness I felt on entering the oratory was so great that it required all the courage I had to force myself in. They say of me that my courage is not slight, and it is known that God has given me courage beyond that of most women, but I have made a bad use of it. In the end our Lord came to my help ; and then when I had done this violence to myself I found greater peace and joy than I sometimes had when I had a desire to pray."

For many years Teresa was to endure this state of privation and desolation. It would require a heart like hers, which had tasted the chalice of divine delights to the full to understand the trials of deprivation. He who had pursued her with His graces amidst the tepidities of past years, retired and hid Himself now that she had begun to seek Him with all her heart. Heaven, which had half opened over her infant head so that she had caught sight of its beauty—the thought of which had supported her in her struggles against her vocation, in the anguish of her sickness, in the perils even of her days of dissipation—Heaven even seemed closed to her; it had retreated behind the clouds ; the skies became as it were of brass. Thus the days and the youth of the saint, the brightest and fairest of life, flowed on without happiness, without joy. Yet nothing tired her constancy ; nothing daunted the ardour of her love. The morning found her prostrate in her oratory in the place which she had bathed in tears the preceding day. She sought for pious thoughts in spiritual books which her mind was incapable of originating. She humbled herself, she submitted herself to God, she prayed, and waited, and hoped, and abandoned herself into His hands. That was the daily prayer of this great saint for fourteen years; a consoling example for the much-tried soul who treads a similar path.

During this long period of time there were few changes in Teresa's outward existence. Family cares, Juana's marriage to Juan de Ovalle, an excellent gentleman of Salamanca, are the only events which can be recalled at this distance of time. The community of the monastery of the Incarnation became every year more numerous. A hundred and fifty nuns formed a society of pious souls whose fervour was a source of edification to the neighbouring city. Unfortunately this number exceeded the resources of the monastery, and left it, in a sense, at the mercy of the friendly externs who supported it with their gifts. Accordingly the parlours continued to be much frequented, and of all whose presence was desired there, none were more in request than Teresa.

In this century in which we live it is difficult to realize the charm that society in ancient days found in their relations with the cloister. But with regard to Avila the explanation is simple. This little city had risen through its faith, and faith was still its food—its daily bread. To Avila, peopled as it was by sons of the Crusaders, and cut off by its situation from the stream of life, with no commercial activities and no easy communication with the great towns, its churches, oratories, and even its monasteries were the centres around which it moved and gravitated. The great ladies, the illustrious knights, disputed, one with the other, the rights of according their protection to the great monastic families ; and, in exchange for favours grVen, they asked for audience with the nuns or monks in order to learn the mysteries of prayer, or to become initiated into the secrets of the cloister—secrets which offered a strange attraction to their austere tastes. These were the entanglements, for the last time let it be said, under the yoke of which Teresa lamented whilst submitting to it, and which for reasons of policy, as well as of gratitude, she found such extreme difficulty in shaking off.

The day which the Lord had chosen dawned at last; and what fourteen years of prayers, tears, and struggles had failed to effect was accomplished in one moment by one look from Him.

The Lent of the year 1555 was about to end with the sweet though sad memories of the Passion. Teresa had reached her fortieth year, when the hour of grace sounded which was to give her wholly to God. This is her account of that great moment:—

" It came to pass one day when I went into the oratory that I saw a picture which they had put there, and which had been procured for a certain feast observed in the house. It was a representation of Christ most grievously wounded, and so devotional that the very sight of it when I saw it moved me, so well did it show forth that which He suffered for us. So keenly did I feel the evil return I had made for those wounds, that I thought my heart would break. I threw myself on the ground beside it, my tears flowing pienteously, and implored Him to strengthen me once for all, so that I might never offend Him any more. I had a great devotion to the glorious Magdalen, and very frequently used to think of her conversion. ... I used to recommend myself to that great saint so that she might obtain my pardon. But this last time, before that picture of which I spoke, I seem to have made greater progress, for I was now very distrustful of myself, placing all my confidence in God. It seems to me that I said to Him that I would not rise up till He granted my petition. I do certainly believe that this

was of great service to me, because since then I have made great progress."

This great and signal grace was soon to be followed by another. Our Lord had first spoken to Teresa's heart through His picture; He now spoke to her through a book. Presently He was to speak to her Himself in the same manner as He converses with His angels. It would appear as if the divine Voice, before making Itself heard directly, wished to adopt more and more spiritualized forms in order to lift Teresa from earth to Heaven by a gradual ascent, whose steps remind us of the words of the Psalmist: ' 'Beatus mr cujus est auxilium abs te : ascensiones in corde suo disposuit. "

" Shortly afterwards," Teresa says, " the Confessions of St. Augustine were given me. Our Lord seems to have so ordained it, for I did not seek them myself, neither had I ever seen them before. I had a very great devotion to St. Augustine . . . because he had been a sinner, for I used to find great comfort in those saints whom, after they had sinned, our Lord had converted to Himself. I thought they would help me, and that as our Lord had forgiven them so also He would forgive me. When I began to read the Confessions I thought I saw myself there described, and began to recommend myself greatly to this glorious saint. When I came to his conversion, and read how he heard the voice in the garden, it seemed to me nothing less than that our Lord had uttered it for me. I felt it in my heart. I remained for some time lost in tears in great inward affliction and distress. God be praised Who gave me life, so that I might escape from so fatal a death ! I believe that my soul obtained great strength from His Divine Majesty, and that He must have heard my cry and have had compassion on my many tears."

On that day of deep repentance Teresa broke for ever all the ties that still bound her to earth. Her great soul was born again beneath the same ray of light and grace which brought life to her brother in genius, tenderness, and sanctity—St. Augustine ; and, more blessed even than that great saint, she could go to her Saviour's arms robed in her baptismal innocence, and take that place amongst His children which He seems to have reserved especially to the pure of heart.

CHAPTER VIII

" TY beloved to me and I to Him >" this was the 1 VI key-note of the song of Teresa's heart during

the days which succeeded the events related in the last chapter. She had passed, to use her own expression, from death to life, and now reposed peacefully on the bosom of her Saviour. A youthful current appeared to circulate once more in her veins, notwithstanding her forty years, and a new existence to open out before her. If Teresa did not at this point of her life herself come to our assistance, what we should have to say about her would be little more than conjecture. B.ut she was obliged (as we shall see later on) to disclose, in spite of her humility, under holy obedience, the inmost secrets of her heart for the glory of God, and the good of souls. It is for Teresa, and for her alone, to tell her story. The instant she takes her flight to the heights of contemplation, God appears to come to her assistance, and to give her power to put her thoughts on the deepest and most abstruse subjects, such as her locutions and ecstasies, in language which is equally brilliant and profound. To this power she adds a scientific knowledge [1] which embraced not only the fruits of personal experience, but of a deep and

1 Vincente de la Fuente, one of the saint's many biographers, gives a high idea of her mental equipment. He says that before going to the Augustinians she was looked upon as a "persona de instruction y de imagination viva y fecunda "/ and at that convent she received the highest education — "/a education mas esmarada" — of the day.

exhaustive study of the writings of eminent divines, both of her own day and of days gone by.

This human science was allied in her with the divine lights which she gathered from her frequent communications with Heaven. Till the epoch in which she lived (the Spanish editor of her works remarks) ascetic literature had been entirely in the hands of the student of the Bible and its commentators, of men accustomed to the use of scholastic language, and of the definitions and controversies of the schools. Teresa speaks her own thoughts in her own language, which, though her words are well chosen, is easy for all to understand. Nothing can exceed the elevation of her thoughts, or the simplicity of her diction. She pleases equally the learned and the unlearned, the pious and the worldly. She has, in short, popularized mystical theology by making it accessible to all: bringing truths home to the many which had hitherto been restricted to the few, to the student, or to the inhabitant of the cloister.

The saint at this period of her history, it will be observed, changes the narrative of her life into a treatise on prayer. She gives the reason in the following words: " If what I have said be not correct, let him to whom I send it destroy it; for he knows better than I do what is wrong in it. I entreat him for the love of our Lord to publish abroad what I have thus far said of my wretched life, and of my sins. I give him leave to do so ; and to all my confessors also, of whom he is one, to whom this is to be sent, if it be their pleasure during my life, so that I may no longer deceive people who think there must be some good in me. Certainly I speak in all sincerity; such publication will give me great comfort. But as to that which I am now going to say I give no such leave, nor if

it be shown to any one do I consent to its being said who the person is whose experience it describes, nor who wrote it. I have written it in the best way I could in order not to be known ; and this I beg of them for the love of God. If our Lord has given me the grace to say things that are right it is to Him I owe it, for I am neither learned or of good life. I have as it were to steal the time, and that with difficulty, because my writing hinders me from spinning; I am living in a house that is poor, and have many things to do." [1]

Even if the secrecy which Teresa asks for so earnestly had been preserved, yet her book would have betrayed her, for she alone could have written it. We detect knowledge gained from her own interior life in every line we read. She knows by experience the labour, the sweat with which the furrow has to be bedewed before it is watered from Heaven. Those aridities, those struggles, those disgusts, are the secrets of her own soul communing with God. She also it is who has wept those tears of consolation, who has experienced those divine touches, penetrating and ineffable. In short, it is the history of the saint's soul ; one must read it in order to know her.

She begins by casting one look, full of sorrow and repentance, on the past. 2 " O Lord of my soul, and my sovereign Good, when a soul is determined to love Thee —doing all it can by forsaking all things in order that it may the better occupy itself with the love of God—is it not Thy will it should have the joy of ascending at once to the possession of perfect love ? I have spoken amiss,

1 The saint wrote this at St. Joseph's Avila, the first convent of the Reform.

2 We give here, and in the succeeding pages, extracts from chapters X. to xxii. in Teresa's Life, which have for their subject the saint's states of prayer.

I ought to have said, and my complaint should have been, why is it we do not? For the fault is wholly our own that we do not rejoice at once in a dignity so great, seeing that the attaining to the perfect possession of this love brings all blessings with it. We think so much of ourselves, and are so dilatory in giving ourselves wholly to God, that as His Majesty will not let us have the fruition of that which is so precious but at a great cost, so neither do we perfectly prepare ourselves for it. I see plainly that there is nothing by which so great a good can be procured in this world. If however we did what we could, not clinging to anything upon earth but having all our thoughts and conversation in Heaven, I believe that this blessing would quickly be given us, provided we perfectly prepared ourselves for it at once, as some of the saints have done. We think we are giving all to God ; but in fact we are offering only the revenue or the produce, while we retain the fee-simple of the land in our own possession. A pleasant way this of seeking the love of God ! We retain our own affections, and yet will have that love, as they say, in handfuls. We make no efforts to bring our desires to good effect, or to raise them resolutely above the earth, and yet with all this we must have spiritual consolations. This is not well, and we are seeking things incompatible one with the other."

The thought returns to her here of those years of indecision and weakness by which, in spite of her natural force of character, she had been so long kept back. She has also known a worse pitfall, that of false humility, which thinks that in " shutting its eyes to God's grace it is performing an act of virtue." For how should these graces excite our love if we do not realize, even, that we have received them, or dare to look

them in the face? The more we see that of ourselves we are poor, and rich only through God's gifts the more we shall advance in true humility, whereas a too great fear of vainglory depresses the soul's strength by persuading her that she is incapable of any good action. The timid, discouraged soul shuts itself up in a narrow rut out of which it trembles to move. " She walks at the pace of a tortoise, and is satisfied with hunting little lizards." The devil persuades such a soul that there would be pride in lifting her desires higher, and hiding from her the example of the saints, in matters imitable as well as admirable, he deludes her into thinking that poor sinners like her have nothing in common with the lives led by them. Such are the snares in which Teresa has been caught. Therefore she indignantly denounces the enemy of our souls : "It would doubtless be wrong in a person who is weak and sickly to undergo much fasting, and sharp penances, to retire into the desert, where he could not sleep or find anything to eat, or indeed to undertake any austerities of this kind. But we ought to think that we can force ourselves by the grace of God to hold the world in profound contempt, to make light of honours, and be detached from our possessions. We may also imitate the saints by striving after solitude and silence, and many other virtues that will not kill these wretched bodies of ours, which insist on being treated in so orderly a manner that they disorder the soul, and Satan helps much to make them unmanageable. When he sees us a little anxious about them, he wants nothing more to convince us that our way of life must kill us ; I have passed through this, therefore I know it. But when it pleased God to let me find out this device of Satan's, I used to say to him when he suggested that I was ruining my health, that my death

was of no consequence ; when he suggested rest, I replied that I did not want rest, but the Cross ; and so on with the rest. My health has been much better since I have ceased to look after my ease and comfort."

The illusion of false humility, it will be remembered, was one of those which helped to keep Teresa from resuming the practice of prayer. For fourteen years, since her father's death, she had resumed it " never to drop it again " ; but these years had passed amidst the trials of desolation. Our saint has already spoken of them, and she returns to them in order to describe the progress of a soul in divine grace, and, as she says, to start with its early beginnings. She has first noted the preliminary points ; she now launches on her subject, which is that of a life of prayer.

"A beginner," she tells us, " must look upon himself as making a garden wherein our Lord may take His delight, but in a soil unfruitful, and abounding in weeds. His Majesty roots up the weeds, and has to plant good herbs. We have then, as good gardeners, by the help of God, to see that the plants grow, to water them carefully so that they may not die, but produce blossoms which shall send forth much fragrance refreshing to our Lord, so that He may come often for His pleasure in this garden, and delight Himself in their midst.

" Let us now see how this garden is to be watered, that we may understand what we have to do. It seems to me that the garden may be watered in four ways : by water taken out of a well, which is very laborious ; or with water raised by means of an engine and buckets; or by a stream, whereby the garden is watered in a much better way, for the soil is more thoroughly saturated, and there is no necessity to water it so often, and the labour of the gardener is much less; H

or by showers of rain, for then our Lord Himself waters it without labour on our part; and this way is incomparably better than all the others of which I have spoken.

" Now for the application of these four ways of irrigation by which the garden is to be maintained — for without water it must fail — and these I apply to the four degrees of prayer with which our Lord of His goodness has at times raised my soul.

" Of those who are beginners in prayer we may say that they are those who draw the water up out of the well, a process which, as I have said, is very laborious; for they must be wearied in keeping the senses recollected, and this is a great labour, because the senses have hitherto been accustomed to distractions. God grant, also, there may be water in it ! By water here I mean tears, and if there be none, then tenderness and an inward feeling of devotion. What then will he do here who sees that for many days he is conscious only of aridity, disgust, and dislikc, and so great an unwillingness to go to the well for water that he would give it up altogether if he did not remember that he has to please and serve the Lord of the garden? What then will the gardener do now? He must rejoice, and take comfort, and consider it as the greatest favour to labour in the garden of the King of Kings ; and as he knows that he is pleasing Him in the matter—and his purpose must not be to please himself, but Him—let him praise Him greatly for the trust he has in Him. Let him help Him to carry the Cross, and let him think how He carried it all His life long; let him not seek his kingdom here, nor intermit his prayer—if this aridity should last even his whole life long." Teresa stops here in order to pour forth her counsel and encouragement upon the hapless gardener. It is now

our task to return to her history, and to confine our quotations to those passages which illustrate her own spiritual life. In the first place, it is of interest to note what were the subjects of her meditation when she was at this early stage.

"As I could not make reflections with my understanding, I used to picture Christ as within me, and I used to like best those mysteries of His life during which He was most lonely. It seemed to me that being alone and afflicted He must needs permit me to come nearer to Him. In particular I used to find myself most at home in the prayer in the Garden whither I went in His company. I thought of the bloody sweat, and of the affliction He endured there. I wished, if it had been possible, to wipe away that painful sweat from His face ; but I remember that I never dared to form such a resolution—my sins stood before me so grievously. I used to remain with Him there as long as my thoughts allowed me. I never dared to start praying without a book. Sometimes I read much, sometimes little, according to the grace that was given me. It was a help to me also to look on fields, water, and flowers. In them I saw traces of the Creator—I mean that the sight of things was as a book to me ; they roused me, made me recollected, and reminded me of my ingratitude and my sins. As regards Heaven and other supernatural objects, my understanding was too unimaginative for me to be able to picture them to myself. Never could I represent to myself what I could not see with my bodily eyes, as some could do. I could only see our Saviour present within me by an act of faith."

Convinced as Teresa was that divine love consists in serving God in justice and truth, with courage and humility, and not in resting on the enjoyment of His

favours, she guarded herself from ever giving way to too great a joy in consolation, or too lively a sorrow when in desolation. And if this interior abnegation appears utterly beyond our powers, the saint tells us what we should do in order to acquire it. By taking care to remain ever in the company of our Saviour, "the soul who sees Him constantly before her, becomes inflamed little by little with a tender love for Him. She speaks to Him ; she intreats Him when she is in want ; she complains to Him when she is in trouble ; she rejoices with Him, and ever her heart is full of joy." By this means the soul makes much progress, and being drawn insensibly from its worship of self, is submerged, with all its pleasures and its pains, in the adorable Heart of Jesus.

With such dispositions nothing is necessary save to proceed with a firm step and a holy liberty of spirit. The saint says : " Some persons are much mistaken in thinking all their consolation will leave them if they cease for a moment to watch over themselves. Doubtless it is always well to mistrust oneself, but there are harmless recreations which we do well to take in order to return to prayer afterwards with the greater ardour. Discretion is necessary above all things ; also confidence in God, and a generous heart no less so. We must not narrow our ideas. If the saints had not had great aspirations, would they have reached the perfection attained by them? God asks courage of souls; He is pleased with them as long as they remain humble, and if their strength fails them—as we see with young birds whose wings are weak—though they are exhausted and have to breathe, yet they have flown great distances."

The dominant note of Teresa's instructions to others as regards a path which she has followed herself,

is that it should be pursued with firmness and courage. To aim ever at the practice of solid virtue, and of generous actions with a humility untinged with discouragement ; to pray fervently in spite of natural repugnance, or the trial of aridity ; to meditate with simplicity on the mysteries of our Saviour's life ; to keep in His presence, expect all things from His love for us, and to abandon ourselves entirely to Him " in order to follow Him even on to Mount Calvary, helping Him to carry the Cross, and never leaving Him alone to bear its burden " : these are the solid foundations on which Teresa bases the edifice of prayer. This is the first degree to which all may attain, and all persevere in, by the ordinary succour of divine grace. A soul who has never soared above this degree may be very holy and perfect, and none should seek to mount higher by their own strength at the risk of being punished for their temerity. For those ardent desires which Teresa loves so much—knowing how pleasing they are to God—have for their object, not sensible joys which our Lord grants where and when He will, and which are a pure gift of His mercy, but a greater progress in self-abnegation and in solid virtue.

Our saint insists, therefore, on the excellence and security of this simple road of prayer. In following it there are less dangers to be feared, and fewer illusions to be apprehended, than in the higher and more advanced paths ; and God, Who is master of the favours He bestows, " leads souls with different graces to an equal state of perfection." 1 Teresa herself, with few exceptions of supernatural favours, had followed this humble path from the commencement of her religious life. We have heard how much it cost her, continually, to get through her hour's meditation, in consequence

of her repugnance and her distractions. It was now God's will to reward her for twenty years' fidelity to prayer ; and very shortly after the time which we will call, with her, her conversion, she was to receive the earliest foreshadowing of those extraordinary graces with which her life was ever afterwards to be inundated. An almost habitual tenderness of devotion began at this time to replace her former aridity, and soon she was constantly seized while at prayer, or even when listening to spiritual reading, with a profound sentiment of the presence of God. 1 The time of rest had come. Teresa had no longer to draw water from the well by the sweat of her brow. " Let us now," she says, " speak of the second manner of drawing the water which the Lord of the vineyard has ordained ; of the machine of wheel and buckets whereby the gardener may draw water with less labour, and be able to take some rest without being continually at work. This, then, is what I am now going to describe, and I apply it to the prayer called the prayer of quiet. Herein the soul begins to be recollected ; it is now touching on the supernatural, for it could never by any efforts of its own attain to this. True, it seems at times to have been wearied at the wheel, but in this second degree the water is higher, and accordingly the labour is much less. I mean the water is nearer to it, for grace reveals itself more distinctly to the soul."

Here Teresa indicates the essential characteristics of this kind of prayer. The precision and correctness of doctrine with which she expresses herself in this treatise was such that the great mystical writers of the eighteenth century treated her decisions as authoritative, and final in their works on mental prayer.

1 This was the supernatural recollection which usually precedes the prayer of quiet, as Teresa explains elsewhere.

To follow her in her admirable dissertation on the rules by which illusions may be distinguished from realities, and the natural from the supernatural, would take us too long. Let us seek rather to penetrate further into the sanctuary of her soul —now enlightened and transfigured under the direct action of the Holy Ghost. If what we are about to relate appears incredible to some of our readers, we entreat of them not to judge of the work of God rashly. Can we set a limit to His omnipotence? Is it not possible that His Hand, which opens in order to " fill every living creature with benediction," should pour forth a greater abundance of grace on those pure and fervent souls who love Him better, and serve Him more devoutly than do the greater number of His children? Is it not conceivable that God should reward, even in this life, exceptional love by privileges which man grants joyfully to a fellow man when he admits him into his confidence, and tells him all the secrets of his life? And if this divine familiarity, this unspeakable union, is a difficulty to the soul that does not love, is it any to the one who humbly adores without pretending to understand?

Let us listen now to what Teresa has to say to us: " In this prayer (of quiet) there is a gathering together of the faculties of the soul within itself, in order that it may have the fruition of that contentment in greater sweetness ; but the faculties are not lost, neither are they asleep. The will alone is occupied in such a way that, without knowing how it has become a captive, it gives a simple consent to become a prisoner of God.

" This simple act, this sweet repose of the will, does not last long without being interrupted by the other powers, the understanding and the memory wishing to break from their inaction trouble the soul instead of

being of use to it; but it should never heed them at all, simply abiding in its fruition and quiet. For if it tried to make them recollected it would miss its way altogether with them, because they are at this time like doves which are not satisfied with the food the master of the dovecot gives them without any labouring for it on their part, and so go forth in quest of it elsewhere, and hardly find it when they come back. And so the memory and the understanding come and go— if it be our Lord's pleasure to throw them any food they stop, if not they go again to seek it. The soul would lose much if it troubled itself with them. The understanding would present it with fine discourses and grand considerations, and the little spark of divine love would soon be smothered under these logs of wood—that is to say, these learned reasonings— whereas with a few bits of straw, namely, some simple acts of humility, and abandonment to the divine will, the spark becomes a great fire. The soul (with the help of the graces she has now received) is already ascending out of its wretched state, and some little knowledge of the blissfulness of glory is communicated to it. It begins to lose the desire of earthly things ; and no wonder, for it sees already that even for a moment this joy is not to be had on earth, that there are no riches, no dominion, no honour, no delight that can for one instant, even for the twinkling of an eye, minister such a joy. The soul which has never enjoyed greater bliss thinks there is nothing further to wish for, and would gladly make its abode there, and say with St. Peter : ' Lord, it is good for us to be here ! '"

What is this state which Teresa describes as being so full of delight? She calls it, as we have heard, the prayer of quiet. The name by which it is commonly

known is that of contemplation, or of passive prayer. One example instinctively presents itself to the Christian memory, as it embodies what may be considered its prominent features. It is that of Mary seated at our Lord's feet, silent, at peace, profoundly attentive to His words, and forgetful of all else in order the better to hear them. There is now no need of long discourses, or of studied petitions; no intellectual efforts are required to master the truth, either by reasoning or by reflection: to look at the Master, and listen to His words is the whole work of contemplation.

But there are degrees even in contemplation. God may at first only allow the smallest rays of His glory to be seen by the soul, and even these may be veiled to her sight; and yet this is enough to capture the love of the favoured one. But the more piercing and direct the divine manifestation the greater will be the increase of her joy, and these joys, too great for human endurance, are the cause of rapture in the saints—effects which we soon shall be called upon to witness in the case of St. Teresa.

As she has just told us, her prayer was nothing but a profound recollection, a blessed peace in which her soul imbibed at the same moment consolation and strength. Our Lord was drawing ever nearer to her, and discovering Himself more to her soul; and as the influence of grace intensifies, our saint enters into a profound agony of inexpressible delight. She is conscious of being almost dead to the things of this world and lost in a rapture of happiness in the thought of God.

"This method of prayer," she says, " is in my opinion a very sure manifestation of the union of the soul with God ; only His Majesty allows the power in

her to be aware of the great work He is doing there, and they only act in order to occupy themselves with Him, and are incapable of any other thought ; and without His orders they would not dare to move. It would be necessary to make a most violent effort to distract them from this divine occupation, and then it would not succeed in turning them entirely away from this divine Object. The soul lifted out of itself by a tender transport would wish to break out into heavenly canticles, so that all in her should testify the excess of her gladness. She longs to praise and bless God for His benefits, but without order or regularity, unless He should put this into them. She says many foolish things, but these follies do not displease Him Who has put her into this state."

The saint owns that whilst writing these lines she is possessed by this celestial folly, and that her soul would remain absorbed in this song of love and praise, but that she remembers the duty of obedience which obliges her to go on with her book.

" The soul," she says, " understands that God is doing His work without any fatigue of the understanding, except that, as it seems to me, it is amazed in beholding our Lord refusing to let the soul undergo any labour whatever, but that of taking its pleasure in the flowers beginning to send forth their fragrance. In one of these visits, how brief soever it may be, the Gardener—being who He is—pours the water without stint, and what the poor soul, with the labour of twenty years in fatiguing the understanding could not bring about, that the heavenly Gardener accomplishes in an instant, causing the fruit both to grow and to ripen. Finally, the virtues are now stronger than they were, for the soul sees itself to be other than it was, and knows not how it is beginning to do great things—it

being our Lord's will that the flowers should open. Now, too, the humility of the soul is much greater, and deeper than it was before."

Humility is ever the touchstone. The saint in seeing its presence recognizes the spirit of God ; all her interior consolations she would treat as delusions unless they left her utterly annihilated in the presence of God, and abased her more in her own sight. To humility she would join the confidence of an infant reposing on its mother's bosom.

"When our Lord raises a soul to this degree of prayer, He asks only of her a simple consent to the graces which He is prepared to pour down upon her, and an entire abandonment of herself to His good pleasure. He wills to dispose of her as of something that is entirely His."

Confidence in God, mistrust of self, a force of character inspired by hope, but kept straight by humility : this is what Teresa understands and teaches admirably, this is what conveys a lesson to which she returns incessantly. They are the soul's wings, whatever may be her state of perfection, or the heights of prayer to which she has attained.

If the privileged souls whose steps we have been following has the happiness of corresponding perfectly with the signal graces God has conferred on her, what more wonders will He work in her? True, the example we have before us is an absolutely exceptional one, but we must also bear in mind the words spoken by our Lord to another saint: "If there were souls in existence in these latter days who had a greater love for Me than the saints in past ages, I should be ready to grant them even greater graces than those which I poured out upon those saints."

Teresa, having surrendered herself entirely to the

divine control, continues her steady flight towards the summit of perfection, and as she ascends, the ever increasing ardour of her soul seems almost to break the bonds of flesh which enclose it.

" In the prayer already spoken of, and in all states of it, the gardener undergoes some labour, though in the latter states the labour is attended with so much bliss and comfort of the soul that the soul would never willingly pass out of it—thus the labour is not felt as labour, but as bliss. In this fourth state there is no sense of anything, only fruition. It understands that the fruition is of a certain good containing in itself all good together at once ; but this good is not comprehended. How this—which we call union—is effected and what it is I cannot tell. Mystical theology explains it, and I do not know the terms of that science.*'

Here Teresa, in default of theological terms, returns to the use of the comparisons with which she has made us familiar; she borrows them from fire and celestial dew, and then, returning to the mystical garden, she finds in its flowers and in the flight of the dove emblems whence she throws fresh light on that mystical theology of whose phraseology she professes her ignorance.

She goes on to say : " What I would wish to explain is that which the soul feels in this divine union. It is plain what union is : two distinct things becoming one. Oh, my Lord, how good Thou art! Blessecl b£ Thou for ever, my God ! Let all creation praise Thee Who hast so loved us, that we can truly speak of this way in which Thou communicatest Thyself to souls in this our exile ! . . . Thus does our Lord advance, step by step, to lay hold of the little bird, and to lay it in the nest where it may repose. For a long time He observed

it fluttering—striving with the understanding and the will, and with all its powers to seek God and please Him ; and so now it is His pleasure to reward it even in this life. And what a reward ! One moment is enough to repay all the possible trials of this life. How shall I describe all that passes in the soul interiorly? Let him describe it who knows it, for as it is impossible to understand it, so it is impossible to describe. When I purposed to write this, I had just communicated, and had risen from the very prayer of which I had been speaking, and while thinking of what the soul was then doing, the Lord said to me : * It undoes itself utterly, my daughter, in order that it may give itself more and more to me. It is not itself that then lives, it is I. As it cannot comprehend what it understands, it understands by not understanding.' He who has experience of this will understand it in some measure, for it cannot be more clearly described. All that I am able to say is that the soul is conscious of being closely united to God j 1 and the certainty she has of this fact is such that nothing could force her to doubt it."

Thus it is that the body succumbs under the weight of happiness and glory with which the soul is inundated. The consciousness of this divine union is such that it absorbs all the powers and the senses. As the flame soars above the hearth below it, so does the soul rise superior to the narrow bonds of the body which encloses it; it is then that ecstasy commences.

We have no desire to waste words and time in combating the arguments of incredulity. It is to the Christian, to those acquainted with the marvels of the Catholic Church—marvels of which these are some of the greatest—that these pages, drawn from St. Teresa's

1 Solo podre decir, que se representa estar junto con Dios.

mystical treatise, are addressed. In the early days God rapt His ardent apostle up to the third heaven, and the Church in its progress through the centuries has produced many saints of both sexes whose supernatural lives have been signalized by such favours as we have here described. St. Teresa shall tell us in her own words what she has seen and experienced.

"The soul while thus seeking after God," she says, "is conscious, with a joy excessive and sweet, and that it is, as it were, fainting away in a kind of trance : breathing and all the bodily strength fail it, so that it cannot even move the hands without great pain ; the eyes close involuntarily, and if they are open they are as if they saw nothing. The ear hears, but what is heard is not comprehended. It is useless to try to speak, because it is not possible to conceive a word ; all bodily strength vanishes, and that of the soul increases, to enable it better to have the fruition of its

joy."

These last words lead to a consideration on the positive side of the principle of ecstasy, or rapture. Teresa, in describing the external phenomena of this state, places the annihilation of the senses specially before our eyes. One objection may be made here which we should like to notice : it is, that ecstasy is a death, a temporary death doubtless it will be urged, but still a death ; and therefore in what way can this state be looked upon as a blissful one, or a state which confers benefit on the soul ? Ecstasy is not death ; if for a moment it suspends the exercise of the intelligence and the inferior senses, 1 the soul expands to its full life

1 This suspension of the senses is only an effect of weakness. When Teresa's soul, later on, was familiarized with these divine visitations, she was able to sustain these supernatural operations of grace without losing the exercise of her exterior faculties.

and vigour during its sway ; it is a prelude to a heavenly life and the beatific vision. "The soul," St. Teresa tells us, " feels her strength increase in proportion to the weakening of the exterior senses, so that she can better enjoy her bliss. She loses herself in God. She no longer exists, but God exists in her. It is true that her powers are suspended, and lose their natural activity ; but a sweet and ineffable feeling replaces the other and absorbs her utterly; this is the consciousness of the Divine Presence.

This is the dominant note of ecstasy. This joy may inundate the soul in different ways : either by a profound sentiment of the Divine Presence such as Teresa speaks of, or by sensible, or intellectual visions, or by voices, distinctly uttered, or spoken to the soul. All these favours were to be conferred in turn, as we shall see later, on our saint. One word more before we conclude this very incomplete sketch of St. Teresa's gift of prayer.

"It is almost impossible," she says, "for the soul in rapture to resist the supernatural attraction. It comes in general as a shock, quick and sharp, before you can collect your thoughts, or help yourself in any way; and you see and feel it as a cloud, or as a strong eagle rising upwards, and carrying you away on its wings. It seemed to me, when I tried to make some resistance, as if a great force beneath my feet lifted mc up. I know of nothing with which to compare it; there is no power against His power.

" Many are the effects of rapture, and one of the greatest is that the mighty power of our Lord is manifested by it. Whether we like it or not, we see that there is One mightier than we are, that these graces are His gifts, and that of ourselves we can do nothing whatever.

"God then so strips the soul of everything that, do what it may, there is nothing on earth that can be its companion. And, though God as it were seems so far away from the soul at that moment, yet He reveals His greatness in an inconceivable way to it. I have seen it myself, and I know by experience that the soul in rapture is mistress of everything, and acquires such freedom in one hour, and even in less, as to be unable to recognize itself. Oh, what power that soul possesses which our Lord raises to this state ! How it looks down upon everything, is entangled by nothing ! How ashamed it is of the time when it was entangled —how amazed at its own blindness. It sees, too, not only the cobwebs that cover it, and its great faults, but also the specks of dirt, however slight they may be ; for the sun shines most clearly, and thus, however much the soul may have laboured at its own perfection, it sees itself to be very unclean if the rays of the sun fall upon it. The soul is like water in a vessel, which appears pellucid when the sun does not shine through it, but if it does the water is found to be full of motes. Before the soul fell into the trance it thought itself to be careful about not offending God ; but now that it has attained to this state, in which the Sun of Justice shines upon it, and makes it open its eyes, it beholds so many motes it would gladly close them again. It remembers the words : ' In Thy presence who shall be justified?' When it looks on this divine Sun the brightness thereof dazzles it; when it looks on itself its eyes are blinded by the dust. The little dove is blinded. So it happens very often ; the soul is often blinded, absorbed, amazed, dizzy at the vision of such grandeur. Blessed is that soul which our Lord draws on to the understanding of the truth ! "

The knowledge of the truth ; this is the supreme

good which Teresa discovers in the heights of perfection to which our Lord has raised her. Noverim te, noverim me. " Lord, that I may know Thee, that I may know myself." The greatness of God, the splendour of His glory, the tenderness of His supreme love ; God the Creator making Himself known to His miserable creature who, entranced, lost, and confounded in her nothingness, has no strength, nor power, nor life to do anything but love Him Who alone deserves it. This describes the state of Teresa's blind dove—of the soul in an ecstasy.

Are we to conclude that she who is thus lifted up to Heaven, is lost to earth ? The treasure of that loving and generous heart, of that gifted mind, are they closed to the world? Is it God's will that the graces which He has showered upon Teresa should be reserved for Himself alone? The saint's history will be a sufficient denial of such an allegation. We shall soon learn when we come to treat of her relations with the outer world, of her works of charity, and of her zeal for souls, whether her contemplation was of no benefit to anyone but herself, and whether the effect of true mysticism is to enfeeble the mind, or dry up the heart of man. Teresa had still to pass through trials before attaining the full height of her sanctity. The apostle said: " Lest the greatness of the revelation should exalt me, there was given me a sting of my flesh, an angel of Satan to buffet me." Teresa, exposed to the same peril, was to be saved from it in a different manner, and the foundations of her soul, tried by cruel anguish, joined to the contradiction of men, were to be sunk ever deeper and deeper on the solid bed-rock of humility.

CHAPTER IX

IN the same year in which Teresa gave herself to God wholly and for ever, Avila opened its doors to the sons of St. Ignatius. Fr. Juan de Padranos and Fr. Ferdinand Alvarez had been sent there by St. Francis Borja, who was at that time general of the Spanish province, and on their arrival they took possession of an ancient hospice, and the church of St. Giles adjoining it, both of which were made over to them by the confraternity of that hospital. They here founded a college, to which before long the parents belonging to the upper classes in the town sent their sons to be educated. Rumours of the holiness of the lives led by these two fathers were soon spread in Avila. Nor were these reports idle ones, for though neither had reached a mature age, they had already acquired piety and experience in an austere noviceship, which had been followed by much labour in the missionary field.

Teresa, though all she knew at this time of the Society was gathered from its motto, and from one or two books written by members of it, could not contain her joy— in her ardent desire of the greater honour and glory of God—when she heard that they had come to settle in Avila. If she had not been kept back by her convent rules, and by apprehensions for which she could hardly account, she would have been amongst the first to seek from these fathers for that direction of which her soul stood at this time so much in need.

The consolations she was constantly receiving in prayer, which pursued her in spite of her not going out of her way in search of them, were a source of terror to her humility. How is it possible, she said to herself, that God can thus treat a miserable sinner? Such graces can only be the portion of the holy and pure of heart. Are they not therefore illusions of the angel of darkness, who seeks to draw me away, by means of them, from the solid practice of dry but meritorious prayer?

These grievous misgivings grew in proportion to God's favours. It was true that Teresa was inwardly supported by the belief that they came from God. " I had even the certainty of it," she says, " because I could see that I was growing stronger, and better since I received them ; but if I was even for a short time distracted after my prayer, they began again to trouble me."

A sad instance, which bore some resemblance to her case, and thus gave a foundation to her fears, occurred about this time. A woman of the name of Clare of Cordova, called in religion Magdalen of the Cross, had by her pretended miracles, visions, and revelations extorted the admiration of all Spain. She was a member of the Franciscan Order, and after many years spent in a convent in Cordova, in which she edified and astounded the community by her austerities, she was made Abbess. Her fame spread outside the confines of her monastery. Kings and Pontiffs consulted her. The spirit of prophecy was attributed to her, by means of which it was supposed that she had foretold the defeat of Francis I at Pavia, and the pillage of Rome by the Imperial army. Finally, after duping the whole of the religious world—it is said by the aid of the evil spirit—grace touched the woman's

heart, and stripping herself of the mask of hypocrisy, she fell at the feet of the Franciscan Visitor, and owned that her life for thirty years had been a lie and a deception. She was condemned by the Inquisition to read an avowal of her misdeeds in the cathedral of Seville, and finished her life in the practice of penance in a remote convent.

The crisis in the above drama took place in 1546. It produced a great sensation throughout the country ; and it was soon after this terrible scandal that St. Teresa began to feel the supernatural attractions we have described, and to enter into the extraordinary ways by which she was henceforth to be led. It was in vain that her conscience testified to her good faith. She felt that Sister Magdalen was probably deceived by the devil before she began to think of deceiving others, and, deeply persuaded that it was impossible for a person leading a sinful life such as hers to receive divine communications, she resisted the attractions of grace, in the same way as Jacob fought with the angel. A glance at Teresa's account of her struggles will mark the difference between the impostor and the saint. Full of humble misgivings as regards her interior lights and her spiritual experiences, Teresa saw herself ever as a little child in the hands of God, and as such she wished to be led by her spiritual teachers. She made no use of the privileges accorded her by our Lord except to give all the glory to Him, and all the shame and confusion to herself.

" These fears so grew upon me," she says, "that it made me seek diligently for spiritual persons with whom I might treat of my state. I had already heard of some, for the Fathers of the Society of Jesus had come hither, and though I knew none of them, I was greatly attracted by them, merely because I had heard

of their way of life, and of prayer, but I did not think myself fit to speak to them, or strong enough to obey them ; and I spent some time in this state. Was there ever delusion so great as mine, O my God! when I withdrew from good, in order to become good ! The devil must lay much stress on this in the beginning of a course of virtue. He knows that the whole relief of the soul consists in conferring with the friends of God. When I saw that my fear was going so far it struck me—because I was making progress in prayer— that this must be a great blessing, or a very great evil ; for I understood perfectly that what had happened was supernatural, because at times I was unable to withstand it ; to have it when I would was impossible. I thought to myself that there was no help for it, but in keeping my conscience pure, avoiding every occasion even of venial sins; for if it was the work of the Spirit of God the gain was clear, and if the work of Satan, so long as I strove to please and did not offend our Lord, Satan could do me little harm ; on the contrary, he must lose in the struggle. Determined on this course, and always praying to God to help me, striving also after purity of conscience for some days, I saw that my soul had not strength to go forth alone to a perfection so great. I had also certain attachments, which, though not wrong, were enough to keep me back."

Teresa had long before broken with those habits of communication with the outer world which had caused her so much remorse. To what, therefore, did she fear to be too much attached at this time ? Probably to ties within the cloister, which, formed by the consecrated link of community life, and founded on the sure basis of unity of aim and aspiration, and, above all, on holy charity, make a true sisterhood of religious life. If Teresa found material for self-reproach in these legiti-

mate ties, it was doubtless on account of the ardour with which she gave herself up to them. This ardour, which was part of her very nature, was one day to be transformed, not destroyed, by divine grace into burning love of God and zeal for her neighbour. The day was to come for our saint, and was not then far distant, when the love of Jesus would take such entire possession of her heart that she should no longer have any fear of such attachments, for it would be impossible for her to love anyone excepting in God and for God.

This mingling of human attachments, supernatural fervours, and deep attraction to a more perfect life, combined to put Teresa's soul on the rack. Fr. Vincent Barren had long before been moved by his superiors from Avila, and she had found no one to replace him in the task of directing her soul. She was forced to suffer in silence, and pursue her solitary path uncertain whither it was leading her. The Fathers of the Society of Jesus inspired her with confidence, but she was unwilling to take the necessary steps to put herself in communication with them. At last circumstances led to her becoming acquainted with Dr. Caspar Daza, an excellent priest, whose name stands first on the list of learned theologians whom Providence thought fit to associate with our saint in the character of spiritual advisers.

Caspar Daza was introduced to the convent of the Incarnation by Don Francisco de Salcedo, an old friend of Teresa's and of her family. Don Francisco hid under his secular attire the heart of an apostle; and his life, wholly given up to prayer, good works, and the study of theology and philosophy, recalls that of his friend Don Alonso de Cepeda. We shall find him associated with our saint for twenty years, during

which time his services were at her disposal, in her great undertakings, and he showed himself emulous of her zeal and fervour. Later on his wife's death left him free to enter Holy Orders, and he became confessor to a convent of Carmelites of the Reform.

Doctor Caspar Daza's first visit did not produce the results hoped for by Teresa. In the first place, confused to find herself in the presence of so learned and holy a man, Teresa gave but an incomplete and inadequate account of the state of her soul, and her manner of prayer. She begged him to become her director, and to hear her confession. This was very necessary ; as, had Doctor Daza done so, he would soon have been enlightened by a more- precise statement of her faults, and would have perceived that her life was not the commonplace one which she otherwise would have led him to suppose. But pressing duties prevented his acceding to her^request. He even told her it was impossible for him to take charge of the care of her soul, and he left her with some general directions only, as to what she should do to attain a state of perfection. In spite of his experience in such matters, Doctor Daza had only half understood the state of Teresa's soul.

" He began," she says, "to direct me as if I was strong—I ought to have been strong, according to the method of prayer which he saw I used—so that I should in nothing offend God. When I perceived that he ordered the affairs of my soul as if I ought to be perfect at once, I saw that much more care was necessary in my case. In a word, I felt that the means he would have employed were not those by which my soul could be helped onwards. I believe that if I had only had this ecclesiastic to confer with that my soul would have made no progress. I wonder at times how it was

that he was not permitted to understand my case, or to undertake the care of my soul. I see now it was all for my greater good in order that I might know and converse with persons so holy as the members of the Society of Jesus." Doctor Daza became one of Teresa's most faithful friends, and she always manifested the highest esteem for him; his failure to understand her was a matter of no importance in her eyes.

"The saintly nobleman," to quote Teresa's words, Don Francisco, distressed at the want of success of the interview which he had brought about, undertook to console Teresa. "He encouraged me," she says, "and told me I ought not to suppose I could give up everything in a day. God would bring it about by degrees: he himself had been unable to free himself for a long time from some slight imperfection." If Don Francisco had been a priest, Teresa would never have sought another director. His patience, moderation, and firmness were the very qualities that she looked for in a director, but he was not yet in the position of being inheritor of the promise Christ reserved for His minister, "He that heareth you, heareth Me." So, in spite of his comforting words, she remained anxious, not being able to say positively : God speaks to me by his lips. Don Francisco, who joined to his other merits that of great tact and delicacy, wished to be of use to Teresa as a friend and adviser, and by no means desired to take upon himself the part of a judge. He used his influence over her to induce her to write an account of her method and gift of prayer, which he then undertook to lay before Gaspar Daza. This is how she speaks of the advice which had been given her: "This,"she says, "distressed me exceedingly. I could tell him nothing of my prayer, for the grace to understand—and understanding it to describe it—has only

lately been given me by God. Certainly I was anxious to please God, and I could not persuade myself that Satan had anything to do with it. But I was afraid, on account of my great sins, that God might leave me blind, so that I should understand nothing. Looking into books to see if I could find anything there by which I might recognize the prayer I practised, I found in one of them the ' Ascent of the Mount,' 1 and in that part of it which relates to the union of the soul with God I saw all those marks which I had in myself, in that I could not think of anything . . . when I was in prayer. I marked that passage, and gave him the book that he, and the ecclesiastic mentioned before, saint and servant of God, might consider.it and tell me what I should do. If they thought it right, I would give up that method of prayer altogether; for why should I expose myself to danger when at the end of twenty years during which I used it I had gained nothing, but had fallen into a delusion of the devil. It was better for me to give it up. And yet it seemed hard, for I had already discovered what my soul would become without prayer. Everything seemed full of trouble."

Teresa placed the book in Don Francisco's hands, together with a detailed account of her life and the faults she had committed. Teresa prayed much while these were being examined, and many prayers were said for her, as she tremblingly awaited a decree which she looked upon almost as a judgment of Heaven. After a short time Don Francisco appeared at the convent, and broke to Teresa, in accents of grief, that in Caspar Daza's opinion and his own, the manifestations she had received were the work of the Evil One. The conclusion they had come to was that she had

1 Subida del inonte Sion, by a Franciscan, B. de Laredo.

better send for a father of the Society of Jesus and put herself under his direction, so that she might be delivered from the dangers to which she had exposed herself.

The anguish with which this decision was received may easily be imagined. " All I could do," Teresa tells us, " was to weep." She did not even dare to open out her heart at the feet of her Saviour, for she now felt bound to consider the consolation she knew she would then receive from her kind Master was but another delusion of the devil's. But in spite of her inward distress our saint prepared to obey by getting ready for a general confession, and sending for Fr. Juan de Padranos to hear it. Teresa showed one last symptom of weakness in taking this step which cost her so much. She begged of the portress, and the sister who had charge of the sacristy, to mention this interview to no one, as (she tells us) she did not wish the community to know of it ; but "this was of little use, after all, for when I was called down there was one at the door, as it happened, who told it to the whole convent."

Fr. de Padranos received his new penitent with the grave and gentle kindness which marks the bearing of the sons of St. Ignatius in their dealings with souls. He made the much-dreaded manifestation of her conscience easy to her, and sounding the depths of her soul at one glance he understood all. Perfect straightforwardness, the candour of a child, great humility, joined to a superior mind, solid judgment, great good sense, a loving heart pure as an angel's and as ardent : this was doubtless what Teresa revealed to her confessor's sight. Added to these natural gifts he discerned great marvels of divine grace, the manifest and direct action of God, and a surpassing love for her

divine Spouse in this privileged soul. What consolation must have filled the soul of this excellent priest at the sight of such holiness ! He had probably been warned by Don Francisco that his mission was to free his penitent from the delusions of lying spirits, and had come with an anxious mind to the convent; and he found himself brought face to face with a saint, and no less one than St. Teresa !

Her happiness equalled that of Fr. de Padranos. She had now found the direction our Lord had destined for her, and she followed it as long as circumstances permitted ; and when this father was moved from Avila, in the course of those changes which are usual in the Society, she replaced his direction by that of another of its members—unity of spirit being one of their strongest characteristics. Thus the sons of St. Ignatius, whether they bore the names of Juan de Padranos, Baltasar Alvarez, or Francis Borja, were ever to lead Teresa by the same path. This path Fr. de Padranos traced out on his very first visit. " He encouraged me greatly ; " she says, " he said that all was very evidently the work of the Spirit of God, only it was necessary for me to go back again to my prayer, because I was not well grounded, and had not begun to understand what mortification meant—that was true, for I do not think I knew it even by name. That I was by no means to give up my prayer, on the contrary, I was to do violence with myself in order to practise it, because God had bestowed on me such special graces as made it impossible to say whether it was, or was not, the will of our Lord to do good to many through me. He went further, for he seemed to prophesy that which our Lord afterwards did with me, and said I should be greatly to blame if I did not correspond with the graces which God bestowed on me."

Thus a new life opened out before Teresa. Instead of being fettered and restrained by fear, she was told to abandon herself with confidence to the divine leading. She was no longer to look upon the extraordinary lights she was receiving as dreams of the spirit of darkness, but as rays from Heaven. The raptures and joys which transported her soul were the work of grace and not of the father of lies. This was indeed peace after the storm! Rest, after long days and nights of anguish.

If Fr. de Padranos' advice brought peace to the heart of our saint, no less did he impress measures of prudence upon her. Teresa was to take daily a subject for her meditation drawn from the mysteries of the Passion, in all humility and simplicity, and dwell on it in a manner to draw practical resolutions from it. With what object, we may ask, if her director was persuaded that her state of prayer came from God ? With the object of trying her obedience, establishing her in humility, and of giving her a more complete certitude of the divine origin of her supernatural favours. In short, she was to aim at rendering her life, which was already so deeply fervent, still more worthy of the heavenly favours which were being poured out upon it. Fr. de Padranos likewise recommended certain practices of penance " which were not very pleasant to me," adds the saint.

A retreat confirmed the good effects of her confession. Fr. de Padranos put the Exercises of St. Ignatius into his holy penitent's hands for that purpose, and taught her how to follow them. 1 Teresa was little given to such methodical meditations, and her use of these could only be a passing one. But she found in that masterpiece of a great saint a solid basis such as her director sought for

1 Ribera.

her, in order to build up her spiritual life upon it. She felt in making this retreat that a new life had begun for her, and later on she exclaimed : "I was to find in the Society of Jesus my training and my spiritual life."

Whilst Teresa was thus following in docility and obedience the spiritual exercises of the saint of Loyola, that valiant soldier of God was preparing to appear before his Master. He had arrived at the last scene of his great and arduous life, and whilst surveying the work of his sons in spreading the faith in two continents could sing his Nunc Dimittis. How innumerable were the sinners to whom he had procured the grace of conversion ! How many weak and tottering souls owed to him a renewal of fervour—how many infidels the grace of baptism ! What triumphs for the cause of God had this valiant soldier won in the field he had chosen as his own ! But among the conquests which he joyfully bequeathed to his mother the Church, there was one taking place in the depths of an obscure monastery of his beloved country of which he was doubtless ignorant. Had he foreseen its astounding fruits his soul would surely have thrilled with fresh joy, and his dying hands would have sent a last blessing to this inheritor of his zeal, his love for the Church, and of his apostolic spirit.

Under Teresa's humble bearing her director soon discovered a great saint; but he did not allow her to perceive the opinion he had of her. After pointing out to her the road he wished her to pursue, he left her to follow out her own will: " I began at once to make a change in many things," she says, " though my confessor never pressed me—on the contrary, he seemed to make light of it. I was the more influenced by this because he led me on by the way of the love of God.

He left me free, and did not press me unless I did it myself, out of love."

She could not have found a better guide ; for Love had already taken possession of her soul, and she could refuse It nothing. She realized that to give oneself, once and for all, is the only response worthy to be made to Jesus Who says ' Come, and follow Me'; and she desired to do so without limit or exception. Fr. de Padranos had suggested another means of self-surrender by the word mortification. The saint tells us it was an unknown one to her. Her still delicate health, her constant infirmities, had only left her sufficient strength to observe the mitigated Rule of her Order. She had not thought it possible to do more ; many in her place would have done less. But the time for nursing herself was over. When kneeling at her meditations at the foot of the Cross a new feeling came over her : it was the desire to suffer. A strange desire in the sight of the world, but a very natural one to the eye of faith. This longing was, as we shall see later, soon to take possession of her heart and to be the guiding power of her life. But these were the early steps in a steep and arid ascent.

Teresa was now no longer satisfied with renouncing all superfluous objects, comforts, and conveniences. She went further and offered our Saviour the sacrifice of bodily suffering. She wore a hair-shirt, and inflicted severe flagellations on herself with diciplines of steel, or nettles. Such mortifications she confesses at first cost her much. Her delicate limbs shuddered before these instruments of penance, but one look at her crucifix, one thought of the holy counsels she had received, enabled her to triumph over the weakness of human nature. She had been told by Fr. de Padranos, " Possibly God has sent you all these maladies because

you did not practise mortification. You need not fear, your health will not suffer from them." Teresa believed, and her health gained rather than lost ; she was better now than she had been for a long time ; and no doubt the peace and interior consolation she now felt contributed to this result. In vain did she try to struggle against God's favours as she had been recommended to do by her director. The more she resisted the more He inundated her with interior joys, and with raptures which she could not conceal, and from which she complains that it was impossible for her to fly. 1 The saint's obedience and humility having thus triumphantly emerged from the trial to which they had been subjected, God's designs on her showed themselves ever in a stronger light; and it seemed as if liberty had been granted to her in order that she should receive His graces in more abundant measure. A fortunate circumstance hastened the term of trial imposed upon her by the prudent counsels of her Jesuit director.

The college of St. Giles received a visit in the spring from its first provincial, St. Francis Borja. This holy Jesuit, who in the world went by the name of Duke of Gandia, and had at one time been a minister of the Emperor Charles and a dignitary at the Spanish court, was now wholly devoted to the service of the King of kings. Whilst he was at Avila he visited the saint in her convent, and Teresa gives the following account of their interview : " When he heard me, he said it was the work of the Spirit of God, and that he thought it was not right now to prolong that resistance. Only I should always begin my prayer by meditating on some part of the Passion, and that if our Lord should then raise up my spirit I should make no resistance, but suffer His Majesty to raise it—I myself not

1 Life, ch. xxiv.

seeking it. He gave advice as one who had made great progress himself. I was exceedingly consoled. He always helped me and gave me advice according to his power, and that power was great."

St. Francis was an instrument in the hand of Providence to take away the last chains which bound our saint and intercepted her flight Heavenward. She could henceforth without fear or combat allow herself to be borne to the highest regions of the supernatural life : the unknown force which gave her this power being nothing less than her love of God; and the word of a saint guaranteed this for her.

CHAPTER X

THE approbation given by St. Francis Borja to Teresa on her method of prayer, and her supernatural manifestations, had consoled her only in order to prepare her for fresh suffering. As the pure grain of the wheat is crushed in the mill, and thus prepared to become the bread of the divine Sacrifice, so was Teresa's soul tried and transformed in the furnace of tribulation, in order that she might be made fit for the work for which God destined her. She was one chosen out of ten thousand, and destined to be a living victim; and God, jealous of the perfection of His beloved, was not yet entirely satisfied with the holiness which she had thus far attained. He continued to pursue her with His inspirations until His love, victorious on all points, should have nothing further to ask of His servant. This is the secret of those successive " conversions" of which Teresa speaks; a word by which she denotes the progress she was ever making in the path of perfection—one which was to end in total self-abnegation.

We have at last reached the last sacrifice asked of her; the immolation of those heart-ties by which she was still so strongly bound that so far she had never been able to break them asunder. When she has done this she will have pronounced her *' consummatum est, " and she will then enter into the last period of her life : K 129

one of even greater joys, and yet of still greater trial and suffering than those which have preceded it.

Directly after St. Francis left Avila, Fr. de Padranos was recalled to another part of the province. This was in the year 1557. " His departure was a great affliction to me," writes our saint, " for I thought I should go back to my past wickedness, and that it was not possible to find such another as he."

The Convent of the Incarnation had not shared Teresa's views, or her desire to lead a life of greater strictness. The community was increasing rapidly, and the majority of the nuns brought good dispositions and solid piety to the religious life ; but the fine convent with its spacious gardens, though it offered its inmates a peaceful and pleasant retreat, could do little without a fixed Rule, or strict Observance, to imbue them with the monastic spirit. The nuns lived much as they pleased ; in the practice of Christian virtues, no doubt, but still not very differently to many devout women in the world. To aim at perfection in their religious life was far from their thoughts. They left such ideas to Teresa without any desire of following her example.

Again, as we have previously mentioned, the revenues of the convent were insufficient for the number and wants of its members. Hence the necessity arose of frequent appeals to the charity of the nuns' relations, and even of sending some away in order to relieve the convent of the burthen of supporting them. Teresa groaned under these abuses without dreaming that God would one day impose on her the arduous task of reforming them. Meanwhile she humbly and patiently accepted a state of things which she looked upon as inevitable. When her superiors, giving in to the entreaties of her relations, told her to

go and stay with them, she obeyed, leaving with much regret the little cell, which she would never have left on her own accord.

" But all things work for good for those who love God." Teresa experienced this when, soon after Fr. de Padranos left Avila, one of her relatives obtained leave for her to go and stay in her house. The saint whilst on this visit found herself in her native parish, close to the church of St. John, and the Jesuit college of St. Giles. She profited by this neighbourhood to put herself once more under the direction of a member of the Society.

Fr. Baltasar Alvarez, who was later on to be her principal guide in the paths of perfection, was then still a novice, but already he had made great progress in prayer and penance. He was concluding his theological studies under Fr. Bafiez at the Dominican convent of Avila, and every evening on his return to the college he used to visit the Blessed Sacrament in that church ; and our saint when going at night to pray there used to see this holy youth absorbed in prayer and insensible to all exterior things. Teresa whilst visiting her cousin was thrown across another holy soul on whom God had designs for the furtherance of His work. This was Dona Guiomar, a young widow who had lost her husband at the age of twenty-five. Heart-broken, and yet not wholly prepared to break with the world and its dreams of human happiness, she had put herself under the direction of a Jesuit father in the hope that peace and strength of mind might come of his guidance. Teresa, who already knew and loved her, believed that she was capable of doing great .things for God. Dona Guiomar opened her heart to the saint, and told her of those cravings which she had not been able to overcome for

earthly joys, but which—had she known it—God alone could satisfy. Teresa spoke to her of the love of God, and pressed her to give herself up entirely to Him in the practice of prayer. A profound and supernatural affection sprung up between these two women, who were arriving at the same end by very different roads. Dona Guiomar parted with Teresa with regret when the latter, as soon as she was able to escape from her cousin's importunities, returned to her convent. Some months later Dona Guiomar was, in her turn, successful in obtaining a similar permission to take Teresa to her house.

This event took place at the end of the year 1558. The holy novice of the preceding year, Fr. Baltasar Alvarez, had been ordained, and already gave evidence of being a consummate master in the science of the spiritual life. Gaspar Daza had entrusted his soul to his hands. Don Francisco de Salcedo obeyed him like a child. Finally, Dona Guiomar had discovered in him the firm and prudent director of which her soul stood in need. Teresa, struck by the progress made by her friend in her spiritual life, wished to profit in like manner by Fr. Baltasar's direction, and accordingly enrolled herself among the number of his penitents. Fr. Baltasar recognized from the moment of his first interview with Teresa the vast designs God had upon the soul He had confided to his care. He thus wisely limited his direction to seconding the divine workings in her soul with wisdom and prudence.

" This father," Teresa says, " began by putting me in the way of greater perfection. He used to say to me that I ought to leave nothing undone, that I might be wholly pleasing to God. He was, however, very prudent and very gentle at the same time ; for my soul was not at all strong, but rather very weak, especially as to giving up certain friendships, though I did not offend God by them. There was much natural affection in them, and I thought it would be an act of ingratitude if I broke them off. And so, as I did not offend God, I asked him if I must be ungrateful. He told me to lay the matter before God for a few days, and recite the hymn ' Veni Creator,' that God might enlighten me as to the better course. One day, having prayed for some time, and implored the Lord to help me to please Him in all things, I began the hymn, and as I was saying it I fell into a trance, so suddenly that I was, as it were, carried out of myself. This was the first time that the Lord bestowed on me the grace of ecstasy. I heard these words : ' I will not have thee converse with men, but with angels.' They made me afraid, though, on the other hand, they gave me great comfort."

*' God's words effect what they say; they are both words and actions," the saint was wont to say later on. Experience taught her this from the moment she heard them. "From that day forth I have had courage so great as to leave all things for God, who, in one moment, was pleased to change His servant into another person. Accordingly there was no necessity for laying further commands upon me in this matter. When my confessor saw how much I clung to these friendships, he did not venture to bid me distinctly to give them up. He must have waited till our Lord did the work, as He did Himself. Nor did I think myself that I could succeed ; for I had tried before, and the pain it gave me was so great that I abandoned the attempt, on the ground that there was nothing unseemly in the attachment. Now our Lord set me at liberty, and gave me also strength to use it. I told my confessor of it, and gave up everything according to

his advice. It did a great deal of good to those with whom I used to converse." It was with these sentiments that Teresa returned to her monastery. Had she to suffer from any unkindness on the part of those nuns upon whom her new way of living reflected, possibly, a certain degree of blame? Did she hear any gentle murmurs on the subject of her craving for solitude, her austerities, and her silence ; or a whisper that she was trying to pass herself off for a saint? Her extreme reserve on such points allows us to suspect this, without, however, in any way affirming that such was the case. The following is the only confidential letter we possess of hers which throws any light upon what passed between her and the community of the Incarnation at this time: "I passed many years," she says, writing at the end of her life to a nun of a different Order, " in a convent where there were a hundred and eighty nuns, with whom I lived as if only God and I existed. This is what one can do when one loves God as you do, my dear Mother. Love your sisters for the virtues you perceive in them ; pay no attention to their defects. Doing this gave me such interior peace, that though my community was a numerous one they caused me no more distraction than if 1 had been alone ; on the contrary, it helped to make me advance in virtue."

This line of conduct was adopted by Teresa no less from prudence than by her desire to die to herself, and to exterior objects in order to lose herself in God. Her apostleship during three years, from 1558 to 1561, was to be exclusively that of example, and she was only to exercise this with humble reserve. Her one occupation was to be that of working at her own perfection ; and our Lord on His side, whilst He was, unknown to her, preparing her for those great undertakings which He

willed to accomplish by her means, appeared during those three years to have no object but that of sanctifying her soul. Thus was Teresa admitted into a divine novitiate, of which our Saviour Himself was Master, in which He instructed her by word of mouth, enlightened her by means of astonishing visions, and led her finally to pronounce the vow of always following the most perfect way, and the sublime desire to suffer or die.

Trials meanwhile increased ; both Master and disciple, Jesus and Teresa, suffered from the cross which is known as the contradictions of well-meaning people. The recollection of the story of the unfortunate Magdalen of the Cross, and similar cases, still tormented the imagination (more timid than enlightened) of Don Francisco de Salcedo, and Caspar Daza, and various other priests and good people who took an interest in our saint. None assuredly doubted her good faith. If the devil deceived her, it was against her will, but her misfortune was none the less great. She tells the story of the solicitude of which she was the object with her usual charity. Neither the reassuring testimony of St. Francis Borja's nor that of Fr. Baltasar Alvarez could stop the warfare these good folk waged against God and His holy will, whilst all the time they thought they were fighting the powers of darkness.

" As a rule," she says, " I only discovered my soul to my confessor, but by his orders I sometimes spoke on such matters to some other servants of God. As these loved me they feared all the more that I was ensnared by the devil. Also they were not careful to be as silent as they should have been. They consulted with various people whom I had confided in about my method of prayer. They had doubtless good intentions, but they caused me much pain by so doing, as they then divulged what should have been kept secret,

which made it appear as if I had published these things myself. Our Lord permitted it, I think, in order to try me without their being to blame. It should of course be understood that I do not speak of what I had mentioned in confession ; I only say that as I felt bound to conceal nothing because I had received the order to tell all my difficulties, it seemed to rne I had a right to count on their discretion. They had many conferences together about my necessities ; for they had a great affection for me, and were afraid I was under a delusion. I too was very much afraid whenever I was not occupied in prayer ; but when I prayed and our Lord bestowed His graces on me I was instantly reassured. My confessor told me they were all of opinion that I was deceived by Satan ; that I must communicate less frequently, and contrive to distract myself in such a way as to be less alone. I was in great fear myself, as I have just said, and my disease of the heart contributed thereto, so that very often I did not dare to remain alone in my cell during the day. When I found so many maintain this, and myself unable to believe them, I had at once a most grievous scruple, for it seemed to me that I had very little humility, especially as they all led lives incomparably better than mine."

It might seem strange that Fr. Baltasar should have passed such a sentence on our saint, which was entirely opposed to his own personal opinion, and the intimate knowledge he had of her interior life. He acted, however, in this manner in conformity with a divine inspiration. He appeared to doubt this much afflicted soul, whose only support he was, and even at times to abandon her to the attacks of her adversaries ; but in reality he was full of admiration for her progress

1 Life, ch. xxin.-xxv.

in perfection, which his rigorism favoured, and he never ceased to recognize the hand of God in her supernatural gifts which were a stumbling-block to the rest of the world.

Before long, in consequence of the indiscreet talk of which Teresa complained, all Avila became acquainted with the events which were taking place in a cell in the Convent of the Incarnation. The saint's extraordinary gifts of prayer were spoken of by some with admiration, by others with contempt. Some went so far as to go to Fr. Baltasar to put him on his guard against his penitent's delusions. The father heard them in silence ; the popular talk did not affect him like the misgivings of the learned.

4 'My confessor," Teresa says, "though he agreed with them for the sake of trying me, as

I understood afterwards, always comforted me ; and alone did so. He told me that if I did not offend God, my prayer, even if it was the work of Satan, could do me no harm, that I should be delivered from it. He bade me pray much to God ; he himself, and all his penitents and many others did so earnestly. I too with all my might, and as many as I knew to be servants of God, prayed that His Majesty would be pleased to lead me by another way." 1

Whilst the good people of Avila were thus troubled in mind about one whose marvellous life would later on redound so greatly to the glory of the city, they agreed in venerating another woman who was celebrated for her sanctity in those days though little is known of her in these. Her name was Maridiaz. She had consecrated her life to God since her early youth, and from that moment it had been one of constant prayer and sacrifice. She spent her days, and even frequently her

1 Life, ch. xxv.

nights, in the church of St. Emelion, where she prayed, hidden from the eye of man. Years succeeded each other, and found her ever in the same place, which had become her tabernacle—her place of rest. A prisoner with the divine Prisoner, she never wearied of remaining near Him, contemplating and loving Him. But no extraordinary graces rewarded this great fervour. The saint of Avila, Maridiaz, had neither visions nor ecstasies. And was Teresa a more privileged person ? Avila refused to believe it, ignoring that God has more than one road whereby He leads His elect to Himself.

Teresa herself held this holy soul in great esteem. She would gladly, had it been God's will, have been led by the same ways as Maridiaz, and she implored her to obtain this grace for her. But her friend's prayers, in spite of her power over the loving heart of our Lord, were not heard, and whilst she continued her round of visits to the Blessed Sacrament and her rosaries, Teresa went on always advancing on her road. Or, rather, our Divine Saviour, paying no heed to the obstacles put in her path, was ever drawing her in His own way nearer to Himself. The struggle in our saint's heart became at times very severe ; on one side there were the wellnigh invincible attractions of divine love which lifted her out of herself, and on the other the charitable warnings of her friends. Fr. Balta-sar's direction also took a stricter turn. Reversing St. Francis Borja's decision, he ordered the saint to resist her supernatural attractions, put a term even to her hours of solitude, and finally deprived her for twenty days of Communion. At last Teresa could no longer contain her anguish. She went to the college of St. Giles in the hope that she would be able to induce her stern director to soften a little the sacrifices

he asked of her. But either because the good father was absent, or because he judged it wiser to continue trying her instead of administering consolation to her, in either case she left the church without having seen him, and as grief-stricken as when she entered it. It appeared to her as she returned to the monastery that she must succumb to her trials ; for how could she continue to live without prayer, without Communion, in the misery to which she was reduced by the alarms of those who still thought her a victim to the delusions of the devil?

"I was by myself," she says, " having no one in whom I could find any comfort, unable to pray or read, like a person stunned by heavy trials, utterly disquieted and wearied, not knowing what would become of me. I have been at times—yea, very often—in distress, but never before in distress so great. I was in this state for four or five hours ; there was no comfort for me either from Heaven or earth, our Lord let me suffer, afraid of a thousand dangers. In this distress, these Thy words alone were enough to remove it and give me a perfect peace : " Be not afraid, my daughter. It is I ; and I will not abandon thee. Fear not." 1

The tortures ceased. Teresa lifted her head bowed down by sorrow, and smiling at her loving Master she asked herself how she could possibly have doubted that what passed in her was the effect of His goodness, and full of new life and strength and light, she exclaims in transport: " Oh, my Lord, how true a friend art Thou ! Oh that a voice might go forth over the whole world proclaiming Thy faithfulness to those who love Thee. All things fail, but Thou, O Lord of all, never failest."

She had much need of this divine encouragement to sustain her under a persecution which increased and

spread rapidly. A parallel was made between her and Maridiaz in order to exalt the former to Teresa's disparagement. Her smallest actions were spied upon, her words treasured up, and if a shadow of imperfection was traced to either, Fr. Baltasar was at once informed of it. Again the saint was interrogated about her prayer ; when she answered with her usual simplicity it was made out that she wished to appear learned, or people professed to be shocked at her frankness. In a word, the inhabitants of Avila who loved her in the days when she delighted the souls of her visitors in the parlour, now looked upon her with ever increasing suspicion, and pursued her with unjust criticisms.

Teresa accepted these trials ; she drew even greater strength from them in order to detach herself from the world, and to hide herself in God. The severity of Fr. Baltasar and the line of conduct he took in her regard were a greater trial to her.

As we already know, Fr. Baltasar was a very holy man, but to his great gift of prayer, his enlightened judgment, and his supernatural lights, he joined a profound humility which was his chief characteristic. Though personally persuaded that Teresa was led by the Holy Spirit, he had difficulty in understanding how the theologians, to whom (under his orders) she had submitted the state of her soul, and her method of prayer, judged her so differently, and he ended in fearing that he was deceived. Without, therefore, allowing his penitent to see his doubts, which would have put the finishing stroke to her troubles, he judged it necessary to try her to the uttermost. He wished thus to obtain the greatest guarantee of her holiness, her obedience, and her spirit of self-abnegation ; and as Teresa was detached from everything except the

divine consolations, he desired her voluntarily to abstain from them. Strange direction, we may possibly think, and as exceptional as the road by which the saint was led, but it is one which can be explained by the above reasons.

Fr. Baltasar at the same time spared no effort to attain that depth of knowledge and divine enlightenment which were required in order to direct a soul such as Teresa's. He prayed much, and studied the works of the most approved mystical writers. On one occasion it is related that, speaking to a member of the Society of the numerous treatises on spiritual matters which he had read, he said: " Well, Father, I have had to read those and more, in order to understand Mother Teresa

God certainly gave him this grace ; he understood Teresa from the first, and remained her constant support in the storm which broke over her. She, on the other hand, had no peace except in obeying him ; and notwithstanding the trials to which he submitted her, she honoured and loved him as a visible guardian angel and as the father of her soul. " Yes," she exclaims, " I am very fond of this spiritual father, in spite of the severity with which he treated me." In another place she writes: " If he had not reached a great sanctity, and if our Lord had not kept up his courage, he would never have been able to endure what he did on my account. On the one side, he had to answer those who thought I was quite off the right road, and who would not believe the assurances he gave them that they were mistaken ; and on the other, he had to comfort me, and cure me of the fears in which these caused me to fall."

Whilst Teresa was acquiring fresh perfection in the

midst of trials and suffering, her divine Master was pursuing His work in her soul. It was in vain that she tried to deprive herself of solitude, and to shorten her prayer, in order to avoid His supernatural manifestations. He was ever at her side, and made Himself known to her whatever she was doing. Whilst she was engaged in conversations in obedience to the orders she received, He ravished her soul to Himself so that she heard no voice but His. This divine language is not heard by the senses, and yet "the soul," Teresa says, "seems to have other ears with which it hears ; and He forces it to listen, and will not let it be distracted." Teresa received many divine teachings through this supernatural sense. When she was sad our Lord encouraged her by means of it, or He warned her if He saw her departing from the path of perfection which He wished her to follow. He even reprimanded her with a vehemence sufficient, as she says, "to make a soul sink into her native nothingness." But whilst He enlightened, consoled, and rejoiced her heart, He also warned her of dangers which threatened her, and threw a prophetic light on what was going to happen to her.

On one occasion she was tempted, when much tried by Fr. Baltasar's injunctions, to leave him for a director who would give her greater liberty for prayer; when on the point of carrying out her intention our Lord reproved her with such severity that all that Fr. Baltasar caused her to suffer was nothing by comparison with it. Another time, when she had brought a similar complaint to her good Master's feet, "Daughter," He answered her, "do not flatter thyself thou art obedient unless thou art prepared to suffer. Behold My sufferings, and it will seem easy for thee to bear anything." A little later her superior

forbade her to read certain spiritual books, in which her piety had found sustenance. " Do not grieve, my daughter," our Lord said to her, "I will give thee a living book." At first Teresa did not understand the meaning of these words ; she was soon to do so.

She had now during the space of two years resisted God's favours ; she had fought with her ecstasies and with her raptures; she had even struggled against the sense of supernatural recollection which was constantly overcoming her. She had multiplied her novenas and her petitions to obtain the grace of returning to the simple meditation of her past years. She had invoked St. Michael, and prayed to St. Hilarion, whose special gift it is to ward off the temptations and delusions of Satan, with this particular intention. And in answer to these prayers, and this heroic exercise of obedience, "this," our saint says, "was what happened to me: I was in prayer one day—it was the feast of the glorious St. Peter—when I saw Christ close by me, or, to speak more correctly, felt Him, for I saw nothing with the eyes of the body, nothing with the eyes of the soul. Jesus Christ seemed to be by my side continually, and as the vision was not imaginary I saw no form ; but I had a most distinct feeling that He was always on my right hand, a witness of all I did. It is not like the presence of God which is frequently felt, particularly by those who have attained to the prayer of union when we seem to find Him with whom we converse. This is a great grace from God, and let him to whom He has given it esteem it much, but it is not vision. But here in this vision it is seen clearly that Jesus Christ is present."

Teresa enjoyed this unspeakable grace almost without intermission for several days. In the gardens of her convent, as in her cell, in recreation, and whilst conversing with the nuns as in deepest solitude, Jesus was ever beside her, following her wherever she went, and nothing could distract her attention from His divine company. Still, we must not forget that she only enjoyed His presence at this time as a blind man who feels, and recognizes by reason and intelligence, that he who is beside him is a father, or a brother, or friend, without being able to see a feature of his face.

But even this favour, great as it is, does not satisfy the love of our Divine Saviour. And thus with what prudence does He prepare the soul of His well-beloved for the bliss He has in reserve for her ! He discovers Himself little by little, as if— true King of Glory—He would only slowly emerge from the cloud behind which He veils the splendour of His beauty.

One day when Teresa was absorbed in prayer Jesus showed her one of His adorable hands, and at the sight of it the saint was rapt into ecstasy. Another time He allowed her a glimpse of His countenance, and permitted her to gaze upon it for some moments. At last, on the feast of St. Paul, whilst she was assisting at Mass with her customary fervour, and preparing to receive Holy Communion, our Lord appeared to her in the glory of His sacred Humanity. He looked at her lovingly, and spoke to her with the greatest sweetness. The saint cannot describe the transports of her happiness; she has no words to paint that divine beauty, that sovereign majesty.

"One thing, however, I would say: if in Heaven itself there was nothing else to delight our eyes but the the great beauty of glorified bodies, that would be excessive bliss, particularly the vision of the Humanity of Jesus Christ our Lord. This vision, though imaginary, I never saw with my bodily eyes, nor indeed any other,

but only with the eyes of the soul. If I were to spend many years in devising how to picture to myself anything so beautiful, I should never be able, nor even know how to do it, for it is beyond the reach of any possible imagination here below ; the whiteness and brilliancy alone are inconceivable. In short, it is such that no man, however gifted he may be, can ever in the whole course of his life arrive at any imagination of what it is." 1

Teresa, in coming out of the ecstasy into which the vision had thrown her, could not shake off her usual fears. What could this vision mean? Were not the faults of her past life such as to render her unworthy of lifting her eyes to the adorable countenance of Jesus? Is it not possible that she may be the sport of her own imagination, or—as everybody wishes her to believe—may this not also be a deception of the father of lies? At every step, as we have seen, of this mysterious ascent which our Lord forces her to take, our saint is deeply troubled ; she dare not place her foot on the unknown step above her, whose very height fills her with terror. She would desire to be left in her nothingness, and before singing her Magnificat with the Queen of Virgins, before blessing Him " who has done great things in her," she is troubled, as Mary was at the salutation of the archangel ; or as the seraphim who cover themselves with their wings and tremble, in the presence of the Most High.

In spite of her repugnance to confide this fresh proof of God's favour to Fr. Baltasar, she took courage to do so ; it would have cost her less to accuse herself of all her past sins. Fr. Baltasar calmed her fears, told her to acquaint him in detail with all that she

1 Life, ch. xviii. L

should experience, and brought back to her recollection the principles on which his direction was founded ; namely, that a soul that is faithful in following our Lord, and seeks to avoid offending Him even in the smallest particular; who is simple and straightforward; confides frankly in her confessor and follows meekly his counsels : such a soul has nothing to fear. If the devil seeks to deceive him, God will bring about that the evil which the enemy tries to effect will be changed into good. Teresa returned to her convent with her conscience calmed, and there her good Master awaited her. Our Lord, having allowed His minister to speak, confirmed by further visions the reality of those which had already been vouchsafed to her.

" Our Lord," the saint says, "who was ever increasing His goodness to me, showed Himself after this time so often to me that I lost all my fears. Sometimes after receiving Communion He showed Himself so much Master of my soul that I remained, as it were, confounded before Him." "Again," she says, "our Lord almost always showed Himself as He is after His Resurrection. It was the same in the Host; only at those times when I was in trouble and it was His will to strengthen me, did He show me His wounds. Sometimes I saw Him on the cross, in the garden, crowned with thorns, but that was rarely. Sometimes also carrying His cross, because of my necessities—if I may say so—or those of others. But always in His glorified body."

One may easily imagine the effect of such graces on Teresa's pure and ardent soul. She found herself utterly changed, on fire with a love of God which became every day more intense ; and this earth would have been a Thabor, if the thorns of contradiction and persecution had not multiplied at the same time,

wounding her feet, nay, oft-times piercing her to the heart.

The storm was ever growing ; foolish tales grew into serious calumnies: these were the reports that spread among the ignorant. Among the learned there were other rumours afloat; they talked of exorcising our saint in order to deliver her from the delusion of the devil. u This idea," says Teresa, " caused me no pain."

What she felt much more was an order she received from a confessor to whom she had recourse in Fr. Baltasar's absence, which moved her soul to its very depths. Having told her that her visions and ecstasies came from the devil, this priest bade her make the sign of the cross whenever the evil spirit should appear to her, and repulse him with a gesture of contempt, as assuredly it was he who presumed to take the appearance of Jesus Christ in order to mislead her.

No trial could have been greater than this for Teresa. She believed firmly that it was Jesus, her Saviour and her God, who deigned to visit her ; she may herself have felt for a moment the anguish of doubt concerning the divine origin of these favours, but never excepting at the time when she was not engaged in prayer. The instant our Lord appeared, that He spoke to her, she recognized Him. Doubt was then no longer possible, and, to use her own emphatic language, she could " be torn to bits " before she could be deprived of this conviction, this certitude that He was really present.

What is she to do? How is it possible to obey a command which obliges her to make a sign of the cross to her Saviour as if He were a spirit of darkness, much more to repulse Him with a contemptuous gesture ! Teresa could have alleged strong reasons for refusing to submit to the order. She had only to recall the

decision of St. Francis Borja, and even the opinion of her ordinary confessor Fr. Baltasar Alvarez. She could at least have resolved to wait for the return of the latter in order to consult him. Not at all, Fr. Baltasar had left her to the direction of the priest who had laid this terrible command on her. Teresa was aware that the path of obedience is ever the surest and the most pleasing to God ; accordingly she obeyed. She obeys ! What the effort cost her, God only knows. When Jesus appeared to her she made the sign of the cross, then with a trembling hand she tried to push Him away from her, but simultaneously she threw herself at His feet, and the thought of the outrages of the Jews at the praetorium and on Mount Calvary occurring to her, she implored His pardon for acting as they had done. "O loving Saviour," she cried, "if I behave in this manner towards You it is only out of love for You, and to submit myself to those whom You have established in Your Church, and who take Your place with regard to my soul."

And Jesus blessing His humble servant testified the value He set on her submission : "Console yourself, my daughter," He said to her, "thou hast done well to obey. I will Myself make the truth known." 1 Frequently Teresa, to avoid making the sign of the cross every moment, held the cross on her rosary in her hands, and presented it to our Lord as soon as He appeared to her. One day our Saviour took it from her hands. When He gave it back to her, the ebony of which the beads were made was replaced by four precious stones more brilliant than any diamonds, and in one of these Teresa saw a marvellous representation of the five sacred wounds. This holy jewel (which was visible only to her to whom it was given) remained in

Teresa's possession for some years. Finally her sister Juana, having pressed her to give it up to her, she made the sacrifice, not wishing to disclose the reason on account of which she held it so dear. 1

Thus the more Teresa abased herself in her humility, the greater sacrifices she made to holy obedience, the more our Saviour overpowered her with His divine favours. So the days and years passed by for our saint—amidst supernatural joys and exterior trials, and she drew from both of them an ever increasing strength which prepared her for the arduous career which awaited her. But the particular sign which gave a divine stamp to all her actions (one more admirable even than her ecstasies) was her perfect submission to the ruling of the Church. She knew well that the most highly privileged, as well as the least and weakest of Christ's flock, can only walk in safety under the guiding staff of the pastors of the one true fold ; thus, rather than fly from it for one instant, she would struggle against her Divine Master Himself. Holy and touching efforts, which served but to unite her soul still more closely to her Conqueror and King! Teresa paints in such vivid colours her devotion to her mother the Church, that we could not do better than close the recital of the wonders she had so far received, and prepare our minds for those that are to follow, with her own words, treating on this subject. These lines seem to set a seal of authenticity on the prodigies of a life which was almost wholly supernatural.

Speaking of herself as of another person, as is her constant habit, she says the following are the signs by which the Spirit of God may be distinguished from that of Satan: "I look upon it as a most certain

1 The cross on this rosary is preserved at the Carmelite convent at Valladolid.

truth that the devil will never deceive, and that God will never suffer him to deceive, the soul which has no confidence whatever in itself, which is strong in faith, and resolved to undergo a thousand deaths for any one article of the creed. To such a one no conceivable revelation, no not even if she saw the heavens open, could make her swerve in the slightest degree from the doctrines of the Church. If the soul does not discern this great strength in itself, and if the particular devotion, or vision, help it not onwards, then it must not look upon either as safe. For though at first the soul is conscious of no great harm, great harm may by degrees come; because as far as I have seen, and understand by experience, that which purports to come from God should be received only in so far as it corresponds with the sacred Scriptures. But if it varies therefrom ever so little, I am incomparably more convinced that it comes from Satan than I am now convinced it comes from God. In this case, there is no need to ask for signs, nor from what spirit it proceeds, because this divergence is so clear a sign of the devil's presence, that if all the world were to assure me it came from God I would not believe it."

CHAPTER XI

VENTS will soon move more rapidly in Teresa's history, but her spiritual life and the inward preparation of her soul for the great works which God was about to accomplish by her means is still the subject which makes the greatest claim on our attention, and to it we propose giving one more chapter before turning to that of her public life.

God's infinite goodness seemed well-nigh to exhaust its powers in the joys and favours conferred on Teresa before she was to quit the life of silence and retirement which she was now leading. The outward circumstances of her life were the same. Her days were spent in her oratory, her cell, or in the accomplishment of the duties to which she was called by community life. She rarely visited the parlour ; she was summoned there occasionally to meet a relative, or some priest wishing to confer with her on spiritual subjects. She worked whenever her continual prayer and frequent raptures allowed of her doing so. A special mark which distinguished her from many other privileged souls was that even when she had only just come out of an ecstasy, and her soul was still rapt in a transport of lovt?, she was able to conceal what was passing in her soul. She resumed her calm, she spoke and acted with perfect simplicity, never betraying outwardly the wonders God had wrought in her ; yet while her gentle charity put itself at the service of all, her soul remained

fixed in the contemplation of God, so that her prayer was hardly interrupted except by sleep.

The world may smile in hearing this language, and may treat the transport of a saint as a folly—an intoxication. Well, may we not own that it is a divine intoxication, the folly of love? The intoxication of a soul which in its exile catches a glimpse of its Eternal Home ; the folly of a heart which is overcome with the joy of loving its God without limit or measure, and being in turn loved by Him with an infinite love ! " Give me a lover," cries St. Augustine, "and he will understand what I say. Give me a man of desires, one who hungers ; give me in this desert a pilgrim who is athirst; give me one who is sighing after the eternal fountain, he will understand what I say." We can say the same with regard to Teresa. Loving, believing hearts, those athirst for God, will alone appreciate the previous history, as they alone will comprehend what is to follow.

This incident, the most sublime, and perhaps the most salient in the mystical life of our saint, has been recognized, and its authenticity acknowledged by the Church, by the permission she accords to the sons of Carmel to celebrate its commemoration every year on the 27th of August under the title of the transfixion of the heart of St. Teresa.

As we have already said, Teresa was consumed with a desire to see God. Devoured with this longing, she was ever repeating with the prophet-king, "O my God, for Thee do 1 watch at break of day : for Thee my soul hath thirsted. . . . Oh, how many ways !" And the earth containing no remedy "to cure a pang which came to her from heaven," she remained confronted with her torment which nothing could appease, unless it was the thought of death, that happy moment

of departure to her true home. Whilst she was in this state, "it pleased our Lord," she said, " that I should have at times this vision. I saw an angel close by me, on my left side, in bodily form. He was not large, of small stature, and most beautiful, his face burning, as if he were one of the highest angels who seem to be all of fire. I saw in his hand a long spear of gold, and at the iron's point there seemed to be a little fire. He appeared to me to be thrusting it at times into my heart, and when he drew it out he left me all on fire with the love of God."

Was this a glorious vision? or an even more marvellous fact? It was left for the future to decide, and the pilgrim to Avila has the power of proving it for himself. The heart of Teresa, miraculously preserved from decay, still keeps the mark of the divine wound, a long and deep cicatrice which divides it almost into two halves, and proves to the minutest detail the correctness of the account the saint gives of the miraculous and mysterious transfixion she received from the angel of God.

Longer and even more irresistible ecstasies followed this astounding prodigy. It was in vain that Teresa tried to hide them. As a giant lifts a straw (to use her own comparison), so the force of the rapture lifted her frequently off the ground in sight of the nuns and of the congregation assembled in the monastery chapel. A celestial beauty lit up her features on these occasions, and her whole person seemed luminous and transfigured. The Lord was exalting the humility of His handmaid, and avenging her for the unjust accusations from which she had suffered. Teresa, longing to escape from the talk and rumours of which she was the object, complained sweetly to her divine Master of the attention which these favours excited, and implored

of Him to let their effects remain hidden. She shut herself up in her cell as much as she was able, to commune with Him in Whose society she enjoyed a foretaste of Paradise. It was at this time that a breath of divine poetry caused her, like David, to break out into inspired canticles. Such hymns as the following (which she composed after her heart had been pierced with a fiery dart) came spontaneously to her lips :

I felt a blow within my inmost heart,
A sudden blow within this heart of mine,
The Hand that made that wound was Hand Divine,
For mighty workings followed from the smart.
That sudden blow, it left me wounded sore;
Yet from that death new life sprang forth once more.
Divine His Hand, of strength beyond compare— Even in the bitterest struggle of our life
He cleaves in triumph through the surging strife
And works the works of might which show Him there.

The dart of divine love by which she had been transfixed left other characteristics, besides a great joy. To those ignorant in such matters it is commonly supposed that divine love is purely a speculative affair, a happy dream enjoyed by elect souls. Those who are consumed by it can easily disprove this contention, for what effort of unaided man can equal the words, and actions, and sacrifices made by the saints? Who can deny that there is a zeal, a devotion, a generosity in the soul animated by divine love unattainable by one urged by a less worthy motive? And the reason is as simple as it is profound, a servant of God 1 gives it, " because love renders friends equal." How should

we love One Whose providence never rests; One Who never ceases working for our good, and creating for us fresh helps and succour on our path to heaven ; how love Him Who took flesh and lived with us on earth only in order to devote Himself to our service ; how love Him without working as He has worked, without sacrificing self, and without suffering cheerfully for His sake? This therefore is the primordial law of love ; all the saints have understood it in this light, and Teresa, whose love was as great as that of any saint, understood it likewise in this manner.

But what could she do for God? Without any authority in her monastery, with no influence outside, her friends—far from being edified—taking scandal at her life ; without prestige or power in the world, or means of acquiring any. There was nothing she could offer God but her heart. But this was sufficient for the accomplishment of an act of heroism which is almost unequalled in the history of the lives of saints. This divine inspiration, which was approved by Fr. Baltasar, and authorized by the Apostolic Visitor of her Order, and by the Fr. General, was nothing less than a vow which St. Teresa made to do whatever she believed to be most pleasing to God. Could she have pushed generosity to greater lengths? All God's commandments, all that the monastic rule enjoined, everything that reason, justice, charity demanded ; what temperance, prudence, strength, patience, sweetness, humility, truth, and every other virtue required, and this not only in any ordinary measure,, but in carrying out their laws to the highest pitch of perfection : that is what Teresa promised to God in her heroic vow. And this chain, this heavy burden, whose weight would be sufficient to stagger even the saints themselves, she took upon her shoulders

with the same joyful alacrity with which she pronounced the vows of her spiritual espousals. 1

The saint, satisfied at last, since she had nothing further to give, only sought henceforth how she could best fulfil her engagement. In spite of her tenderness of conscience she gave way to no scruples, nor was she worried about trifles in its fulfilment. She made it, we are told in the Roman breviary, at our Lord's word ; she depended, therefore, on His divine help to carry it out in a manner pleasing to Him. Twenty-two years of inviolable fidelity were to succeed and justify this sublime promise. Five years after Teresa had pronounced this vow, the formula (only) of it was changed at her director's request, by the authority of the Superior-General of the Carmelites. It was decided, in order to relieve our saint from the uncertainty into which she might be thrown, in hesitating between two courses, both tending to God's glory, the decision in such cases, as to which was the most perfect, should be left to her director ; thus without relieving her from the obligation she had contracted she added to it the further merit of obedience. 2

This was our divine Saviour's finishing stroke to the hidden work He had so long carried on in Teresa's soul. Out of that ardent impulsive nature, that profoundly loving, sweet, and untainted heart, He had created a saint. What treasures of divine grace, what years of patience, and, above all, what oceans of love had not He, as we have seen, put into His divine work ! And also what a masterpiece, what an incom-' parable saint was the result.

The hour was now at hand when she was to be withdrawn from her retreat, in order to work in the service

1 Boll., No. 230.

of God and of His Church. Her public mission was about to begin, and it was necessary that she should be armed with an invincible humility against the glory and renown which were to accompany it. Our Lord provided for this by allowing Teresa's soul to pass through a series of interior trials, and of temptations of the most painful kind. These are words in which she describes the tortures her soul underwent at the time of which we are speaking.

" At times," she says, " I suffered the most grievous trials together with bodily pains and afflictions, arising from violent sickness, so much so that I could scarcely control myself. At other times my bodily sickness was more grievous, and as I had no spiritual pain I bore it.with joy. But when both pains came upon me together my distress was so heavy that I was reduced to sore straits. I forgot all the mercies our Lord had shown me, and remembered them only as a dream—to my great distress ; for my understanding was so dull that I had a thousand doubts whether I had ever understood matters aright, thinking perhaps all was fancy, and that it was enough for me to have deceived myself without also deceiving good men. I looked upon myself as so wicked as to have been the cause by my sins of all the evils and heresies that had sprung up. This is but false humility, and Satan invented it for the purpose of disquieting me and trying whether he could thereby drive my soul to despair. It happened to me once to be tempted in this way, and I remember it was on the day before the vigil of Corpus Christi. The trial then lasted only till the day of the feast, but on other occasions it continued one, two, or even three weeks. But I was specially liable to it during Holy Week, when it was my habit to make my prayer my joy. Then the devil seizes on my imagination in a

moment; occasionally by means of things so trivial that I should laugh at them at any other time, and he makes me stumble at will. The soul, in fetters, loses all control over itself, and accordingly, so it seems to me, the devil makes a football of it, and the soul is unable to escape out of his hands. It is impossible to describe the sufferings of the soul in this state." 1

But the devil, having blunted his weapons against the serene firmness of the saint, was not prepared yet to give up all for lost ; he returned to the charge. " Sometimes," Teresa says, "temptations seemed to press down the soul, and make it dull, so that its knowledge of God becomes to it as that of something which it hears far away. So tepid is its love that when it hears God spoken of it listens and believes that He is what He is, because the Church so teaches, but it recollects nothing of its own former experience. Vocal prayer or solitude is only a greater affliction because the interior suffering is unendurable, and, as it seems to me, in some measure a counterpart of hell. I used to try exterior good works in order to occupy myself partly by violence, and I know well how weak a soul is when grace is hiding itself. It did not distress me much, because the sight of my own meanness gave me some satisfaction. On other occasions I find myself unable to pray or to fix my thoughts with any distinctness upon God. My soul also is occasionally subject to a certain foolishness (that is the right name to give it) when I seem to be neither doing good nor evil, without pain or pleasure, indifferent to life or death, pain and pleasure, marching like a little ass in the wake of others." 2

To what sufferings was our saint now reduced after

1 Life, ch. xxx.

enjoying the divine consolations on her mount Thabor ! Jesus robs her of His presence. He is silent; and in His absence the earth is to Teresa as a desert, without food or water. Far from giving way to discouragement, she proceeds on her way undaunted by the trial, and she explains it in the following manner :

" In this life on earth," she says, " the growth of the soul is not like that of the body. A youth that is grown up and who has become a man does not lessen in size, but as to the soul, it is so by our Lord's will, so far as I have seen it in my own experience—but I know nothing of it in any other way. It must be in order to humble us for our greater good, and to keep us from being careless during our exile." 1

Again are the touching scenes told in the history of Job renewed, in another form, in our saint's cell. Given up, like the patriarch, to Satan's attacks, Teresa sees herself stripped of all her spiritual possessions. Ecstasies, visions, interior consolations—all are gone, and still she continues to bless the holy name of God, and continues with ever increasing fidelity to serve her Divine Master. The devil, furious at his defeat, is allowed to attack her visibly ; having tortured her soul, she is tormented by him under the bodily form of a negro, and under other even more revolting shapes. Teresa sees him close to her, in her cell, she hears his threats, and vanquishes him with a sign of the cross and holy water. Having multiplied instances of the efficacy of the latter, she cries out: " How great is the power of holy water ! As for me, my soul is conscious of a special and most distinct consolation whenever I take it. And I have a joy in reflecting that the words of the Church are so mighty that they endow water with power, so that there should be so great difference

1 Life, ch. xv.

between holy water and water that has never been blessed."

Strange and mysterious pains succeeded these terrible apparitions, and our saint's body seemed on the rack ; but though she came out of them bruised and worn, her soul remained in peace. The nuns of the Incarnation, alarmed by her sufferings, applied every kind of remedy, but she bore all with perfect fortitude, and prayed and offered to God her interior anguish, which was even greater than her bodily sufferings. Satan's efforts to vanquish her constancy but added to the lustre of her crown. She had little fear of the enemy of mankind. On one occasion she says: "I took up the cross in my hand, and it seemed as if God had really given me courage enough not to be afraid of encountering all the evil spirits. It seemed to me that I could with the cross easily defeat them altogether. So I cried out, ' Come on, all of you. I am the servant of our Lord, what can you do against me ?' and certainly they seemed to be afraid of me, for I was left in peace. I feared them so little, that the terrors which until now oppressed me left me altogether—on the contrary, they seemed to be afraid of me. I found myself endowed with a certain authority over them, given me by the Lord of all, so that I cared no more for them than flies. I do not understand these terrors which make us call out Satan, Satan ! when we may say God, God ! and make Satan tremble. Do we not know that he cannot stir without the permission of God. What does it mean ? I am really much more afraid of those people who have so great a fear of the devil than I am of the devil himself." 1

Teresa had but too great reason for holding this last opinion, for the private inquisition of Avila still pursued

1 Life, ch. xxxi.

her with a watchful and suspicious eye. Caspar Daza and Francisco de Salcedo were agreed, and their opinion was backed up by that of half the good citizens of Avila, not omitting the nuns of her own convent, that Teresa's ecstasies were the work of Satan. The saint, without losing any of her peaceful serenity, or engaging in any lengthy and useless controversies, had but one answer for her adversaries : and that was that the proofs that our Lord has given her of His divine presence in her soul were too powerful and too sweet for her to doubt for an instant that He was the author of them. " For," as she tells us in her Life, " I was poor and He has made me rich. He has given me treasures of great price as His love-tokens. Those who knew me before see the change in me. No ! never can I believe that the devil could tear out my faults by the roots, and give me courage and strength to dare all things for the glory of God ; for such are the results of my visions."

Fr. Baltasar Alvarez, without Teresa being aware of it, used the same language in defending her. But the storm did not calm down till the arrival of an angel of peace, whom God sent to console His humble servant in the trials of her Gethsemane.

Spain at this time could hardly keep count of the number of her saints, and the treatment meted out to them by their countrymen was, in most cases, very different from that accorded at this time to Teresa. The sons of St. Francis, of St. Dominic, of St. Ignatius, protected by the glorious name of their founders, freely exercised a great and striking ascendancy over their nation. The inhabitants of Castile received friars such as Peter of Alcantara, or members of the Society of Jesus such as St. Francis Borja, with warmest ovations ; people thronged round them on their journeys

in order to listen to the holy words that dropped from their lips, and to receive their blessing. Thus at the time when Teresa was suffering in heart, and soul, and body in the cloisters of the Incarnation, Providence sent one of the most remarkable living saints of the day to help her. St. Peter of Alcantara, habited in the rough sackcloth of his Order, barefooted and bareheaded, worn and emaciated, with a frame which could only be compared to the rugged bark of some tree, was at this time making a visitation of the monasteries of the province confided to his care. This holy man had nearly reached the termination of a long life consumed in the exercise of an almost preternatural austerity, and of great heights of prayer. He had done a great work in his Order by forming a nucleus of brothers of the strict Observance, and he was now sent by God to our saint in order to reassure her regarding the miraculous events of her past life, and to prepare her for those which were to come. Dona Guiomar, having learned that this holy man was to come to Avila, saw at once the profit that she could gain from this event in her friend's behalf. She obtained leave accordingly from the Carmelite provincial to take Teresa to her house, and there arranged for a meeting between the two saints. Favoured as both had been by the same supernatural graces, St. Peter, with his long experience and his great knowledge of mystical science, was able to enlighten and reassure Teresa on many difficulties which had hitherto troubled her. " In those days," she says, "I had great difficulty in explaining myself, or in giving account of the graces our Saviour had given me ; but this holy father understood me perfectly. He made everything clear and intelligible to me about my visions, assured me that they came from God, and after the great truths of

religion there was nothing I was to be more sure of, or more bound to believe."

Not satisfied with having thus completely reassured Teresa, St. Peter of Alcantara was determined to put a stop to a persecution, which even this humble and holy old man looked upon as one of the greatest trials in life, that of well-meaning men ; accordingly he visited Fr. Baltasar at St. Giles's, and there spoke to him at great length about Teresa's supernatural life.

" My confessor," Teresa confides to us, "did not require to be reassured on these points, but this was not the case with regard to another person." This other person we can easily guess was Don Francisco ; St. Peter of Alcantara, by his reputation for sanctity, and still more by the profound reasons and explanations which he gave, persuaded this excellent but overcautious man to cease his persecutions of our saint. In leaving Avila, St. Peter arranged with Teresa that she was to keep him informed of all that happened to her. He left her consoled, and prepared to pursue her way with a firm tread through the desert in which it had pleased her Divine Master for some time to lead her.

But already this time of trial appeared to be nearing its termination. Teresa's soul began once more to receive the consoling rays of divine consolation, and to expand beneath them ; the desolations were not continuous, and at times our Saviour showed mercy to her, changing her mourning into rejoicing.

" Often," she says, "when my soul was a prey to aridity and my body to infirmity, and it appeared to me that in spite of all my desire it was impossible for me to pray, a sudden ecstasy used to take possession of me in a way that I could not resist."

Thus, consoled at heart by her good Master, sustained by a saint's blessing, and the encouragement of Fr. Baltasar, who no longer feared to give it, Teresa began to breathe again. The murmurs around her gradually abated. Her sisters in religion, who had never ceased to entertain affection for her, began to treat her with less suspicion than they had done for some time past. Those distinguished for their fervour and piety began to consult her, and she rejoiced to see the practice of mental prayer spreading and taking root in the convent. Some of Teresa's nieces about this time had been sent to the Incarnation to be educated ; Teresa was as much attached to them as they to her. Life once more smiled on her, and she enjoyed the peace of monastic life. But she was not made for repose. A terrifying vision tore her from her pious tranquillity, and gave a new direction to her interior life, transforming the holy contemplative into an apostle.

One day Teresa, whilst at prayer, was conscious of being transported into the infernal regions ; how this was done she is unable to say. She tries to describe the horrors that struck her sight, the terror that seized all her members, the unspeakable tortures that transfixed her; but language was wanting to complete the picture. She turns then to the mental sufferings of the damned. Here again the agony of mind, the heart-shattering tortures of these hapless beings, the bitter, despairing sadness of the scene, forces her to give up the description. 1 In her anguish she is made to understand that God willed that she should see the place to which she would have been condemned had she not changed her way of life. This signifies, remarked Ribera, her faithful biographer, that going from little faults into greater she would have slipped into the fatal inclined plane of tepidity, and thence by

one fall after another have reached the abyss ; we know, however, that she was never in actual danger of hell, for God's paternal hand had arrested her on the edge of the precipice.

This vision was to come upon Teresa as a fresh light. "I was so terrified," she says, "that though it took place nearly six years ago the natural warmth of my body is chilled by fear, even now when I think of it." Then directing a glance at herself, she breaks out in thanksgiving and love : " Blessed for ever be Thou, O my God ! and O how manifest it is that Thou didst love me much more than I did love Thee. I see myself out of that hell in which I deserved to burn. The history of my life should have for title : The mercy of God." 1 Then soon after, forgetting what concerns herself, she lifts her soul up to the contemplation of higher things. Those flames and inexpressible tortures from which God had saved her, are every moment swallowing up souls created like hers to see God and love Him for all eternity. " Is it possible that I can take an instant's rest with such a sight before my eyes ? How can I live, or sleep in peace whilst numberless souls are being lost! "

Broken-hearted and beside herself, she throws herself on our Lord's breast, and weeps with Him— " Lloraba con el Senor." She implores Him to tell her what she could do to save unfortunate souls from the misery that awaits them hereafter. Her anguish is augmented by the sad news she hears on all sides. Spain has been ringing with the tidings of the ravages wrought all over Europe by the errors of Luther. It is now said that they are spreading to France, and that that country is torn asunder with religious dissension. What will happen if France, the pre-eminently

1 Letter to Pedro de Castro, Canon of Alba (Boll., No. 275).

Christian nation, rejects the religion of her forefathers? What a misfortune for the Church if she is deserted by her staunchest support, her eldest daughter !

" With the greatest sorrow of heart I clung to our Lord's feet, and I wept and conjured Him not to let such misfortunes happen. I would have given willingly a thousand lives, had I had them, to save one of these unfortunate, misguided people. But alas ! what could a poor weak woman like myself do in the cause of our Divine Master?"

With no other resources than her prayers and her tears, Teresa never ceased interceding for the conversion of heretics and the salvation of sinners. Especially she prayed that France should be preserved to the faith. The blessed germ of missionary zeal, which was the raison d'etre of her Foundations, thus grew in the shade fostered by sufferings endured under the eye, and in the presence of God alone. After the sufferings of hell, the joys of Heaven were successively shown to her by striking figures. She would have wished to have given some idea of what it was permitted to her to see, but human words were wanting to express those supernatural manifestations. "I should like, if I could," she tells us, " to describe even the least striking of these visions, but I do not find it possible to do so. The most vivid and brilliant power of language would be incapable of giving any conception of the smallest of the wonders our Lord revealed to me. Having no words to describe the unspeakable sweetness which filled my heart and inundated my soul, I am forced to be silent."

Thus eternity unveiled its profound mysteries to her ; and by the side of these supreme realities the things of this life appeared but as shadows and phantoms in her sight. The truths of which she had caught a

glimpse in her childhood and shared with her brother Rodriguez, the thoughts on which she had meditated with her uncle Pedro, now absorbed her mind and heart. God and souls—Heaven and hell—eternal happiness or eternal woe—eternal love or eternal hate — these were the thoughts that burnt, as it were, into her brain, and for which alone she lived. The one longing that consumed her was to save sinners from hell and misery, and to give them to happiness, love, and Heaven. For this object she willingly offered up her life. The tranquil existence she led in her convent, the too indulgent laws by which it was governed, began to weigh heavily on her. Was not a true monastic life impossible under the mitigated Rule of Carmel? Were the duties of silence and prayer compatible with the liberty enjoyed by the communities in which it prevailed, a liberty which was ever leading to breaches of the enclosure ? Teresa felt herself surrounded with difficulties, and though prepared for any and every sacrifice, she was ignorant how to set to work to overcome them. Providence was about to show her the way. " One day," we read in the history of the Reform, u Mother Teresa, reflecting on the graces God had given her, and the lights she had received on the eternity of joys and pains, felt herself seized with an ardent desire to live a perfect life, and to give herself up utterly to the service of God. This desire was followed by another— which was to serve God by*keeping the Rule in its perfection." The historian of the Carmelite Order gives us even clearer details of what passed through our saint's mind. " She began to think," he says, " how she could shake herself free from the dispensations of the mitigated Rule, so as to give herself up to God after the example of the holy hermits her predecessors. She longed to bring together a small number of fervent souls who would be

prepared to embrace perfect poverty, complete severance from the world, constant prayer, and the austerity of the primitive Rule. Full of this idea, which was not a pious dream but an ardent resolve, she pictured herself surrounded by a few generous souls, who like her would vow themselves to the more perfect life. As her soul was ravished by these pious thoughts her heart rejoiced, and she seemed to be already enjoying this state of perfection which would have made life a paradise to her. She imagined herself living in a humble and strictly enclosed house, dressed in sackcloth, occupied all day with prayer, and supporting herself by manual labour, she and her companions devoting themselves entirely to the service of their beloved Master." 1

But these happy dreams had their sad awakening. Teresa was perhaps brought back to the realities of life by an importunate request for her presence in the parlour, or by a visit which the orders of her superior obliged her to accept. Again she found herself forced away from her beloved solitude, and with no human means, apparently, of carrying out her wishes. God was, however, working for her. From one little grain of seed, one word whispered in the air like hundreds which the wind carries away with it, He was about to raise up the great tree of a Reformed Carmel.

CHAPTER XII

IT was on the i6th of July, the feast of our Lady of Mount Carmel, that the idea was first mooted by Teresa's young niece, Maria de Ocampo, of founding a convent of Reformed Carmelites. Though the idea did not originate with the saint, it must have chimed in with all her wishes and aspirations. Nevertheless, with that instinct of prudence and common sense which were almost as strongly characteristic of Teresa as ardour and energy, she at first (as she tells us in her Life) held back. Soon afterwards she received a visit from her friend Dona Guiomar; again the subject was discussed, and the saint remarks : " She had the same wish that I had. She began to consider how she could provide a revenue for the house." Here the plan evidently progressed a step further, and before Teresa and Dona Guiomar separated they agreed "to commit the matter with all earnestness to God."

Teresa wished to assure herself before everything what was God's will in the matter, and she was not left long in uncertainty.

" One day," soon after the previous events, she says, " after Communion, our Lord commanded me to labour with all my might for this end. He made me great promises : that the monastery would certainly be built, that He would take great delight therein, that it should be called St. Joseph's, that St. Joseph should keep guard at one door and our Lady at the other, and that Christ would be in the midst of us; that the

monastery would be a star, and would shine in splendour ; that though the religous Orders were then relaxed, I was not to suppose He was scantily served in them, for what would become of the world if there were no religious in it?"

These last words went home. To save souls and to glorify God were motives for which the saint felt herself strong enough to embark on any enterprise, however arduous. Also, since God had promised that she should attain her end, the obstacles she was to encounter were of no importance in her sight.

"Tell your confessor," He had also said, " the command I have laid on you, and tell him from Me that he is not to oppose, or thwart you in the matter."

The order was formal ; there was nothing left for Teresa to do but to obey. Still she could not refrain from casting one look at what she was about to give up, and also one at what she had undertaken. For it meant that she would have to leave behind the fine monastery in which she had passed the early days of her religious life, and where she had received innumerable graces ; those beautiful gardens to whose shady walks and limpid streams she had grown deeply attached ; a cell which she had looked upon almost as a home, 1 an existence without worldly cares—in short, a thousand advantages which she seemed only to begin to appreciate when on the point of losing them. In the future she could only see before her difficulties and contradictions, great isolation, and above all overwhelming responsibilities. Nature indeed shuddered, but grace triumphed ; accordingly Teresa went to her confessor and gave him an account of all that had passed.

Fr. Baltasar refused to decide on his own authority

1 "La casa era muy a mi gusto, y la celda muy a mi proposito" (Life, ch. xxxii.).

on so important a matter. He passed the saint on to Fr. de Salazar, the provincial of the Carmelites, and Teresa, finding that it would be difficult to communicate with Fr. de Salazar without the knowledge of her superior, commissioned Dona Guiomar to inform the latter of her design of founding a convent where the original Rule would be followed. Teresa herself wrote at the same time to her former friend and benefactor, St. Peter of Alcantara, to ask his advice. She also consulted St. Francis Borja, and St. Louis Beltran, the great Dominican theologian, who was then master of novices at Valencia. Three great Orders of the Church were therefore convoked in council by means of their principal representatives, and their answers were unanimous. God, speaking in the person of His saints, praised and blessed Teresa, and encouraged the undertaking.

St. Louis in answering her letter said : " Mother Teresa, I have received your letter; and as the affair on which you consult me is of the highest importance for God's honour and glory, I recommended it to Him in my prayers at the Holy Sacrifice ; for this reason I delayed my answer to you. I now tell you in our Lord's name to arm yourself with courage in order to execute your great enterprise, God aiding ; and I can assure you on His authority that before fifty years are over your Order will be one of the most illustrious in the Church." The approval of St. Francis Borja and St. Peter of Alcantara was no less marked. The latter not only encouraged the saint to pursue her scheme, but gave her much useful advice on the manner of conducting a work of whose difficulties no one had greater knowledge or experience than he had. Finally Fr. de Salazar listened favourably to Dona Guiomar, and promised to take the new Foundation under his jurisdic-

tion. Teresa had feared that the opposition she would meet from the head of her own Order would be the most difficult to overcome, but this was not the case ; and at first it seemed that all she had to do was to find a house and establish herself in it. This at least was the state of matters when her great design was first mooted. Alas ! under the appearance of great calm clouds were gathering all around. We must, in order to understand the violence of the storm which broke over Avila against the saint, give one look at the state of the Church and the Carmelite Order at this time.

Europe had been for nearly half a century a prey to agitations consequent on the rise of the Lutheran doctrines. But Spain, protected in part by the Pyrenees, and still more by a faith which the struggles of eight hundred years had rendered wellnigh invincible, had kept the doctrines of the Church in all their purity throughout every part of her territory. Thus Spain, exempt from the contagion, had none of that need of reform, the necessity of which was so strongly felt by all the other Christian nations, and to which the Council of Trent in her immortal canons so nobly responded. What Luther, the apostate monk, and his abettors professed to do, or rather the pretext they took as an excuse for their revolt—the suppression of abuses, the reformation of the clergy and of the religious Orders — the Council with its sovereign authority and its divinely inspired prudence actually accomplished. Whilst the innovators defiled the world with the scandals of their lives, and appalled it with their blasphemies, the Church, gathering fresh strength from her trials, offered to the world, as pledges of the immortality of her principles and of her life, on one side those admirable decrees, and on the other a legion of great souls worthy of sustaining the dignity of their

Mother, and avenging her from the affronts of her rebel sons by their virtues and the astounding self-abnegation of their lives. These saints, following the great impulse given in that direction by the Council of Trent, were nearly all reformers. They followed the stream of Christian life, of religious life, and of the apostolic life back to its fountain-head; and in the very midst of the pagan self-indulgence and luxury of the Renascence they recalled the days of the early Christians, and of the saints of the desert by the austerity of their lives.

No wonder that, like the earliest pioneers of the religion of the Crucified One, they met with obstacles in their conquest of the world. The sight of their heroism.was an offence and a reproach to the world in which they lived ; still more did it resent their teaching, and Spain in particular—from the circumstances which we have just mentioned—had no wish to join in this crusade of reparation. The shortcomings among both clergy and cloistered monks, the scandals of court life were everywhere of too notorious a nature in France, Germany, and Italy to be ignored ; and the general feeling among Christian peoples was in favour of stern measures of reform, even when in practice they sought to evade them. But the kingdom of Ferdinand and Isabella was free from these disgraces, and, attached to its ancient customs and its time-honoured institutions, it sought to preserve them intact. Spain was proud of its numberless monasteries, and had no thought of reproaching them with a relaxation of their rules which only tended to make them more accessible to the outer world. No crying abuses roused the alarm of the country. If the monks did not work, and the nuns lived too much in the parlour, and austerities were things of the past, at least the morals

of the country remained pure. Why therefore trouble the peace of these pious refugees? Why, above all, enclose them behind the grille? What sort of innovations, they asked, are these? Surely they are but visionary dreams !

Such was the resistance Teresa met with from without ; but she was soon to encounter still greater opposition in the bosom of her own religious family of the Order of Carmelites.

The monastery of the Incarnation, not having yet counted the fiftieth year of its existence, had known no Rule except that of the Mitigation, and the ancient traditions of the Order were therefore but a glorious memory, which entailed no sacrifice on its members. The nuns would no doubt speak with pride of their Father and founder the prophet Elias, of St. Albert Patriarch of Jerusalem, their law-giver St. Berthold, their first general of the Latin race St. Simon Stock the privileged devotee of Mary, of B. John Soreth, the last and most illustrious restorer of the Order in the West. But would these great saints have acknowledged a monastery frequented by seculars, provided with most of the conveniences of life, dispensed from the greater number of the primitive fasts as their heritage, or recognized its sons or daughters as their spiritual children? These mitigations we repeat had not been introduced by the community of the Incarnation. The convent had been founded on the Rule granted by Pope Eugenius IV, and the nuns could therefore enjoy their liberty and peaceful existence and yet remain faithful to their religious engagements. No reproaches were ever levelled against them for their violation of these, and St. Teresa affirms more than once, and the Carmelite historians agree with her testimony, that the convent had the reputation of being

one of the most fervent of its day. If their Rule was not one of great austerity, they had the merit, at least, of keeping 1 it with fidelity. And yet it was but a shadow of the glorious religious monument of which tradition declares Elias laid the foundation, and which legions of saints had laboured to build up in the course of ages. The majestic figure of the great prophet guarding the base of the monument denotes the character and sets a stamp on the whole spiritual edifice. The spirit of prayer and solitude, of contemplation and of zeal, passed down from generation to generation by a religious tribe, the spiritual sons of Elias, had survived till the coming of Christ, Who had given a fresh direction to their lives, and transformed the austere

Essenes into disciples of the Cross. We have no space to relate how the Order of Carmel, after having spent thirteen centuries of the Christian era on the mountain of Elias, and multiplied its Foundations all over Palestine, was exterminated in the East by the fire and sword of the Saracens. The monks who escaped from the massacres passed into Europe, whither many of their brethren had preceded them after the failure of the Crusade led by Richard Cceur de Lion and Philip Augustus fifty years before. They had already eight provinces of the Order at that time in Europe, and in the following century they could count nineteen flourishing communities all animated by the same spirit and the same fervour. The Rule they had in common was that of the patriarch and law-giver, St. Albert;[1] and by its prescriptions the solitaries of

According to the Speculum Carmelitanum, St. Albert, patriarch of Jerusalem, had drawn up the Rule of Carmel at the request of St. Brocard in 1191 or 1207. This Rule, venerated as the primitive one of the Order, dates back to a much greater antiquity. St. Albert's work was to throw light on certain points in the Observance which were submitted to him for his decision, and his approbation gave force to laws and customs which had existed from time immemorial.

France, Italy, and England lived, like their fathers of Palestine, in silence, prayer and seclusion, perpetual abstinence, and almost continual fasting. To a burning love of our Divine Saviour they united a special devotion to the Blessed Virgin, which their forefathers had been amongst the first to cultivate, and which earned for them the name of the Brothers of Mary.

Such was Carmel in the days of her greatness. Her annals were being constantly enriched by fresh prodigies, and the earth was sanctified, and Heaven peopled by her members.

But this glorious period in the annals of Mount Carmel was succeeded by one of decadence. The Order did not escape the universal relaxation of fervour which, beginning in the middle, increased towards the end of the fourteenth century. The scourge of pestilence—the Black death — after having ravaged Asia and Africa, swept over Europe, where it more than decimated the population, and struck terror into every heart. Another still greater evil, because a moral one, the Great Schism of the East, was at this time deeply disturbing men's minds, fomenting religious discussion, and introducing the element of strife even into the cloister. So terrible was the war that raged, that had it been possible for the Church to perish, it would inevitably have perished then. Her bereavements were indeed great; and the sight of her great religious families joining in the universal movement and seeking to throw off the yoke of ancient laws, and asking for dispensations, in short, endeavouring to approximate their lives more nearly to those led by seculars, was not the least severe of her trials. Like the rest of the world, the sons of Elias found their Rule too severe, their fasts and their prayers beyond their strength, and, above all, their seclusion too strict.

They succeeded in obtaining a mitigation of the extreme severity of their Rule from Eugenius IV through their general, John de Facy. Their monastic life, till then beautiful and pure, because it was strict, became weakened under these concessions. The character proper to the Order, the spirit of solitary prayer which converted every monastery into a solitude and every religious into a hermit, rapidly disappeared. In vain were efforts made in individual instances to resist the general current ; honourable as were these exceptions, and much as the souls of these holy men profited personally, they made little impression on their brethren. For what is more difficult than to struggle up stream, or to fight against a crowd, with all the natural forces of man arrayed on the other side ?

To the Blessed John Soreth belongs the distinction of being the solitary exception to the universal rule, and of having given a strong impulse to the work of reform. He has another claim on our interest from having instituted the second Order for women. John Soreth obtained from Nicholas V the Bull Cum nulla in the first year of his election (1442) as general, by which he and his successors were accorded the privileges (granted previously to St. Augustine and St. Dominic) of admitting nuns into the Order under the same Rule—thus enabling them to participate in its indulgences and privileges. This holy man founded six convents for nuns during his lifetime. After his death the Carmelite Order spread in France, the Netherlands, in Italy, and in Spain. But by degrees these convents, being necessarily subject to the provincials of the mitigated Rule, lost sight of the principles of their holy founder; for how could they show themselves more rigid in their Observance than were their spiritual fathers and brethren ? Accordingly Blessed John Soreth's

Reform survived him only in a very few houses ; the mitigated Rule prevailed elsewhere.

This was the state of things when Teresa took up her work, alone, without resources, power, or credit. She had to disinter the primitive Rule, which was buried in the dust of.ages, and to follow it—a weak woman—with the small company of elect souls whom our Lord was to inspire to join her. It is not difficult to guess the reception such an enterprise was likely to meet with both from the world and the cloister. The fury of the Evil One may also be imagined. If the saint had tasted already of the chalice of tribulation when seeking sanctification hidden from all eyes in her cell, she was now, that.her public life was about to begin, to drink it to the dregs. She was, however, prepared for the trial. To a natural courage (which she owns herself was not small) she joined an unalterable sweetness and patience which was the fruit of her deep faith. For one who walks, as she did, with eyes fixed on eternity, the troubles of this life were of but secondary importance. "All things pass!" was Teresa's joyous cry. This, her favourite saying, she wrote with a few others in her breviary ; they were the key-note to her behaviour during the stormy times which were impending.

Let nothing trouble thee, Let nothing vex thee,

All things pass. God alone changes not. Patience obtains all things, He who possesses God wants for nothing :

God sufficeth.

No sooner was the project of the new Foundation known, than, as Teresa says, "a great opposition

People began by laughing at it; it became the topic of the town, and the saint and Dona Guiomar had much to do in answering all the questions put to them. " What an absurd idea!" was the universal cry. "Let the nun stay in her convent, and not trouble her head about anything outside its doors, especially for anything so unnecessary as a new Foundation. And as for the senora, let her mind her own business, and not meddle in matters which will only serve to make her talked about." : Others urged that Teresa was very foolish to leave such a comfortable monastery. The saint owned that, humanly speaking, her critics were in the right. But Dona Guiomar, who was less patient and also more exposed, from living in the world, to harsh remarks, had much difficulty in bearing them. Her discouragement fell upon Teresa, who, falling at our Lord's feet, complained that she did not know what would become of them.

"You can now judge, my daughter," our Lord answered her, "what the founders of Orders have had to suffer. You have yet much to suffer, more even than you can imagine ; but be not disturbed by it." Our Lord also sent a message through Teresa to Dona Guiomar. The two friends took fresh courage to support the trials in store for them. These were first restricted to mockery, and criticisms in which monks, priests, and laymen all joined. Thus hampered in their inquiries, watched in their smallest actions, they could only proceed with great caution. The first thing was to find a suitable house, also to try to get some moral support and good advice, in order to bring the enterprise to a successful conclusion. Of these three things the last two were the hardest to achieve. The

college of St. Giles would have helped them, but Dona Guiomar hesitated about compromising the Jesuits in the matter. They were poor, also the last comers among the religious Orders of Avila; it was all-important for them not to risk the public confidence which they had by degrees gained in the city. After deep reflection Teresa and her friend had recourse to the Dominican convent, which was the principal one of the town, and the same as that in which the saint's brother, Anthony, had received the habit thirty years previously. But his career had been early cut short; it would hardly serve as an introduction to our saint. Nevertheless she asked for an interview with the great theologian of the convent, Fr. Pedro Ibanez, and presented herself with Dona Guiomar before him.

Fr. Ibanez was a clever and learned man, a professor of Salamanca, and a master in the spiritual life. He had other merits greater even than his learning, for he had greatly loved, and had laboured generously in the service of his Divine Master. He was nearing the close of his life, and was looked upon not in Avila alone, but throughout his Order, not only as a holy man, but also as a shining light in the Church. Teresa was therefore disposed on both counts to place her utmost confidence in him.

Dofia Guiomar was the first to speak. She explained their project, and the sum she proposed to give to the new Foundation. The saint then gave her reasons for embarking on the scheme, without making any mention of the commands given her by our Lord, or the favours and lights she had received from Him. " For," she used to say, " I have no wish to regulate my conduct on such things ; I wish to act entirely on obedience, and according to the light of reason and faith." 1

This was not the first intimation Fr. Ibanez had received of their design. The town rumours had reached his ears, and he had already conceived an unfavourable opinion of it. Teresa's straightforwardness, however, the probity of her views, the wisdom with which she faced her difficulties, as well as her irresistible charm of language and manner, insensibly won upon the aged ecclesiastic. He asked her if she was willing to follow his advice in all good faith. Teresa agreed without hesitation, inwardly convinced that she would find a father and a protector in her impartial judge. " Well," he said, " come back in eight days, and you shall receive my answer."

The two friends withdrew full of hope, Dona Guiomar protesting that she would not give up the scheme even if Fr. Ibafiez should condemn it. Teresa, with more prudence, declared that if he should say that she could not go on with it without offending God, she would at once abandon it. The saint and her friend had no sooner departed than Fr. Ibafiez received a message from a man of position in the town who had heard of the saint's proceedings, and wrote to recommend the father to have nothing to do with her rash designs. Fr. Ibanez fortunately had a better counsellor than this friend. He studied Teresa's project at the foot of the tabernacle ; he examined it carefully, he prayed, and asked for light from above. At the end of the week Teresa returned with her companion, and heard to her great joy that the good father believed that her work was from God, and that he was prepared to support it to the best of his endeavour against all opposition.

"The endowment," he told them, "offered by Dona Guiomar is quite insufficient, but we must leave something to God and to confidence in Him."

The situation in which Teresa now found herself

placed was wholly changed ; she could—protected by the most influential ecclesiastic in Avila—go forward without fear. Other unexpected assistance was offered. Her old friend Francisco de Salcedo, cured of his former misgivings, returned to her side with all his former devotion, and rejoiced in seconding a work in which the glory of God was so greatly concerned. Caspar Daza followed his example, and others who began by belonging to the opposition now turned round and sided with Teresa. Her friends found the house small and unsuited, but our Lord whispered to her, " Take possession when you can ; you will see what I will do for you later on." She seemed to be at the end of her difficulties. A few days more, and she hoped to find herself in her hermitage. Alas ! those days were still far off.

The storm from without had begun to abate, but from within—that is, in the Convent of the Incarnation-it increased daily. The nuns appeared to take the saint's conduct in the light of a personal affront; and they went so far as to desire that she should be punished, if not with imprisonment, still with a detention which would prevent her carrying on her " intrigues." Others, but in smaller numbers, defended her ; and so dissensions were rife in the monastery. One complaint after another was forwarded to the provincial, till the latter, tired of the commotion his permission had raised, withdrew it, after informing Teresa that he did so on account of the insufficiency of the endowment and the opposition which the project had raised. Teresa, without being disconcerted, had recourse to her director, told him of the refusal, and asked him what course he recommended as the most acceptable to God. Fr. Baltasar told her to obey, and to give up all thoughts of carrying out her design.

"God knows," Teresa relates, "with what difficulty the affair had been conducted up to this time, but by the grace of God, I gave it all up without disquietude and with as much ease and contentment as if it had cost me nothing. Having done everything I could to accomplish our Lord's command, my Divine Master could require nothing further from my hands. So I remained in peace at the convent, convinced in my own mind that our plans would be carried out later, though how, or when, I knew not."

This holy submission obtained its reward. And thus while the people of Avila thought Teresa was overwhelmed with the bitterness of her disappointment, she was full of joy at the thought of having something to endure in the service of her Divine Master. One trial only she found indeed hard to bear ; it came to her from her director. " I expected some comfort from my confessor in the midst of these trials," she says, u but to increase my trouble our Lord permitted that he should write me a severe letter. He told me that the result of all this ought to be that I should look on my project as a dream ; that I ought to start afresh by ceasing to have anything to do with it in the future, or even to speak of it any more, seeing the scandal it had occasioned. He made some further remarks, all of them very painful. But our Lord, who never failed me in all the trials I speak of, so frequently consoled and strengthened me that I need not speak of it here. He told me not to distress myself, that I had pleased Him greatly, and had not sinned in the whole affair. That I was to do what my confessor required of me, and be silent on the subject till the time came to resume it."

Teresa, ever obedient and docile as a little child, instantly took up her ordinary way of life ; she even, with that astonishing self-command of which she had

the secret, forbade herself to utter a word, or give a thought to an enterprise for which she had previously been willing to make every sacrifice. This silence was not copied by those by whom she was surrounded. Teresa was looked upon with suspicion in the convent, and accused of folly and ingratitude. Nevertheless she took refuge in her cell, and remained there tranquilly and contentedly, finding in the society of our Lord and His angels the peace which was denied her by man's injustice. Meanwhile, what had become of Teresa's friends, of the plans they had made, and the house they had been on the point of purchasing? If she no longer occupied herself with these concerns, they, unlike her, were bound by no vow of obedience and were at liberty to act. Fr. Ibanez accordingly, whilst restraining the too impetuous Dona Guiomar, pointed out that the means of attaining the ends they all had in view was to obtain a Brief from Rome authorizing the undertaking. Dona Guzman (the widow Guiomar's mother) seconded her daughter's proceedings by giving the protection of her name, as well as some pecuniary aid, to these negotiations. Don Francisco de Salcedo and his friend Gaspar Daza seconded their efforts. In short, God worked for His daughter, who was giving greater proof of her love for Him by her inactivity than she could have done by all her efforts.

Five or six months passed without further developments. Occasionally Fr. Ibanez visited our saint, who made no allusion to their great enterprise, but was satisfied with simply consulting him on some subject connected with her spiritual life, or on the meaning of a scriptural text. The influence exercised by Teresa's marvellous sanctity and elevation of soul was such that Fr. Ibanez was led, in consequence of the constant communications he had with her, to make a fresh start

in the spiritual life. Excellent as the life had been which he had hitherto led, he resolved to devote what was left of it to the pursuit of still greater perfection. Leaving, therefore, his blessing to Teresa, and encouraging words to Dona Guiomar, he announced to both that he was leaving Avila, in order to retire to a remote monastery of his Order, so that he might give up his life to prayer.

"I too," Teresa says, "felt his retirement much, because it was a great loss to me, though I did nothing to hinder him from going. But I knew it was a gain to him ; for when I was so much distressed at his departure our Lord bade me be comforted, for he was going under good guidance." Providence brought him back later when his support was of much use to the new Foundation. Meanwhile Fr. Ibafiez's place was taken by one who was equally devoted to Teresa's interests. Fr. Denis Vasquez, the rector of St. Giles's, was replaced by Fr. Gaspar de Salazar, and on his arrival Teresa received orders from her director, Fr. Baltasar Alvarez, to put herself in communication with the new rector, and to acquaint him with the lights and supernatural favours which she was in the habit of receiving in prayer. Our saint had the greatest natural dislike to these manifestations of the soul, but she never refused anything to obedience, and therefore submitted to the order. The following is the account she gives of her interview with Fr. de Salazar: "When I went into the confessional I felt in my soul something I know not what. I do not remember to have felt thus, either before or after, towards anyone. I cannot tell what it was, nor do I know of anything with which I could compare it. It was a spiritual joy, and a conviction in my soul that his soul must understand

The saint was not mistaken ; she drew great consolation from her interview with the rector, and the latter left her much edified, and thoroughly enlightened as to the views she held. These circumstances told in her favour. If Fr. Baltasar had commanded her to give up the

Foundation, and had, as Teresa said, led her " by such a narrow and rigorous path that he had hardly allowed her soul to breathe," he had not done so on his own initiative. His former superior, prejudiced by unjust reports against the saint, had imposed this manner of dealing with her on his subject, and the humble Jesuit had suffered as much as his penitent 1 in carrying out the order. Fr. de Salazar gave both their liberty of action ; and our Lord, breaking the silence He had maintained of late to Teresa on her plans, pressed her once more to execute them. "Tell your confessor,'* said our Blessed Lord, "to meditate to-morrow on those words : ' O Lord, how great are Thy works ! Thy thoughts are exceeding deep ' " (Ps. xci.). 2

The following day the good father saw his last misgiving disappear in the light shed upon him in prayer. He understood the marvels God was prepared to accomplish by Teresa's feeble hands ; and realized that he was standing face to face with one of those mysteries of divine wisdom where faith and humility triumph over human prudence. He answered Teresa the same day that there was no longer any doubt as to what was God's will, and that consequently she was to take up her work again with courage.

The saint's greatest difficulty was the provincial of

1 It is as well to draw attention to the fact that Fr. Baltasar was at the very beginning- of his priestly ministry at this time. He naturally leant on his superior for advice in such an unusual case as that of his saintly penitent.

2 Ribera ; Yepes.

the Order ; to renew the effort to gain him over to their side was to court disaster. It was agreed to do all that the situation rendered necessary without consulting him. The state of affairs at this time would have disconcerted anyone less energetic than was our saint. Her movements were watched at the Incarnation ; she was hampered in all her proceedings. Under such circumstances, what could she do? How was it possible for her to build a monastery, and to gather together a community? Time, liberty, credit, and fortune, all were wanting in her case.

" Ah, my beloved Master," she cried with her usual loving familiarity, " why do you command me to do impossible things, I who am but a woman and not even a free one ? Tied as I am in every way; without money, or knowledge how to procure any ; what can I do? What am I good for?" Having thus poured forth her anxieties to the Heart of her only Friend, Teresa took courage, counting on His assistance ; and the future foundress of innumerable monasteries, and Reformer of a great Order, showed her genius for organization in the measures she took in preparation for her humble commencement.

She first wrote to her sister Juana, who had been married some time previously to Don Juan de Ovalle, and asked her and her husband to come to Avila to help her to acquire a house which she had in view. Juan de Ovalle at once acceded to her request, bought the house in his own name, and he and his wife, who joined him there soon after, took up their abode in it. This enabled Teresa while visiting them to make her plans respecting the future monastery. But the state of Don Juan's purse did not permit of his offering the saint any assistance further than that of his willing concurrence, and it was necessary before long to pay

for the contract, as well as a part at least of the price of the property. " Our Lord provided for this in a marvellous manner," the saint records in the history of her Foundations.

These marvels which Teresa passes over in silence are worthy of more than a passing remark. One day her dear patron saint and father, St. Joseph, appeared to her and told her to begin the work, for that money would be forthcoming. The saint had not at that moment a farthing to pay the workmen, but a few days later St. Joseph's promise was fulfilled by her brother.

Lorenzo de Cepeda having seen twenty years' service in Peru, where he had been in command of one of the king's regiments, was rewarded with the post of treasurer-general of the province of Quito. In 1556 he had married a young heiress of the name of Juana Maria de Fuentes. These temporal successes had failed to harden Lorenzo's heart. He led an exemplary life, and was most generous in his alms, especially to religious Orders. Though ignorant of his sister's plans, he conceived the happy idea of sending her a sum of money, which was large enough to enable her at once to satisfy her workmen and creditors.

" My dear brother," she writes to him, " I pray God to reward you for your great charity. It was certainly through God's inspiration that you sent me so much money. What you sent me before would have abundantly sufficed for all my wants, who, nun as I am, rejoice through God's grace to wear a much mended habit, and have few wants." She then acquaints him in a few words with her great enterprise, and adds: " Dona Guiomar helps me much, but she has no money at this moment, and I had nothing wherewith to pay the most urgent expenses. Nevertheless, confiding in

God alone, I had arranged with the workmen to go on. To all appearance it was great folly, but our Divine Master takes up the matter, and inspires you to come to my assistance when I was at my wits' end. What astonishes me greatly is the forty pieces of gold which you added, and without which I could not have got on at all. I believe I owe all this to St. Joseph, to whom our house will be dedicated, and who, I feel sure, will repay you for your great charity." 1

What a consolation it must have been for our saint to find God making use of different members of her family to found her little monastery; and no doubt the thought must have often occurred to her that Don Alonso and Dona Beatriz, united in Heaven, were blessing their children occupied in this holy work.

The house which had been bought was so small that at first it seemed impossible to turn it into a convent. Teresa, in spite of all her ingenuity, could not find place for a dormitory or recreation-room. As for the chapel, it would have been necessary to buy the adjoining cottage in order to make it of suitable dimensions, and for this the permission of the owner, and money were necessary, and neither the one nor the other were forthcoming. What was to be done? Whilst Teresa was revolving these thoughts in her head, uncertain what to do, her Divine Master said to her: "Have I not told you, my daughter, that you are to enter, and settle yourselves as best you can ? Oh ! human weakness, which fears that the ground even should be wanting to you ! How often have I not slept in the open air without a roof over My head!" Teresa received this reproach humbly, and returned to the little house. A fresh examination showed her how

to manage, and giving instructions to the workmen she begged them to get the work done as quickly as possible.

Another time St. Clare appeared to Teresa on her feast, and promised to render her all the assistance in I her power. 1 Three days later, on the i5th of August, ' the Blessed Virgin Queen of Mount Carmel showed herself in a vision to Teresa while she was assisting at Mass at St. Thomas's. Here (in the church where she had come to confession to Fr. Vincent Barron after her father's death), whilst she ~was lamenting in profound anguish the sins of her past life, Our Lady appeared to her, and, wrapping a spotless robe over her, told her that all her sins were forgiven. Then taking Teresa's hand in hers, she told her in accents of deep tenderness that the saint's devotion to St. Joseph had caused her great joy, that her monastery would be completed and should never lose its first fervour, and that the Holy Family would ever be devoutly loved and served in it. She said this in presence of St. Joseph, who appeared at the same time at St. Teresa's side.

Teresa kept these graces secret, but she could not conceal a miracle which was due to her prayers. Her brother-in-law, Juan de Ovalle, in order to oblige her, continued to live, at great inconvenience to himself and his family, in the house in course of construction. Teresa suffered for the sake of her sister, who was about to give birth to a second child. One day Gon-zalvo, their little five-year-old son, was playing with the materials collected for the building, when a piece of

1 "This promise," Teresa observes, "was faithfully accomplished. A convent of her Order close to ours has helped us to live, and what is more important, it has little by little contributed so well to the accomplishment of my wishes, that the same poverty is observed in this house as in hers."

wall crumbled down on the top of him, and he lay to all appearance dead on the ground. At first he was not missed ; but when discovered by his father, after an absence of some hours, he was stiff, and apparently lifeless. The unfortunate man, after doing all he could to restore his son, lifted the little body in his arms, and taking it to Teresa, who was working in another part of the house, laid it in her lap—his silence and his tears alone revealing what he asked at her hands. Meanwhile a friend of Juana's, who had heard what had happened, was doing her utmost to keep the mother in her own room. But a secret presentiment, or possibly the look of alarm on the faces round her, roused Juana's fear, and resisting her friend's efforts to detain her, she went in search of Teresa, and finding her with Gonzalvo on her lap, she gave vent to her grief in sobs and tears. Teresa calmed her with a gesture, begged of her to wait—to be patient—and then bowing down her head on the marble face of the little child she covered it with her veil, and without saying a word to those around, implored the mercy of God on these people who had made such great sacrifices for her and for Him. After a moment of profound silence Teresa lifted her head. Gonzalvo opened his eyes and smiled upon his aunt, and caressed her. Teresa, radiant with joy, put him in his mother's arms. " Dear sister," she said, "be not troubled. TherQ is your son, embrace him."

Gonzalvo never forgot what he owed to Teresa. When he was older he reminded her that she was bound to pray for him and take an interest in his soul, since he owed his life, under God, to her intercession. Her biographer tells us that Teresa, much touched, blessed him, and acknowledging the miracle by her silence, she promised to watch with a mother's

affection over the existence she had been the means of prolonging. 1

A month after Juana's eldest boy had been brought back to life she gave birth to a second son. Teresa begged it might be called Joseph, in honour of her beloved protector. " Dear little angel," she said to it after its baptism, " I pray God that He will take you to Himself in your innocence rather than you should live to offend Him." Joseph's holy parents took this prayer calmly; their faith differed in no way from Teresa's. The sacrifice of life was a small one to them compared to that of eternity. Joseph only lived three weeks. Teresa, seeing the child about to give up its innocent soul to its Saviour, took him in her arms and gazed on him long with a look impossible to describe. Juana, looking at her sister with anguish in her heart, wondered what was going to happen. Suddenly the saint's face became transfigured, a beauty such as Juana had never seen before shone out of her eyes and lit up her face. She understood all; and when Teresa, coming back to herself, tried to turn away from her, with the child, whom she still held in her arms: "Stay," Juana entreated while weeping softly, "you cannot hide it from me, my little Joseph is with God." Teresa's only answer was to embrace her fondly ; and then, in order to change the mother's anguish into joy, she confided to her the vision she had seen. "O Juana," she cried, "when one realizes the multitude of angels who come to greet the soul of a little child who enters Heaven—innocent as the angels themselves — one can only praise and bless God."

Devoted as she was to her family, this affection never interfered with our saint's great undertaking ; and our Saviour, though he had reproached her in His jealous

1 Vide Ribera, Yepes, Boll., No. 310.

love of her soul for bestowing her affections, perhaps, in too lavish a manner, on the world outside the cloister, seemed only to bless those outpourings of her heart on those bound to her by the natural tie of close relationship.

Affairs still progressed slowly with our saint, notwithstanding all her efforts to hasten them. The necessity for keeping them concealed from the provincial also hampered their success ; and reports again circulated in the town regarding the new Foundation. The evil spirits, opposed to all generous and intrepid souls, likewise redoubled their assaults. Unable to vanquish the saint's courage and perseverance, they attacked her from another quarter. Accordingly one day the news was brought to Teresa that a great wall had fallen in the night. The saint took the news with her usual serenity. "It will have to be rebuilt," she observed. " That will require more money," replied anxiously her faithful friend Dona Guiomar. "The money will be forthcoming," was Teresa's answer ; and shortly after a messenger arrived confirming her words, and bringing the necessary sum with him.

Juan de Ovalle would have insisted on the workmen rebuilding the wall at their own expense ; but Teresa refused to consent to this. She begged him not to blame the men, for she said it was not due to their carelessness but to diabolical agency. " What efforts," she exclaimed, "have been made by Satan to arrest this work ; but in spite of everything it will be carried out." And truly, notwithstanding all the difficulties thrown in the way, the work advanced, and little by little the house assumed the appearance of a monastery. Teresa watched its progress with the utmost interest; she aimed in every detail at copying the simplicity, humility, and poverty of Bethlehem ; and in this she

had no difficulty in succeeding. The chapel was at last finished, the dormitory was divided into cells, the refectory ready to be used, when Teresa received an order from her superiors which put a stop to all the works, and appeared to compromise the future of the new Foundation.

CHAPTER XIII

EFTLE as Teresa's holiness was understood or appreciated in her native city, rumours of it began to spread outside its bounds. It was said that a great saint lived in Avila, in a Carmelite monastery, who had received astounding graces from God and whose prayers were all-powerful with Him. Saints such as Peter of Alcantara or Francis Borja, learned ecclesiastics, Fr. Ibariez amongst the number, bore testimony to the truth of the report. Teresa alone was ignorant of it. Wrapt in the cloak of humiliation, with which those by whom she was surrounded covered her, she sought only to remain hidden from the world. Her surprise and consternation may therefore be imagined when, on the 24th of December, 1561, a letter from the provincial reached her with the order to start at once for Toledo, and proceed to the palace of the Duchess Luisa de la Cerda, a broken-hearted widow, who had begged for her presence there, and hoped to draw consolation from her society.

The saint was at first much troubled with the summons. How could the duchess have heard of her existence? Would not her sudden departure be fatal to the success of the new

Foundation ? The bell rang for matins, and Teresa cut short her 'reflections to go to the choir, to sing the praises of Him Who brought peace to men of good will.

Soon, wrapt in ecstasy, she heard the well-known

voice of her Master speaking to her heart: " Go, daughter," it said to her; "pay no attention to those who would seek to detain you. You will have to suffer on this journey, but your sufferings will glorify Me. It is necessary for the success of our monastery that you should be absent till the Brief arrives. Fear not. I will be with you."

Teresa went the next day to her director, the rector of St. Giles, and told him of the order she had received, and likewise what our Lord had said to her. The rector told her that she had no motive for refusing. Strong in this assurance, the saint paid no heed to the lamentations and appeals of her friends; and confiding the care of the unfinished monastery to her sister and brother-in-law, she set out on the ist of January for Toledo, accompanied by Juan de Ovalle and a nun of the Convent of the Incarnation.

Two days later the little company beheld the imposing buildings of the Alcazar, with its lofty towers rising in the distance. Soon after the town with its crenellated walls and ramparts came in sight, and charmed the eyes of the saint, to whom everything beautiful in nature and art appealed irresistibly. They passed over the Tagus, and entering the city by the eastern gate they went straight to the duchess's palace. Juan de Ovalle then returned home, leaving Teresa with the mourner.

Luisa de la Cerda was a sister of the Duke de Medina Celi, and widow of one of the principal grandees of Castile ; a great lady therefore, but, what was more important, a woman possessed of a great soul. Till the death of her husband, which changed her joys into grief and mourning, her life had been one of unbroken happiness. Like many, therefore, who had never known what it was to suffer, she gave herself

up to her anguish without measure or restraint. No efforts on the part of her young son Don Juan, or of her brother, or of her many friends, could serve to distract her thoughts from her sorrows, or bring her back to a sense of the duties that still remained for her to perform ; all that she could now see of life was its uncertainty and its speedy termination. Whilst in this state she was told about Teresa, and, as our saint remarks, "God permitted that she should hear good of me in order that good should come of it." Accordingly all Luisa de la Cerda's hopes were placed on what this holy soul, who had possibly the secret of conveying consolation to the heart-broken, could do for her. Perhaps she would tell her with certainty that her husband was in Heaven? Thus (the will of the rich and powerful carrying all before it) the duchess addressed herself to the provincial, and obtained from him the favour of Teresa's presence at Toledo.

The saint found Dona Luisa in bed exhausted by her tears, and refusing to be comforted. She devoted herself to the task of inspiring her with resignation, and of leading this uncontrollable anguish into a Christian channel, and succeeded so well that before long the duchess consented to rise and take nourishment. We are told that having made the great sacrifice, and accepted her bereavement from God's Hands, the duchess devoted the rest of her days to good works. She insisted, however, on keeping Teresa long enough to be directed by her in her new way of life, and surrounded her with proofs of her esteem and affection, many of which, the saint tells us, were "a cross and a trial " to her.

Alas for Teresa ! At the moment when all her desires were placed on imitating the poverty of Bethlehem, she was called upon to live in a palace, and to be waited on by servants who were obliged to emulate their mistress's devotion in their behaviour to her. She submitted to everything, and perhaps studied this unknown world with a certain interest before giving it up for ever. We detect a gentle irony with regard to the lives led by these great people, mixed with much compassion for them, in the record of this part of her life. " I kept my soul continually recollected," she says ; " I did not dare to be careless, nor was our Lord careless of me. For whilst I was there He bestowed the greatest graces on me, and those graces gave me such liberty of spirit that it filled me with contempt for all I saw. I derived very great advantages from this. I saw that rank is of little worth, and the higher it is, the greater the anxiety and trouble it brings. People must be careful of the dignity of their state, which will not suffer them to live at ease. They must eat at fixed hours, and by rule, for everything must be according to their state and not according to their constitutions ; and they have frequently to take food fitted more for their state than for their liking. Then as to servants, though this lady had very good servants, how slight is the trust that may be put in them ! One must not be conversed with more than another, otherwise he who is so favoured is envied by the rest. This is of itself a slavery, and it is one of the lies of the world that it calls such persons master, who in my eyes are in a thousand ways but slaves." 1

This great world, which was powerless to dazzle our saint, felt deeply the ascendancy of her character and of her holiness. So attractive was her piety that everyone wished to share its secret. The young girls brought up in the palace, Dona Luisa's friends,

crowded round her, seeking her advice and asking questions of her. Teresa had wise counsels for all. She spoke to the great ladies of working for the glory of God by fidelity to their duties as heads of families, and by their charity to the poor. The young girls she told to obey their parents as they would our Lord Himself, and if their parents wished them to adorn themselves, to do so with simplicity, with the intention of pleasing God by their submission. 1 Maria de Salazar, a relation of the Duchess de la Cerda's, who eclipsed all her companions by her brilliancy and charm, met with a different treatment from the saint. Teresa, seeing her robed in silks and satins, gently reproached her, saying: "This finery is unsuitable for one who would willingly, were it possible, assume the habit of a nun." Maria was astounded at finding that the saint had discovered a secret she had disclosed to none. She was twenty at this time, with the world at her feet, and to all appearance not insensible to its pleasures. But the death of Don Aries, cut off in the prime of life—a death which had plunged his family into anguish and mourning—had made a profound impression on her. She asked herself of what benefit was a happiness which might crumble away at any moment, leaving nothing behind it. And whilst the poor Dona Luisa was weighed down almost to the grave by her sorrows, Maria, calm in appearance, was no less struck by the sudden blow, and was seeking to replace her lost illusions by the solid realities of God's service. Providence having betrayed Maria's secret to Teresa, she gladly owned to the disgust she experienced of the world, and her desire for the cloister. Teresa received these confidences with maternal tenderness, and began at once to train her spiritual daughter to the

1 Ribera, Life of St. Teresa, Book IV, ch. v.

practice of those virtues which she most desired to see in the members of her future community. She was delighted with Maria's excellent judgment, and looked upon her journey to Toledo as a fortunate one, if for no other cause than that she should thereby have become acquainted with this generous soul, whom she foresaw would be so well fitted to carry out her designs. Maria de la Salazar bore little resemblance to the saint in her outward manner, which was calm and reserved. But she resembled her through her brightness and intelligence, and by what Teresa esteemed at a much higher value, her humility, sweetness, and strength of character.

Teresa's stay at Toledo was prolonged beyond her expectation, the provincial ceding to Dona Luisa de la Cerda's earnest desires to retain the saint beside her. She divided her time whilst in that city between her duties to society, prayer, and an undertaking she had commenced the previous year in obedience to an order of Fr. Ibaftez. This was a history of her spiritual life, a work for which the Church has owed her a debt of gratitude for more than four centuries. This task had been a great trial to her, and in sending it to Fr. Ibaftez she writes : " I am much tempted to give you some idea of what I have gone through for your sake in writing the history of my life. I feel I have a right to do it after all I have suffered in seeing myself thus described, and in recalling to my memory so many miseries." But side by side with these sufferings there was the joy and consolation of glorifying her beloved Lord and Master. For our saint's history of her life meant speaking little of herself and much about God. To Him she incessantly returns ; to Him she addresses herself in the touching avowal of her faults and her repentance. Her Life

is but a long outpouring on the bosom of her Saviour. She does not so much write as pray ; she loves, and she sings. She sings, like Mary, of her littleness, and of the greatness of God ; she sings through her tears. But above all she sings of the incomprehensible goodness and tenderness of the King, the Master, the Friend, of her Lord and Saviour Jesus Christ.

Dominated by such exalted inspiration, she was indifferent to the form taken by her literary labours. They were written under obedience, in order to render an account of the state of her soul, her infidelities to grace, and the unspeakable mercies of God in her regard. Accordingly there is no anxiety to express her thoughts properly, no method used in putting the story together ; but on the other hand there is a delightful simplicity about the book, the charm of a natural and unstudied style, an absolute spontaneity, which render it deeply attractive. The pages are living ones, and in reading them one seems to see her and to hear her voice. Sublime and yet most simple, a poet without wishing to be one, eloquent without being conscious of her power, she enchants and carries the reader away with her to those lofty regions where her soul habitually dwells. She convinces the reader of the truth of what she urges, less by her arguments than by the inimitable accents of sincerity and truth which animate them.

Teresa's stay at Toledo was marked by another providential occurrence. Whilst she was there, a nun who was a stranger to her, of the name of Mother Mary of Jesus, asked for an interview with her. Mother Mary was a widow of good family, who, after her husband's death, had become a Carmelite nun, and by a singular coincidence had been inspired to found a Reformed convent of the Order in the same

year and month that Teresa had conceived a similar idea.

Mother Mary had larger resources at her disposal than our saint, but she was less well endowed by nature and education. In spite of these drawbacks, she had so thoroughly mastered the primitive Rule of Mount Car-mel that she was an authority upon it, down to its minutest details. She had received permission from her superior at Granada to leave her convent and go to Rome to obtain a papal Brief approving of her Foundation ; and having succeeded (after a journey of great hardships) in obtaining it from Paul IV, she had just returned to Spain. Then, hearing of Teresa's designs, she had come to Toledo to confer with her on this subject. The duchess gave hospitality to Mother Mary, so that the two foundresses were able, for the space of a fortnight, to hold converse together. Teresa studied deeply the diploma and Brief given by the Holy See, as well as the procedure necessary for the erection of a monastery of the Reform ; and Mother Mary was able likewise to give her other useful information. But these details were not the principal subjects of their conversations. Teresa loved above all to talk of the spirit of recollection, poverty, and penance in which she desired that these beloved solitudes should be steeped. She confided in her newly-found friend the kind of perfection, austere yet sweet and attractive, which she dreamed of as the distinguishing mark of the little group of elect souls whom she hoped to draw round her. Mother Mary had also made her plans, but her spirit was not so wide and far-seeing as that of our saint. The spirit of penance dominated her too exclusively. Teresa noticed this in order to draw subject of edification from it, and she thought herself unworthy of intercourse with one so

mortified and detached. When, however, the time came to carry their plans into execution, we shall see which of these two best understood the human heart, and God's designs upon it, and above all that happy medium which is the test of solid virtue. For in order that Mother Mary's work should take root, it was necessary later on for Teresa to intervene and repress the generous but imprudent direction taken by her Reform, and communicate to it the holy liberty characteristic of the spirit of Carmel.

The meeting of the two Mothers was therefore a blessed one, for both one and the other. They parted with a mutual promise to pray for each other, and Mother Mary of Jesus pursued her way to Madrid, where she hoped to enlist the help of the Nuncio on her side against the opposition raised by the Order—an opposition which was not overcome till after a year of trial and difficulty.

Meanwhile Teresa continued her apostolic work in the society of Toledo whilst waiting for permission from the provincial to return to her convent. The time had passed when contact with the world would have been a source of dissipation to Teresa. At this period it would seem, rather, to have been a time of special grace and favour. Obedience had taken her from her convent to the palace, and accordingly her Divine Master had Himself accompanied her there, and amidst these gilded chambers, as in her oratory at home, He spoke to her soul and ravished her to Himself. Teresa took the utmost care to conceal these divine favours from those who surrounded her, but the curiosity of these good people was not to be denied ; they continually surprised her in ecstasy, her face transfigured with a supernatural joy, her eyes streaming with tears of love and devotion. All in the house, from first to

last, vied in honouring her and in applying to her when in trouble or difficulty. On one occasion a member of the household who had been suffering for a long time from violent pains in the head and ears threw herself at her feet, and implored her to make a sign of the cross on the place from whence her suffering came. Teresa quietly moved her aside, and said : " What are you thinking of! Go and make a sign of the cross yourself on the place, for the good lies in the sign of the cross, not in the hand which makes it." 1 But in gently pushing her away Teresa's hand touched the woman's head, and she was instantaneously cured.

The saint's influence was not exercised on the inmates of the palace alone. It will be remembered that she made acquaintance with a Dominican father who was attending Don Alonso on his deathbed, and had had recourse to him afterwards, herself, in order that he might help her on the road to Heaven. Fr. Vincent Barron had left Avila many years before, and Teresa had never seen him since, but she could not forget what she owed to him. For it was due to him that she had resumed the practice of prayer, had begun to communicate more frequently, in other words, had been brought back to the path of perfection. Providence so disposed matters that the religious and our saint should have the consolation of meeting, by bringing Fr. Vincent to Toledo whilst Teresa was staying there. The Dominican convent adjoined the duchess's palace, and the saint frequently assisted at Mass there. Great was her emotion one day when she saw her former director kneeling before the altar. Her first instinct was to get up and speak to him. " But," she relates, " considering within myself that I might only be losing my time in mixing in the matter, I sat down again.

I did this three times before I could make up my mind. Finally my good angel triumphed, and I sent for the father, and he came and met me in the confessional." 1 The meeting was a source of consolation to both. Fr. Barren had reason to thank God that he had been chosen to interpret the Divine Will to our saint. She, on the other hand, rejoiced in the holy dispositions she perceived in him. Nevertheless our saint, divinely enlightened, was made aware that something was yet wanting to the perfection of his spiritual life. What it was we are not told. We know that he was an excellent man, but Teresa wished to make a saint—and a great saint—of him ; and saints are rare. Directly she left him she set to work to pray, and with that ardent love of souls and confidence in God which was her strongest characteristic, she cried : " Lord, grant me this favour. I know you will not refuse it to me. Consider how meet his soul is for perfect friendship with Thee and me." Her petition was granted in full. He, whom she knew to be holy but whom she wished to see perfect, set out with fresh fervour on the "narrow path," and in a short time he had, by dint of austerity, recollection, and prayer, accomplished marvels such as filled Teresa's soul with joy. Her ardent prayers had gained one chosen friend more for her beloved Master, and for the Dominican Order a shining light. Teresa had many revelations with regard to Fr. Barren's growth in sanctity. On one occasion our Lord showed him to her in a vision surrounded with a brilliant light and borne by angels, and she was told that at the moment when she had the vision he was going through some great trials which he endured not only with patience, but with joy. She said of him on another occasion that "she saw him on fire with the love of God."

1 Boll., No. 317.

Even more grateful, more enchanted at the favours Heaven had bestowed on him than at those accorded to herself, she never ceased thanking God for having heard her prayers and given the Church such a faithful servant. "O my adorable Saviour," she said on one occasion, speaking of the holy Dominican's great zeal, " how powerful is the influence exercised by a soul which is entirely possessed by love of Thee ! " This was indeed a thought which occurred to all those who came within the sphere of Teresa's influence.

Her mission at Toledo was soon to be completed ; but though she was in her element in apostolic work wherever she went, she did not forget that the mission her Divine Master had given to her lay elsewhere. The Foundation at Avila was therefore the first object both of her thoughts and of her prayers. An opportunity of conferring once more with St. Peter of Alcantara on the subject was given her at Toledo. He came to stay at the palace whilst Teresa was there, and she was able to consult him on a point which up to that time had escaped her notice. Mother Mary of Jesus had drawn her attention to the fact that according to the primitive Rule no monasteries were endowed. "I was not aware of this," our saint remarks; "and though I had frequently read our constitutions, I never noticed this till I was told of it by Mother Mary, who could not herself read at all." Strong in these two principles : one that the Rule forbade endowment, and the other that it was more perfect to dispense with it, Teresa resolved to start her Foundation without revenue. But here she met with opposition from everyone of her friends; Jesuits, Dominicans, every theologian with one accord brought arguments, which she found unanswerable, against her. She laid this difficulty before St. Peter, but he was too great a lover of poverty to turn her from the strict Observance, and he used all his powers of persuasion to recall her to the ideal of destitution as exemplified in the Cradle and in the Cross.

Teresa, satisfied with this decision, no longer sought to argue the matter with her other advisers, and before long they came round to her opinion. Our Lord Himself confirmed her in it: "Daughter," He said, "it is My Father's will, and Mine, that you found your monastery without endowment. I will take charge of your affairs."

All this time Teresa was kept in ignorance as to how long her sojourn at Toledo was to be prolonged. Dona Luisa became every day more attached to her friend, and the saint's society became more indispensable to her ; and still the provincial made no sign of withdrawing his order. Meanwhile there was great discouragement at Avila. Juana, tired of waiting for her sister's return, had gone home to Alba de Tormes. Juan de Ovalle, left guardian of the little installation at St. Joseph's, was uncertain what to do next, and impatient to join his wife. At last he determined to go to Toledo to consult Teresa. Her advice was that he had better return to Alba. It was necessary for him, however, to go back first to Avila to make various arrangements. On reaching St. Joseph's he was attacked with high fever, so that all further journey was out of the question. He was laid up accordingly in the unfinished monastery, where he was deprived of all help from his relations, neither his wife nor Teresa being informed of the state he was in.

About the middle of June, a week after de Ovalle's visit to Toledo, Teresa at last received a letter from the provincial, in which he revoked his previous order, and left her free to prolong her stay with Dona Luisa, or to return to the Convent of the Incarnation. This was

a tactful way of himself escaping the difficulty of distressing the duchess, by throwing the responsibility of doing so on Teresa. No stone was left unturned by that great lady to retain her fri,end near her. To Teresa also the parting was not without a pang, as she had conceived a real affection for that generous and affectionate soul whom she had been the means of turning to God. She had been successful, however, in inspiring the duchess with a little of her own spirit of self-abnegation, and after speaking to her in the language of faith of the interests of God's glory which were involved in her departure, she at last persuaded her friend to consent to it. There had been a moment when Teresa had almost been tempted to delay it. She had received a letter from the Incarnation telling her that the time of the election was approaching, and that several of the nuns were inclined to vote for her appointment to the office of prioress. The saint shuddered at the thought ; any form of martyrdom would have been preferable. She dreaded less the prospect of being at the head of a large community, many of whose numbers were strongly opposed to her, than the great responsibility attached to the position, and the increased difficulties it would put in the way of the new Foundation. She hoped to avoid the danger by remaining at Toledo till after the new prioress's election. Our Lord reproved her for these fears, and pressed her to go. " Do not wait a moment longer," He said to her. " You desire crosses; you will meet with one there which you will find hard to bear ; but fear not, I will help you to bear it."

Our saint wept on hearing these words ; she thought the cross our Lord spoke of was her appointment to the office of prioress; but ever submissive, she prepared at once to depart. The heat, great at all times in June,

was at that moment overpowering, and in Teresa's delicate state of health it seemed almost madness to attempt the journey. Her confessor recommended delay. But Teresa felt she was resisting the Divine Will ; she succeeded in getting his permission to depart, and tearing herself away from her kind friends at Toledo, she started on the road to Avila. The fatigues and heat of the journey were the least part of her trials. She could not rest from thinking of the great cross our Lord predicted for her. "I saw," she remarks in her Life, " that I was about to throw myself in the fire ; but I started full of joy, impatient for the moment to come when I should be launched into the combat in which my Master wished to see me engaged, and for which He had given such strength to my feebleness."

Arrived at Avila, she paid a visit to the little newly built monastery of St. Joseph on her way to the convent. There she found to her surprise Juan de Ovalle laid up with fever, and much in need of her assistance. Her duty of obedience obliged her to return at once to the Incarnation ; but she left her brother-in-law with the promise that she would return to him the moment she got leave to do so.

Avila at that moment had some of Teresa's greatest friends assembled within its walls. St. Peter of Alcantara was staying there with Francisco de Salcedo; Caspar'Daza, the rector of St. Giles, and another holy prelate, Gonzales de Aranda, were in the town. Also Mgr. Alvaro de Mendoza, Bishop of Avila, who, acquainted by Peter of Alcantara with Teresa's enterprise, took a friendly interest in our saint, though he had not yet given his consent to the Foundation.

News reached Teresa directly she got back which filled her with joy, besides explaining to her the reason

why our Lord had laid so much stress on the necessity of her speedy return to her convent. The long awaited Brief from Rome had at last arrived ; it was dated the 6th of January, 1562, and authorized the establishment of the monastery of St. Joseph. This Brief, 1 which was addressed to Dona Guiomar and her mother Dona Alonso Guzman, gave them permission to found a house of Carmelite nuns of the primitive Rule, which was to be provided with chapel, bell, cloisters, and cells, and was to be under the jurisdiction of the diocesan bishop, and to enjoy the rights, exemptions, and privileges accorded to all the monasteries of the Order. It was accompanied with a threat to all who should trouble its peace. Cardinal Farnese, Grand Penitentiary, charged the prior of the Convent of Magacela, the Archdeacon of Segovia, and the grand chaplain of the cathedral at Toledo, in the name and by the authority of Pope Pius IV, to carry out these orders of the Holy See. The name of Teresa did not appear in the authorization ; a simple nun, a member still of the community of the Incarnation and still under the orders of the superior of that monastery, it was impossible for her to figure personally in any document of this nature. Dona Guiomar and her mother took all the responsibility of the new departure. There was now no time to be lost. Providence, to the joy and consolation of Teresa's friends, had brought together at this critical moment every one of the chief supporters of her great work. At a private meeting, presided over by St. Peter of Alcantara, it was decided that the first step taken should be that of trying to gain the consent of Mgr. Alvaro de Mendoza. The saint was himself too ill to leave his room, but he sent two messengers to the prelate to speak in his behalf. They

SAINT PETER OF ALCANTARA

returned without succeeding in their mission. The bishop had not understood that the Foundation was to be made without endowment ; as soon as he heard that this was the case he refused his sanction.

As soon as the son of St. Francis had heard the bishop's answer, he only said: "If God permits that we should receive this rebuff, it is only for our ultimate advantage." And so saying he rose from his bed to go to Mgr. Alvarez, but his legs were so weak they refused to support him, and he, who in all his constant journeyings through Spain and Italy had never ridden or driven, had to make use of a saddle-mule to take him into the bishop's presence. When the latter saw the holy man arrive he was deeply moved. He could refuse nothing to the saint: Teresa had gained her cause.

It was no slight duty that the bishop had taken upon himself in consenting to the Foundation and taking it under his own jurisdiction. It meant that he declared himself father and superior of the little community, with the obligation of defending it against evil reports and the displeasure of the Order of Mount Carmel, from whose jurisdiction it was withdrawn. If the influence of the saintly Franciscan was decisive, the eminent piety of the excellent prelate had its share in a decision in which the glory of God was so greatly involved. From that day he ever showed the love and devotion of a father for the community of St. Joseph, and in particular for its foundress. Teresa, on the other hand, profited by his benevolent dispositions by enlisting them in the service of others much more than she did in protecting her own interests. St. Peter of Alcantara was only a few days at Avila. He left soon after, never to return. His life of penance and self-sacrifice was about to receive its everlasting reward.

" It would appear," St. Teresa tells us, " as if God had kept him alive only to finish our undertaking, for he had been very ill for more than two years, and he was to die almost immediately afterwards. He did all he could for us, and without his counsels and his help I do not know how the work could have been done."

The hand of the holy old man had placed the last stone on the edifice which all three of the great Orders of the Church had assisted in erecting. The children of St. Ignatius had dug its foundations, and the sons of St. Dominic had protected its early beginnings ; and now the zeal and charity of St. Francis was to crown the holy work. Teresa delighted to efface herself in the presence of her benefactors, giving them all the credit for what she herself had accomplished. Thus in her delightful history, she multiplies names of founders and foundresses, and protectors of the Carmel Reform. Yet notwithstanding her efforts she deceives no one ; the ascendancy of her genius, the power of her sanctity asserts itself everywhere. If she is able to gain advocates in the most unexpected quarters, and to conciliate even her adversaries, turning them into devoted friends, these were in truth but resources of which she made use, without her personal influence being thereby in the smallest degree diminished.

St. Peter of Alcantara visited the new Carmel before leaving Avila. It was unfinished, but it was already easy to see that the only beauty to which the building could lay claim was its simplicity. The saint who worshipped his " lady Poverty" rejoiced at the sight of it. u This in truth," he said, "is a house of St. Joseph, and another grotto of Bethlehem." 1

Teresa, having received permission to nurse de

Ovalle, was able to watch the finishing strokes of the workmen.

"I had much trouble at this time," she says, "in persuading this person, or that, to allow the Foundation. I had to nurse the sick man, and to hasten the workmen in their preparation of the house, so that it might have the form of a monastery. I saw that everything depended on haste for many reasons, one of which was that I was afraid that I might be ordered back to my monastery at any moment. I was troubled by so many things that I suspected my cross had been sent me, though it seemed but a light one in comparison with that which I understood our Lord meant me to carry."

The election came off at the Incarnation shortly afterwards, without bringing about the results feared by our saint. This gave her more breathing space, and occasions were not wanting to satisfy her love of crosses. July passed amidst much anxiety and fatigue, Dona Guiomar's absence adding a great deal to her labours. Affairs were conducted in the strictest secrecy, for, as Teresa said, a word would have been sufficient to ruin everything. Juan de Ovalle's illness, fortunately, was sufficient pretext to account for Teresa's presence in the house purchased by him. The very day when the workmen left it his fever left him, and on rising from his bed of sickness he thanked his kind nurse, and said to her with a smile : " Now that it is no longer necessary for me to be ill here, I am quite cured!" 1 Accordingly he left the saint to make all her own arrangements in the new monastery, and moved to lodgings in the neighbourhood.

Everything was now finished. All that was seen from the exterior were solid, thick, well-cemented

1 Ribera.

walls, irregularly pierced with windows. Inside there was a narrow vestibule, beyond this two low doors, an image of Our Lady over the one which gave access to the chapel, and one of St. Joseph over the other which opened into the convent. The interior was in harmony with the rest; the chapel was a plain hall, clean and suitable, but without any decoration. Another much smaller room served as a nuns' choir ; a large aperture, protected by a double grille and curtain, pierced the wall which separated the choir from the chapel. It was here, wrapt in impenetrable shadow, that the saint and her companions came to adore and to sing the praises of their beloved Lord and Master, hidden from every eye. Teresa was now perfectly happy. Her childhood's dreams, the aspirations of her youth, the longings of her riper years were realized when she was able to bury herself in her little hermitage and live sola cum solo —alone with Him. Where and who were the chosen souls who were to join her in this retreat, and share her sacrifices and self-immolations with her? Was Juana Suarez, her faithful friend, to be one? or her high-spirited niece, Maria de Ocampo? or Maria de Salazar, her latest recruit from Toledo? It was to be none of these. The first-named, at the age of fifty, found it impossible to break with the habits of a lifetime ; she was to die peacefully and happily at the Convent of the Incarnation. It was necessary that the vocations of the two Marias should take time to mature before they could gain permission to follow our saint. Maria de Ocampo was too young for her aunt to wish to expose her to the austerities and difficulties inseparable from a first Foundation. Also, in spite of the thousand ducats which she had so generously contributed to the building of St. Joseph's, and the vision by which it had

been rewarded, 1 Maria hesitated ; the world still offered her much attraction, she was tried by temptations against faith, and by a desolation of spirit which made prayer a veritable weariness in the flesh to her. On one occasion she was kneeling with her school companions at the Convent of the Incarnation, trying in vain to pray, when Teresa approached and gave her a passage in the Following of Christ to read. Maria gave a careless glance at the page, then suddenly her mind took in the meaning, and the words placed before her eyes seemed to pierce the veil of darkness which enveloped her, and to let in Heaven's light. She renewed her resolution to give up all and become a Carmelite, and hurried to thank her aunt for the help she had given her. Teresa encouraged and blessed her, but she took the wise part of putting her vocation to some months' trial before accepting her.

In place of taking these much-loved friends, whose company perhaps would have been too great a joy to her, Teresa took four postulants providentially chosen for her, who were worthy of being the foundation stones of the reformed monastery of St. Joseph. This is what the saint says of them : " I felt as if I were in bliss when I saw the most Holy Sacrament reserved, and found myself with four poor orphans (for they were taken without dowry), great servants of God, established in the house. It was our aim from the beginning to receive only those who by their example might be the foundation on which we could build up what we had in view—great perfection and prayer—and effect a work which would be greatly to the glory of God and to the honour of the habit of His most Blessed Mother."

1 Vide Mother Mary Baptist's Declaration, History of the Order of Mount Carmel.

Antonia de Henao, one of these privileged women, was a connection of Teresa's, though she had been almost unacquainted with her till St. Peter of Alcantara had brought Antonia before her notice. She had been under St. Peter's direction for some years, and had been prevented by him from seeking a monastery of strict Observance outside Avila, as he had assured her if she waited she would find what she sought, in time, in that city. Antonia was twenty-seven years of age; she possessed a well-balanced mind, the frankness and simplicity of a child, and solid piety. These were sufficient reasons for Teresa to receive her with open arms.

Dona Guiomar and Caspar Daza each had a postulant to recommend to our saint. Dona Guiomar had brought up a child out of charity, whose parents, though of noble birth, had lost everything they possessed. Maria de Paz passed a hidden life in her benefactress's house. She was everybody's servant, and she spent her time in prayers and good works. Her great humility obtained many favours from our Lord, and Teresa rejoiced in giving her the habit of Mount Carmel.

Ursula de Revilla, Fr. Caspar's penitent, had begun life with a taste for worldly pleasures. Her director had small indulgence for these weaknesses in a soul when he perceived in it an attraction to higher things. The young girl humbled herself under his hands, and in time she changed her life altogether for one of great self-abnegation, which obtained for her the grace to embrace the austerities of the Reform.

The fourth postulant was a sister of Fr. Julian d'Avila, a disciple of Fr. Caspar Daza's. This was another Maria, a simple and pure maiden resembling her namesake, Maria de Paz. Teresa gave her the name of

Maria of St. Joseph. Maria de Paz became Maria of the Cross. Antonia became Antonia of the Holy Ghost, and Ursula kept the name chosen for her by the piety of her parents, Ursula of the Saints. This renunciation of family names was new in the Order of Mount Carmel. Teresa desired by renaming her postulants to efface every distinction of rank and title, in order to emphasize what in her sight was their sole distinction, that of being mystic spouses of Jesus Christ. She therefore intended, by giving them new names, celestial and symbolic names borrowed from the saints or angels, or from the divine mysteries, to let them perceive that for them a purely human life had concluded, and another almost wholly divine had begun.

On the Feast of St. Bartholomew, the 24th of August, Antonia, Ursula, and the two Marias arrived one after another at St. Joseph's. Teresa welcomed them with a mother's tenderness, and led them to the chapel where they were joined by Don Francisco de Salcedo, Fr. Julian of Avila, Gonzales de Aranda, and Juan de Ovalle and his wife, who had returned from Alba in order to be present on this great occasion. Teresa's cousins, Inez and Anna de Tapia, professed nuns of the Convent of the Incarnation, were also able to assist at the execution of a project which they had known of and encouraged from the first. Fr. Daza, delegated by the Bishop of Avila, said Mass, and deposited the Blessed Sacrament in the tabernacle. He then blessed the religious habits, and our saint invested her daughters .. w in them. They consisted of a rough stuff dress, a scapular of the same material, a head-dress of coarse linen, a cloak of white wool, and, for the postulants, a white linen veil, till they could assume the black one proper to the professed. The assistants chanted the Te

Deum, the little monastery bell 1 rang loudly, and the happy novices, prostrate before the altar, bedewed the stone floor with tears of joy and gratitude.

The saint, rapt in God her Saviour, seemed to belong no longer to this earth. Her little house had become God's House. Jesus possessed another resting place, where pure and fervent souls, withdrawn from the dangers of the world, would have henceforth no occupation save that of praising, serving, and adoring Him. St. Joseph, her beloved protector, would be honoured with special devotion in this chapel dedicated to him. All these consolations inundated the heart of Teresa with a joy which seemed to be the precursor of the bliss and glory of Heaven. Concealed beneath her veil, she poured out her soul to God in prayer. This moment of almost paradisaical happiness was not to last long, and it was to be followed very shortly, according to the almost invariable conduct of her Divine Master towards His spouse, by a great tribulation.

1 This bell, which only weighed three pounds, represented religious poverty in such perfection that it was kept as a precious relic in the Order. It was taken to Pastrana, and used there at the Convocations, to remind the heads of Chapter of the holy poverty in which the Reform was founded.

CHAPTER XIV

A FTER the morning's ceremony was over, Fr. Daza XX and his assistants retired, leaving Teresa and her daughters to the enjoyment of their solitude. Teresa could hardly tear herself away from her little chapel. Prostrate before the Blessed Sacrament, she tasted something of the joys of Heaven in seeing her Saviour consecrating by His presence the newly-made Foundation and the four dowerless orphans, who though obscure from the world's point of view, were so pleasing to Him, and who had been first admitted to the honour and privilege of embracing the Rule of Carmel in all its perfection. Teresa, in speaking of this day, says with her usual simplicity : " It was also a great consolation to me that I had done that which our Lord had so often commanded me to do, and that there was one church more in this city dedicated to my glorious father St. Joseph. 1 I always looked upon it as the work of our Lord. My part in it was so full of imperfections that I looked upon myself rather as a person in fault than as one to whom any thanks were due. But it was a great joy to me when I saw His Majesty make use of me, who am so worthless, in so grand a work. I was therefore in great joy, so much so that I was as it were beside myself, lost in prayer."

1 The sons of Carmel brought with them from Palestine the cult of St. Joseph, but the glory of propagating it belongs to Teresa. Churches were very rarely dedicated to that saint before the Reform was inaugurated. (Boll., No. 344.)

But God Almighty, who exalts and then humbles, enriches and subsequently reduces to poverty, permitted that an extraordinary change should come over the soul of our saint. All the doors whence she could draw consolation appeared suddenly closed, and instead of them one opened from whence an agonizing recollection of the past, and painful anxiety for the future, came forth to disturb her soul. This terrible attack which, as Teresa tells us, the Evil One made upon her, began three or four hours after Mass. Satan suggested to her the one terror which had power to make her quail: that of having founded her monastery without her superiors' consent. The commands she had received from Heaven, her director's sanction, the encouragement of St. Peter of Alcantara, and of so many other eminent and holy souls, the Brief from the Holy See, everything seemed to be, as she says herself, so completely blotted out from her memory it was just as if they had never existed. Other terrors suggested themselves to her. How would these young girls, delicately brought up, be able to lead a life of austerity such as the one she had persuaded them to embrace ? How would they be able to stand the strictness of the enclosure ? Shall I even, she said to herself, be able to provide the necessaries of life for them, their daily bread? Perhaps after all the undertaking was a piece of folly. "The devil would have me ask myself" (we quote from her Life) "how I could think of shutting myself up in a house of strict Observance when I was subject to so many infirmities? how could I bear so penitential a life, or leave the large and pleasant house where I had always been so happy, and where I had so many friends? I had taken on myself a heavy responsibility, and might possibly end in despair." Here indeed there was every sign of

diabolical temptation, with its lies and darkness. " Oh, my God," she says, turning to Him Who was her sole consolation, " how wretched is this life! No joy is lasting. Only a moment ago I do not think I would have exchanged my joy with any man's on earth, and now I know not what to do with myself. Oh, if we did but consider carefully the events of our life, how little we should make of its pains or pleasures ! This was, I believe, one of the most distressing moments I ever passed in my life. But our Lord would not allow His poor servant to suffer long (for in all my troubles He never failed to succour me). He gave me a little light so that I might see it was the work of the devil. Then I began to call to mind my great resolutions to serve our Lord, and my desire to suffer for His sake. What was I, then, afraid of? If I longed for tribulations, I had them now." 1

With a great effort at self-command Teresa took courage once more, and promised in front of the tabernacle that she would leave no stone unturned to obtain permission from her superiors to shut herself up in her new monastery. As soon as she had made this promise the temptation suddenly left her. "I believe," she says, "that our Lord suffered me to be thus tempted that I might understand how great a mercy He had shown me herein, and from what torment He had delivered me, and that if I saw any one in like trouble I might not be alarmed at it, but have pity on her, and be able to console her."

These interior trials of the saint seemed to be a prelude to the storm from without which was about to break over the little community of St. Joseph.

The tinkle of the monastery bell had announced the opening of the new Foundation to the inhabitants of

1 Life, ch. xxxvi.

Avila from earliest dawn, and it was at first hailed by the good and simple folk, in whose hearts Castilian faith still reigned, with satisfaction and joy. This feeling was, however, of short duration. As soon as the principal inhabitants of the town, who were stoutly opposed to Teresa's undertaking, heard of it, they commenced at once to get up a violent agitation against it. They concerted together to mislead the people by persuading them that a convent which had no endowment would take the bread out of the mouths of the poor, by absorbing the alms which had hitherto gone to relieve their necessities. The indignation soon spread, and became universal; St. Joseph's was talked of as a public evil which it was necessary to suppress. To account for fears so absolutely chimerical, one must attribute the panic of the good inhabitants of Avila, as our saint did, to the machinations of the devil. " If the whole town had been set on fire," was the comment of Fr. Julian, " it would not have created a greater panic."

The excitement was no less at the Convent of the Incarnation. When the news came like a clap of thunder on the community, discretion and prudence were scattered to the four winds. Teresa was heaping affronts on the Holy Order of Mount Carmel by founding a monastery which was to aim at a more perfect life than that led by her sisters in religion. If her health had scarcely permitted her to follow the mitigated Rule, how could she observe the primitive one, in all its rigour? Finally her enterprise was denounced as one only calculated to disturb the public mind, and bring trouble on communities of nuns in general. The upshot was that the prioress /pressure being put upon her both from within and from the secular world outside) sent word to Teresa that she was to leave her house and return at once to the Convent of the Incarnation.

The saint had just finished partaking of her frugal midday meal with her sisters, and had gone to her cell to take an hour's much-needed rest—having kept vigil all the previous night—when the summons from the prioress arrived. She read it with apparent calm, though inwardly she felt deeply for her young novices whom she had to leave behind in solitude, and without the protection of her presence. But throwing her anguish into the heart of her Divine Master, she only waited long enough to bless and embrace her dear children, leaving sister Ursula of the Saints at their head, to prostrate herself at the foot of the altar, and to recommend the monastery to the care of our Lord and St. Joseph, before taking her departure for the Incarnation. She says: " I went persuaded that I should be put in prison at once ; but this would have been a great comfort, because I should have had nobody to speak to, and might have had some rest and solitude which I was much in need of; for so much intercourse with people had worn me out."

Teresa passed through the town accompanied by Fr. Julian, who says he offered himself to her as chaplain and squire, and told her that he would be ready to devote himself, as such, to her service till the day of her death. " Other priests," he says, " also accompanied us, and though she was badly received at her convent she had not to suffer to the extent she feared." The saint on her arrival was led, like a rebel, into the presence of the prioress, who awaited her surrounded by the elders of the community. The sight of her alone had an effect in softening the angry feeling which had reigned in the convent with regard to her. Teresa answered the questions addressed to her, explained her

conduct, and left herself in the hands of her superior. The latter, after consulting the rest of the community, with the advice of the majority appealed to the provincial for his judgment. On Fr. de Salazar's arrival the nuns were re-assembled, and Teresa, peaceful and modest as ever, with the dignity born of deep humility, appeared before her judges.

" When he came," says Teresa, " I was summoned to judgment, rejoicing greatly at seeing that I had something to suffer for our Lord. I did not think that I had offended against His Divine Majesty in anything I had done. I thought of Christ receiving sentence, and I saw how this of mine would be less than nothing. I confessed my fault as if I had been very much to blame, and so I seemed to everyone who did not know all the reasons. After the provincial had rebuked me sharply, though not with the severity which my fault deserved, nor according to the representations made to him, I would not defend myself. I prayed him to forgive me and punish me, and be no longer angry with me."

Disarmed by Teresa's humble sincerity, Fr. de Salazar was disposed to be indulgent, but the nuns returned to the charge with fresh accusations. Teresa excused them as follows: "I saw that they condemned me on some charges of which I was innocent; for they said I had founded the monastery that I might be thought much of, and for other reasons of that kind. But on other points I saw clearly that they were speaking the truth, as when they said I was more wicked than the other nuns. They asked how could I, who had not kept the Rule in that house, think of keeping it in another of stricter Observance. They said I was a source of scandal in the city, and was setting up novelties." These accusations failed to disturb Teresa's

serenity. Nevertheless, she tells us in her Life, she appeared grieved, so as not to annoy her sisters by an appearance of indifference. Fr. de Salazar heard all the nuns' allegations in much perplexity. Was Teresa in truth a visionary and rebellious subject such as they made out? He waited for her to justify her conduct, but the saint, true to her resolution to imitate Christ's silence before Pilate, said nothing. Finally the father bade her tell him in the presence of the community the motives on which she had acted. Thus adjured, Teresa explained the objects she had in view, and her reasons were so conclusive that neither the provincial nor the community had a word more to urge. The provincial then dismissed the nuns, and keeping back Teresa he received a .detailed account from her of all that had passed between her and her Divine Master on the subject of the Foundation, of the advice she had asked and received, and the precautions she had taken not to depart from the path of duty and of obedience. Fr. de Salazar was a just man, and an excellent religious ; satisfied with the explanations she had given him, he blessed her, and promised to authorize her return to St. Joseph's as soon as the tumult in the town had subsided.

The troubles, however, in that direction went on steadily increasing. Anyone would have said that a revolution was brewing in " Avila of the Saints." The people assembled in crowds in the streets, messengers were being sent to and fro between the governor's house and the Convent of the Incarnation. The sudden apparition of an army of Moors at the gates of the city would not have produced a greater commotion. 1 The popular tumult spread to the governor's house ; and on the 26th of August, after a noisy meeting at the town hall, it was agreed that the

1 Julian d'Avila. Q

convent should be suppressed, and the four novices told to depart to their own homes. The little community, when informed of the council's decision by the corregidor, who came in person to acquaint them with it, refused to obey it. They appealed to the tribunal of the King, Philip II, and declared that they trusted their cause to God, the Avenger of the weak and the oppressed.

The corregidor retired, for the moment defeated ; but he convoked a meeting for the following day, in which he set forth at length the, supposed, iniquities of the new Foundation. They were as follows : It was a new departure, therefore to be suspected. It was founded by a woman who gave herself out as the recipient of visions and revelations ; that was sufficient for sensible people to distrust it. Also, Avila was possessed of many religious communities ; an additional one without endowment would be a heavy burthen on the resources of the city. Teresa de Ahumada had opened it without the consent of its chief magistrates, or of that of the community to which she belonged. Consequently it was illegal. He therefore asked of the religious authorities that the Blessed Sacrament should be removed from the chapel and the nuns expelled, and subsequently that the walls of the convent should be pulled down.

The reasons alleged by the governor appeared so conclusive that a large majority sided with him ; the few who differed were silent. Accordingly the order for the immediate destruction of Sft. Joseph's convent was about to be given, when a Dominican, Fr. Banez, rose from his place and spoke as follows :

"I am conscious," he said, " of temerity in opposing the unanimous opinion of so influential a meeting. But my conscience obliges me to support the rights of

justice. I neither know, nor have I ever seen, Teresa de Ahumada, and I am ignorant of her projects. Accordingly I am absolutely impartial in what I am about to urge. You say that this is a new departure ; but because a thing is new, is it therefore reprehensible? Were not all religious Orders new when they first originated in the bosom of the Church? When our Divine Saviour first founded the Church itself, was it not altogether a new thing? If it is the novelty of this new Foundation that displeases you, I will change the word for another. I repeat that the changes, the fresh beginnings that are introduced into the Christian life for the greater glory of

God and for the reform of morals, are not to be talked of as novelties, but as efforts at renewing and infusing fresh fervour into a sanctity which is from all time. The trees are not new because the spring covers them each year with fresh foliage, nor the sun because it rises again every morning ; why, therefore, should you condemn as a novelty the zeal of a soul who desires to clothe an ancient Order with its ancient splendour, or at least to bring forth a young and vigorous off-shoot from its stem ? The monastery lately founded is a reform of an ancient institute ; it seeks to raise that which has fallen to the ground. It restores an enfeebled Rule, and tends to the honour of religion and the edification of a Christian people. It should, therefore, under all those headings earn not only toleration, but the favour and protection of the authorities of the city and of the state. Truly" (he ended by saying) "I am amazed when I think that it should be considered that a few poor women hidden in their cells and occupied with prayer could become a burthen on the place and a public menace. Is that a cause sufficient to rouse a city? Why is it we find ourselves assembled here

to-day in such numbers? Is there an army battering at the gates? Or a fire ravaging it? Or plague or famine laying it waste? By what perils is it menaced ? Four peaceful and humble Carmelites have established themselves in an obscure quarter of the town—that is the scourge of Avila, and the cause of all this agitation." 1

Fr. Dominic Banez, who spoke thus, was a doctor of divinity of Salamanca, a learned man of much influence in Avila. He was listened to at first with surprise, but his arguments finished by convincing all but prejudiced minds. He concluded by regretting the absence of endowment of the new Foundation, less on account of the tax it would be on the resources of the town than because of the privations which it would entail on the nuns.

" The bishop," he said, " alone has the power to decide on the question at issue, the Holy See having put it under his authority. If there has been any irregularity in starting the convent without the agreement of the civil government, they have the power of carrying their complaints to the bishop himself, instead of resorting to measures against which the rights of individuals, the Christian sentiment, and the honour of the city alike protest."

The governor found himself obliged to bow before the general impression produced by this speech ; the instant execution of his judgment was therefore suspended. The meeting dispersed. Fr. Banez had saved the convent from destruction, but that was all. Murmurs rose once more. The saint's opponents did not dare to address themselves to the bishop : their object was to induce the provincial, and prioress of the Incarnation to force her submission. Teresa suffered

much meanwhile, but she continued praying, and hoping that the work in spite of all would one day triumph.

"Do you not know, my daughter," our Lord had said to her, "that I am all-powerful? Rest assured that our monastery shall never be destroyed. I shall accomplish My promises to it." 1

Strong in this assurance, Teresa wrote to her friend Dona Guiomar, and having told her what had happened, she showed no uneasiness about the future, but commissioned her to buy some missals, and a small sacristy bell for the use of the community.

After fresh deliberations it was judged advisable to lay the matter before the king's council. "There is a great law-suit impending therefore," Teresa writes; " the town is sending its deputies to court, we ought to send ours. But where are we to find them, or the money which will be required?" She adds: "God's servants left alone at St. Joseph are doing more with their prayers than I am doing with all my negotiations." 2

Teresa had recourse to the excellent Fr. Julian, who had constituted himself her chaplain and servant from the first day of the Foundation. He was ready to act as messenger and man of business, with a power of attorney from Teresa, and she in turn was her own lawyer and advocate. 3 Nor was this all. He went to and fro between St. Joseph's and the convent of the Incarnation, carrying the mother's blessing to her forlorn daughters, and giving the former daily news of her beloved little flock. Fr. Gonzales de Aranda agreed to act as deputy, and started for Madrid to

1 Our Lord had predicted this persecution to Teresa at Toledo. A vision mentioned in the thirty-ninth chapter of her Life also alludes to it.

2 Life, ch. xxxvi.

defend the interests of the Foundation before the king's council. Finally Fr. Daza and Don Francisco did all in their power to help the nuns, Fr. Daza in providing for their spiritual, and Don Francisco for their material requirements.

It was at this time that a temporary absence of the provincial threatened further to compromise the situation. The prioress profited by his absence to forbid Teresa to take any further steps in the matter. The saint quietly submitted without a word of remonstrance, and determined to let the Foundation perish rather than to infringe on the duty of obedience. " Oh, my Divine Master," she cried, turning to her Saviour, " this house is not mine, it is Yours. Now that nobody is left to defend it, it is for Your Majesty to do so." The return of the provincial shortly afterwards set Teresa at liberty to continue her course of action. vv

The law-suit proceeded meanwhile slowly ana tediously with varying fortunes ; sometimes all seemed lost, and then again a ray of hope appeared. Teresa, looking at the question from the highest standpoint, avoided all bitter views or thoughts with regard to her opponents. She remained always kind and charitable in her intercourse with them, and was persuaded that they acted in good faith, though blinded by prejudice, and believed that they were working for the interests of the town in opposing her project. In her opinion the evil spirit, who misled these good Christians, was alone to blame.

At last Fr. Gonzales de Aranda, by his zealous efforts, obtained a complete success at Madrid. The king's council pronounced in favour of Teresa, and blamed the governor's proceedings severely. The latter had to renounce his plans of destruction of the monastery ; but he maintained that unless it was endowed the

town would never sanction the existence of the Foundation. " I was very wearied," Teresa owns, " of the trouble and anxiety the affair was causing our friends ; thus, rather to give them peace than for my own sake, I thought there would be no harm in ceding the point." But this concession would have been a departure from God's designs, Who desired that the roots of the reformed Carmel should be set in the most complete poverty and detachment. He did not fail to acquaint Teresa with this, and St. Peter of Alcantara was sent to her, with the glory of heaven, which he had just entered, about him, and said to her with a severe countenance: " See that you do not consent to an endowment. Why will you not follow my counsels?" Accordingly Teresa remained inflexible, and difficulties recommenced. Some one whose name is not known, but to whom Teresa alludes as a great servant of God, suggested that a meeting of learned men should be held and the decision left to them. But Teresa remembering that her saintly Franciscan friend had said to her, " In matters that concern the perfect life only take advice of those that follow it," refused the projected conference, and the opposition waxed more bitter from day to day. In the midst of these turmoils and anxieties, when the prospects of St. Joseph were at their blackest, the arrival of Fr. Ibanez, the eminent Dominican divine, who had been Teresa's first help and support in founding her convent, was announced in Avila. Father Ibanez knew nothing of the opposition the saint had met with, and he seems to have arrived at Avila scarcely knowing what brought him thither. But as soon as the public rumours reached him he went at once to Teresa and put his services at her disposal. The Dominicans, and Fr. Ibanez in particular, enjoyed considerable influence in Avila,

which even his absence had not wholly destroyed. He was received everywhere with much deference, and the violent language excited by Teresa's proceedings, and the opposition offered to them, were sensibly diminished when it was known that the venerable religious was her warm supporter. Before he left Avila, after a short stay in that city, matters had taken a more favourable turn. On his return to his solitude he continued the good work, and wrote to the provincial urging him to allow Teresa to rejoin her daughters at St. Joseph's. The Bishop of Avila used his influence in a similar manner. Fr. de Salazar hesitated, he did not dare to refuse, but he found one pretext after another to defer his consent. A fresh Brief from Rome giving permission to the saint to found a convent without endowment 1 removed the last objection to the new Foundation; and Fr. Ibanez's intervention having pacified the public feeling, what reason was there to deprive the community of their mother? Teresa, who felt deeply the trials her daughters were undergoing, herself implored the provincial to fulfil his promises ; and seeing she gained nothing thereby she warned him with holy intrepidity: " Take care, my father," she said, "lest you resist the Holy Ghost." Fr. de Salazar, on hearing these words, was suddenly enlightened by Divine grace. He no longer hesitated ; and besides consenting to her return to St. Joseph's, he empowered her to take with her some nuns from the Convent of the Incarnation. Three professed nuns and a novice followed her. The latter, Isabella of St. Paul, was related to Teresa; she had worn the Carmelite habit for a year, but she had waited to make her profession till she could do so in the Rule of the primitive Order. That solemnity was one of

] Boll., Nos. 362-70.

the first festivals celebrated by the community of St. Joseph.

Thus bereft of all possessions, but happy " as a sparrow escaped from the net of the fowler," 1 Teresa passed through the streets of Avila, which she had traversed seven months before, almost as a condemned prisoner. According to a popular tradition, she stopped on her road at the ancient basilica of St. Vincent. There she descended into the subterraneous crypt, and having prayed before the much-venerated statue of our Lady which is kept there, she took off her shoes and stockings, and assumed the alparagartas •, in order to enter St. Joseph's a discalced Carmelite. 2

What joy must have moved her heart as she passed over the threshold of the door ! Her children awaited her in the nun's choir; but before joining them she went straight to the little chapel to make the first offering of her joy and gratitude to her divine Saviour; and there she remained long absorbed in prayer. She thanked Him for His mercies and graces to her; she offered herself, and the little flock who were about to share her life of self-abnegation to His love and service. She conjured Him to bless the retreat where, as she believed, she was going to be buried for the rest of her days. Jesus listens to His well-beloved servant. Then, in His turn He speaks, and Teresa, rapt in ecstasy, beholds Him stooping down to her with unutterable love, placing a crown on her head, and blessing her for what she has done to please Him, and to do honour to the Blessed Virgin and Queen of Carmel. At last Teresa left the church ; the doors of the convent were opened to receive her. The novices met her with a joy

1 Julian d'Avila.

2 The alparagartas were the sandals used by the poor throughout Spain at that period.

in proportion to the anguish they had gone through at losing her. She embraced them and presented their new companions from the Incarnation to them, and together they all repaired to the choir, where their holy mother offered up, in the presence of the Blessed Sacrament, the following prayer :

" O my God, Thou knowest that I have ever felt that there was no proportion between my littleness and the greatness of the task Thou hast assigned to me. Thou knowest that all I have undertaken has been at Thy command. And without Thy help, how should I have accomplished it, or have surmounted my difficulties ? Being convinced, therefore, that it is Thy work, I am also convinced that it will grow and prosper. Here are the living stones with which Thou hast chosen to build up Thine edifice. Make them worthy to be used in its construction ; and give them such strength and firmness that time will have no power to overcome them. Let all worldly vanity and pleasure be far removed from our hearts. Let Thy love reign alone in Thy house, and may it be accompanied with penance, and humility, and prayer without which no virtue can stand. Thou hast planted this little garden in which to take Thy delight. It belongs to Thy omnipotence to cherish the flowers that grow in it. I know myself too well to think I can do aught to help this work. My nothingness is always before me, and all I ask of Thee is the forgiveness of my cowardice and my sins. Remember, O Lord, Thy mercies of old, and the promises Thou hast made to me ; and may Thy Blessed Mother, and my glorious Father St. Joseph, and all the saints of our Order, protect us now and for ever." 1

Having poured forth her soul to God fn prayer, Teresa got up from her knees, and proceeded to invest

her companions with the habit of the reformed Carmelites. She likewise assumed it herself with great joy. The habits previously worn by the nuns, though plain and worn, had been of good material ; they exchanged these for the coarsest serge, their fine linen garments for woollen tunics, and their long pleated mantles edged with fringe, for mantles of rough white material, without fringe or pleats. Finally they put on the rough sandals of the poor on their bare feet. All distinctions of rank or title were alike suppressed—the nuns choosing for names those of their patron saints. What name was Teresa to choose? That of Him towards Whom her heart turned night and day, Whose love consumed her ; Teresa de Ahumada became Teresa of Jesus.

CHAPTER XV

Carmel of St. Joseph was founded, the primi-tive Rule reinstated, and Teresa of Jesus belonged henceforth to God and her spiritual children only. " What a marvellous sight it was ! " exclaims Fr. Julian of Avila, who, writing the history of the Foundation forty-two years after it was effected, gives vent to his enthusiasm at the recollection of all that had passed. " Who would not be struck with astonishment in beholding what Omnipotence has done for this little house. What was there in it, O my God, which evoked such tenderness on Thy part and such solicitude ? If Thou hadst not been at hand to protect the holy mother, how could she have possibly triumphed over her persecutors? Surely there must have been great importance in this work, a great secret concealed beneath it, or the evil one would not have worked so hard to undo what God had accomplished. Well, let the world learn what this great thing was if it has not yet learned it. It is that God willed to have a house in which He could recreate Himself; a house in which He could take up His abode; a garden in which flowers should grow — not of the kind which expand on earth, but those which bloom only in heaven."

The monastery of St. Joseph was to be, in truth, the paradise of delights, the precious retreat of the Divine Master : rinconcito de Dios, as it was named by Teresa, in her own charming language. It was here that the

saint shut herself up with her daughters in order to console the heart of her divine Saviour by a boundless devotion, a perfect fidelity, and—as this object developed and revealed itself more clearly—by working by means of prayer and penance for the triumph of the Faith and the conversion of sinners.

Fr. Julian was not mistaken ; this work of reparation and atonement was indeed a very great and important one. It was the essential and necessary work of an epoch when the Divine Justice found unceasingly fresh crimes to punish. The tide of heresy was ever rising. The Netherlands were deeply involved ; France lay bleeding from her wounds. Scepticism reigned in Germany ; England, the Isle of Saints, was plunged in the horrors of Henry the Eighth's shameful reign. All these great nations were at war with God. They chased Him from their churches, and proscribed His religion in their dominions. Was it not therefore necessary that He, the sovereign Master, should find one spot, in the garden of St. Joseph, wherein His divine wrath should be appeased? And since our Saviour has so many enemies, and so few friends, should not His friends try hard to please Him?

This was our saint's primary idea in shutting herself up within the walls of St. Joseph's Convent. It was a question of attaining perfection, and of going to work to acquire it with generosity, and yet with wisdom, according to the lights given by God, and not in accordance with human impulses. Teresa was resolved to impose no sacrifice on her daughters but those which personal experience had proved to her were possible and practicable; moreover, to teach principally by example, and to follow the wishes into which the fervour of her nuns led them rather than to forestall them. Thus, before going into the question of the

primitive Rule, or of the Constitutions, as laid down by the saint, or studying the principles of her direction of souls, we will, like her, allow the first few weeks and months to pass by, and take a short survey of the methods she made use of in order to infuse the monastic spirit into the daily life of her little community.

Teresa divided the various duties of the house amongst the nuns on the very day of her arrival, in order that, whilst all should assist in a mutual service of their neighbour, none should be troubled with cares injurious to recollection and prayer. Teresa (to the general consternation) appointed Mother Anne of St. John as prioress, and took herself the lowest place in the house. This act of humility was met by tearful expostulations, which were followed up by an appeal to the bishop who, when he heard what she had done came at once, in person, to rectify matters. He imposed upon her under obedience the office of prioress. Obliged therefore to accept it, she fulfilled to the letter the precept of St. Albert's Rule, namely, that he who governs others should look upon himself as the servant of all. 1 Everything in the monastery had to be organized, and the saint neglected nothing, providing for the wants and necessities of her community with a mother's care. Thanks to Don Francisco de Salcedo's alms, she was able to supply the cells with their simple furniture, a mattress of straw, a footstool, an earthenware jug; a crucifix, with the figure of our Lord traced on paper, and a shell to contain holy water near it hung on the plain white wall. A narrow garden just held room for their little supply of vegetables, and for some tiny hermitages in which the nuns, following the example of the Fathers of the desert, could retire in order to read and pray. Teresa worked unceasingly,

and by degrees the convent began to assume a more regular and monastic appearance.

Her maternal solicitude found another outlet in the care of the refectory. The manual labour of the community ensured their supply of daily bread, and Providence took care that what was required, over and above, was not wanting. Again, Teresa never ceased watching that there should be no excess in acts of penance. She insisted that the frugal meals should be properly prepared, and, notwithstanding her thirst for mortification and sufferings, she partook of an egg, or some fish, or fruit or vegetables, at her meals in order that her daughters should keep up their strength by following her example. 1 If, however, a day of scarcity of more than usual severity occurred there was general rejoicing. " To-day," was the universal cry, " we are really poor." Then the saintly mother would gather together what was left of the previous day's provisions, and, blessing them, distributed them amongst the most weakly of her little flock. But these being quite sure that their sisters' necessities were as great as their own, would refuse to touch their meagre portions. So they were handed from one to the other till they returned to Teresa, who, replacing them on the table, exclaimed, " Evidently we must wait till all can be served." They were never kept long in suspense. On one occasion of this kind a poor man brought them two big loaves and a piece of cheese. Or the outer bell summoned the portress to the door, and silently, without her being able to judge who was their benefactor, a quantity of provisions were passed in at the turnstile. Another time, a lady living at a distance of twelve miles from the monastery, and ignorant of the necessities of the community, sent them at a critical

moment, when they had nothing to eat, all the food they required. Thus they were never left to starve, and the fervour of their acts of thanksgiving to God and their benefactors on these occasions may be more easily imagined than described. 1 When Providence appeared to lend itself to the fervent desires of the Carmelites, and allowed them to feel something of the rigour of extreme poverty, Teresa had the secret of making their very privations sweet. With a blessing from her a dish of fried vine-leaves, acorns served without any seasoning, sufficed for the wants of the community. On one occasion on the feast of Corpus Christi there was nothing to eat but a little bread. Teresa distributed this amongst her daughters, and then, instead of the usual spiritual lecture, she spoke to them herself, and—satisfying their souls with a divine nourishment—she poured forth burning words of love for Jesus hidden under the sacramental veil, so that the nuns forgetting their hunger rose from the table and, inflamed with divine love, went in solemn procession from the refectory to the choir. They sang psalms and acts of thanksgiving there, praising God for having allowed them to taste on that occasion the sweetness of poverty, and the delights of the Heavenly Manna. 2

It was but rarely, as we have already said, that our Lord permitted that they should be reduced to these extremities. Dona Guiomar did not forget the wants of her beloved Carmelites. She would have willingly shared their life had her health allowed her. Not being able to do so, she made up for it by frequent visits, and she never came without bringing an offering with her. The nuns of the neighbouring convent of Poor Clares

1 History of the Order of Mount Cartnel, Bk. II, ch. xvil.

2 Ibid.

delighted in sharing their meals with the sisters of St. Joseph. In short, every prejudice died out of itself in Avila, and the poor little convent became the object of general admiration and goodwill. Teresa received everything that was given her in alms with gratitude ; as she said of herself, " her heart could be gained with a sardine." But she never begged from anyone, and she forbade her daughters to make any appeal to their relations by speaking to them of the necessities of the convent. The rumours of the holy lives led by the recluses of St. Joseph attracted many to the little church ; frequently it could hardly contain the crowd who came to listen to the slow and solemn chanting of the Carmelites of the Reform, true notes of turtle-doves mourning with their Beloved. The saint alluding to it says naively, " It gave people much devotion to hear it." None were more assiduous in their attendance at divine office than Teresa's niece, Maria de Ocampo. As we have already seen, love of God struggled within her soul with love of the world. Finally, God triumphed, and she came in the month of October, 1563, to ask of her saintly aunt the holy habit of Carmel, which she took under the name of Mary of St. John the Baptist. Besides her jewels, which were used for the adornment of the altar, she brought a dowry which relieved the convent of a rent with which it had been burthened. 1 Maria's father would have willingly increased the sum if Teresa had permitted him to do so, but the saint refused, guarding the poverty of the house as its greatest treasure. She may also have feared that her niece's gifts to the convent might have had the effect of causing her to be treated with greater consideration than her less well-endowed sisters, and to avoid this danger she not only stemmed the tide of her family's

generosities, but she treated Maria herself as the last and least important of the community. She seemed to take no notice of Maria's superior intelligence, and set her to work at the lowest and most menial offices of the house. A complete transformation took place in the character of the youthful novice ; the high-spirited girl became the humblest member of the community, and her growing sanctity took the form of a simplicity, and an abandonment of herself in the hands of God, which enchanted and edified the little convent of Carmel. By nature enthusiastic and lively, Maria found the silence of the cloister a little oppressive, but when the time came to break it, at recreation, her playful remarks delighted everyone. Teresa, though she accused her of talkativeness, was frequently seen to smile at her niece's sallies of wit.

St. Joseph's Convent was deficient in one important requirement: the water contained in the only well inside the enclosure was so bad that the supply used for drinking had to be fetched daily from the town. Teresa, thinking that if the water was passed through pipes it might be made drinkable, sent for a plumber to consult him on the subject. He ridiculed the idea, alleging that the source itself was corrupt. Teresa, relating what had passed at recreation time, asked of her sisters what they thought about it. "Let us put down the pipes, dear mother," said Sister Mary Baptist; "as it is, our Lord is obliged to send us to the town for water, so that we have to pay someone to bring it. It will cost Him much less to let us have it straight from the well. Be sure it will all come right." The saint approved of the argument, and gave orders that the men should proceed with the work. Accordingly, they began at first much against their wishes, but soon they found the canal they had dug was filled with

a plentiful supply of pure water. The workmen spread the news of this great marvel—for as such they looked upon it—throughout Avila, and people asked to drink of this astounding spring, which came to be known before long as the fountain of Mary Baptist.

Another novice, Maria de Avila, who was also nearly related to our saint, rivalled Maria de Ocampo in her fervour and piety. Young and beautiful, and the possessor of a great name and a large fortune, she had many aspirants to her hand, whom in her pride of race she repulsed as unworthy of it. When at last the King of kings asked her for her heart she could no longer urge this excuse, but appalled at the thought of the solitude and obscurity of a cloistered life, she implored to be let-off this sacrifice. Vain was the prayer ! Jesus loved her too dearly to give her up. Accordingly, after days and nights spent in tears and inward combats she parted from her relations, broke the chains which bound her to the world, and came to ask for admission in the poorest and humblest convent in Avila. Teresa, warned of her arrival, met her at the door of the cloister. The saint smiled when she saw Maria robed in satin and adorned with jewels, as if she had been dressed for some great function. She held out a crucifix to her, and Maria kneeling before it kissed it, and then turning to the crowd who had accompanied her to the monastery door she bade them farewell, and following Teresa into the house she stripped herself of her gay apparel. Soon after she returned to the church clothed in the rough habit of Mount Carmel. The woman of the world was transformed into the humble spouse of Christ. In answer to the usual questions put to her by Mgr. de Mendoza she answered in a firm voice : "I ask three things—the mercy of God, the poverty of the Carmelite Order, and the com-

panionship of the sisters." She had chosen the name of Mary of St. Jerome, and to the love of penance, and the mortifications of her patron saint, she joined a humility and meekness which made her look upon herself as utterly unworthy to be associated with her sisters in religion. Teresa, astounded at this young girl's progress in sanctity, made it an occasion of self-humiliation before God in prayer. " How many years it is, O my Lord, that I have given myself up to prayer and Thou hast overwhelmed me with Thy favours," cried the humble saint, "and yet Thou hast not received from me a return such as these generous souls have made to Thee in three months with far fewer graces ! what do I say? even one amongst them, in three days." These words applied to Mary of St. Jerome, who was in truth a perfect nun almost from the day in which she put on the habit. Teresa gave her charge of the novices directly she had pronounced her vows, reserving for her at a later epoch a post of even greater responsibility. It was to Teresa's prayers, and to the influence she had over her, even in the days of her worldliness, that Mary of St. Jerome felt that she was indebted for her vocation ; and she used to repeat in her later days that she owed her conversion, her vocation, and her eternal salvation to " Our mother Teresa of Jesus." [1]

The church of St. Joseph's Convent was enlarged with Mary of St. Jerome's dowry. Other postulants presented themselves, and though penniless our saint received them with open arms, so that the number of thirteen, which she had determined not to exceed, was soon reached. She had fixed on that number because experience had taught her the disadvantages of a large community to a contemplative life. Active Orders can

never number too many in community, their united efforts being more useful than if they lived apart. But it is not so in a cloistered one, where the soul goes in search of solitude in order to give itself up to prayer. Doubtless the contemplative nun requires a mother to watch over her and to direct her footsteps, sisters who rouse her fervour by their example, a religious family towards whom she is able to exercise the duty of charity ; in short, a life in common is necessary, so as to give her constant occasion for self-sacrifice, for patience, and the other virtues. But a small religious family will furnish all these requirements without the distractions consequent on a numerous one. Also few souls are able to stand an unbroken life of contemplative prayer. Action should take turn with contemplation ; and as the cloistered life prevents the Carmelite nun from devoting herself to works of mercy, it is necessary to provide her with an outlet for her energies inside her own enclosure, in manual labour, and work for her sisters. This outlet Teresa found for her daughters in the discharge of the various offices of community life, where each contributed her services to the general good.

The fervour of these novices at St. Joseph's equalled that of their predecessors. Teresa prudently put them through a long trial before admitting them to their profession. She wished to make sure that their courage was of the kind that would carry them through the trials of solitude, and the austerities of monastic life, and would last to the end, and was not the result of a passing fit of fervour. Ursula of the Saints, the eldest of the novices, had before leaving home had the management of her father's house, and would have been well fitted for a similar post at St. Joseph's. But our saint wished to make a humble and

perfect nun of her, not a good housekeeper. Ursula submitted to this training with the simplicity of a child. On one occasion Teresa sent her to bed in the middle of the day, and when her sisters in religion came to visit her, and sympathized with her supposed ailments, she answered : " I don't feel anything the matter with me, but as our mother has sent me to the infirmary, she must know best." Teresa made no remark, but she was satisfied with the way Ursula stood the test, and she showed a particular regard for her ever afterwards.

Mortification and humility, next to obedience, were the favourite virtues of this fervent novitiate, and Teresa had to be on the watch to restrain her novices in the imprudences to which they were led by their spirit of penance. If she had permitted it they would have mixed cinders, or bitter herbs with their food, the use of the discipline would have multiplied, and nature would have succumbed under the weight of prolonged fasts. The garden was pressed into their service, and not satisfied with the discomfort of straw palliasses, they would sleep, when allowed, on roots and thistles. Ingenious devices of this kind were constantly resorted to by the community, and though not one of these were unknown to their saintly mother, she wisely directed the ardour of their piety into a safer channel, reminding them that Jesus preferred obedience to sacrifice, and that it was in the pure and, above all, the humble heart in which He took His delight. Humility was the virtue which she preached incessantly by word and example, accusing herself of the smallest fault on all occasions, and obliging the nuns, including the novices, to reprove her for the smallest imperfection. She thus earned the right to expect her daughters to receive reprimands without attempting to excuse them-

selves and to receive with gratitude penances imposed upon them.

There were no lay-sisters at St. Joseph's Convent at first, and Teresa would have wished to have dispensed permanently with their services. Accordingly the different offices of the house, cleaning, cooking, and so forth, were distributed weekly among the nuns. Our saint gave an example to all by the cheerful alacrity with which she applied herself to her work. She never allowed her attraction to prayer to excuse her from taking her part in these occupations. One of her historians relates that when it was her week to be in the kitchen, she took the greatest trouble to make some variety in her preparation of the simple food put before the community. 1 On the days when the Sisters communicated she used to return to the kitchen directly she had made a short thanksgiving, feeling sure that by doing so she was accomplishing the Divine Will. 2 Ribera says that when her turn came to be cook nothing was ever wanting ; provisions poured in. " How good God is !" she used to exclaim. " He sees my desire to feed the community well, so He gives me everything I want." Let us add that in taking such care of her daughters she never forgot the Divine Host. " He is always there," she says. " Whatever my occupation, He is in the midst of it, helping me exteriorly and interiorly." Our Lord used to choose these times to visit her. One day a sister entering the kitchen saw the holy mother wrapped in ecstasy, her face radiant, her feet raised above the ground, and still grasping the pan in which she was frying some fish ; though her soul was far hence, she still continued her work of cooking the dinner. She carried on all the other occupations of

1 Ribera.

2 Hist, of the Order.

the house in the same spirit, especially if it was one from which human nature would naturally shrink. As soon as she got back to her cell Teresa used to begin to spin or work. Her earnest desire was to live the life of the poor, and—with Jesus the Divine Workman of Nazareth—to earn her bread with the sweat of her brow. She never allowed herself a moment for rest, or contemplation outside the hours fixed for prayer. This was so well known at St. Joseph's, that no one would have dared to waste a moment in her presence. Even her work bore the mark of the spirit of Mount Carmel, for it was of the plainest description : sewing, mending, and spinning. Teresa whilst at the Convent of the Incarnation had shown a great talent for needlework; in her skilful hands the needle became a paint-brush. She had produced some pictures from the life of our Lord, which, as Ribera tells us, were masterpieces. To look at them, he says, was to be filled with devotion. But such artistic embroideries, which in those days were the pastime of queens and great ladies, were unsuitable for the solitaries of Mount Carmel. Teresa renounced them for herself and her daughters. She advised them to occupy themselves with plain and useful work, such as could give rise to no vainglorious thoughts, and which, whilst occupying their hands, would not interfere with the recollection of their minds in God.

" Could a more beautiful sight be witnessed," asks an ancient chronicler, "than that of this little flock led by such a mother, bound by the ties of charity, and ever advancing in union with God and love of Him ! All these fervent nuns might have been said to be animated by one spirit. Their diligence and punctuality at the various religious exercises, especially at

choir, where they emulated one another in praising God, was a joy to behold. In their modesty and attention during divine office they might almost have competed with the spirits above." Teresa herself was enchanted with them. " All my wishes," she says, "were fulfilled in the daughters whom God first gave to me. My most earnest desire was that the first to join should by their example lay the foundation of this spiritual life by leading lives of prayer and perfection." They had no difficulty in keeping the rules of cloister, nor in living in absolute poverty. The yoke of penance was light to them ; they even looked upon themselves as unworthy of bearing it. Many amongst them had passed their youth in the world in the enjoyment of the best it had to offer. None were happier here than these. God seemed to repay them with true joys for the false ones they had given up for His sake. " I cannot describe," Teresa writes, "the happiness it was to me to live amidst these innocent souls, detached from all earthly things." This great fervour, however, we repeat, was directed by our saint's maternal prudence, which was ever on the watch against the shoals and pitfalls of an excess which is almost inevitably followed by reaction.

The fame of the sanctity of Pius V (who had lately been appointed to the papal throne) was on the lips of all; it reached the solitudes even of Avila. His piety and austerities became the talk of the recreation room. No one was more enthusiastic in his praise than Sister Mary Baptist. It was said that he wore coarse sackcloth next to his skin, and accordingly Sister Mary, backed up by another novice, persuaded Teresa to allow her daughters to follow his example. The experiment was tried, but it led to results which the saint judged to be of a nature to make it unsuitable in

a climate like that of Spain. When writing the Constitutions later on, she specially notes that the habit alone is to be made of sackcloth, and the under garments of serge. Many other instances could be given showing the happiness of this united family, living together as they did in an atmosphere of holy liberty of spirit and of unbroken austerity.

The Bishop of Avila, who fulfilled his duty towards St. Joseph's with paternal kindness, visited the convent frequently. On one occasion he brought a beautiful crucifix with him to show Teresa, who in her turn asked his permission to exhibit it to the community. The bishop consented, and Teresa took it inside the enclosure, and returned to the parlour to entertain her guest. A few minutes later sounds of chanting were heard. Teresa listened, and the bishop did the same. They opened a door by which a view was obtained into the cloisters, and there they beheld a procession headed by the youngest postulant carrying the crucifix, whilst the nuns chanted the litany of the holy Name. A little alteration, however, had been made in the responses, and instead of the usual "have mercy on us," the community was heard to sing at the top of their voices "stay with us." Teresa was moved to confusion at her nuns' audacity; but the bishop, possibly amused, certainly moved to kindness, by this appeal, presented the crucifix on the spot to the community.

The holy mother was accustomed on the great feasts of the Church to give pleasure to her daughters by composing verses appropriate to the occasion. An ardent faith was allied in these compositions to the deepest devotional feeling. The Carmelites sang of the poverty of the Son of God in the stable of Bethlehem, and of His first tears. Or they rejoiced when the angels announced His coming to the shepherds,

and they left their flocks to adore the Lamb of God. At the Circumcision they wept with Him at His first blood-shedding, and vowed to follow Him on the road of penance and self-sacrifice. There were other great days to be celebrated, such as the joy of the days of profession, the delights of the cloister, the sweetness of an ascetic life, the tenderness of Jesus, " Who puts us in a prison in order to free us, and to lead us by a happy life to a forever blessed eternity ! " [1]

Days passed rapidly at St. Joseph's. This little monastery was in truth, as their chaplain told us, a house of recreation, and of joy to their Divine Lord. Nowhere did He possess purer or more loving hearts, or souls more faithful to His service. Thus Teresa saw Him in a vision confiding them to His Mother, and saying to her: "This is My paradise of delight." And on another occasion our Lady appeared to the community after compline, and first looking down upon them with much love and tenderness, she then spread her mantle over their heads in token of having taken them under her protection.

There remained still something more for Teresa to undertake ; a work of difficulty which required both knowledge and skill. This was to write a commentary on the primitive Rule, and to adapt its Constitutions to the special requirements of female communities.

1 See Poems by St. Teresa. V. de la Fuente, p. 501.

CHAPTER XVI

THE ancient spirit of Carmel—the Carmel of Elias and of St. Albert—was, as we have already pointed out, that of contemplation, accompanied by manual labour and fasting. The Carmelites were true hermits, and emulated the lives of fasting and prayer led by their brethren the monks of the desert. Teresa, in resuscitating the Order at Avila, changed nothing of its spirit; her work was to give a particular bent to its objects, such as the ancient Rule had left undefined. A new element, that of zeal for souls, was under her directing hand to transform this life of prayer and recollection, by turning all the forces of the new-born Carmel on to the conquest of souls.

Let us hearken to Teresa, explaining in her own words to her daughters what God expected of them : " Help me, my sisters in Jesus Christ," she says, "to pray for all the sinners who are being lost. It is for this object our Lord brings you all here together. This is your vocation—your business. All your desires should tend to this end. For this should your tears flow, for this you should multiply your prayers . . . what shall I say? The world is in flames. Those unhappy heretics would condemn our Lord, so to speak, once more to death, since they raise a thousand false witnesses against Him, and seek to destroy His Church. Can we lose a moment's time over trifles with this thought before us? When I think of these great evils, which are ever increasing, it seems to me

the only way would be to raise an army of chosen souls ready to die in the cause of God's Church ; souls who would never acknowledge a defeat." The saint explains her meaning by saying that she would not seek a place for herself, or her daughters in this army of defence of the Church; this was to be the privilege of apostolic men, of bishops, religious, and saints. All she desired for the Carmelites of St. Joseph's was to march in the van of the army, and sustain them by the ardour of their prayers. " Let us help," she cries, " the servants of our King. But, you may rejoin, why go to the help of those who are much holier than we are? I will tell you the reason. Do you understand what you owe to God, my daughters, for having delivered you from the dangers of the world? It is a great happiness and privilege, and one that these apostles of God have not got, in these days least of all, for they have to strengthen the weak, to encourage little ones. Would soldiers fight without their captain ? It is necessary, therefore, for them to live amongst men in order that they should speak to them, appear in their great houses, and even sometimes live the same lives, exteriorly, that they do. Does it require, think you, but a small exercise of virtue to live in the world, treat with it, adopt even its ways, and yet remain in heart and soul not only apart from it, but an enemy to it, and so live on earth as if in exile? I implore of you work in such a manner as to become so pleasing in the sight of God that you may obtain great graces for His defenders. If we could contribute to this success by our prayers, we also shall have fought, we, in the depths of our solitude, for God's cause."

We should like, did our space permit of it, to have quoted at length these pages which seem on fire with

divine love. Teresa longs to make her daughters burn with the same zeal. These are the motives of self-abnegation on which she wishes to see their life of prayer founded : " Do not imagine, my sisters, that it is a useless task to be incessantly occupied in praying to God for His Church. I know that there are some who find it is hard not to be allowed to pray for themselves, and yet is there a better prayer than the one I have set before you? Are you afraid that your purgatory may be prolonged on this account? I answer that prayers such as these are too pleasing to God for Him to leave them unrewarded. But supposing our time of expiation is prolonged thereby? Well, let us consent to this also ! What would it matter to me supposing I remained in purgatory till the day of judgment, if by that means I had saved one soul, or procured an increase of glory to my God by the spiritual advancement of any of His children? Despise, my sister, these sufferings which will end in time, when it is a question of rendering a service to Him who has suffered so much for love of us."

Teresa concludes the chapter thus: "This, my daughters, is the object towards which all your prayers, your penances, iyour desires should tend. The day in which you cease to consecrate all you do for these ends, know that you will no longer be fulfilling God's wishes in your regard, or the objects for which He has brought you together to Mount Carmel. 1 It is not only necessary to please God by a pure heart, fervent prayers, and great fidelity; expiation for sin must be joined to purity, sacrifice to prayer. Joys must, at times, be renounced in prayer, repose in contemplation, in order to implore, to entreat, to storm Heaven in behalf of those who do nothing for them-

selves, and will not even take the trouble to knock at the gate of Divine Mercy." Teresa tells us that in the beginning she had no idea of founding St. Joseph's in such extreme poverty and mortification ; it was only later on, when, struck with consternation at the progress of heresy, that she resolved to neglect no means of helping preachers and theologians to defend the Church of God. This Observance, of which she then conceived the general idea, was to be as strict as was compatible with human frailty, and was to be incorporated with the Rule of St. Albert. She was, however, in no haste ; she began where the wisdom of man usually terminates. Instead of laying down the law and formulating rules from an a priori point of view, she began by making a trial of customs such as were adapted to bring about the object she had in view. Her only programme was the ancient Rule of Carmel, and she waited till experience had taught her, little by little, the best way of fulfilling, or even of excelling it, could this be done without imprudence. During these days of trial she constantly received her daughters' confidences, and this gave her a profound insight into the feminine heart—the deeply religious feminine heart. 1 She learned what were the wants of a soul vowed to a life of renunciation, of separation from the world, and of death to self. She carried this practical knowledge to the feet of our Lord, she deepened it with prayer; and her intelligence, enlightened by divine wisdom, completed her acquired knowledge.

The primitive Rule, given by the patriarch St. Albert, to the hermits of the mountain of Elias, is only a short summing-up of the great monastic precepts on poverty, chastity, and obedience, which are put under the

1 V. de la Fuente, Vol. I, p. 281.

guardianship of solitude and silence, and joined to the following three points which confer on it the character proper to the Order:

1. As regards prayer: Let the religious remain in their cells, and meditate day and night on God's law, watching in prayer, unless prevented by necessary and legitimate occupation.

2. As regards fasting: The religious should fast from the feast of the Exaltation of the Cross until Easter daily, excepting on Sundays, unless prevented by illness or other valid causes for which " necessity knows no law." They shall never eat meat unless it is for some special reason of health.

3. The Rule prescribes manual labour as incessant as is their prayer. It proposes St. Paul for their imitation, who worked day and night. " Labour in silence," it enjoins, "for this road is a good and holy one ; follow it." 1

The Rule, after giving advice on the subject of humility, the spirit of faith, of mortification, the recitation of divine office, and correction of faults, terminates with these words : " We have treated these subjects briefly, laying down rules for your way of life ; and if any of you should do more than is required of them, God will reward you when He comes to judge the world. Let, however, discretion be observed, which is the rule of all virtues." A great field was opened to our saint by the last-mentioned words. She explored it both in the character of an adept in the spiritual life, and in that of a mother of many children. The Brief of Pius IV which had approved of the foundation of St. Joseph, had authorized Teresa to make any change or alteration she saw necessary for the good of the monastery when drawing up its Constitutions. She

made use of this right in her " Constitutions of Carmelite Nuns," a masterpiece little known to the world, but appreciated by her daughters at its true value. We do not propose to lift the veil under which this sacred treasure has ever been carefully guarded by the saint's spiritual family. The Constitutions are an heirloom belonging to Carmel which it does not share with the crowd, not even with the pious crowd. Teresa herself recommended her nuns to abstain from discussing the ways and customs of community life in the parlour, or when writing to friends. " Avoid," she told them, " giving wrong impressions of the life you lead; if the world knew you did such and such a thing they would take you for saints. Would you be the gainers by it?" These Constitutions, let it suffice to say, bear the mark of her broad and wide spirit, as well as her desire for great heights of perfection. There is nothing superfluous in them, nor do they descend to trifling details, nor vague theories. They are practical and simple, going straight to the point— which is the faithful observance of the fundamental precepts of the Rule, religious vows, penance, prayer, and work. The saint first of all lays down the order to be observed in spiritual matters. Then she gives regulations for the day's work, by which the Carmelite A is led through a judiciously combined series of exercises, from prayer to work, divine office to manual labour, from the moment of her rising at five, to eleven at night when she retires to rest. The manner of her clothing is also specified, and the kind of grille to be used in the convents. The duties of the nuns with regard to their intercourse with each other ; the charity to be displayed to the sick ; the respect due to the superiors, and finally the distribution of the various

offices in the house : all these points are gone over in detail. Certain precepts which Teresa laid down in the primitive text of her Constitutions she afterwards modified, owing either to the wishes of her ecclesiastical superiors, or to the results of personal experience which convinced her of their unsuitability. They were as follows :

(i) She had first limited the members of each community to thirteen ; this number she raised to twenty, (ii) She began without lay sisters ; but later on, recognizing the necessity of making use of their services, she allowed two or three in each of her convents, but this number was never to be exceeded, (iii) Finally, in spite of her personal views and her ardent desire for complete poverty, she consented, as we shall see later, to the endowment of her convents, in compliance with the advice of certain eminent theologians.

These Constitutions were submitted to the Bishop of Avila, who, after having approved of them, submitted them to Pius IV, by whom this approval was confirmed. It was likewise enacted, that should the saint find it necessary to make any alteration or addition to them later on, she was at liberty to do so. 1 Teresa, in her maternal solicitude for her daughters, was not yet satisfied by what she had done for them. The exterior framework of regular life, as traced by the Constitutions, was laid down, but the great work of developing the interior spirit of Carmel in the souls of her children remained to be accomplished. No two souls are alike; and thus, though all lead the same life in common, it is necessary for a superior to be acquainted with the character and attainments of every soul under her charge, so that she may guide them on the road to perfection. This was the special

work Teresa carried on from her cell. It was by this means that she initiated her children into the secrets of the spiritual life. Yet, in spite of the community being few in number, the life of constant prayer and work, the hours of silence, all interfered with the much coveted moments of confidential intercourse between the mother and her spiritual children. The latter accordingly besought her to commit her thoughts to paper, so that they might treasure up her counsels, and refer to them for guidance. Teresa owns that it was with difficulty that she yielded to their entreaties. It cost her much to write ; she could only find time in her rare moments of leisure. She sighed for her distaff whilst using the pen, and complained sadly that it kept her from spinning. Fortunately the Carmelites' petitions were backed up by others. The Dominican Order, after coming to our saint's assistance at the time of the foundation of St. Joseph's, had kept on terms of fraternal charity with her. Father Baltasar Alvarez having left Avila, Teresa took Father Bafiez as her director, and he was replaced, in his absence, by Father Garcia. Father Garcia induced her, under obedience, to complete her autobiography by an account of the foundation of St. Joseph, and when this task w r as completed he asked her to undertake a fresh one. This was to be a treatise embracing the counsels she daily gave her daughters on prayer, and the virtues belonging to the religious state. The community of St. Joseph, aware of Father Garcia's wishes, gave Teresa no peace until she carried them out. Teresa then wrote (with little more method or care than she had previously bestowed on her own history) another spiritual masterpiece, under the name of The Way of Perfection. There are possibly fewer brilliant passages in this work than in the earlier one, for a reason which is not far to seek. It is not here a question of

describing the flight of an eagle, it is rather that of directing the movements of a little child who has but lately learnt to walk. The path she traces lies alongside the valleys ; from time to time the eye is directed towards the mountain tops, but at every step the prudent mother stops to point out the hidden pitfalls, the yawning precipice, or deceptive mirage ; in short, all the dangers of the road. Encouragement also is not wanting. The saint stops at times in order to cheer the faint-hearted, to raise up the weary. To travel under her guidance is to walk without fatigue, and to find oneself speedily at the wished-for end. The Way of Perfection was intended in the eyes of the holy mother for her children of the convent of St. Joseph, and for them only. Hence the simplicity of its language. She never seeks to cover up the little frailties from which life even in a cloister is not exempt ; all is put down without weakness or flattery. If the evils to which she alludes do not exist, she provides against the possibility of them, because (as she tells us) she has herself been exposed to these dangers without knowing how to defend herself from them. Her task is to enlighten her daughters, to save them from foolish illusions built upon virtues which are only skin deep. She attacks self-love even to the last barrier behind which it lies entrenched. The piety aimed at by the Carmelite, according to her teaching, should be ardent yet solid, tender but above all profound. This is the gist of her book. She would persuade her daughters of the nothingness of the perishable joys which they are asked to give up. " All things pass away." Teresa, who so often has said this to herself, repeats to them : " What folly to attach oneself to what to-morrow will be gone ! We have but a few hours to live, and what a recompense awaits us ! Life is but as a night which we have to pass in a bad inn. My daughters, let us make no effort to live at our ease. What consolation shall those find in death who during life have done penance for their sins ! " The saint goes on, after showing the vanity of earthly desire, to describe the realities of eternal happiness. Teresa's reason and common sense preserved her from the excesses which later on were so vigorously denounced by Bossuet, who uses her as a witness when combating the errors of Quietism. If she accepts, and pleads with others to accept, sacrifices of all kinds (a possible prolongation of purgatory included) in order to forward God's glory, never was she misled by a false mysticism into pretending indifference to her eternal salvation. She is ever holding out the sight of Heaven to her nuns ; she presses them to fix their eyes on it, in order to support the fatigues of the journey ; and recommends them to think constantly of the blessed moment which will unite them to their Beloved. "O my daughters," she exclaims, " how sweet it will be for us, at the hour of death, to go before Him to be judged whom we have loved above all ! With what confidence we shall present ourselves before Him, sure of hearing a favourable sentence. What happiness to think we are not going to a strange country, but to our own country, since it is to the home of that much loved Spouse whom we love so much, and by whom we are so much loved !"

The foundations of the spiritual life being thus solidly laid, the holy reformer builds up the religious virtues of poverty, obedience, humility, and mortification upon them. She offers her daughters the support of prayer and the crowning grace of charity. Her knowledge of human nature is displayed in the way she tracks its defects and weaknesses to the ground ; and

then with what force and vigour does she slay them ! She will have nothing 1 narrow nor petty in the souls of her daughters. If the spirit of the world creeps in, they must be armed at all points to resist it. The things of this world have no part in the objects which have drawn the nuns of Carmel together at St. Joseph's. She has much to say about poverty. " Poverty," she tells them, "is our badge, our coat-of-arms. Let us keep it intact, and let everything, our houses, our garments, our desires, and our thoughts, show it forth. The greatest honour a poor man can have is to be truly poor. Take care never to build huge monasteries. Remember they will all crumble away at the last day. Would it be seemly that the house of a few poor nuns should shake the earth when it comes down ? " The virtue of obedience was so perfectly kept at St. Joseph's that Teresa said she never knew what it was like till she saw it practised by her daughters. It was unnecessary to recommend it, so the saint only says a few words about it. '' Obedience, " she tells them, *' sees God in the superior, and submits unreservedly to his commands. A soul bound by this vow and neglecting to fulfil it loses her time in a monastery. She will never become a contemplative, or acquit herself well of the duties of an active life." Mortification meets the nun at St. Joseph's at every turn ; it is not necessary for her to go in search of it. Yet is it astonishing if at times, when the first fervour had passed, that nature should try to reassume her sway? This Teresa will not permit : she ridicules the idea that a Carmelite could seek her comfort, or be preoccupied about her health. No one knew better than their holy mother what it was to bear the weight of infirmities, and to have to drag about a weak and exhausted frame, but she knew also by experience that except in the case of serious malady

the best remedy is to pay as little attention as possible to these physical miseries, and to bear them bravely. Her daughters suffered from no ailments such as those which she had endured for many years. She therefore asks nothing unreasonable of them when she exhorts them to bear trifling indispositions with fortitude. Her prudence, no less than her maternal tenderness, points out the happy medium to be observed. "It would be an imperfection," she says, "to complain about little maladies of no importance. If you can endure them in silence, do so. Remember you are few in number here. If any of you got the habit of making the most of your sufferings and complaining of them it would be enough to trouble the peace of the rest, to whom you are bound by the tie of charity. I beg of you therefore, my daughters, to bear your little ills in silence. They are sometimes only the effect of the imagination. They come and go ; if you once begin to talk of them you would never have done. The more we give in to the body the more it asks of us ; it deceives the poor soul, and prevents its advance in virtue. The nun who is really ill should mention it and take the necessary remedies. If she is free from self-love she will be so distressed at receiving any kind of indulgence and dispensation that there is no fear she will take therr without cause, or complain without reason."

Teresa esteems this penance, with justice, higher than any. " To suffer something for God," she says, "alone, without anyone knowing anything about it; to vanquish the body, to free oneself of fear of death, and of the loss of health—this is to be rid of a heavy burthen, which will make our march lighter and more rapid. But this is not enough for a true Carmelite. She should, besides this, smile at the occasions which continually present themselves of practising mortifica-

tion on her path through life, and pick up with alacrity the smallest crosses with which it is sown. Let her have constantly before her the example of her Fathers the hermits of Carmel. She will see them endure cold, hunger, heat, solitude. ' Were they made of iron ?' she may ask herself. 'No, not more than I am,' and she will try and follow in their footsteps. Then, preferring the austerities enjoined by the Rule to all others, she will seek not to injure her health by excessive mortification which will render her incapable in consequence of keeping the regular penances. Above all, she should apply herself to interior mortification." The holy mother does not mince matters on this point. She speaks with perfect frankness to generous hearts capable of understanding and obeying her. " If you wish to be true nuns, my daughters, intimate friends of our Divine Lord, you must be prepared to live the life of martyrs. . . . We should have the courage to say once for all that we have come here to suffer, not to rejoice. Let us therefore renounce in all things our own satisfaction, let us accustom ourselves to conquer our natural desires, so that the flesh may be entirely subject to the spirit. When we have learnt to curb our desires in all things we shall have reached the heights of perfection." Self-love, the desire of pre-eminence, is trampled underfoot with the same vigour. Teresa is wroth with feeble souls who would associate their interests or their honour with God's service. The very idea of a proud and ambitious Carmelite causes her to shudder. "No poison could kill the body," she exclaims, " more promptly than pride kills perfection in a soul. Do not tell me that I am speaking of little defects which are common to all the world. This is far from being a subject you can treat lightly. There is nothing small in cases where great dangers are menaced."

Points of honour, thoughts prompted by self-love, attempts to get appointed to particular posts, all these human miseries, born of pride, are to be utterly banished from St. Joseph's Convent. Teresa desires that such words as "I was right," "Such a one was wrong," should never be heard. Temptations such as these may present themselves; they are inevitable. What should be done? To those who are tempted by them the saint recommends that they should act at all times in a manner absolutely opposed to these defects ; that they should ask for the humblest employment in the house, practise acts of humiliation, and never excuse themselves when rebuked, even when conscious that the rebuke was not merited.

This is the austere side of the perfection which Teresa requires of her children : poverty, obedience, mortification, self-abnegation carried to heroic lengths, not only on great occasions, performed at the cost of a momentary pang, but in the thousand obscure details of everyday life, when renunciation, more trying because inward and unseen, becomes a true martyrdom. How is it possible to put human nature to such a severe trial ? Should we not augur that a mortal sadness would weigh down these young hearts thus burthened in the spring-time of their existence? No, for this yoke is that of the Divine Master, Who lightens it for those who bear it lovingly. Teresa does not add to its weight; her counsels, her rules, her constitutions, are but a generous application of the teachings of the Gospel. By the pathway of strong virtues she leads her daughters to the possession of the beatitude which is promised to those who are poor, humble, meek, persecuted here below, valiant in their opposition to the world and their own frail natures; who thirst after justice, are persecuted, and are ready to persecute them-

selves, voluntarily, for love of God and His glory. The divine promises were literally fulfilled in the Carmel of St. Joseph. This hard and penitential life was a continual feast there. The love of Jesus enraptured every heart, and poured a flood of joy into them. Prayer more than compensated for every sacrifice. These holy souls drew courage from this source to conquer themselves, and found a recompense therein for their victories. The saint with the authority of her long experience made the road, which she knew so well, easy for her daughters to follow. She led them gently from simple meditation to the early beginnings of contemplative prayer, carefully following, not anticipating, the attraction of divine grace in the hearts of each one. She knew how to put herself on the level of all, murmuring little words of prayer into her novices' ears as a mother, leaning over her infant's cradle, whispers to it in broken language the accents she wishes it to pronounce. If she saw them discouraged by trials or aridity, " Know well, my daughters," she said to them, " you may become perfect by acquitting yourself of your duties without reaching the heights of contemplation. It is right you should give yourself up to prayer, but you will not all receive equal favours in it. The one, however, who receives the fewest may surpass the others in merit, because she has exerted herself the most to acquire it, God treats her as a valiant soul, and He will add those consolations which have been wanting to her in this world to her joys in the next. St. Martha was a saint, though we are not told that she was a contemplative one. And can we desire a happier fate than to imitate this holy soul, who was reckoned worthy of receiving our Saviour so many times into her house, of giving Him food, and waiting upon Him, even of sitting at

table with Him, and eating out of the same dish? If she had been rapt in prayer like Magdalen there would have been no one to prepare His repasts. Well, my daughters, you should look upon Carmel as the house of Martha. . . . Whether it is by prayer, mental or vocal, by waiting on your sick sisters, or in any of the other offices of the house, however humble and low they may be, think that we are always and at all times serving our Divine Guest who condescends to lodge and take rest under our roof." Teresa, in order to console her daughters in their trials, used sometimes to confide her own past difficulties to them. With what fresh courage her novices must have been inspired when their holy mother owned to them that for fourteen years she had never been able to meditate without using a spiritual book! Our Lord did not, however, treat Teresa's children with the same severity. Prayer for them was nearly always a food of whose sweetness they were never satiated, and she had frequently to moderate their ardour in giving themselves up to it. She used to recommend to them the simplest subjects for their meditation, especially the words of the Gospels. The Paternoster was her special choice, " for," she said, " there is always a great advantage to be derived for establishing one's prayer on the one which came from the mouth of Jesus Christ Himself. If our weakness were not so great, and our devotion so cold, we should never require any other method of prayer, or book of meditation." And joining example to precept, she then began her commentary on the Lord's Prayer, to each petition of which she attaches a short meditation, simple, luminous, almost like those of the Divine Master Himself. Teresa identifies herself with the thoughts and desires of our Lord when He taught His prayer to man. She keeps close to His

side, and she brings with her, to the feet of this indulgent Teacher—this Divine Friend 1—not only her Carmelite children, but all those desirous of saying this prayer properly. First of all she teaches them what is the only right way of praying, which is to pray with Jesus Himself. She recommends great confidence. " For the angels who surround the King of kings never turn anyone back, for they know that the simplicity of the humblest suppliant, who would speak better if they knew more, pleases God infinitely more than great thoughts beautifully expressed by learned people who are wanting in humility." This book should be read in order to learn from the great contemplative saint how the least of God's children, no less than the holy nun, can find food for their piety, consolation and encouragement in their needs, in the Lord's Prayer.

Who would not have lived happily and attained sanctity under such direction as Teresa's ? She had the secret of making the life of prayer and recollection which was led by all, and was the very focus of the life at St. Joseph's, both easy and attractive. Joys of the heart went hand-in-hand with joys of the soul, in that little corner of the earth which was so visibly blessed by Heaven. Love of Jesus filled the existence, and was the breath of life, of these dwellers on Mount Carmel. The angels, saints, above all the Blessed Mother and St. Joseph, came in for a share of their love. The nuns were bound to each other, and to their mother, by an affection which she returned with equal love—a truly solid and enduring one. There was nothing earthly in these ties, or anything which recalled the world, its sentiments or language. The holy mother would have vigorously opposed all that threatened to

bring a human element into affections which she desired to be wholly supernatural. " Believe me," she tells them, " those who love God above all things, and all men in Him, love their neighbours with a greater, a truer, and even a more ardent love than do the rest of the world : for this alone is love."

Friendship thus understood lightened the labours, and charmed the solitude of the monastery. Everything, joys and sacrifices, work and suffering, was shared in common ; it was a true family life with all its opportunities of mutual devotion. At recreation time all assembled around their mother, and took their turn in contributing to the general entertainment. Teresa was the first to set an example, delighting the sisters with the genial wit of her conversation. She attached much importance to these moments of relaxation, being convinced that prudence required that human nature should not be kept always on the stretch, and that it was a necessary part of religious life to unbend at those times provided for by the Rule. " What would become of our little house," she says on one occasion, " if each one of us hid all the little wits she possessed? No one has too much ! Let each one produce whatever, she has in her with all humility, in order to cheer up the others. Again, do not imitate those unfortunate people who the moment they have got a little good out of prayer shut themselves up and hardly dare to talk or breathe for fear it should fly away." The intercourse of the nuns with the world should be short and rare. " I know better than you do," Teresa tells them, " the drawbacks of long conversations in the parlour. Trust my experience." She forbade her daughters, however, to show themselves ungrateful or discourteous. She excepted parents and brothers and sisters from the severe restrictions she placed on con-

versations behind the grille, and she was desirous that these should have all the consolations in their troubles that could be given them. When, however, it was necessary out of charity, or for any just reason, to receive a visitor Teresa wished it done cheerfully. " Do not," she says, " be tongue-tied, my daughters, out of scrupulosity. Try to show yourselves as affable as is possible without offending God, and to conduct yourselves in such a manner in your interviews with worldly people that they may be attracted by your way of life, and that, instead of going away discouraged and disgusted, they may feel the charm and attraction of goodness." The saint would thus pursue the work she has begun in the oratory to the parlour. Having asked in prayer for the salvation of souls, she seeks it wherever she goes, attracting them by her amiability and kindness in order to give them to God. The same width of views characterizes her at all times. Faithful to the Rule to a heroic degree, she yet sacrificed its observance in minor matters before a greater good. When such a case occurs she never hesitates ; she knows neither scruple nor indecision. She goes straight wherever God's greater glory, or the duty of charity to her neighbour, calls her, and she wishes her daughters to unite, as she does, rectitude of judgment with generosity in the practice of virtue.

" Rest assured," she says, "that God does not consider trifles. Keep your souls free from little anxieties which have no real foundation, but which will interfere much with your doing good. Preserve an upright intention, and a firm desire not to offend God, and then do not fear to allow yourselves a holy liberty of heart and spirit. . . . Scrupulous fears, far from doing you good, will cause you to fall into imperfections and stop the good you could do to others." There is nothing

narrow, no constraint nor tediousness, in this summit of Carmel, however steep the ascent. The child of St. Teresa in her little cell, behind her impenetrable grille, is no hapless prisoner weighed down by her chains. She is a joyous, a free soul, who sings with her seraphic mother the mercies of God, Whose beauty she contemplates from a nearer standpoint than the rest of the world. And if this blessed contemplation detaches her from worldly pleasures, it is only in order that she may keep her heart more open to a tenderness which embraces all human sufferings and sins, and a vigour of character which will serve to fortify the weak, and bring back the wanderer to the feet of God.

This is,therefore the straight and simple road, austere and yet sweet, by which Teresa conducts her children to the heights of religious perfection. But whilst she was thus descending to their level, and keeping step with them in order to permit of their following her, her soul was ever continuing its flight Godward, she enjoyed almost habitually the sensible presence of our Lord, and His interior direction. She describes the divine familiarity of this relation in which she stands to her adorable Spouse thus : " I saw that though God, He was man also, 1 and I could speak to Him as to a friend, though He is my Lord, because I do not consider Him as one of our earthly lords who affect a power they do not possess, and to whom only certain persons may speak. O King of Glory, and Lord of all! Thy dignity is not hedged in by trifles of this kind. We require no chamberlain to introduce us into Thy presence." If our Lord hid Himself from her for a time, the saint sought to redouble her humility and good works in order to hasten His return, and when

that happy moment arrived how quickly it made amends for all the weariness His absence had occasioned ! " To-day it is true I have been rejoicing in our Lord, and have dared to complain of His Majesty. I said: " How is it, O my God, that it is not enough for Thee to detain me in this miserable life, and that I should have to bear with it for the love of Thee, and be willing to live where everything hinders me from enjoying Thy presence? where besides I must eat and sleep, transact business, and endure all these things for love of Thee? How is it then, that in the rare moments when I am with Thee, Thou hidest Thyself from me? How is this consistent with Thy compassion ? How can that love Thou hast for me endure this? I believe, O Lord, if it were possible for me to hide myself from Thee, as Thou hidest Thyself from me, such is Thy love that Thou wouldst not endure it at my hands. But Thou art with me, and seest me always. O my Lord, look to this, I beseech you ! It must not be. A wrong is done to me who love Thee so much." The good Master, Who takes pleasure in such reproaches, responded to them by fresh favours. One Saturday, on the eve of Pentecost, the saint had retired, after having communicated, to a hermitage, and was employed there in reading the life of our Lord by Ludolph of Saxony. She was reading the meditation on the feast which was to be held the next day, and recognizing in herself the marks by which the author had laid down that the actions of the Holy Ghost might be discerned ; also remembering the dangers and vanities of her past life, the punishment of hell which had threatened her ; and contrasting this with the holy joys with which it was now transfigured, she was wholly overcome with a sense of gratitude to God for His mercies. At this moment she saw a Dove above her head, utterly unlike

any she had ever seen before. Its wings, which appeared to be made of rays of glory, were quietly agitated, and Teresa was conscious momentarily of a divine thrill. Then, ravished in God, she was aware of nothing more, remaining absorbed in her Sovereign Good, with whom she was wholly united. When the ecstasy passed away she was left with a sensible increase of love of God, and a greater strength for the practice of virtue. Thus the feast of Pentecost passed in the midst of a plenitude of heavenly joys.

" One night," she says, "I was so unwell that I thought I might be excused from making my meditation, so I took my beads that I might employ myself in vocal prayer. ... I remained but a few moments thus engaged, when I was rapt in spirit with such violence that I could make no resistance. It seemed to me that I was taken to Heaven, and the first persons I saw there were my father and my mother. I saw other things also, but the time was not longer than that in which the Ave Maria might be said." This vision was renewed several times, and on each occasion our Lord deigned to reveal secrets to her concerning His Kingdom. " Behold," He said to her, "my daughter, what they lose who are against Me ; do not fail to tell them of it." From the Heavenly abode, and the assembly of saints, the Divine Master transported the soul of His servant to the throne of His Divinity. He penetrated her with the awe-struck love of the seraphim. Teresa, when approaching Holy Communion afterwards, is confounded to the depths of her being at the thought that He, of whose inexpressible greatness she has had a glimpse, should humble Himself under the appearance of a Host, and come to repose Himself in the frail heart of His creature. More graces were to follow. Sometimes they came under the

form of symbols of profound signification; 1 at other times by the halo of a ray of supernatural light, it was given to her to understand how, in the words of St. Paul, all things are contained in God, and how God lives in the faithful soul. How God is truth, truth in itself, and how all truths depend on this Truth, in the same way that all love depends on this Love, and all greatness on this Greatness. Finally, a wisdom is imparted to her from the mystery of the Blessed Trinity, which leaves her divinely "consoled," and " amazed at the marvels of God." 2 And by an infused science which she draws from these contemplations she receives a great increase of knowledge of theological truths, and an even greater increase of fervour and zeal.

That God should be more and better known ; that He should be loved as He deserves ; that the spread of heresy should be arrested ; that the grace of forgiveness for the sins of men and their pardon from their Judge should be obtained by prayer and expiation : these are the desires which Teresa brought with her to earth when she came out of her ecstasies. These were the fires which consumed her heart, and which she sought to kindle in the souls of her daughters, and all those whom she came across, or had power to influence.

Proofs of the efficacy of her prayers were constantly coming to light. 3 People came to her to recommend sinners to her prayers, or to ask her to intercede for religious people who had fallen away from their first fervour ; or to pray for the sick, or the dying ; or sometimes for temporal benefits. Even for the last —though these appealed to her less—she had a ready

1 Life, ch. XL. 2 Ibid., ch. xxxix.

sympathy, "for," she says, "one should feel for man's weakness which rejoices at receiving succour in its necessities." 1 But on these occasions she had no assurance of being heard, unless the glory of God was involved therein. Human suffering, whether of mind or body, appealed to her more closely. On one occasion, a man suffering from violent pains no sooner came into the saint's presence than he was delivered from them. Another was cured from almost complete blindness by her prayers. A few words of hers addressed to persons in great trouble and affliction gave them strength to bear their crosses, or was the cause of their receiving unhoped-for blessings and consolation. But it was specially in the domain of men's souls that she wielded a great power, in her influence over the loving Heart of Jesus, for she could truly say, with Him, "My kingdom is not of this world." Teresa's apostleship had begun with life itself. From the time when, as a child of seven, she had led her brother to the siege of Heaven, never had she ceased preaching, by word and example, and above all by prayer, for the progress of the just and the conversion of sinners. Never, however, had these fervent intercessions produced such fruits as they had done since the time they issued from the solitude of St. Joseph's. Numberless conversions obtained in an extraordinary manner, and many more known to God alone ; heroic sacrifices and generous resolutions formed, which owed their inspiration to her ; a renewal of fervour in the case of priests and religious; the deliverance of innumerable souls from purgatory: these were some of the answers to prayer, admitted even by Teresa herself, which signalized the foundation of the reformed Mount Carmel. We do not

1 Way of Perfection,

propose multiplying instances of this sort. The saint gives us an example by saying as little as possible about them, on the plea that such narratives are tedious. Also, in many cases, where the cures were moral ones, besides the recipients they were known to God and His angels alone, and will only come to light at the last day. Teresa had a special leaning towards the Religious Orders, and frequently received lights in prayer regarding them : these she sometimes communicated to those Orders at our Lord's desire, or kept them in her own heart, where they were made the subject of her prayers. 1 The Society of Jesus was ever the first object of her solicitude, and her Divine Master gave her great joy by revealing to her the glory of some of its members, and showing her the services they had rendered Him, or were to render Him in the course of ages. The sons of St. Dominic and St. Francis held an equal place in her esteem. The duty of gratitude obliged her frequently to recommend the sons of St. Peter of Alcantara, and the Fathers Ibanez, Vincent Barron, and Garcia de Toledo, to God. The saint saw Fr. Ibanez enter Heaven almost immediately after his death, which took place about this time ; our Lord rewarding him in this way for the assistance he had been to her in her Foundations.

One day when Teresa was invoking the mercy of God on behalf of a woman threatened with an incurable disease, she feared that her own sins might stand in the way of her prayers being heard. Whilst she was praying our Lord appeared to her, she says, "and began to show me the wound in His left hand ; with the other He drew out the great nail that was in it, and it seemed to me that in drawing the nail He tore the flesh. The greatness of the pain was mani-

fest, and I was very much distressed thereat. He said to me that He who had borne that for my sake would still more readily grant what I asked Him, and that I was not to have any doubts on the subject. He promised me that He would grant all I asked of Him, adding that He knew I should ask for nothing that was not for His glory, and that He would grant me what I was now praying for. ' Remember,' He said, 'even when you did not serve Me I granted you all, and even more than all, you asked of Me. How much more shall I do it now that I am sure of your love." Frequently her Divine Master used to say to her," Now thou art Mine, and I am thine." 1

The history of a saint is, above all, the history of her soul. Thus if we interrogate Teresa upon what at this time was passing between her and her Divine Spouse, she answers as follows : 2 "It seems as if our Lord had been pleased to bring me to a haven which, I trust in His Majesty, will be very secure. Now that I am out of the world with holy companions, few in number, I look down on the world as from a great height, and care very little what people say, or know about me. I think much more of one soul's advancement, even if it were but slight, than of all that people may say of me. He has made my life now a kind of sleep, for what I see seems to me to be seen as in a dream, nor have I any great sense of either pleasure or pain. If anything happens to occasion either, the knowledge of

1 "Estas me dice su Magestad muchas veces, mostrandome gran amor: ' Ya eres mia, y yo soy tuyo.'" Hence probably the origin of the following legend, of which, however, the Bollandists deny the authenticity. It is said Teresa met a most beautiful child one day in the cloisters, and, astonished to meet him there, asked his name. " Tell me first yours," was his reply. "Teresa of Jesus." " And I," he answered, "am Jesus of Teresa."

it passes away and leaves an impression on me similar to one made in a dream. Accordingly, if I wished afterwards to delight in that pleasure, or to be sorry over that pain, it is not in my power to do so ; just as a sensible person feels neither pain nor pleasure in the memory of a dream that has passed. . . . Thus I have never had any real affliction since the day when I decided on giving up my life to the service of my Divine Saviour and Master. If He sometimes allows me to suffer a little, He makes up for it in a manner that makes me feel I have no merit in asking for crosses. Without them it seems to me I could not endure life. How many times do I cry from the bottom of my soul, * Lord, to suffer or to die : this is all I ask of Thee.' Whenever I hear a clock strike I rejoice at thinking that I am nearer to the hour when I shall see God, and have an hour less to spend on earth. May God take me to Himself or give me the power of serving Him."

CHAPTER XVII

TERESA, late in the autumn of 1566, was called to the parlour of St. Joseph's in order to speak to the Missionary Apostolic, Fr. Maldonado, who had lately returned from the West Indies. Encouraged by the saint's eager interest, Fr. Maldonado told in burning words the story of the ignorance and vices of the natives of those lands—lamenting all the difficulties that stood in the way of their evangelization. Teresa was profoundly moved by the account, and when he had concluded, she invited the good missionary to go to the church, and there assembled the rest of the community in order that all might have the opportunity of hearing him. The nuns were likewise deeply impressed by Fr. Maldonado's discourse, which turned on the fruits of repentance; but Teresa most of all. After the priest's departure she had recourse to solitude in a hermitage in the garden, and unable (as she herself says) to contain her feelings any longer, she cried aloud to her Divine Master, imploring of Him to give her the means of saving souls, " since the devil carried off so many," and to make some use of her prayers for this object, "as they were all I had to offer Him." Teresa continued to pour out her soul to God in prayer thus for many days. One night He appeared to her whilst she was praying, and manifesting His love to her, as if to console her, He said: "Wait a little while, my daughter, and great things shall be revealed to you."

Six months elapsed before the divine promise was fulfilled. Teresa kept the words in her heart without being able to understand their significance. The means God intended to use for their execution never even crossed her imagination. She thought in building her little convent she had accomplished all Heaven's decrees in her regard, and wished for no other future for herself, or her nuns, than to live and die in obscurity within the four walls of the cloister. In the spring of the following year (1567) it was notified to Teresa that Fr. John Baptist Rossi, General of the Order of Mount Carmel, had arrived in Castile and was on his way to Avila. " This was something quite unusual," our saint remarks, " for the Generals of our Order always reside in Rome, and it was unknown for any of them to come to Spain." Teresa would have been not unwilling to dispense with this visit; she feared that Fr. Rossi might be opposed to the Foundation, and would use his authority to send her back to the Convent of the Incarnation. She trembled, therefore, in spite of her courage. To her community, however, she only said that they were to look upon the General as their father; and directly she heard of his arrival she sent a very humbly-worded request to him to ask him to visit her little house. Fr. Rossi did not keep her long awaiting his arrival. He entered the cloister, and directly Teresa saw him her fears were dispelled, for she saw she had to do with a true servant of God. Kneeling at his feet, she gave him an account, in all frankness and simplicity, of the origin and history of the Foundation. Far from blaming her in any way, the General was enchanted at all she told him, and even more so when he had made a visitation of every part of the monastery. It was the living image of the first solitudes of Carmel—

another grotto of Elias, consecrated to poverty, austerity, and, at the same time, to holy joy. He shed tears of consolation, and promised Teresa that he would never oblige her to leave her house of St. Joseph. 1 He told her that his ardent desire was that this germ of reform should grow up in the bosom of the Order, and spread through all its branches. The convent of St. Joseph, in fact, realized precisely the views which Fr. Rossi had come to Spain to advocate. Himself a fervent religious, he longed to apply the decisions of the great Council, which had so lately been held, to his own Order. With this object he sought to rouse attention to the ancient traditions of Mount Carmel amongst his brethren, though without requiring from them so searching a reform as the one Teresa had inaugurated. It was this mission which Philip II had imposed upon him when inviting him to his kingdom. This monarch, desirous of restoring discipline in the innumerable monasteries in Spain, had first addressed himself with this object to the secular clergy. Later on he invited the superiors of the Regular Orders to undertake the task. Pius V had just mounted the papal throne, and in February, 1566, he authorized Fr. Rossi by a Brief to undertake the much needed reform. Accordingly the General started at once for Madrid, where he was welcomed by the King ; he then proceeded to make a visitation of the houses of the Order in Andalusia, returning to Madrid in February of the following year. The Carmelites, many of whom were opposed to the reforms of their General, succeeded in turning Philip's mind against him in the interval, with the result that on this occasion he met with but a cold reception at court. On leaving Madrid Fr. Rossi went to Avila,

where he held a Provincial Chapter, and where, without abandoning his measures of reform, he succeeded in calming the opposition which he had raised. Under these circumstances the Father-General found much consolation from the peaceful retreat of the little convent of St. Joseph. Whenever his occupation allowed him a moment's leisure he had recourse to it. The saint became the confidant of his anxieties. He consulted her on the affairs of the Order ; and he never left her without an increased esteem for her enlightenment, and her force of character.

The somewhat delicate question of the jurisdiction of St. Joseph's had now to be considered. The General saw that there were strong reasons for putting it under the authority of the Ordinary, and on this point he submitted ; but he informed Teresa that as a professed nun of the Incarnation she remained under obedience to him. Teresa then showed him the papal Brief which dispensed her from this obedience. Fr. Rossi, after reading the Brief, found some defect in its form, and maintained that with the double claim of Visitor Apostolic and General of her Order he had the right to resume his authority over her. The saint seeing that he was bent upon it, and reassured by the promises he gave her, fell in with his views. Bishop de Mendoza who loved Teresa as a daughter, when informed of the change, was much distressed ; this, in turn, afflicted Teresa, who looked upon him as her greatest benefactor. She used so much tact, however, in smoothing matters over that she succeeded in restoring peace between the Bishop and the General. The former even asked Fr. Rossi to authorize him to found some monasteries of the primitive Observance for men on the same lines as the one Teresa had started for women. But the General, fearing that the project would raise

too much opposition among members of the mitigated Rule, answered that the moment for doing so had not come. The saint tells us, however, that he gave her authority without her having asked for it to erect convents for nuns. These patents were dated the 27th of April, 1567, and contained severe censures on all provincials who would oppose their execution. They declared that the monasteries of Mother Teresa of Jesus were to hold their authority straight from the Generals of the Order, and that she was to have a right to establish them in any part of Castile, without permission of anyone but the Ordinary of the diocese. 1

After the Provincial Chapter had finished its work Fr. Rossi returned to Madrid. Here he was not long in discovering that he had been restored to the royal favour, the king manifesting his satisfaction to him for the profit the Order had derived from his visit to Spain. The Father-General took advantage of the favourable moment to interest him in the Reform of St. Joseph's, and spoke to him about the holy foundress. Philip II, much edified by what he heard, asked Fr. Rossi to recommend him and his family to her prayers and those of her community. 2 St. Teresa, on receiving Fr. Rossi's letter, read it to her daughters; and we are told, in the annals of the Order, that henceforth the king had a special share in their prayers and their suffrages. Soon afterwards the General set off on his return to Rome. When he had got as far as Valencia he received an express letter from Teresa, which was to lead to great results. The saint, after his departure, reflecting on the importance of the request made to Fr. Rossi by the Bishop and refused by him, once more urged him to consent to the foundation of monas-

1 History of the Order, Book III, ch. 11. 2 Boll., No. 400.

teries of the Reform for men. The General could refuse nothing to his dear daughter ; accordingly his answer was accompanied with authorizations for the foundation of two monasteries of friars of the primitive Observance. The only condition annexed to the permission was that they should be made with the consent of the provincial and his predecessor in office. This consent Mgr. de Mendoza undertook to obtain, and succeeded in doing so. Teresa thus found herself confronted with an entirely new situation : she was commissioned by Providence and authorized by her superiors to found an Order for men and women ; for to carry out this thorny reform, which was to strip a degenerate Carmel of all its mitigations and many of its abuses, was it not, in a sense, to found it anew? And to do this it was necessary to start houses, then to find subjects, and to train them to a life of penance and contemplation. " And in order to attain these results," Teresa tells us, " there was only one discalced nun, armed with patents and good intentions, but without the smallest resources with which to start the work, or any support except from God." 1

Teresa knew well what her first Foundation had cost her, in spite of much help from her friends in Avila, Dona Guiomar and de Salcedo in particular. But these had already assisted her so generously that she hesitated at making fresh appeals to them. Also as soon as they heard of the new projects they were much dismayed, and did their utmost to dissuade her from carrying them out. All Teresa could expect from her friends, therefore, was that they should abstain from active opposition. Adverse rumours were again current in the town. Thus Teresa found herself once more face to face with similar difficulties to those she

had encountered on her first Foundation, and with even less prospect of material support than she had had on that occasion.

Nevertheless the time was at hand when "the grain of mustard seed sown in the soil of Avila was to become a great tree, in whose branches the birds of the air—that is, chosen souls who are lifted to heaven on the wings of contemplation—should shelter; also under whose shade the beasts of the earth, in other words sinners and infidels, should take refuge." 1 Our saint had a presentiment from this time of the greatness of the mission entrusted to her. She knew she had no time to lose. The Master of the Household had sent her out to work in the apostolic field at an age when the servant, weary of the day's work, is accustomed to ask for rest. With her bad health, and the burthen of her fifty-two years upon her, she thought she had reached the evening of life. But she had received her orders, and she was ready to obey. She had to bid adieu to the dearly bought peace of the convent of St. Joseph, to the little religious family, the sweet intimacy, all so dear to her heart, and to the long hours of prayer and contemplation. Her life henceforth would have to be spent in the world, taking charge of affairs, treating with men. She will be involved in endless work and an incessant correspondence. This was to be the programme of her future existence. We shall note whether, during this later period, her ecstasies have enfeebled her powers ; whether mysticism has clouded or obscured her intelligence ; or, finally, if mortification has dried up her heart.

The holy foundress began by casting her eyes round her to see where she should first direct her footsteps.

1 Yepes.

Medina del Campo, situated at a distance of twenty miles from Avila, its fertile environs watered by an affluent of the Douro, offered her more than one attraction. The Jesuits had been settled twenty-five years in the city, and Fr. Balthazar Alvarez had lately been sent there as rector. The certainty of finding a firm support in that quarter decided the saint's choice. She wrote to Fr. Balthazar to acquaint him with her design, and he answered in the name of his colleagues that they would second her efforts to the best of their power. Teresa at once sent Fr. Julian d'Avila, the excellent chaplain of the convent, to Medina, and corn-missioned him to look out for a house, and to take measures to obtain the necessary authorization from the diocesan authorities, and magistrates of the town. The saint, whilst these negotiations were being carried on, proceeded to set her house in order, so that nothing should suffer from her absence at St. Joseph's. She appointed Sister Mary of St. Jerome to take her place, her previous charge of mistress of novices, and afterwards of sub-prioress, having given her to a certain extent the necessary experience. She bought a neighbouring piece of land (a most urgent requirement, Ribera tells us), in order to add to the size of the garden. In short, before leaving Avila she settled her affairs on a thoroughly satisfactory basis.

Fr. Julian met with considerable opposition from the authorities at Medina. He was called upon to prove not only that the penniless condition of the new community would not be prejudicial to the temporal good of the city, but that it would derive great spiritual benefit from the new Foundation. A testimonial was then got up in behalf of the Carmelites, which Fr. Baltasar and his colleagues were the first to sign. Some

magistrates of good standing followed their example, and finally the permission was granted. The next thing to be done was to find a house. " I had not a penny," Teresa writes, "with which to buy one!" Her envoy was no better off; but, like the saint, he trusted in Providence. Accordingly he hired a house in the town next door to an Augustinian convent, signed the lease, and returned to Avila, in order to prepare to start again with Teresa and her companions for their new abode.

Shortly after Fr. Julian got back to Avila, a young girl of that town applied to the Carmelites to be taken as a postulant to Medina. The girl had already asked for admission into the novitiate at St. Joseph's, but the number being already complete, her application had been refused. Teresa now received her gladly, and the tiny dowry which she brought with her sufficed to cover the expenses of the journey, and to pay the first year's rent.

Teresa had secured support in another quarter at Medina ; this was from the Carmelites of the mitigated Rule. Far from hiding her purpose from them, she had written direct to the prior of the monastery of St. Anne, Fr. Anthony de Heredia, asking him to try and find them a house. Fr. Anthony set to work with such good will, that he succeeded before long in buying one for her which was well situated, though in a bad state of repair—an arrangement being concluded that, whilst Teresa and her companions lived provisionally in the hired house, the other should be made suitable for their future occupation.

The start from Avila was made on the i3th of August, 1567. The saint assembled her daughters together; embraced them, confided them to the care of Sister Mary of Jerome, and then, with much sorrow in her

heart, she betook herself to one of the hermitages in the garden, and prostrating there before a picture of the flagellation of our Lord she cried, " My God, I confide this little monastery to Thy care ; since it was erected by Thine orders, deign to preserve it in the same fervour in which Thou seest it now." Teresa only took two nuns from St. Joseph's with her, though all would have been ready to follow her. These were Sisters Anne of the Angels, and Mary Baptist. Four nuns from the Incarnation who desired to embrace the Reform had been given permission by the Father-General to accompany her. They got into their rickety carriages, the last of which carried their baggage, Fr. Julian mounted his horse, and the party set out for Medina. The journey was made under the pitiless sun of a Spanish August, the so-called carriages progressing along rocky roads by a series of jerks and bounds. After a most fatiguing day they were met at Arevalo, where they had arranged to spend the night, by a messenger from Fr. Julian. He brought the worst possible news; no less than that the proprietor of the house which Fr. Julian had hired begged of the travellers to give up their journey, as it was impossible for him to fulfil his contract, the Augustinians having objected to the Carmelites as neighbours. 1 "As these religious are my friends," he added, " I do not wish to cause them annoyance." When this news was broken to the saint, " in spite," Fr. Julian remarks, " of her courage, she was much upset by it." What was to be done? she must have asked herself, stranded as they were, six nuns without resources, or a roof over their heads, in a town where they were unknown. To return was

1 Fuente remarks that the Augustinians were justified in their resistance, and quotes from the canon law: " Monasteria puellarum longius a monasteriis monachorum . . . collocentur."

not to be thought of. There was a dozen reasons against it. Accordingly the party entered Arevalo, and dismounted at the house of some pious women. Teresa watches and prays. " O Lord ! " she beseeches, " this enterprise is Thine, not mine. If Thou wishest it carried out, Thou canst easily do it, if not, let it be according to Thine adorable will." 1 In order that her nuns might have a good night's rest, Teresa kept the bad news from them till the following morning. Fortunately Fr. Banez happened to be passing through Arevalo, so the saint sent at once to him to ask his advice. The Father consoled her by his assurances that all would end well; but recommended her to wait till the present difficulties could be overcome. Whilst the saint was hesitating, wishing to proceed on account of the following day being the feast of the Assumption, and yet not daring to do so, a visitor was announced. This was the prior of St. Anne's, Fr. Anthony de Heredia. When Teresa had told him of her dilemma, the prior recommended her to go straight to the house he had purchased. " No doubt," he said, " the house requires repairs, but it is habitable. You can make a chapel of the vestibule, and then the convent can be founded without further delay." He also advised the saint to divide her forces, so as to travel quicker and more quietly. Teresa agreed to his suggestions, left four of her nuns at Arevalo, and started once more with Fr. Julian and the rest of her little company for Medina. She visited on her road the castle of Dona Maria de Heredia, who had sold to her, without purchase-money or guarantee, the old house in Medina. The saint wished to show her gratitude by this visit, and Dona Maria was so pleased to see her that she presented her on the spot with some tapestries, and some

1 Julian ci'Avila. U

bed-hangings of blue damask belonging to the house at Medina. When they reached Olmedo the saint stopped again to ask Bishop de Mendoza's blessing. The hour was already late, and the bishop offered a night's hospitality to the travellers, but Teresa asked permission to push on. At last, when it was close on midnight, the carriages stopped at the gates of Medina, near the monastery of St. Anne, which was situated outside the walls of the town. Fr. Julian ran to acquaint the fathers of their arrival, and had much difficulty in rousing them from their sleep. Finally, having procured from St. Anne's all that was required to start a chapel in the new convent, they started on foot (in order to make less noise) to traverse the town. The prior accompanied them with two of his religious ; the saint and her companion, Fr. Julian, and another priest who helped to carry the luggage, completed the procession. " We were so laden," Fr. Julian says, "that we might have been taken for gipsies carrying off the spoils of a church, and have been put into prison. Fortunately we met with no opposition on our road." They hurried their footsteps, taking byways to avoid the crowd which circulated in the streets notwithstanding the lateness of the hour, in preparation for the festivities of the following day. The bulls destined for the fights next day were being driven through the streets—another danger to avoid. Finally they reached a dark and dilapidated-looking house. This was the future monastery. The guardian was so sound asleep that it took a quarter of an hour's efforts and repeated knocks at the door to rouse him. It was two in the morning before they effected an entrance. Teresa visited the building, and found it in a deplorable state. "Our dear Lord must have prevented Fr. Anthony using his eyesight," she exclaimed, "other-

wise he would never have said that such a ruinous abode was fit to receive the Blessed Sacrament!"

Supported by her confidence in God, Teresa never dreamed of giving way to discouragement. It was necessary that the chapel should be prepared by daybreak, so she would see that this was done. Assisted by her nuns, she quickly removed the rubbish which littered the ground, swept the court, and cleaned the walls. The guardian brought out, according to the orders he had received, his mistress's fine tapestry and blue damask hangings; but here another difficulty arose : there were no nails ! It was impossible to procure any at that time of night, so all they could do was to use a few which they found on the walls ; with these they nailed the hangings on the walls of the sanctuary and made all ready. Fr. Anthony prepared the altar, another friar hung the bell, Teresa's friends vying with each other in rendering her assistance. 1 The space, however, was so confined, the porch so dilapidated, that in the obscurity of the night it was hard to see whether the chapel was in the house or the street. Suddenly Teresa remembered a formality which had to be observed ; this was to have a statement drawn up by a notary that the convent was authorized by the diocesan council. Fr. Anthony started off at once to interview the vicar-general, and Fr. Julian went in search of a notary. The act was drawn up ; all was ready, and at break of day a little bell—of even more humble dimensions than the one at St. Joseph's—rang for the Angelus, and for the first Mass. Teresa assisted at it with her daughters, hidden behind the door of the staircase. The little chapel was filled with people, who flocked in from the neighbouring district at the sound of the bell, and who were astounded to

1 Julian d'Avila.

find that a new convent had been founded in the night. The saint's soul was rapt in ecstasy all the time of Mass, " rejoicing that the Blessed Sacrament should be honoured in one more church." x Trials awaited her on leaving the chapel. The darkness had prevented her realizing the state of the house; she was horrified at the sight of the crumbling walls which daylight revealed to her. How could she allow her Divine Master to inhabit an abode so unworthy of Him ? The sense of discouragement which she had felt on the opening day at St. Joseph's again came over her. The work having been accomplished God withdrew His protecting arm from His servant, lest its success should be a peril to her, and allowed her to feel her natural weakness and frailty. "Lord," she cried to Him, " how is it possible that Thou canst make use of such a broken reed!" Prayer before long calmed this interior trial : and abandoning herself and her daughters to God's good pleasure, she occupied herself, with her usual energy, in providing what was urgently required. First of all she made inquiries (this time through the Jesuits) for a hired house which she and the community could inhabit, till the necessary repairs could be effected in their present abode. " I passed days, and above all nights, of great anxiety," she relates. "Every night I engaged men to take it in turn to watch in the church ; and even then I was not at ease. I was afraid they might be overcome with sleep. So much alarmed was I that I used to rise from time to time and look out of the window, where I could see by moonlight that they were at their posts. The people, however, still continued to crowd the church. Instead of blaming us for what we had done, the good folk were moved to devotion at seeing our Lord inhabiting, so to speak, a

1 Foundations, ch. in.

stable once more, and His Divine Majesty, who seems never too weary of humbling Himself for our sakes, seemed in no hurry to leave it."

The octave-day of the Assumption put an end to our saint's anxieties. On that day a rich merchant of the name of Bias de Medina, who owned a large house at the extreme end of the street in which the future monastery was situated, came to put the upper floor of his house at the Carmelites' disposal. This floor he offered to make over to them for their exclusive use, whilst the workmen were employed in building up the ruined walls of their present abode. Teresa accepted the good man's hospitality with much gratitude; and she and her daughters were soon installed in his house. A gilded chamber was turned into the chapel; thus the nuns were able to assist at Mass, recite divine office, and even keep the enclosure, as the merchant and his family respected their presence as if they had been angel visitors. Teresa alone was immersed in business, but she was full of hope and therefore of courage. Fr. Anthony did his best to repair his mistake by superintending the works in St. John's Street. A pious widow of the name of Dona Helena de Quiroga, who lived in the same street, watched the progress of the new building with interest, and wishing to associate herself by her alms in the new Foundation offered to build the chapel at her own expense. As an interchange of benefits, Dona Helena begged the saint's prayers for herself and her five children. Teresa obtained many graces for her. Dona Helena had the happiness of seeing two of her sons priests, she gave her youngest daughter to the Order of Mount Carmel, her two remaining daughters lived saints' lives in the world ; finally she herself, after overcoming great obstacles, became a Carmelite at Medina before Teresa's

death, and lived there fifteen years afterwards till her own death. Other benefactors contributed their alms to the new monastery, and towards the end of October it was ready for occupation. Like the house at Avila, it was dedicated to St. Joseph. The good people at Medina were well disposed from the beginning to the new Foundation, and soon novices came to be received. Teresa passed several months at Medina, her time being wholly occupied with the spiritual training of her daughters. " These," she says, "follow in the footsteps of their sisters at Avila, and seek no other happiness than that of rendering all the glory which they are capable of giving to their Heavenly Master."

Meanwhile the saint had not lost sight of the other work which she had undertaken. The friendly relations between her and the monastery of St. Anne, of the mitigated Rule, continued, and their prior was struck every time he visited the convent with the recollection and austerity of its inmates. Thus no sooner had Teresa acquainted him with her intention of founding two similar monasteries for men, than he at once promised to be one of the first to embrace the Reform. This was almost more than the saint was prepared for. She wished his support, would have been glad of his counsels, but could have dispensed with his person. She temporized, therefore, and gave him to understand that she did not take his proposition seriously. The prior was an excellent religious, pious and learned, and a lover of solitude ; but Teresa, in order to launch her great undertaking, required a saint, and her knowledge of Fr. Anthony's character showed her that on certain points he was not up to her standard. Did she feel uncertain whether his constitution, which was a delicate one, would stand the severity of the Rule P 1 Or had she

remarked a tenacity in clinging to his own opinions and a rigour in dealing with his subordinates, in her interviews with him, which made her doubtful whether he was fitted for so exceptional a post ? We incline to the latter opinion. In any case the saint asked him to put his resolutions to the test of time, and to await the course of events. Fr. Anthony submitted, but he embraced from that moment the Rule of the Reform. God permitted that during the following year he should become the butt of calumny, and even of grievous persecution. He emerged from these trials greatly advanced in the path of perfection, and, as Teresa gladly recognized, also much better disposed to carry out her designs. The shadows we have pointed out in the character of this great and holy man were more than redeemed by his spirit of self-abnegation, and the intrepidity of his faith, virtues which contributed greatly to the extension of the Reform. A true son of Elias, he belonged to the purest type of the Carmel of the Old Law ; but he was wanting in the suavity, the tenderness of heart, in short the unction of divine grace, which distinguished Teresa, and it was these virtues which were pre-eminently required for the leadership of the Christian Carmel, the Carmel of our Saviour Jesus Christ and His Blessed Mother.

Thus Teresa accepted Fr. Anthonyf though she had neither asked for, nor desired, his services. Shortly afterwards she received a visit from Fr. Pedro de Orozco, an aged religious of the Order who was much revered for his learning and piety. He had heard of Teresa's designs from Fr. Anthony, and though too old to cooperate with them personally he came to recommend to the holy foundress a young religious whom he looked upon as perfectly fitted for the task. Teresa, in listening to Fr. Orozco, instantly felt a secret conviction that

this young man was the one she was in search of, and that he was intended to serve as the foundation-stone of the edifice of the Carmelite Reform. She asked that he should be sent to her the following day, and spent the whole night in prayer, wrestling with God, as was her wont, when she had some favour greatly at heart, and which she desired to obtain from Him. 1 The next day Fr. John of St. Mathias, as he was then called, presented himself at the parlour. " The instant I saw him," the saint tells us, " I was enchanted with his appearance." His modesty, the wisdom he showed in his speech, the piety which his very countenance expressed and which gave him an angelic look, his manners and even his child-like stature, delighted her. Fr. John, in answer to Teresa's questions, told her in a few words about his way of life, and the exercises of penance which he had embraced in order to approach more closely to the primitive Rule. He added that God had inspired him with an irresistible attraction for a life of solitude, and that he was about to respond to this call by joining the Carthusians. " My father and my son," the saint joyfully exclaimed, "I implore of you to be patient and wait for awhile. You must give up your present idea, for a Reform is in contemplation in our own Order which will satisfy all your desires. If you will join in this great work, I will answer for your acquiring much grace by its means, and in addition to this you will be rendering a great service to our Lady, the Mother of Carmel."

Fr. John received the news with joy equal to Teresa's, and promised her everything she asked on condition that he should not have to wait too long. She was able to satisfy him on this point. Accordingly the holy mother, having now two religious ready to carry out

1 History of the Order.

the great work, already looked upon it as an accomplished fact, and could not thank God enough for having sent her such a treasure as this young priest. She recognized under his youthful and fragile appearance, a great soul, much generosity of character, and a wide spirit ; and she used to call him playfully her little sage—her Seneca. Later on, comparing his diminutive height to Fr. Anthony's fine presence, she was wont to say, in joke, that she had had but a religious and a half wherewith to start the Reform of the Order of Carmel. Though she did not acknowledge it, doubtless she thought that her half-religious was alone worth a whole province. Teresa was as anxious to set to work as Fr. John was to follow her; but she judged it prudent to wait till Fr. Anthony's year of trial was concluded. Also she had as yet no house ready for them ; and business of a pressing nature required her presence elsewhere. She therefore left her " little Seneca" to pursue his theological studies for awhile, and occupied herself with the two Carmelite Foundations, which for some months she had been called upon to undertake.

Don Bernardino de Mendoza, a brother of the excellent Bishop of Avila, though a man of the world, and apparently not too exemplary in his habits, shared the bishop's sentiments about the Carmelites. He offered Teresa a fine property which he owned at Rio de Olmos, near Valladolid, with its gardens and vineyard, for the foundation of the new convent. The saint hesitated on account of the distance between his property and the town ; but touched by the generosity of the young man, and " not wishing," she says, " to disappoint his piety, nor deprive him of the merit of his good work," she ended by accepting his offer, postponing, only, taking possession to a favourable

moment. Scarcely had the saint agreed to Don Bernardino's wishes when Dona Luisa de la Cerda arrived at Medina to beg of her to make a Foundation at Mala-gon, a little town on her property. This proposal was even less attractive to her than the former one, there being too few inhabitants in Malagon to support a monastery which was dependent on alms. Dona Luisa, it is true, had foreseen this difficulty, and promised to endow it; but an endowment was opposed to the strict vow of poverty, and the saint refused, in spite of her affection for her friend, to give in to her wishes. A message from Dona Leonor de Mascarenas, former governess to Philip II, reached Teresa whilst she was in the midst of these negotiations. It will be remembered that it was this great lady who had given her support at court to Mother Mary of Jesus, and who had afterwards made over to her a property at Alcala as a Foundation for a Carmelite monastery of the Reform. This Foundation was at this moment in a tottering condition, owing to Mother Mary's pious imprudences, and Dona Leonor invited Teresa to go to Alcala to make some much needed changes in the way of life of the community, and to instruct the nuns in the true spirit of the Order. Mother Mary of Jesus, with great humility, joined her entreaties to those of her illustrious friend. Teresa, therefore, in spite of her own anxieties and her other important engagements, started at once for Alcala. Little it mattered to her whither she went as long as she was working in her Master's service. Don Bernardino, with his sister Dona Maria de Men-doza, accompanied her to Madrid. He profited by this journey (in consequence, one would be tempted to think, of a secret presentiment) to settle his affairs, and accordingly made over to Teresa, on parting, a deed of gift of his property at Rio de Olmos. Rumours regarding our saint had preceded her, so that numbers of great ladies attached to the court came to make her acquaintance at Dona Leonor's house; some attracted by sentiments of piety, others from curiosity, hoping to see her in ecstasy, or to be witness of a miracle. Teresa received one and all with her accustomed amiability ; and tactfully eluding their attempts to draw her out, she talked of the beauty of the streets in Madrid, and such-like commonplaces. Her visitors withdrew, with their curiosity baffled. The greater number protested that Mother Teresa was certainly no saint, though doubtless an excellent nun; report had endowed her with qualities which she was far from possessing. Teresa's humility had never gained her a greater triumph* The discalced Franciscan nuns of Madrid had greater discernment than the court ladies. Their prioress, a sister of St. Francis Borja, persuaded Teresa to spend a fortnight with them, and with this fervent community she might have given free vent to her piety. She preferred, however, to conceal her spiritual gifts under the most ordinary appearances. This time she deceived no one, and her modesty and humility edified the nuns more than miracles would have done had she performed them. ' l God be praised!" the prioress exclaimed after her departure, "for having allowed us to know such a saint. She ate and slept and behaved like the rest of the world, and yet she was a saint; for her soul resembled that of her Divine Master in its humility, simplicity, and sincerity. She lived amongst us as He lived amongst men, alarming no one and consoling all hearts." 1

Teresa was taken by Dona Leonor from Madrid to Alcala ; where she found Mother Mary weighed down by her excessive austerities and by the cares of her

office. Pale and worn out, surrounded by daughters who were equally depressed by burdens whose weight she did not dare diminish, she hailed the saint as a messenger from Heaven. On Teresa's arrival she handed over to her the keys of office, and proceeded to disburthen her soul to her. How was it possible, she asked, that Teresa had succeeded in causing that perfect life which they had dreamed of together to flourish in her monasteries, whereas she could only produce ruined healths and vocations in hers ? Teresa comforted her friend, and pointed out to her the drawbacks of a rigidity which sticks to the letter of the law, and ignores those lawful dispensations which are dictated by prudence and charity. She also explained to her the Constitutions she had drawn up for her Foundations, and above all impressed upon her that the spirit of Carmel was that of love and joy in self-sacrifice. The humble Mother Mary longed that all her daughters should profit by Teresa's instructions. Accordingly the saint regulated their penances and their hours of prayer, and cheered up every heart with her gentle gaiety, so that when she left Alcala, after a stay of two months and a half, she carried with her the blessings and gratitude of the whole community, as well as those of its foundress.

Dona Luisa de la Cerda, meanwhile, had not abandoned her project of founding a Carmelite convent at Malagon, so she pursued Teresa with letters ; and the latter, passing through Toledo, stopped there to discuss the question. We have already seen how Teresa was especially told by our Lord Himself to found her monasteries in the strictest poverty, and how St. Peter of Alcantara had twice enforced this order. But it was impossible to found a convent at Malagon without endowment. What was she to do ? Was she

to refuse God the glory He might acquire from a fervent convent of Carmel, or withdraw herself from a course of conduct which had been traced out for her by wholly supernatural means ? Teresa had recourse in her difficulty to Fr. Banez, and to other equally learned and pious theologians — her great and humble soul ever placing the decisions of the Church and her ministers above her own private revelations. They answered in the words of the Council of Trent: that it is considered advisable for the spiritual welfare of monasteries that they should possess some endowment, so that the extreme destitution of a community should not give rise to worldly cares and relaxations. " You would do well therefore," she was told, "to accept the endowment which has been offered you. Otherwise you would appear to put your own inspirations before those of the Holy Ghost who presides over the deliberations of Councils." Teresa submitted in silence. "There is reason to think," Ribera informs us, "that our Lord told Teresa to follow the advice of His servants, and in this we need not necessarily see any contradiction, for God's providence merely recommended two different courses of action to her under the different circumstances in which she was placed. If she had waited for an endowment in founding her first convent it would never have been founded. But later on, as her monasteries multiplied in number, it would have been difficult with their Rule, and rigorous enclosure, to have subsisted entirely on alms. Experience proves that convents possessed of some endowment, and therefore not dependent on alms, are less exposed to suffer from exterior relations, and live in greater recollection. Thus," her biographer concludes, "though the absence of revenues was correct in principle, it was necessary to modify it afterwards in practice."

Difficulties having been thus solved to Dona Luisa's satisfaction, Teresa returned to Medina. She appointed a prioress and sub-prioress to the convent there, and, satisfied with the state in which she found the community, returned shortly afterwards to Toledo, accompanied by four nuns whom she had sent for from Avila. Teresa was detained some days at Toledo by her friend, whose young cousin, Maria de Salazar, seized this opportunity of asserting her wish to follow God's call to a religious life. Dofia Luisa gave her consent, and Maria was the first to be professed, under the name of Mary of St. Joseph, at the monastery of Malagon. The solemn installation took place amidst the rejoicing of the townspeople on Palm Sunday. The clergy, followed by all the congregation, came to meet the nuns on their arrival. They were conducted first to the principal church, " where a sermon was preached," the saint relates, " then they took the Blessed Sacrament, which was carried in great state, to the convent." Like the two preceding ones, the new Carmel was dedicated to St. Joseph. Teresa was only able to spend two months at Malagon. She suffered much whilst she was there from constant encroachments on the time she could give to prayer and solitude ; but to suffer for God became more and more the element in which she lived, as to work for Him became her only repose. She left Malagon towards the end of May, thanking God for her daughters' fervour, especially of that of her young novice, who was already noted for her singular merit and piety.

Unfortunately, Teresa's physical powers were not always equal to her mental activity. She wished to hasten to Valladolid to fulfil her engagements with Don Bernardino, engagements which his sudden death had invested with an almost sacred character. He had

died without the last Sacraments, and Teresa, having been informed by a revelation of the double misfortune which had befallen her benefactor at the very time of its occurrence, recommended his soul to God with all the ardour of her gratitude and her charity. " Daughter," our Lord said to her, " his salvation was in much danger ; but in consideration of the service he rendered My Mother by giving you his house in which to found a convent, I have shown compassion to him. Nevertheless, he will be detained in purgatory till the first Mass is said in the new convent."

From that moment Teresa could not rest till the work was carried out. She was separated at Malagon from Valladolid by a distance of sixty miles ; she was wanted at Toledo, and anxiously awaited at Avila ; the roads were bad, the heat great, and means of transport were slow and inconvenient. She required all her strength to surmount these obstacles, and, unfortunately, in addition to her usual infirmities, she was suffering from fever brought on by overwork. She refused to postpone her departure, but her illness increasing she had to stop at Toledo, and there to submit to a course of remedies, of which one was blood-letting. She accepted these trials with her usual patience, for the love of God. Dona Luisa was absent, but she had left orders that Teresa's wants should be provided for. Accordingly the saint writes a grateful letter to her friend, in which we can trace no sign of the trials which were weighing on her. "The care you have lavished on me, dear lady," she says, "from the depths of Andalusia really fill me with admiration. Your people have done all they could for me, so that I am now well, though weak." Teresa was starting the next day, but, in spite of weakness, she spent half the night writing. It was necessary for her to arrange

with Dona Luisa certain affairs connected with the Malagon Foundation, such as the choice of a chaplain. Also she must needs console Doiia Luisa in her troubles, telling her she must not on any account add to them by thinking her friend will be laid up on the journey. The saint, in order to set her mind at rest, assures her that the journey—though, alas ! neither carriage, nor coachman could be found—will be safely accomplished. Failing these, " I am carrying off, and I trust you will approve," the saint adds gaily, "a saddle with a back to it which you have at the castle. As no one is making use of it, I feel sure you will be delighted that I should take it for the journey. It will at least be a pleasure to me to think I am making use of something belonging to you. 1 Farewell, dear lady and friend ; I grieve to conclude my letter, and to think that I am going far from one whom I love so tenderly." Teresa passed Avila on her way to Valladolid. The same fervour met her at St. Joseph's, and a joy which was increased by her presence. Illness detained her here for nearly a month, during which time another important proposal was made to her. " Don Rafael de Mexia had learnt, I know not how,"she says, " that I wished to found a monastery of discalced Carmelites for men, and with this object he has offered me a house he possesses in a small village. This house had been used by an agent of his. I could guess the kind of dwelling it would be ; nevertheless I praised God, and thanked the gentleman warmly. He told me that the house lay on the road to Medina, so that I could visit it on my way to Valladolid." Teresa left Avila at the end of June, very early in the morning, accompanied

1 This was one of the few occasions in which the saint rode. Her journeys were always performed in shut carriages, in which she kept the Rule as strictly as she did in her convents.

by Sister Antonia of the Holy Ghost and Fr. Julian. They went in search of the village indicated by Don Rafael, but no one could tell them where it was situated. At last, after a long day's journey in the burning sun, they reached, towards dusk, the tiny hamlet of Duruelo. The house was a miserable one, consisting, Teresa tells us, of " a porch, one bedroom, a garret, and a kitchen, all more dirty than words could describe. This was the fine building, out of which we were to construct a monastery ! " The saint, however, made her plans. The porch could be turned into a chapel, the bedroom into a dormitory, and so on. Sister Antonia, notwithstanding her mortified spirit, and confidence in her holy mother, protested that no efforts could make it habitable, and in this Fr. Julian agreed. Teresa, however, maintained her opinion, and would have spent the night there ; but the presence of a number of harvesters rendered this impossible. Our travellers, having no other shelter, took refuge in the church, and remained there till daybreak. " It must be admitted," the saint remarks, "that, fatigued as we were, we had more need of sleep than of vigils."

Teresa sent Fr. Julian the following day to Olmedo, to ask the Bishop of Avila for letters of recommendation for the Valladolid Foundation. Mgr. de Alvarez was deeply interested in this work on his brother's account, and in giving the necessary letters he charged his secretary to invoke the goodwill of the ecclesiastical administrator at Valladolid in favour of the Carmelites. Whilst these negotiations were going on, Teresa and Sister Antonia remained at Medina.

As soon as Fr. Anthony and Fr. John heard of the .saint's arrival, they hastened to see her. The holy mother described the monastery she had found for them without softening any details, and asked if they

had the courage to go there for a time. " God will certainly come to our assistance," she said; "the important point is to make a beginning. Are you ready to go?" The fathers answered with a fervour equal to her own, that they were willing to shut themselves up in a stable for the love of God. It was arranged, therefore, that Fr. Anthony should resign his office of prior into the hands of the provincial, and set his affairs in order ; and that Fr. John should follow the saint to Valladolid, and learn from her own lips the Rule of the Reform.

Early in August Teresa left Medina. " Make haste," our Lord had said to her whilst she was at prayer, " for the soul you will deliver is suffering grievously." Accordingly she made long stages on her journey in spite of the great heat. She was accompanied by Sister Antonia, two nuns from Medina, and two more from the Incarnation, as she relied on finding accommodation in Don Bernardino's house ; but more misfortunes awaited her there. She found a large and fine garden, but an unhealthy house at the edge of the river. Her poor daughters would certainly lose their health in such a spot; and, moreover, the house was uninhabitable till some indispensable repairs had been carried out. It was the Feast of St. Lawrence (August loth), and the Mass bell was ringing in a convent of Carmel of the mitigated Rule at the entrance of the town. Teresa began by taking her daughters there, and seeking at her Master's feet the light she required for her future guidance. On her return she set to work to improvise cells and make all necessary changes, and before long monastic life was resumed, the cares and anxieties falling, as they always did, to her share. Fr. Julian was still making efforts to get his negotiations carried through. The vicar-general, however,

could only hold out hopes ; he was awaiting the consent of a prelate of a neighbouring diocese who had jurisdiction over Valladolid. Sunday arrived, and Fr. Julian was allowed, on that day only, to say Mass in the temporary chapel. ' ' I believed, " the saint observes, "that when our Lord promised me to deliver the soul of Don Bernardino at the first Mass, these words would apply to the Mass which should be said when the Blessed Sacrament was reserved in our church. But at the moment of the Communion, when the priest gave me the sacred Host, Don Bernardino appeared at His side with his hands joined and his face radiant and shining. He thanked me for what I had done to get him out of purgatory, and I then saw him go up to heaven." Don Bernardino appears to have kept up his interest in the new Foundation, as he inspired his sister Dona Maria with a truly maternal love for the Carmelites ; and when some of the sisters were taken ill, in consequence of the unhealthiness of the site, she offered them a house in the town in exchange for that at Olmedo. Moreover, this generous benefactress took Teresa and her daughters to live with her whilst the house was being prepared for them, and even arranged that Fr. John should have a separate apartment in the neighbourhood, in order that the saint's instructions might not be interrupted.

The Carmelites' stay with Dona Maria was prolonged till February, and Teresa profited by the time of rest to occupy herself with her soul, her Foundations, her daughters, and her friends. Gratitude and affection have never stirred the heart, or found more vivid expression by the pen, of any human being than in the case of our saint. Witness the following letter to her old and faithful friend Don Francisco de Salcedo:—

" God be praised that, having written seven or eight letters on indispensable matters, I have a moment left to recreate myself with you, and to assure you of the consolation I receive from your letters. Do not think, I beg of you, that writing to me is time lost — I can assure you I feel the want of them, but it is on condition that you do not repeat so often that you are getting old, as that distresses me. Have young people any assurance of life either? I pray that God may preserve you till my death ; then once I get to Heaven know that, in order not to be there without you, I shall do my best to get our Lord to take you as quickly as possible. . . . What shall I say now about the six ducats you would give to see me? It is indeed a great deal, but I would give more (if I had it) for the pleasure of paying you a visit. In sober truth you are worth much more than I am. What is a little nun worth, who has nothing in the world? Who would think twice about her? But a gentleman who, besides all the good things and good drinks he gives us, can also supply us with radishes and lettuce out of his garden, and who, when he brings potatoes, will not employ any servant, I am told, but brings them himself, is worthy of much esteem. Apropos of drinks, I am told there are some excellent ones here, but as we have no Don Francisco de Salcedo, we have no idea how they taste, and are without hope of ever learning." 1

Teresa was much preoccupied at this time by a personal matter. When she had written her first history of her life at Fr. Ibanez's orders, it was with the intention of submitting it to Fr. John d'Avila, a holy Doctor of the Church whom Spain honoured under the title of the Apostle of Andalusia. This wish was not fulfilled at the time ; but when her second account was

1 Letters of St. Teresa, Valladolid, September, 1558.

written three or four years later, it was destined expressly for Fr. John d'Avila's approval. When she had finished it, therefore, she kept it till an occasion offered to send it to him. Dona Luisa de la Cerda's journey to Andalusia gave her this opportunity ; but apparently that lady did not use much diligence in acquitting herself of her task. She wished to become acquainted with the treasure confided to her care. Teresa reproaches her gently ; then she presses her ; finally, she conjures her to make haste over her commission, and above all to hide this precious deposit. " Remember," she says, "that it is in truth my soul which I have placed in your hands." She adds, " It would distress me greatly if he died before seeing my manuscript. Send it to him at once, I beg of you, well-sealed, by express." At last Dona Luisa performed her duty to Teresa's satisfaction, and the latter writes at once to her : " As for the book, you could not have done better, and I have instantly forgotten all my anger against you, caused by your delays. Fr. John d'Avila has written to me at great length. He is pleased with everything. God reward you for this good work."

This great man's decision in her favour reassured our saint. When she heard of his death, which occurred the following year, she expressed so much grief that her daughters asked her what made her mourn for one who probably at that moment was enjoying the happiness of Heaven. " Nothing is more true," she replied, "than that at this moment he sees God ; nevertheless, I weep because the Church has lost one of its pillars, and many souls, mine amongst the number, their guide and support."

Meanwhile the works at the convent of Carmel at Valladolid progressed by the aid of Dona Maria de

Mendoza's alms, and under her supervision. On the 3rd of February, 1569, the Carmelites went there in procession, preceded by the clergy and followed by all the people, whose enthusiasm equalled that shown by the inhabitants of Malagon. The monastery, by Dona Maria's desire, was dedicated to the Conception of Our Lady.

Teresa only waited long enough at Malagon to establish her daughters there. She was happy at leaving them in a good house — a community of excellent nuns all trained to a religious life; and, having appointed a prioress, she was able to give herself up to other works which then engaged her attention. To console Dona Maria, however, for her absence, she called her niece Sister Mary Baptist to Valladolid, and made her sub-prioress.

CHAPTER XVIII

FR. JOHN of the Cross, having followed the saint to Valladolid, began his novitiate at once under her direction. Assuredly it was a new thing to see a priest, and a religious, trained to the monastic life by a woman. Even more new and strange was it to see a woman undertake with her disciple's concurrence the reform of an Order for men. But this can only be explained—apart from the supernatural character of her mission—by the astounding force of character of the holy mother. An eminent ecclesiastic, 1 after an interview with her, had said : " They told me she was a remarkable woman ; it is nothing of the sort. She is a man, and a man such as I have never met before." To sum up her share in the foundation of the Order of discalced Carmelites, male and female, it might be said that the Carmelite nuns owed everything to their mother and foundress. The friars owed to her the idea and inspiration of the Reform, the initiation in the arduous enterprise, the spiritual training of their father St. John of the Cross, and finally the happy results of an influence which she exerted till the last day of her life over their monasteries. The trials of persecution and injustice which followed close on her death passed away, leaving the halo of martyrdom on her beloved sons, John and Gratian, but the saint's authority recovered all its power, and has never since lost it. Friars and

nuns of the Order of Carmel speak of her to this day with equal veneration and love as "our Mother" St. Teresa. Though she had therefore the greater share in the work of the Reform, she did not accomplish it alone. She performed it (as the Church's decrees set forth) Joanne adjutore; and what concerns us now is to trace the formation of a saint in the school of a saint.

St. John of the Cross was born in the poverty and obscurity which through life was so dear to him. His father, Gonzales de Yepes, though well born, had lost' whatever fortune he possessed, and was reduced to gaining his livelihood as a weaver; and his mother, Catherine Alvarez, was a simple peasant. John lost his father at an early age. Marvellous stories are told about his youthful piety and precocity, and on more than one occasion he was saved from imminent death by providential intervention. His pious and devoted mother gave him a good education, and at twenty-one he applied at the monastery of St. Anne at Medina for the habit of Mount Carmel. He was professed in 1564 at the age of twenty-three, and having showed great distinction in the schools, was sent to the university of Salamanca to finish his studies there. His life at Salamanca was divided between study and prayer, and as the day was not long enough to satisfy his fervour, he gave up the greater part of the night to prayer. The account given by his biographers of his austerities seems almost incredible to the modern mind. We read that he slept on faggots, and habitually wore a hair-shirt next to his skin, and an iron chain, bristling with rough points, round his waist. When the moment came for him to be ordained, like St. Francis of Assisi he alleged his unworthiness of this supreme dignity, and implored his superiors to pass him over, which, however,

they refused to do. He then returned to his convent at Medina del Campo to give his mother the consolation of assisting at his first Mass. Later on he resumed his theological studies, at the university—at which he had already gained the highest honours—by order of his superiors. But his soul was intent more on prayer than on learning, and it was at this time that he formed the project of joining the Carthusians. We have seen how his interview with Teresa at Medina led his thoughts into another channel. Whilst, therefore, Fr. Anthony was arranging his affairs, and occupied with the necessary formalities for the Foundation at Duruelo, Teresa took Fr. John with her to Valladolid, " in order," as she says, " to instruct him fundamentally on our Rule and usages. I spoke to him about the austerities in use with us, upon the fraternal charity which united us, the manner in which we spent our recreations—where all is regulated in such a manner that those hours of meeting help to open our eyes to our own defects, and yet serve to unbend the mind so that it may afterwards work all the harder to keep the severity of the Rule. Fr. John was so holy that I had much more to learn from him than he had from me. But that was not the question for the moment. I only thought of instructing him in the way of life led by our nuns." 1

The holy mother did not spare her fervent novice. She wished to assure herself of the stability of his character, to sound the depth of his incomparable humility, and to test him with a view to ascertaining whether he would be equal to the trials which awaited him in the poverty and solitude of Duruelo. Fr. John came forth triumphantly from this severe probation, as we read in a confidential letter from Teresa to Don Francisco de

1 Foundations, ch. Vin.

Salcedo: " I beg of you show every kindness in your power to Fr. John. He is small in appearance, but, in my opinion, very great in the sight of God. He is a very wise man in spite of his youth, and it is impossible to doubt that the grace of God is with him. For though we have been tried in many ways by all these affairs, and I myself have been on more than one occasion annoyed with him, yet we have never discovered the smallest fault in him." The saint finishes the portrait she draws of the young priest with one characteristic touch : " He is full of courage/' Courage is what she always asks of her sons, as well as of her daughters. The Reform, she says, is a work of pain and difficulty : without courage and energy it is useless to embark upon it. " As for Fr. John, he will require all the gifts God has conferred on him to go and start his new life alone at Duruelo." Teresa accordingly judged her " half-religious" capable of beginning, alone, the Foundation; but she was still met by one obstacle. It was indispensable that she should, in accordance with the patents granted her by the Father-General, obtain permission from the late provincial of the Order as well as that of the one then in charge. Her recollections of the past did not inspire her with great confidence in Fr. Angelo de Salazar. However, it so happened, God permitting, that Dona Maria de Mendoza was in a position of being able to render service to the late provincial in some other matter, and she accordingly used this power to obtain the authorization desired by her friend. The Bishop of Avila was no less successful with Fr. Gonzales, an excellent old man who occupied the position of provincial at that time, and to whom Teresa wrote in such forcible terms-representing the account he would have to give for good hindered, should he oppose it — that he yielded at once to the bishop's request.

At last Fr. John started for Duruelo, accompanied by a young workman who was to make the house habitable. He took with him the habit of the Reform which Teresa had cut out and got ready with her own hands. " Since, Mother Teresa," he said upon taking leave of her, "you have had such a large share in the work I have undertaken, ask our Lord's grace and benediction upon me. I beg that you will give me your blessing as well, and that you and our sisters will sustain me by your prayers." Teresa, touched almost to tears, promised in her own name, and in her daughters' that they would recommend him each day to God ; and kneeling at his feet she, in turn, asked his blessing. 1

Fr. John on arriving at Duruelo made it a duty to follow out carefully the plans sketched by the saint. The porch was turned into a church, the garret into the choir, the bedroom was divided into two cells, which were so low and narrow that it was with difficulty that anyone could turn round in them. He made beds out of straw, with stones for pillows, and having made a cross out of two bits of rough wood, he hung it, with a skull, to the wall. The kitchen utensils consisted of two broken pitchers which had been thrown away as unserviceable. A trunk of a tree served as table in the refectory, and a broken jug and two pieces of calabash as a bottle and glasses. The night surprised him before he had finished his work, or thought of his dinner. The workman who accompanied him went into the village to beg a few bits of bread ; and so great was the charm of the saint's conversation, and his kindness, that the man never thought of complaining of his hard fare. Fr. John passed a part of the night in prayer. The next morning he said Mass at day-

1 Foundations; ch. xin.

break, and then after blessing the habit of the Reform, which consisted of a tunic, and scapular of rough serge, and a narrow short cloak of white material, he assumed the humble garb with the same pride that a courtier might take in putting on his king's uniform. He resolved also to go barefoot instead of wearing the sandals, or alparagatas, which Teresa had adopted for herself and for her daughters, and which was the footgear of the Spanish poor. The inhabitants of the hamlet were at first astounded at this strange figure, but it was not long before he found his way to their hearts, and soon his hermitage became a place of pilgrimage for miles around. They assisted at his Mass, examined every corner of his little abode, and then, forming in a circle round him, used to ask him to speak to them about the love of God.

Teresa followed the early beginnings of the young friar with a mother's interest, and praised God for them. Fr. Anthony came at the end of November to take the saint's orders ; he was in haste to join Fr. John and to take him the alms he had collected. The holy mother laughed heartily when she found that these alms consisted of five hour - glasses. "What on earth will you do with so many hourglasses?" she exclaimed. "I shall use them to mark the time, so that the hours of the community may be well kept," was his answer. " Yes, but the hour-glasses will be no use in telling you the dinner hour, or the time to go to bed !" Fr. Anthony had not provided himself with more furniture than money. He had not even a mattress. He set out for Duruelo, however, as cheerfully as if he expected to reach heaven the same day—his fifty-seven years and all his memories of the past forgotten ! Scion of a great family, consecrated to our Lady by a holy mother at ten years of age,

a prior at twenty-six, and since then charged successively with the government of more than one monastery, favoured also by the king, and enjoying a reputation of being a great preacher and a worthy religious—his life till then had been wanting neither in dignity nor in independence. His prudent friends advised him to take time and thought before definitely embracing the Reform, but his fervour admitted of no suspense or delay.

The day after his arrival at Duruelo was the first Sunday in Advent. Having said Mass he knelt with Fr. John at the foot of the altar, and both, in the presence of God and His angels, and of our Lady the Queen of Carmel, solemnly renounced the mitigated Rule, and vowed to live henceforth according to the primitive Observance. Then, following the custom introduced by cur saint, they adopted fresh names, Fr. Anthony calling himself Anthony of Jesus, Fr. John Mathias, that of John of the Cross, and a brother who had followed Fr. Anthony from Medina calling himself Joseph of Christ. Three months later circumstances enabled Teresa to visit her "dear little house at Duruelo."

" Being in that neighbourhood," Teresa relates, " in the Lent of 1569, I stopped to see them. I arrived in the morning, and found Fr. Anthony, cheerful as usual, employed in sweeping in front of the church. t What is this I see?' I exclaimed; * where is now your regard for appearances ?' ' A plague upon the time when I used to trouble my head with such ideas,' he answered, laughing. I then entered the chapel and was moved to tears when I saw the spirit of poverty with which our Lord had filled him. I was not the only one who was touched by it. Two friends of ours, merchants who had accompanied us from Medina del

Campo, who went over the house with us, could not keep back their tears. There was nothing to be seen in it but crosses and deaths' heads. I shall never forget a little wooden cross suspended near the holy-water stoup on which a print of our Saviour had been pasted ; this picture was of paper, but it inspired more devotion than if it had been beautifully carved. The choir was the former garret, which was raised in the centre, so that the fathers could recite their office with tolerable ease, but they had to stoop in order to enter it. They had contrived to fit in two little hermitages in the angles of the choir on each side of the church, but they were so low that they could only sit or lie down in them, and then they almost touched the roof with their heads. The ground was so damp that it had to be covered with hay. I was told that instead of going to bed after Matins our fathers used to retire to these hermitages, and remain there till Prime, and such 'was their recollection that when the snow fell upon them from holes in the roof they did not even so much as notice it."

These pious excesses had the effect of alarming the holy mother. She was in favour of great austerity, but she would have wished to have seen it regulated by prudence. The fathers having consulted her on several points of the Rule, she gave them her advice, "then, weak and imperfect as I am," she adds, "I thought it right to conjure them to moderate the severity of their penances. . . . For, seeing the work so well started, I feared that the devil might urge the fathers to excessive austerities, injurious to their health, and so bring it to nothing. Such fears, as I have said, came from my want of perfection and little faith. As they had those virtues in which I was wanting, they paid little attention to my words, and went on with

their practices. I bade them farewell, and went away greatly consoled by what I had seen."

Before following Teresa to Toledo (whither she was going), let us give one glance at the subsequent history of the discalced Order of Carmel. Speaking of this Reform the saint says : " What acts of thanksgiving I owe to God on this matter, for to my thinking this was a much greater favour than to be allowed to found convents for nuns ! " Who realized better than she did that the flame of divine love, the spirit of prayer and self-sacrifice, burned no less in the heart of the friar than in that of the nun. Prayer was likewise the food of his soul— silence his strength, penance his armour ; but he was an apostle as well as a contemplative. It was his mission to leave his cell, and go forth to the world, where the austerity visible in his appearance, and the holiness of the life he led, added tenfold to the strength of his words. His vocation was to mix in the thickest of the fight, and bear himself as a valiant leader against the enemies of God and His Church. In the future he was to take part in the labours of the ministry in distant lands, as well as in the cities of Christendom. Can we wonder that the heart of the saint bounded with joy at such a prospect, for who appreciated the double vocation of her sons as she did? Henceforth she might console herself, for, though but a woman, and incapable of announcing God's truth to man, she was destined to be the mother of many generations who would continue this great work through the centuries with equal learning and zeal. But the enterprise would succeed at the cost of great suffering. She will have to suffer, as we shall read later on, from violent persecutions raised by the mitigated Order of Carmel against the reformed. She will also suffer from the inflexibility

of character of some of her own children. These are the shadows in a great picture — shadows caused by a frailty which is never absent from human undertakings, but which only causes the holiness and beauty of God's saints to shine out with greater brilliance. In summing up the difficulties Teresa had to encounter, we must also take into account the advantages she was to enjoy. She built her Reform on a soil watered by the blood of martyrs. Spain had but lately emerged from the trials of Moorish oppression, and at that time offered a splendid field to anyone who knew how to capture its resources in order to utilize them for the service of God. The saint found no difficulty, therefore, in implanting the primitive Rule in the Order of Carmel. The zeal and penitential fervour of her children, as we have seen, went far beyond her expectations, or even her desires. Other monastic virtues were practised with equal fidelity. Excess, want of discretion, were the defects Teresa saw in these early leaders of the Reform. She fought long against the dangers she foresaw in this direction, but it would have been an easier task to make martyrs out of these fiery Castilians than meek and submissive men. St. John of the Cross was ever to be her chief hope and consolation in these trials. She was also to find support later on in Fr. Jerome Gratian, her last spiritual director, and her well-beloved son. In Fr. Anthony she also found a valuable auxiliary. Many others were of the utmost assistance to her, and though not all were perfect, still, she saw so much good in all, that she was wont to thank God till her latest day for the helpers she had found for her great work of Reform ; and to say that she had no greater desire than that it should preserve the fervour of its first members.

The monastery of Duruelo was transferred the following year to the village of Manzera, Don Luis de Toledo, a wealthy nobleman, having offered them a house and church there. The fathers continued to lead the same penitential lives at Manzera that they had previously done at Duruelo, preaching in the neighbouring hamlets wherever spiritual succour was needed, and walking great distances barefoot, even in the depths of winter, through snow and ice, to instruct children and carry consolation to the sick. Their days were spent in preaching and hearing confessions. They only returned at nightfall to the monastery in order to partake of their frugal meal. The recitation of the divine office occupied a great part of the night, and the early mornings were given up to prayer.

Novices, who came to them in great numbers, were handed over to the care of Fr. John of the Cross. The Foundation at Pastrana took place in the year 1571, and the noviceship was transferred there shortfy afterwards.

CHAPTER XIX

TERESA set out for Toledo on the 2ist of February, 1569. She visited the monasteries of Medina del Campo and Duruelo on her way, spent some days at St. Joseph's, Avila, and started again on the 15th of March, taking with her two nuns from the last mentioned house, and accompanied by a firm friend of the Reform, Don Gonzalez d'Aranda. Her chaplain, Fr. Julian d'Avila, had been detained by business at Valladolid.

The journey was a lengthy one, as they had to go out of the direct route in order to reach Madrid, where Teresa was awaited by Princess Juana, a sister of Philip II, who had asked for an interview with her. It was accomplished, like the other journeys which she was constantly undertaking, in such a manner as to interfere as little as possible with the exercises of religious life, and the life of prayer habitually led by her. St. Gregory of Nyssa, when travelling with his companions through the deserts of Arabia to the sounds of psalms and canticles of praise, said that his chariot served him as church and monastery. It was the same with Teresa and her daughters ; the interior of her humble coach, or litter, was for the time a convent. She carried holy water with her, a statue of the Infant Jesus, and a bell to ring when the time came for prayer, divine office, or silence. An hour-glass measured the time. As soon as the bell rang, the saint's companions, whether religious or secular, ceased their conversations. It was an amusing sight to wit-

ness the rejoicings of the latter, Ribera remarks, when the bell rang to announce the end of silence; and Teresa would sometimes reward them for keeping it well with little gifts, or an addition to their modest fare.

The nights were spent in the inns. The nuns on descending from their coaches covered their faces with their veils, and shut themselves up together in one room, a nun being stationed at the door as portress to receive communications, so that the recollection of the rest had not to be disturbed for every trifling occur-ence. Teresa watched over everything, was the first to rise to waken her daughters, the last to seek repose. The priest who accompanied them said Mass every day, and the nuns communicated on the days appointed by the Rule. Their holy mother kept their fervour alive by her example and her words. The sense of the presence of God in her soul appeared to strengthen in proportion with the distractions which multiplied outside her. Her words and looks, the expression of her countenance, seemed to say at all moments to her daughters: God is present. The incidents of the journey—whether it was a river they had to ford, a mountain which they had to climb on foot, a beautiful view, a sunset, a storm, even the dust and inconveniences of travel—served as occasions for her to raise her soul to God in praise of Him, or in acts of resignation to His Will. On one occasion she composed a hymn, in which she recalled the journey of Moses through the desert, and the travels of the Divine Master on the road of penance and poverty. The refrain was as follows : —

Caminemos para el cielo Monjas del Carmelo. 1

1 Nuns of Carmel ! Onwards march to Heaven.

To travel with Teresa was indeed a joy ; so that, in spite of the hardships which attended each Foundation, the nuns whom she chose for this office looked upon it as a favour of which they deemed themselves unworthy. She carried alone the weight of the sacrifices which these undertakings involved, and whilst she was nourishing the souls of her companions, and watching over them with a mother's care, her own soul was harassed by business of every kind, and she was sighing for the solitude of her little cell at Avila, and asking God when it would please Him to recall her there, and leave her to peace and recollection.

One day when this desire was pressing heavily on her, our Saviour found fault with her for it. "Daughter," He said, "understand this, that merit does not consist in enjoying great consolation in prayer, but in doing My will." Only a short time previously her Divine Master had explained what was His will in her regard. "It is not time now for you to take your rest," He had said to her whilst she was making her thanksgiving, "but to hasten to found more monasteries in which I may take My repose in the souls which shelter there." 1

With Teresa, as she had been heard to say with holy pride, to know the Will of God was to obey it, in spite of every obstacle which could be thrown in her way. Her path was sown with hardships and obstacles in every fresh undertaking, and these she encountered with the same calm serenity as she did the applause which followed these achievements when her efforts had been crowned with success.

Teresa, on her arrival in Toledo, was received by Dona Luisa de la Cerdawith her usual cordiality; but having already endowed the convent at Malagon, that lady made

her no offer of assistance in her new enterprise at Toledo. The saint, who was averse to importuning anyone, especially one who had already conferred great benefits on,her, had recourse to Alonso Ramirez, a merchant of Toledo, with whom she had already been in correspondence with a view to the proposed Foundation. Alonso Ramirez, in pressing Teresa to build a convent at Toledo, was following out the wishes of his brother Martin, who six months previously had on his death-bed laid this injunction upon him. She found a good friend in Alonso, but unfortunately he was much under the influence of his son-in-law, Diego Ortiz, who was less easy to deal with. The latter was a man of property, with literary tastes and a turn for theology, and much wedded to his own opinions. The result was that his stipulations for the Foundation were quite inadmissible, and Teresa left him in despair, being unable, as she says herself, to bring him to reason. Whilst waiting to come to terms with Ramirez and Ortiz, the saint set to work to find a temporary abode, and also to get the necessary authorizations from Don Gomez Tello Giron, who governed the diocese at that time, the Archiepiscopal see being vacant. She was met at first by a refusal, and, to complete her misfortunes, Alonso was induced by his son-in-law to withdraw his promise of assistance. What was to be done? Struggle on, suffer, endure wearisome delays, or retreat ? Teresa never hesitated, for were not the interests of God involved? Accordingly she set to work to overcome the greatest obstacle by gaining the consent of Don Gomez. In this she was helped by Dona Luisa and other influential friends, but the Governor showed no signs of yielding. Finally, Teresa asked an audience of him at a neighbouring church. Don Gomez consented, and as soon as the

saint saw him she went straight up to him: " My lord," she said, " here have I been waiting for over two months, not in order to take my pleasure in your town, but in order to seek God's glory in it, and the good of souls. It would have been worthy of you, and of the authority in which you are invested, to protect poor women who only ask to lead penitential lives. Truly it is hard to find no one who will support us, but to see, on the contrary, that those who live for their own pleasure seek to put obstacles in a work so pleasing to God. Know this, my lord, that we have nothing to lose by going away and taking up our abode elsewhere, but you will have to answer before the judgment seat of God for the loss sustained in this town, if you do not cease struggling against a work of God, and one which you are bound to support."

Don Gomez, far from resenting Teresa's plain language, was so much struck by it that he granted her the necessary license at once, on condition that the convent should have neither endowment, patron, nor founder. The saint willingly consented. She had but three ducats in the house, but money with her never counted for anything in her difficulties. " Teresa and three ducats," she said, "are good for nothing. But God, Teresa, and three ducats can do all things." It was on these principles that the saint founded the convent of Toledo. More disappointments were in store for her. A merchant came to her assistance, and undertook to provide her with a house. But before he could do so he was taken ill. Teresa redoubled her prayers, but it appeared as if God wished to try her even at the very foot of the altar. One day, when she was making her thanksgiving after Mass, a peasant woman attacked her by showering blows upon her head with her wooden clogs. Teresa, roused

from her prayers, looked at her without even remonstrating, and then, turning to her two companions who rushed to her defence, remarked with a smile : " May God forgive the good woman ! I had quite enough pain in my head already." The explanation was simple. The poor woman had lost one of her shoes, and seeing the poverty of the saint's garments, took her for the thief.

After this adventure Teresa might have had reason to distrust another encounter, which took place shortly afterwards in the same church. A poor youth of modest but unattractive appearance came up to the saint and put himself at her service, explaining that his confessor had told him to help her in any way in his power. Teresa appears to have been puzzled to know what she could do with him. "Andrado," she says, "had nothing in his appearance suggestive of his being of any use to Carmelite nuns." Nevertheless she thanked him graciously, and to please him took his address. She and her daughters amused themselves afterwards with the recollection of the grand protector who had been sent them. Still, an instinct told her that the young man had not been sent her by a holy religious without a secret design of Providence. Her daughters continued to make jokes about Andrado, but without paying attention to them Teresa sent for him and asked him to find them a house. Nothing was more easy, he declared ; and the following day, the I3th of May, whilst Teresa was assisting at Mass, Andrado came in search of her, told her that he had found a house, and presented her with the keys, so that she might ascertain at once if it were suitable for her purpose. Teresa was enchanted. "Praised be God!" she cried; "here have the rich people of Toledo been looking about for a house for

us for three months, and never found one, any more than if there had not been a house in the city. This young 1 man appears, who had nothing to recommend him but his poverty, and God so arranges that he finds one at once." Andrado then offered to help the nuns to transport their furniture to their new abode. " As to that, my good Andrado," answered Teresa, " it will not take you long ; two mattresses and a quilt is all the furniture we possess."

Teresa with her three ducats bought two little pictures for the chapel, and paid for her mattresses. One of Dona Luisa's ladies, who seems to have better realized the state of Teresa's affairs than her mistress, offered her on parting a loan of a hundred reals. This sum was all that our saint took with her to her new abode, and it enabled her to employ some workmen to make ready the chapel, the same night, for Mass on the following day. An altar was improvised, and decorated with a few ornaments borrowed from a neighbouring church. One difficulty remained : it had no door open to the public. It was found necessary to make an entrance through the wall of a neighbouring cottage. More difficulties presented themselves. Finally, Teresa was successful in appeasing the wrath of the neighbours by promising indemnification. Peace was restored, and all was ready when morning came. The prior of the monastery of Carmel celebrated Mass. Each successive Foundation was marked by a progress in poverty and humility. The bell which weighed three pounds at St. Joseph's was replaced here by a sacristy bell. Its little tinkle attracted some passers-by, amongst whom was a little child, who called out loudly, "God be praised, what a fine sight!" Teresa was much touched. " Yes, my daughters," she said, " let us praise God. If we had only gained this praise

to God which has just come from the lips of this little angel, we should be well recompensed for all our trouble." The news of the Carmelite Foundation was soon spread far and wide. It is said that a great disaster to the town had been prophesied, and its accomplishment was expected on that day. Many had been to confession and prepared for death as if the end of the world were at hand. When instead of the destruction of the town they heard that a new monastery of Mother Teresa's Reform was founded, they gave thanks to God. 1

Troubles soon recommenced. The council, in the Governor's absence and unaware of his permission, were indignant at Teresa's audacity in opening her chapel, and refused permission for Mass to be celebrated a second time in it. The saint submitted with her usual meekness. Don Manrique, however, took her cause in hand, and laid the patents before the council by which Teresa was authorized to found monasteries in any part of Castile. A Dominican friar, a friend of the Governor's, made himself responsible for the promise given by the latter. By degrees matters settled down, and the Carmelites were allowed to live and pray in peace. Their poverty did not cease so quickly; for months they were left wholly without resources. One blanket was still all the bedclothes they possessed. At night the two young nuns spread it on their mother's bed, assuring her that with her fifty-five years it was impossible for her to dispense with a covering, and contented themselves with their choir mantles. One night, noticing that Teresa was shivering in an ague-fit, they covered her up with their mantles as well. Teresa, not perceiving what they had done, and still shivering, remarked, " My daugh-

1 Hist, of the Order.

ters, could you not give me some blankets to cover me? I feel so cold." "Alas! reverend mother," they answered, " do not ask for any more, for you have got all the warm clothes of the monastery upon you." The saint could not refrain from laughing, and used often to tell this story against herself in after days.

The food was on a par with the furnishings. One dav an egg, on another a sardine, had to be divided into three. On one occasion, when there was no wood in the house, a faggot was deposited by an unknown hand in the chapel. They had to borrow a pot in order to boil the water ; the salt had to be ground with a stone. They had no lights ; in fact they had nothing, absolutely nothing, and this poverty was a cause of intense joy to them. Teresa gives us an account of the privations they endured, in order to praise God for the generosity of her daughters ; to complain of anyone does not enter into her head. On the contrary, she seeks to excuse her dear friend who allowed her to suffer want within a hundred yards of her palace. "God permitted it," she says, "in order to acquaint us by experience with the sweetness of poverty. It is impossible to explain otherwise what happened, for this great lady was very fond of me, and had always treated me very generously. But I asked nothing from her, for I could not endure being a trouble to her, and luckily for us she never discovered our utter destitution. We found such interior consolation and joy in this poverty that I can never think of it without admiring the manner in which God has hidden all true riches in the practice of these virtues."

God having thus tried the courage of His servants showed that He was watching over their Foundation. Alonso Ramirez, who had riot ceased regretting the

way our saint had been treated, persuaded his son-in-law to be more conciliatory, and himself sent them large alms. Teresa received them with as much sadness as if she had been robbed of a treasure, and her daughters partook of her regrets. 1 She more than once refused gifts which did not accord with her love of poverty. When a novice who wished to join the community sent her furniture beforehand, Teresa returned it, saying that if she filled the convent with her tables and chairs there would be no room for her in it.

Alonso Ramirez, besides his own personal gifts to the monastery, wished to carry out his brother's intentions with regard to it. The monastery had, however, been started without his concurrence, and on conditions stipulated for by the Governor ; it was therefore impossible for Teresa to confer the title of founder on him. She, however, proposed to allow the Ramirez family to build the chapel attached to the future monastery, in which the Masses founded by the late Martin Ramirez should be said in perpetuo. Fresh obstacles intervened, this time from the aristocracy of Toledo. A personage of high rank having made a similar offer to Teresa was indignant at being passed over on account of the claims of a simple merchant. Teresa cared little for this opposition. " Thanks be to God," she exclaims, "I have ever put virtue above rank." Nevertheless, the Ramirez family now put forward a claim to the right of sepulture in their chapel. Assailed by all these conflicting appeals and by contradictory advice, Teresa had recourse to our Lord in prayer. "Tell me," she implored, "what am I to do?" The answer she received was: "What folly, My daughter, to trouble about worldly vanities! Cast your eyes upon Me.

Behold My poverty and how I was despised by the world ! Do you think the great ones of this world are great in My sight? And you, is it by your titles or your merits you will be judged? Ah, My daughter, what attention will be paid at the last day to pedigrees and possessions ? " " This rebuke confused me utterly," Teresa relates. "I resolved to conclude my arrangements with Alonso Ramirez, and to allow him to build the chapel; and I had no reason to regret it, as by reason of his help we were able to buy one of the best houses in Toledo." 1

The Carmelites were unable to transfer their abode to this new house before April, 1590. Teresa took some nuns from Malagon to the new Foundation. She also received, at their own request, some nuns from the Convent of the Incarnation. Only one of these persevered, the others renouncing after a short trial a life to which they were unsuited, and the severity of which was beyond their strength. The holy mother, enlightened by experience, later on added a clause to her Constitutions whereby admission was refused to nuns coming from any other Order, including that of the mitigation.

Teresa received much consolation from the novices who presented themselves at the convent at Toledo. One of these she had objected to, though her admission from a pecuniary point of view would have benefited the community, on account of her delicate health ; she was also forty years of age. In spite of these misgivings, which Teresa did not hide from her, the novice made over all her fortune to the Foundation some months before her profession. When the saint asked her what she should do at her age, if, in consequence of her generosity, she was left penniless, the

answer she received was: "I shall beg my bread for the love of God." Her fervent desires were heard, and she received her recompense ; for her health improved in spite of the austerity of her new life, and she lived for many years afterwards to edify her sisters in religion.

Teresa was not able to take pleasure for long in the fervour of her daughters of Toledo. She was called to other Foundations which required her care at this time ; but her journeys often recalled her to their midst, and whether absent or present she was ever occupied with their welfare. Few other Foundations gave her more cause of anxiety. Diego Ortiz continued to show the same obstinacy, and pious greed that he had done from the beginning. At one time he stipulated for sung Masses ; at another he desired that the hour of vespers should be altered. Again, he asked for other things incompatible with the Constitutions. Teresa maintained her rights with firmness, and yet with a tact which her position with regard to Ortiz, and her obligations to him, rendered absolutely necessary.

On one occasion, after receiving a letter from Ortiz written in his usual rapacious style, she sends him the following charming reply: " You do me so much favour, and show such charity in writing to me, dear sir, that even if your letter had contained severer remarks I should have received it with gratitude. The reasons you give are so powerful, and you put them so strongly, that I have nothing to urge against them. I do not wish, therefore, to allege reasons. But like one whose case is weak I wish to seek protection by asking for an arbiter, and I desire no one else but yourself for that post. It is a consolation to me to believe that we could not do anything more advantageous than to place our interests in your hands

and those of Senor Ramirez. Will you then be so good as to decide after consulting with him? I shall never be displeased with any letter I receive from you, as I know with what good intention it is written. Only one thing would pain me, and that is to cause you any pain or that my daughters should be the cause of any pain to you." [1] By degrees difficulties were smoothed ; Diego Ortiz found it impossible to hold out against such tact and amiability. As for his father-in-law, nothing could shake his feelings of veneration for the saint, and her letters to him are full of grateful affection. " May God preserve your health, dear sir," she writes on one occasion, " so that you may live to enjoy the church, which I am told is going to be so fine. . . . How often I think of you, and how often I bless you, remembering that with you a promise made even in jest one may look upon as good as accomplished. I pray our Divine Master to preserve you for long years, and to grant me the pleasure of seeing you again, for I love you in Him. I embrace in spirit your little angels, and pray that they may become great saints."

The tact and firmness which Teresa showed in the above correspondence were no less needed for the Foundation which followed closely on that of Toledo.

Much remained to be done after the Carmelites had moved into their new house. "It was necessary," Teresa writes, "to arrange the church, put up the convent grille, and get things in order. We found much to do, and I was looking after workmen from morning to night. At last, on the eve of Whit-Sunday, all was finished, and on the day of the feast, when I went into the refectory to dinner, I felt much consolation in the thought that, having no longer anything on my mind, I could rejoice a little in our Lord's

presence. My soul took such pleasure in this that I could scarcely eat. I was unworthy of such happiness. They came to tell me that a courier had arrived from the Princess of Eboli. I went to speak to him, and he told me he had come to take me to the Foundation at Pastrana—one which had been already agreed upon between us, but which I did not think I should have to carry out so soon. This unexpected message surprised and distressed me. It appeared very difficult to me to leave a monastery which had only just been founded, and founded under such difficulties. I made up my mind to refuse, and told the envoy so. The man remonstrated strongly, protesting that it would be an insult to his mistress if I did not go, as she had come to Pastrana on my account, and was expecting to meet me there.'" [1]

Teresa promised to explain her reasons to the princess in a letter, but apparently she had some difficulty in satisfying her messenger, who " stood upon his dignity," as the saint informs us. Before writing she went to prostrate herself before the Blessed Sacrament, to implore our Lord to dictate the terms of her message, so that she might not offend this personage whose favour, or disfavour, might influence greatly the cause of the Reform. The Princess of Eboli occupied a great position at Philip IPs court; her husband, Prince Ruy Gomez, was the king's chamberlain, and both enjoyed that monarch's favour. Whilst Teresa prayed with this intention, our Lord signified to her that it was His wish that she should start at once for Pastrana, and take the Rule and Constitutions with her. " For," He said to her, "it is question of a matter of even greater importance than the foundation of a Carmelite convent."

1 Foundations, ch. XVII.

Teresa then consulted her confessor, without, however, confiding to him what our Lord had said to her, and on receiving the same advice from him she started the following day for Pastrana. She passed once more through Madrid, and received hospitality from Dofia Leonor de Mascarenas, who, at that time in her character of foundress, lived at the convent of our Lady of the Angels. Dona Maria took occasion of the saint's visit to make her acquainted with Ambrogio Mariano; and Teresa, as soon as she had heard the history of this remarkable man, felt he might be of use to her in her great undertaking.

Ambrogio Mariano was an Italian of'high birth, who had as a young man occupied an important post at the court of Queen Katherine of Austria. Disgust of the world, and a desire for military distinction, caused him to leave her service. He joined the Knights of Malta, was made a commander, and his exploits, especially at the battle of St. Quentin, when he headed the Spanish troops, covered him with glory. But God had designs on his great soul, and as He had previously weaned him from the world's pleasures, He now detached him from its honours. He was falsely accused of complicity in a murder, and thrown into prison, in which he languished for ten years, and during which time he made no effort to defend his cause, esteeming himself happy in imitating his Divine Master. When his innocence was brought to light he spent large sums in trying to defend his accusers. Philip II, having become acquainted with his history, called him to his court and made him governor to his son ; but God had a better recompense in store for His servant. Mariano made a retreat under the Jesuits at Cordova, and on coming out of it he renounced his appointment, and fled to the desert of Tardon to join a company of

hermits under a holy superior, Fr. Mathias. Teresa shall tell us the result of her interview with him.

" Fr. Mariano told me about the holy life led by the hermits. They had their cells apart, and took their meals in it. They did not recite divine office together, only meeting in the oratory for Mass. They had no endowment, nor were they allowed to ask for alms ; they lived in great poverty by the work of their hands. Fr. Mariano had lived thus for eight years when he heard of the decree of the Council of Trent, which obliged all hermits to join a religious Order. When we met him he was on his way to Rome to beg the Pope to make an exception in favour of the hermits of Tardon. When he had finished speaking I showed him the primitive Rule, and pointed out to him that in joining the Order of Carmel he might go on with the same way of life he had led in his desert, particularly as regards manual labour, a practice to which he specially clung. He told me he would take a night to think it over. I saw that he had almost made up his mind, and I remembered the words our Saviour had addressed to me. . . . During the night our Lord spoke in such a manner to him that he came the following day to announce his decision to me. He told me he could not understand the change that had come over him, especially through the instrumentality of a woman. He repeated the last word several times—as if it was not God alone who changes and moves the hearts of man ! " Mariano was accompanied by another hermit, a young man who, though simple and ignorant as a child in some matters, was very enlightened on divine things. His name, Fr. John de Miseria, was as humble as his person. Fr. John adopted Mariano's plans directly he was informed of them ; the two religious, however, asked Teresa if she would not found a new

monastery at Pastrana, in a fine hermitage which had been given them by Prince Ruy Gomez, instead of sending them to Mancera. Teresa was delighted at the suggestion, and wrote at once to the two provincials for the necessary authorization. Meanwhile she left Mariano at Madrid, and went on to Pastrana.

The princess gave her at first a good reception, and the prince showed her much deference and genuine satisfaction at the proposed Carmelite Foundation. They begged her to occupy an apartment in a retired part of the castle, while the workmen executed the necessary alterations in the convent under her eye. Difficulties soon arose. Teresa sums up the matter in a few words. She says: "I had no little to suffer, as the princess's demands were quite contrary to our Constitutions." It took the saint three months of struggle with the princess's whims to arrive at some tangible result. She first wished her to receive an Augustinian nun, who had left her convent at Segovia, without examination. Then, annoyed with the firmness displayed by the intrepid foundress, she refused to endow the convent, saying that it might live, as that of Avila had done, on alms. But, urged the prudent mother, in a village of the size of Pastrana, whence would the alms come? From their capricious benefactress? (she no doubt asked herself). In that case they would have a superabundance one day, and starve the next. In short, the saint declared that unless enough was settled on the convent for the Carmelites to live on, no Foundation should be made at Pastrana. The prince at last interfered. " He was a sensible man," Teresa observed, "and gave in to my reasons, and then caused the princess to do so likewise. I yielded on certain points because I was much more anxious about the establishment of a convent of friars

at Pastrana than I was about the one for nuns." She had also not had the same difficulty about the former. The provincials gave their consent. Fr. Mariano and Fr. John arrived soon-after and asked to be clothed. Teresa begged Fr. Anthony, who was then at Mancera, to come and give them the habit; at the same time she sent for two nuns from the convent of Medina. The nuns were accompanied by Fr. Baltasar, of the mitigated Rule, who wished to embrace the Reform. Teresa, having examined him, thanked God for having sent her a man of such merit and sanctity ; and, as Fr. Anthony still delayed his arrival, she begged Fr. Baltasar to give the habit to Mariano and his companions. When Fr. Anthony at last arrived, he found a. nucleus already formed by the holy foundress awaiting him at Pastrana. The Carmelite nuns were solemnly installed in their new convent on the gth of July, and the friars in theirs four days later.

The kind and generous dispositions of the prince and princess towards the new Foundations continued till the death of the former, which took place shortly afterwards. The princess, left to the guidance of her own fancies and a prey to grief, was soon to justify Teresa's misgivings in her regard.

Leaving an experienced nun from Avila, Mother Isabella of St. Dominic, at the head of the new community, the saint returned to Toledo. Here she refused to take the place of prioress, and Sister Mary of the Angels had to submit to occupy this post under the eye of the holy mother, who gave an example of humility and obedience to the young novices by joining them in choir and at recreation. Admirable object-lesson which she never ceased to render till the last day of her life ! Having used her talents and her untiring energy in founding a monastery, no sooner was the

work accomplished than the saint retired to the background, effacing herself before a simple nun whom she called mother, though she had but a little while before received her as a daughter, and trained her to the spiritual life. From this daughter she asked such permissions as were necessary to the performance of the duties of monastic life, and took pleasure in submitting her affairs and those of the monastery to her ; thus attaining a double end. In humiliating herself she initiated the young prioress in the government, and in the still more difficult task, the direction, of souls. She taught her to command with gentleness, and yet with firmness, and to make allowance for difference of character without diminishing the force of authority. She communicated to them her own breadth of views and her exquisite tact. It was thus she formed those great souls who, under the name of Mary Baptist, Mary of St. Jerome, Anne of Jesus, and countless others, governed the first convents of the Reform in a manner worthy of their holy mother herself.

During the six months Teresa spent at Toledo under obedience to Mother Anne of the Angels, her time was much taken up with her many Foundations. Many questions had to be settled and difficulties to be solved. Accordingly, writing to her brother, Lorenzo de Cepeda, she says : " It is well I should let you know that since God has given me the charge of establishing these houses—which indeed are His—I have become a woman of business to the extent that I know a little about everything. ... I must tell you that your money arrived just in time to free me from certain scruples. For I have frequently had difficulties in all these Foundations, upon which I make a point of consulting the best lawyers wherever I happen to find myself. I make it a duty to do this in all cases in which my

conscience is concerned. And though I try to be exact, and to do all for the best, nevertheless I reproach myself for being a little too generous as regards the fees of these consultations ; also in other little ways when I find it necessary to make presents. From this point of view, therefore, your money gave me pleasure in proportion to the annoyance I was spared had I had to borrow it, though plenty of people would have been ready to open their purses to me. However, I prefer being independent in order to be able to say what I like to these good folk. Would you believe it? My credit is so good that people trust me to the extent of one or two thousand ducats. Thus, in spite of the horror I have of money and business, it is our Lord's will that I should be occupied with nothing else. That is no small cross! Please God that I may procure Him some glory by carrying it." 1

Teresa was still occupied with the buildings which were being put up by Ramirez at Toledo, when she received a letter from Fr. Martin Gutierrez, rector of the Jesuit College, suggesting to her a Foundation at Salamanca, a town no less remarkable for its piety than for its learning. This proposition offered much attraction to the saint. In placing her modest house under the shadow of the great university, she ensured, what in her sight was no secondary concern, the direction of her nuns, in spiritual matters, by the first Spanish theologians, "for," she says, " piety without knowledge may lead to delusions ; and it likewise fosters silly puerile devotions in souls ; and from childish devotions good Lord deliver us ! De devo-ciones a bobas nos libre Dios! Again, Teresa perceived another and a most striking advantage which was likely to accrue from this scheme, and that was that it

1 Toledo, January i7th, 1570.

would pave the way for a Foundation of the friars of the Reform ; a college for the training of their students in this centre of learning being essential for their success. In addition to this, though Fr. Gutierrez was unable to assist them pecuniarily, he put his credit and his advice at their service. This was worth more to them than any fortune, for the name of the holy and learned rector was venerated throughout Salamanca as that of a saint. Teresa answered that she would go to Salamanca as soon as circumstances made it possible.

When she had got all in good order at Toledo, she began a round of her other convents, so as to assure herself that nothing would suffer in her absence during the labours of the new Foundation. She revisited Medina del Campo, Valladolid, and Pastrana. Whilst she was at the convent of Pastrana she assisted, on the loth of July, at the professions of Fr. Mariano and Fr. John de Miseria. Fifteen days later she returned to Medina, where she had the following vision, which she confided to Fr. Baltasar Alvarez. 1

Whilst engaged in prayer on the Feast of St. Anne, 1570, she was transported in spirit to the Pacific Ocean, where a terrible scene of carnage was unveiled before her eyes. She saw forty sons of St. Ignatius, priests, scholastics, and novices, being massacred on board a ship which was taking them to Brazil. One commanding figure stood out amongst the crowd encouraging his brothers to suffer martyrdom for the faith, his voice dominating the cries of fury of the murderers, and the groans of the victims. " Let us die," he cried, " rather than surrender, as becomes children of God and sons of the Crusaders." Teresa recognized a relation in this sainted hero ; it was Francisco Perez Godoi, a

former pupil of Fr. Baltasar's. A little later she beheld, in a vision, his entrance into heaven, where he and his companions were gloriously rewarded with the crown of martyrdom.

News of the massacre of forty Jesuits reached Spain a month later. The ship they sailed in had been attacked near the Canary Islands by John Soria, a furious Lutheran who commanded a fleet of corsairs. In his zeal against the Catholic Church he did not allow any one of her faithful defenders to escape him. Fr. Baltasar, comparing the official account, which he received later on, with the one Teresa had given him, recognized the accuracy of her words in all particulars.

The saint's last halting-place was Avila. It was ever a fresh joy to her to return to her Bethlehem. The nuns, no less happy than their mother, came one by one to render an account of their souls to her. Some had difficulties in which they required her advice; others humbled themselves by confiding the weaknesses of which they had been guilty. Others asked her advice about prayer. Teresa gave each as much thought and attention as if she were occupied with the care of her soul alone. 1

The prioress, Mother Mary of St. Jerome, had received three novices in Teresa's absence. The saint had been interiorly enlightened about one of these, Anne de Lobera, besides knowing her slightly by reputation. Anne had been suggested as novice to Teresa by Fr. Rodriguez three months before her arrival. Contrary to her habit of receiving a postulant with prudent reserve, the saint had welcomed this one less as a subject than as a coadjutrix. Their first interview took place at St. Joseph's. Teresa, who loved great natures

1 Foundations.

only less than great virtues, found both one and the other in Anne of Jesus. She promised herself that in cultivating this valiant soul she would have one on whom she could depend in her old age, and who, God helping, would prove a powerful support to the Reform.

'THERESA spent three months at St. Joseph's Avila, 1 during which time she prepared for the Foundation at Salamanca. She wrote to Mgr. Gonzales de Mendoza, a prelate of illustrious birth and great personal merit, 1 for an authorization, which the bishop, having heard much in her favour from Fr. Gutierrez, granted her very willingly. A good-sized house was hired without any difficulty. Having been occupied by students, it was divided into many small rooms all opening into an inner court. The description given to Teresa of the building pleased her, as she saw some resemblance in it to the plan of a monastery. Unfortunately no one mentioned to her the neighbourhood of a sluggish stream which rendered the house damp and unhealthy ; a grave drawback, which her maternal eye was the first to discover. Everything being thus prepared beforehand, Teresa started at the end of October, taking Sister Mary of the Blessed Sacrament, an elderly nun of a somewhat timid disposition, with her as her sole companion. The night of the 3Oth was passed in a rough, covered litter ; the weather was cold, and the saint in a more than usually suffering state. Arriving about noon at Salamanca, she went straight to the inn, and sent for Nicholas Gutierrez, the father of two nuns of the Incarnation, and a very good friend

1 He had taken part in the Council of Trent, and on his return to Spain had exerted himself with as much zeal as prudence in executing its decrees.

to the Reform, to meet her there. This excellent man put himself entirely at her service. The first thing to be done was to get rid of the students, who still inhabited the house hired for the Carmelites. This being done (though not without difficulty), Teresa and her companion took possession of their new abode at nightfall. The students, we are told, had left the house in an indescribable state of filth and disorder, and the saint spent the night, in spite of her ill-health, in cleaning and sweeping. Sister Mary tried to be of as much use to her as her terror and her years permitted, but, as Teresa tells us, " she could not get out of her head that possibly some of the students, whom the people had such trouble in dislodging, were hidden in the many corners and garrets of the house." The situation had certainly a comic side to it, and Teresa, in spite of her fatigue, was amused at the idea u that the good sister at her age should be in such a mortal fear of students." The following night the saint had great need of rest. She was accustomed to provide herself on these occasions with straw, which she spread on the floor to sleep on, and Gutierrez having lent her blankets, she prepared two beds for herself and her companion. Instead of sleeping, however, Sister Mary appeared to be still a prey to fears. " What ails you, my daughter?" asked Teresa. " No one can possibly get in here ! " " Doubtless, mother," she replied; " but what troubles me is the thought of what you would do alone in the house, supposing I were to die to-night." It was the eve of All Souls, and at that moment every bell in Salamanca was tolling mournfully for the dead, and their sounds had, no doubt, impressed themselves on the imagination of the Carmelite nun. The saint admits she was not altogether insensible to their influence ; nevertheless, her answer was dictated by her

usual common sense. "Well, daughter, when this happens it will be time enough to think about it; meanwhile let us go to sleep." 1 This Foundation was attended by the usual difficulties. Winter set in, and the brook which flowed, or rather stagnated, close to the house made it insupportably damp, and its old and crumbling walls threatened to fall in and crush its inhabitants. It was impossible to offer our Lord a suitable abode in such a ruin, so that whilst the nuns stayed there, though Mass was said daily, it was only in the hearts of His servants that He could find a resting-place. Teresa sent to Medina for three nuns with whom to begin the new Foundation. Ana de Tapia, one of these nuns, had, with her sister Inez, embraced the Reform three years previously. Teresa had no hesitation in separating the sisters, for she knew them capable of any sacrifice, and leaving Inez de Jesus at Medina as prioress, she confided the same office to Anne of the Incarnation at Salamanca. She also sent to Avila for two novices; Teresa thought so highly of one of these, Anne of Jesus, that we shall find her henceforth constantly associated with the holy mother in all her undertakings. She gave Anne a bed in her own cell, thus admitting her into a most enviable intimacy ; by this means she became the recipient of the inmost confidences of a soul which she cherished in a special manner because she believed it to be one of predilection in the sight of God. This strong and supernatural affection, moreover, far from blinding her to her daughter's weaknesses, gave her an even greater insight into them, and a double courage in correcting them. We may be permitted to think that a ray of that prophetic spirit which the saint so often manifested, revealed to her that it was the destiny of

1 Foundations, ch. xix.

Anne of Jesus to carry the first light of sacrifice, and intercession and expiatory prayer, to that unfortunate country France, which the saint had so often wept over— a light which she had herself lit in Spain, and which had in all probability saved it from the heresies and divisions which overran Europe at this time.

The saint did not, as a rule, leave a new Foundation till it was provided with what was absolutely essential to its well-being ; but Salamanca, owing to the great pressure which was put upon her, was an exception ; and early in the year 1571 she left it for Alba de Tormes, where she established her eighth convent of Carmel. " She was about to erect her own sepulchre," an ancient biographer of Teresa tells us, "and to prepare, unknown to herself, a sanctuary in which pilgrims from Spain and other countries for succeeding ages would come and venerate the relics of her blessed body."

Scarcely fifteen miles separate Alba from Salamanca. This little town, situated on the western slope of a high hill, overlooks the majestic flow of the River Tormes. The castle of the Alba family, represented at that time by the conqueror of Miihlburg and viceroy of the Netherlands, stood on a high cliff to the right of the town. The peaceful waters of the great river washed the foot of the left slope, whilst the last spurs of the Guadarramas on the horizon must have recalled to Teresa the situation of her own town of Avila.

The installation of the Carmelites took place without obstacle, all the preparations having been made before the saint appeared on the scene. Her sister, Juana de Ahumada, and her husband, who had long been settled at Alba, had seconded the efforts of the founder, Francisco Velasquez, in preparing for Teresa' arrival.

Francisco Velasquez occupied the post of steward

to the Duke of Alba's vast estates. He and his wife, Teresa Laiz, having given up hope of posterity, resolved to consecrate their fortune to building a convent, whilst leaving the Carmelites their sole heirs. Teresa, in her Foundations, gives us the whole history of this excellent couple. Their lives had been passed in affluence and honour, but they had one drawback to their happiness, and it was a grievous one: they had no children. The desire for this blessing, which had been denied them, left them no rest. They multiplied their devotions, especially to St. Andrew, in order " to obtain children who after their deaths would continue praising the Lord." Finally, a vision gave a fresh direction to Teresa Laiz's desires. She saw herself seated in the balcony of her house at Salamanca, having in front of her the streets of the city. Suddenly the scene changed to a meadow enamelled with exquisite flowers—flowers such as were never seen blooming out of paradise. She saw a court on one side of the meadow surrounded by a gallery, a well, and various objects which she was to see later on. An old man of mild and venerable appearance, the Apostle St. Andrew, stood near the well, and, looking at her—who for so long had implored one favour from him—said, pointing to the flowers : " Here are indeed children, though not those you asked of me."

The heart of Teresa Laiz was filled with joy, and simultaneously the craving to become a mother left her. She confided the vision to her husband, and they both agreed in its interpretation. Accordingly they commenced searching for a community of nuns who would carry out the design which owed its inspiration to this heavenly dream. Six years passed, and still they were no nearer finding what they, sought. At the end of that time Francisco Velasquez, having been

appointed to the management of the Duke of Alba's affairs, took up his abode with his wife at Alba. Teresa Laiz had a great dislike to the town of Alba, and her distaste was not diminished when, on arriving at nightfall, she was inducted into a huge and ill-arranged house. Great was her joy, however, when the day broke, and she looked out of the window and recognized the well, the gallery, and all the other features of the scene she had been shown in her vision six years before. Teresa at once renewed her search with fresh ardour, and her confessor, who till then had been opposed to her designs, having, in the course of a journey he had undertaken about this time, heard of our saint, told his penitent that she could, not do better than make over her house to the Carmelites. Teresa Laiz, in this juncture of affairs, had recourse to Juana de Ahumada, who gladly undertook to serve as intermediary between the founders and her sister. Some preliminary difficulties intervened, but in the end Velasquez and his wife made over their own house to the Carmelites, taking up their abode in a much inferior one in the town. The Blessed Sacrament was solemnly carried into the chapel on the feast of the Conversion of St. Paul, January 25th, 1571, and the monastery was founded under the title of the Annunciation.

Teresa would willingly have spent a little time at Alba in her sister's society, and surrounded by kind friends. But a lengthened residence there was impossible to our saint when she thought of the privations which were being endured by her daughters at Salamanca. She wished to rejoin them early in February, and after summoning to Alba five or six nuns from the monasteries of Toledo and Medina, and appointing Mother Juana of the Holy Ghost prioress,

she set out for Salamanca. On arriving in the town, she was obliged to go first to the house of the Count de Monterey, by order of the provincial, the countess having obtained leave to receive a visit from the saint. This visit, which Teresa accepted out of obedience, God blessed by two miracles. On her arrival the countess begged of her to go and see a woman who had been long in her service, and who had been attacked by a violent fever, and was given over by the doctor. The instant Teresa laid her hand on the sick woman's forehead, she seemed to wake up from a deep sleep. She rose in her bed and exclaimed: " Who touched me? My illness is gone ! " Teresa, confused by the suddenness with which her prayer was heard, tried to pass off the invalid's exclamations as the ravings of one in delirium ; but the joy and gratitude of the poor woman, and the testimony of those who surrounded her, testified to the miracle which had been granted to the saint's prayers. Directly afterwards the countess's youngest daughter was attacked by the same fever. Again they had recourse to Teresa. This time Teresa's humility caused her to take precautions. Whilst she was praying for the child's recovery, St. Dominic and St. Catherine of Siena appeared to her, and promised the child's cure on condition she wore the Dominican habit for a year. Fr. Banez was living at Salamanca, and the saint confided the vision to him so that the conditions might be fulfilled without anyone suspecting whence the knowledge came. The good father undertook the commission ; the promise was made, and the precious child was restored to its parents' arms. Notwithstanding the care with which the secret was guarded, the child, when she was grown up to be a woman, always attributed her cure to Teresa's prayers ; and she transmitted to her son, the celebrated Olivarez, a devotion to the patron saint of Spain, and a love for the Carmelites of the Reform. 1

Teresa returned to her monastery as soon as she could escape from her kind friends. Though their generosity followed her there, nothing could remedy the evils from which the convent suffered. Nowhere was the situation of the Carmelites more deplorable ; a fact which decided Teresa to stay at Salamanca as long as circumstances permitted. Other crosses, and heavier ones, awaited her elsewhere, but God, before imposing them on her, wished to strengthen her by a succession of graces, thus preparing her for the ineffable joys and sorrows which the Lent of the year 1 571 was to bring her.

It is time for us to return to Teresa's interior life. Let us picture her to ourselves for the moment as having shaken the dust of the roads off her feet. The noise of trafficking is now far from her. Even the Foundations are for the moment forgotten. In the cell at Salamanca, at the foot of the tabernacle, Teresa of Jesus belongs to Him alone. She is His in prayer, as before she was wholly His in action. The saint passed the last days of Holy Week in that agonized state to which she gives the name, in mystical language, of "the absence of God." It is an indescribable pain, she says, one which it is in the power of none to invoke or to escape. The soul feels itself penetrated with so ardent a desire to see God that she is taken out of herself ; she longs to get rid of all creatures. God puts her interiorly into a desert —a desert of such a nature that it appears to her that nothing in the whole world could be any source of consolation to her, and that she has only one wish : to die in this solitude. Though God appears to be far removed from her, He sometimes discovers His sovereign grandeur to her in a manner

that goes beyond all imaginable thoughts of man, and this not to console her, but to show her how much reason she has to afflict herself for the absence of the Sovereign Good, Who embraces all good within Himself. Thus her sorrow grows with the light; her desire becomes so great, her solitude so profound, her torture so piercing, that she can say in truth with the royal prophet: " Vigilavi et factus sum siciit passer solitarius in tec to." 1

On one occasion, at the end of a day spent in this interior martyrdom, Teresa, having been told that the hour of collation was past, went out of obedience to the refectory. In spite of her loathing for food, " I tried," she says, " to overcome myself and took a piece of bread, and our Lord, appearing to me, broke and put it to my lips, saying : ' Eat, My daughter, so as to have strength for this time of trial. I suffer in your sufferings, nevertheless it is good for you to endure these things.' My sufferings soon left me," % Teresa says ; " I felt we were at one, and for the time all my longings were appeased." On the Feast of Palm Sunday, while still under the impression of this favour, she went to Communion, and it appeared to her as if her mouth, after receiving the sacred Host, was filled with the Precious Blood, and that all her being was immersed in it, and at once her soul tasted ineffable sweetness and joy. This sacred blood seemed to flow warm from the wounds of our Saviour. " Daughter," our Lord said to her, " I wish to apply the effects of My Blood to you ; fear not that My mercy will ever be wanting to you. I have shed it with much suffering, and it shall be a cause of great joy to you. This is My recompense for what you have done for Me this day." For thirty years Teresa had made a special preparation for

1 Life, ch. xx. 2 A

her reception of our Lord on Palm Sunday, so as to make up by the warmth of her welcome for the cold-heartedness of the Jews, who, though they greeted Him with Hosannas, neither invited Him into their houses, nor gave Him food to eat. "These were very childish considerations," she says, "yet our Lord deigned to show that He was pleased with them." 1

Holy Week passed in silence and recollection. She looked forward for consolation to the day of the Resurrection. It came, but still she mourned the absence of the Beloved One ; prayer was without consolation ; no divine light illumined her soul. The saint kept silence about her sufferings. She came to recreation with a smile on her lips, so as not to trouble her daughters with her trials. As was her custom on great feasts, she asked one of the community, Isabella of Jesus, to sing them a hymn. Unconsciously the young novice, in the exquisite verses "on the suffering of living without God," put the torture that pierced Teresa's heart into words. At the refrain—

Only to see Thee, O Beauty Divine ! For this I would gladly die —

Teresa became rapt, as it were, out of herself, from excess of agony. Sobs and cries escaped her lips, and she had no power to restrain them. Her daughters carried her to her humble cell, where she remained prostrate till the following day, plunged in an agony in which love fought with bitterness and desolation. How describe the pains she was suffering? Bossuet has attempted to do so. "Who," he says, "will give me words to express the ardour that fires Teresa's soul . . . to describe how day and night, without intermission, she sighs for her Divine Spouse? How her love—

ever increasing—makes it impossible for her to support existence? . . . Thence come these tears, these sobs, these excessive pains, which no doubt would have consigned her to the grave, had not God miraculously preserved her life in order to render it even more worthy of His love."

When Teresa came to herself, the hymn known as her "gloso" rose spontaneously to her lips from the depths of her pierced soul. It would be necessary to have her heart, and her genius, to translate it into any* other language. In this poem we have the cry of the exile mingled with the accents of the lover; hope and desire are both there. "I die because I cannot die! I live transported out of myself." Our Lord, touched doubtless by the ardent aspirations of His servant, desired to show her that, though He left her on earth because He had still need of her services, yet that she was ever with Him as He was with her, and this union was as close as was possible whilst she was in a land of exile. Accordingly on the following day, Monday in Easter week, Teresa, whilst ravished in spirit at prayer, was transported to Heaven, and Jesus Christ took her to His Father's feet, and presented her to Him, saying: " This is her whom Thou hast given Me. I, in My turn, give her back to Thee " ; and the Eternal Father accepted the offering that was made to Him. Then, the hour of Communion arriving, she was sensible of the divine Presence closely united to her. Jesus overwhelmed her with favours, and said to her, amongst other things, "Thou seest Me, My daughter. It is indeed Me. Show Me thy hands." Taking them in His own He placed them in the wound in His side, saying: "Look at My wounds; thou art not alone, and life is short."

The recollection of this week, and especially of the

transpiercing of her heart on Easter Sunday, was ever cherished by Teresa. But she did not rest on her sorrows or her joys. She fed her strength on God's gifts, in order to set an example of the lesson which she never ceased inculcating, namely, that love is proved by actions. The occasion soon came for her to suffer, to act, and to be humbled.

Difficulties had arisen at Medina between the community and the provincial of the mitigated Order with regard to the admission of a novice, Isabella of the Angels. The provincial had no right to interfere, the Carmelites of the Reform being (it will be remembered) under the jurisdiction of the General of the Order ; but the girl was an orphan with money, and her uncle had appealed to the provincial to support certain claims he had put forward to be considered patron of the church built by the girl's money. This was not the first time that an attempt had been made on the part of the friars of the mitigated Observance to interfere in the government of the convents of the Reform. Teresa, therefore, took this occasion to assert their independence by writing a firm but respectfully worded letter to the provincial, asking him to leave the regulation of her novice's affairs to her. The letter having produced no result, she went herself to Medina, and transferred Isabella to Salamanca. It happened to be the moment of the elections, and the community had just re-elected Mother Inez of Jesus. The provincial, determined not to suffer defeat, arrived without warning at the monastery, cancelled the election, appointing a nun from the Incarnation as prioress, and ordered Mother Teresa and Mother Inez, under severe censure, to leave at once for Avila.

The saint submitted in silence. Though her houses were not under the provincial's jurisdiction, she con-

tinued personally to look upon him as her superior, having made her profession as nun of the Convent of the Incarnation. It was the same with regard to Mother Inez. It was late on a winter's day, and the cold threatened to be severe, when the saint and her companion started on their journey. They could find neither coach nor litter to convey them, but were forced to borrow two mules from a water-carrier, on which to cover the distance of twenty miles which separated Medina from Avila. If the holy mother required consolation, the affection of her daughters at Avila, and the solitude there, would have sufficed to give it; but rejoiced as she was at being humbled and turned out of her own house, she suffered deeply for her daughters at Medina, left to the mercy of an incapable ruler. Providence was soon, however, to apply a remedy as complete as it was unexpected.

Pius V had been pursuing the difficult work of the Reform of the religious Orders with equal energy and gentleness, a work in which he was seconded by Philip II. That king, not satisfied by the results obtained by Fr. Rossi, asked to have the Carmelite Order submitted to a second Apostolic Visitor. The Pope this time appointed two Dominicans, Fr. Vargas for Andalusia, and Fr. Pedro Hernandez to Castile. Fr. Hernandez was a man of great learning and consummate prudence, and of even greater virtue. He travelled with the utmost simplicity, making no use of vehicle or saddle-horse, accompanied by another friar of his Order. To some who expressed their astonishment at seeing him thus traversing on foot the roads of Castile, he answered that " having come to visit saints it would not become him to travel at his ease." His first visit was to the monastery of Carmelites of the discalced Rule of Pastrana. He established himself

there during the Lent of 1570, following the exercises of the friars, and partaking of their fastings and their rude fare. He was astounded with the virtues he saw practised there, and found nothing to add or to retrench in their Constitutions, which were stamped with the wide and generous spirit of their holy foundress. To a novice who came to tell him that he thought of joining a more austere Order, he said, " Trust to my experience ; from all I have seen and read, I do not believe there exists a monastery in the Church of God which excels this one in austerity and perfection." 1 After he had spent some days with the fathers he assembled them in Chapter, and asked them if they were ready to recognize his authority. They answered that they were quite ready to do so, conscious that the Reform would gain in the Apostolic Visitor a powerful advocate and protector. Satisfied with the reply, Fr. Hernandez authorized the Foundation of a third monastery at Alcala de Henares before his departure ; and from that time the Order of the discalced began to spread rapidly. Before leaving Pastrana, Fr. Hernandez visited the convent of Carmelite nuns. More and more edified at what he saw, he became anxious to make the acquaintance of our saint, and as soon as opportunity permitted he went to visit her at the convent of Avila.

Fr. Hernandez having in his capacity of Apostolic Visitor examined Teresa on her interior life and practices, she answered with her usual straightforwardness, explaining to him the affairs of her Reform, her trials and her consolations, all with a force and simplicity which filled him with admiration. As regards her personal conduct, she referred to it in a manner which brought out rather the errors she saw in it than the

good ; but her humility spoke more in her favour than all the praises he had heard of her.

Fr. Hernandez hearing whilst he was at Avila that the prioress of Medina was already weary of her charge, and about to return to the Convent of the Incarnation, he set off at once for Medina, and presided at a fresh election. With much tact, instead of recalling Mother Inez, whom the provincial had rejected, as prioress, he caused Teresa to be elected, and sent for her at once to put her at the head of her little flock.

Fresh journeys and fresh fatigues were in store for our saint; but she offered all willingly to God for the good of her daughters. On her return journey she found herself at nightfall on the edge of a river, and her guide was unable to find a fordable place. Discouraged by his failures the man pulled up, but the saint accosted him gently, saying, "We cannot spend the night in the fields, my friend ; let us recommend ourselves to God's care and go on." She led the way and pushed her mule into the stream, and passed over it without any difficulty—a ray of light miraculously illuminating her passage, so that the rest of the little company were able to pass over in safety.

Teresa gave two months to the work of re-establishing order in the convent at Medina, which had suffered from as many months' misgovernment. She had restored peace and joy to all hearts, when she received an order from the Visitor to return to Avila in order to take up a cross which human weakness had caused her to dread so deeply nine years before, and which threatened to have increased ten times in weight during that interval. For, using the authority delegated to him by the Pope over the whole Order of Mount Carmel, Fr. Hernandez had nominated the holy mother prioress of the Convent of the Incarnation.

CHAPTER XXI

ABUSES had multiplied at the Convent of the Incarnation since Teresa left it. Whilst poverty —generously accepted, and joined to manual labour, penance, and regularity of life — had produced miracles in the Carmelites of the Reform, the nuns of the Incarnation dragged it as an intolerable burthen, or sought to lighten its weight by asking hospitality for indefinite periods of their friends, alleging that the revenues of the convent were insufficient for their support. Disorder, moral and material, reigned, and relaxation of discipline was carried to such lengths that little more was needed to complete the ruin of the community.

The effect produced on the Apostolic Visitor by the Convent of the Incarnation after his visits to those of the Reform may be easily imagined. He saw at once that it was idle to attempt to remedy evils so deep-seated by rules and regulations. One sole means of salvation suggested itself to him : to find someone with a character of sufficient firmness to make the necessary reforms, and a heart sufficiently gentle, and merciful, to do so in a manner that would make their acceptance possible to these poor souls, already so opposed to regular Observance. Fr. Hernandez recognized in our saint the possession of these qualities. Without announcing his intentions to the nuns, he summoned a Chapter of the mitigated Order, and

having obtained a majority of votes he named, in virtue of his authority as Visitor Apostolic, Mother Teresa of Jesus prioress of the Incarnation.

The news of this appointment was as great a blow to Teresa as it was to the community. A desperate resistance was organized at the Incarnation, and Teresa was not less desirous of inducing the Visitor to change his mind. How would she find it possible to abandon her eight Foundations ? she asked herself. All were but newly established; her counsels and decisions, and even her presence, were continually required by them. Novices, nuns, all were led by her direction. Temporalities also required her constant supervision. She had difficulties of every kind, including exacting benefactors, to contend with. On the other hand, it was clear that a charge such as that to which she had been appointed would rob her of her liberty, and absorb all her time and her strength. It was impossible also not to take personal reasons into consideration. How could she think without shuddering of having to recall a community of nuns to obedience, and to adherence to their Rule, whose minds were prejudiced against her, and the majority of whom probably looked upon her as a traitor? The feast of the Visitation found Teresa still a prey to interior anguish and uncertainty. She was also unhappy about her brother Pedro, to whom she was tenderly attached, and who was at this time in the West Indies. She took refuge in these anxieties to a little hermitage in the garden, and appealed to our Lord to help her : " Why, O Lord," she cried, " should my brother be in a place where his salvation is endangered? Ah, my Lord, if I saw Your brother exposed to such risks, what should I not do to deliver him from them?" Our Saviour answered her: "And yet you hesitate about

going to the help of the nuns of the Incarnation, and they are sisters of Mine. Take courage! and know that it is My wish. The undertaking is not so difficult as you believe it to be, and what you think will be hurtful to your Foundations will turn to their advantage, as well as to that of your former monastery. Cease, therefore, your resistance, and never forget how great is My power."

Teresa was vanquished. She confided her brother to the mercy of God, her convents to His Providence, and told Fr. Hernandez that she was ready to obey his orders. Teresa did not start at once for Avila, as the Visitor thought it prudent she should delay her arrival a few days in order to give the nuns time to conquer their resentment. Teresa also issued an order before arriving that the young girls who were being educated at the convent should be sent back to their parents— a very necessary precaution in view of what was to follow.

The saint's installation was fixed for the 6th of October. Fr. Hernandez, in order to add to the solemnity of the occasion, had charged the provincial, Fr. Angelo de Salazar (who had been lately re-elected), and another eminent ecclesiastic to accompany Teresa to the convent. The provincial on his arrival convoked a Chapter. The scene was an exact reproduction of that which had taken place in 1562 ; only instead of being the culprit, Teresa was now in the place of honour. Who knows, however, whether the holy mother in her own heart was not suffering a greater trial and humiliation on this occasion than on the former one? The provincial proceeded to read the act of election establishing Mother Teresa of Jesus prioress of the Order, by authority of the Apostolic Visitor and election of the heads of the Chapter. As soon as he had ceased the storm broke loose. A hundred furious voices protested against what they chose to call an act of violence and a crying injustice. 1 Too angry to be careful of their dignity, the nuns shouted and pushed, when a voice—that of Catherine de Castro—was heard above the tumult crying : " Yes ! we recognize Mother Teresa as our prioress." And she began to intone the Te Deum. A small number followed her lead, and taking the cross they tried to force a way through the crowd in order to conduct the new prioress processionally (as the rule prescribed) into the choir. The provincial, sought to come to their aid through the opposing crowd. On the one hand the chant of the Te Deum was heard, on the other sobs and abuse. Disorder reigned. The provincial menaced the censures of the Church to deaf ears. Teresa alone remained cairn, occupied in imploring God's assistance. She succeeded at last in escaping from the crowd and proceeded to the choir, where she prostrated herself before the tabernacle. Whilst the storm waged round her she prayed with that ardour which had ever opened Heaven to her petitions: " Lord, send peace to this house, and either send it a superior less displeasing to the community, or dispose their wills to submit." She then returned to the Chapter-room, where the provincial was still trying to impose silence and submission on the nuns. Teresa approaching him said: " Pardon these poor souls, father, it is not surprising that they should accept a prioress ungraciously who is so unworthy of the office." Then going to each of the nuns in turn, she spoke to them with her usual kindness. Several had fainted in consequence of their own fury, and the pressure of the crowd. The saint, taking their hands in hers, brought them back to consciousness. When

1 Hist, of the Order. Yepes ; Ribera.

someone shouted "A miracle !" the saint produced a relic of the true Cross which she bore. " Here is the author of the prodigy," she said, " Our Lord has had pity on these poor sisters."

Thus, without the support of the provincial, Teresa triumphed by her kindness ; and after a struggle which lasted some hours, she was left mistress of the situation. Some gentlemen, friends of the recalcitrant nuns, who, in opposition to all rules and regulations, had been admitted into the convent in order to foster the rebellion, were forced to retire without having effected their object. The nuns dispersed to their cells, and silence was restored.

Peace was made, but in appearance only. The community but awaited the first Chapter to tell Teresa in so many words that it would be useless for her to impose fresh rules on them, because they would not be obeyed. Her presence would be endured because it was impossible to get rid of her, but her authority would never be recognized. Whilst plans of resistance were being organized, Teresa made hers. The monastery bell assembled the nuns in the Chapter-room on the day fixed for the first Chapter to be held. The saint had been in the room before them, and had placed a large statue of the Blessed Mother in the stall occupied by the prioress, and, having put the monastery keys in Mary's hands, she seated herself at her feet. As the nuns one after another trooped into the room their eyes took in the scene, and their faces fell ; already a glimmer of remorse found its way into their hearts. Teresa's idea could not fail to be grasped. Under her sway of peace and love the honour and superiority were all to be laid at the feet of the Queen of Carmel; the humble prioress, desirous only of ruling under her orders, had come to the Incarnation

to obey her, and to serve her sisters. When all had taken their places, Teresa opened the Chapter in the following words :

"Your reverences, my mothers and sisters. Our Lord has sent me out of obedience to this house to occupy a post which I was far from desiring, or meriting. This election has afflicted me much, not only because I feel myself incapable of worthily acquitting myself of the duties which it imposes, but also because you have been deprived by it of your ordinary rights of election, and because your prioress, chosen contrary to your wills and inclinations, would do very well if she followed the good example of the least amongst you. I come accordingly amongst you to serve you and console you, as much as it is possible for me to do, in doing which I trust our Lord will assist me with His divine grace. In all other matters there is not one who has not the right to teach me or to reprove me for my defects. See, my mothers, what I am ready to do for each one of you ! If the sacrifice of my life or my blood would help you, I am ready to make it. I am a daughter of this house, and your reverences' sister. I know the character and wants of all here, or at least of the greater number. Why should you look upon me as a stranger, who am yours under so many rights and titles? You need have no fear of my rule ; though I have lived among the discalced Carmelites and governed them, I know by the grace of God how to lead those who do not belong to the Reform. My wish is that we should all serve God in meekness, and carry out the small amount our Rule and Constitutions ask of us out of love for Him Who loves us so much. Our weakness is great, I know it well; but if we cannot attain our object at first by our actions, let us reach it by our desires. Our Saviour is merciful. He

will come to our assistance, and by degrees our actions will equal our good-will." 1

Who could resist such lovingkindness? The nuns, better punished by the mercy Teresa showed them than by any chastisement she could have inflicted, promised her obedience with one accord, and begged her to reform whatever customs she found in the convent which were opposed to the Rule, and the religious spirit. The following day all the heads of the departments brought her their keys, and asked her to dispose of the offices as she thought best. 2

Teresa was in no haste to make changes. She contented herself for some time in merely noting the abuses which had crept in since she left, and in strengthening her position by a truly maternal kindness. It was necessary first of all to make cloistered life bearable, even attractive, to souls accustomed to fly from it; and in order to effect this, to create a family life such as made the little solitude of St. Joseph's so peaceful and happy. The difficulties she encountered in order to effect this, with so many and such divers characters to conciliate, would have seemed insuperable. But Teresa threw her genius and her heart into the work. She did all from motives of love, and her success was such that she could only safeguard her humility by ascribing all the glory to "her Prioress the Blessed Virgin Mary." 3

vShe was always ready to put herself at her daughters' disposal, and gave free access to all, so that each one might come and confide, their troubles and wants to her. Her conversations were so delightful that the nuns no longer sought for distractions in the parlour ; and at recreation her playful talk, and the hymns which she

1 V. de la Fuente, Vol. I, p. 522.

loved, took the place of profane songs, unworthy of a religious house. One of the saint's greatest difficulties was to suppress, or at least diminish, the time given by the nuns to conversations in the parlour. A gentleman of Avila, a friend of one of the nuns, having been continually refused admittance through Teresa's orders, asked to see her, and abused her soundly for the changes she had made. Teresa waited in silence till he had. finished, and then forbade him in her most authoritative manner ever to trouble the peace of the monastery again ; and threatened, should he disobey her orders, to report him to the king. After this she had no further trouble, and the governor of Avila hearing of it came to congratulate her on the firmness with which she kept order in her monastery.

The numerous abuses in the monastic life required also a stringent reform. Teresa made use of the tried fidelity of the little band of holy nuns whom she found at the Incarnation to introduce, by example, customs which she wished to be loved, before they were enforced upon the rest of the community. It was to these nuns she confided those posts which required zeal and tact. She also invited to her assistance the prioress of Valla-dolid, Mother Isabella of the Cross, a professed nun of the Incarnation, and made her sub-prioress; so that when she was confined to her cell by one of her violent attacks of tertian fever, Mother Isabella took her place in the choir. The rest of the community followed insensibly the lead of the two mothers, and of the group who supported them. Divine office devoutly sung, spiritual reading, pious practices which the saint knew well how to vary according to the seasons and feasts ; recollection, prayer, the practice of penance, all contributed to restore a vitality to religious life to which it had long been a stranger.

Thus Teresa succeeded in carrying out her programme without going beyond it. She had come to the Incarnation not to impose the austerities of the primitive Rule on nuns not bound to observe it, but to cause those imposed by the mitigated Rule to be kept with fervour. In short, she taught them how to sanctify the life they were leading, and in this she succeeded in a measure far beyond the hopes conceived by the Apostolic Visitor. Thanks to the saint's prudent administration, and to the nuns' industry, to which her example gave a fresh impetus, and to alms sent to her by friends, the temporal prosperity of the convent also returned. The alms she distributed amongst the poorer nuns ; bread was all she would take herself from the convent, her small expenses being covered by Juana de Ahumada, whose purse was always at her sister's service.

Teresa had scarcely six months' health, even of the precarious kind which went with her by that name, during the time she was at the Incarnation. She was attacked by fever and sore throat, followed in the Christmas of the year 1571 by quinsy, but she accepted these troubles with her usual courage. She felt herself too necessary to her daughters to absent herself more than she could help from choir or recreation. " When I see," she writes to her sister Juana, "the progress wrought by our Lord among the nuns here, I try never to keep my bed except when I have fever." Again, writing to Dona Maria de Mendoza, she says : " I tell you my aches and pains in order to excuse myself for not having written to you. God, in order to show rne, as St. Paul says, that in Him we can do all things, has deprived me of the little strength I ordinarily possess ; and yet in spite of this I have been able to do all He requires. I sometimes laugh at myself. . . . As far as anything can be done for my body, it must be owned I

want nothing. I am surrounded with care and compassion. Our nuns are so good and peaceful. I cannot thank God sufficiently for the change He has worked in them. Those who gave most trouble at first are now the ones who are the most contented, and the kindest to me. There are in truth some great servants of God here, and the majority are making progress in perfection. My prioress it is who has worked these wonders. So that there should be no doubt about it, our Lord has willed that I should be in such a state that it would appear as if I came here in order to fly penance. My time is taken up in nursing myself."

The saint's humility deceived no one but herself. The nun's of the Incarnation soon learned to appreciate the mother who had been sent to them. She had not long been prioress before they applied to her to choose a confessor for them. Teresa was fully aware of the importance of this appointment, and had waited for them to express a wish on the subject in order that she might transmit it to the Apostolic Visitor.

After consulting with her, Fr. Hernandez appointed Fr. John of the Cross, and Fr. Mathias, who was also a religious of the discalced Rule, to the post of confessors to the Convent of the Incarnation. Fr. John of the Cross was at this time rector of the college of Alcala, which had been recently founded. Learning and piety flourished under his rule, for this holy priest was as much in his element in forming the character of the students under him, and training them to the spiritual life, as in instructing them in philosophy and rhetoric. To many, conscious of possessing talents such as his, it would have been no small sacrifice to give up this important post to become confessor to a community of nuns. But Fr. John of the Cross had no thought except for God's glory; and, pleased to 2 B

second Teresa in a work for souls, he put himself at once at her orders.

A wooden hermitage outside the enclosure was made over to him and his companion, and the life led there by these two holy religious recalled in their poverty and penance the early beginnings of the Order at Duruelo. The Carmelite community, with Teresa for their mother, and Fr. John of the Cross for their spiritual father, bid fair to rival before long their sisters of the Reform in their fervour and love of self-sacrifice. An interesting document preserved in the archives of the Order gives us an idea of the virtues held in honour in a convent which but one year previously was a prey to abuses, and given over to tepidity.

The discalced Carmelites of Pastrana had lately admitted a young man of distinguished birth and talents, and of great piety, Fr. Gratian of the Mother of God, into their novitiate, of whom we shall hear much, later, in connection with the saint's undertakings. Fr. Gratian had been brought in close relations with Fr. John of the Cross, the latter having been his first master of novices. It was therefore probably through the medium of Fr. John that he sent a "cartel " to the nuns of the Incarnation challenging them, in knightly fashion, to enter the lists against him and his brethren of Pastrana—each party having to declare what sacrifices they were prepared to make in the service of their Master. The idea delighted Teresa. She communicated the contents of Fr. Gratian's letter to her daughters at recreation, and after consulting with them returned the following charming answer to him :

JESU MARIA,

"Having read the challenge, it appeared to us that our strength would never be able to allow of our entering into single combat with such valiant and

intrepid knights. Their victory being assured they would leave us stripped of all our possessions, and perhaps even discouraged to the extent of giving up the little we were able for. In the presence of these facts no one has signed, least of all Teresa of Jesus. This is absolute truth and no fiction. But for all this we have made up our minds to try our strength, and engage in this pleasant pastime ; and thus, possibly, some day, with the help of those who take part in the encounter, we may feel ourselves equal to accepting the challenge."

The saint then draws up the conditions. She asks for victuals (namely, counsels and encouragement), for "if we were starved out, what honour or credit would there be to the conquerors?" Then she allows her daughters to enter the lists, assuming always that the conditions will be fulfilled.

" Every knight, or son of the Blessed Virgin who will pray daily that Sister Beatriz Suarez may preserve the grace of God, and that He will accord her the favour of never speaking without reflecting beforehand, and always acting for His honour and glory, shall receive in exchange two years of the merit she may gain in nursing some very troublesome invalids.

"Sister Ana de Bergas declares that if the before-mentioned knights and brothers will ask from God that she should be delivered from a contradiction that she endures, and give her the grace of humility, she will surrender to them all the merit she will gain if her prayers are heard.

" Mother sub-prioress says that if they will obtain for her that she should renounce all will of her own, she will make over to them all the merit she gains by this sacrifice for two years. Her name is Isabella of the Cross.

1 «To that member of the Order of our Lady and knight

who, considering the poverty in which Jesus Christ was born and died, should obtain for her that interior poverty which she has vowed to the Divine Master, Sister Ana de Miseria offers the merit she will acquire before Him for repentance of her sins."

The engagements continue in the same strain ; sweetness, humility, obedience, the graces of a lively faith and a perfect contrition, are those specially asked for; graces are also asked for the Order. A long life for Mother Teresa is the only temporal blessing asked for. Prayers, and part of the merit asked for by humiliations, interior trials, or bodily sufferings, are promised in exchange.

Our saint concludes with her characteristic challenge: "Teresa of Jesus gives to that knight of our Lady who once a day forms a firm resolution to put up all his life with an incapable superior of the worst possible character, half of what she will merit on that same day from the many pains she endures, and everything else, which after all is but little. The contract is signed for a month and a half."

Notwithstanding the cares of her office, the holy mother watched closely over her convents of the Reform. The prioress of St. Joseph's Avila never gave an order of any importance without submitting it beforehand to her. Amongst the papers signed by Teresa, and preserved in the archives is one authorizing Sister Anne of St. Bartholomew to pronounce her vows. This privileged soul, who from her earliest years had received astounding supernatural favours from God, was specially cherished by our saint. In the last years of her life Teresa seemed hardly to be able to dispense with her services, and it was leaning against her heart — pure as that of an angel — that Teresa breathed her last. All the other houses of the Reform had recourse

equally to her for directions. The prioress of Valla-dolid was involved in difficulties with the excellent foundress Dona Maria de Mendoza, who wished to saddle the community with two undesirable subjects, in spite of their obvious disqualifications. 1 Teresa, with her usual gentleness and tact, persuaded Dona Maria to withdraw these novices.

At Alba de Tormes the saint exercised her vigilance over the prioress, Mother Juana of the Holy Ghost, whom she reproved for excessive austerities, such as were likely before long to cause injury to health. "I am much displeased at these fasts," she writes. "God deliver m,e from those who prefer their own will to holy obedience."

It is not the first time we have had occasion to notice that excess in penitential exercises was almost the only defect which Teresa found necessary to reprove in the monasteries of the Reform. If, however, she reproaches them for want of prudence, her heart doubtless rejoiced at seeing them consumed with the same desire which filled hers—" either to suffer or to die." And we know that in her own case, as soon as her fever left her, she returned to her hair-shirt and discipline, owning that her worst penance was to be forced to dispense with it.

If we reckon up the occupations that filled the saint's life, the correspondence, religious conferences, indispensable visits to the parlour, direction of her monasteries, and many other matters joined to a health always deplorable, we are tempted to ask what became of her interior life?

Within a few months of the saint's arrival at the Incarnation, on the eve of the Feast of St. Sebastian,

1 Letters, Avila, March 7th, 1572.

2 Ibid., September 27th, 1572.

1572, the nuns were assembled in the large oratory where the first Chapter had been held, in order to sing the Salve. The statue of our Lady still occupied the prioress's stall, and as Teresa advanced into the middle of the room to intone the anthem, she suddenly perceived that the statue had disappeared and the Blessed Virgin had taken its place. Teresa remained standing, rapt in ecstasy, with eyes radiant and fixed on her holy Mother. A multitude of angels surrounded their queen, and were ranged in a circle above the nuns' stalls. The oratory seemed transformed into paradise. Teresa's vision lasted all the time the Salve was sung. When it was over Teresa, at the pressing entreaty of her nuns, communicated the words our Lady had addressed to her: "Thou hast done well, daughter," she said, " to put me here. I shall be present at the praises in honour of my Son sung by the nuns* of this monastery, and will present them to Him." 1

The Carmelites, in gratitude for Mary's protection, kept the prioress's place vacant in her honour, and, esteeming themselves unworthy to occupy stalls which angels had graced, sat on footstools below them. These precious recollections survive to this day. The pilgrim to Avila looking through the curtains of the grille beholds a statue of our Lady with the monastery keys in her hands, and a row of empty stalls to right and left, still piously decorated with flowers.

It was at the little communion-table in the nuns' choir, below the oratory of which we have just spoken, that Teresa used daily to receive the Bread of Angels from the hands of St. John of the Cross. She had said to him on one occasion with her usual simplicity, " I know, Father, it is not a matter of the smallest importance; but I do love large hosts." On the

octave of the feast of St. Martin, 1572, Teresa was kneeling at the grille waiting to receive Holy Communion when she saw that Fr. John was breaking the host in two, reserving one-half for one of the nuns. She thought he was doing it in order to mortify her. u At that moment our Lord," Teresa says, " appeared to me in an imaginary vision, as He had often done before. He gave me His right hand and said : ' Behold this nail; it is a symbol of our espousals ; from this day you shall be My spouse. Up to this time you did not deserve this favour, but henceforth you shall look upon Me not only as your Creator, your King, but you shall have a care of My honour as My true Spouse. My honour shall be yours and yours Mine.' This grace produced such an effect upon me that I could no longer contain myself. ' O Lord,' I cried, ' change my baseness, or do not bestow so many favours on me.' I passed the rest of the day immersed in spiritual joy. Great profit accrued to my soul therefrom, and a greater confusion at the thought that I had nothing to give my God in return for His benefits."

This signal favour marks the first beginnings of the highest and last period of St. Teresa's spiritual life. A transformation has taken place in her. We shall no longer see her swoon away in ecstasy at our Saviour's voice, or when He discovers Himself to her sight. She now rests in a silence, and calm which can only be described as being full of strength. A perfect harmony has been established within her between the gifts of grace and her natural faculties. It is the noon-day of her sanctity, a period which was to last for a term of ten years in which she will have to endure trials crucifying to the heart, but which will leave her soul in peace. On one occasion our Lord appeared to her and said : 44 What would you ask of Me that I am not willing to do for you? You know the bond that unites us. All that I possess is yours. I give you My labours and My Passion. You may claim everything you wish from My Father as if it was already yours." Once, when a violent headache prevented her going on with her prayer, He said, " Think you that merit consists in enjoyment? No, daughter, but in working, in suffering, and in loving. The souls the most beloved of My Father are those whom He has the most tried, and the greatness of His trials is the measure of His love for them." Sometimes He gave her advice according to the circumstances in which she was placed. " If it is a question between poverty and charity, since love is best, you should neither deprive yourself nor your nuns of that which will excite it in your souls. Keep therefore the statue you thought of giving up." Another time He said : " To found safety on spiritual sweetness is to deceive yourself. The true testimony is a good conscience. . . . The truly humble are they who know what they can accomplish, and what I can accomplish." One day when Teresa was distressed because she was unable to keep abstinence, He said : "Have a care, daughter; there is sometimes more self-love than fervour in these desires for fastings." Another time, when she was unhappy at being always at work, and thought how much purer her soul would be if it was not taken up with worldly cares, our Lord answered : " It is true; it could not be otherwise. But exert yourself to have a pure intention and great detachment from creatures. See how I Myself acted, and your actions will become conformed to Mine." 1 Sometimes, instead of conversing with her, our Lord held her absorbed in contemplation, and in one of

1 These citations are taken from Teresa's Relations^ Nos. in. and iv.

these moments she enjoyed, in an intellectual vision, the presence of the most Holy Trinity. 1 Fr. John of the Cross shared Teresa's devotion to this great mystery.

It is related that on Trinity Sunday the two saints were conversing, separated by the convent grille, and that as St. John held forth in burning language about the mystery which the Church celebrates that day, the heavens appeared to open, and their two souls, united in this sublime contemplation, soared upwards to the supreme Good, a glimpse of which had been vouchsafed to them. Whilst they were thus rapt in ecstasy, Sister Beatrice of Jesus, the portress, came to give a message to the prioress. She knocked ; no one answered. She opened the door, and beheld the two saints lifted up into the air in an ecstasy ; St. John holding on to the chair, vainly attempting to struggle with the force which impelled him upwards, St. Teresa still on her knees, and also miraculously raised above the ground. News of the wondrous sight spread rapidly through the convent, and many came to witness it. The saint, interrogated afterwards by her daughters, answered : " That is what comes of talking with Fr. John. Not only does he fall into an ecstasy, but he carries others away with him !" In tracing the events of Teresa's earlier life, and following her from one prodigy to another in her upward ascent, we may sometimes have marvelled what God reserved for her later years. The treatise on prayer, which she wrote five years before her death, is an answer to such questions. This work reveals that on which her humility would have fain kept silence. The seventh abode in

1 Spiritual writers are agreed that revelations with regard to the Blessed Trinity belong to the highest degrees of the mystical life. See seventh abode in her Castle of the Soul.

her Castle of the Soul is a true picture of the state of her soul during the last ten years of her life. Her habitual reticence is insufficient to conceal the facts, for no one could write as she does on matters above all human ken without having learnt them by experience. We have given an account already of the vision which introduced her into this new state ; the saint described it under the name of spiritual espousals, making use of that word, she says, for want of a better one. Human words translate God's secrets imperfectly. To express them properly we should require the tongues of angels. It is therefore only possible to convey the ideas through imperfect images and similitudes.

In the first place, we see the great difference which the saint makes between this favour and those that preceded it. At that sublime moment, when our Saviour gave her a token of His espousals with her, under the form of a nail, mystic symbol of His sacred Passion, she was made to understand that His Sovereign Majesty deigned to unite itself to her lowness by so close a bond that the saint does not hesitate to call it indissoluble. Thus immersed in God, "as a little stream flowing into the sea mingles its waters with those of the ocean in such a manner that they cannot be separated," she died to herself, and could say with the Apostle, "I live now not I, but Christ liveth in me."

The effects of this grace were even more admirable than the grace itself. "I have said," 1 Teresa writes, " that the soul, raised by this divine alliance dies to her own life in the unspeakable joy of finding her true repose, and that Jesus Christ lives in her." Let us now see what this life is, and by what signs it manifests itself. The first is a self-oblivion so great that it

would truly appear as if being had no meaning for her. She no longer knows herself ; with regard to herself, heaven, life, honour have no meaning ; all her interest is centred in gaining glory to God. Our Lord's words to her, " Occupy yourself with My interests, I will take care of yours," are words and works with her. The second effect is a great desire for suffering, but one which no longer afflicts her as it previously did. She desires so ardently that the will of God should be accomplished in her, that whatever seems good to Him pleases her likewise. . . . But this is what most astonishes us: this soul who formally endured life as if it was a martyrdom, so impatient was she to enjoy God's presence, is now so consumed with the desire to serve Him, to cause His name to be praised, to make herself of use to other souls, that far from desiring death, she would fain live long years in the midst of the greatest sufferings, happy if she could at that price purchase for her Divine Master the smallest increase of that glory which He deserves. Her happiness and her glory is to immolate herself for the Crucified One, when she considers how many offences are committed against Him, and how few souls there are detached from creatures who seek His honour alone. It is true that the desire of going out of the desert of this life, to find herself with God in Heaven, appeals very tenderly to her at times ; but she soon renounces it, satisfied by possessing Him in that intimate manner I have described, and offering Him the voluntary acceptation of a long life as the greatest proof of love that she can give Him. " In this soul," Teresa concludes by saying, " there are no aridities, no interior sufferings, but a sweet and constant joy. If she is but inattentive for a moment to her Saviour's Presence, He Himself reveals it to her. He labours at her per-

faction, and teaches her without the smallest disturbance in a peace so profound that it recalls to me the building of Solomon's Temple. The soul is, in truth, God's Temple, in which God and the soul enjoy each other's presence in the midst of a great silence."

Thus total self-abnegation, the assemblage of all the human faculties in one perpetual act of love : this in all its grandeur and simplicity means God's reign in the human soul. Happy the soul to whom this kingdom comes !

u Formerly," the saint goes on to say, " when the soul was consumed with ardent desires to be united to God, the smallest occasion, such as pious hymns, or a holy picture, sufficed to raise her into an ecstasy. But now circumstances most fitted to excite her devotion cease to produce these effects on her. Whether it is that she has now found a place of rest, or, for some reason of which I am ignorant, she is delivered from this weakness which was formerly as habitual as it was distressing to her. It may be that the reason is because God has strengthened her, enlarged her soul, and so rendered her capable of supporting His favours !"

Yes ! It is because she has become stronger, greater; because every day she is more closely united to God that the rays of divine grace enlighten her now without dazzling her. The gaze of the dove has now acquired the strength of the eye of the eagle, and can contemplate the sun of justice. Instead of being absorbed by contemplation, it can give itself up with equal facility and ardour to the Master's work.

4 'The company she enjoys gives her a strength such as she had never possessed. If ' by living with saints one becomes a saint,' as it is said, how would it be possible that the soul who is one with the strong God should not participate in His power? This super-

natural strength is often communicated to the senses and faculties, so that the body itself profits visibly by this mysterious vigour." This is the explanation of the change which we perceive in St. Teresa. God consummated His union with her soul when she was on the eve of a crisis that required all her powers ; and we shall see her, strong in the strength of God, tread with a holy joy a road sown with thorns, which though they may pierce her feet will never arrest her progress.

CHAPTER XXII

EARLY in the summer of 1573 the saint received a letter from the prioress of Salamanca, informing her that an opportunity offered of giving up the unhealthy house which they had inhabited so long for one which was both convenient and well situated. The proprietor of this house, Pedro de la Vanda, was not able to sell it without permission from the king's council, it being entailed, but being pressed for money he was ready to take steps to do so. The Visitor authorized Teresa's departure at the nuns' entreaty, her concurrence to these proceedings being urgently required. Accordingly, leaving the sub-prioress in charge of the convent of the Incarnation, the saint set out for Salamanca early in August.

The little company included one of the nuns of the Incarnation, Fr. Anthony, and Fr. Julian, chaplain and biographer to the saint. They were mounted on donkeys and mules, and, as Fr. Julian relates: "The sun at midday being very trying to the holy mother, we set off towards evening ; and at the first start, before reaching the nearest village, Fr. Anthony fell off his saddle, without, however, injuring himself, thanks to God's mercy." This was not their only misfortune. Teresa was taking the sum of five hundred ducats, the amount of Anne of Jesus's dowry, to Salamanca, having destined it as first instalment for the payment of the new house. The money, and some ornaments required for the altar, were loaded on a

baggage mule which formed part of the cavalcade. Unfortunately the night was dark, and everybody being occupied in keeping out of the many pitfalls which lined the road, it was only on their arrival at the inn that it was discovered that this particular mule was missing. Search was made for it in all directions, but to the general consternation no trace of the animal could be found. The saint alone was unmoved, and in the morning she despatched a child to look for it. The boy had not far to go; he found it browsing at a short distance from the inn, its valuable burthen intact. The following night there was still greater cause for alarm, for when the travellers arrived at the inn where they were to sleep, it was discovered that the holy mother was not of the party. It was not till the night was far advanced that their anxiety was relieved. No greater mishap had occurred than that of the mule on which she was mounted having wandered off the path ; finally, on meeting an honest peasant he had put her on the right road, so that she was enabled to rejoin her companions. 1

On arriving at Salamanca Teresa visited de la Vanda's house, and finding it suitable for her purpose concluded the bargain. No time was to be lost, as considerable changes had to be made to the building before it could be used as a monastery, and unless the community were able to take possession before Michaelmas Day they would have had to pay a year's rent for the house they were then occupying. To the joy of her daughters Teresa now shut herself up in the cloister, leaving the task of carrying out her plans to Fr. Julian. She found much cause for consolation in the little community at Salamanca. If austerities of an astounding nature were less sought after there than in some of her

other convents, she perceived in these holy souls a spirit of penance no less edifying, which caused them to accept fastings, and privations, and the discomforts of a damp and insalubrious house with joyous and intrepid hearts. Glory for God alone, consolation for the sisterhood, sorrow and suffering for self: this might have been the motto of each one. " In suffering," a young nun, Anne of the Trinity, was heard to say, "one must never stop to take breath, one must go straight on." Isabella of the Angels asked only one thing of Jesus — His cross ; and on one occasion Anne of Jesus, having reproved her for hurrying over the words "Quando consolaberis me" whilst reciting her Office, she said, " Forgive me, mother, but how should I ask consolations of God when I am conscious I only deserve punishment?" 1 Teresa received the confidences of these youthful souls, encouraged them in their interior life, and helped them. Anne of Jesus she specially singled out in this way ; the holy mother had a maxim that great virtue is a very dangerous thing unless it is accompanied with great humility ; accordingly she never lost an opportunity of trying her, and yet, in spite of rebuke and humiliation, not a word of excuse or impatience ever passed her daughter's lips.

It was about this time that Teresa began the history of her Foundations. Like all her other works, it was written in obedience to her confessor. When he gave her the order she was occupied with so many things, and in such bad health, that she thought it would be impossible for her to execute it. "Daughter," our Lord said to her, " obedience gives the necessary strength." That same day she took up her pen, and "with a great desire to contribute thus to the glory

of God," she began to tell the story of the wonderful things God had accomplished on behalf of the seven monasteries founded since that of St. Joseph of Avila.

Fr. Julian meanwhile had not been idle. The case was urgent, and the workmen had laboured under his supervision with such goodwill that, on the eve of the feast, only fine weather was required to enable them to put the last finishing touches to the building. Unfortunately the morning of the 28th broke in torrents of rain ; and it was under this watery sky that the Carmelites transferred themselves to their new abode. They there discovered that the roof was not finished, and accordingly that the sanctuary, where it was necessary to prepare three altars for the morrow, was inundated. "Eight o'clock struck," Sister Anne of Jesus, to whom we owe an account of the day, relates, "and our holy mother was still anxiously looking at the roof of the chapel, through which the rain was penetrating. I came to her with two other nuns, and said to her very firmly: ' You know, reverend mother, how much there is to be done before tomorrow ; you really might beg of God to stop the rain, so as to give us time to arrange the altars.' 1 Then if it is so necessary, you should pray hard,' she said, a little annoyed at the confidence I had so openly expressed in her prayers. I left her, and had hardly returned to a neighbouring courtyard when I looked out and saw a cloudless sky, looking as if it had never rained before. I went straight back and said to her before the same witnesses, 'Your reverence might really have asked for this fine weather a little sooner.' This time the saint could not help laughing, and went away without saying anything. The next day, fine weather, a great crowd, and an excellent

sermon made the ceremony of installation a very impressive one."

The troubles of the community were not, however, concluded. The proprietor, de la Vanda, returned to Salamanca directly afterwards and insisted on being paid in full for the house, instead of by instalments. The saint managed to pacify him for the time by her gentleness and tact, but he recommenced giving trouble later on, and the community had to suffer for ten long years from his humours and his exactions. "My poor daughters/' Teresa wrote to them, on one occasion, " may God help you to suffer joyfully. It matters little whether our habitations in this life be convenient or inconvenient, as long as, when we leave them, the eternal mansions are open to receive us." 1

Teresa, with Fr. Hernandez's permission, prolonged her stay at Salamanca for some months longer; there was, indeed, little necessity for her return to the Incarnation when her mission was accomplished, and where the sub-prioress ruled peacefully in her place. On the other hand, several monasteries of the Reform were in trouble, and the saint could help them only by her presence amongst them.

At Valladolid the convent had to combat the resentment of a powerful family, that of the de Padillas. The cause of this enmity deserves a few words of explanation.

Casilda de Padilla 2 was the youngest of three children ; her father had died when she was in her infancy; her eldest brother, heir to the family honours and property, left all in order to join the Company of Jesus. Her eldest sister, called likewise to a higher life, stripped herself of her right to the succession in favour of Casilda. The relations, fearing possibly that

the latter might follow her brother and sister's example, affianced her, according to the strange custom of the country, at eleven years of age to her father's youngest brother. Casilda, the chronicler relates, pleased with the gifts and attentions showered on her, and attached to her bridegroom, seemed at first perfectly satisfied with her fate. But God spoke to her heart as He had done to that of her brother and sister. One day the young girl presented herself at the grille of the Carmelites to ask admission. The nuns refused to take her on account of her extreme youth, and, backed up by her confessor, persuaded her to return to her family. A second time, two years later, and yet a third time Casilda returned to ask the same favour. Finally her perseverance was rewarded, and she was given the habit. The reproaches of her family followed her, and the community had much to suffer from the outcry raised by her powerful and influential friends for long years afterwards. The anxieties endured by the Carmelites of Valladolid and Salamanca were more than equalled by those at Pastrana. The Princess of Eboli had been left a widow in July of this same year, I5731 The shock of her husband's death was great, and with a mind almost unhinged by sorrow she insisted on being clothed in the habit of the Carmelite Order in the very room where the prince was laid out previous to his burial. When all was over she left her palace, got into a carriage, and gave orders that she should be taken straight to the convent. Fr. Baltasar, learning her intention, had preceded her there, in order to acquaint the prioress with the news. " What, my father," she exclaimed, " the princess a nun here! Then the community is lost indeed !" Mother Isabella had undoubtedly grasped the situation. The princess

1 Boll., No. 596.

showed directly on arriving that she had not changed her character with her garments, and she began at once to impose her imperious will on the community. She insisted, first of all, on two of her waiting-women being clothed on the spot. The prioress said it was impossible without the superior's authorization. The princess was furious at the reply, and the prior of the convent of the discalced was sent for. He gave his permission, and this time the princess was satisfied. But her satisfaction did not last long. Nothing pleased her. Never in her own palace even had the great lady showed such caprices and such temper. It sufficed for anyone to offer her anything for her to reject it, and the smallest refusal necessitated by the Rule threw her into a fury. The day after her arrival the governor, and magistrates and other dignitaries of the town, requested an audience of her, in order to present their condolences. The princess insisted on receiving them in the cloister, and when the prioress offered to give up the monastery to her to make use of as she pleased, if she would allow the community to follow their Rule in any little corner of the building, her answer was, that "She thanked the prioress for her advice, but as the monastery-belonged to her she would make what use she chose of it."

Teresa, informed by Mother Isabella of what was going on at Pastrana, tried in vain to extricate the nuns from their terrible dilemma without hurting the feelings of their foundress. Finally, a new fancy led the princess to establish herself in a hermitage in the garden. After spending a few weeks there she went to stay at a neighbouring house, and at last betook herself home. Conscious that she had covered herself with ridicule by her caprices, the princess took her revenge by giving orders that the church, which was

being built at her expense, should be stopped. She also withdrew her alms, as well as those given by the prince, to the support of the community, thus reducing them to dire distress. The saint was deeply concerned at these tidings, though less (as she said) at hearing how much her poor daughter had to suffer, than from fear for their souls oppressed by these chains of slavery. -

Whilst she was at Salamanca, Teresa was inspired to make a Foundation at Segovia. A pious widow of that town, Ana de Ximena, offered what was necessary to make a beginning, and her cousin Andres undertook to arrange matters with the authorities. Not long afterwards Teresa received an invitation from the rector of Veas to make a Foundation in that town, which was supported by several members of his congregation. The saint forwarded all these petitions to the Apostolic Visitor who surrendered to the reasons she gave in favour of these proposals, though he had been previously opposed to her starting any more convents.

Teresa's farewells to Salamanca were not made without deep regrets. In the first place it cost her much to leave a young nun, Isabella of the Angels, who was dying. Then the interminable disputes with the proprietor were far from being settled, and the young prioress was scarcely able to cope with these difficulties. At Salamanca too the saint enjoyed consolations which she ranked as next in importance to divine ones: namely, the learned and enlightened counsels which the eminent doctors of the University placed at her disposal. Fr. Baltasar Alvarez, "the true father of her soul," had recently been appointed rector of the Jesuit college there. He not only visited her occasionally, but he had brought her a young student, a scion of the house of Braganza, to initiate into the

secrets of the interior life ; this youth Teresa soon got to love like a son.

The saint left Salamanca in February 1574, taking sisters Isabella and Mary of Jesus with her. The Duchess of Alba had obtained permission from Fr. Hernandez to receive a two days' visit from Teresa on her way to her convent at Alba; and the latter, accustomed to the bareness of her convents, was struck by the grandeurs of the palatial residence. " When I was first shown into a magnificent hall," she writes, " crowded with works of art, and an infinite variety of rare and precious objects, I marvelled to what use such treasures could be put; then the thought came to me that the beauty and variety of all these works of art should lead me to praise God." 1 Passing on to the monastery two days later, she writes with the same directness and simplicity: "I have a hermitage here whence I see the river, and I have the same view from the cell where I sleep, so that I can enjoy the prospect from my bed, which pleases me much." Thus we see that Teresa was equally sensible of the beauties of art and nature, but she used them as a means of leading her thoughts from the contemplation of finite things to the infinite. She profits by a messenger to send tender letters from Alba to her daughters at Salamanca ; also to send a present to a Dominican Father whom she esteemed for his learning and piety, but of whom she had not so far been able to make a friend. " Here, my dear mother," she writes to the prioress, " is a trout which the duchess sent me yesterday. It appears to me so good that I am sending it to my dear Fr. Bartholomew de Medina. I trust it will arrive in time for his dinner. Let it be taken to him directly with this card. Even if it is too late, send

it all the same. Let us see now if this will produce a letter from him." 1

A good man of the name of Antonio Gaytan, hearing of the troubles undergone by the saint at all her Foundations, asked leave to go with her; "for," he said, "nothing pleased him more than to undergo fatigue and suffering for the love of God." Fr. John of the Cross and Fr. Julian were also of the party. " On our way," the latter relates, " I asked our mother if she had got the Bishop of Segovia's permission in writing. ' No/ she said, ' his promise is all that is necessary.' I then became very uneasy, as I knew the bishop was away from home, and I feared we should get into trouble with the vicar-general."

The Carmelites arrived at Segovia on the i8th of March. Ana de Ximena had hired a house and prepared the chapel for them, and on the following day, the feast of St. Joseph, Fr. John of the Cross said Mass, and reserved the Blessed Sacrament in the tabernacle. A little later in the day a canon on his way to the cathedral passed by, entered the chapel, and, touched by its simplicity, was moved to the desire to say Mass there. He was still at the altar when the vicar-general arrived, much displeased. "What is your reverence doing here?" he said. "Can you not find a better place in which to say Mass?" "At these words," Fr. Julian tells us, "however great the canon's devotion had been previously, it departed very quickly !" The vicar-general inquired who had presumed to found a monastery and open a chapel without leave from him ? He looked about for the culprits. But the moment was unfavourable for finding them,

1 Letters, Alba, Feb. 1574. Whether the saint's amiability produced a response we know not. But V. de la Fuente remarks : " Fr. Bartholomew, who began by censuring- Teresa, ended by becoming her panegyrist."

Fr. Julian having hidden under the staircase, and Gaytan, notwithstanding his courage, having likewise disappeared. The nuns were invisible behind the grille. Only Fr. John, tranquil as usual, remained to face the irate dignitary. " Who has placed the Blessed Sacrament in the chapel, Father?" he asked. Then, without waiting for an answer, he said, " Go all of you, or I will put you into prison." He left without carrying out his threats, but posted a beadle at the door to watch the chapel, and see that his orders were carried out, namely, that the Blessed Sacrament should be taken away, and no public act of worship performed. 1 The saint lost no time in acquainting the vicar-general with the fact that she had been authorized by the bishop to make a Foundation in Segovia, and after a time he showed himself amenable to reason. Before, however, the nuns could get out of the hired house (where they were not allowed to reserve the Blessed Sacrament), and into another which they were enabled, in consequence of the dowry brought by two postulants, to purchase, they had many trials to undergo. Teresa extricated herself from these strifes and contentions less by the help of powerful friends than by her charity, and love of peace. The secret of conciliating adversaries is never wanting to those possessed of these last resources. Meanwhile Teresa had not forgotten the troubles of her daughters at Pastrana. She had taken counsel with the Apostolic Visitor, the provincial and Fr. Banez, and all were unanimous in advising her to recall them. She therefore confided to Fr. Julian and Antonio Gaytan the mission of helping them to escape. The prioress, acquainted of this design by Teresa, sent for the governor of the town, and confided various gifts, formerly given to the con-

vent by the princess, to his care. The governor consented to their departure, but the townspeople resolved to oppose it, and the princess threatened to put a guard at the doors, so that no one should leave her monastery. The prioress continued to work quietly at her preparations; and the day and hour when their plans were to be carried out being agreed upon with Fr. Julian, she and her nuns slipped out of the convent in the dark, joined the carriages which were waiting for them at the other side of a hill, and were soon out of danger of pursuit. Teresa meanwhile was praying hard for them. At one moment her daughters at Segovia saw her clasp her hands in anguish. " Pray," she said, u pray for our sisters of Pastrana." Two days later Teresa had the consolation of welcoming the much-tried sisters at Segovia. Mother Isabella confided to the holy mother that they had been in imminent danger whilst crossing a river in high flood ; and the nuns at Segovia, comparing notes, found that it was at the exact moment when the saint had implored their prayers. 1 A short time afterwards Teresa assisted one of her daughters at Salamanca in an even more marvellous manner.

Isabella of the Angels, after months of suffering, was in her last agony. The peace which up to that time she had enjoyed had deserted her, and she was torn with anguish, mental and physical. The community who had prayed round her bed since daybreak left her for a short time for Mass. On their return a great change was visible ; joy and peace once more shone on her countenance. Interrogated by the mistress of novices as to what had happened, she answered: " During Mass Mother Teresa came to me, and blessed and caressed me ; she consoled me in my pains and

1 Julian d'Avila, Boll., 600.

delivered me from my fears, saying to me, ' Daughter, do not give way to idle fears. Place all your hope in the Blood and merits of your Spouse, Jesus. God has great glory in store for you, and this very day you shall enter into it.'"

She remained in this state, for the consolation of all who approached her, till after matins, when, with crucifix in hand, and the Credo on her lips, after pronouncing in a distinct voice the words " et vitam eternam" she expired. Whilst these scenes were taking place at Salamanca, the saint was rapt in so deep an ecstasy that her daughters at Segovia spoke to her several times without being able to rouse her from it. Sister Anne of Jesus, besides testifying to this circumstance, seized an opportunity a year later to question Teresa about it. "And," she says, "as our holy mother was very fond of me she admitted it was true." A declaration to this effect was made by Mother Anne of Jesus in St. Teresa's process of beatification.

Evidences of her prophetic spirit and miracles multiplied during her stay at Segovia. She revealed to the provost, Mgr. Covarrubias, the great destiny which God had in reserve for him. 1 She read her daughters' most intimate thoughts, and dissipated their temptations. Another time she condescended to bless the innocent wishes of a poor little lay sister whose piety and goodness appealed to her heart. Finally, on the yth of August, the feast of St. Albert, Teresa had a vision of that holy Reformer, and was encouraged by him to pursue her work for the good of the Order.

The saint's term of office as prioress of the Incarna-

1 He was afterwards made archbishop and president of the king's council.

tion expiring on the 6th of October, she left Segovia on the 3oth of September, confiding the community there to the care of the late prioress of Pastrana. Before leaving the town, moved by devotion to St. Dominic, she went to visit the church of Holy Cross, where the saint had spent many years of penance and prayer. She received great consolations whilst kneeling at this shrine. St. Dominic appeared to her, and told her of the sufferings he had endured, of the assistance he had received from God, and promised to help her in her undertakings.

The holy prioress found on her arrival at Avila that the community of the Incarnation were determined to re-elect her; and she had much difficulty in dissuading them from doing so. "I love this house as my mother," she told them, " and you all, my most dear daughters, as sisters; but it is impossible for me to stay longer with you. Our other houses require my care."

The nuns then begged of her to choose a successor who would carry on her work. Teresa designated the sub-prioress; a choice which was confirmed at the elections. 1 She returned to St. Joseph's directly afterwards as prioress, the community there having, meanwhile, elected her. Her stay at her " Bethlehem " was of short duration, as her presence was required at Veas and Valladolid. God alone knew what these constant changes cost her; whilst ignorant and prejudiced people accused her of leaving her enclosure under any pretext, she owned to a friend that these journeys were her greatest trial, " but," she added, " when I consider how faithfully our Lord is served in these convents, all my pains are as nothing to me."

Her stay at Valladolid was a source of great consola-

tion to her. " There are," she said, " souls in this convent who give me occasion continually to praise God." There was, first of all, Casilda de Padilla, who was known to Teresa by the name of "the little angel," and who from the day of her clothing had received great gifts of prayer. Then there was a humble lay sister, Stephen of the Apostles, whose soul was insatiable in its desire for penance, and consumed with love of God. But it was in Sister Mary Baptist that Teresa found all the perfection that her soul ardently desired to see in her daughters. It was in the long talks they had together, which were frequently prolonged far into the night, that the young prioress learnt from her holy mother how to govern souls without relaxing the care of her own. Proposals for four fresh Foundations came to Teresa whilst she was at Valladolid. u Time is wanting," she writes to Teutonia de Braganza, "for all I have got to do. ... I leave here after the Epiphany. Then I go by way of Medina to Avila, where I spend a day or two ; and then from Toledo to Veas. Recommend me to our Lord, I implore of you."

Our saint gave the habit to Geronyma de Quiroga at the first resting-place of this long expedition of a hundred leagues. Dona Helena came with her daughter, and asked only one grace of God in return for her sacrifice : that of being able one day to follow her example. The sight of the joy of the young novice served as inspiration to Teresa, and she composed verses which were sung in the evening of the feast, of which the refrain was : "Maiden, who has brought you here out of the vale of tears? God, and a longing for happiness !"

The path she followed on her hurried journey was marked by miracles. On leaving Malagon she was attacked by fever, and remembering Elias in the desert

she was not afraid to complain with him, " What shall I do, my Lord? See the state I am in." And at once she was cured. 1

At Almodovar she blessed the eight children of her host, Mark Garcia. Then, lifting her veil to consider them more attentively, she said to the mother, pointing to one little boy: " Senora, that child will be a great saint, the reformer of an entire Order." And to another: " As for you, my little Anthony, you will have to arm yourself with courage, as life has great trials and afflictions in store for you." Then fearing for the effect her words might have on him, she said : " Poor child, you will have troubles, but what will you do to bear them?" The boy, encouraged by her caresses, said firmly: "I will take courage, reverend mother, and suffer them with as much patience as I can." Then turning to one of the little girls, she predicted that she would have much honour after death. These prophecies were verified to the letter.

Later on, whilst passing through the Sierra Morena, the drivers of their coaches lost their way, and found themselves in a narrow defile with a precipice on either side, equal danger threatening them whether they advanced or retreated. "Pray hard," ejaculated the saint; "ask God to save us through the intercession of St. Joseph." Instantly a powerful voice was heard telling them to retrace their steps in a particular direction. The drivers, following the orders given, to their astonishment found themselves on a good road, and looked about to find their guide in order to show their gratitude to him. Teresa turning to her daughters said: "There is not much use in looking; the voice we heard was that of St. Joseph, and they will not find him!"* Again, when they reached the banks of the

Guadalquivir they were transported to the other side without knowing how they got there; this is the testimony of Anne of Jesus, an eye-witness, from whose narrative we quote. Rumours of the last miracle had preceded them to Veas ; accordingly when they reached that town a great number of knights and ladies, as well as the clergy of Veas, came to meet them, and escorted them to the church, and afterwards to the house of the foundresses, Catherine and Maria de Sandoval. Teresa gives us the history of Catherine at length in her Foundations^ and we feel, as we read it, that she was in truth a woman after her own heart. As a young girl Catherine was remarkable for her pride and ambition ; but once God had touched her heart there were no bounds to the heroism she displayed in His service. Six years before St. Joseph's convent was founded, wh£ti she was still hesitating, and praying to God to show her the life to which He called her, she had a dream. In this dream she saw herself led into a monastery, where the nuns were dressed in white with bare feet. The prioress met her and took her by the hand, telling her that she was called to that house, and she then read the Rule and Constitutions to her. As soon as Catherine awoke she wrote these down from recollection, and sought in all directions for an Order corresponding to the one she had heard of in this mysterious manner. Many years passed ; her father and mother died, and yet she was no nearer realizing her aspirations. Finally she came across a Jesuit Father, to whom she confided her history, showing him also the notes she had written down. When he saw them he instantly recognized that they were those of the discalced Carmelites, and recommended her and her sister, who shared her hopes and intentions, to apply to Mother Teresa. But a fresh

difficulty presented itself, for Catherine had meanwhile fallen into bad health, and was at that time a martyr to dropsy and gout, so that it seemed out of the question that any convent would receive her. Full of faith, however, Catherine cried to God to help her, and she was rewarded with an instantaneous cure.

Teresa on her arrival at Veas, finding her strong enough to keep the Rule, gave her and her sister the habit on the feast of St. Matthias. Both one and the other made over all they possessed to the convent without a stipulation of any sort, and when Teresa asked as she had done before to the novice at Toledo, " What will happen to you if we cannot keep you?" like the novice they replied: u We will serve you at the door as portresses, and if you cannot feed us we will beg our bread in the city for the love of God."

When the saint prer^nted her companions to Catherine, she went straight up to Anne of Jesus, and said to her: "This is my prioress. She it is whom I saw in my dream. I give her my obedience." Without knowing it she confirmed Teresa's choice, for the saint had brought Anne of Jesus to Veas with the intention of making her prioress. 1

1 This Foundation was Teresa's first in Andalusia ; without knowing it she had crossed the frontier of Castile.

CHAPTER XXIII

'"THERESA was now sixty years old. Her infirmities, X joined to the extreme fatigues of the last thirteen years of her life, had aged her physically before her time. Though her ardent heart, her indomitable energy, and an intelligence which seemed to become always more luminous, enabled her to thank God for renewing each year her youth, it did not restore her worn-out body. It was in this state of health, therefore — which had always been precarious, but was now ruined —that she entered into that course of trials to which her biographers have given the name of her Gethsemane. The hour had come for her, as it had done for her Divine Master, to drink the chalice of bitterness to the last dregs. But as Jesus condescended to receive help in His agony from an angel, so He gave Teresa a support in those last years worthy of herself. Before embarking on this part of her history, it is necessary that we should know something of the religious to whom was granted the privilege of partaking the sufferings of the holy mother, and of softening them by his filial devotion.

Fr. Jerome Gratian 1 of the Mother of God had worn the habit of our Lady three years at this time. He was one of twenty children born to Don Diego Gratian de Aldarete and his wife Dona Juana Dantisco. His father had been secretary first to Charles V and then to his son Philip II ; he was also a man of letters, a poet, and

1 History of the Order, Vol. II, Bk. I, chs. xx. and xxi. 400

a historian. His mother was the daughter of a Polish ambassador, and a woman of great piety, as well as of considerable mental gifts. Fr. Gratian was brought up at the Jesuits' College in Madrid, from whence he passed to the university of Alcala. His talents showed themselves at an early age, and his college and university career were marked by a series of triumphs. His piety and goodness were proof against successes which would have turned weaker heads; and his studies, far from leading him away from the practice of prayer, showed him the insufficiency of learning to satisfy the cravings of the heart. At an early age he was conscious that God called him to a religious life, and at twenty-four he was ordained, and shortly afterwards made a Doctor of Divinity. His intention at that time had been to join the Jesuits, but circumstances having intervened to postpone his admittance into their novitiate, his thoughts turned to the Order of Carmel. His biographer tells us that this attraction was due, in the first place, to a great devotion to our Lady which he had had since childhood, and because as a student of Alcala he had constantly come across members of the discalced Order of Carmelites, who had a convent there, and was partly repelled and partly attracted by what he heard of their austere way of life. A great struggle then took place in his heart. Our Lady seemed to attract him with irresistible force to her Order, and human nature fought against the life of penance to which he would be condemned by such a choice.

Grace triumphed. He was asked by the prioress of the convent at Alcala to preach on the feast of our Lady of Mount Carmel. To do justice to the subject he had to study the origin and privileges of the Order, which necessarily increased his veneration for it. So 2 D

eloquent was he, and so persuasive were his words, that his great friend, Dr. Juan Rocca, who came to hear him, made a resolution to give up the world on the spot, and soon after entered the Order of Carmel. Though he was delighted to hear of the conquest he had made, Fr. Gratian allowed his friend to go alone to Pastrana. Shortly afterwards he went himself to the Carmelite convent at Pastrana to arrange about the admission of a novice.

St. Teresa tells us the outcome of this visit. " Oh the marvellous secrets of God ! Fr. Gratian, led by our Lady to Pastrana, went there quite in error as to the object of his journey. He only thought of arranging for the reception of a novice, and our Lord intended to give this grace to him. . . . Fr. Gratian has such a charm in conversation that it is impossible to speak to him without conceiving an affection for him. What happened elsewhere occurred at Pastrana ; the prioress was so delighted with his good qualities that she had a great wish to secure them for the Order. She spoke of this afterward to the nuns, and showed them the importance of the affair ; for at that time there were few or none belonging to the Reform who united all his merits. . . . All took the matter to heart, and set to work by fasts, and disciplines, and constant prayer to obtain it. Their prayer was heard. Fr. Gratian visited our fathers' monastery at Pastrana, and he was much struck by the regularity and recollection he saw there, and the facilities given for serving God ; also at the thought that the Order was specially dedicated to our Lady whom he had ever wished to honour with all his power. He resolved not to return to the world. The devil put great difficulties into his mind, representing to him the distress it would occasion his parents. But Fr. Gratian, confiding the care of those he was about

to leave to God, asked for our Lady's habit. The discalced Fathers hastened to give it to him. It was a great joy to all, and especially to the prioress and her daughters, who knew not how sufficiently to thank God." 1 Fr. Gratian—happy conquest of Mary's—embraced the Rule in all its rigour, with a courage to which his strength was not always equal. Before he was out of the novitiate his prior employed him to preach and give conferences, and even confided the direction of the other novices to him. With bare feet Fr. Gratian used to scour the neighbouring hamlets, preaching and instructing the ignorant, then returned to a dinner of herbs or vegetables, and bad fish. His health gave way under these trials, and he was strongly tempted to give up his vocation. Again grace triumphed, and he made his vows, with restored joy and peace, on March 28th, 1573. Teresa was fifty-eight on that day. " If our Lord," she writes, " had permitted me to choose one who would set our newly established Foundations in order, I should not have known how to have asked Him to give us such perfection as He was pleased to give us in sending us Fr. Gratian. He came at a time when, if it had not been for my great confidence in God's mercy, I should have regretted more than once that our Reform had been begun. I allude to the friars' houses only. As for those of the nuns, through the goodness of God so far they are doing well." 2

Already the discalced friars were a cause of the deepest anxiety to Teresa, though not on account of any sign of decay in fervour amongst them. In the Foundations of Altimora, Granada, Seville and La Penuela, which had succeeded those we have already mentioned, there was the same thirst for penance,

humiliations, and work in God's service. True sons of the anchorites of old, they had scarcely any food but the herbs of the field, no beds but bare earth or planks. They opened their lips only for the praise of God, or to preach His gospel. Unfortunately the bond of unity was wanting to the monasteries. Teresa in the following words gives us the key of the situation. She says: " The Reform (amongst the friars) carried the seed of speedy decay in its bosom. In the first place, they remained under obedience to the superiors of the mitigated Observance, and belonged to no special province. In the second, they had no Constitutions. Each monastery lived according to its own rules. Some thought one way, and some another ; the Reform underwent great perils from this cause." 1

St. John of the Cross, meanwhile, went on with his hidden work for souls at the Convent of the Incarnation. His gifts lay more in the direction of souls than in those of law-giver or organizer. He had trained the souls of the greater number of the religious in the novitiate. It was to him they owed their spirit of prayer, their self-abnegation and humility, and an example which all tried to follow, though they despaired of equalling it. But the Reform required an exterior action of a different nature from this. Fr. Gratian, with his learning and eloquence, his natural dignity, his firmness tempered with sweetness, and even his court influence and connections, was, as Teresa affirmed, the man chosen by God to save the friars of the discalced Order, both from the above mentioned disintegrating elements in their midst and from the storm which was about to break with fatal violence over them.

Very few months after his profession Fr. Gratian

found himself invested with unexpected powers. Fr. Vargas, who had been named Visitor to the Order of Carmel in Andalusia, at the same time that Fr. Hernandez had been appointed to the same office in Castile, had invited the discalced to his Province in 1572, and had helped to settle them at Granada, La Penuela, and at St. Juan del Porta, where they had taken the place of the friars of the mitigated Rule. Encouraged by their success, he decided upon sharing his authority with Fr. Baltasar of Jesus, which was almost equivalent to making the latter provincial. 1 The following year Fr. Vargas invited Fr. Mariano to assist him in a new Foundation of the discalced friars at Seville, and told him to bring a coadjutor with him. Fr. Mariano made choice of Fr. Gratian, and very shortly after he had done so, Fr. Baltasar made over the powers which he derived from the Apostolic Visitor to that young religious. Fr. Vargas, instead of objecting to this somewhat summary proceeding, when he got into personal relations with Fr. Gratian, conceived such a high opinion of him, that he took the momentous step of handing over to him the powers he derived from the Holy See, alike over the mitigated and the discalced. Fr. Gratian, far from coveting such a post, saw only its grave inconveniences, and at first refused to accept it, pleading his youth and inexperience, and the offence it would give to the legitimate susceptibilities of the friars of the Observance. Unfortunately, Fr. Vargas, though a zealous man, was not a prudent one, and he persuaded himself that Fr. Gratian, with his exceptional powers, would overcome an opposition to measures of Reform which he had himself found insuperable. He would therefore take no refusal. Fr. Mariano also joined his entreaties, for he realized the great services that his

1 Boll., No. 568.

confrere would be in a position to render to the Reform in his new capacity. Finally Fr. Gratian submitted, resolving to occupy himself with the convents of the discalced, and to leave the others in ignorance of the powers he possessed, unless urgent circumstances arose to give him occasion to use them. In spite of these precautions the friars of the Observance became alarmed, and wrote to Fr. Rossi, General of the Order, that the partialities of the Visitor Apostolic for the Reformed branch menaced the ruin of the mitigated Rule, giving Fr. Gratian's appointment as proof of their allegations. 1

It will be remembered that when, seven years before, Fr. Rossi had visited Spain in order to forward the cause of Reform, he had been deeply impressed by what he saw at the convent of St. Joseph at Avila. Teresa had not failed to keep up these favourable impressions by a correspondence in which she acquainted her superior—for as such she looked upon him—with matters affecting the interests of her convents. The imprudence of Fr. Vargas, and the displeasure of the friars of the Observance at what they conceived to be troubling the peace of the Order, operated, however, very unfavourably on the General's opinions. Too far from the seat of action to have a complete knowledge of the facts, he asked the Holy See to revoke the power of the Visitors ; which was accordingly done on August i3th, 1574. Fr. Rossi waited till the convocation of the General Chapter in the following spring to publish this Brief. Though he kept it secret, yet the news of the change reached the ears of the Papal Nuncio at the Spanish court.

Mgr. Hormaneto, who occupied the post of Nuncio, was a man of great zeal, and so ardent a Reformer that 1 Boll,, No. 586.

when he occupied the see of Padua it gained for him the somewhat ironical title of Reformator Orbis. From his first arrival in Spain he proclaimed himself a protector of the Carmelites of the Reform; and realizing the influence that had been brought to bear on the Holy See in order to carry this measure of repression, he resolved to use his best efforts to counteract it. After examining the Brief he saw that though the Pope revoked the powers granted to the Visitors, he had not limited those which he, as Nuncio, exercised over the Religious Orders in Spain. Consequently, on his own authority he re-appointed Fr. Vargas, and gave him Fr. Gratian as coadjutor. This masterstroke completed the dissatisfaction of the friars of the Observance. They were ready to accuse the Nuncio of insubordination to the Holy See, but Mgr. Hormaneto had already put his case in influential hands, and obtained the assurance that he was acting within his rights.

We do not propose entering into all the details of the lamentable struggle that ensued. In retracing its salient features we shall see our saint dominating the storm by her energy and her sweetness. Though this page in the history of our Lady's Order is a painful one, it should not scandalize us to find it subjected to a trial from which Holy Church herself has not been exempt. The holiest works here below have been founded by human hands, and humanity carries frailty and imperfection in its train. God triumphs in the end in His Church, whose youth and beauty He is ever renewing in spite of the storms that break over her, and so, in their measure and proportion, He triumphs in the work of His saints. He was to triumph in the Reform of Carmel, and it is to God's glory and the honour of our saint that we should see at what cost this was effected.

Encouraged by the Pope's approval, the Nuncio proceeded to gain that of the king, and also that of a council of high dignitaries of the Church convoked with the same object. Philip II, who was well acquainted with Fr. Gratian's family, gladly sanctioned his appointment, and told the Nuncio to send for the young coadjutor to Madrid in order that he might be presented to him.

Fr. Gratian was then at Seville, and on his way to obey the royal summons he stopped at Veas in order to see and consult the holy mother. " When his arrival was announced," she says, "I was filled with joy, for I had never seen him, and from all the good that I had heard about him I longed to know him. I was even happier after we had talked for some time together." She adds:

" Never have I seen such perfection joined to so much sweetness." In these words the saint hit upon Fr. Gratian's strongest characteristic. He hid under the mantle of Elias less of the fire of the prophet, and more of the meekness of the Saviour of mankind.

Fr, Gratian opened his heart to the saint, and confided all his fears and anxieties to her. Teresa, recognizing him as her superior, consulted him on the affairs of the Order, and on her own interior life, with equal straightforwardness and candour. 1 Fr. Gratian's stay was prolonged at Veas beyond his intentions. " He is waiting for Fr. Mariano,"Teresawrites, "who, much to our satisfaction, delays his arrival." Fr. Gratian made use of this interval to persuade Teresa to undertake a new Foundation at Seville. She had hitherto restricted her convents to Castile on account of the General's authorization having been limited to that province, assisted possibly by a repugnance which

1 Hist, of the Order, Vol. TI, ch. xiv.

she had to leave her own country and go into Andalusia, but Fr. Gratian relieved her fears on the former point. "God has permitted, reverend mother," he said, "that you should have come under my jurisdiction without intending, or even knowing it. You are therefore bound, in this province, to obey me, and to do all that I ask of you in God's service."

Teresa was ready to obey, but she had strong reasons for wishing to undertake the Madrid Foundation first. She was expected at Madrid, and could rely there on powerful friends, such as the Princess Juana and Dona Leonor de Mascarefias, to help her. Moreover, she would then be in the neighbourhood of her other houses, which in the event of difficulties arising was a point of some importance. Fr. Gratian asked her to consult God in prayer. She did so, and told him that our Lord wished her to go to Madrid in preference to Seville. "And yet," Fr. Gratian persisted, "I am strongly in favour of your going to Seville." Teresa said nothing, and began her preparations to obey him.

Edified by her docility, the father allowed her to go on for two days; then he asked her: "Reverend mother, it is possible I am mistaken. How is it that you are willing to follow my wishes in opposition to a revelation which you know comes from God? " " Because," the saint replied, " I might be mistaken about a revelation, but I can never go wrong in obeying my superiors." 1 Humble and beautiful answer, coming as it did from one of the saint's age and experience to one of less than half that age.

Fr. Gratian urged her to lay the matter again before God in prayer. This time the answer was: "Thou hast done well, daughter, to obey. The affairs of the Reform and Madrid will lose nothing by it. Go to

1 Yepes, I, II, ch. xxvu.

Seville; you will succeed there, but you will have much to suffer."

Accordingly Fr. Gratian started for Madrid, and Teresa took the road for Seville in company with five other nuns, one of whom, Mother Mary of St. Joseph, in the world Maria de Salazar, she destined to be prioress. Teresa suffered much from the heat on the journey, as she tells us in her delightful and spirited account of it. The covered coaches became " a species of purgatory," but the courage of her daughters was such that in their company she would be willing to go to the country of the Moors. On the eve of Pentecost the saint was attacked by high fever. " Never in my life have I had such a fever. I became unconscious, and our sisters in order to bring me back to my senses threw water on my face, but the water was so heated by the sun that it was not of much use. ... I will describe what our inn was like : a little hut in which we were given a tiny room under the roof, without shutters, into which the sun — and the sun of Andalusia —

poured straight whenever the door was opened. They laid me on the bed, but I would rather have been on the floor, as it was so high at one end, and so low at the other, that I could hardly keep my place on it. ... At last I made up my mind to get up and leave it, for I found the sun more endurable in the open air than in the room. Two days earlier we were exposed to great danger in the passage of the Guadalquivir. The ferry-boat which took us and our carriages over was obliged to go in a slanting direction instead of crossing the river where the rope was stretched. They made use of the rope all the same, but those who were holding it let go, so that the boat was carried away without ropes or oars by the current. I was more grieved for the boatman, who was in despair, than alarmed by

the danger. We nuns set to work to pray, and the rest to shout. By great good luck a gentleman saw the danger we were in, and sent quickly to our assistance. ... I shall never forget the touching way in which the boatman's son, a child of ten or eleven, sympathized with his father's distress. It was enough to make one praise God to see his loving little heart sharing the paternal anxieties. The boat grounded at last on a sandbank, whence we were rescued. Another misadventure which we had on Whit Tuesday put me out much more. We had hurried our journey in order to arrive early at Cordova, in time to hear Mass without being seen by everybody, at a church beyond the bridge. We had chosen this church as the quietest one in the town. When we reached the bridge we were stopped ; our carriages were forbidden to pass without the governor's permission. The guard went to get it, but the governor being in bed we were kept two hours waiting for it. During this time a crowd surrounded the carriage in order to discover who was inside. That did not trouble us much, as the carriages were well closed. The permission came, but we found ourselves in another difficulty : the passage on to the bridge was so narrow that something, what it was I know not, had to be sawn away before we could pass through. This took more time. At last we arrived at the church where Julian of Avila was going to say Mass, but as the church was dedicated to the Holy Ghost, the days of Pentecost were celebrated with greater pomp there than elsewhere. There was even to be a sermon. When I saw the crowd with which the church was filled, I was so troubled by it that my own feeling was that it would be better to go without Mass than to encounter this multitude. Fr. Julian was of another opinion, so as he is a theologian I followed

him. We got out of the carriages with our veils covering our faces, and at the sight of our white mantles of coarse stuff and our sandals the people were roused to enthusiasm. We, on the other hand, were not a little put out. As for me, it gave me such a shock that my fever left me. One really might have thought from the tumult that the bulls were being driven through the town. This grand reception was in truth a great trial to us. " 1

The good chaplain gives us some details which are wanting in the saint's narrative. One day they were taking a midday rest in the fields when they saw some men at a little distance, disputing. From words the men proceeded to blows, or rather to one side attacking the other with knives and daggers. The nuns crowded round their mother, but the saint, who never wanted courage in the service of God, put them aside, and going up to the men implored them in burning words to remember God, in Whose presence they were fighting, and the judgment which would follow them after death. Struck by the faith and courage which breathed from every word she uttered, they dropped their knives, and one by one slunk away—let us trust to meditate upon the saint's advice at leisure.

The distractions of the journey did not prevent Teresa from keeping the " Easter of the Holy Ghost" with her usual devotion. She spent Whit-Monday in a hermitage near Ecija, and calling to mind the signal graces God had bestowed on her many years before, on that day, and which had been followed up by such innumerable ones since, she became a prey to what she herself calls a " tormenting " sense of gratitude. What return could she make to her Divine Master for all He had done for her? She had sacrificed everything to

1 Foundations, chap. xxiv.

Him ; but had she kept nothing back? She asked the question of God, and it seemed to her then that in the midst of her pains and labours, in spite of the vows by which she is bound, she had kept a certain degree of independence. Instantly she takes this last possession, and joyfully surrenders it to the Holy Spirit. Henceforth she will own no will of her own ; she will follow God's will in all matters, as it is signified to her by her superiors.

Teresa shall tell us in her own words what this sacrifice meant to her. " On one side," she says, "it seems giving up little ; on the other, it appeared to me a very difficult thing to do. I saw that I should have no exterior, or interior, liberty for the rest of my life, and I was conscious of a profound repugnance to binding myself in this manner. Except for the agony I felt in leaving my father's house, nothing, not even my profession, had cost me so much. At the moment Fr. Gratian's good qualities and the affection I bore him were nothing to me. I looked upon him as a stranger, and only asked myself if my promise would be pleasing to the Holy Ghost. After a struggle our Lord filled me with confidence. ... I knelt down and promised to obey my superior in all things till death." 1

A great inward joy followed this fresh promise. On May 26th the saint arrived at Seville. Here again the usual trials awaited her. The friars of the discalced Order had preceded them in that city, and had received such a friendly welcome from the excellent Archbishop de Roxas, that Fr. Gratian assumed that a similar welcome would be accorded to the Carmelite nuns. Unfortunately the Archbishop had made a rule, in consequence of the number of poor convents already in existence, that no fresh one should be founded in

the town without some means of support; and as Teresa tells us, "in the way of funds we had not one penny left of the small sum we took for our journey. All we possessed in the world was our habits and some coarse stuff to cover the waggons."

A month passed in negotiations. Finally, Fr. Gratian's letters decided the Archbishop to call on Teresa, and from that moment the Carmelites' cause was gained ; he could not resist such charm and goodness. On leaving her he blessed her heartily, and said : " You shall do everything you wish, reverend mother. I agree to it all beforehand, for the honour and glory of God." 1

That very day the Blessed Sacrament was installed in the little house which had been hired for them. The community was enclosed, and Teresa appointed Mother Mary of St. Joseph prioress. The regular exercises of convent life began. The house was small and inconvenient, and the destitution so great that the nuns slept on the bare ground. For some time they lived like birds, on crumbs of bread which the Heavenly Father let fall from His hands, a few vegetables, some fruit, even herbs from the field, was all they had to eat. Amongst all the rich and pious families in Seville not one came to their help. A charitable lady, Dona de Valera, knowing their extreme poverty, wished to assist them, but in order to hide her good actions she confided her alms to a faithless servant who disposed of the money otherwise. This was not all. The health of the community suffered from the climate, and their privations. The saint even passed through physical and mental trials, so that, as she says, she hardly recognized herself. "Lord and Saviour," she cried, "I ask myself what is become of Thy servant? She who thought she had received graces sufficient from Thee to face all the storms in the world, is now weak, miserable, bowed down by a trifle." This weakness did not last long.

Besides the trials we have enumerated, the saint had yet another, and a very serious one to endure. It will be remembered that, prior to the Foundation at Pastrana, Teresa had stayed for some days with the Princess of Eboli in her palace. The latter having heard that the saint had written the history of her life at her confessor's orders, insisted on seeing it. Teresa refused; but her refusal redoubled the princess's curiosity. She urged that both the Duchess of Alba and Dona Luisa de la Cerda had read it. Why was the favour denied to her? After a long resistance Teresa gave in, hoping by this concession on a point which only concerned herself, personally, to gain the imperious foundress's consent to other measures on which she could not yield, as the good of the Order was involved in them. She lent her the book, therefore, but on the condition it should be shown to no one. The princess, incapable of understanding the book, made a jest of its contents. It was passed from hand to hand, and finally reached the court at Madrid. There it was admired by a few, but laughed at by the greater number of its frivolous readers. Teresa tried all this time in vain to recover possession of it. Meanwhile the reports about the book came to the ear of the Holy Office, together with some malevolent gossip which the princess, since her breach with the Carmelites, had not scrupled to spread about them. Finally she handed the MS. over to Inquisitors, hoping possibly that the vengeance which she had not been able to wreak on the nuns would fall on their mother's head.

Teresa, acquainted of these facts by her old and

faithful friend the Bishop of Avila, was much distressed. Her humility had always caused her to fear that there were many errors in her book, the result of her want of learning, and she dreaded the scandal which the denunciation of these would cause, and consequent loss to the work of Reform. She was lamenting this to Mother Anne of Jesus, prioress at Veas, who answered her that if she prayed hard "and enlisted God on their side " the trial would turn to good. They agreed accordingly to communicate with this intention. After Teresa had made her thanksgiving she returned to the prioress, and said to her: " Let us thank God, my daughter. Our Lord has assured me that He will Himself take charge of this affair, and that my cause is His." 1 Thus consoled she left for Seville, where she heard that the Holy Office had given a favourable judgment on her book. But this triumph was followed by further anxieties. A young novice, said by her friends to be possessed of astounding qualities and merits, presented herself for admission to the novice-ship at Seville. Teresa took her with some misgivings, for she was a little afraid of perfection that had been the subject of so much praise ; and to one of the postulant's admirers, who had indulged in exaggerated phrases, she remarked with gentle irony: "Take care, Senora, if, after all you tell me about her, this good soul does not perform miracles, where will be your reputation ?" The reputed saint was in reality a disappointed and fanciful girl much attached to certain puerile devotions of the kind which Teresa could not endure, as she believed them to be the ruin of true piety. Discouraged in her inclinations, the novice gave herself up to feelings of dissatisfaction. The practices of convent life appeared insupportable to her,

and when she was asked in Chapter (according to the Carmelite custom) what were her interior dispositions, and whether she was in want of spiritual help, she objected to what she called a sacramental abuse, and denounced the prioress to the chaplain for wishing to " hear the nuns' confessions." The chaplain, though a worthy man, was scrupulous to excess, and without taking any trouble to inquire into the accusation, he thought it his duty to denounce the

Carmelites to the Inquisition at Seville. Accordingly shortly afterwards, carriages drove up to the little monastery in the Plaza, and various members of the Holy Office stepped out of it. After subjecting the community to a minute examination, they exculpated them from blame and departed. The cause, however, was not dismissed at once. The Inquisition caused an enquiry to be held on the saint's direction of her nuns, and her states of prayer.

Meanwhile reports were spread of the most calumnious kind. Teresa writes thus to Mother Mary Baptist 1 on the subject: " You know, my dear child, about the falsehoods of which I have already told you, published by the novice we dismissed. Well, they were nothing in comparison to what she has since said. She pretends that we fasten the nuns by the hands and feet and then scourge them. And would to God she had said nothing worse, but many other things have been invented about the community. I see well that our Lord wishes to try our hearts for a short time, in order afterwards to turn matters to our profit. Let us therefore not be disturbed. God gives me the grace of keeping up my courage. It is a good thing to have the heart free, and peace in one's conscience."

The Inquisitors deputed a learned Jesuit, Fr. Rodriguez Alvarez, to inquire into Teresa's method of

1 Letters^ Seville, April agth, 1576. 2 E

prayer. At his request the saint wrote two long treatises, both of which, after submitting them to a rigorous examination, he highly approved of. Henceforth the Rule of the Carmelites and their holy foundress met with nothing but honour from the Holy Office, and we are told that the priest who had denounced them was severely reprimanded.

At the same time that these events were taking place at Seville, the General Chapter of the Order of Carmel convoked by Fr. Rossi was sitting at Placentia. It was opened on the 22nd of May, 1575, and was numerously attended by delegates from Spanish monasteries of the Observance, who came to protest against the wrongs they had received at the hands of their discalced brethren. What these were we have already seen. They may be summed up under two headings: that the discalced had withdrawn themselves from the jurisdiction of the heads of their Order in Andalusia, and that, owing to the partiality of the Apostolic Visitor, a young man of twenty-eight (Fr. Gratian) had been given almost unlimited power over them in that province. No representative of the discalced Order was present, accordingly nobody was heard in defence. Fr. Rossi, though an excellent and single-minded man and earnest in the cause of Reform, could only judge from the one-sided account of it that was placed before him by the friars of the Observance. Severe decrees were accordingly drawn up and launched against the " rebels," and a Portuguese of the name of Tostado, a clever and somewhat unscrupulous man, was deputed to go to Spain, armed with full powers from the General, to turn the discalced out of their monasteries in Andalusia, and afterwards to visit the houses of the mitigated and reform abuses.

The conflict had now reached an acute stage, Fr. Gratian having received power from the Nuncio, ratified by the king, precisely similar to those that Fr. Tostado had received from Fr. Rossi and the Chapter. Teresa, not yet informed about the decrees of Placentia, was exceedingly anxious about the expected decisions. She knew how divided minds were on the subject to be discussed, and would have wished to soften matters by frank and conciliatory explanations. The more minds were divided, the more she sought to unite their hearts in the charity of their Divine Master. If people could not be made to understand, let them at least, she urged, love one another.

This thought is the predominant one in a letter which she addressed to the Fr. General, whom she venerated as a saint and loved as a father. It is dated the 18th of June.

"May the grace of the Holy Ghost be ever with your Paternity. Last week I wrote to you at great length on the same subject on which I now write, and sent this to you by two different routes, so anxious was I that one at least of these letters should reach you. Yesterday two letters from your Paternity were handed to me ... the date of them was not so recent as I should have wished, nevertheless I was much consoled to learn by them that you were in good health. May our Saviour keep you in it. All your daughters ask this of Him. It is the almost continual prayer of these monasteries which are also yours. Our sisters know no other father than you, and all bear you the same affection. This is not surprising, because we have no greater good on earth than to be under obedience to you; and as all are well pleased, they are never tired of expressing the gratitude they owe you for having helped the Reform in its first beginnings. . . . Please

God that the differences between you and the discalced may be softened, and that they may no longer be a cause of trouble to you. Though they are able to justify their conduct and I know them to be true sons to your Paternity, submissive, and anxious not to give you displeasure, yet on several points I consider they were to blame. . . . There have been great disputes, especially between Fr. Mariano and me, for he is very high-spirited. As for Fr. Gratian, he has behaved like an angel. If he had been alone matters would have turned out differently."

Teresa then implores the Fr. General not to visit the faults of individuals on the entire Reform. That there have been faults she is ready to confess ; she owns that Fr. Mariano, though a man of great virtue—austere, upright, without ambitions—yet is led by his fervour into great acts of indiscretion. She sees that Fr. Vargas has gone too far ; she would have preferred that he should have followed the prudent example of the Visitor of Castile. But are these errors sufficiently grave to cause the Fr. General to close monasteries peopled by fervent religious, whose lives are divided between study and prayer? religious who are in no way occupied with worldly matters, and are quite blameless as regards Fr. Vargas's or Fr. Mariano's actions. The friars of the mitigated Rule, on the other hand, are they faultless? Something must clearly be said about them; but how charitably the saint slips in the little word which has to be said in the interests of truth : " Oh, my dear and venerated father, you cannot see what goes on here. But I see it, and I tell you because I know your holiness and love of virtue. The friars of the Observance say one thing to your Paternity, another here. They tell you they cannot understand how you can treat virtuous men in such

way. They go to the archbishop and make out that they are innocent of all designs against our monasteries, and then they have recourse to you. . . . As for me, reverend father, I see both one and the other, and God knows I am speaking the truth. I think your sons of the discalced Order are those who are the most faithful to you, and will always be so." Then she allows Fr. Rossi to see the powerful support the Reform can count upon, not in order to intimidate him but to spare him further trouble, and concludes thus : The sole wish of the friars is " to be assisted by you as your sons, and it is one that reason demands you should accord them. To do otherwise would be to displease God. Let your Paternity recommend the matter to our Divine Master. Forget the past, as a true father should. Remember that you are a servant of the Blessed Virgin, and that she would be displeased if you abandoned her sons who are working for the increase of her Order at the price of their utmost endeavours."

This letter [1] only reached Fr. Rossi after the promulgation of the decrees of the General Chapter. Perhaps had he received it earlier these might have been less severe on the Reform ; meanwhile the holy reformer Teresa, ignorant of what was passing in Italy, only saw that the relations between the friars of the two Observances was getting more and more strained. Fr. Gratian was still in Madrid awaiting the king's pleasure. In this juncture the saint, realizing that in order to have peace it was necessary that the Reform should be erected into a separate Province under the Fr. General, wrote the following letter, direct to Philip II:

1 'May the grace of the Holy Ghost be ever with

1 Seville, June i8th, 1575.

your Majesty. Whilst I was recommending, my heart plunged in pain, the Order of our Lady to our Saviour, it came into my mind that the best way of supporting our Reform was to acquaint your Majesty with the means which will tend to give it peace and prosperity. As, Sire, the affair is in your hands, and you have been chosen by our Lady to be the support and protector of her Order, I venture to write to your Majesty, in order to implore you, for the love of our Lord and His glorious Mother, to command that we should be made into a separate Province. The devil has so much interest in preventing this being done, that no doubt he will be the cause of many obstacles being raised ; but in reality there are none; on the contrary, much good will come of it. The best thing would be if in the beginning Fr. Gratian was given the post of provincial. It is true that he is young, but one cannot thank God sufficiently for the grace He has given him, and the great work He has accomplished by his means in the last few years. ... I implore your Majesty to forgive my boldness, which I know is great."

Apparently Philip was not displeased with Teresa's frankness. She wrote this letter on the iQth of July, and on the 3rd of August the Nuncio transmitted to Fr. Gratian a Brief, appointing him Apostolic Visitor to the mitigated branch of the Order in Andalusia, and superior of the discalced in Andalusia and Castile. The saint learned, not without dread, of the first of these two appointments ; but to oppose the king and Nuncio was impossible, and, God helping, she believed that Fr. Gratian was capable of doing much good among the friars of the Observance. She begins her efforts at once amongst these at Seville, in order to smooth the way for the young Visitor. " I had a visit yesterday," she writes to Fr. Gratian, "from the

provincial of the Observance, and soon after the prior arrived. ... I found them all determined to obey you, and to second you in the reform of abuses, provided in other matters you do not go too fast. I assured them that you would go to work gently, knowing you as I do. I hope by the grace of God all will prosper if you begin quietly, reverend father, with prudence, and do not expect to accomplish all in a day." 1

The meeting between Teresa and Fr. Gratian did not take place till November. They thought alike ; and Fr. Gratian was prepared to invest his authority with meekness and humility, to avoid rigorous measures, to use tact with regard to the rights of the Fr. General, and, in short, to humour all legitimate sentiments, and to take up his difficult post in the character of a brother, or father, rather than that of a master. Fr. Gratian's disposition was admirably suited to this task, and the saint, having heard his plans, joyously encouraged him, saying: " Courage, my father; in behaving in such a manner you will ensure success."

Unfortunately, Teresa and Fr. Gratian were not masters of the situation. A fiery soldier, now a heroic penitent, like Fr. Mariano; proud Castilians like Fr. Anthony and Fr. Bartholomew could not so easily give up their instincts, though they had bowed their necks to the yoke of Carmel. And they were the heads of the Reform, its priors and elders. Accordingly, at the Chapter held to discuss these burning questions, after Fr. Gratian had explained his pacific views at length, Fr. Anthony got up to speak. He was opposed to humouring their opponents; and his long experience in the affairs of the Order lent weight to

1 Seville, September 27th, 1575.

his words. He was followed by Fr. Mariano, who, with a voice like one calling on an army to advance, said, " Tempus pacis, tempus belli. If there is a time for peace, no less true is it that there is a time to fight, and the present is such a time." He then described the situation at length, and declared that, in spite of differing from their saintly mother Teresa, which he deeply lamented having to do, he considered the moment had come for acts of vigour, without which nothing could be accomplished. 1

The unanimous opinion of the Chapter was on Fr. Mariano's side, and Fr. Gratian found himself obliged to yield to it. Bitter experience was needed to show them how much better Teresa had grasped the Providential mission of her sons. To pray, suffer, expiate the world's sins ; to glorify God and edify their neighbour by leading lives of perfection ; to gain souls by charity and by preaching the gospel—that was the work of her children, such as she understood it to be. Her aim had ever been that the Reform should be a young and vigorous offshoot of the ancient tree, taking away nothing of its strength or sap. If the king's commands outstepped the aims of the Reform, the latter should bear in mind that they were the children of a great Order, and bear themselves respectfully towards their Mother. In this way she would have counted on a victory such as she had achieved at the Convent of the Incarnation. As for Fr. Mariano's way, it was to be watered by Teresa's tears.

1 History of the Order, Vol. II, ch. I.

CHAPTER XXIV

THE little monastery at Seville, sheltered from these grave anxieties, enjoyed great peace in spite of its poverty. Mother Mary of St. Joseph, under Teresa's guidance and helped by her advice, almost realized the ideal prioress such as the saint has depicted her. " Lady and sovereign of her daughters' hearts" 1 (thus she describes her) she gains these less by fond words, of which she is sparing, than by the boundless confidence inspired by her goodness. She makes the practice of penance attractive, labour sweet, and prayer fruitful and consoling. Recreation with her is full of delight. Words of correction on her lips have no power to wound, though they speak strongly to the conscience of the guilty. She takes as much pains in forming the least of her novices to a religious life as a king would to govern his kingdom ; for to govern a soul, the saint tells us, is to reign over a world.

Mother Mary of St. Joseph, trained on the maxims of a saint, showed such high qualities in the discharge of her office, that Teresa could not contain her admiration for her. Writing to her niece, the saint says: "Our prioress has a courage that astounds me; it is much superior to mine. Moreover, she has an excellent

1 See treatise on the way of governing convents, Vol. II, Letters of St. Teresa, p. 495.

judgment. In short, she possesses in the highest degree all the qualities necessary for a prioress." 1

The crosses which marked their early beginnings at Seville were now succeeded by consolations. A postulant came to them whose parents were rich and charitable, and whose alms relieved the pressing wants of the community. Providence gave Teresa a great joy in welcoming back her beloved brother, Lorenzo de Cepeda, and his family from South America. This excellent man had recently lost his wife, and the loss of earthly happiness having turned his thoughts more than ever to God, he resolved to throw up his appointment —which was that of treasurer-general to the province of Quito—and retire from the world, in order to occupy himself with his children's education and his own salvation. Teresa was tenderly attached to her relations, and was full of joy at meeting them once more. Don Lorenzo was accompanied by another brother, Pedro ; the eldest, Ferdinand, and the youngest remaining in Peru. Teresa transmits the news to her sister Juana thus: " God be praised that you will have the happiness of seeing our brothers. They are already at S. Lucar. . . . Alas ! there are no joys without sorrows. Our good Jerome died like a saint. Do not mourn the death of one who is in Heaven : rather thank God for having brought the others home to us." 2

Lorenzo and Pedro arrived soon afterwards at Seville, and Juana de Ahumada and her family came to join them there. " My brother is delighted to meet my sister and Juan de Ovalle," Teresa writes to her niece, "and they are no less pleased to see him. Thus I have the happiness of seeing them all living together

1 Seville, April 29th, 1576.

in perfect amity." 1 It is obvious from this same correspondence that Lorenzo opened his heart wholly to his sister, and leant on her for advice. She had disapproved from the first of the idea he had formed after his wife's death of joining a religious Order. His children required him. That was a sufficient reason for him to remain in the world ; moreover, she did not think him fitted for that kind of life. She advises him to give all his attention to the education of his two sons. Avila is his native town, the air is pure ; he should settle there. If he finds it cold in the winter he must buy a little country place, well sheltered from the cold winds, and spend the winter in it. The Jesuit College of St. Giles will provide education for his sons, or the Dominicans, if they require a course of theology. They will want a page, and their aunt will provide them with one. She will find him a boy of high character and good family, but poor, so that it will be a charity to employ him. 2

Teresita, the little motherless girl, seems to have been the object of the saint's special affection. This child was but seven years old, but her intelligence was far above her years. She attached herself so strongly to her aunt, as soon as she got to know her, that it was with difficulty she could be separated from her. Teresa, full of compassion for Teresita's loneliness (for father and brothers could not take her mother's place) would willingly have brought her up. But the difficulties in doing so seemed insuperable. In a happy moment Fr. Gratian interposed, and gave Teresa the order to take her into the monastery and keep her till such time as she should be of an age to choose her vocation. The saint writes to him thus in answer to his

1 Seville, December soth, 1575.

letter: "Teresita is already here in her habit. Her father is enchanted, and all the nuns are very fond of her. There is something about her which is quite angelic. She delights us at recreation by what she tells us about the sea, the Indians, and so forth. She says it all better than I could myself. I am longing for you to see her. She owes you much gratitude for this great favour. I recognize, reverend father, the charity of what you have done for me. It is a great one, and in doing it in such a way as to free me of all scruple you have made it greater still." 1 Teresita therefore stayed with her aunt, who showed herself a mother to her ; and the child, by her charming disposition and unquenchable gaiety, became not only a cause of joy to the saint, but to all around her.

On the Feast of the Presentation of the same year, 1575, Fr. Gratian began the difficult task which had been assigned to him, commencing with the monastery of friars of the Observance at Seville. He convoked a Chapter, and read the decree by which he was constituted Visitor and superior of all monasteries \of Carmel in Andalusia. The friars asked for a copy of the Brief. This he refused to give them, 2 and a scene of great confusion followed. Finally, though not before the archbishop and governor had been sent for to support Fr. Gratian's authority, an appearance of peace was restored. The sub-prior alone took the Visitor's side, and though the rest of the community submitted to the Nuncio's threats of censure, they were prepared to shake off the yoke of obedience to the new-comer on the earliest possible occasion.

1 Seville, September 27th, 1575.

2 "He refused much against his own wishes, and contrary to his conciliatory disposition, but this refusal was the cause of much bitterness and heart burning." (History of the Order, Vol. IT, Book III, ch. I.).

His powers recognized, Fr. Gratian managed before long to introduce some measures of Reform. His charitable and conciliatory spirit prompted him to correct with moderation, and to pardon more than he punished. He regulated the hours of prayer and divine office, put the principal charges into the hands of capable religious, and left the great monastery to all appearance pacified, in order to visit the other houses under his authority.

The holy mother meanwhile was under no illusions. She realized the thorny path on which the Visitor had embarked, and followed him anxiously in spirit.

•The affairs of her convent at Seville were also giving her trouble. Don Lorenzo on his return found the community still living in a hired house, and with his wonted generosity he set to work to find a house to give them. His first choice fell on one which turned out to be so badly built that it would have been necessary to rebuild it almost from the foundation. '' I was not happy about it," Teresa writes in her " Foundations." " I had implored our Lord to provide us with a house. He had answered, * Your prayer is heard, daughter, confide in Me.' These words signified, I consider, that He would choose us a good house, and this one did not accord with His promise."

An error in the contract prevented its being signed at the last moment, and Don Lorenzo was able to withdraw from his engagement. Shortly afterwards he found another much more suitable house, which was well built, with a large patio and garden. Difficulties again presented themselves ; the owner declined to turn out, and a convent of Franciscans situated opposite objected to the new arrivals. Teresa was ready to give in, but it was too late, Lorenzo having concluded the bargain.

Whilst still engaged with the Foundation at Seville, the saint was preparing the way for another at Caravaca. She was invited to make it by a holy woman of the name of Dona Catalina de Otalora, 1 in the interest of three young girls who, though all owning to the Christian name of Frances, belonged to different families. These three maidens were bound by one tie only : that of feeling themselves equally called by God to embrace the Rule of Carmel. They formed a little community in Dona Catalina's house, whilst awaiting the moment when Teresa would found a convent in that locality. Before deciding to do so, the saint sent Fr. Julian and Antonio Gaytan to see whether the matter could be arranged.

Their journey was not without incident. They arrived late at a miserable village, and finding they were still far from their destination, took a guide to show them the way. Fr. Julian (who liked to improve the occasion) began to preach to the man. The road seemed interminable, and at last Fr. Julian exclaimed : " Surely we have lost our way ?" " Certainly we have," the guide answered cheerfully. " No wonder," called out Gaytan : "how could you expect him to pay attention to the road whilst you were preaching contemplation." " It was not precisely contemplation that I was teaching him," observed Fr. Julian ; u I was talking of the Ten Commandments which are the road to Heaven, and, strange to say, it made him lose his way on earth." Many obstacles stood in the way of this Foundation. The saint was overwhelmed with other undertakings; this one appeared surrounded with difficulties, but finally they were overcome. Antonio Gaytan, the faithful envoy, was so edified by the fervour of the three Frances, that he supported their cause himself,

1 Foundations, ch. xxv.

and prepared a house for them. Teresa gives him the name of her " very dear Founder," as " assuredly," she says, " without him there would never have been a monastery at Caravaca."

When all was ready and the necessary permission obtained, Teresa, by Fr. Gratian's orders, sent Mother Anne of St. Albert to replace her at the new convent, her presence being indispensable at Seville.

It was about this time that Teresa learned that the last decree of the General Chapter attacked her personally, and condemned her "for her disobediences " to choose one of her monasteries as a permanent abode, forbidding her to leave it, or to occupy herself with fresh Foundations. The saint's letter to the Fr. General shows us in what spirit she took this order : " I have learned, very reverend father," she writes, " the decree of the General Chapter by which I am forbidden to leave the house which I have once chosen. Fr. Angelo de Salazar sent the order to Fr. Ulloa telling him to acquaint me with it. The latter, fearing it would cause me great pain — as no doubt those who drew it on me likewise thought — delayed for some time acquainting me with it. A little more than a month ago, having heard of the decree through another channel, I obliged him to notify my arrest. I can assure you, father, that, as far as I can answer for myself, I should have looked upon this order as a great favour and recompense had your Paternity told me of it in one of your letters ; or if, for example, knowing how fatigued I am with my long journeys, and my little strength, you had given me orders to rest myself. The proof that I speak the truth is that I am even now very well pleased to remain quiet, though the command has come in a very different manner. But if the order fills me with joy from one point of

view, from the other, on account of the filial affection I have for you very reverend father, it is a very severe blow ; because you address me as if I was a very disobedient person; this is the interpretation that Fr. Angelo gave of it before the court before I knew anything about it. He thought he was imposing constraint on me, for he wrote that I might, if I wished, appeal to the Pope, as if it was not an advantage to me. But, indeed, if it had not been so, and if instead I had been deeply distressed by it, never would it have occurred to me to be wanting in the obedience I owe to you. ... I can honestly say, very reverend father, and God knows it, that if there was one thing that consoled me in the anxieties, sorrows, contradictions, and labours which I have endured in the past, it was to have known that I was obeying and pleasing you. At this moment, even, I have some comfort in doing what you tell me. I should have wished to have obeyed you instantly ; but on account of the Feast of the Nativity being at hand, and the road a long one, they would not allow me to go, believing that to injure my health would be contrary to your intentions. For this reason I remain here till the end of the winter."

Thus it was in vain that Fr. Rossi chastised his daughter ; she inclines her head to the blows, and kisses a hand which will ever be to her that of a revered father. But in spite of her submissiveness she is not afraid to stand up for the rights of justice, or to speak out in the cause of truth. From the beginning of the disputes she had recognized that on some points the friars of the discalced Order were to blame, and she had unhesitatingly admitted their faults, whilst imploring their forgiveness. Now that she sees them condemned with the greatest severity, and menaced with complete annihilation, she rises up with all the feelings of a mother cut to the quick for injury inflicted on her sons, forgetful that these had drawn their troubles upon themselves by neglecting her wise counsels. Further on in the same letter she says: " No longer daring to write to you themselves, they (the discalced) have asked me to act as mediator, and I implore you, very reverend father, with all the fervour of which I am capable, to take them back into your favour again. ... I spoke to you in my last letters of the commission Fr. Gratian has received from the Nuncio. ... I should have wished, as the saying is, to make a virtue of necessity; I would, therefore (before opposing the commission entrusted to Fr. Gratian), have wished he had been given a chance of seeing whether it was likely to succeed. It seems to me, moreover, that it was much less mortifying for the Order that this task should have been confided to him rather than to a stranger. . . . Why should you not be pleased that the reform should be carried out by one of your own children ? even had there been many in the Order to whom this commission could have been entrusted ! But as there are none with Fr. Gratian's talents, as your Paternity would be the first to acknowledge if you knew him well, is that not sufficient reason for you to support him with your authority, so that all may know that, if the Order is reformed, it is through your counsels and with your sanction? . . . Once more I implore you, very reverend father, for the love of our Lord and His glorious Mother, whom you love so much, and to whom Fr. Gratian has such devotion, to answer his letters kindly ; to forget the past, and the faults he may have committed, and receive him as your subject and your son, as he is in truth, as well as Fr. Mariano—against whom nothing can be

said, unless it is that he does not always judge the effect of his words." 1

Teresa received no answer to this letter, and the storm continued to rage. Fr. Gratian, in virtue of his authority as Commissionary Apostolic, could have dispensed her from obeying Fr. Rossi's orders; the Nuncio also would have readily intervened; but, as she said, it would have been in vain that the Pope would have offered her powers to withdraw from obedience to the General. The question of the place of her captivity had now to be considered. Her natural inclination would have led her to prefer Avila. For a moment her niece, Mother Mary Baptist, hoped to have her at Valladolid. She writes in answer to the latter : " How could you think seriously of my going to Valladolid? Is it for me to make choice of a house ? Have I anything to do but to go where obedience calls me?" She left the decision to Fr. Gratian, without showing any wish in the matter.

The saint was anxious that the community should be settled in the new house Don Lorenzo had bought for them before she left Seville. The purchase of the house had not been effected without troubles to the generous donor; for having given his person as surety, claims were made upon him which he was unable for the moment to satisfy ; and, being a stranger in Seville, he was obliged to go into hiding till Teresa was in a position to make terms with the creditors. At last, on the 29th of May, a messenger came to announce that the house was free, and all obstacles removed. It was in the middle of the night that the saint, and Mother Mary of St. Joseph, with some other devoted followers, took possession. There was some doubt still whether the Franciscans were likely to offer opposition. * ' Those

who accompanied me," Teresa relates, "took every shadow in the street for Franciscans. 1 Once we got there nothing more was to be feared. The friars opposite were as still as death."

Teresa took advantage of the few days that were left her to give her last injunctions to her successor. From a letter written by the saint to Mother Mary Baptist after she left Seville, it would almost appear that the latter had not responded to the deep affection the holy mother entertained for her to the extent that she desired. " I was moved to tears, dear child," she says, " by the joy your letter caused me. I cannot think why you ask my forgiveness so often. As long as you love me as much as I love you, I willingly forgive everything you could have done in the past, as I do all you might do in the future. What I felt most was the little inclination you had for my company when we were together, but I am convinced this came not from your fault but by God's permission. I should have found too much consolation in your affection in the troubles I went through at Seville; and He willed to deprive me of it . . . but your letter has effaced all from my memory ; you may take this for certain. Nothing remains but my affection for you, and it is so deep that it needs all the remembrance of the past to moderate it."

Thus it was that Teresa loved ; and this cloud which for a moment obscured perhaps the deepest of her friendships, soon passed away. Mother Mary Baptist by her virtues, her admirable character, and her exceptional talents, deserved the place she held in the holy mother's affections ; for if she was not the eldest daughter of the Reform, she was first in Teresa's heart.

Thanks to Don Lorenzo's generosity, the new monas-

1 Foundations, ch. xxv.

tery was all Teresa could wish. " Everything is so satisfactory," she writes to Fr. Mariano, "that our sisters have never tired of thanking God for it. We are in one of the best parts of the town. ... I do not think we shall feel the heat here. The patio is as brilliant as if it had been made of alabaster ; we have a delightful garden, with beautiful views from it. ... We owe all this to my brother ; without him we could have done nothing." 1

The saint wished the installation to take place quietly. In spite of the respectful silence of the Franciscan friars, she had not forgotten the objections they had made, and her desire would have been that her little church should remain modestly silent opposite their great convent. "The prior of the Trappists and Garcia Alvarez," she writes, "were of a different opinion to mine, and they went to the archbishop to ask for his. The three decided to take the Blessed Sacrament from the parish church in procession to our chapel. . . . Nothing was wanting to beautify the feast, or to rejoice our hearts. The solemnity was so great and the streets so well decorated, with so much music and chanting, that the prior told me he had never seen anything like it in Seville. Contrary to his habit, he took part in the procession. The archbishop himself carried the Blessed Sacrament in the presence of a great multitude, who praised God, and cried out that the Foundation was in truth the work of God."

Teresa omits to mention a touching incident which occurred on the same occasion. After the procession was over, the archbishop entered the enclosure, where he was met by the holy mother, who on her knees begged for his blessing. The venerable prelate, emulating her humility, knelt himself before the saint.

" Oh, my daughters," she said afterwards, "think of the confusion which overwhelmed me in seeing the holy bishop kneel before a poor little woman like me." As soon as the archbishop had withdrawn, the Carmelites returned to silence and recollection. But the Andalusian seizes on every excuse for a merry-making, and thus the event was celebrated with fireworks, and fusillading which were prolonged far into the night. A serious accident was on the point of troubling the general hilarity. A packet of gunpowder exploded in the hands of one of the crowd, threatening not only the man's life, but the safety of the monastery. Providence, however, would not permit this day of rejoicing to end in mourning ; and not only no loss of life resulted, but the beautiful damask hangings, lent for the occasion by Garcia Alvarez, escaped, though the walls and ceiling of the chapel were blackened by the explosion.

Directly afterwards Teresa left Seville, uncertain whether her destination was to be Avila or Toledo. Her brother accompanied her, and was naturally keenly desirous that her residence should be fixed at the former place, where he was about to settle with his family. Teresa, however, expressed no opinion, and Fr. Gratian, in spite of his wish to please Don Lorenzo, decided in favour of Toledo. The saint, therefore, was enabled to satisfy the desire of her heart, ever athirst for sacrifice ; for if one thing could still have given her earthly consolation, it would have been to return to St. Joseph's, the birthplace of the Reform, never more to leave it.

The nuns of Seville had obtained leave from Fr. Gratian to have the saint's portrait painted by the holy lay-brother, John of Miseria, before her departure. Brother John, though a great contemplative, was but

a moderate artist. Teresa submitted out of obedience, but with great repugnance, to the sittings which this necessitated. When the picture was finished and shown to the saint, she exclaimed: " God forgive you! my good brother John. He alone knows what you have made me suffer, and at the end of it how ugly you have made me ! " Though the portrait but imperfectly reproduces the fine physiognomy and dark eyes of which her contemporaries speak, yet the artist has managed to infuse into it some spark of the seraphic expression and serene majesty of brow, such as we should have looked for in a portrait of the saint. 1

Leaving Seville early in June, Teresa spent the Feast of Pentecost at her convent at Malagon. From there she and her companions proceeded to Toledo; but before taking up her abode in that town permanently, she paid (at Fr. Gratian's orders) a last visit to St. Joseph's at Avila.

1 Several convents in Spain dispute the honour of possessing- this portrait. The most competent authorities assign it to the convent of Seville.

CHAPTER XXV

FR. TOSTADO, the Father-General's delegate, arrived in Spain provided with plenary powers, and full of zeal for an enterprise which he looked upon in the light of a holy war. It was a question in his eyes of sustaining the honour, and even safeguarding the existence of the Order, in defending it against an offshoot which threatened to devour the sap of the parent stem. The religious of the discalced Order, on their side, were prepared for a vigorous resistance in order to defend a divine right to live a poorer, a more penitential, and a more perfect life; one also which was more in conformity with their ancient Rule, and resembled more closely that of their Divine Master. On each side there were excellent intentions reciprocally misunderstood, and prejudices defended with a native ardour which even heroic virtues had failed to master. Circumstances likewise combined to push matters to extremity between brethren worthy, for the most part, of understanding each other, and uniting in God's service.

Fr. Tostado disembarked at Barcelona in the month of March, 1576. He assembled a Provincial Chapter at La Moraleja, to which the priors of all the convents of the mitigated Observance were invited, and the priors Frs. John of Jesus, Didaco of the Blessed Trinity, and Elias of St. Martin, who belonged to the three first convents established by the discalced with the

General's consent ; those founded without it were looked upon as unauthorized and ignored. On receiving their notification to attend the Chapter, the three priors went to Madrid in order to take advice of the Nuncio, who recommended them to refuse consent to anything that would contravene the spirit or Observance of the primitive Rule, or the obedience they owed to

Fr. Gratian. The fathers having received their instructions, proceeded on their journey ; but they discovered on their arrival that the decision on all important points had already been made ; nothing remained except to impose them on the latest comers. The decrees contained in substance the programme given to Tostado by the General Chapter, and its object could only be described as the total destruction of the Reform. Concessions to a brotherly spirit were mentioned, it is true ; but what were they? The mitigated were asked to change their black habits for brown ones, and to abbreviate slightly the length of their capes., The discalced were ordered to wear the same habit, consequently to give up their sandals and their sackcloth. Also, what was infinitely more important, the latter were ordered to live with the brethren of the Observance, or with their own, indifferently, according to the will of their superiors. The friars in these mixed monasteries were to be allowed to live each in accordance with his own Rule. So that the contemplatives (the name given to the discalced by the Chapter) could choose the meagre food prescribed by his Observance from the well-filled table put before the friars of the mitigation. In a monastery frequented by seculars the discalced were to keep their perpetual silence ; and they would have to rise in the night to recite divine office, as directed by their Rule, but without being roused by any bell. None knew

better than the mitigated that this plan was an impracticable one. 1

The three priors having vainly protested against the decisions of the Chapter, returned to their own monasteries. Philip II being informed of the decrees cancelled them, and ordered Fr. Gratian to refer in matters appertaining to the Order to Mgr. Covarrubias, President of the Council, and Mgr. de Quiroga, Grand Inquisitor. 2 Assured of the support of the king and of the Nuncio, Fr. Gratian then convoked the first Chapter of the discalced Order of Carmel for the 8th of September at Almodovar del Campo. In his opening discourse he showed firmness, mingled with much charity. " War has been declared with us," he said, "not by enemies, but by our brethren; not by the wicked, but by just men and saints. For this reason the war will ever be a pain and a grief to us. The General Chapter condemns us. Our Father-General repulses us. On their representations our holy father Gregory XIII revokes the bulls pronounced by his sainted predecessor in our favour. . . . I wish to believe that those who have persecuted us have done so with a good intention. They have done it to protect their Order, that of the mitigated Rule. But we on our side, have we not a greater right still to defend the primitive Rule? Is it not the most ancient, the most perfect? Thus, supposing each has a cause to defend, that of our brethren is good, but ours is better. Courage and confidence, therefore ! Let us put our faith in God. He it is who, by the hand of the holy Mother Teresa, has founded our houses. He will not permit that they should be overthrown. Let us not give in. Let us oppose the meekness of our Saviour Jesus Christ to the attacks of our

adversaries. Let us take heed that no word should escape us unworthy of the disciples of the Divine Master. Let us pray for those who persecute us, and suffer in silence. The day will come when, won over by our conduct to them, our enemies will be our best defenders. Patience obtains all things." 1

Meanwhile Teresa, whose favourite maxim Fr. Gratian had quoted, was united in heart and in spirit with the deliberations of the Chapter, and never ceased from invoking the light of the Holy Ghost on her sons. "Our fathers," she writes to Fr. Gratian, "have come back enraptured with the success of the Chapter, and I am equally pleased with it. To God be the glory ! But this time your paternity will not escape from praise. It gives me extreme pleasure to hear that you have appointed a zelator for our houses. This is an excellent and most useful measure. I have recommended him to lay great stress on manual labour. This is of the utmost importance." Then with regard to the burning question, Teresa says, " they tell me, also, you have proposed forming a separate Province through our very reverend father-General, and are going to employ every means in your power for this object. It is truly an intolerable struggle to have to fight the superior of the Order. If money is required God will give it to us ; and we can use it for those who are to go to Rome in our interests. For the love of God hasten their departure. This is no secondary matter ; it is the principal point. "-

The saint here indicates the one path by which peace could be restored, e.g. the formation of two separate Provinces with separate jurisdictions, administered according to the spirit and Rule of the

1 History of the Order, Vol. II, Book III, ch. vin.

two families, under the government of the Father-General. After four years' disputes this measure was at last adopted ; but how much agony might have been spared had the saint's voice been earlier heard and obeyed !

Frs. John of Jesus, and Pedro of the Angels, the deputies chosen at the Chapter to represent their case at Rome, delayed their departure. Fr. Gratian, distracted by counsellors, and overpowered with the cares of the visitations which the Nuncio still insisted on his making, allowed the matter to lapse. But few possessed, in the same degree as our saint, the gift of distinguishing the essential from details in matters of conduct, and without neglecting the latter to throw all their energy into the former. She alone, from her poor cell at Toledo, mastered perfectly the situation ; but the difficulties of communication, the slowness of the couriers, delayed her correspondence, and frequently interfered with its usefulness. She felt that her hands were tied, and uniting her will with the Divine Will by a continual fiat, she accepted her isolation, and the obedience by which she was morally chained, which prevented her from flying to the assistance of her deeply-tried children. "The little we can do," she writes, " let us do with all our hearts." And so she ceased not praying for the work of the Reform, and in directing her sons and daughters by means of her letters. All her character, the human element in it as well as the divine, comes out in this correspondence. We read in it the wide views of the foundress; the mother's tenderness; the charity, the burning zeal, the absorbing love of the saint.

In order to disguise her meaning to her adversaries (should any of her letters reach their hands) she had established a code which adds a touch of playfulness to

their contents. Thus she calls herself Laurentia, or Hope, or poor Angela. Fr. Gratian is her dear Paul, or Eliseus ; the Nuncio Mathusalam ; Father Anthony Macharius. The discalced are the Eagles, the Carmelites Butterflies, and so on. She writes most frequently to Fr. Gratian as her superior; but if Fr. Mariano loses his temper, or Fr. Anthony appears to her to be too rigorous, she hastens to remonstrate with them. Thus her letters form a continuous history of every phase of the Reform.

After the Chapter of Almodovar, the priors returned to their monasteries. Fr. Tostado meanwhile had gone to Portugal, and the discalced breathed again. Teresa, however, had no confidence in this temporary lull, and she writes: " We have much to do in order to acquire a solid peace, for this we shall never be able to enjoy as long as our Father-General is opposed to the Reform." To Fr. John of Jesus she writes : " I had hoped you would pass this way, as it is but little out of your road. It is clear you have not much wish to see me. As for the journey to Rome,

I must tell you I can do but little to help you. I have asked for it for so long, and so far I have not even succeeded in getting a letter written to one to whom it is certainly due. Let us do what we ought to do, and then let things happen as they may. Many advise differently, so that my counsels are not of much weight. I am grieved not to be able to do more. May God cause this plan to succeed. I implore of you, my father, never to cease from working for it." 1

The delays continued, in spite of all that the saint could urge ; and the march of events soon made the departure of the deputies impracticable. Fr. Gratian's difficulties with the monasteries of the mitigated friars

had recommenced. When he had presented himself once more at their house at Seville they refused to receive him, alleging that Rome had cancelled his powers. Backed up again by the archbishop and authorities, he had triumphed over the opposition, but the question of exhibiting the Nuncio's Brief came again to the front, and the refusal of Fr. Gratian to produce it embittered the community against him. 1

Teresa, with her usual love of peace, writes to him : " Would to God you could be relieved of this heavy burthen, and could give all your time to the discalced, friars and nuns." 1 Fr. Gratian had this desire equally at heart. Wherever he went in his quality of Visitor he encountered opposition and discontent. Not satisfied with disputing his authority, his opponents spread libels of a scandalous nature about him. Fr. Gratian refused to justify himself, leaving his good name in the hands of God ; but he implored the Nuncio to relieve him of an office which (as he urged) the state of matters prevented his discharging to any useful end, and to allow him to give himself wholly up to the service of the discalced. The Nuncio refused to listen to his appeal. His opinion of Fr. Gratian was so high that he thought him capable of surmounting all difficulties ; and accordingly he confirmed his powers, on the plea that they were for the good of the Order. The father, therefore, had once more to shoulder his burthen, consoled by the thought that God alone placed it upon him. Some unhoped-for successes followed this obedience. " For God's sake," Teresa writes to Mother Mary of St. Joseph, "tell me all you hear about Fr. Gratian. May He reward you for the care you take to pass on his letters to me ! I live for them."

1 History of the Order, Vol. II, Book III.

2 Toledo, October 2ist, 1576.

When he succeeds beyond her hopes, under critical circumstances, she writes: "Thank God for having given such marvellous talents to Fr. Gratian ! Really the success of his visit was quite miraculous. He has behaved with admirable gentleness and tact. In truth the zeal that animates him is so pure that it is impossible God should not come to his assistance." Then with her desire to give all the glory to God, and to Fr. Gratian all the merit of his good works, she writes to him with a mother's authority and a daughter's devotion : " If God did not give us His light to see that all the good we do comes from Him, and that of ourselves we are capable of nothing, I own I should be tempted to take pride in your success in Andalusia . . . one sees that all this is His work ; therefore never forget that all comes from God, and continue to distrust yourself. The great God of Israel wills to be praised in His creatures. We should then—after your example-have His glory always in view, and never seek our own. What becomes us is that our nothingness should be known, and that it should serve as foil to His greatness. Am I not ridiculous to talk thus to you ? You will laugh at me, father, for doing so." 1 Her motherly heart makes her anxious about the fatigues to which Fr. Gratian is exposed. She writes to Mother Mary of St. Joseph thus: " My daughter, our father has told me of the care you take of him. You have endeared yourself to me more than ever by obliging me in this matter, and what pleases me most is that I recognize your prudence in everything you have done." To Fr. Gratian she says: " You must remember you are not made of iron, and that we must not ask God to keep us alive by miracle ! " Not satisfied with general directions, she enters into various details, recommending

him more sleep, and advising that he should be careful to keep his feet covered at night, and allow himself a more substantial diet. But if she is interested in his health, even more so is she in the state of his soul. She continually asks for prayers for him, tells him without hesitation the smallest imperfection she notices in his conduct, and is only satisfied when she can say: "It is clear, very reverend father, that our Lord is well pleased with you." Whilst thus leading him, as it were, by the hand, she is ever the humblest, most respectful of daughters.

To govern Fr. Mariano was a far more difficult task. Candid to excess, with a heart of gold, he treated others as roughly as he did himself. On one occasion the holy mother writes to him: " God have you in His keeping in spite of your faults. . . . You are indeed one with whom it is impossible not to lose patience !" She had constantly to deplore his wrangles with the religious of the mitigated Rule, which undid frequently all the good results brought about by Fr. Gratian's patience and charity. In this Fr. Anthony was not far behind. " May God forgive the disturbance they have raised ! " she writes. " It seems to me that they might behave differently with their brethren. They cause our father much anxiety." l In spite of all she loved them as her sons, made allowances for the faults of their early training, and recognized their great virtues, and was never happier than when she could say, (Fr. Mariano and I are the best of friends. As for Fr. Anthony, I am envious of the way he has stopped offences against God by what he has accomplished." Fr. John of Jesus gave her anxieties of another kind. Fr. Gratian having given him the charge of visiting the houses of the Reform, he marked his progress by

the innovations that he left behind him. Finding nothing to put right, he sought to impose fresh obligations under the pretext of these being conducive to greater perfection. The saint complains to Fr. Gratian: 4 < Only to read all Fr. John's regulations is a fatigue to me, what would happen if I had to follow them! Believe me, father, our Rule does not accommodate itself to these austere people ; it is sufficiently severe of itself." 1

Meanwhile the Carmelite communities of nuns, buried in their impenetrable retreats, were a source of much less anxiety to our saint. Fr. Gratian's attention had been called about this time to a community of the mitigated order at Paterna ; rumours had been busy with their names, and though the worst of what was said about the nuns was disproved, the Visitor saw how deeply they required instruction in the duties of their vocation. With their superior's consent he sent two fervent nuns from the convent of Seville to reform their sisters at Paterna. Teresa followed her daughters from afar with vivid interest, not unmingled with anxiety, and rejoiced when their efforts were crowned with success. u How I envy our sisters," she writes to Mother Mary of St. Joseph, "who have been called to Paterna ! . . . May God be with them, we implore here with all our strength. Take care to write to them very often to counsel and encourage them. It is a severe trial to them to be there alone. Oh, what consolation fills my heart when I see members of our Order contributing to God's honour and glory !"

The successful termination of this affair was Teresa's last joy before her great tribulation began. In the commencement of the year 1577 she had sent some papers to the Nuncio with the object of hastening the

appeal to Rome, and she writes still hopefully: "Our affairs seem to be taking a favourable turn. The Nuncio has sent for our Fr. Visitor. The Order requires all our prayers.

Never was prayer more necessary, for we may soon see, by the grace of God, a favourable solution of our difficulties, or the destruction of our hopes." God permitted that it should be the latter, for the Nuncio dying soon after left them without a friend. Mgr. de Sega, Bishop of Plasencia, his successor, was in many respects a worthy one, but unfortunately the Cardinal Protector of the Order, Buon-compagni, and Fr. Rossi, both strongly prejudiced against the discalced, addressed themselves to him before his departure, and conjured him to put down the Reform with a strong hand, representing its heads to be rebels against lawful authority, bent on destroying the unity of the Order. Mgr. Sega, considering the complaints legitimate, promised to satisfy them in due course. Tostado did not wait for the Nuncio's arrival to recommence hostilities. He launched fresh decrees against the discalced, forbade them to take any more novices, and ordered them to recognize as their superior the prior of the religious of the Observance in every town where they were established. Philip 11.was once more applied to on behalf of the Reform. He took their side, but the arrival of Mgr. Sega complicated everything ; and with many other matters on his hands he declined to meddle any longer with the " monks' quarrel." Abandoned by all, the discalced gave themselves up for lost. Fr. Anthony hid himself in the vaults of the cathedral at Toledo; Fr. Mariano took refuge with friends at Madrid; and Fr. Gratian appeared or disappeared as events made it necessary. In addition to Tostado's severe and repressive measures, various members of the mitigated Order, unworthy

religious, who had long chafed against the Reform and its holy supporters, seized the opportunity of blackening the character of their opponents. Every kind of libel was circulated against them. The saint's great work seemed on the point of being destroyed. This at least was the despairing judgment passed by the discalced themselves on the situation. A number of friars of the mitigated Rule who had embraced the Reform returned to their former houses ; others advised their brethren to submit to Tostado. This was the state in which Mgr. Sega found the Reform on his arrival in Spain.

Our saint's courage alone never faltered. She prayed, and caused her daughters to pray incessantly; and alone, with all the world against her, she set to work to defend her flock. Till then she had given no heed to the stories spread against the Order, she had not even allowed Fr. Gratian to defend himself when his reputation had been attacked. " To contradict such things," she said, " would be to lower oneself." But if she was patient and humble she was also strong — strong in God's strength. " If all the nations gathered together to attack me," she said, "I should not fear, because God is with me." This was her song of hope ; and she added: "If creatures reward me in this manner, it is because my Creator is pleased with me." l In the first place, she sent a strongly-worded appeal to Philip II on behalf of Fr. Gratian. Calumny had outstepped all limits with regard to him. Members of the mitigated Order had extracted false testimony against him by violence, some unfortunate members of a community of the discalced having been terrorized into signing a paper with charges against him. The saint asks for a judicial inquiry ; for here the glory of

God is at stake. In simple but respectful language such as becomes a nun who is yet addressing her sovereign, she asks this less as a grace than as an act of justice. "Sire," she ends by saying, "forgive the length of this letter. Since our Lord endures my indiscreet complaints, I trust your majesty will suffer them no less. May the God of mercy preserve you many years, for you are our only support." 1

Philip ordered the inquiry to be made, and the libellers were forced to withdraw their false statements.

Directly after Teresa had saved Fr. Gratian's reputation, an attack was made from another quarter. The three years tenure of office of the prioress of the Incarnation had expired, and the community had resolved on re-electing Teresa as their prioress. The saint, in order to avoid a conflict with Tostado, begged them to choose a nun of the mitigated Rule; but, true Castilians, they were determined to have their own way. She describes the result to Mother Mary of St. Joseph thus: "The provincial of the mitigated came a fortnight ago to the Convent of the Incarnation in order to preside at the prioress's election. He menaced with censures and excommunication all who | should give me their suffrage. These menaces had no effect, and fifty-five nuns voted for me. With every vote which was handed to him he uttered all kinds of malediction on the nun who presented it, and declared her excommunicated. . . . For fifteen days, now, these have been deprived of Holy Communion, and are not allowed to go to Mass, or to enter the choir, or even to sing divine office. . . . Then, assembling together the forty-four nuns who had not voted, he made them make another election, and sent the papers to Fr. Tostado for confirmation. The

confirmation has already arrived, but the nuns who are opposed to it hold their ground, and say they will not accept the prioress thus elected except as their sub-prioress. Theologians say they are not excommunicated, and that the mitigated have gone against the Council of Trent, which ordains that elections should be carried by majority."

Teresa, in great distress at the punishment inflicted on the nuns, whose only crime was their loyalty to her, moved heaven and earth to get the sentence reversed. This was done at last, but in such a manner as to leave them in almost as sad a plight as they were before.

Not satisfied with treating the community in this manner, Tostado turned his attention to their confessors, Fr. John of the Cross and Fr. Germain. In obedience to his orders they were hurried out of the hermitages they occupied, in the middle of the night, their papers seized, [1] and they themselves dragged, with hands tied like malefactors, to the convent of the Mitigated Observance, where they were scourged and shut up in separate cells. Fr. John confronted his gaolers with his usual serenity, and agreed with their verdict. When some one pitied him, he said : " I am even now treated better than I deserve." His firmness, however, equalled his resignation. To all the menaces or representations that were made he gave but one answer : " I have embraced the Reform, which consists in a life of prayer and penance. I have taken a habit of sackcloth, and I go barefoot. The Nuncio and Apostolic Commissionary have forbidden me to obey the orders of the General Chapter or to change my way of life. I owe them obedience, and

1 It was owing to this circumstance that all Teresa's correspondence with St. John of the Cross was destroyed.

would sooner die than disobey them, so certain am I that such is the Will of God." The following morning Fr. John was sent to Toledo, and given over to Tostado's hands, and Fr. Germain was taken by the prior of Avila to La Moraleja. The saint, on hearing the news, exclaimed : " I would rather see them in the hands of the Moors than of these people."

Not satisfied with praying and causing her nuns to pray, Teresa once more carried her complaints to the king. She began by relating the wrongs of the nuns and of their confessors, and then goes on to say: "I am profoundly afflicted to see our friars of the Reform in such hands. That great servant of God, Fr. John of the Cross, is so exhausted by his sufferings that I am uneasy about his life. I implore of your Majesty, for the love of God, to set him at liberty, and to put an end as quickly as possible to the persecution of the discalced friars by those of the mitigated Observance. Those of the Reform suffer and are silent, thus having great merit in the sight of God ; but what a scandal to the world! Our adversaries declare that Fr. Tostado, having given orders that the Reform should be destroyed, they will see the decrees are carried out. May God be blessed! Unless an order from your Majesty brings some remedy to this state of things, I know not what will become of us! "

Philip, who had ever befriended the Reform, and in particular our saint, caused his council to arrest Tostado and to force him to surrender his powers. As soon as he was set at liberty he started for Rome to obtain redress and fresh authorizations; but his absence made no difference, as the Nuncio, displeased at the interference of the king's council, carried on the same policy in his absence. St. John of the Cross was shut

up at Toledo in a cell, where the light hardly penetrated, for nine months, and was beaten and treated like a criminal, though divinely comforted by grace. He was so well concealed that his friends could not find out the place of his imprisonment. Fr. Gratian took refuge in a grotto at Pastrana and refused to make use of his powers, in order not to increase the Nuncio's displeasure. Teresa alone, standing at the breach, cheered the hearts of her children and raised their hopes. "It is true," she told them, " God is very hard on His children ; but He does them no injustice, for He treated His own Son in the same way." 1 With one hand she closed the mouth of Fr. Mariano, unable to contain his indignation; with the other she sustained Fr. Gratian, worn out by the fury of the storm.

To the first she says: "I implore of you, reverend father, to be silent. You are so candid, that I always tremble for some outburst on your part. Please God that what you have said may not be found out! Do not forget that our duty at present is to obey and to suffer." She reproaches the other affectionately for his dejection: "My dear Paul is rather foolish to have such scruples : your Paternity may tell him so from me. He was certainly rather morbid when he wrote to me last. . . . May God be with you and deliver you from the Egyptians. May He give you strength to come victorious out of the conflict." 2

She longs to find out the place of Fr. John's captivity, and to deliver him. "What does this spiriting away of Fr. John of the Cross signify? Pray see if it be possible to do something for him. If some one of position asked his deliverance of the Nuncio he would not dare to refuse it. ... Could not Fr. Mariano, who has frequently occasion to speak to the

king, represent the state the poor little saint is in, and the length of time he has been languishing in prison?" 1

Fresh complications added to the troubles of the friars of the Reform. Don Maurice Pardos, who had recently succeeded Covarrubias as head of the king's council, commanded Fr. Gratian to take up the work of visitation again. As soon as Mgr. Sega heard of this he issued a decree revoking the commission given by his predecessor to Fr. Gratian, on the plea that that commission had been transferred to the provincials of the mitigated Observance. Philip II cancelled this decree on the gih of August, 1578, by another, in which he forbade any monasteries in his realm to take orders from the Nuncio, alleging that the latter had not submitted his credentials to be verified by the Royal Council.

Who could see clear in such an entanglement? True, the Nuncio represented the Holy See, but it was said that he had exceeded his powers. The saint writes in the following terms to Fr. Gratian directly this decree was known: "Try, my dear father, without being wanting in loyalty to the king, to keep out of this business as much as you can, whatever Fr. Mariano may say to you. Your conscience is not fitted for accommodating matters between two opposite opinions. ... If you have occasion to speak to the Nuncio, and he will listen to you, justify yourself, and tell him that you would willingly submit to his authority, and that if you have not done so it was only because you knew that Fr. Tostado was bent on destroying our Reform. Follow up our plan for a separate Province, that is the one important point. You should press this upon the king, the president, and the archbishop, as well as on

1 Avila, August i4th, 1578.

all the others, and make them understand that all these disputes and scandals come from the Reformed branch of the Order not being constituted into a separate Province." The saint, with a hopeful glance at the future, adds: "If our Saviour grants us this grace it would be right to send deputies to Rome without delay. Perhaps one day we may be the favourite children of our Father-General. Let us first be those of the divine Master, the rest will be as He pleases." 1

Peace and obedience came first in her thoughts, but she adds one word of prudence : " It would be folly to put yourself in the hands of the Nuncio before the president has appeased him. If possible your first interview with him should take place in the presence of Don Pardos."

The saint was ignorant of the scene that was taking place at that time at Pastrana. Whilst Fr. Gratian was living in the monastery of that town, he received an official visit from two friars of the mitigated Observance with powers from the Nuncio. Fr. Gratian received them with much deference, and after showing them into a separate room proceeded to take advice of the community. What was to be done? Was he to obey the Nuncio or the king? The religious differed. Finally he put the same question to a humble lay-brother who had a great reputation for sanctity. Brother Benedict answered: " By refusing to obey the Nuncio we should displease the Pope, who, if he is displeased with us, will withhold the permissions we require. As for the king, he will certainly forgive us when we explain that as religious we are bound to obey the Pope's representatives." Acting on this advice, Fr. Gratian behaved with equal respect and

humility to the visitors, and they departed much edified with all that they had seen. This was but a lull in the storm, but Frs. Gratian, Mariano, and Anthony, trusting that their submission had somewhat mollified the Nuncio, thought the moment favourable to go to Madrid and plead their cause in person. No sooner had they arrived there than they were seized, by the Nuncio's orders, and imprisoned in the convent of the mitigated Observance in that city. Their detention, however, did not last long, as we find them back in their former retreats directly afterwards. 1

Teresa meanwhile had enlisted the help and sympathies of the learned Dominican Fr. Hernandez, and in a long and eloquent letter she implores him to use all the influence he possesses to obtain justice for the cause of Reform. Little came of his intervention, nor of that of Fr. John of Jesus, though great hopes were entertained of both. The latter had tried, equally with Fr. Gratian and his companions, to obtain an audience of the Nuncio, and had shared their fate in being imprisoned. He wrote many letters from his cell imploring to be heard. At last Mgr. Sega sent for him and asked him what he had to say. Fr. John began at once to try and remove his prejudices against the Reform by justifying the saint's actions. " Don't tell me anything about her," the Nuncio exclaimed, "she is an ambitious and disobedient woman, who goes from place to place and meddles with the instruction of others like a doctor of the Church, in spite of St. Paul's commands." Fr. John of Jesus, mastering his indignation at hearing the holy mother maligned in this manner, proceeded to vindicate her, producing the strongest evidence for all he said. Mgr. Sega listened attentively to Fr. John's arguments, and dis-

1 History of the Order, Vol. II, Book IV, ch. II.

missed him with kind words, though without giving him his liberty. 1

Soon afterwards the discalced, sick of the interminable strife, resorted to a desperate measure. The heads of the Order met in Chapter at Almadovar, and — on the strength of a Brief given them by the Apostolic Visitors, Frs. Vargas and Hernandez, to assemble a Chapter and elect a provincial when they should judge that the fitting moment had arrived — erected the Reform into a separate Province, and elected Fr. Anthony of Jesus as provincial. The moment was badly chosen to act upon powers whose value was so strongly open to doubt. Teresa saw this at once, and tried in vain to stop them. "We shall have much greater difficulty in getting the Pope to confirm our choice of a provincial, than of the preliminary measure of forming a Province apart. . . . And the most important point in these matters of jurisdiction, which are so grave and delicate, is that the heads should be appointed by lawful authority."

Fr. John of the Cross, who had been miraculously delivered from his prison at Toledo through the Blessed Virgin's intervention, arrived at Almadovar whilst the Chapter was being held. He was likewise opposed to the measure. But in spite of this double opposition it was carried, and two friars were deputed to go to Rome to obtain the sanction of the Holy See.

At the same time that this news reached Teresa, another courier acquainted her with the death of Fr. Rossi. "The death of our Father-General has deeply afflicted me," she writes to Fr. Gratian. " How much I regret the distress we have occasioned him ; he was most undeserving of it. If we had only had access to him all the difficulties would have been

smoothed away. May God forgive those who stood in the way of our being heard."

This was not the moment to send deputies to Rome, though, by a strange unreasonableness, the heads of the Order decided on carrying out a project which Teresa had never ceased urging when it would have been of use, but which the death of the Father-General now rendered inopportune. Again Teresa writes in forcible terms to represent the mistake that was being committed ; but the decision had been made, and shortly afterwards Fr. Pedro of the Angels, accompanied by a lay-brother, started for Rome. Fr. John of the Cross, on taking leave of Fr. Pedro, said sadly: " Your reverence starts a discalced friar. Take care you do not return with shoes on your feet." These words were almost prophetic ; as Fr. Pedro, demoralized by the hospitality he received at Naples, gave up his life of penance, neglected the objects of the mission, surrendered his papers to his adversaries, and returning to Spain joined the mitigated branch of the Order.

To return to the Chapter. Fr. John of Jesus, who had meanwhile escaped from detention, arrived just as it concluded. He did not hesitate in representing to the fathers the imprudence of which they had been guilty. His warnings were fulfilled ; as shortly afterwards the Nuncio, informed of what they had done, passed a decree of suppression on the whole of the Reform. He excommunicated the heads of the Chapter, and condemned the leaders, Fr. Gratian, Fr. Anthony, and Fr. Mariano, to imprisonment in different monasteries of the mitigated Observance. Teresa was commanded to return to Toledo never to leave it again. 1 All the members of the convents of the

1 The saint had been sent by order of her superior the previous year to Avila.

Reform, friars and nuns alike, were to be placed under obedience to the superiors of the mitigated Rule, and deprived of the right of taking fresh novices. The decree meant the total destruction of the work of the Reform. 1

When the news arrived at the convent of St. Joseph, Teresa for the first time broke down under the blow. She remained the whole day alone without taking food. She wept, and she prayed. Was all the work swept away? Had God rejected her labours? Those blessed solitudes where fervent souls consumed themselves in sacrifice and divine love; those beloved convents, abodes of peace and joy—were they about to be dissolved? Was the Church about to lose the prayer, the unceasing immolation which the Carmelites were ever placing at her service? Moreover, were the holy traditions of the primitive Rule once more to fall into neglect? Was our Lord to lose that little number of chosen friends who placed all their happiness in remaining close to Him, and following His footsteps?

Thirty years before St. Ignatius had asked himself, or had been asked, what he would do if he heard of the destruction of the Society? His answer was that armed with a quarter of an hour's prayer he would be able to accept it with perfect resignation. Teresa, with the knowledge that the imprudence of her children had contributed to their fall, required a longer period. After many hours of anguish her faithful daughter, Sister Anne of St. Bartholomew, knocked at the door of her cell. The night was already advanced ; but, respecting the agony in the mother's heart, she had not dared to interrupt her sooner. But it was Christmas night, Teresa would have to chant the long Office, and Sister Anne came to implore her to come down to the refectory before she went to matins. Teresa obeyed, and

her daughter placing her frugal meal before her, withdrew to a little distance. She there saw the Divine Master approach the table, and, blessing the bread, give it to the saint, bidding her eat it for love of Him. [1] We know not what passed on that blessed night between Teresa and her Beloved. But the next morning the holy mother with fresh hope had recovered all her strength, and. expecting success from God only, she set to work as if God relied on her to effect it. She once more sent couriers in all directions, with letters to the king, the council, and to the monasteries of Castile and Andalusia. She asked her daughters to redouble their prayers and their penances. It is probable that one of the first effects of her intervention was the attitude taken by the Count Tendiglia. A friend of the saint's and a sympathetic witness of the good done by the Reform, he was indignant at the severe treatment Frs. Gratian, Mariano, and Anthony had received, and remonstrated so vigorously with the Nuncio that the latter complained to the king. Philip had by a providential coincidence received at the same moment a letter from Teresa, acquainting him with what had taken place, and accordingly he received Mgr. Sega somewhat coldly. " Count Tendiglia," he is reported to have said, "owes you an apology, and I shall see that he makes it. But I am not ignorant of the hostility borne by the friars of the mitigated Rule against those of the Reform. There is great reason to believe that it is unmerited, and that the latter lead holy and austere lives. To protect virtue is a duty ; and if rumour is to be believed, you have no love for the discalced, and you make them feel it only too strongly." [2]

The Nuncio was greatly troubled at these remarks

which the king pronounced with considerable emphasis, and he withdrew somewhat crestfallen. Shortly afterwards Philip fulfilled his promise to the Nuncio, and charged the president of the Council to reprimand Tendiglia and insist on his giving satisfaction for the language he had used. The count acknowledged his fault, but he wrote to excuse his conduct to the king, and in doing so laid before him a faithful picture of the persecutions the discalced had suffered at the hands of their foes. Philip transmitted this letter without comment to the Nuncio.

As we have already had occasion to observe, Mgr. Sega was a good man. He had every wish to act justly ; he now saw that he had taken a one-sided view of the question. Instead of having (as he had been made to believe) to do with rebel and defiant religious, it was possible that he was by his rigorous measures seeking to destroy a work blessed by God, protected by the king, and by many other great and worthy personages, and secure of ultimate success.

Accordingly, when the Count Tendiglia presented himself in his house soon afterwards he cut short his apologies: "I protest to you, sir," he said, " that my intentions in this matter which interests you so deeply were absolutely upright; and to prove this I am willing to associate myself with any arbitrators chosen by the king to consider the matter. I have no greater desire than to see evil punished, and virtue triumph." The matter being laid before Philip, he appointed four assessors, Don Louis Manrique, Grand Almoner, Canon Villavincentia, and two Dominicans, one of whom, Fr. Hernandez, was a warm friend and supporter of the saint's. The Reform was saved, and Teresa could begin her hymn of thanksgiving. 1

" May God reward you," she writes to Roch de Huerta, "for your good news. As soon as I heard that those two dear and venerated Dominicans had been given as assessors to the Nuncio, all my fears left me. I know them well, and know that in all they will ordain they will have God's glory alone in view. We wish for nothing more."

The Nuncio published a decree on the ist of April, 1579, at the request of his councillors, exempting the discalced from the jurisdiction of the mitigated Rule, and giving them as superior Fr. Angelo de Salazar. It is true he was a former provincial of the Observance, but he was a just and holy man, and Teresa rejoiced at his appointment. " Please God," she wrote to Fr. Gratian, "that our new superior does not retain his authority long ; I do not of course mean to refer to his length of life. He will be very kindly disposed towards us, and his wisdom will teach him how far to go." Then resuming her usual tone of playful wit, she says: "Is it not true that in our character of perfect people we could not have wished for anything better than the Nuncio? He has added to all our merits. You make me smile with your desire for fresh tribulations. For the love of God do not ask for any at present, because you must not forget that you would not be the only person who would have to endure them ! Give us at least a few days to breathe freely." 1

Fr. de Salazar's first act of authority was to set the holy mother at liberty. He sent her a respectfully-worded permission to go wherever the wants of her Order required her presence. He likewise took Fr. Gratian as his assistant and secretary. Teresa's desires were at last heard, and Fr. John of Jesus, and Fr. James of the Trinity were sent on a secret mission

to Rome to plead their cause there. The negotiations were lengthy, for the delegates took a year to collect the documents which their judges required to see before passing their decision. Warned by the previous failure, the discalced friars kept absolute silence on the objects of their mission, and passed themselves off for lawyers, so that their affairs were well advanced before they reached the ears of the friars of the mitigated Observance. Teresa, meanwhile, had obtained letters of recommendation from the king to the Holy See. These, and various other important documents, were laid before Gregory XIII, who sent them to be examined by the Congregation of Regulars. The decision reached by the Congregation was strongly in their favour, but before sanctioning it, the Pope wished to take the opinion of the General Chapter of the Order. The matter thus came before the newly-elected General, Fr. Baptiste Cafardo, who, not unnaturally, sought to save the credit of his Order by a compromise. This was, that the discalced should be separated from the mitigated, but that the former should be governed alternately by one of their own Observance and one of the mitigated Rule.

The Cardinal Protector accepted this proposal as an eminently satisfactory one, and persuaded the Pope to sanction it. Fr. John of Jesus, on the contrary, saw that it would open the door to every sort of fresh difficulty ; but in spite of his protests the proposition was on the eve of being carried when a new ally to the cause presented himself in the person of Cardinal Sforza. The cardinal used his influence over the Pope, to whom he was related, to induce him to put the matter before a Consistory; urging as a reason that, as the Father-General of the Order of Carmel had come to a different decision from the Congregation of

Regulars, it would be a wise measure to bring the question again before a Papal Consistory, so that this last would be final, no further appeal being possible.

The Pope assented to this argument, and in order to acquaint himself with the subject under discussion, sent for a cardinal who had sat on the Commission, and asked him what motive could have influenced the General of the Order to oppose a Reform by which it would greatly benefit. " Holy Father," answered the cardinal, " The Congregation examined in detail all the reasons urged by the friars of the mitigated Observance, and they resolved themselves into this: the mitigated are in dread that the Reformed branch should end by reforming them."

Gregory XIII, at the Consistory which was held shortly afterwards, did full justice to the Reformed branch, both of friars and nuns. He decreed that in future their monasteries should be formed into a separate province governed by a provincial of their own Rule, and elected by them. 1 This Brief was published on the 27th of June, 1580.

1 Boll., No. 878.

CHAPTER XXVI

WHILST the friars of the two Observances were agitated by bitter dissensions, Teresa's daughters, in their happy and peaceful enclosures, took no part in the struggle except by their prayers and their sacrifices. Each one of these Carmels, following the example of St. Joseph's at Avila, was a true Paradise of the Lord—His dear retreat, rinconcito de Dios. In these favoured spots the holy mother's work attained perfection without having to submit to the terrible trials to which her second Reform had been subjected. Living under the same Rule, and animated by the same spirit and the same fervour, these convents had nevertheless each one its special character; or rather, like the personality of the saints, its distinctive traits, which without effacing the rest surpassed them.

The great virtues of religious life, joined to the spirit of prayer and penance, formed the groundwork of all, but at Medina del Campo 1 the community was distinguished by a love of silence which was so great that it was never broken save by pressing necessity ; and it could be said of these faithful souls that they were ever ready at all moments to seize the faintest whisper that came to them from the lips of the Spouse. At Malagon fraternal charity gave rise to actions so heroic that our fastidiousness almost recoils from hearing them de-

1 For this and following details see Foundations, the saint's Letters, and the History of the Order.

scribed. A nun in that convent was suffering tortures from an abscess in her ear which remedies failed to alleviate. Her infirmarian, finding her efforts to ease the pain unavailing, applied her lips to the ear and sucked out the poisonous matter—God permitting that her devotion should lead to her patient's cure without her own health suffering thereby.

Valladolid, under the firm and gentle government of Mother Mary Baptist, was marked by the perfect and joyous performance of the duties enjoined by obedience. The convent of

Toledo, which had suffered perhaps more than any of Teresa's foundations from the pangs of poverty, was full of compassion for suffering which came from the same cause. Accordingly, in a time of great scarcity, when great crowds came to the door to beg, the prioress gave orders that none should be sent away empty-handed, and though the provisions in the house were hardly sufficient for the nuns' own sustenance, the people were fed and yet there was enough left for all.

In describing many of the characteristics of the Carmelites, which we meet with in the early annals of the Order, we feel we might be describing those of the holy mother herself: "for," as one of her contemporaries says, "to see her daughters was to see Teresa."

Such, for instance, was the story told of Sister Isabella of Jesus, whose confessor, in order to try her, refused her permission for daily Communion. Though the priest was stern, her Divine Master was more merciful, and while Isabella remained in her place— her heart the while yearning for union with her God— the Host left the ciborium and came and deposited itself on her lips.

Again, a story is told of a good lay-sister, Frances

of the Mother of God, who had a great love of cleanliness. One day she looked at her hands blackened with her work in the kitchen, and cried sadly to the crucifix hanging in the refectory, " Alas, my Lord, why is it necessary for me always to have dirty hands ? " The Divine Master deigned to answer her, saying : " And I, Frances, what have I not suffered in My hands for your sake?" Such was the obedience, the faith, the simplicity of Teresa's children. And now what shall we say of their courage and love of penance ? In this self-indulgent century what are we to think of her daughters sleeping on thorns or briars ; how speak of their long fasts, their scanty food, mingled sometimes with ashes or bitter herbs? The holy mother herself was alarmed at their penances, and sought to moderate them ; or perhaps it would be more just to say that she tried to turn this heroism into other channels, especially those of humility and interior mortification.

Death was welcomed at the convents of Carmel with the same joy as suffering ; and it pleased God at times to change that time of mourning into one of rejoicing. Thus, whilst the nuns were chanting the Requiem round the coffin of Sister Catherine of Mary, the choir of angels responded with Alleluias. Sometimes delicious perfumes, and an indescribable atmosphere of peace, came to console a community for the loss of one of its members. The holy mother was ever kept informed of these manifestations of God's grace, and was with her daughters in heart and sympathy, even when prevented from visiting them in person. The time of her captivity was perhaps that in which her maternal direction reached to its utmost degree of expansion. Far from allowing the anxieties which she endured to engross her thoughts to the exclusion of other duties, her correspondence shows what she found

means to accomplish for God and for souls, whilst directing her sons in their conflict with the friars of the Observance.

" Exert yourself, my daughter, to acquire little by little great liberty of spirit," she wrote to Mary Mother Baptist on the eve of the crisis. " Thanks to God's grace, I possess it, and in very large measure." In the light of this liberty of spirit, trials and afflictions assumed their true aspect, as transitory incidents in life's journey, having no power to deflect it from its true end. Whilst she was a prisoner at Toledo, it was necessary for her to give up making fresh Foundations, or visiting those which already existed. As God did not permit her to serve Him in that way, she tried to do so in other ways, such as by an apostleship of prayer, and of the pen. Fr. Gratian told her to continue her history of her Foundations ; and it was at that time that she described those of

Segovia, Veas, Seville, and Caravaca. These pages, written when she and the Order of the discalced were the objects of savage persecution, are perhaps the brightest and most vivid in her book. She finds place in it for every little passing adventure, and brings light and beauty out of all. Sometimes it is by a mere expression, a cry of the soul, such as : " Oh, ravishing secrets of God ! with what sweetness He disposes us, frequently against our inclinations, to receive His favours." Or : " Yes ! my Lord, to crush a person to the earth in order to raise him up to a new life is for Thee but the work of a moment! " Another book was to follow that of the Foundations. The manuscript of the saint's life was still in the hands of the Inquisitors, who judged it inexpedient that it should be published in her lifetime. But meanwhile, many souls longed to be initiated by Teresa into the secret of prayer; and Fr. Gratian, seconded by a learned doctor of divinity, Fr. Velasquez, ordered her to write a treatise on the union of the soul with Christ. " Amongst all those things which obedience has imposed on me," Teresa writes, " there are few which have appeared more difficult to me than to write about prayer. But as I know that obedience gives incredible power to smooth away difficulties, I set to work cheerfully, in spite of all the feelings that nature opposes to it. I shall not, I think, add at all to what I have written before on this subject; I fear, indeed, that I shall have nothing further to say about it, for I am exactly like one of those little birds which are being taught to speak, and which, not knowing what they are taught, or what they are saying, repeat the same sentence from morning to night. ... I submit all I am about to say to the judgment of those who have given me orders to write. If it should happen to me to depart in any way from the teaching of the holy Catholic Church, it will be from ignorance, not from malice, as I submit myself to her from the bottom of my soul."

This is the humble preamble of Teresa's Interior Castle; and as God loves humility He came to the assistance of His servant. The saint had conceived a great desire to understand the beauty of a soul in the state of grace, intimately united to God. Accordingly, on the feast of the Blessed Trinity, whilst rapt in contemplation, she saw, in answer to her prayer to have the plan of her book traced out for her, a vision of a resplendent globe of crystal. This globe was divided into six parts. In its inmost depths was seated the King of Glory, and thence, as from a luminous centre, rays were shed whose brilliancy varied according to their proximity to Him. Whilst Teresa was gazing enraptured at the sight the light disappeared, and she

saw the crystal darken, and many loathsome reptiles appear on its surface, whereby she was made to understand the effects of mortal sin on the soul.

It was under the impression of this mystic vision that the saint drew out the plan of the Interior Castle, or Las Moradas; and, basing her views on the Scriptures and on Christian tradition, she sees the true principle and foundation of interior life in the presence of God in the souls of the just. In this crystal, as in Heaven, there are many abodes. The saint is acquainted with all; who can therefore, better than she, reveal the beauties of this splendid mansion which every Christian in a state of grace bears in his soul, though so few seek to enter it. How she compassionates those who are satisfied by admiring it from outside! " With regard to those who lean on thoughts, affection, looks—they but rest on the material setting of the crystal, on the miserable body. Shake off your apathy, poor paralysed souls ; enter into your delightful castle. But perhaps I may be told, ' You are dreaming. If the castle is the soul, how is one to enter it?"

Teresa explains the mystery; the soul recollected within itself alone inhabits this divine castle, and prayer is the only door into it. Once this truth is grasped, we have only to follow the saint from mansion to mansion, that is from one degree to another in the upward ascent of the path of prayer. The soul begins with humility and advances by sacrifice ; then, climbing by perseverance, arrives at last in that blessed region where, with purified heart, she enjoys the delights of union with God. Even when the soul has reached this goal Teresa reminds us that her merit does not consist in the favours she receives, but in the virtues she has acquired ; and that the true spiritual life consists not in enjoying divine consolations, but in

carrying the impress of the cross of Christ. "It is," she tells us, "to belong so utterly to our crucified Saviour, to make so complete a sacrifice of our liberty that He should, at His good pleasure, dispose and sacrifice us for the salvation of the world, as He Himself chose to be sacrificed and disposed of for the same end." 1 Thus we see at every turn, in spite of the effort the saint makes at self-effacement, the reflection of her own beautiful soul in her book. We see that the happiness of suffering for God is in her eyes the greatest of any. Man's abuse, disappointments, and the trials of the soul have no power to injure "that profound peace in which she dwells alone with God." Is Teresa, then, indifferent? Has her heart ceased to love, and to suffer? No; her heart will ever be the tenderest possessed by woman ; she will ever be the most loving saint in our religion of love. But she reposes in the arms of her Beloved, and as all she endures is for Him, and her will is perfectly united to His, she wishes with joy all that He wishes, and accepts without demur what He ordains.

Teresa began her book on the Feast of the Blessed Trinity, 1577, and she finished it on the 2Qth of November with these words : "I have said with what repugnance I began this work. Now that it is finished I am well pleased with it, and look upon the labour I gave to it as well bestowed ; I must own that the labour was very slight. If, my sisters, you find any good in it, know that our Saviour put it there for your benefit ; on the other hand, whatever you find in it that is defective comes from me. In return for the great desire I have to help you a little to serve my Sovereign Lord, I ask one prayer of you. Every time you read these pages praise our Divine Master in my name ; ask

1 Seventh Mansion, Interior Castle.

of Him the increase of His Church, light for heretics, and for me, pardon and deliverance from Purgatory."

Fr. Gratian, and a learned Dominican, Fr. de Yangues, were the first to read this book, and the latter wishing to have certain passages in it explained, went with Fr. Gratian to Avila, and re-read the whole work in the parlour in her presence. His minute questions showed'the importance he attached to it; and, satisfied with her answers, he declared afterwards that the light infused by God supplied in her what was wanting in dogmatic learning. He then left her consoled with his approbation. With her usual straightforwardness she confides her satisfaction to her old friend, Fr'. de Salazar. This priest had alluded to her autobiography as a "jewel," and she answers in her usual playful style, " The jewel you speak of is still in the hands of the same person. But if M. Carillo (this is her name for Fr. Gaspar) came here, he would see a far superior jewel; at least, that is my opinion. The second being detached from all extraneous matter permits of its native riches being seen." 1 Ignoring the share she had taken in producing this masterpiece, the saint could well afford to admire it. As Yepes says, "With the exception of her pen, and the hand that held it, there was nothing of her own in it, for the inspiration came entirely from on high. God, in furnishing her with the matter, the arrangement, and even the title of the book, showed her that He willed Himself to be its author."

Her daughters relate that she was so much occupied in the daytime with her correspondence and the affairs of the Order, whilst she was writing this book, that all the time she could devote to it was stolen from the night; and that more than once, noticing a brilliant

1 Avila, December 7th, 1577.

light coming through the chinks of her door, they had quietly opened it, and found her rapt as in one of her former ecstasies, her face shining and rays of glory coming from her head. Whilst in this state her pen never ceased moving, as if at the dictation of a hidden voice. When midnight struck, having no doubt fixed on that hour as the term of her vigils, she ceased writing, the flames slowly died away, and the nuns could see her stretching out her arms in the form of a cross and praying thus before she sunk to sleep. The following day she was, as usual, first at divine office and at work, and when the time for recreation came none of her daughters were more cheerful than Teresa, so that they marvelled how she could hide under so natural and simple an exterior such astounding heights of sanctity.

The saint had written some years before (we are not told precisely at what date) a commentary on " The Canticle of Canticles" at the order of "one who had a right to her obedience." But instead of giving a fresh masterpiece to the world, she was to give, by means of it, a lesson of humility and submission. Fr. Yanguas hearing that she had a manuscript of the kind in her possession, without having seen it, and with the object of trying her, said somewhat brusquely: " Throw it into the fire ; a woman has no business to write commentaries on the Scriptures." Scarcely had he left the house when she had committed it to the flames. The saint to whom the pleasure of performing an act of self-abnegation equalled that which she would have had in publishing her book for God's glory, was silent about the sacrifice she had made. One of her daughters, however, had copied some pages of it, and Fr. Gratian hearing of it in this way, told Teresa to bring it to him, thus forcing her to confess what she had done. She

had refused to say by whose orders she had destroyed it, but Fr. Yangues, miserable at the result of his hastiness, owned that he had only spoken to her thus in order to try her humility, and had returned to retract his orders, too late to save them from being carried out. We can see by the pages that have been preserved the loss the world has sustained by the act of destruction. To the saint the matter probably was of small importance. She had no idea that she was doing more in her writings than to preserve in a permanent form her instructions to the Carmelites. " It is a great consolation to me," she said, "to confide to my daughters what our Lord has deigned to say to me." Her work as an author was to her but an accessory to her maternal duties. She studied the difficulties of the present times and foretold those of the future. Thus she had said that if ever the love, and faithful practice of prayer, declined amongst her daughters, the retreats of Carmel would be no more than an abhorred tomb. To use any influence outside the cloister was never once in her thoughts.

Thus the subject of prayer—prayer of the heart— humble, confiding and generous; the prayer which embraces all necessities, all sorrows ; the ardent prayer which renders our weakness all-powerful even in the presence of God's justice, was at the root of all her writings and exhortations. Her correspondence was directed to the same end. Whether she writes about the health of her daughters, or tells them what is happening to the Reform, or answers their questions, she yet never ceases from reminding them that the first object of a Carmelite should be to lead a life of prayer.

" May God ever preserve you in His blessed company," she says to a prioress, much troubled with

the cares of office, having solved in a few and trenchant words the difficulties submitted to her. " Prepare," she continues, " to give much to our Lord. . . . Remember the best made prayer is the one which leaves most results : I mean results which show themselves in actions. I desire no other prayer for myself than that which causes me to grow in virtue. I should prefer it even, if it be accompanied with temptations and aridity, because it would make me more humble, and consequently more pleasing to God."

Her piercing glance distinguishes, in the same way as her heart embraces, all the special wants of these divers and much loved souls. In one she sees a shadow of sadness, in another a little excess in fervour, or a love of singularity much opposed to her taste, and all these are so many obstacles to a life of prayer. Through what door could sadness dare to show its face in Mount Carmel ? The devil alone could introduce it, and he must be opposed with courage and contempt. Nowhere was this better understood than by Mother Mary of St. Joseph, the most tried of any of her prioresses. The little convent at Seville laughed and sang in the midst of the storm. " How delighted I am," Teresa writes to her, "that you know how to sustain your daughters in holy cheerfulness and joy." Another time she writes: 1 "I am very pleased with your verses, I have sent the first, and some of the concluding ones, to my brother. I think you might also show them to the holy old man (the prior of the Trappists). . . . Nothing could be better than to give this little pleasure to one to whom we are so greatly indebted. ... It requires much faith to keep this perfect equanimity of soul. But truly, if we found nothing to suffer in our convents, we should have

Heaven on earth, and there would be little occasion of merit. In order to be happy with our Crucified One in Heaven, let us carry the cross after Him on earth.' After the community had gone through great trials she writes to the prioress. "What gives me much cause of rejoicing is that your soul made great advance in perfection ; and, my daughter, the soul never makes so much progress except at a great cost." It was a sufficient reason for dismissing a novice if she showed signs of melancholy. If this disposition showed itself after a nun was professed, she was treated charitably, as one in bad health, and every effort was made to cure her. The holy mother herself prescribes remedies for it, 1 and thanks to her a holy gaiety has been an inheritance in her Order. A want of discretion in penance and devotion was, next to sadness, the greatest - object of her attacks. If the health is ruined, how is the Rule to be followed? she asks. " Observe, father," she said to a Visitor, "I wish to incite to the practice of virtue, not to bodily mortification. Doubtless that results from my doing so little penance myself." She severely reproves prioresses who overload their nuns with works of supererogation, and keep them in choir when they ought to be sleeping. " Pray do not lead your daughters by such a rigorous path," she writes to one. "Never forget that mortification should serve for spiritual advancement only." She recommends great prudence to those who have the direction of nuns favoured with extraordinary graces. " I do not approve," she writes to Mother Mary of St. Joseph, " of the nuns writing down what happens to them in prayer. I see great drawbacks in doing so, even if it was only on account of the loss of time. One may easily imagine things 1 Foundations.

which have never happened. . . . The safest way is to praise God for what He has done, and be satisfied with that. Let the soul draw its profit therein ; that is the chief point." 1 Carmelites could never be her real daughters without being simple and straightforward, in their virtues, their practice of prayer and their exterior relations with each other, or the world. Teresa passionately loved simplicity, realizing that there was no surer road to union with God. It has been said : The more a word resembles a thought, a thought a soul, and a soul God, the more these things are beautiful." These words might have been used by Teresa. "Your letter was a true pleasure to me," she wrote to the prioress of Seville, "and helped me to get over the disgust I felt at that of Sister St. Francis. How little humility was displayed in hers ! Beg hei to give up that exaggerated style. People may think there is no falsehood in those fine phrases, but truly they are much opposed to religious perfection, which demands frankness and simplicity. Tell her this from rne, it is all the answer I have got for her. I shall riot be satisfied until she has cured herself of this defect." Another time she says: "What you say of Sister St. Elias's prayer is good. As, however, I am not so learned in the scriptures as she is, I do not understand her allusion to the Assyrians." " Please to say," she writes another time, to sister St. Jerome, who signs her letter Muladar* "that I beg of God with all my heart that her humility may not be in her words only."

Mother Mary of St. Joseph, though the saint was generally "beyond measure" pleased with her, also gets a word of advice. "Your letters, far from fatiguing me, my dear daughter, are the greatest pleasure I have. Only I am amused at your dating all your letters. God grant that you did so in order not to be spared the little humiliation of writing such bad figures. Before I forget it, I must tell you that I should have much approved of your letter to Fr. Mariano, if you had not quoted so much Latin in it. God preserve my daughters from wishing to become Latin scholars!"

Though the holy mother does not refrain from home-truths, she is ever ready to follow them up with a kindly word : " Bad as you are, my daughter, I should not be sorry to have others who would resemble you," she says to one of her correspondents. And to another " you tell me you have no one to reprove you. Well, for fear you should be tempted to give way to vanity, I will try and come to your help." She never concludes her letters without her mother's heart revealing itself in a tenderness which is deep, rather than expansive. " My daughter, my dear daughter," she says to one, " with what reason I can give you that name ; I love you beyond your belief. I love you so much that it would be impossible for me to forget you, or to cease from praying for your advancement in virtue." Again, she says to Sister Mary of St. Joseph: " If you have a great affection for me I return it, I can assure you, and I love to hear you say it. Oh, how true it is that instinct teaches us to long to have our love returned! This cannot be wrong, because our Saviour Himself asks this of us. And though there is an infinite distance between the love we owe to our adorable Master, and that which we give to His creatures, yet it is good for us to resemble Him in something, if only in this." This ardent tenderness comes from the Heart of Jesus, and Teresa returns it to its source. " My dear child," she says, " I offer the

Divine Master the pain I suffer in being separated from you. . . Please God, we shall be united in eternity. Everything here below passes quickly ; this thought consoles me." [1] Nothing could be more touching than her maternal solicitude for both souls and bodies. "My daughter, "she says to one, " I suffer from your pain ; I implore of you to write and tell me how you are." To another: " May God protect you, my dear child. Take the greatest care of your health, I implore of you ; your illness causes me greater anxiety than anything else. Take everything necessary to give you relief. Wear linen and suspend your practices of penance in this time of trial. Borrow some money in order to live ; you can pay it back later, but pray do not expose yourselves to privations ; that would cause me too much pain."

Not satisfied with tender recommendations, Teresa sometimes sends for her invalids in order to nurse them. Mother Brianda of St. Joseph, prioress of Malagon, was said to be attacked with phthisis, and to be slowly dying. "The physicians hardly give me any hope about her," Teresa says, "but God is life; He may give it to her. Let us not cease imploring Him to do so." Her letters are full of her dear invalid at this epoch. " Our prioress of Malagon told me lately she was better. She said so, dear child, to comfort me, as I see no improvement in her." To Mother Brianda herself our saint writes the most affectionate letters: "May God give you," she says, "at these feasts of Christmas a great love for Him, so that you may not feel your sufferings. You are gaining great glory in Heaven for these days you spend in bed. God be praised, it is something that you are not worse in this cold weather." Is not a mother gifted

with an insight, a genius, such as no one else can possess? Teresa therefore being persuaded that the prioress would recover if she was under her care, sent for her to Toledo, and took entire charge of her. She occupied herself day and night with her patient, and consoled and delighted her with her company. She was ever trying to tempt her delicate appetite, and studying what suited her enfeebled digestion. She mentions her thus in a letter treating otherwise of business matters : " I did not give Mother Brianda the preserves sent by my brother, as in her high fever it would only have done her harm. Do not send me anything for her which would be of a heating nature. I have great hopes of the water of Loja for her ; I have arranged that it should be fetched for her. . . . What our dear patient fancies, most at present, are little cakes made of sugar and butter." 1

God blessed the saint's care of her dear prioress, and after a time she was cured ; but Teresa did not send her back to Malagon. Difficulties which had supervened in the convent, after she had been taken away, made the holy mother feel that Mother Brianda's still delicate health might suffer by her return thither. The community had not taken to the sub-prioress, who ruled in Mother Brianda's absence, and their petitions that the latter should be sent back to Malagon were too urgent for our saint to listen to them.

Teresa was as firm as she was kind, but she blamed her daughters at Malagon for an attachment which she considered excessive. Later on she visited the convent, and left them pacified under the rule of a new prioress who had learnt better how to gain their confidence.

The trials undergone by the community at Seville,

1 Toledo, January 26th, 1577, 2 I

about the same time, were a cause of much greater anxiety to the saint. That convent, it will be remembered, had been subjected from its foundation to injurious rumours and suspicions. In 1578, whilst Fr. Gratian was in Madrid, the heads of the mitigated Order in Seville, deceived, themselves, by a miserable impostor, insisted on having the doors of the cloister thrown open to them, and on examining one by one every member of the community. The intention of the religious of the Observance was to collect evidence against Fr. Gratian by means of the nuns' depositions, especially with regard to his relations with the holy mother, and Mother Mary of St. Joseph. The nuns protested indignantly against this treatment, and the accusations involved in it. A poor lay-sister, and Sister Beatrice of the Mother of God, had the misfortune, after a long examination, to break down under threats of excommunication, and signed a paper full of falsehoods which had been drawn- up under their names. The provincial, furious at the firmness of the rest, deposed the prioress, confided her office to a nun without any experience, and forbade her to hold any communication with the saint. The holy mother writes thus to her friend the Carthusian prior on the subject :

" What do you think, my father, of what has happened in our house, and of the manner in which the nuns have been, and still are, treated? As for me, I can only say that if they have asked crosses and suffering of God, He has in truth heard them. I am not so unhappy about those who came with me when the Foundation was made ; there are moments, indeed, when I rejoice at the great benefits which they will reap by this warfare which the devil has raised against them, but for those who have since taken the habit. To these such a beginning may do much harm. May

God remedy it! I implore you, reverend father, to see that this letter which I take the liberty of sending you reaches the former prioress, and the nuns who came from Castile. You doubtless know the manner in which they deposed the mother and replaced her by a young nun, and you are aware of all they made those poor souls suffer, forcing them even to give up the letters they had received from me in order that they should be sent to the Nuncio. ... I beg you, therefore, once more, reverend father, not to abandon my poor daughters, and, above all, to help them in their trials with your prayers." 1

The letter Teresa encloses for her daughters begins as follows :

" May the grace of the Holy Ghost be with you, my daughters and my sisters ! Know that never have you been so dear to me as you are now, and also that there has never been a time when you owe our Lord greater gratitude than you do now; for He has vouchsafed you a great grace in letting you taste of the bitterness of His Cross and of His abandonment during His Passion. . . . Courage, my daughters! Remember, God never sends greater crosses than we are able to bear, and that He says He is with those who are in tribulation. Pray hard, my sisters. May humility and obedience reign amongst you, and may all, including the former prioress, give the others an example of perfect submission to the new superior. If you help yourselves, Jesus will help you. Though He appears to sleep whilst the storm rages, when it is at its worst He will command the waves and there will be a great calm. . . . What gives me great pain is to hear that in the depositions drawn up for the provincial assertions have been made with regard to facts which

I know to be false, as they took place in my presence. For the love of God, see what motive could these sisters have had for maintaining such falsehoods. Was it fear or anxiety? If God is not offended, the rest matters little. But to lie, and to lie to the prejudice of one's neighbours, that, my daughter, is to do something which breaks my heart."

These falsehoods, dragged from the evidence of girls of twenty, were to be used to add to the catalogue of delinquencies which Fr. Gratian's enemies in the mitigated camp had drawn up against him. The Royal council (as we have already seen) did full justice to Fr. Gratian, and the calumniators were brought to deserved shame.

When peace was restored and the community enjoyed their liberty once more, the first use they made of it was to re-elect their former prioress. The saint writes her congratulations in these terms : " You have given me great pleasure in the letters which I have received from you, my dear daughters, and I should have wished to have answered each one in particular had I the leisure to do so. ... It would appear as if God intended to make you more perfect than the rest of us, since He has sent you such trials ; take care you do not lose the merit of them. May His holy name be blessed for the happy inspiration you had in making your election. I was much consoled when I heard of it." The holy mother has also a word for the poor culprits. " I pray Sister Beatrice and Sister Margaret to forget the past, unless in the presence of God or their confessor. Our Lord often permits us to fall in order that our souls may increase in humility, and when we rise up with upright intentions, and the conviction of our own weakness, we draw fresh strength from our falls to advance in the paths of virtue. This

has been the case with many saints. Thus, my daughters, as you have our Lady for your mother, and you are all sisters, love one another ; and as for the past, let it be buried in oblivion. I say this to all of you without exception." 1

Thus did Teresa realize and carry out her duties as mother, carrying the feeble and the little ones in her arms, in order to bring them back to the fold. This was how she encouraged the strong, healed the sick, and, in short, led every soul to the summit of Carmel, which was, it is true, surmounted with a cross, but a cross transfigured by love and bathed in the rays of Heaven.

1 Malagon, January, 1580.

CHAPTER XXVII

T)EFORE resuming the history of the saint's XD Foundations, and seeing her succumb to them— as a soldier falls on a battlefield where he has won his dear-bought laurels — let us consider her from the point of view of a sister and a friend, and follow her through the trials that her faithful and loving nature entailed upon her.

For Teresa to love a man was to love his soul, and to love a soul was to long to see it beautiful, holy and great, and to long for it with a holy and impassioned longing. God was indeed the first and moving principle of her affections, but that did not prevent her taking human means, such as kind words and a little condescension to man's weakness and wants, in order to lift his heart on high. Thus, far from being sparing of marks of affection, she bestowed them with a lavish hand on those she loved. She took part in their troubles, interested herself in the state of their affairs, their healths, and their families. True, she passed quickly over the preliminaries in order to get to the essentials, but not before she had gained her point ; so that her appeals to consider the nothingness of life, and the importance of prayer were afterwards taken in good part.

It is of prayer, before and above all, that she speaks to all the world. Not in the same manner, of course ; still, in her letters to men and women in the world, as

in those to her nuns, she never ceases to carry on the work, which above all others our Lord had confided to her, of praying- and teaching others to pray.

Though called by God to this mission, Teresa was, by nature and on principle, so much opposed to all singularity that she never went out of her way to exercise influence in this direction. She accepted the opportunities Providence put in her way. She reserved the first place in her affections (after the supernatural ones of the cloister) for her own family. In this she was following out our Lord's own commands ; for on one occasion, fearing that she was transgressing the Rule by receiving visits too frequently from her brother, and laying this difficulty before Him in prayer, she received this answer : " Do not fear, daughter ; for your conduct should be regulated in accordance with My laws-" 1

Her family circle had grown smaller with her advancing years. Rodriguez, the companion of her childhood, was gone, and after him Anthony, the Dominican friar. Then again Teresa had to mourn the loss of Jerome, " the good Jerome " of whom she ever spoke so kindly ; and of Maria de Cepeda, her eldest sister. The latter had had the great misfortune of losing her husband by so sudden a death that he was not given time to receive the last sacraments. Teresa shared deeply in her sister's sorrow, and did her utmost to console her and turn her thoughts wholly to God. Our Lord having revealed to her that Maria would likewise die suddenly, Teresa, without telling her sister, represented to her the importance of approaching the sacraments frequently, and being always prepared to appear before God. " My sister followed my advice," she writes, "and having lived four or five

years in great purity of conscience she died alone, and without being able to make her confession. Thanks to the habit she had of going often to the sacraments, it was only a week since she had confessed. She remained but a very short time in purgatory, barely eight days, when our Lord appeared to me just after I had been to Communion, and deigned to show her to me going up to Heaven with Him." 1

Of all Teresa's brothers and sisters there only remained Juana, Lorenzo, Pedro, and Augustine. The last-named was a distinguished soldier, having been victorious, it is said, in seventeen fights. He had received in reward for his services an important post in the Government of Peru ; but the saint could not endure the thought that he was participating in the despotism which the conquerors of America exercised over the vanquished races, and she never ceased imploring him for his soul's sake to return to Spain. Augustine obeyed, and directly after he had given up his post the Indians sacked the town of which he had been Governor, and massacred his successor in that office. Augustine remained in his own country till Teresa's death, and then, irresistibly attracted back to the scenes of his early life, returned to Lima, where he died soon after landing. Teresa, according to his confessor's attestation, appeared to him in his last moments, consoled and assisted him, and received his last sigh.

Pedro de Ahumada was a source of even greater anxiety to his sister. He had run through all his fortune, and was entirely dependent on his elder brother ; and unfortunately his temper and trying character made it difficult for him to share a home with any of his relations. On one occasion, in a fit of melancholy,

1 Life, ch. xxxiv.

he ran away from Don Lorenzo's house, and appeared pale and in despair at the parlour of the Carmelite convent at Toledo. Teresa sought with great tact to make peace between the two brothers. In a letter to Lorenzo she first does justice to his natural resentment, and goes on to say : " The poor fellow owns that you have a right to be angry with him, but he says he cannot behave better. He understands the mistakes he has made, and he must be weary of making them ; but in spite of all, he says he would rather have died than remain as he was. ... I shall keep him here until I receive your answer, though he says he is convinced of the uselessness of my proceedings. But as he is beginning to see the situation in which he has placed himself, he consents to wait. Answer me quickly, I implore of you." The saint then suggests that Lorenzo should increase the sum he allows his brother, in consideration of his no longer being at the expense of his maintenance, adding that with this sum he will be able to arrange to live with their sister Juana, or a nephew, Don Diego de Guzman, neither of these being rich enough to take him in gratuitously. " But," she prudently adds, " do not pay the whole of the sum at once, but give it successively to those with whom he stays, as I foresee he will not long remain in one spot. No doubt it is very sad . . . but if this poor brother is foolish on one point, though upon no other, it is clear from the point of view of perfection you are more obliged to help him, and to give him alms in preference to others on account of the tie of relationship. Believe me, when God gives graces such as He has given you, He expects much in return." Teresa adds this charming touch: " Look upon this sum as if it was to me you were giving it, as you certainly would if you saw me in misfortune ; and in truth I shall take it as if

it was done for me." 1 Don Lorenzo gave gladly the sum asked for by Teresa, and continued to provide for his brother in the different houses whither he was led by his vagabond humour. Pedro had met with cruel disappointments on his return from Peru, the king having refused certain honours and rewards to which he considered he was entitled ; hence this morose temper which made him a trial to all around him. His love and veneration for his sister, however, never ceased, and though his career seems to have been a sad and wasted one, he ended it by a peaceful and happy death.

If the saint had her share of those trials and anxieties from which no large families are exempt, she had also her joys and consolations. Juana de Ahumada and her husband, in their little home at Alba de Tormes, led a truly Christian life, occupied in the service of God and the duties of their state of life.

The saint's relations with her brother Lorenzo were more intimate. Lorenzo had bought a property in the neighbourhood of Avila called La Serna, where he led the life almost of a hermit, observing literally the command in the Book of Wisdom to the rich man to use his wealth in God's service. Yet neither his alms to the Carmelites, to the Church, and to the poor, nor his generosity towards his own family, or his practices of piety wholly satisfied him. He was devoured with that holy thirst after justice of which our Lord speaks. But a certain scrupulosity was mixed with his piety which threatened to paralyse it, and made him feel the necessity of a wise and firm direction. Enlightened confessors were not wanting at Avila, but Lorenzo's desire was to submit his soul to his sister's guidance. The saint hesitated much before undertaking such a responsi-

bility. Her humility shrank from the idea of directing a soul outside the precincts of the cloister, and she feared to usurp powers which the priesthood alone confers. Her confessor, however, decided in Lorenzo's favour. "My dear brother," she writes, "I have spoken to my confessor about your wish to put yourself under obedience to me, telling him I thought it quite uncalled for. He approves of it, nevertheless, as long as you do not bind yourself by vow, either as regards me or any other person. I consent therefore on this condition only, and even thus not without repugnance, which, however, I overcome in order to comfort you." 1 Teresa, relieved from doubts suggested by prudence, gave herself up to the happiness of opening out her heart to one to whom she was so closely united by ties of blood, and by the attractions of divine grace. What she was ever in search of, in the cloister or outside of it, a heart whose one desire was to seek God and please Him, she found now in her own brother. Thus in what transport she writes to him : " May God be praised now and for ever ! We have both of us, at last, the happiness of being in His good graces. Oh, how good our Lord is! It appears to me that He wishes to show His power by raising poor people such as you and me —for I know no one worse—into such high favour. We should, my dear brother, thank God each of us, one for the other; I beg of you at least to do so for me, as I can never be sufficiently grateful to Him ; so I greatly desire that someone should help me." More than one motive contributed possibly to provoke this outburst from Teresa. Knowing her brother as she did, her first instinct was to draw him from his habitual melancholy. Their mutual friend, Francisco de Salcedo, who was as pious and timid as ever, had begun to play the

1 Toledo, January lyth, 1577.

same part with Lorenzo that he had formerly done with Teresa. In his opinion Lorenzo was not on a safe path, because he was enjoying consolations reserved for more advanced souls. The saint, fearing his influence on her scrupulous brother, warns him thus : " The good Francisco de Salcedo's humility is worthy of all praise. God leads him by the road of fear. I look upon him as a saint, but God leads you by quite a different path. He treats him as a strong soul, and you and me as feeble ones."

A little later she writes: "You are charitable indeed, my dear Lorenzo, to wish to take all the trials and leave consolations to others. Thank God for inspiring you with the wish. But, on the other hand, do you not see that it is rather foolish, and even a want of humility to think it would suffice to have Francisco de Salcedo's virtues without the helps you receive in prayer? Believe me, you had better leave the Master of the Vineyard to do as He likes ; He knows the wants of each one. Never have I asked Him for interior trials, and yet this has not prevented Him sending me many. These kinds of troubles depend much on character and temperament." 1 Lorenzo's scruples reappear perpetually under one form or another. Sometimes it is his transports of devotion that frighten him, at another his aridities with which he reproaches himself, or his appetite and the time he gives to sleep. He tries to waken himself at night to pray, and covers himself with instruments of penance, or binds himself with imprudent vows. The care of his household and his children's education weighs him down. A very little more, and he would be of the number of those "who," according to his holy sister, "do not dare to move or stir, for they feel that if even they give themselves time to breathe all their

devotion will vanish." Happily for Don Lorenzo, he had to do with our saint; and in spite of his resistance, she soon persuaded him to give a looser rein to his piety, encouraging him to walk in the path of prudence and common sense, without taking up practices incompatible with his temperament or his paternal duties.

" Do you know," she writes, " who makes you regret having bought the property of Serna? It is the devil, and it is in order to prevent you thanking God for having done so. ... Make up your mind once for all that in many respects this is the very best thing you could have done ; for it assures a property, and what is more important still, a good position for your children. Did you think you could get your rents paid without trouble? And as for those evictions you say you are always having to make, every one who has a property has to do the same thing! Again I warn you to take care ; this is a real temptation. Instead of regretting what you have done, thank God, and do not imagine that if you had more time you would pray more. Time so well employed as in looking after one's children's interests could never interfere with prayer. God often gives more grace in one moment of prayer than He does in others which have lasted hours. His works are not measured by time. Try, therefore, as soon as these feasts are over, to see to your affairs, and get them in good order. Exert yourself to improve your land. Abraham was not the less a saint because he looked after his flocks ; the same can be said with regard to Jacob, and St. Joachim. But, naturally inclined as we are to avoid work, we weary of everything."

The advice Teresa gives him with regard to the education of his sons is equally marked with wisdom and prudence. After devoting the necessary time to

study, and to practices of piety suitable for their years, they are to be allowed time for recreation, to be looked after, and amused. Lorenzo, in striving after perfection, must not cease to be a father. Once more she pursues him with her gentle raillery. " By the way, before I forget, is it true you make vows without saying anything to me about them? This is a pretty obedience ! As for me, I look upon such a vow as pure childishness. Never should I dare to promise what you have, knowing that the apostles themselves have sinned, only the most holy Virgin being exempt. To undertake under vow to avoid faults into which one may easily fall, without perceiving them even ! Heaven preserve us from doing such a thing. This must be remedied at once; change your promise to something else, and never attempt to tie yourself up in such a manner again. 1 ... I tell you, and I also order you, my dear brother, not to give less than six hours to sleep. If we old people overburthen the body we depress the soul, which is the cause of great suffering. Sleep then, I insist upon it, and be sure that you will please God by your obedience. . . . Believe me that your giddiness has nothing to do with what you eat or drink ; you should, therefore, take a good collation. One may go too far in one's desire to surfer for God, and one does not find it out till the harm is done." 2

Don Lorenzo, forced to sacrifice his views on so many points, tried to make up for doing so in other ways; by dint of pressing his sister he got leave from her to wear a hair-shirt. She sends one to him in fear and trembling. " You may wear it," she says, " when you have difficulty in recollecting yourself in prayer, or when you feel a great desire to practise penance. . . .

1 Toledo, January 2nd, 1577.

Wear it only long enough to give yourself a feeling of discomfort; and, indeed, I am afraid of allowing so much. However, let us at least try it, as there is much happiness in suffering for the love of God, even if it should be only in a trifling way. I laugh when I think of it! You send me money and preserves, and I send you a hair-shirt in return. . . . As for your disciplines, let them be of short duration ; they hurt more in that way and do less harm. Mind you do not strike too hard. I told you to wear the hair-shirt twice a week. How well you know how to count the days! The Carmelites are nothing like so clever as you are in that respect!" Don Lorenzo, overjoyed at getting these permissions, was prepared to make use of them in such a manner as to reproduce the flagellations of St. Paul in the solitude of La Serna. Again Teresa writes: " I really cannot understand what you mean about the discipline you take for the length of some Paters. Never have I permitted any such thing. Read my letter again, and see if I am not right. . . . You will do more penance in using it moderately, because you will renounce your own will. Don't forget when you use the hair-shirt to let me know if you are the worse for it. ... Our Lord does me great favour in giving your good health. May our Divine Master preserve you in it many years, so that you may employ them in His service."

Teresa's recommendations would have carried no weight unless she preached by example. She makes, therefore, such an avowal as this one in her letters: " In order to write you to-night I had to infringe on the time I give to prayer. I have no scruple in doing so, though I frankly regret much not having more leisure." Or else: "I was very unwell lately, now I am getting better every day. I say this as you might be worried

if you saw one of my letters in someone else's handwriting. Do not be uneasy. I take great care of myself." Again: "My last letter procured me one advantage. I was obliged to dictate my letters. I like it so much that I think I shall go on doing it. Still, what I have suffered shall not deprive me of the consolation of writing to you to-day myself, as I do not wish to mortify myself first in order to mortify you !"

We are reminded, in reading these lines, of St. Francis of Sales' advice : " Let us be saints here below, not in the manner of the angels, since that is impossible, but as good men and women." Both saints understood that nature should be taken into account in the work of the sanctification of souls ; to do otherwise would be to risk crushing the soul instead of super-naturalizing it. Their words and actions were within reach of all, after the example of Him Who said, ' l Learn of Me —not how to create Heaven or earth—but how to be meek and humble of heart."

The solitude of La Serna soon became a place of meeting for Teresa's and her brother's friends. The saint was charmed for Lorenzo's sake when she heard of it, and recommended him to encourage and make the most of these visits; for " one cannot always be praying, and the society of spiritual-minded people is very good for one."

On one occasion she invited her brother to write some reflections on the meaning of the words, " Seek thyself in Me," which the Lord had spoken to her in prayer. Lorenzo, much puzzled, asked the assistance of Francisco de Salcedo, Fr. Julian d'Avila, and also of St. John of the Cross, who was living at that time at the Convent of the Incarnation. The four professors agreed each to write separately, and to send their compositions to the Carmelites of St. Joseph, to ask

their opinion before submitting what they had written to the saint. But the Bishop of Avila thought the subject above the nuns' comprehension, and settled that Teresa should be sole judge. The four treatises were, therefore, sent to Toledo. The moment was ill-chosen as regards Teresa, for " she has such a violent headache she can with difficulty see to read." Would anyone guess it from reading her reply ? l

" Unless I were obliged, my lord, under obedience, I should not answer; and for good reasons I should refuse to judge the subject under discussion. Not, however, as our sisters here will have it, because my brother being one of the rival competitors my affection for him would give reason to suspect my impartiality. No! for all the competitors are dear to me, having all helped me in my labours. Moreover, my brother was the last comer, who only appeared as we finished drinking the chalice ; but he also shared it, and he shall have an even better share later, by the grace of God. May God grant too that I say nothing which may cause me to be denounced to the Inquisition ; for my head is tired out with the number of letters, and other things, which I have had to write since last night. But as obedience can do everything with me, I am going to comply, well or ill, with your lordship's orders. I should have liked to have taken a little time to read over and enjoy the papers; but you are not satisfied with my doing this, and I must obey.

" First of all, it appears that the words in question come from the Spouse of our souls, Who says to them, 'Seek thyself in Me.' I do not require more to conclude that Don Francisco is beside the question

1 This celebrated letter goes, in Spain, by the name of La carta del •veyameri) the bantering letter. 2 K

when he says that it signifies God is present in everything. Truly a grand discovery ! But here is something more, and unless Don Francisco does not contradict it I shall have to denounce him to my neighbour the Inquisition. He is ever saying and repeating in his paper, * St. Paul says this': "the Holy Ghost expresses Himself in this way ' : and after that he says— by way of conclusion—that his essay is full of follies. He will certainly have to retract as quickly as he can, or he will see what will happen !

" As for Fr. Julian, he begins well but ends badly ; thus he will certainly not get the prize. He is not asked here to explain how the uncreated and created light became united ; nor what a soul feels who is perfectly united to her Creator; nor whether in this state she differs or not from her divine Objective, etc. Again, what does he mean by the expression, 'when the soul is purified?' As for me, I believe virtues and purification of the soul are insufficient here, because it is a question of a supernatural state, and a gift which God confers on whomsoever He pleases ; and if anything could predispose the soul to receive it, it would be love. But I forgive him his digressions, because he has at least one merit: he is less lengthy than my Fr. John of the Cross.

" The doctrine of the last named would be excellent for one who wished to make the Exercises of St. Ignatius ; here they are out of place. We should be much to be pitied if we could not seek God before being dead to the world. What! were the Magdalen, the Samaritan woman, the Canaanitess, already dead to the world when they found their Saviour ? He enlarges greatly on the necessity of uniting one's self with God in order to be made one— wholly —with Him. But when that happens, when the soul has received this signal favour from

God, He can no longer tell her to seek Him, for she has already found Him. The Lord preserve me from people who are so spiritual that they wish, without choice or examination, to bring all back to a perfect state of contemplation. We must, withal, do him the justice of acknowledging that he has explained remarkably well what we never asked to know. This comes of discussing such a subject: the profit one reaps from it is the one we least expected to get.

" This is precisely what has happened to Don Lorenzo de Cepeda. We are much obliged to him for his answer and his verses. He was speaking somewhat out of his depth. But in consideration of the little treat he has given us, we willingly forgive his want of humility in treating upon subjects which, as he himself acknowledges, were so much above him. He would deserve, however, to be expostulated with for the good advice he gives to devout souls—without their having asked for it—to practise the prayer of quiet, as if it depended on them ; God grant that he may get some good of his intercourse with such spiritual-minded people. Still his work did not fail to please me, though I think he has great reason to be ashamed of it.

"In short, my lord, it is impossible to decide which of these writings is the best, as one cannot say, in justice, that any are faultless. Will you please to tell their authors to correct themselves; and perhaps I should not do amiss to correct myself too, so that I may not resemble my brother in being wanting in humility? I conclude, my lord, for fear of fatiguing you with my extravagances. I will answer at another time the letter you do me the honour of writing to me, for which I thank you heartily." 1

The bishop delighted with the criticism, insisted on

1 Toledo, March, 1577,

Teresa competing with her friends. She sent him in answer the following lines :— 1

My beloved, passing Fair, Love has drawn thy likeness, see In My inmost Heart, and there — Lost or straying unaware — Thou must seek thyself in Me.

Well I know that thou shalt find This thine image in My Heart Pictured to the life with art So amazing that thy mind Sees thy very counterpart.

If by chance thou e'er shalt doubt Where to turn in search of Me— Seek not all the world about, Only this can find Me out— Thou must seek Myself in thee.

In the mansion of thy mind Is My dwelling-place, and more There I wander, unconfined, Knocking loud, if e'er I find In thy thought a closed door.

Search for Me without were vain, Since when thou hast need of Me Only call Me, and again To thy side I haste amain. Thou must seek Myself in thee.

Very soon afterwards the saint was again in correspondence with the bishop— this time on the subject of withdrawing the jurisdiction of St. Joseph's convent from his hands, and placing it (like the rest of Teresa's

1 The original poem is given in the Appendix. The translation is by A. Stirling. The first verse is omitted.

Foundations) under that of the provincial of the Order. Mgr. de Mendoza's paternal affection for the little community made him at first disinclined to the change, but he gave in to the strong reasons urged by the saint in favour of it. The sacrifice was minimized by the fact that the bishop was about to be promoted to the diocese of Valencia. Though he gave up his other rights, he retained that of being buried in the little church at St. Joseph, obtaining at the same time a written promise from Fr. Gratian that Teresa's body, in whatever part of Spain she should die, should be brought back to Avila and laid in an adjoining grave to his own. The saint's fidelity to her friends is shown in the following letter which she wrote to him shortly before he left the diocese: "I hesitate, my lord, how I shall approach your grace on the subject of Master Daza's affair. I much wish you could do something for him, and however little it was it would always be a joy to me. I know how attached he is to you, and I have heard him say that his affection for you was such that rather than give you the smallest annoyance by asking for a favour, he was ready to serve you cheerfully without ever asking you for anything. This does not, however, prevent his being a little hurt, and complaining a little of his want of luck, when he sees the favours you have bestowed, and bestow every day on others. ... In short, my lord, everyone is not obliged to love you in the same manner as your Carmelites, who ask nothing of you except that you should love them, and that God should preserve you for many years." 1

One point, which illustrates a very interesting side of Teresa's character, is the time she found for her huge correspondence, the four hundred letters extant

1 Avila, August, 1577.

forming but a fraction of it. Whether she writes to women of the world like Dona Luisa de la Cerda, or to soldiers such as Don Diego de Mendoza and the Duke of Alba, to priests, bishopsj or members of her own community, or presents her petitions to the king, we are conscious of the same characteristics in them. Her tact, and the charming instinct she has of what is due to each person to whom she writes, never robs her letters of their spontaneity. She is humble with all, respectful when necessary, but never servile. Even in treating with great people, she keeps a certain freedom of expression quite in keeping with her character ; and whilst honouring in them a dignity with which Providence has invested them, she reserves the right of reminding them that true greatness consists in serving God and humbling oneself before Him.

That the saint could speak out indignantly when necessary the following correspondence shows. Fr. Suarez, provincial of the Jesuits of Castile, wrote to reproach her with trying to persuade Fr. Caspar de Salazar, a member of the Society, to leave it in order to join the Order of Carmel. She begins by repeating the accusation, and then says: " Far from having advised him to make this change, I have never even wished it. When the news reached me it did not even come to me straight from the father. I was so distressed by it that it almost made me ill. . . . As for the revelation, I am unaware if Fr. de Salazar has had one, having had no letter from him. But supposing I had myself had this dream, as your Paternity calls it, I am certainly not so imprudent as to advise a change of such importance on similar grounds. I can also answer for this, that Fr. de Salazar would never have heard of it. ... I wish to prove to your Paternity that I treat with the Society of Jesus

as one to whom it is very dear, and who would give her life for it. No ! I cannot believe that our Lord would ever permit that His Company even on a grave subject, much less on a trifling plea, should take action in any way against the Order of our Lady. . . . We are all vassals of this Sovereign Lord. Please God, whether we are the one or the other, His companions, or the children of His Mother, that we may be soldiers of His, desirous only of serving under His standard, and obeying His orders." She finishes by saying: "In any case, I give your Paternity my word that neither in the future, any more than in the past, shall I ever say a word to Fr. de Salazar to induce him to carry out such an intention." 1 The provincial regretted his suspicions after reading this letter, but he charged the rector (whom he had already made use of as intermediary), whilst excusing him to the saint, to beg her to ask the heads of her Order to refuse to admit Fr. de Salazar into it. To this singular demand Teresa answers with a firmness tempered by her usual benignity: " God knows, reverend father, that I have spoken the truth to you without dissimulation, this being what religion and honour requires of me. To go further would be to show myself wanting both in one and in the other, and would be equivalent to committing a great injustice to one to whom I owe much friendship, being convinced as I am that Fr. de Salazar will do nothing without his provincial's consent. Therefore let that reverend father stop him and refuse his consent. I should be doing an ill service to one who is a true servant of God by taking away his character amongst our monasteries, as it would be nothing less than a grave injury to say that he wished to undertake something which he could not carry out without offend-

ing God. I venture to say this to your reverence, and — having done what I thought it was right for me to do — may God give me courage to support the results, however trying they may be. I have committed offences against His Divine Majesty which deserve punishments greater than any to which I can ever be subjected. It does not appear to me, however, that I have given cause to the Company of Jesus to draw them upon my head." 1

The dispute was settled before long. Fr. de Salazar, in spite of his attraction to the Order of Carmel, gave up his wish to belong to it, and remained faithful to his first vows. He abandoned his design, but remained Teresa's friend, and a devoted servant both of the friars of the Order of Carmel and of the Carmelite nuns.

CHAPTER XXVIII

THE Nuncio's Brief which freed the religious of the discalced Rule from the jurisdiction of those of the Observance was published on the ist of April, 1579. Fr. Angelo de Salazar, who had been appointed temporarily to the post of provincial, whilst the case was being heard in Rome, left the management of the affairs of the Reform in Teresa's and Fr. Gratian's hands. 1 A worthy man, though weak in the presence of opposition, he now looked upon himself as fortunate in being able to support a work which he had hitherto regretfully opposed. 2

Early in April Teresa bade adieu to her daughters at Toledo, and set off for Avila in order to spend Easter at St. Joseph's. The holy mother's triumphant return to her first solitude was indeed typical of Easter joys. She came to rest soul and body after the storm ; and feeling her worn-out powers ebbing away, to ask God in silence and seclusion what more He required from her before taking her to Himself.

Her ordinary infirmities had increased tenfold within the last fifteen months, and were accompanied with great weakness in her limbs. Thus at the end of December, 1577, when mounting the steps leading

1 Boll., No. 878.

2 Fr. A. de Salazar lived to an advanced age, and was cited to appear at Valladolid as witness in the first process of the saint's canonization, where he gave a powerful testimony to her sanctity, and to the religious spirit which prevailed in her convents.

to the choir, she was seized with giddiness and thrown by an invisible power to the foot of the staircase. The nuns who, hearing the noise of her fall, ran to help her, at first thought her dead, and hardly dared to move her. The saint reassured them : her left arm only was broken. One of the sisters exclaiming that it must have been the work of the devil, "Yes," Teresa answered, "and had God permitted it he would have gone further."

A woman said to have the gift of setting broken limbs was sent for from Medina. But she was ill and was not able to come for four months, during which time Teresa suffered tortures. The slightest movement she made was painful to her, but this did not interfere with the attention which she gave to the affairs of the Order, or to her religious exercises. She was never at a loss for a pleasant answer to those who asked after her, and with her usual habit of seeing the bright side of everything, she thanked God that "by a special grace her right arm was not affected by the fall." At last, in the month of April, an attempt was made to set it. The saint, guessing what awaited her, and anxious to spare her daughters the sight of her sufferings, sent them to the choir to pray for her, whilst she gave herself up, alone, to the tender mercies of the Medina doctress. The woman had brought another peasant to assist her; and, together, they pulled the arm, which meanwhile had set, with all their strength, in order to get the bones to unite. Though the agony was great, the saint never uttered a groan ; her mind being wholly occupied with the thought of what our Lord's sufferings must have been when His arms were stretched out on the cross. The nuns on their return to the infirmary noticed a great look of joy on her face. " I would not have lost, for any-

thing in the world," she said, "such an opportunity of suffering." 1

This opportunity was not to be merely a passing one. Teresa only partially recovered the use of her arm, and an accident which followed a little while later completed its disablement. With this broken arm, and the weight of sixty-four years upon her, it would have been only natural for the holy mother to have looked forward to a time of rest. Without leaving St. Joseph's convent, she might have occupied herself with the work of superintending her Foundations, and have still enjoyed the peace of Carmel and the delights of solitude. If she allowed herself to indulge in such a hope, it was not for long. On the eve of Pentecost she had retired to one of the hermitages in the garden to pray. The Holy Ghost had frequently chosen this feast as a day on which to shower great and special favours on the saint; and on this occasion, whilst she was rapt in prayer, God spoke as follows to her: "Daughter, I desire that you should tell the friars of the discalced Order from Me to observe well these four precepts :

" First, that the superiors should be as far as possible of one mind and one heart.

" Secondly ', that there should only be a small number of religious in each monastery.

" Thirdly r , that they should have little communication with seculars, and only with regard to matters affecting souls.

"Fourthly, that they should teach by example rather than by word." 2

1 Ribera.

2 Boll., No. 837. These words have been written in golden letters on the walls of the hermitage, and they have been inserted likewise in the Constitutions of the Order of the discalced,

Thus did Heaven appear to foreshadow to the holy mother that her work for souls was about to recommence. After four years spent in an all-absorbing resistance, much was necessary for the re-organization of the inner life of the Order of the discalced. There were troubles to be redressed from wrongs inflicted in the struggle, and there were agitations and memories of the past to be buried, so that the religious might once more breathe the serene air of the heights of Carmel. No one was more alive to these truths than Teresa. With regard to the friars of the discalced Order she could count on the gifts of Fr. Gratian, and the holiness of Fr. John of the Cross to carry out God's designs ; and she had prioresses such as Mothers Anne of Jesus, Mary of St. Joseph, and Mary Baptist, in whom she placed the greatest confidence, for the guidance of the Carmelite nuns.

Fr. de Salazar, hearing that the community at Malagon had suffered from the withdrawal of Mother Brianda, wished Teresa to go there and occupy, at least temporarily, the post of prioress. The other convents, hearing that this favour was to be accorded to Malagon, clamoured likewise for a visit from the holy mother. Fr. de Salazar therefore traced out a journey for her which would include the convents of Medina, Valladolid, Alba, and Salamanca.

On the 25th of June, therefore, Teresa set forth afresh on travels which were practically to last till the day of her death, taking with her as her companion Sister Anne of St. Bartholomew. At Medina and Valladolid she received nothing but joy and consolation. Guessing that efforts might be made to celebrate the occasion, she had begged to be allowed to come and go quietly. "I implore of you," she wrote, " receive me without noise or preparation. The longer

I live, the more trying I find this parade of reception ; it mortifies me instead of giving me pleasure, and I am humbled by it when I think how little I deserve all that is done for me. Pray tell this to our sisters." 1 The nuns obeyed, and suppressed their verses and complimentary speeches ; but the holy mother could not stop their transports of filial joy, which, if they humbled her equally, pleased and touched her more.

Fr. de Salazar's orders allowed of her spending only a short time in these two houses. Every member of the community wished to speak to her in private, and the month she spent in each house passed quickly. Teresa had home-truths for all. To her beloved niece, Mary Baptist, she expressed the wish that the time she spent with her would be of some use "in rendering her less attached to her own will."

The last day of July arrived, and everything was arranged for Teresa to leave Valladolid on the ist of August, when Sister Anne of Bartholomew was attacked with high fever. It was impossible for the saint to postpone her departure, and equally impossible for Sister Anne to accompany her. Though it cost Teresa much to leave her behind, she settled to take another sister in her place. The night before her departure Teresa went into the infirmary, and stood by the invalid's bed. * ' Are you sleeping, my daughter? " she asked. Anne, awaking out of a fevered sleep, said, "Yes, mother, I slept." "Get up," continued Teresa, "and we will see how you are." Sister Anne obeyed. At the same moment the fever left her, and she knelt rejoicing at the saint's feet. " Rise, my child, and let us thank God. I have been praying hard that He would cure you. We will start together." 2

Teresa passed by Alba de Tormes, where she only

1 Avila, June 2ist, 1579. 2 Boll., No. 845.

spent two days, her fervent community there scarcely requiring her supervision. She was in haste to reach Salamanca, where the nuns were still suffering from trials from the former proprietor of the house, Pedro de la Vanda. " It is incredible," wrote the saint, "all the annoyance which that man has given us. Pray that our Lord may find us another, and a cheap house." The saint spent the two months during which she remained at Salamanca in negotiations about another house, but nothing came of them. Teresa was overwhelmed with correspondence whilst there, her letters having accumulated in her journeys from one convent to another. One evening Sister Anne, a witness of the holy mother's labours, looked at her table covered with papers, betokening a night which would have to be spent in work. "Well, my child," remarked the saint in answer to her silent remonstrance, " if you could write, you would be able to help me." Sister Anne, full of faith and confidence, answered that if Teresa gave her the order she certainly would be able, or could learn, to obey it. The holy mother smiled at her daughter's simplicity, and gave her some letters to copy. The poor girl had everything to learn, she could not even spell, but having copied two letters she was able to write a third alone, and ever afterwards she assisted the saint in her correspondence. 1

Whilst Teresa was at Malagon the community changed from a small and dismal house into a new and well-situated one. " The joy of our dear daughters is great," she wrote to Fr. Gratian ; "one is reminded in seeing them of little lizards coming out of the shade in summer to enjoy the sun." There had been trouble in the community owing to the young prioress (Mother Brianda's successor) not having succeeded in gaining

the confidence of her nuns. " Paul and I," she writes to Fr. Gratian, "were quite wrong. Please tell him to accuse himself of it in confession ; as for me I have already done so. We ought not to have trusted completely anyone so young. With her love of action she upset everything . . . and in spite of her excellent intentions has made a great mess of things." 1 Teresa replaced this fidgety prioress by another, who soon re-established matters on a satisfactory footing.

An attack of paralysis prostrated the saint for two months whilst she was at Malagon. The contact of suffering, so liable to incapacitate weakly souls, seemed only to increase the strength and ardour of hers. Providence accordingly chose this moment for making her take up once more the work of founding convents.

Nine pious women had been living for five years in a little house on the confines of New Castile, close to a chapel which went by the name of St. Anne's Hermitage. They lived a life of prayer there, reciting the divine office in common, which in their case was a work of extreme difficulty, as all their breviaries differed, and only one of the nine could read fluently. They fasted, worked, and observed—as far as they knew it—the Carmelite Rule. Hearing the holy mother was at Malagon, they sent repeated messengers to her, begging her to admit them into her Order. Teresa was at first prevented by her illness from going to them. She saw difficulties also in the way of the proposed Foundation ; their resources were insufficient, and she feared that women who had so long had their own way would not easily bend their necks to the yoke of obedience. Whilst she was hesitating and praying for light, her " Adorable Master*' after Communion

addressed to her, she says, " lively reproaches, and pressed me to undertake the Foundation. Oh, sovereign power of God's words ! Not only do they enlighten the spirit, and allow it to perceive the truth, but they impress the heart with an irresistible impulse to execute what His Divine Majesty commands. This is what I experienced. I accepted the Foundation with great joy. I recognized my fault in having hesitated so long for human considerations — I, who had so often seen the Divine Master work wonders in favour of our Order before which human reason remained confounded." 1

Having made up her mind, Teresa wrote to Fr. de Salazar to ask for the necessary authorization, which he sent her, together with the order to go herself to Villanueva, and to take with her the nuns she required to start the new convent. The saint sent for two from Toledo and two from Malagon, one of the latter, Sister Anne of St. Augustine, having already attained great heights of perfection. Teresa got up from her sick-bed to undertake this journey. It was the 1 3th of February, 1580, and a spring temperature softened the trials of the journey to the saint. Fr. Gabriel and Fr. Anthony of Jesus, deputed by the inhabitants of Villanueva, came to meet her, and the little company passed through the plains of La Mancha amidst the enthusiasm of the worthy inhabitants. The news passed from village to village that Mother Teresa was on her way through their midst. Groups collected on the road to greet her as she passed, and the honour of offering the nuns a meal, or a resting-place for the night, was disputed by the people of the villages which they traversed. At the first resting-place Teresa took refuge in a peasant's cottage, hoping to escape the pious curiosity of which she was the object. This was

easier said than done, the crowd pursuing her, and invading the room where she and her nuns were dining. Teresa, half displeased, half smiling, scolded them for their intrusion, yet avoided hurting their feelings by a discourteous reception. She preferred eluding such ovations to rejecting them by a humility whose only result would have been to procure her more and greater ones. The next morning she left before daylight. A rich farmer a little further on her road had assembled all his family, his children and grandchildren, and even his flocks, in the hope of being able to give her hospitality and of obtaining her blessing. He had likewise decorated his house and prepared a great dinner for her. The saint sent him her thanks, but avoided the village where he lived. The farmer, however, was not to be defeated, so leaving h-is house he went with all his train to meet her, and Teresa, touched with the sight of the patriarch, surrounded by his family and household, blessed him and all belonging to him, and promised to recommend him to our Lord in her prayers. 1

On the fifth day of her journey she saw the monastery of our Lady of Help crowning the heights above her. "This monastery," the saint writes, " is raised above the plain and situated in the midst of a delightful solitude. The religious with their prior came to meet us in procession. They walked with bare feet, wrapt in their coarse white habits, and we were all filled with sentiments of devotion at seeing them. As for me, I was touched to the heart, for I felt myself transported to the blessed times when the first saints of our Order lived. . . . They conducted us to the church, where they sang the Te Deum. The entrance of the church is underground, and reminded us of the cavern of our

1 Ribera ; Yepes. 2 L

holy father Elias." Teresa, at the entreaty of the religious, spent three days at the monastery, delighted with the beauty of the spot—a true home of Carmel hidden amongst the hills, and remote from worldly sounds and distractions. 1 She spent long hours in the chapel prostrate on the stone which covered the mortal remains of the great penitent, Catalina de Cardona, foundress of the monastery. She represented to herself the touching scenes of the life that had been spent there ; Catalina's heroic exercise of penance, her tears of love and repentance ; and, penetrated with the sense of her own unworthiness, Teresa protested that she was unworthy to have known so great a saint and so true a penitent. The Divine Master, before Teresa left the monastery, allowed her this consolation. Catalina appeared to her resplendent in glory and accompanied by angels, and said to her: " Teresa, cease not from your labour of founding monasteries, but pursue the work with ardour." s

The following morning, on the 2ist of February, 1580, the holy mother and her nuns arrived at Villa-nueva de la Xara. The bells of the little town announced to the nine anchoresses that their longings were about to be fulfilled. A procession, headed by little children, and composed of the clergy and notabilities of the town, and the Franciscans and religious of the discalced monastery of our Lady of Help, came to meet them at the entrance of the town. They first conducted the Carmelites to the principal church, where they sang the Te Deum ; then the head priest, Fr. Ervias, taking the Blessed Sacrament, they started once more for the hermitage of St. Anne. "The joy of the people," Teresa writes, u was so striking that it moved me much. As the distance to be traversed was

considerable, altars of repose had been prepared along the way, and at these the procession stopped, and hymns were sung. It moved our hearts to hear our good God praised so heartily, and to think of the honour the people were showing, for love of Him, to seven poor Carmelites."

High Mass was then celebrated at the chapel of the hermitage, and Fr. Ervias placed the Blessed Sacrament in the tabernacle; the saint then entered the little house where the nine solitaries awaited her on their knees at the threshold. Their emaciated appearance and look of recollection denoted the lives of penance which they had been leading. Teresa examined them on various points, and, satisfied by the docility of spirit and humility manifested by all, she admitted them to the habit of our Lady. There was but one soul and one heart at the hermitage from that day. The country shared in the blessing of God, and reaped recompense for its devotion to our Lady's Order. No rain had fallen for five months, and a famine seemed inevitable, when, directly after the procession had dispersed, welcome clouds appeared in the heavens, and were followed by torrents of rain. The people, recognizing that their crops were saved, almost by a miracle, and attributing it to the prayers of the saint, came to thank her for them. Teresa acknowledged their faith and piety with her usual sweetness, and told them that they owed this favour to God's mercy and their own piety, and that she rejoiced and thanked God with them.

The holy mother remained two months at Villanueva, and employed herself in doing what she could to transform the cottage into a monastery. It required a Carmelite and a saint's courage to make the best of such a hovel. The cells were divided from each other

by wattled walls, and the anchoresses had hung rugs in the apertures to serve as doors; a cockle-shell served as a holy-water stoup, two pieces of wood crossed for a crucifix. The food consisted in herbs from the garden. Water, even, was procured with difficulty, on account of the depth of the well, and the absence of means of raising it to the surface. Teresa remedied the last inconvenience, but unfortunately, whilst she was superintending the workmen, the handle of the windlass which they were putting into it getting loosened, struck her broken arm, and besides causing her tortures, resulted in an abscess which was of so serious a nature that it gave rise to fears for her life.

Fr. de Salazar's orders recalled the saint to Toledo at the end of March; she was also awaited at Valladolid in order to make arrangements with Bishop de Men-doza, who was desirous of starting another convent of St. Joseph's in his new diocese. Before leaving Villanueva, Teresa sounded the nuns on the subject of the hardship and privations of their life there, and their wishes with regard to it. Would they, she asked, have the strength to support such total destitution? She encouraged them to confide their misgivings, if they had any, to her, so that she might make arrangements to disperse them amongst her other monasteries should they prove insurmountable. The nuns answered this appeal by saying that they were all prepared to remain joyfully in their tiny monastery for the rest of their lives. The saint then made a distribution of offices. She assigned that of prioress to Sister Mary of the Martyrs; and knowing Sister Anne of St. Augustine's astounding gifts of prayer, and the power she had over the Heart of her Divine Master, she made her sacristan and purveyor of the wants of the little family. Then giving Sister Anne a little statue of the Infant Jesus,

to whom the sister had a special devotion, she told her to have recourse to the Divine Infant at all times —in her pressing necessities, as in her smallest difficulties. " Believe only, daughter," she said, " and nothing will be wanting to you."

Sister Anne received the gift in the same spirit with which it was given to her, and putting a real at the foot of the statue she told the Divine Infant that she placed this sum at interest in the hands of His Divine Providence, and expected, in the name of His beloved daughter Teresa, that He would give her all she required. A succession of miraculous answers to prayer followed, and was our Lord's response to His servant's appeal. On one occasion money was required to pay workmen, on another to provide sacred vessels for the altar ; petitions for these and many other favours were granted to the prayers of the community, and thus, though their poverty was great, they bore all the trials it involved with joy and confidence in their Divine Master.

Teresa meanwhile reached Toledo, after six days' journey, and was again attacked by illness. A stroke of paralysis on Maundy Thursday was followed by fever and violent sickness. For two months she was unable to continue her journey. "Accustomed as I am to suffering," she wrote to Fr. Gratian, " even when I am in great pain it appears easier for me to endure it on foot, and going about my daily duties." She reassured her daughters about her health, and wrote to them : "I am still weak, which is only to be expected after the terrible month I have spent. I am paying now for my good health at Malagon, and when I was travelling; I had not been so well for many years. Now the state I am in matters little."

A second appeal arrived from Fr. de Salazar, who

did not know how ill she had been, and wished her to hasten to Valladolid to conclude arrangements for the new Foundation in the diocese of Palencia. Though quite unfit to travel, Teresa prepared to obey ; for the work was one which concerned the glory of God, and she was urged to it, by her gratitude to the bishop. Before leaving Toledo, Teresa had the consolation of seeing once more the holy and austere director of her early spiritual life, Fr. Baltasar Alvarez, of whom she had said that " her soul owed more to him than to any one in the world." Our saint spoke to him of the Foundation she was about to make, and Fr. Baltasar blessed and encouraged her to work without ceasing, at all cost, for the extension of her Order.

During an interview which Teresa had with the Grand Inquisitor, Archbishop de Quiroga, whilst she was at Toledo, he told her that he had read her Life, and submitted it likewise to other theologians, and that not only they had found nothing to object to in it, but he added: "I have been so much edified by what I read that I beg you will ever look upon me as your servant, and as one who is ready to help you in your Reform." 1

Teresa's humility raised her far above all feelings of natural satisfaction at receiving the archbishop's praise ; doubtless, however, as she thanked him her heart rejoiced, and she gave praise to God for having preserved her from error and delusions—dangers which she had ever so greatly feared.

A week's fatiguing journey among the spurs of the Guadarrama mountains brought Teresa to Segovia. A courier reached her at a halting place on the way, bringing her a sad farewell letter from her brother Lorenzo. He was filled with presentiments of his

approaching death, without, however, having any special grounds for them. His sister answered him with mingled encouragement and reproaches: " Whence did he get such an idea? Besides, had he not God for his Friend, and would this true Friend ever be found wanting, either to him or to his children ? I cannot go and look after you," she continues, " but as for you, I wish you would come and join me. Let me tell you, also, that you do wrong in not going oftener to St. Joseph's. It is so near you. A little exercise would be very good for you; you should not be always alone. For charity's sake do as I ask you, and tell me about yourself. I am in agony till I hear from you." 1

A week later, whilst Teresa was at Segovia, she was engaged in spinning at recreation when suddenly the nuns saw a great change come over her countenance. She became pale, and with a look of anguish, she rose, and went straight to the choir, where she remained a long time absorbed in prayer. After a time she told them that she had seen Lorenzo die, but that when kneeling before the tabernacle her Divine Master had consoled her by showing her her brother in glory. He had only passed through purgatory before going to his reward. A second apparition a few days later confirmed the first.

In spite of this vision Lorenzo's death afflicted Teresa deeply. She missed in him a friend, as well as a loving brother ; and she grieved deeply for his children. His death left a great void in her life. Writing to Mother Mary of St. Joseph at this time, she says : "I see clearly that our Lord does not wish to leave me long without suffering. You must know it has pleased Him to take His good and dear servant, Lorenzo de Cepeda to Himself. He was taken with a violent hemorrhage

1 Segovia, June, 1580.

which lasted six hours, and suffocated him. He was quite conscious, and died recommending himself to God. He had been to Communion two days before. It could be said of him that he was always praying, for he never lost sight of the presence of God. Can I repay his affection for me better than by rejoicing, as I do, that he has left this miserable life, and entered into his Saviour's rest? Do not think that this is a flower of speech, it is indeed true. I rejoice in his happiness. I feel only for his poor children ; but God will help them for their father's sake." Teresa was obliged by affairs connected with her nephew's succession to return to Avila. Lorenzo in his will divided his money between his children and the convent of St. Joseph. The saint, to whom he had confided his wishes, intended to carry them out with a care which was as virtuous as it was disinterested. The orphans' rights were no less dear to her than the interests of her convent, but to reconcile the one with the other was to cost her much solicitude. She was also much pressed for time ; and after a few days, leaving her niece with the nuns at St. Joseph, she took her nephew Francisco with her to Medina. "Till his future is provided for, we shall both spend an anxious time,"she writes. " If I were not told that I am doing a service to God by taking these two children's cause in hand, the repugnance I feel at occupying myself with business would have made me give it all up."

At Medina Teresa heard with deep emotion of the holy death of Fr. Baltasar Alvarez. Seeing her distress, one of the nuns ventured to ask her the reason. " Ah, my daughter," she answered, "I weep over the great loss the Church has sustained, both now and in the future, over his death." She spent two hours afterwards rapt in prayer. One of the nuns at Medina was

dangerously ill with erysipelas, her face being a running sore which resisted all the remedies that had been tried upon her. She was in the infirmary, and no one had mentioned her illness to Teresa. One day, having a great wish to see the holy mother, she came to recreation. Teresa, on seeing her, exclaimed with horror, " Dear daughter, what is the matter with you?" Then taking her poor head in her arms, she stroked her gently, whispering into her ear, " Have confidence, and say nothing. I believe our Lord will cure you." At the same moment the nun's face was completely cured. Teresa, a little confused by what had taken place, asked everyone to go at once and thank God for the favour He had conferred on His daughter. 1

From Medina she continued her journey, worn with fatigue and in high fever, to Valladolid, which she reached on the i5th of August. There she fell so desperately ill that she was not expected to live. Once more her daughters' prayers obtained her cure, if that name could be given to the state of health which she usually had, and which enabled her to say : " For me it is to get better, not to be worse." Her convalescence was accompanied with great interior trials, which she describes as follows: "I cannot, in truth, see without sadness and astonishment, and without complaining to our Lord about it, how the poor soul shares in the body's maladies, and suffers from the reaction of its infirmities. That is one of the greatest torments and miseries of this life, it seems to me, when the soul has not the fervour to take the upper hand. It is something to be ill, and endure violent pains, no doubt; but I look upon it as trifling when the soul remains full of courage and blesses God whilst it is being tried by His hand. ... I see no remedy but patience, the

consciousness of our misery, humility, and resignation to the Divine Will. May He do with us what He wills, and as He wills. This was the state in which I found myself at Valladolid, convalescent, but so weak that I had lost that confidence which God usually gave me to commence a Foundation ; everything seemed impossible to me." 1

The prioress Mother Mary Baptist, with more zeal than discretion, pressed her to continue her journey to Palencia. An old friend, Fr. Ripalda, joined his entreaties to those of the prioress. " He told me," Teresa mentions a year later, "that my cowardice came from my advanced age. As for me, I knew well that it did not come from that cause ; the proof of which is that, though I am now older, I have not the same feeling of depression." The Master of the Vineyard could alone give her strength to work in it. This she never ceased telling Him, and she implored Him, " since He kept her in exile, at least to give her strength to render Him some little service." Her prayers were heard at the hour which our Saviour generally chose for granting them. Having received Him in Holy Communion, she heard these words of gentle reproach : " What dost thou fear, my daughter? When hast thou found Me wanting? I am with thee now, as I have been in past times. Do not stop ; continue thy Foundations."

Grace triumphed. Teresa remembered that if she could do nothing, Jesus with her could do all things. In vain she was told that Palencia was so poor that her nuns would want the necessaries of life. Her confidence was unshaken ; and in spite of the weather, which was bitterly cold, accompanied with a thick fog which made the day nearly as dark as night, she

started for the town. A good canon of the name of Reynoso had got a house ready for her, which was lent to her till the Feast of St. John. The following day Mass was celebrated there, and as soon as the Divine Friend reposed under her roof Teresa's heart was at rest. Palencia's welcome of the Carmelites was as warm as that of Villanueva. The bishop was the first to visit them, and he provided largely for their first wants, besides promising to supply them yearly with their provision of corn. His people, who " though poor in worldly goods were noble in generosity," flocked to make their offerings. Even the governor, though opposed to their coming, was forced to give in. The holy mother had deputed Fr. Gratian to visit him. When he saw him he exclaimed : " Do whatever you want, my father ! Mother Teresa, in order to get on as she does, must have a decree of the Royal Council of His Majesty our good Lord Himself, by virtue of which she causes us all to do what she wants, in spite of ourselves."

When it came to the question of buying a house, serious difficulties presented themselves. Mgr. de Mendoza suggested to the Carmelites to establish themselves near a large chapel called our Lady of the Street, and the Chapter gave them the right of opening a grille into it, and thus being able to assist at the Masses said there. The neighbouring houses, however, were so small that a monastery made out of the space occupied by three or four would still have been insufficient for the accommodation of the community. After some days of uncertainty Teresa decided to acquire them, our Lord having revealed to her that many sins against Him were committed there, which would be stopped by the convent being established on the spot. Canon Reynoso, and a friend of his, Canon

Salinas, took all the necessary steps to acquire the property, even providing the funds for this undertaking ; and as their own slender means were insufficient, they persuaded the Vicar-General to give his name as guarantor. They likewise repaired the building at their own expense. Teresa, deeply touched by such devoted service, named them " Our Lady's two holy friends," and she honoured them with a special regard. " I have nothing to do but to rest," she said, "and let them work." Few Foundations cost her less anxiety. When the canons had finished their preparations, with the aid of their bishop they organized a great feast, in which all Palencia took part. The road which the Carmelites traversed to go from their hired house to their new monastery was strewn with flowers, and choirs of musicians sang the praises of the Queen of Heaven. The Bishop carried the Blessed Sacrament, preceded by a long procession in which every family in the place was represented. Teresa, hidden under her deep veil, shed tears of thanksgiving. "No! never have I seen anything equal to it!" she wrote later on; "I do not know how to praise God sufficiently. What charity, what piety there is in this town ! Assuredly such things are rare in this world, and remind one of the days of the primitive Church. We arrived without funds, without even being able to provide ourselves with the bare necessities of life; and instead of repulsing us, these good people declared that God in giving us to them to maintain were doing them a great favour." 1

Another proof which the people of Palencia gave to our saint of their tact and good will towards her was, that knowing her devotion to the foster-father of our Lord, and yet not wishing to change the name of the

chapel, which it had borne long years, they bethought themselves of the plan of uniting once more St. Joseph to our Lady ; so the convent was given the name of St. Joseph's of our Lady of the Street.

Teresa united all her daughters with her in testifying her gratitude to the bishop and her two friends the canons. She caused a detailed account of the Foundation to be written, and sent it to all the other Carmelite convents. She who ever sought to hide her own labours loved to publish those of others, and to hear God praised for the zeal of His servants. She concluded her letter to her daughters by these words : " As for me, I am now no longer good for anything."

been lost. A covering letter is, however, extant, in which she begs, amongst other things, that the Constitutions should be printed. " For," she urges, " sometimes a prioress, without realizing the importance of the fault she is committing, takes away or adds as she thinks proper in making a copy of them. This must be formally forbidden. It is said that the Chapter is going to make various additions in the recital of divine office and to order two ferias a week to be observed. My advice, which I submit to you, would be to exempt nuns from these changes, and to allow them to say their office according to their ordinary rubrics." A few words then follow, with a view, clearly, of easing scrupulous minds about the kind of sandals which should be worn. She then remarks : " I should wish, with regard to fasting, that bread should be allowed at collation. It is enough to observe the law of the Church without adding anything to it. This is a source of disquiet to nuns, and injures the health of many who think they have strength to keep both the one and the other, and are in reality mistaken." Having disposed of scruples and exaggerations, she insists with her usual vigour on points essential to the regularity of cloistered life. She recalls the recent Brief of Gregory XIII, in which he forbids nuns to go into the exterior portion of their churches. A few words are given to the question of opening the grille in the parlour, of revenue, Masses, and prayers for the dead, and as regards the punctuality which should be observed in infirmaries. In the concluding remarks we see a mother's tenderness mingled with the wisdom of the foundress. " There is nothing I fear more than to see my daughters lose that great supernatural joy in which up to this time our Saviour has preserved them. I know what it is for nuns to be discontented ;

and unless there is cause for it, more should not be required of them than what they themselves have promised and undertaken. ... A soul which has not full liberty cannot serve God well, and the devil takes advantage of this to tempt it, whereas when there is absence of constraint people never think of using it, or going in search of it."

The saint was not oblivious either of the other portion of her family, the friars of the discalced Order ; but they had their own Constitutions, which were now to be nrvised by the

Heads of the Order and the general sense of the Chapter. She had, however, a mother's word of advice for them : it was to implore prudence, and breadth of view of the superiors; and order, and charity in their administration of temporalities. Thus she says: " The Heads of the Chapter should not forget to lay down the precept to the priors that they are to give suitable food to the friars, and in greater abundance than has been commonly done hitherto. If this matter is not attended to in all their houses they will see to what it will lead. God will never fail to supply necessary food ; but if priors give little to their religious He will give them little. For the love of God let your Paternity recommend cleanliness ; decidedly I should wish it was commanded by the Constitutions." The first matter placed before the Chapter was the election of a provincial ; their choice interested the Carmelite nuns almost as much as it did the friars of the Order. To Teresa it was a point of great importance ; and from the first she saw there was only one man in the Order capable of filling the onerous post of first provincial: and that was Fr. Gra-tian. There were many learned and holy and zealous religious in its ranks, likewise a saint, Fr. John of the Cross ; but none of these possessed that special tact

been lost. A covering letter is, however, extant, in which she begs, amongst other things, that the Constitutions should be printed. " For," she urges, " sometimes a prioress, without realizing the importance of the fault she is committing, takes away or adds as she thinks proper in making a copy of them. This must be formally forbidden. It is said that the Chapter is going to make various additions in the recital of divine office and to order two ferias a week to be observed. My advice, which I submit to you, would be to exempt nuns from these changes, and to allow them to say their office according to their ordinary rubrics." A few words then follow, with a view, clearly, of easing scrupulous minds about the kind of sandals which should be worn. She then remarks : " I should wish, with regard to fasting, that bread should be allowed at collation. It is enough to observe the law of the Church without adding anything to it. This is a source of disquiet to nuns, and injures the health of many who think they have strength to keep both the one and the other, and are in reality mistaken." Having disposed of scruples and exaggerations, she insists with her usual vigour on points essential to the regularity of cloistered life. She recalls the recent Brief of Gregory XIII, in which he forbids nuns to go into the exterior portion of their churches. A few words are given to the question of opening the grille in the parlour, of revenue, Masses, and prayers for the dead, and as regards the punctuality which should be observed in infirmaries. In the concluding remarks we see a mother's tenderness mingled with the wisdom of the foundress. " There is nothing I fear more than to see my daughters lose that great supernatural joy in which up to this time our Saviour has preserved them. I know what it is for nuns to be discontented ;

and unless there is cause for it, more should not be required of them than what they themselves have promised and undertaken. ... A soul which has not full liberty cannot serve God well, and the devil takes advantage of this to tempt it, whereas when there is absence of constraint people never think of using it, or going in search of it."

The saint was not oblivious either of the other portion of her family, the friars of the discalced Order ; but they had their own Constitutions, which were now to be nrvised by the Heads of the Order and the general sense of the Chapter. She had, however, a mother's word of advice for them : it was to implore prudence, and breadth of view of the superiors; and order, and charity in their administration of temporalities. Thus she says: " The Heads of the Chapter should not forget to lay down the precept to the priors that they are to give suitable food to the friars, and in greater abundance than has been commonly done hitherto. If this matter is not attended to in all their houses they will see to what it will lead. God will never fail to supply necessary food ; but if priors give little to their religious He will give them little. For the love of God let your Paternity recommend cleanliness ; decidedly I should wish it was commanded by the Constitutions." The first matter placed before the Chapter was the election of a provincial ; their choice interested the Carmelite nuns almost as much as it did the friars of the Order. To Teresa it was a point of great importance ; and from the first she saw there was only one man in the Order capable of filling the onerous post of first provincial: and that was Fr. Gra-tian. There were many learned and holy and zealous religious in its ranks, likewise a saint, Fr. John of the Cross ; but none of these possessed that special tact

2 M

and wisdom in the art of government, joined to great spirituality, which she discerned in Gratian. Thus she writes to him with her usual straightforwardness : 4 'The nuns are all longing for you to be appointed provincial. Anne of St. Bartholomew says that, in spite of your desire to escape the burthen, their prayers will be sufficiently powerful to impose it on you." She finishes, however, with her usual Fiat: " May God conduct all so that it may lead to His greater glory. The rest matters little, even though it should give one much to suffer. ... If after so much praying God should permit some one else to be elected, no doubt it will be for the best. His judgments are inscrutable. May He be for ever blessed !"

The saint had much to do to conquer Fr. Gratian's profound reluctance to take up (in the event of his election) a charge from the weight of which he had already suffered so heavily. She told him that, though for his sake she might have been tempted to wish that he should have the rest he so greatly desired, the general good of the Order surmounted every private feeling; and she ends with the pathetic appeal : " Please God, my father, that such a great misfortune should not happen as for our houses to be deprived of your government." She wrote strongly to Fr. Juan de las Cuevas, and to all the religious who consulted her, in furtherance of this view ; and when Fr. Mariano wished to vote for Fr. Anthony she scolded him vigorously, and " treated his view as a temptation." Again she wrote to Fr. Gratian : " If you are not elected, and Fr. Nicholas is in your place, as long as you are always at his side you would supply what is wanting in him. . . . It would be infinitely better, however, if you were appointed ; then you could take Fr. Nicholas as companion and assistant. It would be very useful in the

beginning if he was with you. He is a man of judgment, and would give you nothing to suffer." 1

The holy mother was soon—alas !—to lose the illusion contained in her last remark. The efforts she was making to cause these two religious to work together in the cause of the Reform show her insight into the difficulties of the situation. It is true that the sweetness and charity of Fr. Gratian caused her to prefer him to all others for the government of an Order of which she had said that it was sufficiently austere in itself to be able to dispense with severity in its administration. Nevertheless, she perceived that this benignity might degenerate into weakness, and with this object she chose as his coadjutor a man whom she knew by reputation as a learned and austere religious.

A descendant of the celebrated Dorias of Genoa, Fr. Nicholas enjoyed a great reputation for learning and virtue. Teresa, though she was personally but slightly acquainted with him, had noticed his zeal for Observance, his energy and the perspicacity of his mind ; and these qualities were those, in her judgment, which pointed him out as one who would make a fitting colleague for Fr. Gratian.

Events were to show that he was wanting in some other equally important qualifications, and more especially in self-abnegation, both as regards judgment and opinion. Having thus given her views according to her lights, Teresa thought only of joining her prayers to those of her daughters whilst the fathers assembled in their convent of St. Cyril.

On the 3rd of March, Fr. de las Cuevas solemnly opened the Chapter in the presence of many learned and distinguished ecclesiastics and laymen. He first read the Papal Bull declaring the separation of the

Order of Carmel into two provinces, those of the mitigated and discalced Observance. " Let us call it," he remarked, "a day of union, not of division; for today the brethren separate only in order to preserve greater peace and union with each other." 1

The next day the election of the provincial took place. Fr. de las Cuevas sang the Mass of the Holy Ghost, and a sermon was preached by Fr. Mariano, in which he hailed the springtide of the Order after it had passed through the inclement season of persecution. 2 The fathers then retired to the Chapter House. When they came out Fr. Gratian was walking beside the Apostolic Commissioner. The religious chanted the Te Deum. Teresa's prayer had been heard, and Fr. Gratian was provincial.

The other offices were divided between Fathers Nicholas, Anthony, John of the Cross, Gabriel of the Ascension, and Mariano — the four first as Advisors, the last as secretary. Couriers were despatched to the king to acquaint him with the news, and Fr. Gratian received a complimentary mission from him in return, consisting of two officers of his court charged to congratulate him on his appointment. The Heads of the Chapter presented in return their humble acknowledgments to his majesty, and undertook that prayers and a daily Mass should be offered up in perpetuo for the prosperity of the royal family, and of the kingdom. Public rejoicings were held at Alcala in honour of the auspicious event.

On the 7th of March the examination of the Constitutions began. Those of the nuns were first read. The Chapter, led by a filial respect for the holy mother as well as by admiration for the ripe wisdom displayed in her Rules, solemnly approved of them, without suggest-

ing any emendations. Certain administrative details were added ; moreover, important changes necessitated by the last Brief were introduced into the government of the Order. Instead of the Constitutions of Fr. Rossi (the name given them by Teresa) they were henceforth to go by the name of the Constitutions of the Chapter of Avila. The saint's daughters observe them in every particular to this day.

The Constitutions as drawn up by Fr. Gratian then underwent revision. They were published on the i3th, and on the i;th Fr. de las Cuevas, having written to the Fr.-General to ask his confirmation of the acts passed by the Chapter, formally closed it, and made over all his powers to the new provincial.

Fervent acts of thanksgiving rose to Heaven from every monastery of the Reform, accompanied by great rejoicings. The religious of the mitigated Observance received their defeat in silence. Fr. de Salazar, whose services to the Order merited and received Teresa's and Fr. Gratian's gratitude, contributed no little to waken the spirit of union amongst his brethren ; and the Fr.-General showed on his side great goodwill to the new family of Carmel. Universal peace, and a solid and durable one, was established between the two branches of the Order of Carmel. "God alone knew all the bitterness," Teresa says, writing at this time, "as He alone knows the immense joy that fills my soul at seeing the termination of those sufferings. I wish that the whole world would join me in thanking Heaven. . . . Now we are all at peace, discalced and mitigated alike, and there is nothing to prevent us serving our Lord. Let us hasten then, my brothers and sisters, to devote ourselves to the honour of His Divine Majesty, Who has so mercifully hearkened to our prayers."

The saint was the first to give an example. Leaving the community at Palencia to the paternal kindness of Bishop de Mendoza, and Canon Reynoso, she started for Soria, where she was expected by Mgr. Velasquez, the new Bishop of Osma. He himself offered her a fine church, and (in the name of Dofia Beatriz de Viamonte) an adjoining house and an endowment. Under such promising conditions, the undertaking, to use Teresa's expression, took the form of a pleasure-party. The journey was made under favourable circumstances. The road lay alongside a beautiful river, and the landscape was lit up by the sunshine of June ; all was beauty to the eye and consolation to the heart, for wherever they went they heard the praises sung of the holy bishop. For instance, they were told how he led as poor and simple a life as the humblest peasant, how he spent his time in instructing his flock, and traversed his diocese on foot, so as to be more within reach of those who wished to speak to him. The holy man met them at Soria, and blessed them from a window as they passed in front of his house escorted by the nobility and people, who welcomed them as if they were angels from Heaven.

Teresa appointed Sister Catherine of Christ as prioress to her new Foundation. She was a most fervent nun, but very ignorant on worldly matters ; she could not even write. " On the other hand," Teresa said, "she has great love of God, and is very holy ; nothing more is required to make a good prioress." The saint, before leaving the convent, regulated in detail the order to be observed in the relations between the Carmelites and their foundress. They were to give her every possible proof of their gratitude. "Try and please her," she writes, "whenever it depends upon you to do so. This is only just. With her

virtues she will help you rather than otherwise to observe your Rule."

Soria had given Teresa too friendly a reception to keep her long. God would not leave her long without that " delicious bread of tribulation which the soul having once cheerfully partaken of prefers to any other." She was summoned back first to Avila, where difficulties of a spiritual, as well as a temporal, character had arisen. Before leaving Soria she was visited by Fr. Ribera, a spiritual son of Fr. Baltasar Alvarez, and therefore one who bore a sure passport to Teresa's favour, and who was afterwards to become one of her best-known biographers. At Osma, where she arrived late one night, she met Fr. Yepes, whose name was likewise associated with hers in the same capacity. At their first meeting the saint hardly spoke to him ; when, therefore, they met the following day, Fr. Yepes ventured to ask her if she had forgotten her former confessor of Toledo. " No," she answered, "only in seeing you I was troubled with the thought that you ought to be here in penitential retreat." "This was quite true," Fr. Yepes remarks. "Then, being aware that she frequently knew all about my interior dispositions, I said at once : * I am quite afraid of speaking to you, Mother Teresa, as I believe you know all that passes in my heart, and I wish to have been to confession before coming to see you.'* 1 She smiled, and I saw that though humility prevented her assenting, she could not deny the truth of what I alleged for fear of telling a falsehood." Fr. Yepes gave her Communion at the church at Soria, where he says: " I notice two things which I should never have discovered through her convent grille. One was that her face, discoloured as it had become by her sufferings and penances, and also by her advanced age, when she

approached the holy table became suddenly beautiful, and her aspect so full of majesty that I was moved to devotion by the sight. Also I observed a delicious perfume exhaling from her lips and clothes. Afterwards I inquired from Sister Anne what scents were used by the holy mother, and she told me that not only she used none, but she had a great dislike to them, as they gave her a headache." Like Fr. Ribera, Yepes treasured up these remembrances in order to publish them when the fitting time should come, for the glory of God and the good of man.

Teresa arrived at Avila on the 6th of September. She was anxiously expected by her daughters, who looked forward confidently to her return for the restoration of order in spiritual and temporal matters. At the conclusion of Mary of St. Jerome's three years' tenure of office, a young nun with no experience, called Mary of Christ, had been elected. Don Francisco de Salcedo had recently died, leaving his patrimony, which had been considerably diminished by previous generosity, to the Community. The report spread in Avila that the Carmelites had become rich, whereas in reality they had inherited next to nothing. The alms from the town ceased. Lorenzo de Cepeda's legacy was of no use to them either, as nearly all he left was to be spent in building a memorial chapel. Added to these financial difficulties, there were some in the spiritual order ; some of the nuns were tormented by scruples, and good Fr. Julian did not understand the treatment of that infirmity. The result was that sadness, and discomfort, and ennui crept by degrees into this little sanctuary of our Lord ; after that came illness, and then relaxation. l

Directly the holy mother found herself once more

amongst her daughters they all recovered strength to keep the Rule, and to devote the necessary time to manual labour in order to earn their daily bread. There was, in fact, a general resurrection. Teresa, too happy to obey, taught only by her example, and first of all she gave that of submission to the prioress. Meanwhile Mother Mary of Christ lost no time in sending in her resignation to the Provincial. Fr. Gratian came at once, and after deposing the prioress in accordance with her request, assembled a Chapter in order to elect her successor. "Our holy mother," he relates, " received every vote. When she found she was elected she tried in the kindest way possible to be angry with us all, saying it was time we should leave her in peace, and so on. I told her to kiss the ground, since she was making excuses, and as soon as she prostrated I intoned the Te Deum. The nuns then triumphantly led her to the prioress's seat in the choir."

The saint's election accordingly fixed her residence at Avila, but God, meeting her desire for suffering half-way, took away the joy her return there might, under other circumstances, have caused her, and left her only the pain. "It costs me much," she owned to Fr. Gratian, "to return to this country and to find none of my faithful friends of former days here, nor my brother Lorenzo. The worst part is the unavoidable communications with the survivors. ... But all this I look upon as a mere nothing, if I am able to set things going, satisfactorily, here."

Teresa succeeded beyond her hopes. The convent of Avila recovered its first fervour, and with j success that it has been maintained there to the present day Felix Ciilpa ! exclaims one of Teresa's historians; happy the faults that obtained the holy mother's care for this community and her presence amongst them.

As for Teresa, she allowed no one but the provincial to see the trials which she was enduring. The loss of those who had preceded her, the weight of years, a growing detachment from all things here below, contributed to make life a bare and arid solitude, in which she languished absent from her Lord. The thorns were growing under her feet — those interior sufferings which God had reserved to the last, in order to consummate her heart's martyrdom, after that of her soul. A holy soul once said : " I love my family more than myself, my country more than my family, the human race more than my country, and God above all things." Thus it was with Teresa. She loved the Order of Carmel more than her family, holy Church and souls more than Carmel, and God in all, and above all. And she loved with an ardour which the flight of years seemed to increase rather than diminish, and with a generosity which nothing but the entire gift of herself could satisfy. But these affections, supernaturalized as they were by grace, were as so many open doors by which anguish found its entrance into her soul. Herein the crucifixion of her heart consisted. It began in early youth and was consummated only in death.

Teresa's family at this time caused her many anxious thoughts. Lorenzo's eldest son was in America when his father died ; the two younger ones, Francisco and Teresita, had no nearer relation than their aunt, and as she says: " For the glory of God I took their affairs in hand." Teresita, who had grown up in the shadow of the cloister, had no aspirations beyond it, and sighed for the moment which would unite her even more closely to her Divine Spouse. Francisco had, under the impulse of sorrow, wished to become a friar of the discalced Order, but a short residence in the world

cured him of this passing fancy. 1 He then wished to marry, and under his aunt's guiding hand he made an excellent choice in the Dona Onofria de Mendoza of Castilla, a young girl of high birth, and as good and charming as she was well-born. Unfortunately her mother was a woman of a worldly and grasping disposition ; and under her influence Francisco tried to get the saint to agree to measures to which her conscience forbade her consent. His mother-in-law even tried to get Don Lorenzo's will annulled in order to evade the payment of his legacy to the convent. Teresa was thus involved in the painful difficulty of having to withstand her nephew in the interests of her convent.

In another direction Teresa's sympathies were called forth, and in a most painful manner. Her sister Juana de Ahumada wrote in great anguish to say that her daughter Beatriz was the victim of a calumny of so serious a nature that, to escape the shame of loss of reputation, they would both have to leave their home at Alba. Teresa, much distressed, writes thus to Fr. Gratian : " Please God that you have some remedy to suggest for this affair of Beatriz's. I suffer much for her. As for the honour of her name, it is already lost. I am resigned, though it costs me much; but wish to save her soul; I am longing to get this dear family away from Alba. But badly off as they are, how are they to do it? May God come to their assistance Teresa could not but feel these aspersions cast on t spotless name of Ahumada and Cepeda, but remembering that she bore that of her Divine Master she drank patiently of the chalice of humiliation. Later on, wher Beatriz's innocence was brought to light, the saint had the hope of giving her the habit of Carmel, and

thus assuring her happiness in this life as well as in the next. Beatriz refused; though disenchanted of the world, she was too much attached to it to bid it farewell, and she waited till her saintly aunt was in Heaven to break the chains that bound her to it.

Her convents gave her also many anxious moments. At Medina the troubles came from the foundress, Dona Helena de Quiroga, who had for a long time wished to become a nun. Unfortunately, her family, including her uncle the Archbishop of Toledo and Grand Inquisitor, were violently opposed to it. Teresa at first did her best to discourage Dona Helena. She felt herself bound by a duty of gratitude to the archbishop not to oppose him in a question in which both as priest and near relation he had every right to be heard. She was also quite aware that to provoke his resentment would be to put a serious obstacle in the way of the work of the Reform. But Dona Helena would not give in. For twenty years she had asked the favour of God of being allowed to consecrate herself entirely to Him. Her two sons were priests, her daughter was awaiting her at the convent, and her two remaining sons were happily married. There was nothing to keep her in the world. At last her persistence, and no doubt the saint's prayers, had their effect ; the archbishop yielded his consent, and Dona Helena was admitted into the Carmelite Order.

At Valladolid the convent suffered a loss which Teresa felt very deeply. The Padilla family had never ceased their opposition to the entrance of Casilda, "the little saint," as Teresa loved to call her, into the Order of Carmel. But as, in spite of all obstacles, she remained firm, they sought by means of a Papal Brief (obtained on the plea that her health was suffering from the austerity of the Rule) to oblige the young nun

to go as abbess to the Franciscan convent at Burgos. Though Teresa felt the loss very acutely, for not one of her spiritual children was dearer to her than Casilda, she not only resigned herself, but sought to console others. Thus she writes to the provincial: u For the love of God do not be distressed about it. ... I pity the poor little soul with all my heart, for she well deserves it. Our Sovereign Master and King doubtless does not wish that we should find honour amongst the princes of the earth, but with the poor and little ones, in the same way as the apostles. Let us not be unhappy therefore. May God's will be done." l This great sacrifice was not without compensation. For the holy young abbess, torn away in spite of her wishes from her beloved solitude of Carmel, took its spirit of fervour with her to the convent of St. Luis of Burgos. She made children of Teresa of the nuns there, not by habit or profession, but by their religious spirit; and faithful to the memory of her seraphic mother, she joined her testimony to that of the Carmelites in the process of canonization, which took place after Teresa's

death.

Another, and a far greater, trial than those which we have enumerated now loomed upon our saint, o-reat was it that hardly did she dare, with all her courage, sound it to its depths. It was an anxiety which she hid from all; there were moments, however, wh« a sound of terror escaped her, showing that she never without it. We have seen how the Chapte Alcala joined Fr. Nicholas's name with Fr. Gratians in the work of the government of the Reform, had the former received his brethren s votes * adviser and assistant to the provincial, than his chara showed itself in an entirely new light. A rigid observer

i Avila, September 28th, 1581.

of the Rule himself, he assumed the role of critic of the words and proceedings of his provincial, and even permitted himself to inflict, in public, a severe censure upon him. 1 Whilst the holy mother was imploring Fr. Gratian to husband his forces and moderate his fasts, the other accused him of leading too easy a life and introducing relaxations, by his example, into the Order. Teresa, first astounded, then in consternation, exclaimed that there were " certain sanctities that she could not comprehend ! " No ! a sanctity that crushed human nature and the affections, instead of super-naturalizing them, was one with which she could have nothing in common. Unfortunately, Fr. Nicholas's merits (which were undeniable), his zeal, and his spirit of penance, gave him a great ascendancy among his brethren—an ascendancy which he used to undermine Fr. Gratian's influence and authority. This persecution, for it was no less, to which Fr. Gratian was subjected, and which was shared by St. John of the Cross, only reached its height after the saint's death ; but it was sufficiently apparent in her lifetime to cause her the deepest anxiety. " Oh, if they would only spare my sancta sanctorum," she was heard to cry, "I would cheerfully endure every blow on my own shoulders " ; and for her mother's heart, as well as her anxieties as foundress, this, her last sorrow, was perhaps the most cruel of all.

In Teresa's eyes Fr. Gratian was the very soul, the chief support, or, as she phrases it, the Holy of Holies of the Reform. He alone had perfectly seized the idea of the foundress, and sought, in his actions and by the authority with which he had been invested, to carry it out to the utmost limit of his power. Fr. Nicholas's great fault was that he wished for a Reform according

to his own conception of the words—rigid, severe, and inflexible, as he was himself. Hence a life and death struggle, which ended in the complete triumph of the principles laid down by the holy foundress—in short, of the Teresian Reform.

WITH the Chapter of Alcala a new epoch commenced in the history of the Reform. The holy mother, having borne " the burthen of the day" and the heat of the combat, was to see—amidst the shadows that were closing in around her — a faint glimpse of the future greatness and fecundity of the work which had cost her so dear. The last months of the year 1581 were filled with projects of Foundations which, for the most part, were carried out in the following year. Houses of religious of the Order were established almost simultaneously at Valladolid and Salamanca ; from thence they passed to Portugal, and, following in the footsteps of the hardy navigators of that country, they volunteered in an expedition to the Guinea coast. 1 The convents of nuns meanwhile continued to spread in Spain. Preparations were being made for a Foundation in Madrid, another was under discussion for Pampeluna, a third for Ciudad Rodrigo, a fourth at Orduna. 2 Fr. Gratian had laid his views before the saint and had discussed these matters with her, and she was still considering them and praying for light, when Fr. John of the Cross arrived at Avila charged with the mission of getting nuns for Granada. At the same time another messenger arrived from Burgos, begging of her to start without delay for that town. At Granada, as at Burgos, the saint's presence

1 Hist, of the Order. 2 Boll., No. 942.

was urgently required ; but it was mid-winter, and her health had been even worse than usual, she therefore deputed Sister Anne of Jesus to take her place at Granada. Sister Anne protested that to found a convent without the holy mother's presence was an impossible thing, and that " she could not endure the thought of being entrusted with a work in which her mother was not all in all." 1 Fr. John of the Cross got the better of her humility, and her obedience was blessed by a complete success in the new Foundation, where the fervour and regularity of observance of its members almost equalled her own. Teresa, satisfied with the state of things at Granada, turned her attention to Burgos. The Jesuit Fathers six years before had invited her to go to that city, and "the reasons they urged," she says, " had given me a desire to do so. But the trials our Order was undergoing, and other Foundations, prevented my occupying myself with this one. In the year 1580 I was at Valladolid at the time Mgr. Vela, former Bishop of the Canary Islands, was passing through; he had been appointed to the archbishopric of Toledo, and was on his way to his new See. I had recourse to Mgr. de Mendoza . . . and begged him to speak in our name to the archbishop, and ask leave of him for us to establish ourselves at Burgos. He promised me willingly to do so, as he knows how our Saviour is served in our houses, and he is quite pleased when he sees another founded. . . . The archbishop answered that he would give his consent with pleasure, that he already knew the life that was led by Carmelites, and that he had even wished to establish them in his episcopal town in the Canaries, etc. Mgr. Alvarez transmitted this answer to me ; he added I had nothing further to wait for, and

1 Manriqxie. 2 N

that I need not be anxious about the permission, as the Council of Trent did not insist on its being in writing." l Shortly afterwards the archbishop wrote to the Bishop of Palencia and, without revoking his promise, said that his clients would have to obtain the permission of the town, and that he was doubtful if they would get it. Dona Catalina de Tolosa, a pious widow of Burgos, undertook, with the help of her friends, to obtain it. Negotiations were carried on for some time. Finally Dona Catalina sent Teresa the governor of Burgos's authorization, accompanied with a letter pressing her to come instantly, and warning her of obstacles which were likely to arise with any delay. The saint saw there was no time to be lost; but (as she tells us) she thought it was impossible to start in midwinter, ill as she was, on such a long journey ; she therefore deputed the prioress of Palencia to take her place. "Thus I had quite decided not to go when our Lord said to me : < Pay no attention to the cold ; I am the true heat. The devil is making great efforts to stop this Foundation ; work, therefore, on your side to make it a success. Do not fail to go there in person. Your presence will be very necessary.' I at once changed my mind. If nature shudders sometimes when it is presented with a great trial, I had ever, at the bottom of my heart, a firm resolution to suffer all things for the sake of our great God. I conjured Him to pay no heed to the repugnances of my weakness, but to order all things according to His good pleasure, as, assisted by His grace, I should not fail Him."

It had been settled since the Chapter of Alcala that the saint should be accompanied on her journeys by two friars of the Order, instead of by secular priests such as Fr. Julian ; Fr. Gratian on this occasion accom-

panied her. Before leaving Avila he asked her if she had a written authorization from the archbishop, but this she assured him was unnecessary. 1

Teresa left Avila for the last time on the 2nd of January, 1582, accompanied by her niece, by Anne of St. Bartholomew, another lay-sister, and Mother Thomas of the Baptist. The travellers encountered snow and an icy wind on their way to Medina del Campo, and they took three days to get there. Teresa arrived with a violent inflammation of the throat which delayed her departure nearly a week, a wound forming in the part affected so that she could not swallow anything without agony. She paid no attention to her own pains, and occupied herself with her fellow-sufferers, especially with little Teresita, whose health also suffered from the rigours of the journey. She found the prioress, Mother Alberta Baptist, very ill on her arrival with pleurisy, accompanied by high fever. " How can you be ill, daughter," Teresa said to her, " when I come to pay you a visit? Get up and dine with me. You are all right now." Mother Alberta arose ; the moment the saint's hand touched her the fever and pain in her side left her. She went down to the refectory and dined at Teresa's side, and resumed her ordinary occupations the same day. 2

On the Qth of January the party set out again and reached Valladolid. Teresa, who was in high fever, could neither sleep by day nor by night; moreover, she had a slight return of paralysis which affected her tongue, so that she could only speak with difficulty. In this state she reached Palencia. The townspeople, who were devoted to the saint, allowed neither snow nor frost to prevent them from giving her a hearty reception. The

* Hist, of the Order, Vol. II, Bk. V, ch. xv. 2 See Acts of Canonization, Boll., No. 1104.

crowd thronged round her litter, and rushed to see her when she stepped out of it in order to hear her, touch her habit, and get her blessing. She took refuge from them into the convent, amid the sounds of Te Deums and bells ringing. The Carmelites had decorated their cloisters, and prepared altars of our Lady, and St. Joseph, and her favourite saints in honour of their mother. They hoped to keep her with them till her health was re-established, but nothing could stop her. " Accomplish your journey, daughter," our Lord said to her'; " I am with you."

Teresa describes the journey thus : " We had to run many dangers. At no part of the road were the risks greater than within a few leagues of Burgos, at a place called Los Pontes. The rivers were so high that the water in places covered everything, neither road nor the smallest footpath could be seen, only water everywhere, and two abysses on each side. It seemed foolhardiness to advance, especially in a carriage, for if one strayed ever so little off the road (then invisible), one must have perished." The saint is silent on her share of the adventure, but her companions relate that, seeing their alarm, she turned to them and encouraged them, saying that "as they were engaged in doing God's work, how could they die in a better cause ? " She then led the way on foot. The current was so strong that she lost her footing, and was on the point of being carried away when our Lord sustained her. " Oh, my Lord !" she exclaimed, with her usual loving familiarity, " when wilt Thou cease from scattering obstacles in our path?" " Do not complain, daughter," the Divine Master answered, " for it is ever thus that I treat My friends." " Ah, Lord, it is also on that account that Thou hast so few ! " was her reply.

followed her across the dangerous part of the road, and soon after they reached a church, where they heard Mass and communicated. As soon as the sacred Host came in contact with Teresa's tongue the difficulty in speaking left her. Later on the carriages stuck in the mud, and they had to resort to every sort of device to get them extricated. The saint's comment was: "The presence of the father provincial soothed me much. He took care of everything ; and his calmness was such that nothing could trouble it." 1 They reached Burgos on the 26th of January, and on their arrival Fr. Gratian took them first to venerate the crucifix in the cathedral; this crucifix is still an object of devotion to the faithful. On leaving the cathedral they went straight to the house of Dona Catalina de Tolosa, a holy widow, mother of seven children, who had already had the consolation of seeing four daughters embrace the Rule of Carmel, and whose two sons were before long to follow their sisters' example and join the same Order. In staying with such a family Teresa felt herself in no strange house. Dona Catalina had prepared a fine room for her, and she showed the saint a hall close to her own which the Jesuits had previously used as a chapel, and in which she assured her Fr. Gratian would have no difficulty in getting leave to celebrate Mass. Then perceiving that Teresa's habit was soaked with rain, she brought her close to a large fire. Unfortunately the sudden change brought on a violent return of fever, and after a bad night the saint found herself incapable of rising. She could not even move her head. Fr. Gratian, who had gone to stay with an Alcala college friend, the Reverend Doctor Manso, went at an early hour to solicit an interview with the archbishop in order to present the holy

foundress's respects to him. Meanwhile Canon Salinas, and several members of the council, and other persons of distinction who had received letters of recommendation for the saint, came to call upon her. She tried in vain to rise; her paralysed head and members made all movement impossible. Accordingly she caused herself to be moved on her bed to a little grilled window opening into a passage, and there received her visitors, on whom her gratitude and the charm of her conversation made their usual favourable impression. So far all appeared to be prospering, for her own health was, with Teresa, a matter of no importance; but Fr. Gratian returned from the palace bringing with him " severe reproaches in the place of authorization." The archbishop showed himself as displeased with the nuns' arrival as if he had forbidden them to come. Fr. Gratian in vain reminded him of the promises he had made to the Bishop of Palencia. " I shall never give my consent," he told him, "to the Carmelites establishing themselves at Burgos till they have got a house of their own, and means of subsistence ; if they have no resources they had better return home."

The saint was not one to surrender at the first obstacle ; still, to buy a house at a moment's notice was out of the question, and to find a revenue equally so. It was necessary to exercise patience, to struggle by means of prayer, and to trust to time to bring round the excellent prelate, who was only influenced by prudence, and had no unfriendly feelings against the Carmelites. It was thus Teresa argued with Fr. Gratian. " He showed no displeasure," she writes; " in fact, he seemed quite content. God permitted this in order to spare me the trial it would have been to me had he been displeased with me for not having followed his advice in getting the archbishop's consent in

writing." Teresa's friends did their utmost to gain permission at least for Mass to be celebrated in the former Jesuits' chapel; but this favour was also refused on the plea that the street was too noisy, and the hall damp. Accordingly the saint, as soon as she recovered the use of her limbs, was forced to go out, with her nuns, to the neighbouring church. On one occasion, when she was walking alongside a little stream on her way there, a woman stood on the pathway. The saint asked her gently to let her pass. The wretched woman loudly reproached her for "her hypocrisy," and pushed her into the gutter. The nuns who accompanied her were naturally furious, but Teresa said : " Leave the good woman alone. She has spoken and acted truly; that is just what I deserve." Another day whilst she was kneeling in church her infirmities prevented her moving out of the way of some men who passed her, and one of them gave her a push which knocked her down. Anne of St. Bartholomew, who records these things, said she only laughed at her misadventures. The joy of the Holy Ghost in her heart enabled her to accept these, and many other little trials, with perfect equanimity.

On the 6th of February she wrote to Mother Mary of St. Joseph: " We have now been twelve days at Burgos, and the Foundation is not even begun. There have been many difficulties ... by which I can see that God will be served as He should be in this monastery, and I am convinced all is for the best. The obstacles opposed to us will have the effect of making the discalced Carmelites known. If we had made our entrance into this big city without opposition, no one would'have so much as thought of us. ... Already several postulants have asked to be received as soon as we are settled."

Never, indeed, had Teresa met with more formal opposition than she had done from the archbishop, nor had she ever met, in an unknown town, such lively interest and sympathy. Nowhere had friends flocked to her assistance in the same manner, and their devotion touched her to the heart. Fr. Gratian had brought a former college companion of his of the name of Aguiar to see the saint, and try if he could be of use to her in her suffering state. Not only did Dr. Aguiar put himself entirely at Teresa's service, but as " he had much common sense and excellent judgment" (to use her own words), he made himself very useful to her. March was approaching, and Fr. Gratian's presence was required at Valladolid to preach the Lenten sermons, and discouraged by the want of success of their negotiations, he was much tempted to give up the Foundation and take away the nuns. Teresa, however, having received orders from our Lord to persevere, saw matters in a different light. Secure of ultimate success, she begged of the provincial to leave her at Burgos. He answered that he would consent only on condition that it was no longer necessary for her and her nuns to hear Mass without going through the streets, on account of the curiosity excited by their appearance. Driven to a last extremity, Teresa tried, herself, to get the archbishop to yield, and went to plead her cause in person. Whilst she was with him her daughters were employed in praying and taking the discipline " in such a manner that there was always one who was scourging herself all the time of the holy mother's interview with the prelate." [1] God permitted that she, also, should fail. She was at her wits' end, when Doctor Aguiar came to her assistance. With the concurrence of a colleague he offered the little

community a garret at the top of the hospital of the Conception, where they would be next door to the patients' chapel. The room was under the roof, and so dirty and uncomfortable that the cause for its being vacant was that no one would consent to live in it. But the hospital was crowded; with this exception there was not a single vacant room in it, so the saint joyfully exchanged her grand apartment for the garret, which owed its attraction to being close to the spot inhabited by her Divine Master.

Though still anxious about the future of the community, Fr. Gratian, as soon as he had seen them settled in their garret, left for Valladolid. " His departure comforted me greatly," said Teresa, "for the greater part of my anxiety came from his. . . . I relied on being successful, but I was not able to raise his hopes.- Before leaving us he advised us to look out for a house and buy it; but this was not easily done." The Carmelites spent a month at the hospital. Fr. Manso was their spiritual director, and Doctor Aguiar their physician, man of business, and counsellor, and in return for their services they asked the favour of personal interviews with the saint, when the one talked theology with her, and the other discussed practical questions of everyday life. Both were astounded with her wisdom and holiness, and said that never had they had the same feeling of devotion as when they had the happiness of speaking to her.

"When I came near her," said Fr. Manso, "I felt penetrated inwardly with such a profound respect, that I said to myself: "In truth this is a very great saint and a great friend of our Lord's to whom I am speaking ; and I already looked upon her as a pillar of God's Church." The other went to work quite simply; he cross-questioned the saint on all her many under-

takings, and followed her with ever-increasing interest from Foundation to Foundation. " Soon," he remarks, " there was so much intimacy between us that she told me about all her troubles. She even confided the whole history of her life to me, with the exception of her revelations and the favours God had conferred upon her, about which she never said a word. I cannot describe the benefit my soul derived from these conversations." [1]

The patients at the hospital implored her to visit them. The numerous communities at Burgos begged her to go and see them. It seemed as if God, before taking her to Himself, wished to lift the veil which covered her humble and obscure life, and to permit the world to look into this sanctuary, which had hitherto been inaccessible to it. The archbishop's resistance was but an instrument in His hands to expose the saint's life to the broad light of day. Though still suffering severely she visited the sick daily, and if she found any in great pain she returned to them again and again. " When the holy Mother Teresa is here we no longer suffer," they used to say. " The sight of her alone comforts us." One day she heard loud groans coming from some unfortunate man who was enduring agonies; when she approached him he was silent; but she chid him gently, saying, " Why were you crying so loud, my poor fellow; are you not willing to suffer cheerfully for the love of God?" She then prayed for a few seconds near his bedside, and left him cured of his pain.

On another occasion her daughters, anxious about her loss of appetite and constant nausea, asked Dona Catalina — who continued providing for their wants — for some oranges. She sent them directly, and the saint, delighted to get the fruit, took them instantly down to her dear patients, and distributed every single one amongst them. The nuns remonstrated, but it was no use. She only smiled, and told them that the pleasure she had experienced in giving them away had done her a great deal of good. Another time someone sent her some fine lemons, and again she rejoiced. " It is for my poor sick people," she said, "that they are sent to me." The little garret she and her companions inhabited was cold and draughty, and her sleepless nights were spent on a hard and uncomfortable bed. When her nuns expressed their sympathy with her she said, " Dcta't be unhappy about your mother; remember our Saviour suffered much greater torments when they gave Him gall and vinegar to drink; and see how luxurious my bed is in comparison with His ! " This same charity which filled her heart caused her to visit the convents at Burgos at the earnest desire of their communities, and wherever she went similar results were produced. A secret virtue appeared to come out of her which pierced the souls of all whom she came across, and attracted them to God. Above all, it was impossible to come under her influence without feeling the attraction of that perfect simplicity which gave such charm to all she said and did. Affectations of speech or manner, attachment to superfluities, and other remains of worldliness vanished from many religious houses after she had visited them —such was the general verdict in Burgos. An eyewitness, alluding to her visit to the royal convent of Las Huelgas, said: "Mother Teresa of Jesus only entered this house once, but her poverty, her humility, her religious spirit, her frank and straightforward way of speaking, the advice she was good enough to give on the severity nuns should use towards themselves in

order to please God, made such an impression that that single visit reformed the entire monastery." 1

In spite of all these holy occupations in God's service, Teresa by no means lost sight of her great undertaking. Her generous benefactor, Dona Catalina, had made an arrangement with her two Carmelite daughters at Tolosa, by which they gave up their patrimony in favour of the new Foundation. Dona Catalina would willingly have added to this donation, but her family reproached her already with her too great devotion to the Order, by which they declared she was bringing ruin on herself, so she was obliged to leave to Providence the care of completing her work. Teresa, alluding to the anxieties Dona Catalina had undergone on her account, says : " I saw what she had been made to suffer, and was deeply distressed by it. Still she had acted as she had done on the advice of very enlightened theologians, and if she had gone against it I would never have accepted anything from her had my refusal cost me not one, but a thousand, Foundations." The saint rewarded Dona Catalina's noble generosity with her gratitude, and even her admiration, saying of her that she was "a worthy daughter of a noble house."

Matters therefore progressed but slowly. The nuns, however, never ceased from praying to St. Joseph to find them a house in time for his feast. Two days before it (on the i7th of March) Dr. Aguiar came to visit Teresa. He had no good news to impart, but in the course of their conversation the saint suddenly remembered having heard of a house which was on sale, though she had been told it had little to recommend it; still, she suggested, it might possibly serve as a temporary abode till they could get something to

suit them better. The doctor went to inspect the house, was delighted with it, and returned to take Teresa to look at it, to whom it gave equal satisfaction. The domain comprised a house, to which a chapel was attached, and a garden looking on to the river; in fact, it appeared exactly suited to their requirements. No time was to be lost, as others were in treaty for the possession of the property. The price asked was thirteen hundred ducats, but when Teresa hesitated she was rebuked by our Lord.[1] Accordingly the bargain was struck and the contract signed, whilst the nuns were singing vespers for the feast of St. Joseph. At last the saint thought she had got to the end of her troubles. She acquainted the archbishop with the success of her efforts, and his answer was, " Mother Teresa owes the fine property to me ; if I had been less firm with her she would never have got it." Teresa took this message as a consent. " I wrote at once to thank his grace," she says, "and I told him that I was getting the house ready to receive us as quickly as possible, so that he might put the finishing touch to his favours. . . . Scarcely had we got into it than we heard that he was very angry with us. I softened him as much as I could, and he is so good his displeasure soon passed. He visited us, and seemed pleased with the house, and was very gracious to us. Still he left us nothing more than our hopes. It was less his fault, I believe, than his vicar-general's. . . . We had many troubles before our affairs were settled. First they required guarantees, then some money down. Such incessant worries !" Still, in time the worries were disposed of, and the saint ends cheerfully with the remark: " The devil who is fighting us here is really a very stupid one. He doesn't know his own business.

1 En dineros te detienes ? were our Lord's words to her.

One would fancy he tried to take us like flies in spiders' webs."[1]

The saint, satisfied that things were progressing favourably, left to her friend, Dr. Aguiar, the care of superintending the workmen who were employed in getting the house in order, and retired to her cell. When the good doctor complained to her that he missed very much his conversations with her, she answered, " Doctor, you know my correspondence takes up a great deal of my time ; also I am writing at this moment the account of this Foundation. This very day I am telling about what you have done for us. I say that your charity prevents you taking food, or rest, as long as we have need of your services ; and that we owe you much gratitude, whilst awaiting the time when God Himself will reward you."

It is highly probable that besides concluding the book about the Foundations, she was also writing her Manner of Visiting Religious Houses at this time. Fr. Gratian, who was charged with this duty, had asked her to prepare a manual for him and his successors, which would serve them as a guide, in what, in some ways, was one of the most delicate tasks entrusted to superiors. In this masterpiece of supernatural wisdom and common sense she completed her works on the Constitutions of the Reformed Order of Carmel.

One letter, in her interminable correspondence, had to be written ; but the saint, disliking much to have to write it, put off doing so from day to day. The archbishop still withheld his permission, and it was a question of employing a decisive weapon against him by asking the Bishop of Palencia to remind him of his former promise. To extort favours in such a way was

not at all to the saint's taste. She had already heard with pain a remark made to her by Mgr. Vela: " Our Lord's death, Mother Teresa," he said, " changed enemies into friends ; your arrival here has had the contrary effect, for from being friends it has changed the Bishop of Palencia and me into enemies." Teresa's answer was characteristic: " That shows you, my lord, what I am."

She exhausted every possible method of persuasion before having recourse to this last expedient. Finally she wrote to the bishop and asked him to intercede for her. Mgr. de Mendoza—who had been much annoyed already by what he had heard of the archbishop's treatment of Teresa—sent the saint an open letter for her to forward to the archbishop, expressed in such forcible terms that to forward it would have been to forfeit every chance of success: "I kept the letter," Teresa says, "on Dr. Manso's advice, and wrote once more to the bishop imploring him to send me a second letter, kindly worded, for the archbishop. He did what I asked him, for the glory of God and in order to help me, but it was much against the grain. He told me afterwards that writing that letter cost him more than all he had ever done before for the good of the Order. When the archbishop received it he was delighted with it, and no less with Dr. Manso's remarks when he presented it. He sent us the authorizations at once, through our good friend Ferdinand de Matanza. The latter arrived full of joy. Our sisters were getting more and more discouraged. Cata-lina de Tolosa was in such despair I did not know what to do to console her. I had myself since the previous night lost the confidence which had hitherto sustained me ; it appeared as if our Lord wished to try us more than ever, before finally consoling us." The

holy sacrifice was offered up the following morning, the i8th of April, at daybreak in the little chapel, and our Lord took possession of His tabernacle. Dona Catalina wept with joy; the Carmelites blessed the Lord. Burgos took part in their rejoicings. A choir of musicians came self-invited to sing at the High Mass, which was celebrated by the Dominican prior. To complete the general satisfaction the archbishop got into the pulpit, and expressed his regrets for the delays made over the Foundation, [1] and spoke in terms of highest veneration of the holy Mother. Teresa all this time was ravished in God, crying to Him : " Lord, what do Thy servants desire in life except to serve Thee, and to see themselves prisoners for love of Thee in this spot from whence they will never go out? Oh, Jesus, divine Spouse of my soul, true man and true God! Is it a small thing to belong to Thee? Mayst Thou be blessed for ever and ever. Amen ! Amen ! "

The holy mother and her daughters shut themselves up once more in the solitude of their cloister: "like poor little fish who, after having been thrown out from a net on the river-bank, were enabled to scramble back once more into the water."

A month later an alarming accident threatened to devastate their peaceful abode. The River Orlanzon, on the feast of the Ascension which was kept that year on the 24th of May, swollen by heavy rain, rose to a great height, and became transformed into a foaming torrent. The whole district in which the convent was situated assumed the appearance of a sea, whose stormy waves uprooted trees and carried away houses. The inhabitants fled to the higher parts of the town, begging the Carmelites to follow them ; but Teresa was satisfied with the precaution of taking the Blessed

Sacrament to the top storey of the convent where she assembled the community under our

Lord's guardianship. The nuns never ceased praying, but still the river continued to rise. The first floor was submerged, and an icy cold seized the unfortunate nuns who were thus suspended over a watery abyss, into which every shock threatened to submerge them. The saint alone remained calm, but she, also, was deeply anxious. Was she to see her beloved daughters perish ? Ignorant of the character of the locality she had not foreseen the danger, and having no one to advise her, she had thought herself obliged to respect the law of cloister, and remain in her convent instead of taking flight with her neighbours. Her anxiety was great, but so also was her resignation. She offered her life with the lives of her children to God, and abandoned them and herself to. His will and pleasure; but her stress of mind, joined to her infirmities, caused her to feel very faint. She asked Sister Anne to give her a little piece of bread. " I wept to hear these words," Sister Anne relates, "for what was to be done? The bread was under water! In this difficulty a strong young novice offered to try and get some. She plunged into the water up to her waist, and seized a loaf, which we gave to the holy mother, who little knew at what price the bread had been procured!"

In the night the waters began to fall, and the townspeople, who were in terror as to the fate that had befallen the Carmelites, made an attempt to rescue them. They broke through the doors of the ground floor, and let out the water and rubbish which had collected there, and brought food and assistance to the poor prisoners.

This was to be the last scene in the history of the Foundations. The saint had commenced twenty years

2 O

before with an account of the disturbances at Avila; she was now to close it with the description of a great storm, after a weary period of trials and persecutions levelled against her by the invisible enemy of souls, furious at Teresa's victories. Far, however, from destroying her great work his efforts had but contributed to consolidate it. Only an edifice firm as the rock on which it was built could stand trials such as those to which Teresa's Reform was subjected. In the year of which we are writing the discalced Order numbered sixteen convents of nuns and fourteen of friars, and it was to pursue its way through succeeding centuries, multiplying its Foundations in every country, and carrying with it, whithersoever it went, the spirit of its holy foundress.

CHAPTER XXXI

THE events related in the last chapter did much to increase Teresa's reputation for sanctity in Burgos. She went throughout the city by the name of "our saint," the archbishop and the people alike attributing the rapid fall of the inundations to her prayers. A friar of the discalced Order ventured to bring the popular rumour to her ears. " My son," was her answer, "when I was young they told me I was beautiful,- and I believed it. Later on I was told I was prudent, and this also I, too easily, believed. I have also confessed these two sins of vanity. As for what they say about me now, I can assure you I have never been deluded to the extent of believing it for a single moment."

St. Bernard says to be esteemed a saint by others, and to remain in one's own eyes a sinner and an unprofitable servant is a miracle. May we not call this miracle, which is great in proportion to the greatness of the temptation to think otherwise, the most striking of Teresa's life? To some who have, perhaps, only known the saint by her motto, "to suffer, or to die," or by some ecstatic expression of the divine love by which she was inflamed, or by her pictures, in which she is represented transfixed by a seraph's dart, the preceding chapters may have been the cause of some astonishment. They might ask: This strong-minded woman, this intrepid foundress, whom we have fol-

lowed from town to town, and seen worn out with business and cares, having hardly time for prayer and contemplation, who, in short, travels, builds, works, speaks, and smiles like the rest of the world, is this, indeed, the seraphic St. Teresa? In answering in the affirmative we bring home to ourselves the chief lesson of Teresa's life. For, if from some points of view her sanctity is wholly beyond our imitation, from others, and especially from that of her single-mindedness and candour, she stands as a model to all.

The primary gift Teresa received from Heaven was that of an upright soul. This upright, firm, and single-minded character not only guided her in the ordinary actions of her life, but in the path of perfection. She had her moments of weakness in her youth —her humility has recorded them in the strongest light—but she never was led away by delusions. The heights which she sought to attain were ever before her, and she made straight for them; consequently she never lost time in fruitless endeavours. She seized at once the idea of what was essential in the law of God. "Thou shalt love the Lord thy God with thy whole heart, and with thy whole soul, and with thy whole mind, and thy neighbour as thyself." She was utterly penetrated with the sense of this divine precept; she made it the soul of her soul. And as holiness is only the development of those two loves, Teresa of Jesus, because she loved God as He desires to be loved, and because she loved her neighbour in Him, and as God wishes he should be loved, became a great saint.

" Lord ! " was her cry, " Let others serve Thee better and be rewarded with greater happiness in Heaven, of this I would never complain. But I know not how I could endure that any should love Thee more than

I do." 1 To realize something of the fervour by which she was consumed one should have listened to the saint praying. Sometimes after Holy Communion, when her heart was on fire with divine love, she would let fall some of those aspirations which were published after her death under the name of her ejaculations.

With the prophet she groaned over the length of her exile : " Oh, life of my life, how canst thou live without Him Who is thy true Life? What consolation hast thou, my soul, in the stormy sea of this world? I weep, and my tears are redoubled when I think of the days I lived without weeping. My soul would fain rest in the thought of what her joy will be when Thou in Thy mercy wilt, perchance, one day give her the happiness of possessing Thee. But first I wish to serve Thee, for it is in serving her that Thou hast acquired for her the happiness to which she looks forward. What can I do, my Saviour? What can I do for Thee, my Lord? Oh, how late did I learn to inflame my desires for Thee, and Thou, on the contrary, how early didst Thou call to me ! "

More often still she weeps over sinners. Like her "most sweet and compassionate Saviour"- she is bowed down by the world's iniquities : " Oh, my God, how I suffer when I think of what passes in a soul, who, after having been the object of every loving care and adulation, sees itself, when death comes, on the point of being lost." Then those truths of faith from which she has sought to escape seize hold of her. "Oh endless torments! What blindness! Oh, my God, what sorrow ! Ah ! since in the excess of their folly they will not come to Thee, come, O Lord, to them. I ask it in their name. The greatness of Thy

1 Ribera, I, IV.

2 Piadoso y amoroso Senor de mi alma.

divine compassion is revealed in proportion to the depths of their misery. May God have pity on those who have no pity on themselves. Lazarus did not ask Thee to be raised from the dead. Thou didst work the miracle at the prayer of a sinner. Behold another, and a greater sinner, at Thy feet. Show forth Thy mercy ; I ask it for those who will not ask it for themselves. Look not on our blindness; only look on the Blood which Thy Son shed for us."

These groans and sobs of exile are mixed with others —accents of hope, and faith, and love. The saint dares to tell her Lord how she loves Him ; the desire she has in her heart that He may be adored, praised, and glorified. She unites herself with the blessed in Heaven, and then she descends to the thought of her own nothingness, and one feels she is only really at peace when she is humbled at the feet of her Well-beloved, and forgetful of herself so that she may think only of Him, and immolate herself for Him. " Never will I cease," she says, "to confess my sins and publish Thy mercies. I desire to attract Thee by my sighs. Those are my canticles of praise. ... I would rather live and die in working for eternal life than possess all creation and all the goods of this life. O my God, increase more and more the martyrdom of my soul by wounding it with Thy love, or let it cease by giving Thyself to it in Heaven."

" To suffer or to die," this is ever the cry of Teresa's soul. And her love was as pure and disinterested as it was burning. " If I love Thee, it is not, Thou knowest, because of the Heaven Thou hast promised ; if I fear to offend Thee it is not because Thou threatenest me with hell. What draws me to Thee is Thyself alone ; it is to see Thee, Jesus my Saviour, nailed to the cross, with pierced and bleeding body in the anguish of

death. Thy love has got such possession of my heart that should there be no Heaven I should love Thee, and if there was no hell I should fear Thee. Thou canst give me nothing to provoke my love, for even did I not hope for what I now hope for, I should still love Thee as I love Thee."

But with the saint we should add that love consists in something besides sentiments, however great and ennobling. " The love of God does not consist in tears, nor tenderness, nor emotions; to love God is to serve Him in strength and humility and justice." It was thus Teresa loved. With the native ardour which belonged to her race and country, she joined an energy and patient perseverance which was wholly supernatural.

Her courage never failed her, neither in the presence of difficulties, nor of opposition such as she was constantly to encounter from all ranks of life, the lowest as well as the highest. As she once said : " I am ready to yield if my conscience declares a thing to be wrong ; but except for the fear of sin I am afraid of nothing." Those interior desolations in which God appears to abandon the soul had no terrors for her. She suffered from them—God alone knows how much —but she loved in spite of all. Writing to a much-tried soul, she says: " Understand, my daughter, that the divine Master is one of those who rewards great services with great sufferings, and He could not better repay them than by so doing, because it is through them that real love is acquired. Let Him work His Will upon your soul. Place your glory in carrying His cross; attach no price to sweetness and consolations. It is fitting indeed for private soldiers to be paid daily wages—aim for your part at giving your service free, in the same way as nobles serve their king ; and may the King of Heaven be always with you."

If love of God is generous and intrepid, it watches unceasingly, and even when sleeping slumbers not. Teresa's heart never knew rest. When great occasions were wanting, and circumstances prevented her going in search of them, she made the most of trifling ones. Sometimes when too ill to do any work she would rise from her bed to sweep the oratories, or to ornament them with flowers — accompanying these humble offerings with a fervent prayer which told her Lord how willingly she would do more had it been possible. She even profited by occasions which would have been a source of distraction to those less advanced in the spiritual life. Thus she willingly left her prayer to console afflicted souls, or to assist her sisters, certain that her sacrifice would be acceptable to Him who said, " What you have done to the least of these my little ones you have done unto me." This tender and solid love, ardent and yet practical, was founded on a mighty faith. God preserved her from a trial from which He had spared few of His saints. Teresa's faith never knew a moment's doubt. The eye of her soul reposed in perfect peace on the " Infinite Truth, in which all other truths are contained." 1 "The soul," she once said, "is raised more wholly to God, and is animated with a deeper sense of worship by mysteries which she cannot fathom, than by those which are accessible to her low and weak understanding."

"Lord and Saviour," she cried, "miserable and wretched as I am, I believe firmly that Thou canst do all that thou wiliest to do. The greater the wonders that I hear said about Thee, more do I feel certain that Thou couldst do even greater; and the more is my faith strengthened thereby, and the more confidence I feel that Thou wilt do what I ask of Thee." Another time

she said : " The less I understand the more I believe. The longer I live the greater is my faith." She did not care for curious investigation into sacred dogmas. " It is good for theologians," she wrote on one occasion, "to study these things for they have to defend their faith by their knowledge ; it is enough for us to receive those lights from God which He chooses to give us. If He refuses them, let us humble ourselves without being discouraged, and rejoice that His greatness is such that one word of His embraces a thousand mysteries." She had so much devotion to the credo that she could hardly sing it without her voice betraying it, and she owned she could never say those words— cujus regni non erit finis —without a thrill of joy.

This lively faith was the moving spirit of her interior life ; thus her piety though so ardent had a grave and prudent side to it. She had a horror of childish devotions, and those only were admitted into her convents which were approved of by the Church. Amongst them she ranked first everything that concerned the worship of the Holy Eucharist; she cultivated also a filial piety towards the Mother of God, and to her good father St. Joseph, to the angels, the saints of the Order, and in an especial manner to the great penitents, Magdalen and Augustine.

Her appearance before the tabernacle was more that of an angel than of a terrestrial being. Absorbed in an adoration which rendered her insensible to all earthly things, she tasted the delights of being close to Jesus, of being " in His good graces." Her greatest consolation in founding a new monastery was in the thought that she was "offering a home to the Blessed Sacrament " which heresy had turned out of so many places. However poor were her convents, the chapels attached to them were always remarkable for their perfect neat-

ness and order, and if any of her friends wished to present her with a valuable gift she always asked that it might be for the decoration of the altar; and then, whether it was sacred vessels, incense, or vestments, nothing could be too costly to please her. 1

Though permission for daily Communion was rarely given in those days, it was granted to her before she started her Reform. She prepared with fresh fervour every time she approached the holy Altar, and no human obstacle could ever have kept her away from it. Only the duty of obedience had power to stop her, and then she refrained without a word of remonstrance. Thus her confessor more than once, in order to try her, used to stop her daily Communions, and she only thanked him for sparing our Lord the indignity of entering the "wretched hostelry of her heart." On one occasion, severe illness having prevented her communicating for a month, she said, in answer to her daughters, who were sympathizing with her for her loss: "God wills that it should be so, and that is enough to set my heart at rest." Her fervour in reciting divine office infected all her nuns who said it with her. She took much care to inspire them with the spirit of each feast in the liturgical year ; and she identified herself with the intentions of the Church in following it from scene to scene in the life of our Lord. She cultivated with equal devotion the glories of Mary, her maternity, her purity, and the victories of the saints and martyrs. The Church's feasts were held as family feasts in her convents, and they were not only celebrated by more solemn offices, but by more joyous and festive recreations. Teresa, as we know, loved singing and poetry, and there was much of both in the convents of Carmel. She liked to see this bright and

joyous piety in her children. On one occasion she asked a nun to sing a hymn to the community on Easter Sunday. The nun excused herself, saying, "On such a great day as this, dear mother? Would it not be better to return to prayer?" " You may go and contemplate if you like in your cell, my daughter," was the saint's answer, " but leave your sisters to rejoice with me and our dear Lord ! " Teresa's spirit was that of her Order: very austere in appearance, in reality very sweet, and large.

Teresa's piety towards the members of the Church in Heaven was joined to limitless devotion to the Church militant on earth. It was with the object of putting more abundant graces and merit at its disposal that she had introduced practices of penance and austerities into her Constitutions. No dogma was dearer to her heart than that of the Communion of saints. She had no greater happiness than to pour her labours, her sacrifices, and her prayers into the common treasury whence the Saviour may draw those graces which He loves to dispense on sinners, and abandoned souls in purgatory.

The pious Bishop of Tarazona, Teresa's confessor and biographer, says of her, " If I had to relate all I know of Mother Teresa's humility I should have to begin a fresh volume. Perhaps some idea might be given of it, by saying that God wished by means of it to establish a necessary counterpoise to all the marvellous gifts with which He had ennobled her, and the astounding graces and favours which He had heaped upon her." Nothing in truth is more striking when one penetrates into the secrets of her heart than its touching humility. Our Lord pours His gifts on her, and she can only see her own nothingness and misery, and weeps with anguish at the thought of

His stooping to so vile a creature. The honour and consideration shown to her by people in the world was a true torture to her. Compliments, marks of deference, discreetly worded admiration were all so many crosses and afflictions to her. For a nature like Teresa's it was far easier to bend under a load of humiliations than one of honours. Thus, when she was at Seville, hearing of the calumnies that had been spread about her, " God be praised," she writes, "in this country they know me as I am, and esteem me according to my deserts." In another place she writes to her confessor: "At last, father, I have found a happiness here which I have desired for many years. No one pays any more attention to Teresa of Jesus than if she did not exist, accordingly I hope not to leave this monastery unless I am forced to do so by obedience."

A clever man, who was also a good Christian and a man of high birth, speaking to her on one occasion, and anxious to try her humility, said to her : " Mother Teresa, people talk a great deal about you ; you should be careful. Magdalen of the Cross performed even greater marvels than you have done, and she was a slave of the devil." "You are indeed right," exclaimed the saint. " I never think of her without trembling."

The higher the source from which she received insult or humiliation the more she esteemed it; and if nature received any repugnance she quickly subdued it at the feet of her meek Saviour, and implored Him to let her follow Him on the road of ignominy. It was on an occasion of that sort—when an involuntary recoiling followed on an heroic prayer—that she heard these words of gentle irony from the lips of her divine Master : " My daughter, you ask me incessantly for sufferings, and then you refuse them. And I, reading

your heart as I do, dispose of events according to your goodwill, and not according to your frailty." 1

It was from the depths of that " love of her abjection " —to use a word with which St. Francis of Sales has familiarised us—that those actions which astonish us so much proceeded. Thus the holy mother loved to kneel at the feet of the humblest of her daughters and accuse herself of her trifling imperfections ; and used to insist on their telling her of any that had escaped her notice. When any of the nuns, even the youngest of the community, had performed this work of charity, she thanked her graciously, saying : " May God bless you, my daughter. I hope with the assistance of your prayers to correct myself of my faults." In the last years of her life, under the pressure of her ever-increasing sense of her unworthiness, she begged of Fr. Gratian to deprive her of her habit, which she said she had profaned with so many faults. The provincial gave in to her wishes, and the saint stripped herself of her habit and asked the nuns to take her back in to the novitiate, and there she started again as the youngest of the community. 2

She used frequently to accuse herself of her faults at refectory, asking pardon of the community for the bad example she gave them ; then collecting the scraps of bread left after the nuns' dinner she ate them seated on the floor, though in doing so she had to vanquish a feeling of nausea which was increased tenfold by her habitual disgust of food. In general, however, she preferred to seek humiliation in the ordinary way, in order not to be distinguished from the rest even by acts of humility. Thus she was constantly to be found dusting, sweeping, and working in the kitchen in her convents, or serving at table in the refectories.

THE

When her nuns begged of her to desist from these menial tasks, she used to ask them to leave her alone to work in God's house. " We cannot be always in the choir in a state of contemplation," she used to say; " but we can at every moment find occasions of humbling ourselves in little things."

She never consented to the wish of the prioresses, in whose convents she stayed in the course of her visitations, to take their place whilst she remained with them. She used, on the contrary, to ask their leave for the smallest permission she required, and enjoy to the full the happiness and merit of obedience. What made her humility so touching and attractive was the amiability which served as a cloak to it. She was so persuaded of her own nothingness and misery that humiliations came quite naturally to her. She rejoiced in them, and found herself completely in her element whilst practising them ; for she was persuaded from her inward standpoint that nothing so bad could ever be said of her than she deserved should be said, and that she could never be worse treated or more humbled than her conduct merited. She said on one occasion : " One virtue is never opposed to another. Humility therefore should never be in opposition to the knowledge of truth. But truth teaches us that though God may grant us great favours, we are, in ourselves^ less than nothing."

If she committed a slight imperfection from human frailty, far from disguising it, she wished to let it be known. Thus, in one of her letters she remarks, "I have a great difficulty in believing poor Fr. Castailo is a good preacher ! Present my compliments to him, and tell me if any one listens to him." Then, evidently reproaching herself for what she had said, she continues : " See how curious I am! No, don't tell me,

and tear up my letter." It was not sufficient for her to humble herself before men, and to annihilate herself before God, she had also a deep desire to suffer for His sake, and in their behalf. Her life was one long sacrifice, consumed by illness, infirmity, penance, and labour. She had seldom a day's cessation of pain. Constant fevers, frequent paralytic attacks, continual sickness, violent headaches, not to mention accidental maladies, left her, for forty-seven years, hardly a day free from pain. She made a joke of her sufferings, saying that the less attention that was paid to them the less trouble they gave her, and that penance, even in illness, was the best remedy. When deprived of her instruments of penance she would scourge herself with a bunch of nettles, and she used carefully to hide her hair-shirt in order to put it on again the moment her fever left her. However ill she was she would never sleep on a mattress, but insisted on resting her worn-out limbs on a hard straw pallet similar to those used by the other nuns.

Her superiors found it necessary to moderate these austerities which were beyond her strength, and they even obliged her more than once to break her abstinence. She obeyed then with her usual humility, and when the prioresses of some of her convents used to send her little delicacies, such as orange-flower water, or preserves, she accepted them always gratefully, and said how good they were, without adding that after tasting them she generally distributed them among the poor, or sick people.

Always careful to efface herself, she never refused the care lavished upon her by the infirmarian for fear of hurting her feelings, or drawing attention to her mortifications. On the other hand, if she had to suffer from awkwardness or neglect she allowed no one to see

it. In one of her many illnesses Sister Anne, on coming to her in the morning, saw by her parched lips and her tongue almost glued to her palate, the agonies of thirst she must have suffered in her feverish night. " Oh mother ! " she exclaimed, " why did you not call me. A little water would have relieved the torture your thirst must have made you endure." The saint thanked her, and answered that she gave her quite sufficient trouble in the day without keeping her awake at night as well.

But the self-abnegation which attracted her most —because she knew it was most pleasing to God-was that which concerned the duty of charity to her neighbours. She knew all her daughters' wants, and necessities, and sufferings thoroughly ; she was, above all, a mother in her treatment of them. She wished to make them happy; she longed to make them saints. We have already noticed how full of benignity and prudence was her direction of souls ; how enlightened with perfect knowledge of God's requirements, as well as the wants of man ; also how strong, and how tender. Her vigilance increased in proportion to the number of her Foundations. She watched over the doors of the cloister, so that none but those who were worthy should enter them ; or those who were capable of leading the life of solitude and penance of a true Carmelite. She did not ask for extraordinary virtues, but she insisted, in the first place, on good judgment and docility. To a priest who was praising the angelic piety of some girl whom he recommended as postulant, she said: " You see, Father, our Lord will give her piety when she is here, and she will be taught to pray ; but if she has no judgment, she will never get it; and instead of being of use to the community, she will be a drag upon it." " An upright soul," she said, "is straightforward and submissive. She recognizes her faults and allows herself to be guided. A narrow one does not see her faults even when they are pointed out to her, and being always satisfied with her own way, never goes straight." She asked, above all, for uprightness of character in her nuns; the smallest dissimulation alarmed her more than great faults, and in coming across an instance of it she was heard to say: "How far is this from true religious sincerity !" A pretentious or affected letter, or a conversation in which she detected a desire to shine, were defects she could not get over, and were sufficient to make her get rid of applicants who thought that in consequence of their fine phrases the doors of Carmel would be thrown open to them.

She took the greatest pains to cultivate this spirit of simplicity amongst her daughters. On one occasion, at recreation in order to make a true story more interesting, a nun added some details of her own invention. The holy mother reprimanded her severely, and told her she would never attain perfection unless she corrected herself of this defect. With regard to truth, Teresa preached by her example. She would rather that all her Foundations should have perished than to have committed the slightest breach of this virtue. At her last Foundation at Burgos, when the obstacles to it appeared insurmountable, an expedient was suggested to her by which she would have at once conciliated the archbishop; and in order to do so she would not have had to say anything herself, only to allow a slight untruth to be said in her behalf. She refused indignantly, saying, "What! Are we not taking the greatest pains to make this Foundation, and for what reason unless it is for the glory of God? and should we not give Him more glory by opposing this

2 P

falsehood than by making use of it to further that undertaking." Some of her nuns had been astonished at the perfect openness which she displayed in talking to lay people about what happened inside the convent, and remonstrated, saying, it might lower their opinion of religious life. " Oh, as for that, my daughter," the saint answered, " don't be alarmed. Truth can never be injurious to the children of God."

Humility, obedience, mutual charity, and application to work, were the virtues she recommended to her nuns. As regards corporal austerities, though she applied them vigorously to herself, she was, as we have already seen, very prudent in imposing them on others. "Our Rule gives us enough austerities," she used to say; "if our sisters keep it, they have done well." But if she came across one of those timid and indolent souls who think "anything will kill her," she did her best to laugh her out of her fears. " No, my daughter," she used to say to her, "your observance of the Rule will do you no harm ; your headache or sickness will pass away at divine office. To-day you will not go because you are feeling ill; to-morrow you will not go because you were feeling ill the day before ; and the next day because you might be ill three days later." To soften her sarcasm she adds, "I have gone through the experience myself, and I know the ideas the devil puts into one's head in order to prevent one from serving God. I also know that since I pay no attention to my maladies I am in better health."

If, however, the illness was a serious one nothing could exceed her tenderness to the poor sufferer. She would have preferred to allow those who were well to go without the necessaries of life rather than that the sick should be wanting in every alleviation they required. She went to the furthest limit which holy poverty allowed; and Providence appeared to take her part and to multiply its gifts at such times. The holy mother's presence was the greatest alleviation to her children's sufferings ; thus when any of the nuns were seriously ill she took upon herself the office of infirmarian, and never left their bedsides till they were either cured or safe in their heavenly Father's arms. Even when very ill herself, she would rise in secret and visit and console the sick in the infirmary. Her maternal charity was never displayed to greater advantage than on behalf of her children who were in affliction. She encouraged their confidence and—divinely enlightened—anticipated them, by dissipating their grief with a single word. Passing her hand gently on one occasion over a nun's face, she said to her: "Poor child, do not be so foolish, your sorrow will be changed into joy." And at once the nun experienced the truth of her words. But this extreme tenderness never degenerated into weakness. The sanctity which shone from the saint's brow invested her with a kind of majesty, so that her daughters' affection for her was mingled with deep religious respect; some, indeed, hardly dared to raise their eyes in her presence ! Perceiving this, her direction of their souls became ever more sweet and gentle, as if she wished to temper by her kindness the awe she involuntarily inspired. "The longer I live," she once said to Mother Mary Baptist, "the more I see that one should do all things through motives of love. I no longer govern with the same severity that I did formerly. I do not know whether the reason is that there is not the same occasion for me to exert it now as in former times, or because experience has proved to me that the latter course is the better one."

She adapted her behaviour with astonishing wisdom to the particular wants of souls. Sometimes encourag-

ing with a smile a poor culprit who came to own a breach of the Rule, she would at another arrest with a look an indiscreet or useless word ; and though severe in the presence of pride or excuses, she was ever ready to show mercy when she saw symptoms of humility and repentance. Her daughters used to say of her that she had the gift of reading their very souls. One of them longed to go with her to make a new Foundation, and had hidden this desire from her. Teresa meeting her, gave her one of her gentle penetrating looks, and said to her : " No, my child, you will never leave this place. Think no more of it." Again she said to the same nun : " My poor child, you will have much to suffer later on ; " and she pointed out to her what she should do to accomplish God's will in these trials, all of which happened as she had foretold. She was able frequently to clear up difficulties in her daughters' minds, even in cases when they were unable themselves to define the troubles from which they were suffering. On one occasion a nun came to her, who for three years had been enduring an interior martyrdom, and the saint blessed her, and told her to take courage as she was convinced our Lord would come to her assistance. The following morning Teresa offered up Communion for her, and from that day the nun was delivered from her trials. Again she told many what their temptations were, or saved them from undergoing those trials by tracing a plan of conduct to them which would deliver them from their difficulties. In short, she carried them all in her heart, and there was not one of her children who did not feel that in surrendering themselves to her guidance they were being put on the straight path to Heaven.

Her charity found likewise a field in which to exercise itself, outside the cloister, in acts of mercy and

compassion to the poor, and gratitude towards her benefactors. Speaking of the latter quality in one of her letters she says : " I see clearly that gratitude is no merit in my case. It is natural to me. It is sufficient for anyone to give me a sardine for them to be able to do what they like with me. 1 She recommended to God every day of her life a poor man who had once given her water on one of her journeys. 2 She received a gift of a picture of the sacrifice of Abraham for the chapel at Seville, which was not a great work of art. One of the nuns joked about it, and said the angel looked as if he was taking the discipline. Teresa rebuked her for her want of gratitude to a kind benefactor, and told her she was never to indulge in such witticisms at the expense of people who had befriended them. On another occasion a man who had rendered them great services in a Foundation afterwards became a source of great trial to the community, and the prioress wrote to Teresa that she was trying to get rid of him. " For God's sake," the saint answers her, " whatever suffering . . . has caused you do not talk of shaking him off, since God is not offended thereby. I cannot endure that we should show ingratitude to one who has been good to us."

Some of her most attractive and charming letters were dictated by this sentiment of gratitude; but she did not always restrict herself to words. A little picture, an Agnus Dei, or some trifling present, frequently accompanied her letter, as if to satisfy the longing she had to testify her feelings in something besides words. But it was above all in prayer that she sought to return the benefits that had been conferred upon her. Her charity for the poor, and all

1 Letter to Mother Mary of St. Joseph, 1578.

souls in affliction, was even more touching. Like the saint of Assisi, she looked upon them as the living representatives of her divine Master and His suffering members. Thus she not only loved and honoured them, but she did her utmost to share their lives. Religious poverty was so dear to Teresa's heart that she made it the badge and happiness of the Order of Carmel. It was poverty that the claimant into its ranks asked for, kneeling, at the threshold of the cloister. The saint having taken the vow of poverty according to the primitive Rule, did her utmost to keep it in the same spirit. She reserved, whenever it was possible, the oldest and most patched habit for her own use, rejoicing in thus wearing "the Lord's liveries." Never was she happier than when she found herself deprived of the actual necessities of life, or when she made a discovery of something which she could dispense with. There was also another sense in which she understood poverty. The rigours of destitution which she rejoiced in for her own part she loved to alleviate in others. The little fund raised by her own privations, or labour, went to soften their misery. When she had given everything she took her own food or clothing. Thus she stripped herself of her own sleeves to cover the bare arms of a beggar on a winter's day in the streets of Toledo. If money was wanting to her she carried an inexhaustible store of charity in her heart, which she poured out at all times, and without measure. It is told of her that on one occasion when coming out of choir to the midday repast after a long fast, which her health rendered additionally trying, that she heard of a poor woman asking to see her in the parlour. The nuns pressed her to go to the refectory saying: "She can easily wait until you have partaken of food." "No, my daughters," was the

saint's answer, " let me go to her ; my best food is to console one in trouble." 1

If she had an even greater predilection it was for those who had done her an injury. " In order to enjoy Mother Teresa's good graces," Bishop Alvarez de Mendoza used to say, " it is enough to have abused her or to have given her something to suffer." 2 Nothing could be truer. It was sufficient for anyone to injure her character, or that of her convents, to obtain special marks of gratitude from her. If anyone accused such people of their misdeeds in her presence she would defend them, and find something to say in their praise. She would also seek opportunities of doing them a service. And thus though at different times of her life she had many enemies, there was not one who was not vanquished by her charity, and who did not end, sooner or-later, by becoming her friends and protectors. This picture of Teresa which we have placed before our readers shows us the saint as her daughters have depicted her in their depositions drawn up at the acts of her canonization ; or rather it is a sketch of that picture. To complete it we must call to mind the miraculous graces of which she was the recipient ; also the astounding supernatural lights shed on her interior life. Besides this, we must remember that her soul, enlightened by the Holy Ghost, dwelt habitually on the heights of contemplation ; that Heaven opened, and granted miracles in answer to her prayer, and that for twenty-three years she bore in her heart the mysterious wound inflicted by the seraphim. Again we have to admire in her "a luminous intelligence, a vivid imagination, an ardent soul—three great powers which by a rare gift of God were united in her, and moreover reached in her their utmost perfection." 1

i Boll,, No. 1233. 2 Ibid., 1231. 3 Dupanloup.

Or, as the same writer says in another place, "we should salute a genius such as this, though manifested by a woman, for no greater gift than hers has ever been given to humanity." 1 " We must also recognize in her the possession of the noblest, the purest, the tenderest, the strongest heart with which woman has ever been endowed." 2 But in the sight of God all these merits are but as the setting of the diamond. It is with Teresa as a saint that we are here concerned, and it is under this aspect that we have endeavoured in the foregoing chapter to place her before our readers. One word more before we conclude. A young nun asked her one day what she should do in order to become a saint. "Daughter," Teresa answered, "I am shortly going to start on a journey to make a new Foundation; I will take you with me, and teach you what is required." They started ; many months passed in sufferings, fatigues, in great isolation, and many anxieties. At first the poor nun suffered in silence. Then, finding the trial somewhat prolonged, she gently complained to the Mother. Teresa's answer was, " Did you not ask me to teach you how to become a saint, daughter? It is thus one becomes a saint. Sufferings endured for the love of God are the true road to sanctity."

CHAPTER XXXII

THE holy mother having achieved her object in coming to Burgos, had now but one wish : to escape from the veneration in which she was held there, and retire to the peace and obscurity of her dear retreat at Avila. She suffered much, and her malady was, as Sister Anne remarks sadly, unto death. She was never free from fever. She dragged herself wearily from the cell to the choir, and the sisters followed her tottering gait with equal grief and alarm— though her great and majestic soul, piercing its frail covering, shone with ever-increasing vigour. The peace and holy joy which seemed to come out of her, and of which all around were sensible, seemed to foretell the approach of Heaven.

About six days after the inundation, and shortly before leaving Burgos, Teresa wrote a letter of reprimand to Mother Anne of Jesus, which the humility of the culprit has preserved to us. Mother Anne, whilst engaged in the Foundation at Granada, had been guilty of various indiscretions. She had desired to go too quickly and climb too high. Thus, having started with a fine convent and a picked community, she had become, in a sense, a celebrity in the town. Postulants presented themselves in crowds, 1 but Mother Anne found fault with some for the absence of one qualification, and some for another, and continued to

1 See Foundation at Granada, described by Mother Anne of Jesus.

live on the alms of her benefactors, with the nuns she had brought with her from Veas. This was certainly not the way in which the saint understood establishing a new convent; and to think of Mother Anne of Jesus, her coadjutrix, her chosen friend and daughter, whom she looked upon as a pillar of Carmel, falling into such errors was indeed a trial to her maternal heart! She does not hesitate to give her a lesson, however much it may cost her. She points out to Mother Anne her want of prudence, and of consideration to her benefactors, to her harshness to those whom she had sent away; she complains even of her want of obedience to the provincial. She finds fault with her for having favourites amongst the nuns.

" I ask of you, for the love of God," she says, "to remember that you are training souls to be the spouses of Christ crucified. Let them be crucified so that they may have no will of their own, and may not lower themselves to the follies of children, for an attachment of any sort, even for the prioress, should be foreign to the spirit of a true Carmelite. Such things are ties, and God wills His spouses to be free and bound to Him alone. . . . You have, I know, had many difficulties to start with. This need not astonish you ; no great work can be accomplished without difficulties, and they will have their reward. Please God that the imperfections, of which for my part I am always conscious in establishing these Foundations, should not make me worthy of punishment rather than recompense. This is my constant fear." She sums up the letter in the spirit of the mriliter agite of Holy Writ. " Act," she says, "in a manly spirit, and not after the ways of silly women." 1

1 Como varones esforzados y no como mujercillas (Burgos, May 3oth, 1582).

Teresa was not able to leave Burgos as soon as she had intended. The negotiations respecting a Foundation at Madrid were reopened, and, in spite of her I exhausted state of health, the saint resolved to under-\ take it, should she be allowed to do so, instead of returning to Avila. The months of June and July passed in indecision, Cardinal Quiroga declaring that j he must await the king's return before opening the doors of the capital to the Carmelites. At last the saint, who was meanwhile getting every day more feeble, began to make arrangements for departure. The time was approaching for her dear niece Teresita to make her vows, and she was taking her with her in order that she might make them at St. Joseph's of Avila.

This holy little soul realized all the saint's aspirations in her behalf, and loved and served the divine Master as Teresa wished to see Him loved and served in the monasteries of Carmel. "Pray for Teresita," she wrote to some of her communities; *' she is a little saint, and is longing for the hour of her profession. May God support her with His hand. Ask Him to give her all the graces she requires, as, though she is so holy, she is still very young." 1 The saint's farewell to the community at Burgos was a more touching one even than usual. As a rule, in spite of feeling these partings acutely, she hid all manifestations of what she underwent in order to spare her daughters' feelings, offering all in silence to her adorable Master. This time, either because her feelings were more acute, or because she was less mistress of them, she was visibly affected; and when at the last moment the prioress, Mother Thomas Baptist, followed by the nuns took her hand, and insisted on kissing it, contrary to her

1 Burgos, July, 1582.

habit, she gave in to their importunities, while her parting with each one of them was accompanied by kind and tender words.

The saint took with her, besides Teresita, her faithful infirmarian Anne of St. Bartholomew. She left Burgos at the end of July, and the Foundation at Madrid having again been postponed, she would have wished to have gone straight on to Avila. The provincial's orders, however, were that she was to go first to Palencia, Mother Isabella of Jesus having obtained permission from him to keep her for a month. The young prioress surrounded the saint on her arrival with filial attentions, and got ready a cell for her in which she was well protected from the heat of the August sun ; and here she found herself in better health than she had been for some time.

The saint's leisure was much occupied while she was at Palencia with the affairs of her monasteries and with her correspondence. Never had she been more precise in her decisions or more firm in her warnings, and yet never had she, withal, mingled a greater sweetness with her admonitions. She lays the greatest stress on the spirit of abnegation, and on that elevation of ideas, thoughts, and views which should form the groundwork of her daughters' lives. " No littlenesses," she repeats more than once, "no childish follies," 1 and what she means by this is a last remains of human attachment to those vanities which ensnare the hearts of great men as well as those of the idle and frivolous. She recommends them a joyous love of poverty, gratitude to God and a holy gaiety. She does not forget her benefactors. Faithful to the obligations of affection to the last she begs Mother Thomas Baptist to replace her beside her devoted friends at

Burgos. " I must make use of another hand than my own to acquit myself of this duty to them," she writes. " If I do not write to my dear doctor (Aguiar) he will understand that it is because I have not time ; give him my kindest remembrances. . . . Do not forget always to remember me to our friends. I authorize you to do so in my name even when I do not mention it." A few days later she says : " Pray tell Doctor Aguiar especially that I feel very much not seeing him, and that his letter was a great pleasure to me." Her daughters, however, have always the first place in her heart. She loves them ever more and more in God, and sends them her habitual salutations and farewells with a redoubled tenderness: "May Jesus be with you, dear mother," she says to one, "and may He make a saint, a great saint of you. May the God of goodness preserve you to my affection ; may He sustain you with His hand. ... I beseech Him to preserve you in His love, and sanctify you as much as I wish! " " May our Lord fill you with His graces," she says to another, "and may He give you strength to support with courage the trials He sends you. . . . Listen, my child. He treats you as a valiant soul. Let us praise Him in all things. It cost me much I can assure you to leave your house, and you in particular." 1 Teresa continued her journey at the end of August, in overpowering heat, and arrived in an exhausted condition at Valladolid. Sister Anne remarks : " God so willed that she should have nothing but suffering all along the road."

In reaching this convent Teresa looked forward to a time of rest such as she enjoyed at Palencia, when she would be able to console her heart with a last intimate talk on the love of God and salvation of souls with her beloved niece, the warm-hearted and high-spirited

Mother Mary Baptist. Instead of this, she found her preoccupied and agitated by ideas which had been put into her head by a lawyer on the subject of Don Lorenzo's legacy. The prioress, in short, had been misled into espousing the cause of Lorenzo's sons against the holy mother's views and opinions. The lawyer likewise urged his case in an interview with the saint; but her only answer to his insulting language was: " God reward you for the favour you do me." Though Teresa bore the man's taunts unmoved, she could not but feel deeply the insinuations of a tenderly loved daughter, who accused her of injuring the interests of Lorenzo's children. Who loved the young Francisco as she did ? Had she not been a mother to him since his father died ? If she defended Lorenzo's will it was assuredly only because she desired to carry out her brother's last wishes, and to ensure the perpetual help of the prayers of the Order for him and his descendants ; as well as to attract God's blessings, promised on those who honour their fathers' memory, on the young heirs. These reasons, in which faith had so large a share, were apparently misunderstood by Mother Mary Baptist and by Francisco's mother-in-law, Dona Beatriz de Castilla, who had instigated the distressing altercation. Teresa sought in vain to open their eyes. "It appeared to me," she writes to the latter, u that when I besought of you to let this correspondence cease between us, you would understand this referred only to the subject of business. It would be folly on my part to tell you that I receive your letters with pleasure—attaching as I do so much value to them. What afflicts me much is that your letters are concerned with matters to which I cannot in conscience consent, and to which, as many agree with me in thinking, Francisco could not himself consent with-

out being wanting in honour. As other people tell you the contrary, I understand that you doubt my goodwill. This is very painful to me, and I cannot express how great my desire is to see these questions terminated. May God dispose of it in the way to give Him the greatest glory, as you desire yourself. Never have I from the first moment desired anything else. May God spare us such a thing as a lawsuit, for that would be a terrible thing; and may He preserve you, madam, for many years for the happiness of your children."

Dona Beatriz remaining inflexible, Teresa preferred to make every sacrifice rather than resort to a lawsuit. She therefore left the care of carrying out, sooner or later, Don Lorenzo's intentions in God's hands. " If I had not been told it was a duty," she wrote in one of her letters at this period, "I should long ago have given it all up. I feel such a repugnance in mixing myself up in these matters. ... Oh how it has all wearied me, and wearies me still. You would be alarmed, my daughters, if you were witness of the sufferings I endure here on account of these affairs, which are killing me." 1 These last words, written by Sister Anne of St. Bartholomew in Teresa's name, reveal her sufferings in a stronger light possibly than the saint would have desired. They do not exaggerate, however, the bitterness of the chalice of which she was made to drink, of which the bitterest drop was her much-loved niece's attitude towards her. Other cases of no less painful a nature were as so many thorns in the crown which pressed on her brow. Accusations against Fr. Gratian for breaking the Rule and of alienating exemplary religious from motives of self-interest—namely, from fear of their rivalry of his authority—had recently come to her knowledge.

» Valladolid, August, 1582.

Though the saint knew these rumours were wholly without foundation, she had the courage to warn him to be careful in the presence of the attacks with which he was menaced. " I know well," 1 she says, " there is nothing in it, but as the time for the Chapter approaches I warn you of this rumour which has been circulated, as I do not wish that anyone should have cause of complaint against you, even wrongfully." Then dropping, as it were, a tone of advice, she takes up that of a daughter, and of a subject as she loved to call herself. She is uneasy about the affairs of the Carmelite convent of Salamanca. The prioress, who had for many years suffered from a troublesome landlord, of whom we have heard before — Pedro de la Vanda — wished to buy a house which had been lent provisionally to a novitiate of the discalced, who were studying at the university; she had, moreover, persuaded the rector to turn out at once, and transfer the students into a damp and unfinished house. Accordingly Teresa continues: "I have much to say to you, Reverend Father, on this affair at Salamanca, which has been a great anxiety to me. May God find a remedy to it. I cannot understand matters. Our prioress is so thoroughly feminine in character that she negotiates in this affair, neither more or less, than if she had your permission.

She tells the rector that she is acting by my orders in what she is doing, although I never understood she was going to buy this house, or wished her to do so. She makes out to me that the rector is behaving as you have told him to do. There must be some pitfall of the devil in all this ; and I cannot think on what the poor mother grounds her behaviour, as she is incapable of lying. I am tempted to believe her great desire to acquire this house has upset her

mind. Listen to this advice, father, which I venture to give you. It is never to put trust in women—not even in nuns—when you perceive too great keenness in ^ them, for their desire to succeed will make them think a hundred reasons good which are all abominable. Let our sisters of Salamanca, therefore, buy a small house, as befits poor people, and enter humbly into it, instead of getting into debt with a big one. . . . Another difficulty is, that if they were to go to the house in question your students would have to take possession at once of the new buildings of St. Lazarus, which would be enough to kill them. I am writing to the Father Rector to beg him not to give his consent. ... He only agreed by dint of the prioress's importunities; and I know through Brother James, who arrived yesterday from Salamanca, that the father had a scruple afterwards, and accused himself of doing so in confession. Do not be uneasy about the eight hundred ducats your religious owe our sisters. I am glad they are not able to repay them, so that they have not got the money for the purchase of the house."

It was with vigour such as this that the gentle and holy mother conducted the affairs of her convents. This particular negotiation was only settled a very short time before Teresa's death. The rector himself came to plead the Carmelites' cause with her at Alba, but the saint still maintained her position, declaring to him " never would our sisters set their foot in that house." The accuracy of her words was proved in the event; for the Carmelites reconsidered the matter, and bought, two years later, the Rosary hospital, which they only left in 1641 to go to a house which they still occupy.

The saint's sad sojourn at Valladolid ended in the middle of September. She allowed no one to suspect

the sorrow that filled her heart, and ignoring the cold displeasure in the prioress's face, she turned to the community before leaving and blessed them, saying :

"My daughters, I depart much consoled with the state in which I leave this house ; at your fidelity to the duty of obedience, your spirit of poverty, and the charity which unites you one to another. If you persevere thus, God will always be with you. May none of you, I implore, ever depart from what is prescribed by our holy Rule. Do not perform your religious exercises from habit, but with fervour, and each day with greater perfection. Be filled with good desires, for our Lord takes account of our good will even when we cannot accomplish all that we wish."

She then embraced them with tears in her eyes. The nuns wept, and kissed her hands and her habit. Mother Mary Baptist alone appeared unmoved, and, according to an eye-witness, impatient for the scene to be concluded, thus preparing for herself a lifelong remorse.

Unfortunately, the saint was to meet with a similar trial at Medina. "The evening of our arrival," Sister Anne writes, "our holy mother found fault with the prioress for some breach of discipline, and God permitted, to increase His servant's merit, that the prioress should take her words ill. She retired forthwith to her cell, and our holy mother spent a sad night without sleep. The next morning we left at an early hour."

What a mystery, we are tempted to say (as, indeed, others have said before us), is hid in these crosses which redoubled about our saint in the closing scenes of her life.

These two excellent and virtuous nuns who had hitherto been a source of nothing but joy and consola-

tion to Teresa, now when she blesses them for a last time with a tenderness increased by the knowledge of her approaching end, for a mere nothing —a question of money, an imagined affront—shut their hearts against their mother, thus inflicting a cruel wound on her. This is, indeed, a mystery which human frailty only partly explains, but which we understand more easily by sounding God's dispensation with regard to His servant, Teresa. Our Lord was pleased before the supreme hour arrived to detach the saint from her purest and most legitimate affections. He crucified her in the only spot which hitherto He had spared, so that, like her divine Master, she might die pierced to the heart and in total abandonment.

Instead of taking the road to Avila, the saint made a last sacrifice of her desires, and by order of Fr. Anthony (who was invested with Fr. Gratian's authority in his absence) went instead to Alba de Tormes, where the Duchess of Alba was eagerly expecting her. This new divergence was another cross to the saint in her exhausted and suffering state ; but, obedient to death, she allowed no sign of unwillingness to appear, and i humbly followed Fr. Anthony, who came to meet her, | to Alba. During the journey her maladies assumed i a more grave character. A serious complication reduced her to the last extremity of weakness. Half-fainting and wholly exhausted she dragged herself from one halting-place to another, though the state she was in did not prevent her trying to console her faithful infirmarian and her niece Teresita, who wept to see her sufferings.

"At night," Sister Anne relates, " we arrived at a wretched inn where we could find nothing to eat." The saint, feeling very weak, said, "Give me something to eat, daughter, as I feel very faint." I had

nothing for her but a few dried figs. I gave them to her, and she eat one, though she was in high fever. At the same time I gave a woman who was present four reals to buy eggs, telling her to get them, cost what they might. But when she came back saying she could not get any with all that money, I looked at the saint, who seemed more than half dead, her face quite livid, and I burst into tears. It would be difficult to describe the anguish which pierced my heart in seeing her thus dying of inanition without being able to help her. But, with a sweetness which was quite celestial, she said to me: " Do not cry, my daughter; those figs were very good ; many poor people have not anything so good. It is God who allows this to happen." 1 The next day there was a similar famine. They stopped at a village which was as poor as the one in which they had spent the previous night, and could find nothing to eat there but vegetables boiled with onions. The saint, exhausted from her want of food, tried to eat a few mouthfuls, but such nourishment did her more harm than good. " The hour of her blessed end was approaching," Sister Anne remarks, "and our Lord was trying her in all ways, and she bore these trials in the manner in which the saints bear them. As for me, I suffered from seeing her suffer, and being less mortified, she had to come to my assistance to help me to bear them. She assured me that she was quite happy, and wanted nothing more."

The Duchess Maria Henriquez, hearing of the state of the saint's health, sent one of her own carriages to meet her. With this help she managed to reach Alba at six o'clock in the afternoon of the 2Othof September.

1 Informaciones, No. 96. V. de la Fuente, Vol. II, p. 122. The Castilians still reproach the village of Peneranda with the death of the saint, saying 1 , " Los de Peneranda mataron la santa."

The duchess was expecting Teresa at the castle, 1 but Fr. Anthony judged that it would be more prudent in the saint's exhausted state to take her straight to the convent.

The community made up by the warmth of their reception for the sufferings the saint had endured on the journey ; but their joy at seeing her was checked by the look of death which they saw written on her countenance. The prioress, seeing that she could hardly stand, through weakness, implored of her to go at once to bed. She did as she was asked, smiling, and saying: " I am very weary, my dear daughters. It is twenty years since I went to bed so early! I thank God for having fallen ill whilst in your hands." The next morning she got up at the usual hour, assisted at Mass, and communicated. Later on she received the duchess, and even made the round of the convent, saw each one of the nuns in private, and joined in the religious exercises. In spite of this rally the prioress sent for two doctors, and these, after an interview with Teresa, gave as their opinion that her condition was such as to leave no hope of her recovery. Her habitual energy and determination seemed to give her strength to go on as usual for a little while longer. She went to choir, received Communion, and only rested for a short time in the afternoon. On Saturday, 29th of September, the feast of St. Michael, she was taken worse during Mass, and had to go back to bed after communicating. She begged her daughters to take her to another cell, her own being at some distance from the choir. She was therefore carried to a little infirmary on the top storey, which was quite close to the chapel. A grilled window in the room looked into

1 The duchess had obtained leave from the provincial for the saint to stay with her every time she came to Alba.

the sanctuary, thus permitting its occupants to assist at the Holy Sacrifice. The saint could find no greater consolations than the neighbourhood of her beloved Saviour, and the joy of suffering close to Him, and dying in His presence. Having drawn fresh courage, all her life, at the foot of the tabernacle, and taken refuge there in all her trials, she came for a last time to unite her dying moments with those of the Lamb of God, immolated for love of her.

The saint spent the day of the 2Qth of September in prayer. She was calm and silent, though in great pain. An indescribable anguish filled all hearts. Sister Anne never left her for a moment, and Teresita, to whom she had been more than a mother, sat in a corner of the cell, weeping silently. The nuns succeeded each other in the infirmary, and in the chapel, praying with fervent hearts, their arms outstretched in the form of a cross, for this precious life, and almost disputing its possession to God. Meanwhile she, whose prayers had so often evoked miracles, abandoned herself to the divine Will, and hailed the speedy moment of her deliverance. Her recollection became deeper with the approach of night, and she was seen to become rapt in God. The nuns learned afterward that the tidings of her approaching end were then revealed to her. She spoke little, her only answer to the assistance lavished on her was a kind and loving smile. She prepared for this last journey with the same calmness and simplicity that she had done for so many others; and, but for the joy visible in her expression, no one would have guessed that anything unusual was passing within her soul. God nevertheless wished to testify to His servant by glorifying her body before it had received the consecrating touch of death. The doctors had prescribed that she should be rubbed with

some kind of oil of which the smell was so strong and nauseous that it permeated Teresa's cell directly the infirmarian opened the bottle. At the same moment a visit from the Duchess of Alba was announced. The saint, distressed at her inopportune arrival, bade the infirmarian cover her up, so that her kind benefactress might not suffer from it. The duchess was already on the threshold, and, deeply distressed at the state in which she saw her saintly friend, she embraced her, and held her to her heart. " Your excellency should take care," Teresa said, trying to disengage herself from her embrace, " the doctors have been trying a remedy on me which emits such a bad smell that I fear it may make you sick."

"The only scent I notice is a most delicious one, and the thought even occurred to me that it was perhaps hardly prudent for you to use such a strong one in your state of health," was the answer.

The saint alone was not conscious of a perfume which was perceptible to everyone who entered her cell. 1 A little later one of the nuns who had been suffering from violent pains in her head came to her bedside, and, taking Teresa's hand, applied it to her forehead, and the pains left her instantly. 2 Sister Catherine Baptist, a holy nun of the same community, saw a star of great magnitude above the chapel adjoining the convent. Other signs and marvels appeared, betokening that Heaven was making ready to open its gates for the admission of God's servant. 3 On the 2nd of October Teresa, after a sleepless night of prayer, sent for Fr. Anthony to hear her confession. The venerable religious implored of her to ask God to leave her a little longer on earth. " My son," she

1 Deposition made by Sister Mary of St. Francis. V. de la Fuente.

2 Ibid. :t Ibid -

answered, " do not be unhappy; I am no longer necessary here below." Then, when she was left alone with her infirmarian, she said to her, " Daughter, the hour of my death is come."

Sister Anne could not contain her grief, which was shared by all the community. The doctors were again summoned, and perceiving that her malady was rapidly gaining ground, they imposed a last sacrifice on the saint by suggesting her removal from the room she had chosen to a warmer one on the ground floor. They also tried fresh remedies — blisters amongst others. The saint, ready as ever for suffering, agreed with an expression of gratitude to everything that was suggested, well knowing that in spite of all the Will of God would be accomplished.

Towards the evening of the 3rd of October she asked for Holy Viaticum. An icy sweat bathed her forehead, and she had not been able since the previous evening to move in bed without the help of two of the nuns. Watching calmly the gradual extinction of her strength, she wished before entering her agony to fortify her soul with the Bread of Life. It was five o'clock in the afternoon ; the sun was stooping towards the horizon, and only shed a dim light on to the saint's death-bed scene. She was clothed once more in her mantle and veil. The nuns brought flowers — the last flowers of autumn— and candles to adorn her cell, and themselves dressed in their choir mantles, with tapers in hand, pressed round the holy mother's bedside, anxious to catch every sound falling from her lips. The saint prayed, and as they were a little time before bringing the Holy Viaticum she stopped for a moment, and looking round at all the nuns kneeling before her, she stretched out her hands imploringly to them, and said: " Forgive me the bad example I have given you, my daughters.

Do not imitate my example, for I am a great sinner, but keep well your Rule and your Constitutions. Obey your superior, I beg of you, for the love of God." She was answered by sobs and tears. The sounds of the bell announced directly afterwards the arrival of Fr. Anthony bearing the most Holy Sacrament. In spite of Teresa's extreme exhaustion, which for two days had prevented her making the slightest movement, the saint raised herself in bed to a kneeling posture, and would have knelt on the ground unless she had been prevented. Her look became inflamed, her face lit up with a heavenly brightness, her whole being was transformed. With a loud and vibrating voice she cried: " Oh, my Lord, and my well-beloved Spouse! the long-wished-for hour is then arrived! It is time we should see each other. Oh, my Saviour, and my only Love, it is time to depart; it is time I should go out of this life. Blessed a thousand times be this hour, and may Thy will be accomplished. Yes, the hour is arrived when my soul shall go to Thee, be united to Thee, after waiting for Thee so long." 1

Fr. Anthony laid the Sacred Host on her lips, and first she remained silent, wholly taken up with the joy of her act of thanksgiving ; then remembering she was still on earth, and had not undergone the judgment of Him "whom she had so much loved," the words of the prophet and penitent rose to her lips, and she cried with him : " Sacrificium Deo spiritus contribulatus; cor contritum et humiliatum^ Deus, non despicies. Ne projicias me a facie tua et spiritual sanctum tuum ne auferas a me. Cor mundum crea in me Deus"

She repeated these verses many times in Latin, especially the last words " Cor contritum et humiliatum Deus non despicies. No! Oh, my God, Thou wilt not

despise the heart that has ever humbled itself before Thee." And she brought faith to the support of her confidence, faith in the promises of our Lord Jesus Christ. "At least," she exclaimed, " Oh, my God, I am a child of Thy Church. I die a daughter of Thy Church." Thus this great saint, this Reformer of Mount Carmel, had nothing stronger to rely on to find favour before God than that she was one of the children of His Church. In no action of her life, no sufferings, no labours, could she find support in that supreme moment when she was about to appear before the sovereign Judge, only one thing she could recall with humble assurance—that she had ever been the most submissive of His children. " My sisters," she said again, "I conjure you ask of God the pardon of my sins. I trust to be saved through the merits of our Saviour. Do not forget me when I am in purgatory."

Fr. Anthony, fearing that she would exhaust herself, told her to cease speaking. She was instantly silent, and relapsed into prayer and recollection, leaving her daughters deeply moved.

The night began with frequent fainting fits. At nine o'clock the saint asked for Extreme Unction. She helped the nuns to recite the psalms prescribed by the liturgy, and answered the litany and prayers in a firm voice. When the ceremony was concluded, Fr. Anthony asked her if she wished her body taken to Avila. This question appeared to distress her. " What, my father! " she said, " is this a thing for me to decide? Have I a will in such a matter? Will they not give me, out of charity, a corner of earth here ? "

The rest of the night was spent in intense suffering. At times the sound of the name of Jesus rose to her lips, or she called on God to help her, or repeated her

constant prayer: "A contrite and humble heart, O God, Thou wilt not despise."

Sister Anne of St. Bartholomew changed all her linen at early dawn, even to her sleeves and coif. The holy mother thanked her with a smile ; they were the garments she was to wear at her heavenly espousals. 1 A little later Fr. Anthony sent Sister Anne to take some food. Teresa, not knowing what had become of her, sought her with her eyes, and appeared to have no rest till she returned. Then, motioning her to her side, she took her hands, and leant her head on the shoulder of her dear infirmarian, her grateful heart wishing to show her by signs, when her lips were no longer able to speak, all she felt for the thirteen years' devoted service which Sister Anne had lavished on her.

At seven o'clock in the morning the saint turned on her left side, and, with a crucifix in her hand, she became absorbed in a profound contemplation, in which she neither spoke, nor saw, nor gave any further attention to outward things. Her agony began without groans, or sighs, or sufferings, joyous as if rapt in ecstacy, she lay in her Saviour's arms, waiting for the moment when Heaven should open to receive her. Her daughters, kneeling round their mother, contemplated her with an admiration which stopped their tears. The little cell had become a place of paradise. An ever-increasing brightness dwelt on the saint's countenance, and lit up Sister Anne's face, who supported her. Her features were invested with a super-natural beauty; the brilliancy of youth was united to the majesty of death and old age. The rays of light which encircled her forehead, the crimson on her

1 We have already noted the saint's love of cleanliness. It is more than once mentioned by her infirmarian. It appeared to be the exterior reflex of the purity of her soul.

cheeks, the unutterable joy of her expression, were all divine. God was present there, and His beloved already enjoyed a foretaste of the joys of the blessed. The day passed without the saint making any movement of her feet or hands, no painful contractions giving appearance of the smallest suffering. The same sweet smile played upon her lips, only this smile was emphasized from time to time, and her features assumed an expression of deeper awe, as if our Lord had unveiled some fresh mystery to her sight as — breaking the bands that held her to earth with the ardour of her desires — she mounted from the world of shadows into eternal light. 1 Towards nine in the evening three gentle sighs escaped her, so light that they were scarcely heard, so soft that they resembled rather those made by a person absorbed in prayer, than one in her agony, and she gave up her soul to God.

CHAPTER XXXIII

THE glory of the saints commences where oft-times the glory and pomp of man ends—when the tomb has closed over them. No sooner had Teresa died than God showed by striking portents and miracles the honour in which He held His faithful servant. Two of her daughters saw the saint's soul rising to Heaven, one under the figure of a white dove, and the other under the appearance of a shining crystal globe. 1 Sister Catherine of the Conception heard sounds of exquisite music, and beheld a procession of virgins clothed in white escorting the saint to Paradise. Again, a tree beside the convent chapel which had been dead for years, and was half buried under a rubbish-heap, put forth anew leaves and flowers. 2

So beautiful was Teresa's body after death that the nuns could with difficulty tear themselves away from contemplating it. Her members were as flexible as if she were still in life. Her brow was white as alabaster ; all the lines which time had impressed on her countenance had disappeared. A sweet and gentle smile lingered on her lips. The exquisite fragrance which had pervaded her cell before her death became even more marked after it. Her flesh, her clothes, everything that touched her was penetrated by it. Her daughters were not left long to weep beside her blessed body. Fr. Anthony, accompanied by the Franciscan Fathers and other clergy of the town, came on the morning of the day after Teresa's death, and, taking

1 Bull of Canonisation, Boll., No. 1397.

2 Ibid., Deposition of Sister Catherine of the Angels.

the body, deposited it in the outer chapel. The news had already spread of her death, and there was but one cry: "The saint is dead! The saint has gone to Heaven." The little convent church could not contain the crowds which flocked to do her honour, to pray by her coffin, to praise God, and to ask favours of Him through her intercession. She was buried the following day, and, as great fears were entertained by the foundress, Teresa Laiz, and the Duchess of Alba—fears which were shared by her daughters and the inhabitants of the town—that claims would be raised by Avila to the precious remains, the body was buried at a great depth and the cavity filled up with a large quantity of stones and mortar. For nine months it was left undisturbed. At the end of that time Fr. Gratian visited Alba, and he and another friar of the Order, after four days of incessant labour, reached the coffin and exhumed the remains. The wood of the coffin was found to be split and decayed, and the coffin was filled with earth and water, but the body of the saint was intact, her flesh white and soft, as flexible as when she was buried, and still emitted the same delicious and penetrating smell. Moreover, her limbs exuded a miraculous oil which bore a similar perfume, and embalmed the air and everything with which it came in contact. Fr. Gratian, before leaving Alba, enclosed the body in a strong coffin, and re-interred it in the same spot, but nearer the surface. Two years later, at a meeting of the General Chapter of the Order, he laid before the fathers the following reasons for moving the saint's body to Avila:—It was her native city; St. Joseph's Convent was her first Foundation ; he was bound by his promise to Bishop de Mendoza, who, relying on it, had built a mortuary chapel there, where his own body at his death was to be buried beside the saint's. The Chapter, con-

vinced by Fr. Gratian's arguments, agreed unanimously to the transfer, and he was charged, in company with Fr. Gregory of Nazianzus, to carry out their decision. Accordingly, he returned to Alba armed with letters for the prioress, and on the 24th of November, 1585, the body was once more exhumed and found to be in every respect unchanged. Silence was enjoined on the community, and to console them for the sacrifice which obedience imposed on them, an arm of the saint was cut off and left in their possession. 1 The body of the saint was then carried to Avila. Here, instead of being buried as heretofore, it was enclosed in a long case lined with purple velvet, and was deposited in the chapter-room of the convent. Though, for fear of the opposition which these measures were certain to rouse, silence had been imposed on the members of both communities, the news rapidly spread both in the Order and outside of it that Alba had been made to surrender its treasure. Accordingly, powerful representations were made to Rome by the Duke and Duchess of Alba, and by the Head of the Order of the Mount Templars, who was nearly related to the latter, to reverse the decision of the General Chapter. Their voices prevailed, and the community of Alba had the happiness of regaining possession of the saint's body and of giving her "the little corner of earth" which she had asked of them.

Again and again, at the appeal of holy souls, of members of her Order, such as Mother Anne of Jesus, of dignitaries of the Church and of great people, the

1 This was not the only mutilation of the blessed body of the saint. A lay-sister extracted her heart which is now exposed to the devotion of the faithful in a crystal reliquary at Alba de Tormes. The wound inflicted by the seraphim is visible in it, as well as the three thorns formed from dust which has collected at the bottom of the reliquary, and whicl have given rise to so much controversy. One of her hands is in the possession of a convent of Carmelites at Lisbon.

shrine containing the saint's body was opened, and again the same phenomena were manifested— her incorrupt body and the sweet smell testifying to the honour in which God holds the bodies of His saints. The last time this was done was in the year 1750, when the church was enlarged and re-decorated by the generosity of Ferdinand VI and Queen Maria Teresa. The body was then clothed in rich vestments, a collar of the Order of the Golden Fleece hung round the saint's neck, and her remains were deposited in a new shrine of embossed silver, lined with crimson velvet. The ceremony was performed by the Cardinal Archbishop of Seville.

The saint's death was followed by many miracles. And as if Divine Providence wished to enable her to continue her loving care of her daughters even after she had gone to her reward, she appeared to many and consoled them with words full of heavenly wisdom, " My child, if I enjoy the blessed vision of God," she said to the prioress of Veas the day after she died, " it is due not to revelations and ecstasies, but to the practice of virtue. Too much attention should not be paid to extraordinary graces. . . . He who keeps the law of God and the commandments alone shall be saved."

A short time afterwards she appeared to a young nun at Veas who was undergoing great spiritual trials ; "My child," she said, " your divine Spouse retains your will in order to dispose of it according to His— that is ever in opposition to your own." " Mother," the sister cried, "what you say is much too sublime for me who am so weak, even in the smallest matters." "God will give you strength when you least expect it," was the saint's answer. "To suffer and to overcome one's inclinations in small things is the way to overcome one's self in the greatest."

Fr. Gratian, who was left in charge of the holy foundress's spiritual family in consequence of her death, had a large share in her consolations. Teresa appeared several times to him, and prepared him for the trials which awaited him. " My son," she said to him, " if anything could recall me to earth, it would be the desire to suffer more than I have hitherto suffered." On another occasion she uttered these remarkable words: " We who are in Heaven, and you who are on earth should make but one in purity and love—we in Heaven in contemplating the divine Essence, you in exile in adoring the most Blessed Sacrament: we in rejoicing, you in suffering. It is in this that we differ ; but the more you suffer in this world the greater will be your joy in the next. Tell this to my daughters."

The saint's devoted affection to her family did not cease with her life ; after the example of her divine Master, she loved them to the end. She left her niece Beatrix no peace till she followed the interior voice which called her to a religious life ; and when she had obeyed it, Beatrix was heard to say that she never knew another regret: excepting that of not having listened to it sooner. Teresita, the special object of Teresa's loving care and affections, was more than once visited by the saint after her death. She comforted her in her interior trials, and in the sufferings entailed by her frail health, and left her filled with joy and consolation.

Four years after Teresa's death, Mother Anne of Jesus having been sent to Madrid to found a convent, collected there the original MSS. of her Way of Perfection, her Advices, her Interior Castle, and her Exclamations. She also procured a copy of her Life, the original being still in the possession of the

Grand Inquisitor. [1] These Mother Anne made over to Friar Luis de Leon, a learned doctor belonging to the University of Salamanca. Dr. de Leon performed his work of editing these writings with the greatest care and assiduity—carefully adhering to the saint's own words in the numerous instances when others had been substituted with the idea of improving Teresa's diction. This first edition of the saint's works appeared in 1588. The History of the Foundations was not published till the following century.

As the knowledge of Teresa's gifts, of her sanctity, and the astounding miracles which followed in quick succession after her death was spread in Spain, and from thence to other countries, so also the desire spread and increased that the Church should raise her to its altars by a decree of canonisation.

The preliminary juridical processes were begun within a few years of Teresa's death, and were terminated in 1597 and sent to Rome by the Nuncio. They were accompanied by a petition from Philip II, the royal princes, the Cortes of Spain, the municipalities of many of the great towns, as well as by the Spanish hierarchy, and the provincials of the Order of Mount Carmel, to ask her beatification of Pope Clement VII. This request was favourably received, but it was not till the reign of his successor Paul V that a Brief was published declaring her Blessed, and authorising members of her Order to keep her feast on the 15th of October. She was canonised, in company with St. Ignatius, St. Isidore, St. Francis Xavier, and St. Philip Neri, in the year 1622, in the pontificate of Gregory XV. Though the Church has reserved to

1 The provincial of the Order, at the special request of Philip II, made over the saint's MSS. to hirn, so that they might be preserved at the Escurial. After the canonisation of the saint they were deposited in the chapel of relics in that building 1 .

her sons the honour of a doctorate of divinity, and therefore this dignity cannot be claimed for St. Teresa, she has, nevertheless, set the seal of her approval on her writings ; and if we sought for a title which would express the feelings of her devout clients—and they belong to every race and every nation, and to every age—we should find it in that which is inscribed on her statue at the entrance of St. Peter: "Mater Spiritualium." Yes ! this is her fitting rank. This is the title she has won in the hearts of thousands who look up to her as the mother of their souls—as their guide and leader in the path to Heaven.

And now to conclude with a humble address to our divine Master, let us cry out in the words of St. Teresa's first biographer : * " Miserable wretch that I am. How have I dared to speak of such great sanctity ! Lord, may not the contrast between my deeds and those which I have described recall to Thy mind my many offences against Thee. Rather may they be pardoned through the intercession of Thy servant, and give me a new heart and a new spirit, so that I may imitate her whom Thou lovest so much, and whom I also love. Finally, deliver me from the fear I have that her life will lose its efficacy from being written by a hand such as mine."

And you, O blessed Mother Teresa of Jesus, kneeling for the last time at your feet, we thank you for the blessed hours we have spent in your company, for the instructions you have given us, and for your assistance. Bless these pages ; fill up the voids left by our weakness and ignorance. Put a little of the fire which consumed your heart into our cold words. Bless those who will read this book. Place them amongst the number of your friends, and ask from our divine Saviour for them and for us the gift of a great love of Him.

1 Ribera.

Alma, buscarte has en mt Y a mi buscarme en ti.

De tal suerte pudo amor, Alma en mi te retratar Que ningun sabio pintor Supiera con tal primor Tal imagen estampar.

Fuiste por amor criada Hermosa bella, y asi En mis entranas pintada, Si te perdieres, mi amada. Alma buscarte has en mi.

Que yo se que te hallaras En mipecho retratada, Y tan al vivo sacada, Que si te ves te holgaras Viendote tan bien pintada

Y si acaso no supieres Donde me hallaras a mi, No andes de aqui para alii, Sino, si hallarme quisieres A mi, buscarme has en ti.

Porque tu eres mi aposento, Eres mi casa y morada, Y asi llamo en cualquier tiempo, Si hallo en tu pensamiento, Estar la puerta cerrada.

Fuera de ti no hay buscarme Porque para hallarme a mi. Bastara solo llamarme. Que a ti ire sin tardarme, Y a mi buscarme has en ti.

THE END

CPSIA information can be obtained
at www.ICGtesting.com
Printed in the USA
BVHW012201101220
595458BV00015B/408